"Mademoiselle," he whispered.

She bent over him. Her dark bright curls touched his cheek.

"There is no one for me, but—" she whispered in return.

Their eyes were close together. They held their breath. Their lips came closer, met, clung. At that touch, they were both swept into a veritable agony, blinding, disintegrating, blown upon by winds of savage harmony. They felt nothing, saw nothing, but this. The universe swirled about them, filled with bursting stars and blazing nebulae. They heard a roaring in and about them, and did not know that it was the beating of their hearts.

They drew apart.

Then, at last, shuddering violently, Louis sprang to his feet. A horrible coldness ran over him. He cried out.

"Mademoiselle, I am a priest!"

The Arm
and the Darkness

Taylor Caldwell

"Three things only can reach beyond the world:
the sun in its light, the darkness of night,
and the long arm of God."—EASTERN PROVERB

A FAWCETT CREST BOOK

Fawcett Publications, Inc., Greenwich, Connecticut

To
PIERRE VAN PAASSEN,
a man of good will, whose works have been a constant
inspiration to me.

AUTHOR'S NOTE

The events and the characters in this novel were not invented by me. To critics, I refer the evidence of history. If
there appears too much violence, I recommend a study of
the Massacre of St. Bartholomew, and the acts of that
most Catholic Christian gentleman, Philip of Spain, in
Holland. To those who believe the Roman Hierarchy is
uniformly vicious, I refer the lives of many heroic priests,
without whom the cause of civilization would long have
perished. Men of good will are not confined to one creed
or race, but can be found in the most unlikely places. To
these men this novel is dedicated with reverence.

THE ARM AND THE DARKNESS

THIS BOOK CONTAINS THE COMPLETE TEXT OF THE
ORIGINAL HARDCOVER EDITION.

A Fawcett Crest Book reprinted by arrangement with Charles
Scribner's Sons

Printed in the United States of America

CHAPTER I

THE TUMULTUOUS STORM had passed over Paris, and behind it there came a hollow silence, in which there were no echoes. But a moist and livid patina formed on the chaotic rooftops, which an uncertain moon, shrouded with tattered veils, turned at intervals to a dull silver. A mist was rising rapidly from the river, its upper reaches brightening into pale bright clouds in the vagrant moonlight, its lower depths swirling like dark smoke over the city. Here and there, the roofs of higher buildings resembled the outlines of wrecked ships drifting under the illusive moon, and the towers of Notre Dame, in a deceptive distance, loomed as soft vast shadows, somber and unreal.

The fog came in with remorseless silence, engulfing the streets, flooding them. It had not yet reached this street. The houses were old and dilapidated. The upper stories projected over the silvered stones of the street, and their narrow shuttered windows were dark. The filthy gutters gurgled chokingly. The street went into darkness and out again into vague light, as the moon flung herself behind clouds or leapt out as if pursued.

There was no light of any kind in this narrow and crooked street, which was hardly more than an alley, leading to other and more narrow alleys. But, yes, there was a single glimmering light after all, flickering through a slit of a window on the street level. So faint it was, so spectral, that only a desperate or seeking eye could have discerned it.

The city, at midnight, might have been dead, at least from this street, where there was no sound at all, and only a breathless and sunken quiet. Yet, all at once, there was the thin echo of running feet, and harsh breath and stumbling steps. The breathing had already taken on itself the quality of sobs, spent and agonized. The moon came out again, shining with wan brilliance down the length of the street. A man was

5

running, staggering, his wild eye leaping ahead of him, as if to find refuge and shelter.

He was in terrible distress, panting and dishevelled, carrying in his right hand a drawn sword. The night was cool, too cool for his coatless condition. His white shirt was torn, and on the right sleeve there was a wet dark stain, and from his right cheek there dripped a tiny rivulet of blood. Mud and water had drenched his doublet and boots; his long hair was matted close to his head, as though recently dipped in water. He had just emerged from the river, into which he had plunged in order to escape his pursuers. But he had not escaped them; now, in the near distance, still hidden from him by the corner of the street, he could see the red shadow of a torch, and could hear the slapping of running feet.

He was young, and his eye was keen, and by the light of the moon he could discern that the end of the street was a cul-de-sac, and that at right angles to it there was another alley. He leaped forward, stumbling, then halted, trembling. He would have no time to reach that alley. His pursuers would see him. He was already exhausted. He could go no farther.

His wild eye struck the shut and bolted doors of the miserable houses. He crept, shivering, under the shelter of a projecting balcony, trying to assuage the bursting pain of his heart, looking backwards, as he did so, to the corner which he had just recently rounded. He would be slaughtered in this street, right where he stood. There was no help. In a moment, his enemies would be upon him.

Suddenly, he saw the wan glimmer of the candlelight near at hand. Instantly, he leaped towards it, and glanced within. An old man sat at a table in a bare and wretched room. A single candle in a wine bottle stood near his right elbow. He was reading from the pages of a large book. The young man could peer through the cracks in the shutters. So sharp and intense were his emotions then, that he could be impressed, even in his mortal danger, by the slow and thoughtful manner in which the old man turned the pages, and the meditative bend of his head.

There was a door near at hand. The young man pressed his palms desperately against it. It yielded, with a dolorous squealing. He had hardly expected it to yield, and he sobbed aloud a word of gratitude. He found himself in a dank dark passage smelling of mice and dust. At his right hand was a door leading to the chamber which he had seen. It was slightly ajar. He pushed it open, sprang into the room, closed it. There was a bolt upon it, and he shot it into place.

The old man, startled, glanced up, half rose with an expression of alarm. He saw before him a young man, white and ghastly of face and lips, bleeding, armed with a sword. He saw the distraught dark eyes, the dripping garments. He uttered a faint cry.

But the young man was already glancing beyond him to the curtained doorway of a dark windowless room. A young girl, aroused by the old man's cry, appeared in the doorway, in her shift, braids of light brown hair on her shoulders. She gripped one of the ragged curtains in her hand as she saw the strange and ferocious visitor who had just precipitated himself into the room.

In a moment he had sprung the three or four paces towards her, had jumped behind her. He lifted his pistol and pressed it into the small of her soft young back. The old man stood by his table, staring. The young girl did not move or turn, but her face turned gray and still, and her hand clenched the curtain tightly.

The young man spoke through his teeth, softly, and with a deadly intonation.

"I am pursued," he said. "They will see your light. Blow it out!" He listened. "No, it is too late. They are already in the street. They have seen your candle. They will be suspicious— In an instant, they will knock upon your door. You will tell them I am not here. If you do not obey me, this girl will die. Instantly."

The old man slowly sank back into his chair. His hand, wrinkled and swollen, fell heavily upon the open book. Terrible fear appeared on his bearded face. He could not see his visitor, but he saw the wide strained eyes of the girl, fixed steadfastly upon him.

"Who are you?" he whispered.

The invisible man did not answer. But it was evident that he was listening. In the street outside there was a subdued tumult, the hoarse infuriated voices of men, and in through the shutters there came lances of red light. The young girl still did not move or speak, but the knuckles of her gripping hand had turned a pearly white.

Now there was a thundering upon the door. The door opened, and men catapulted themselves into the little passageway. They struck at the barred inner door.

"Open! Open in the name of His Majecty, and the Cardinal!"

7

"Open the door," said the invisible man, very softly.

The old man forced himself to his feet. For an instant, he looked at the girl, and his bearded lips shook. She returned his regard with desperate gravity. He tottered towards the door and opened it. Two musketeers, in the livery of Monsieur the Cardinal, forced themselves into the room so violently that the old man was hurled back. In the passageway outside, he saw the flushed coarse faces of other men. One held a torch high. Drawn swords were in every right hand.

"What is it? What do you wish, messieurs?" asked the old man, in his faint cracked voice.

They were panting. They did not answer him for a moment, but they looked at the young girl. Then one spoke.

"Have you seen a man? Has he taken shelter in here?"

"There is no one here but my granddaughter, and myself, messieurs."

He looked at their heavy bodies, at their brutal faces, and a strange gleam came into his pale and sunken eyes.

"Who is the man? A thief? A murderer?"

One of the men laughed savagely. "Worse, old man. He is a Huguenot. Worse than that, he is conspiring against the King and the Cardinal. You have seen nothing of him?"

Now the old man spoke in a stronger, more controlled voice. "Nothing. I have heard nothing. I was reading to my granddaughter, and was about to go to my bed."

The musketeers, by the light of the candle, glared at him suspiciously.

"It is strange," one of them, evidently, the leader, said. "He had not time to reach the end of this alley. He has taken refuge somewhere, in one of these houses."

There was a shout behind him, from the street. "Here is blood, on the doorstep!"

The leader scrutinized the old man with narrowed eyes. "Blood upon your doorstep, grandfather. The criminal halted there for a moment. Are you certain you have seen or heard nothing?"

"I have said," answered the old man, with strength and tranquillity. "If you doubt my word, search my poor house. There are three rooms. It will not take you long. That is my granddaughter's bedroom. Beyond her room is the kitchen, where I sleep. Beyond that, is a passageway into a back alley. You are welcome to search."

He glanced at the young girl. For a moment, her full white lids drooped over her eyes. But she did not stir. He saw a faint convulsion pass over her pale mouth. But he compelled her to silence and motionlessness by the hard and direct impact of his glance.

The men hesitated. One took a step forward, then stopped. The harsh and ferocious eyes of the Cardinal's men scrutinized him. But he looked at them calmly.

"Why do you not search?" he asked them.

A look of doubt passed over their faces. Then the leader said impatiently: "We are wasting time. It is evident that he is not here. In these moments, he can have hid himself securely in another of these cursed houses."

He turned towards the door, and his men followed him, scowling threateningly at the old man. The young girl's face changed, and she moved slightly as though about to swoon. The old man stood quietly, the candlelight on his cheek and bearded lips. The door closed behind the Cardinal's men. Outside, they could hear their angry altercations, the sound of their hurrying feet. The red torchlight wavered over the shutters. They could hear the voice of the leader.

"You, Armand, will stay near this house, and watch, and you, also, Jean. I and the others will search at every house. He cannot have gone far, curse him!"

There was silence in the miserable bare chamber, whose plastered walls were leprously spotted with decay and moisture. The candlelight wavered. The old man went back to his table, trimmed the candle, bent over his book. His lips moved in a whisper.

"Cecile, return to your bed, my child."

The girl stirred, waited, her eyes fixed helplessly on her grandfather.

"Yes, return to your bed," murmured the invisible man. "It is best."

The girl slowly moved, stepped backwards. There was a poor bed in the dark chamber. She fell upon it; the straw creaked and rustled with her slight weight. She sighed deeply. The visitor remained behind the ragged curtains.

The old man turned a page. He was actually reading, his lips moving soundlessly as his eyes followed the printed lines. Then, as if he had forgotten the stranger, he began to read aloud, murmuringly, and the man behind the curtain subtly knew this was his usual way:

"He is free who lives as he wishes to live; to whom none can do violence, none hinder or compel; whose impulses are unimpeded, whose desires attain their purpose, who falls not into what he would avoid. Who then would live in error? None. Who would live deceived and prone to fall,

9

unjust, intemperate, in abject whining at his lot? None. Then doth no wicked man live as he would, and therefore neither is he free."

There was a mysterious and tranquil grandeur in the low melodious words, which followed each other like the measures of some lofty music sung by the soul to itself in the depths of some radiant peace. The effect was extraordinary. The bare chamber, cold and gloomy, lit only by the light of that wan and flickering candle, which caused gigantic and unformed shadows to drift over the spotted and broken walls, was filled with quietness and majesty. It was impossible to believe that violence had recently erupted into this room. The stillness of ages appeared to overflow in it. And the man behind the curtain listened, as if amazed, and overcome.

"Epictetus!" he said at last, in a loud whisper. And he laughed, softly and incredulously.

"It is evident that you are familiar with the philosophers," said the old man, and his lips hardly moved. He did not glance up. "It is also true that a loud voice can be heard from the street." His eyes did not leave the printed page, and again, he slowly turned another page. "Moreover, I suspect an eye is still watching me through the shutter."

The visitor did not answer. The old man bent closer over his book. His face had a thin and singular nobility in its outlines, in its high narrow nose. Even the gray unkempt beard gave him a classic look, aristocratic and melancholy. He was almost bald, and a fringe of gray hair outlined his slender and fragile skull. His clothing was of the poorest and meanest, and much patched. His hands were twisted and calloused, but the fingers were long and delicate, and faintly trembling. As his eye swiftly travelled down the pages, the candlelight caught gleams of their pale blueness and quiet intensity.

"What and who are you?" whispered the young man.

The old man did not answer for a moment. He finished the page, turned another. He did not glance up.

"My name is nothing. But it is François Grandjean, if you will. I am one of those employed to care for the Palais Justice. I am also a Breton." He hesitated, asked gently, his lips scarcely moving: "And you?"

There was a long hesitation. Then the answer, still whispered: "My name is—Arsène—" The whisper ended abruptly.

"And evidently not a sweeper. Not even a burgher." A tired smile passed over the old man's eyes and lips.

He leaned back on his stool, sighed, rubbed his hand over

10

his eyes, yawned, drooped his head. He looked wearily at the candle, got to his feet. With tender hands he closed the book. The cover was of the finest leather, but old and flaking, and there was a dim golden crest on it. His hand touched it reverently. He yawned again, took the bottled candle in his fingers and lifted it. He could feel the sharp round eye watching him through the shutter.

He turned his back to the window and whispered. "I am coming into my granddaughter's chamber, and then I shall go into the kitchen. You may follow me."

He moved quietly towards the curtain, holding the candle high. He heard the young man falling back. The candle dimly cleft the darkness of the bedchamber. The old man looked only at his granddaughter upon the poor bed. She had drawn the tattered covers up to her chin, and her blue eyes shone silently in the light. There was no fear in them, but only steadfastness. Now it was to be seen that she was very young, scarcely more than fifteen, with her grandfather's nobility of feature, and with it, a great beauty. The old man bent over her, and kissed her forehead with deep love.

"Goodnight, my child," he said. "God keep you through the night."

He went to the rear of the bedchamber, opened the door, leaving it ajar. The candlelight disappeared. Both the front room and the bedchamber were in complete darkness.

The young man could hear the soft irregular breathing of the girl, and the dripping sound of the renewed rain.

"Thank you, mademoiselle," he whispered. "I am sorry that I was forced to frighten you."

He waited. She said nothing. "My deep regrets," he murmured. Then he slipped silently towards the rear door, opened it, closed it behind him.

CHAPTER II

WHEN ARSENE entered the kitchen, he found the old man kneeling on the hearth, blowing on incandescent old embers, and adding small sticks to them. He had set his candle upon a bare stained table, and it revealed the misery of the little windowless room, with its slanting plastered ceiling and cracked distempered plaster walls. Moisture ran in quicksilver drops from the ceiling and down the walls, and the drops caught the light of both fire and candle so that they glittered like tiny silver balls. The room contained a wooden cupboard, leaning sideways, and filled with mugs, jugs and wooden plates, and there was a bare and broken table, and a wooden bench. On the floor, in a corner near the table, there was a straw pallet, covered with tattered quilts. The floor itself was of uneven stone, the cracks filled with moist mud and dirt.

Arsène stood in the doorway for a moment, leaning against the side, for he was weak and exhausted. He panted audibly. He still carried his sword and pistol in his hands. The old man continued to blow on the fire, as if he were alone and unaware of the stranger in the doorway. The fire now crackling to his satisfaction on its ashen stone hearth, he put upon it a deep iron vessel filled with water. Arsène, after a moment's hesitation, laid his pistol and sword upon the table. The firelight shone on the hilt of the sword, which was of gold, elaborately twisted and set with twinkling gems. The young man hesitated, sighed, sank upon the bench, leaned his elbow on the table and dropped his head on his hand. The blood still moistened his sleeve, and a slow drip of blood from his cheek filtered its way through his white fingers.

He closed his eyes, then opened them, and stared at the old man curiously.

"You are brave," he said, in a faint forced voice.

François Grandjean looked over his shoulder as he knelt

12

on the hearth. His pale blue eyes had an inscrutable gleam in their depths, as if he were amused.

"Not so brave," he said, in his quiet and composed voice. "I knew, after an instant or two, that you would not kill little Cecile even if I had betrayed you. You would not even have killed me."

The young man stared again, then laughed abruptly. "That is a singular conclusion. Why should you have had that opinion?"

The old man rose, rubbed his hands free from ashes. "I have lived a long time, and I have known numerous men. There is no reckless murder in you."

The young man did not speak.

"Nevertheless," said François, "you have killed before. Perhaps several times. Is that not so?"

Still, Arsène said nothing. His eyes were dark and intent as they studied François, and more than a little hard, and coldly haughty.

"I, too," said François, composedly, "have killed. But, like you, I kill only upon necessity, and then with regret."

Arsène made no comment on this. Instead, he asked with curiosity: "If, then, I would not have killed the girl, or you, why did you protect me?"

François dipped a finger into the iron kettle, to test the temperature of the water. The red flames of the fire and the yellow flame of the candlelight mingled together in the dark and fetid room. François said: "I am a Breton, and my people have, for ages, been seamen. Those who love the sea have mysteries in their heart, and they are never deceived."

Arsène contemplated these odd words, which seemed no answer to his question. But he was very tired. He closed his eyes again.

"Neither are they dupes for liars," added François. He approached Arsène, and touched his white and silken sleeve, torn and stained with blood. "Monsieur, if you will remove your garments—"

Arsène looked without interest at his arm. "It is nothing. I was grazed by a ball." He tried to rise, sank back on the bench. "I must go," he said, in a dwindled voice. "They will search for me. I am a danger to you here."

"But more than a possible danger if you leave," said François. "They are still outside, those paid devils of Richelieu. They will catch you, and then there will be no mercy for those who hid you." He smiled. "I would not have even the excuse of your threat, for I would be told that for the glory of the Cardinal and Our Lady I should have betrayed you at the cost of my life."

His tone was filled with mockery and some bitterness. Arsène scrutinized that smiling Roman face, and his interest quickened.

"You find life, then, so valuable?" and his eye passed swiftly over the room.

"I find it less fearful than death," replied François.

Arsène's mind was drained of coherence by his recent danger and his present suffering. The old man's face floated, disembodied, before him. He said, childishly: "It is strange to find a student of the philosophers in such a den."

"No stranger than to find you here," answered François, with a significant look at the gold-hilted sword with its crust of intricate jeweling.

He unfastened the gemmed studs of the shirt with gentle hands. Arsène resisted for a moment, then fatalistically resigned himself to having the shirt removed. Resistance seemed at abeyance in him. François noted how white and silken were his shoulders and chest and body, yet how strong and well-formed. The candlelight glimmered on the face of the young men. He seemed about twenty-six years of age, with excellent and well-bred features. His eyes were large and dark, but ungentle, and there were wrinkles of cynicism, shrewdness and bold hardness about them. Nevertheless, their expression was both intelligent and quick, and humorous. He had a good broad forehead with sharp black brows under his thick long hair, the color of his eyes. His nose was long and aquiline, with curved and distended nostrils, and his cheekbones were wide and flat. His mouth, large though it was, was not soft and too sensitive, though the corners seemed more used to smiling than drooping. It was the face of a grand seigneur, but not that of a decadent nobleman, for there was no weakness in it, no languor, no daintiness nor perfumed elegance. His flesh was clean and pampered, but it was not scented, and the handkerchief which he withdrew from his doublet to wipe his sweating face had no lace edges upon it, but was clean and crisp, and of the finest linen.

He winced when the strangely gentle fingers of the old man examined his wound, but he did not cry out. There was no false bravado in this restraint, but rather an indifference. Nevertheless, he watched the old man intently and with detachment.

"You are quite right," said François. "The ball grazed, deeply, but is not in the wound. You have lost much blood.

14

But you are young, and the young replace their blood with new, rapidly, just as they replace their dreams with reality."

His voice had a queer note in it, touched with bitterness.

"You prefer the dreams to reality, then?" asked Arsène.

"There is no reality without dreams," murmured François, abstractedly. He dipped a clean rag in the hot water, sponged the wound, bent over it. The young man winced again, stiffened. The wound was very deep, and bubbled with blood. François drew the edges together and held them tightly with his fingers. With his other hand he pressed firmly an area near the wound. He smiled down at Arsène with his deep blue eyes.

"I learned this in caring for the animals on my mother's farm," he said. "In a few moments, the blood will clot, and there will be less bleeding."

There was silence in the kitchen. The firelight and candlelight danced together. The old man's fingers were strong and steady. The pain lessened. Long moments passed. Arsène felt his flesh grow numb under the pressure of François's fingers. The wound slowly ceased to drip.

"Dreams, and mysticism," said Arsène, "should be left to priests and other liars. They are not for honest men."

"On the contrary," murmured François, studying the wound. "They are only for honest men. Liars and mountebanks use them only for oppression and for manipulation of the defenseless and the ignorant. Until honest men take them for their own there can be no justice in the world, no faith, no enlightenment. Without a dream, honesty, mercy, indignation and courage must remain impotent."

He took a strip of cloth and wound it tightly above the wound. Then he washed away the blood from Arsène's cheek with touches as gentle as a woman's. And again, he smiled down at the young man, and his smile was a little sad. But he said: "The cut on your cheek will leave a scar, unfortunately, monsieur. However, your mistress will not find it disfiguring. To the ladies, an unscarred man seems wanting in virility."

Arsène began to smile, but his weakness had returned. He panted again. The old man put a smaller vessel on the fire, removed a bottle from the cupboard, and a pewter cup, and set them on the table.

"In a moment, there will be good hot broth. In the meantime, drink this wine. It is not of a good vintage, or excellent bouquet, but it has strength in it."

He poured a cupful of the acrid wine, and held it to

15

Arsène's lips. The young man obediently drank, made an excruciating face, choked, and pushed aside the cup.

"It is vile," he said, frankly.

François was not offended. He held the cup again to Arsène's mouth, and Arsène drank again, and groaned.

"I have drunk poison," he spluttered, wiping his mouth with his kerchief.

François lifted the bottle, and regarded it with regret. "Worse, you have lessened my own ration."

"I am sorry for that," said Arsène, ironically. However, he felt the strong and acrid wine flowing through his body, and giving it strength again.

"The poor have need of strength, and violence," remarked François. "Especially in these days. But they have always needed them. Strong wine for the oppressed, sweet wine for the oppressors. In the end, this will have significance."

He pointed to the pallet. "Now, after you have had your broth, you will rest there for the night. Tomorrow, we will find some escape for you."

"That is impossible, my good friend. I must leave immediately."

François shook his head. "As my guest, you endanger me. But you endanger me more by leaving. You would not go far, after this night's work. Either they would discover you, or you would drop in some gutter."

He dipped a cup in the hot soup and gave it to Arsène. The young man found it hardly less obnoxious than the wine, but he drank it. "It is strange," he murmured, glancing about the chamber again. "I have always espoused the cause of the wretched, but purely from an intellectual platform. I never knew you lived like this."

François studied him piercingly, but did not answer. Then, after a moment, he said: "There is no reality, or dream, without knowledge."

Arsène protested when he was led towards the pallet, which he regarded with open disfavor. He privately thought the gutter less undesirable than this. But François forced him down upon it, and threw the odorous rags over his legs. "Rest," he said. "Tomorrow is another day."

"But where will you sleep, mon ami?"

"On the hearth. I have slept in worse places."

He laid his old emaciated body on the stones before the fire. The young man watched him from the straw pallet. His wounds no longer pained him. He was conscious of drowsiness and great weariness.

16

"But you have also slept in better," he murmured.

François did not reply. He curled himself towards the fire, and closed his eyes.

Arsène closed his eyes, also. He heard the dripping and the wind of the renewed storm outside. But he could not sleep for a while. The night's events rose up vividly before him. He did not like to kill, not from any squeamishness, but because murder was a violation of human dignity. The faces of the two men he had killed that night painted themselves on his closed eyelids. One had been young and very ardent, and full of laughter. He had been very adventurous, and Arsène doubted his passionate adherence to the Cardinal. He sighed. He had plunged his sword deeply into the youth's side, and the youth had fallen, still faintly smiling, and had died only with a regretful moan for the ending of adventure. The older man had been fanatical, full of fierceness and hatred, and had tried to kill Arsène out of some mystical compulsion. Arsène did not regret killing him. Such men were dangerous.

Still sighing for the youth, he fell asleep, into a maze of troubled and uneasy dreams. Toward dawn, the dreams had become nightmares, filled with pain and fever.

CHAPTER III

ONE OF THE DREAMS of Arsène was not really a dream, but a recollection, strangely mingled, at the last, with nightmare.

It seemed to him that he was a child again, and that he was standing before an enormous rosebush, covered with large dark-red roses. He must have been very young, for he was only vaguely conscious of intense white sunlight, grass, arbors, a swan-filled pool, rose walks and great trees. Somewhere, there was a white old wall, the back of his father's house. Even in the dream, now, he felt a deep pang of sadness and nostalgia. He felt the silence, as he had not felt it as a child, and saw the long blue shadows of the trees, and heard the thin sweet callings of birds. He did not know why the rosebush, with its large red flowers, fascinated him so. It was not that he liked these particular roses, for their darkness and secretive thickness of petal revolted him. Moreover, they had no scent, and he had always had a peculiar love for perfumes.

It was very hot, in that country garden, and the sun was too whitely brilliant. It burned on his head and shoulders. But for some reason, he did not return to the purple cool of the house. He had seen his young mother weeping that morning. He could not bear to see her in tears, so he had run out here, and remained, though his nurse had called him several times. He felt sullen and full of inexplicable hatred.

He heard the murmuring of voices, and glanced over his shoulder. Behind him, to the left, there was a long yew walk, and the voices came from the passageway. One of the speakers, he knew, was his father. The other was both strange and a stranger. Arsène felt his childish rage and aversion rising at the thought of that stout and elegant man, Monsieur the Archbishop of Paris. His black garments, the white ruffles at his neck and wrist, his round red face with its syrupy wet sly smile, and his little fiery blue eyes, were all

18

repulsive to the child. The archbishop had patted him on the head only an hour ago, had studied him shrewdly, had shaken his head with a fond but sorrowful sigh. "Ah, sad, sad," he had muttered. "But not too late, Monsieur le Marquis du Vaubon." He rolled the title unctuously on his tongue, and with a certain significance.

"I trust not," Arsène's father had replied, with a furtive and uneasy smile on his dark, fox-like face. He was a nervous and very thin man, restless, capricious and distrustful. He did not look directly at Arsène when he spoke. But he rarely looked directly at anyone with his glittering, ball-like black eyes. His nervousness manifested itself in his almost constant dry sniffing, his jerking head, his crooked meaningless smile, his manner of rubbing his right ear with one sallow forefinger, his twitching shoulders, and his rapid, disjointed walk. He dressed with almost too fastidious an elegance, but his legs were stringy, with knobbed knees, and his wrists were bony. There was a febrile quality about him, a certain incoherence of attitude, which aroused suspicion in others. His voice was high, and sometimes broke ignominiously, his features were long and unprepossessing, with a thin wide mouth and receding chin. His tempers were unpredictable, hysterical and womanish, and so he was both feared and despised by his household. When he laughed, his laughter had a note of shrill hysteria in it, and a meaninglessness. It was also very unexpected, and was aroused by the most inexplicable things which did not cause laughter in others. Moreover, he was abnormally suspicious. He suspected everyone of falseness, hypocrisy, knavery, plottings and meannesses, or, in the matter of servants, of thievery and slyness. He suspected his young wife less than he suspected anyone else, but even she, poor pretty creature, was not exempt from his accusations at times.

Even when he was very young, Arsène knew that his father lived in a chronic condition of universal hatred and terror and suspicion. Because of this, he had few visitors. The family was immured behind the white walls. Sometimes, Armand went to Paris, secretly, but always alone. His wife, Sabina, never accompanied him, though Arsène knew she was Paris-born. Arsène wondered, as a child, what caused his father's constant and active fear. Later, he knew that some were born this way, and lived their lives like rats watching, glittering-eyed, from a hole. From the first, he smiled at his father, and despised him for his causeless terror. He hated his elegance, his simpering mannerisms, his capricious and

19

violent tempers, so feminine in their unreason, his sickly sentimentality which rose from his self-pity and self-adoration. Even when he was hardly more than a babe, Arsène knew that his father felt himself a victim of all mankind, a martyr both to imagined physical delicacy and the viciousness and plottings of other men. Every man was either a rascal or a fool, and he, Armand, had to be eternally on his guard lest he be betrayed. Arsène could not recall that he had ever shown true kindness or compassion to a single soul, except his wife, and even then it was tempered with watchful falseness and amorous exigencies.

Undeceived by his father, and never forbearing to show his childish aversion on every occasion, though tempering this aversion with the respect of a child for its sire, Arsène was yet his father's favorite, and his great pet. Perhaps it was because in coloring and in a certain vehemence of manner on occasion, the child resembled him. For his younger son, Louis, who was fair, blue-eyed and nervously silent, like his mother, he had only indifference, and a sharp irascibility. It was Armand's opinion that Louis lacked spirit and fire, two attributes which he considered he, himself, possessed in large quantity. Arsène's fits of temper and violence pleased him, assured him that the child was of a valorous and aristocratic temper. And, like many men of his kidney, Armand was given to capricious spasms of demonstrative affection, when in less nervous moods. Louis and his mother, Sabina, shrank from them with uncontrollable fear and timidity, whenever they were infrequently offered, but Arsène, who was less sensitive of temperament, and possessed, even in childhood, by a certain cynicism, endured them with composure. This further endeared him to his father, who showed his maudlin gratitude by spoiling and lavish gifts. As a result of copious neglect of discipline, Arsène developed his naturally haughty, selfish and overbearing faults to a prodigious degree, and with them, his increasing contempt for his father. Had he not also possessed a strange sense of justice, a humorous disposition, an odd independence and cold logic of mind, he would have become insufferable, and one of those pampered young wretches who make life untenable for more gentle folk.

He had only a vague suspicion of the meaning of the presence of the Archbishop de Paris this morning, in this Huguenot household. He had heard his mother cry only last night, on one of the rare occasions of her revolt against his father: "I shall not have the monster in this house of my father's, my father who died at La Rochelle! I shall not have his memory defamed, or his ghost uneasy in its grave!"

"You forget, Madame, that I am your husband," Armand had replied coldly, yet with the ominous note of hysteria in his voice which never failed to cow the gentle Sabina. "You forget that men have reasons for what they do, which women cannot comprehend."

"I comprehend that you are ambitious," Sabina answered, with stern tears.

Armand had been silent a moment, and she thought he would say nothing, in contemptuous indifference to her. And then all at once he had burst out into incoherent cries, and had gestured violently.

"Madame, have you thought how much longer I can endure life in your accursed Gascony, among your peasants?"

Then Arsène had seen terror in his mother's large blue eyes. She had risen, putting her hand to her cheek, as though consumed with incredulous fright. But her whisper had been low, unbelieving:

"You would sacrifice the memory of your father, and mine—these two who fought together and gave up everything —for ambition? You would compromise with the devil, and give worship to the fiend?"

Armand had looked about him uneasily, and had wet his jerking lips. For a moment, he had seemed ashamed, and uncertain. Then he spoke furiously, and Arsène knew that the fury was partly for himself: "You speak like a traitorous fool! Henry of Navarre has said: 'Paris is worth a mass!' Am I less than that great king?"

Sabina had looked at him for a long moment, and had stood there, tall, slender and beautiful, and her eyes were blue lightnings.

"It is not for Paris, it is not for France, that you would betray our fathers. It is for yourself, for your mean ambitions, for your pride, for your longing for favor and gaiety and a return to a corrupt court, and a smile from that foul demon, Richelieu. I have long known this. I can say nothing to dissuade you, I know. But beware the maledictions of the dead!"

She had raised her trembling white hand then, as if to curse him, and had stood there, shaking but unafraid, and filled with proud hatred and scorn. Between the profuse and tumbling masses of her golden curls, her face quivered with a pale light.

Armand had left her presence, infuriated. The Archbishop

had come, but had delicately refused Armand's invitation to occupy a suite at the château. He and his entourage were uncomfortably established at the mean little tavern in the village, whose proprietor, a Huguenot himself, was overwhelmed by the honor, and dusted off his plaster images and crucifixes, which he had hidden scornfully in his garret, and placed them in conspicious places throughout the house. Then he had assiduously studied old broken prayer-books, relics of his youth, and was seen to cross himself frequently and assertively on every occasion, to the bewilderment, but gratification, of his devout wife. "Only a fool," he said, "wears the same coat in every weather."

The stout and elegant Archbishop, who always considered the prejudices of those he intended to seduce, did not drive up to the château in his gilded carriage the next morning. Nor did he wear his more elaborate garments. He walked to the château, climbing the dusty, stone-strewn road in solitary humility, though had any one been present to observe him, he would have seen the Archbishop stop frequently to wipe his florid brow and curse with more color than restraint. He was, to all appearances, a humble and reverent abbé, coming to call upon some recalcitrant sinner out of Christlike gentleness and sad concern. The heat and dust of the summer morning did nothing to soothe his temper, but his smile was fixed and gentle on his rotund countenance when he observed Armand du Richepin waiting for him at the gates, unable to conceal his nervous excitability.

They had walked then, in the garden, murmuring assiduously together.

"You can be sure, my dear Marquis, that His Eminence will not hold the sins of the fathers against their sons," said the Archbishop. "I have already told him of your invitation, though he inquired, naturally enough, why you had not come to Paris to see me. Permission would have been granted easily, upon your application."

Armand muttered something unintelligible. He was miserably ill at ease. The lessons of his youth, the admonitions and warnings of his father, still influenced him, and he felt only suspicion and fear of his visitor. But more than these, in his febrile ambition, he wished to please, to conciliate. Whenever his resolution faltered he had only to glance at the white bare château, and over the burning countryside which he hated. Miserable, horrible place of exile! To a temperament like his, which could be happy only in the midst of approving fellows, which achingly longed for excitement and gaiety and the intrigues of courts and the presence of many lovely women, the quiet life of a country gentleman was obnoxious, unendurable. In his childhood and boyhood, he had lived in La Rochelle, and the memory of gaiety, lightness and laughter and bustling streets was a burning nostalgia in him.

Arsène, though very young, dimly knew these things, for he had immense intuition of a shrewd rather than a subtle kind. He tried to be indifferent, and scornful, but he was excited, nevertheless. He had the soul of an adventurer, and the peace of quietness of his rural life had begun to gall him, and he was frequently conscious of a loneliness that the presence of his gentler brother did nothing to dispel. He knew that in a moment the Archbishop and his father would discover him, waiting there, and that again the Archbishop would pat him on the head, and sigh, smilingly, over him.

Now, in his dream, he was waiting there. But all at once, the dream began to darken, the hot air to chill. A great terror seized him. Some Horror was approaching through the yew walk. He could not move. He could only tremble and try to move legs paralyzed and heavy with nightmare. The Horror was coming closer. He heard the tolling of a mighty bell, slow and deathly. It was the tolling for the dead. Now a wind blew, violent and frightfully cold. It blew through his body, but aroused fire in his flesh, rather than chill. He struggled against the incubus, but he could not move. He cried out. He heard the murmuring voices, closer to him, and he shrieked aloud. And woke.

His first consciousness was of immense pain, flaming and enveloping. He had a faint memory that his screaming voice had been hoarse and painful. His throat was swollen, choking with phlegm, transfixed with burning blades of steel. His right arm, when he tried to move it convulsively in his extremity, could not be lifted. Darkness and sparks of red lights floated before his eyes.

So intense had been his memory, and his nightmare, that he expected to see his father's face, and the countenance of the Archbishop when he could see clearly. But, by wavering candlelight, he saw old François's concerned features bent over him, the shadow of a pale female face, and the faces of two strangers, one an old man, and the other young. The memory of recent events had not yet risen to the surface of his consciousness. He could only stare blindly, out of his fever, his breath struggling with agony in his tortured throat. Then, dimly, he remembered François Grandjean, and the girl, Cecile. He looked at them, speechlessly. He was still lying on the straw pallet in the miserable kitchen, and he was alternately deathly cold and flaming hot.

"The wounds are well enough," murmured the strange old man. "You have done excellently, François."

"Thank you, dear abbé," said François. "But it is the throat that disturbs me. He woke before dawn, yesterday, delirious and fevered, unaware of his surroundings. I thought it his wounds, but when I heard his crying voice, I knew it was some disease that had seized him. He became rapidly more ill, and that is why I called you, knowing your skill in these matters."

Arsène heard these words as from a tremendous distance, so that they had a hollow echo in his ears. They thought him still delirious. He saw the old men, and the young one, move aside. The girl, in her poor garments, knelt beside him, and applied some unguent to his throat on a rag. It stung, and it smelled vilely. He struggled to move, to speak, and his voice was the voice of a stricken crow. He saw the girl's young face, shrinking but compassionate, and very beautiful. She was only a child, but she understood suffering, and her expression was mature with grief.

"We must lift him and carry him to Cecile's bed. A poor bed, but better than this pallet," said François. "He cannot remain here, on the cold floor, with his fever. Would you consider him dying, abbé?"

The old abbé hesitated, looked sorrowfully at the stricken man. His face became anxious. "It is in the hands of God," he murmured. "You say you do not know his name, or his condition?"

"No. I have told you how he came to be here. But, it is evident that he is not of our kind. His garments, his sword, his manner of speaking. He is a great gentleman, of some sort. He told me his name is Arsène, but would say nothing else. One can understand his suspicions, and reserve."

The old abbé sighed. "Have you considered what might happen to you, and Cecile, if he died on your hands?"

"I have considered," replied François, calmly. "But I know no one to call, no one to identify him. And if there is danger to us, in sheltering him, in allowing him to die unknown, then we must trust to God. The Cardinal's guard was pursuing him. Inversely, should we call the Captain of the King's Musketeers? It is evident he is no musketeer, no soldier. He was a fugitive. How can we trust the King's men, then? Would they be kinder to a Huguenot gentleman, though it is evident that he is one? I know nothing about him."

"He may be a criminal," said the abbé, with hesitation.

François shook his head, but he said: "And, if so, must we throw a dying man into the gutter? Suffering has call upon our compassion, no matter the sufferer."

"You humble me, François," said the abbé with humility. "But I was thinking of you, my friend."

The three men, the old and the young, lifted Arsène in their arms. At this moment, he screamed again in his agony. They bore him to Cecile's chamber, and laid him on her bed. He became faintly conscious that they had removed his garments, that he was wearing a coarse white shirt, and that his legs were bare. He must have swooned again, for when he opened his eyes he was conscious of wet hot cloths being applied to his swollen and choking throat. The old abbé was ministering to him, and the girl stood beside him, a steaming iron pot in her hands into which the abbé kept dipping his cloths.

"I trust he has nothing contagious," said François, who stood at the foot of the bed.

"We must only pray," said the abbé, sighing. "But I have seen little children die of this, strangling. He has a young man's strength, however."

Arsène's icy feet became aware that a hot comforting stone lay between them. He was shaken by chill, consumed by fire. His toes eagerly sought the comfort of the stone. They had piled blankets, tattered and dusty, upon him.

"No one must guess at his presence in your house," said the abbé. "I know a physician, but in this case we can trust no one. We must do what we can for him, and pray for him."

François was holding a candle. It was night. The candlelight flickered over the leprous ceiling with its cracked plaster, and the dripping walls. The abbé continued his ministrations. Arsène, overcome with weakness and nausea, closed his eyes, which ached abominably. He gave himself up to sole consciousness of his throat, which seemed to be closed inexorably. His breath struggled to reach his lungs, struggled to leave it. He could hear the frantic laboring of his smothered heart. There were twining ropes in his throat, and he tried to cough them loose. He tasted blood in his mouth.

"I am dying," he thought, with complete detachment. His mother would be overcome. Ah, no, his mother, the pretty Sabina, was dead, these ten years, of grief and loneliness. Would his father, that lying, terrified hypocrite, be grief-stricken? Or would he feel a welcome, if miserable, relief? Relief that he would be called upon for no more frenzied concealment, for hasty falsehoods, for placating and pleading and promising? Arsène smiled to himself, with scornful compassion. He had been a burden, a strain, upon his father, who still slavishly adored him. Now, his death would be a release from terror. But he would grieve. At the thought of that womanish sorrow, Arsène's compassion lost its overtone of contempt, and became sad and regretful. He had never felt sadness for his father before. He did not think of his brother, Louis, at all.

Now, all at once, he was alone, and there was only a peculiar grating sound in the dank chamber. It was some moments before he knew it was his own breathing. The stone was hot against his feet. The pain was a little less in his throat. He fell into a deep sleep.

CHAPTER IV

HE AWOKE to such profound weakness that he thought, for a horrible moment, that he was paralyzed. There was a nervelessness in his body, a numbness, which terrified him even before he opened his eyes. He tried to speak, but there was only a faint fluttering in his throat, from which, however, pain had blessedly departed.

There was a milky film over his vision, not to be dispelled for several moments after consciousness. But at last the film began to lighten, to move aside, and he saw clearly.

He was still lying on the young Cecile's bed, in the windowless miserable chamber with its stained cracked walls and stone floor. But from the front chamber there came a shaft of brilliant yellow light, in which floated sparkling dust-motes. The shutters had been removed from the window, with its diamond-shaped little wedges of glass, and the sun streamed through it, fretted with sharp black lines. The air was warm, and very still. He heard the far and unfamiliar crying of a fishmonger in the narrow street outside, and the rumble of a cart's wheels over the cobbled stones. The weakness was heavy upon him, and he again tried to call out. His breath left his lips in a shrill rustle.

There was a movement in the lightless kitchen behind the bedchamber, and the young Cecile entered the room. He saw her quiet pale face, and her head, bound about with its braids of light-brown hair which were half-concealed by a white frilled cap. He saw the still nobility of her expression, sad and too mature for her age. She was tall, for a young girl, and her slenderness was almost emaciation. But she moved with dignity, and when she smiled her small teeth were bright between the rosy outlines of her soft lips. She wore a black neat bodice, tight and smooth across the high and immature outline of her pretty breasts, and a full black skirt which slipped back at the instep to show her little

27

foot in its rough shoe. Her dress, her demureness, her soft manner of walking, were all the mark of a servant girl, a mark he recognized.

She came to his bedside, and laid her cool hand on his head. He felt its callouses and roughness, and he winced involuntarily. The girl looked down at him, without fear or respect, and fully, with her deep blue eyes. This antagonized him, and his whisper was abrupt:

"I have been ill?"

If she marked his tone, and the cold arrogance of his eyes, she was not disturbed. She smiled again.

"Yes, Monsieur. Very ill. I have nursed you for fourteen days."

He was silent. Now he vaguely recalled nightmare nights of pain and fever, drifting with black and red shadows, and, always in them, always ministering to him in them, this quiet steadfast girl. It was her hand which had held the pewter cup brimming with cold water to his lips. It was her touch, gentle and sure, which had soothed him, and her strong young hands which had moved his body from its hot trough of pain to a cooler spot on the coarse white sheet. He thought of the sleepless nights she must have spent, after days of drudgery; he thought of the score of unpleasant tasks she must have performed for him, all full of nastiness and danger to herself. It was evident she was only a servant, but she did not know him, and had ministered to him devotedly, a stranger, a fugitive, and nameless. Why? But, ah, certainly, she and her grandfather must have known he was no vagabond, from the evidences of his sword, the remnants of his rich clothing, and his manner and voice. His mind, only lately ridden of fever, was still preternaturally sharp.

She looked down upon him, watching intently, and a thin beam of light lay on her cheek, and brightened her hair to braided gold. Her intensity increased. All at once she seemed to be reading his thoughts as clearly as though he had spoken them aloud. She flushed, but her face was still calm. She returned the cold hardness of his regard without flinching, but her own eyes became proud and a little angered.

However, she said: "The fever has passed. The abbé has said you are convalescent, and need only nursing. I shall do what I can for you, Monsieur, when I return at night from my work."

She turned away from the bed, and from a wooden bench she lifted his britches. Under them lay his sword and his torn white shirt. He saw the studs in the shirt, jewelled and brilliant in the shaft of sunlight. She thrust her hand into the pocket of his breeches, and drew out his silken purse, which he had forgotten.

She approached the bed again, the purse in her hand. He was surprised at the look on her face, hard and still, the sharp light in her blue eyes. She laid the purse near his nerveless hand.

"Monsieur," she said, calmly, "my grandfather has given you of all he had. That is almost nothing. He has deprived himself, for your benefit, of the little food he can afford, the little milk and wine, the bread to soak in them. He has bought you unguents for your wounds, and salve to help rub away your fever. He is old and feeble. And good. Most excessively good."

For a moment her hard expression softened into one of uncontrollable sadness. Then it tightened again, and she met his eyes with a look amazingly like contempt.

"You came to this house, unbidden and threatening. We have taken you in, hidden you, nursed you, dying with weariness though we were, and afraid of every sound. We have kept tallow candles burning at your bedside, and sat with you, controlling you with our strength while you threshed on my bed, and shouted in your delirium. What we have done for you has been done without hope of reward, and only with the wish that we be not punished for it." She paused, looked at him with penetrating straightness, and resumed, still quietly, and with heightened contempt and impatience:

"We owed you nothing. I have demurred with my grandfather, but he has a gentle heart, which pities even a wounded dog in the gutter. You came from the gutter into this house, did you not, Monsieur?"

He had been listening, amazed at her effrontery and impudence. A servant girl, whom even the law hardly regarded as a human being, a creature to be enslaved and beaten when uttering an impertinent word, or when daring to lift its eyes! But she was not only impudent, she presumed to look into his own eyes without fear, and with frigid disdain.

Then, in spite of his weakness, and his outrage, he could not refrain from smiling. But she did not answer his smile. She thrust the purse closer to his hand.

"There are fifteen golden crowns in your purse, Monsieur. I counted them the night you came. None has been touched. But now you need good meat, much milk, and delicacies, if you are to get well as rapidly as possible. We cannot afford them. It is you, Monsieur, who must make the choice between a rapid or a painfully slow convalescence. I beg of you to make the more sensible choice, for we shall the sooner be rid of the danger of your presence, and the exertion of your care."

Arsène was more and more amused and full of curiosity. His cold and trembling fingers fumbled with the purse. Then he paused, and looked up at the girl, who waited, her hands folded calmly before her. He saw that her blue eyes were full of stern bitterness.

"My grandfather," she said, coldly, "would ask you for nothing. He would be stricken to know of my conversation with you. But my grandfather is a gentle old child, and he must be protected, from, you, and from himself. That is clear, Monsieur?"

She opened the purse, and poured the golden coins over his fingers. Her smooth pale cheek was flushed now. Arsène laughed, and his laugh was hardly a murmur, weak and struggling.

He whispered, with mocking irony: "Mademoiselle, you are too good. I am not ungrateful, however. I recognize in you a lady of excellent sense. Take all of this money, and do with it as you wish. I shall ask no accounting."

If he thought to goad her, he failed. She picked up the coins and the purse, and calmly deposited them in the pocket of her skirt. Then, briskly, she shook up the pillow under him, holding up his head firmly in her left hand. He felt her young strength. She ran her hands under his body without embarrassment, smoothing the sheet, and pulling the tattered quilts into place. Then she went into the kitchen, returned with a bowl of soup. She sat down on the edge of the bed, and put the bowl to his lips, again lifting his head in the hollow of her arm.

He looked up into her stern young face, with its firm pink lips and the blue eyes, which were so deeply and beautifully set in large deep sockets. Her expression was stern and repressed.

But he would not drink for a moment. He smiled up at her, and shook his head.

"No, Mademoiselle, I cannot drink with such a face bent over me. Parbleu! Such a face would give a well man a fever."

She looked down at him with young hard exasperation, and pressed the bowl to his lips. "Monsieur," she said, sternly, "it is nearly six o'clock. I am very late. You will please

30

drink, and save me displeasure from my lady." She added: "That is the least you can do for me."

He drank, obediently, with an exaggerated air of meekness. Once or twice he choked, for she poured too hastily, as though wishing to be rid of him. Her eyes looked not at him, but at the lengthening beam of sunlight on the stone floor.

The soup was hot and thin, tasting of mutton and onions. He felt strength returning to him. She laid his head back on the pillow, not too gently. She stood up.

"I shall buy good wine for you, tonight, better wine than we have given you before," she said, ironically. "And there will be white bread, and butter, and perhaps a rabbit from the market."

She went into the kitchen again, returned with an empty bowl, some slices of cut black bread, and a jug of wine. She poured the wine into the bowl.

"Not the fare to which you are doubtless accustomed, Monsieur. But it will have to serve until I return."

She caught up a black cloak from the foot of the bed, threw it over her shoulders. He lifted his hand, feebly.

"May I ask," he said, in his weak voice, "why you have done all this for me, Mademoiselle, when it is so evident that it is done unwillingly?"

She had reached the doorway between the two rooms, and there paused, looked back at him over her shoulder. Her face expressed both sadness and scorn.

"There is no thanks to me, Monsieur. I despise what you are, and have no heart for you. It is to my grandfather that you must give your gratitude, for I obey him in everything, though he is an old child, and defenseless."

She left him then, but she heard his faint sick laughter, as though he were greatly amused. Her face flushed, and she muttered something as she closed the door behind her, and locked it.

He must have slept, for when he awoke the bedchamber was in total darkness, and the room beyond it was flooded with a gray dim light. His senses more acute, now, he could discern the acrid odor of dust. The silence pressed against his ears in mournful insistence.

But he was more conscious of urgently returning strength, and was able to sop pieces of bread in the bitter wine and eat them. A vile concoction, but he was surprised at his own voracious enjoyment. These poor people had given him of their best. This, then, was their best, this dreadful habitation, this miserable starveling food.

He lay back on his musty pillow, meditating. It came to him, with a childlike amazement, that millions of Frenchmen lived like this, millions of anonymous souls who knew nothing of the Tuileries and the Louvre, of the Court and the theatre, of ball-rooms and châteaus, of perfumes and jewels and gilded coaches and great gardens cool and indigo under the sun. They knew nothing but guttered streets, filth, starvation, pain and disease. But surely he must have known! He had not been that completely stupid.

Yes, I have known, he thought, with wonder, yet I did not know. It was because I did not care. To me, as to many others, France meant the Court, the intrigues of scented rogues and cavaliers and statesmen and Jesuits, country estates and laughter in candle lighted midnight, exciting wars, gallantry, laces and women. These millions of wretches, dumb and driven, silent and oppressed, were not France. They were not human beings. They lived only to serve us, seigneurs and priests, rich rascals and smooth liars. They carried no swords, made no legs, were no connoisseurs of excellent wine, engaged in no artful plots, were authorities on no fashion, conspired in no wars, wore neither lace nor lacquered boots, read no foul novels nor made gay epigrams. In short, they existed only as dark unmoving sea upon which floated our carved barques and tinted sails. A dark unmoving sea! Nay, perhaps a dark motionless chaos waiting for the lightning!

Even as a Huguenot, vehement, contemptuous and violent, he had not thought of the masses of the French people. Like all his class, his caste, the people had not existed. The people who were France.

Cardinal, le Duc de Richelieu, had been a frequent visitor to his re-established father in his hotel on the Champs-Elysées. Arsène remembered that subtle and satanic countenance, with the eyes that seemed both supernaturally fiery and inhumanly cold. The man fascinated him, filled him with wild but cunning hatred, and he had watched his father's servility, his nervous ingratiating smiles, with scorn and detestation. He, Arsène, had sat in smiling and courteous silence, and had listened. He knew that Monsieur the Cardinal suspected and disliked him. Worse, he knew that the Cardinal held him negligible, a young man of crude young passions, not to be taken seriously. (But how much did Monsieur the Cardinal know of him?)

There had been some discussion, but Arsène could not

remember its elegant careless phrases. But he did remember one utterance from the Cardinal:

"Men do not make castes. Mankind tends to sink and rise to certain strata by the force of inherent endowment, given by the mysterious will of God."

Unwillingly, Arsène had acknowledged to himself the acuteness of his observation. Now, as he lay in Cecile's bed, he was enraged by his former simplicity. He was amazed by his juvenility. In one phrase, the Cardinal had disposed of millions of lightless and hopeless people, had discounted the dark and moveless chaos, had ignored the faint sound of the distant earthquake. (But he did not know then how much of this new rage was rooted in his hatred and fear of the Cardinal.) He was shaken by new revelations. His Protestantism had been for himself and others like him, a materialistic creed springing not from passionate indignation, but from hatred of the wily and the subtle, the superstitious and the absurd. In its essence, it was revolt against his foolish father, and a loathing for lies. Moreover, it had become, for him, an exclusive doctrine, not concerned with religion or dogma, but a social doctrine pertaining only to himself and others of his kind. It was a way of life, suited to his temperament. It was a clean, hard emancipation from sickly elegance and intrigue.

Now, dimly (and not for a long time to become clear and powerful), he saw it as a liberation for all men, a liberation from slavery and oppression, from suffering and exploitation, from serfdom and starvation and cruelty. It was the coming-of-age of countless multitudes, bent under whips, sightless and tormented.

For the first time in his life he felt the stirrings of universal compassion, of impersonal anger and indignation. His was a temperament shrewd, and by turns, cold and violent, reckless and cautious, loving adventure for its own sake, an adventurousness stemming from vengefulness. He remembered, with some humiliation, that when he had thought of the people at all, it had been with a contempt and loathing as great as the Cardinal's and the Jesuits'. So had the German princes, embracing Protestantism, felt. Their Protestantism had not sprung from indignation at the misery of the people. It had come from their temperamental dislike for restriction and supervision and commands for obedience, and forced tribute to Rome. It was a personal revolt, and had nothing at all to do with compassion for their serfs and the dumb anguish of their people. It was the revolt of simple and violent Teutonic minds, disgusted with black intrigue and the wiliness of the Latins, against which their childlike simplicity and crudeness had no defenses. The rebellion of great children, who hated French and Italian diplomacy, so subtle and adult, which they could not understand, and, not understanding, could only distrust and fear.

His mind, sharpened by its recent fever, and now ascendent because of the weakness of his strong body, rose up like a wind full of passionate and fiery shapes. His was not the philosophical or meditative mind. Rather it had been a quick and energetic mind, ebullient and sensual, yet calculating and hard. It had never known any spirituality, any poesy or gentleness and intuition. Robust and active, it had delighted in movement and danger. (But under it, as yet unknown to himself, there had been the tides of justice and logic and disgust for falsehood.) He had despised almost everything, yet his life had been full of the gusts of his hearty laughter, and his lustfulness. Kind yet arrogant, selfish yet full of the potentialities for love, egotistic, yet humorous, greedy, yet at times abnormally generous and openhanded, he had found existence colorful and exciting, full of friends and gay companionship. Among those associated with him in a dangerous plotting, were men of brilliant eyes and noble words and self-sacrifice. Only a few there were, and he had felt only disdain and humor for them. A turn of the wheel, and they would have been enthusiastic Jesuits, he was certain. His nature made him distrust all fanatics, whether they were good or evil.

Now he felt in himself the first vague but gigantic shadows of conscience, pity and impersonal fury. They were only shadows, however, and like shadows, the bright sharp sun of reality might still disperse them. He was conscious that his heart was beating rapidly, and his weakness increasing as his mind strengthened and stood astride his emaciated body.

He thought of François Grandjean and Cecile. He was still full of simplicity, and in his new enthusiasm he fatuously thought that all the people were like these. His was a nature so emotional that impersonal stability and calmness were to be a lesson hardly learned. He had prided himself on a certain cynical detachment, and it would have humiliated him to have discovered that he really did not possess this detachment.

The rooms were very dark now. He heard the faint grating of a key, and saw a small bent shadow enter the outer chamber. There was something cautious and silent about its movement, and he waited, curiously. He heard the striking of flint against steel, then the light of a candle bloomed suddenly in the dusk. He saw that his visitor was a very small, very old priest, bowed and shuffling. Faintly, he remembered having seen this priest in his fever, and having heard his soft voice.

Carrying the candle, the old abbé approached the bed-chamber. In the light, which he held high and timidly, his face was vividly illuminated. Arsène saw its ancient sad gentleness, its diffidence and childlikeness. There were the brown sunken eyes, the large Roman nose, the sweet tired mouth, all set in a gaunt and cavernous face like a death's-head. His sparse hair was silvery white, his garments coarse and patched. Yet, there was an heroic quality about him, steadfast and quiet.

But Arsène observed him with a rising of the loathing he felt for all priests, a loathing which was actually physical as at the approach of some noisome and disgusting creature, full of venom and noxiousness. He waited in silence while the abbé put the candle down upon a bare table near the bed. The old man approached the bed, bent over Arsène anxiously. And Arsène stared back at him, with his cold disgust sharp in his eyes, and his old contempt and aversion.

The abbé smiled. "Ah," he murmured, "we are much better today. We are conscious. That is well."

He stretched out his hand to feel the young man's fore-head, but Arsène jerked his head aside, wincing. The abbé stood there, stricken immobile, his hand still outstretched. Then, after a moment, he dropped his hand. His gentle smile was a trifle fixed, as though he were bewildered.

"I am well," said Arsène, in his hoarse, weak voice. (The foul and wily old priest, the stinking old vulture in carrion-clothes!)

"Yes," said the abbé, softly, "you are well. And this is because of the devotion and sleeplessness of your friends, and the goodness of God. There were hours when we could do nothing but pray, pray for a nameless and dying man." He paused, and smiled as though slightly ashamed: "I am afraid, though, that I was more concerned with the danger to my dear friends, than with you, Monsieur."

Arsène was silent. His eyes glowed contemptuously in the candlelight.

The abbé sat down on a bench, and studied the young man anxiously.

Arsène forced his voice to reach his lips, and he said, coldly: "Why are you here?"

The abbé sighed. "It is a promise I made to my friends, that after Vespers I would sit with you until one of them returned."

"That is not necessary," said Arsène, turning away his head.

The old man said nothing. Arsène was suddenly conscious of thirst. As if he had spoken, the abbé rose, went into the kitchen, and returned with a cup of cold water, which he held to Arsène's lips. Arsène drank. He glanced up over the rim of the cup, and was startled at the intense sweetness of the other's understanding smile. His antagonism, his loathing, subsided, involuntarily.

"You must sleep, my child," said the abbé. And Arsène slept.

CHAPTER V

ARSENE DREAMT that he was riding gaily in the rosy morning in the gardens of the Bois. Everything was still, crystal sharp and bright, and there was no one but he abroad. He saw the long flung shadows of the sparkling trees, heard the poignantly sweet murmurings of the birds. He felt the soft morning wind in his face, heavy with the odor of thousands of flowers. He thought to himself: I have never been so happy. But what caused his happiness, he did not know.

His horse cantered merrily along the silent, sun-fretted path. A branch brushed his plumed hat. He removed that hat, let the wind blow through his hair. He began to sing, aware of his youth and his joy. The blue sky, through the trees, glowed in turquoise squares and diamonds, melting into each other. How fresh and pure was the morning! This seemed a world apart from the corrupt Court, the dead scent of powder and fetid perfumes, the meaningless mirth and the evil eyes, the intrigues and the moribund elegance. It was a world of life, and the world of corpse-like postures and silken attitudinizing had existence only in death and night. "I am free," he cried, aloud, and the birds and the soft laughing wind murmured in reply: "Free! Free!"

But, as if the words held in themselves a spell, a frightful enchantment, the light fled from the land, the light darkened from the trees, the flowers, blinding and joyful in their color, lost all their tints and became gray as ashes. The fountains he had heard in the distance, singing and glittering as they fell into their marble bowls, suddenly became the menacing roar of cataracts of doom, loud and thunderous in the near distance. Now the wind blew cold as if roaring over frozen seas. The air, a moment ago so warm and silken, became icily bitter, with a smell in it as if it had come from burned cities. He felt the ground tremble under him; the trees bent, screamed, and leaves, suddenly withered and blighted, fell from the branches and spun in dry stinging whirlpools all about him. Dust rose, twisted into ropes of gray smoke, choked him. Everything was uproar, thunder, quaking, groaning and desolation. An enormous fear leapt into his heart; he looked about him in terror, expecting some awful destruction to leap upon him. He saw the aisles of the trees, shaken, and torn, bare as bones, and the long grass ran furiously before the gale.

He looked about, with dread, for the coming of murderous enemies. But he was all alone. And as he realized this, that no one else but he was in the midst of this horror of destruction and death and ruin, he was the more terrified. His horse stood under him, trembling, his head bowed.

And then, he heard a muttering, which was part of the whirlwind. It was some moments before he discerned that the muttering was that of thousands of hoarse voices, rising and falling, crying and shouting, threatening and dolorous. "Free!" they screamed. "Free! Free!" A multitude of voices, a world of cries, springing up from the bowels of the earth, rushing through the twisting aisles of the trees, leaping downwards from the sky, echoing back from space, blowing in the wind and shrieking through the fountains and the thunder. Then Arsène could hear nothing but those voices, and his terror became like death in his body.

Arsène felt a tremendous shaking under and about him, as though the universe shuddered on its pillars and in its orbits. The air was darkening; it had become dusky and choking, as though the earth was rolling in smoke. "Free!" cried the countless voices, and now there was a stern and deadly sound in them, inexorable and appalling. A universe of voices, sweeping implacably through sky and through the world. Now the black sky reddened, as if reflecting the light of a hundred flaming cities, and the whirlwind increased and there was a hissing quality in it.

"Doom!" thought Arsène, and waited for annihilation. The sky, scarlet with flames, brightened savagely above him, in the abysmal blackness of the night.

"Free!" bellowed the voices, triumphantly, and now he heard the rushing of millions of released feet, though he could see nothing. But he felt the breath of countless armies and multitudes hot in his face, panting, searing with destruction.

"It is the end," thought Arsène.

Then, as he thought this, he was no longer afraid. A frightful joy leapt in him, and a stern exultant anger. He flung up his arms. "Free!" he shouted, his voice mingling with all the other voices. This was not death upon him, but the furious prelude to morning, the storm that presaged a calm, the ruin and chaos that came before life.

He awoke. Even while he opened dazed eyes, he could hear the last echoes of the thunderous voices, drifting far into space among the stars. Then there was silence, but his eardrums rang, and the silence was the more intense after the chaotic and overwhelming uproar.

The dream was more real than what he saw as his eyes opened. It was very dark now, and in the candlelight near him sat the old abbé, crouched in his chair, his withered lips moving, his eyes closed. His rosary dripped slowly through his gnarled fingers, and there was a look of solemn ecstasy on his face. Arsène watched him. He could not feel his old contempt. Suddenly, the ecstasy on the old man's face subsided, and his lips ceased their moving. The rosary slipped into his tattered bony knee, and lay there, like black tears. Now his face took upon it an expression of terrible sorrow and exhaustion. He sighed deeply, bent his head. One by one tears crept from under the lids of his closed eyes, and each tear was a globule of pain and suffering, shining piteously in the candlelight. He clasped his hands to his breast convulsively, and the gesture was unbearably moving, for it betrayed despair and hopelessness and immeasurable sadness.

Arsène did not stir on his straw bed. To have allowed the old man to become aware that his naked torment has been seen by alien and unsympathetic eyes would have been inexcusable. But Arsène wondered, with a strange pity. He had known, mysteriously, that this sorrow, and these tears, came from no fanatical meditation, no mystic contemplation of the forgotten tortures of Christ. It was not the gesture of priests, removed from men, not the formal outpouring of deliberately induced rapture. These were the tears of an old man, burdened and suffering, the tears of earth and grief and bitter pain, the tears of all men, acrid as gall and cleansed of mysticism, and purely unconscious of God.

He weeps, thought Arsène. He weeps as a man, and there is no faith, no hope, in his weeping. It is as though reality had become, to him, more exigent than superstition, and had made it impossible for him to pray, had swept away all belief. His pity became stronger; it ran through his veins, like painful blood through paralyzed limbs. Never had he felt such pity, and the remembrance of his dream mixed with it.

Arsène closed his eyes. He stirred his weak body deliberately on the bed, so that it creaked. He muttered, sighed,

39

imitating the movements and sounds of an awakening man. He groaned, faintly. He opened his eyes again. The old abbé was bending over him with his sweet smile, anxious and solicitous. On his sunken cheeks gleamed the thin streaks of rivulets of pain. His hand, feeble yet kind, pressed itself on Arsène's brow. So gentle was the smile, so calm, as the old man satisfied himself that there was no return of fever, that Arsène would have doubted what he had seen had it not been for the marks of the tears on the old abbé's face.

Arsène returned the smile. "I am well," he repeated.

"Yes," said the abbé. "And it is time for your broth, my child."

He said this, not unctuously, in the manner of priests, but with loving sincerity. He crept from the bedchamber, and once Arsène saw him grasp the lintel of the doorway, as if to sustain himself. He returned with a pewter bowl of steaming soup, and a pewter spoon. He sat beside Arsène and dipped the spoon in the broth. He smiled again, and Arsène was painfully moved. He allowed himself to be fed, docilely. Moment by moment, he was conscious of the return of his youthful strength. The abbé did not speak, but he was openly pleased at Arsène's appetite.

Arsène lay back on his musty pillows, life tingling in his body.

"Why have you, all of you, done this for me, a stranger out of the night?" he asked, and his voice was full of unaccustomed gratitude.

The old abbé was truly surprised. He gazed at Arsène incredulously.

"That is an odd question, my son," he said. "You were wounded and a fugitive. You were sickened. What else could we have done?"

Arsène considered this, then he frowned, cunningly. Ah, but you all knew that I was not some homeless wretch, he thought. There was my sword, and my pistol, my garments and my money. These are evidences of wealth. But, had I been a beggar, perhaps you would not have done these things for me.

He glanced swiftly at the abbé. The old man's face had become stern and dignified, as he watched Arsène. He had clearly read the young man's thoughts.

"No," he said, quietly. "It is not that we suspected you were not of us, but a great lord. Moreover, we knew that you were in danger, and that in taking you in, we endangered our lives. François told me that the musketeers of Monsieur the Cardinal were searching for you, and that he hid you."

Arsène was both embarrassed and ashamed. Then he said: "And you, a priest, were not disturbed by the fact that His Holy Eminence's men were seeking me, with bared swords?"

The old abbé sighed, and he glanced away. The terrible sorrow sharpened again on his face, but he said nothing. Finally, he whispered: "You were a fugitive, and wounded, hunted and desperate."

Arsène's shame increased. There was some mystery concerned in this. He was sure of it, from the expression of the old man's sorrowful eyes.

"I thank you all, from the depths of my heart," he said, gently. "And I shall not forget it, I promise you."

The abbé's face became stern and dignified again. "We ask nothing of you, Monsieur, but that you regain your health quickly, and leave this place. You are a constant danger to us."

"Do not fear," replied Arsène, with some contempt. "I assure you that even if the Cardinal's rascals knew of my real identity they would lift no finger against me." But he wondered, cynically, if this were entirely true.

"Even if they knew you were a Huguenot?" asked the priest, with a direct look.

"Ah, then, you know," smiled Arsène, looking at him keenly. "And even that does not disturb you? You do not, as all priests do, hate Protestantism?"

The abbé rose, picked up the bowl and spoon, and carried it into the kitchen. He came back, and sat again on the bench near Arsène. He regarded him straightly, and his sunken eyes shone in the candlelight.

"Nothing is evil which makes men think," he said. "And a sword cuts away gangrened flesh. A fountain of cold water can wash away corruption."

Arsène was perplexed, for there was no subtlety in him. The old man's words annoyed him with their ambiguity. Ambiguity, he knew, was the very essence of the priesthood, the chant of the deceivers, and the liars.

He said, somewhat childishly: "I am your sworn enemy."

The old man regarded him with genuine surprise. Then he began to smile, as at a child, with true mirth.

"No man is my enemy," he said, "unless I admit him to be so."

"That is a mystical sophistry," remarked Arsène, with disdain.

"No," said the priest, "it is a living truth. No man can hurt

41

another, unless that other admits his enemy's capacity to hurt him. There is no evil if we deny its existence, there is no menace to the soul unless that soul has conceded the reality of evil."

"And you refuse to believe there is evil?" asked Arsène, with pitying scorn and amusement.

He was again ashamed at the sight of the old man's sudden sadness. The abbé glanced away and fixed his mournful eyes on space.

"I am frail, and old, and sinful," he whispered. "Had I true faith, I would know that evil lives only in the imagination of men, in the corrupt hearts of the enemies of God. God has created no wicked thing, therefore, good is the only reality. How can one, then, believe in the existence of evil?"

His face brightened, became suddenly ecstatic, as though some rapturous secret had been revealed to him by another voice. His emaciated frame appeared to expand, as a prisoner's body expands after being released from chains. Heroic joy appeared in his eyes, shone like the reflection of the sun. He turned upon Arsène the full beam of his transformed face.

"My son," he said, in a shaking voice, "you have done a miraculous thing to me!"

Arsène, the unsubtle, was amazed, and regarded the old abbé suspiciously. Was he making game of him? He knew the tricks of priests. Moreover, he felt himself a dull lout in the presence of a man of full stature. This did nothing to restore his good humor.

Then he had another thought. Vaguely, he recalled that often in the day there had been another here, a young man like himself, moving about with bowls and basins and administering to him, and washing him. He had a faint memory of a thin taut countenance, of considerable attenuated beauty. He looked at the abbé. The unearthly light had died on his face, leaving a steadfast and radiant peace.

"There was another here, at times," said Arsène, irritated at the other's rapturous detachment. "Who is he?"

The old man looked at him, bemused. Then another light came to his eyes, fond and sweet.

"That was my nephew, a young man, from Toulouse," he said. "A student. He keeps my poor house, and I teach him what I know. He is also a poet." He hesitated, became saddened. "His mother, my sister, died of starvation. There was a drought on their land, and my nephew came to me."

He looked again into space, with a mournful sigh.

Arsène watched him with interest, and unusual curiosity. This poor old man reminded him of the wretched curés of more wretched villages, creatures whom he had not considered human beings. He marvelled at himself, that in the past humanity had seemed to him, and others like him, the exclusive attribute of the gracious and the cultured, the noble and the aristocratic. Beyond this perfumed and sophisticated circle had lived a vast world of sub-beings, starving, oppressed and blighted, the concern of priests only. Yet, today, he saw humanity in these poor wretches, the stamp of his own race in their tortured lineaments, his own capacity for life and joy and suffering reflected in their eyes.

If this is so, he mused, then something is most frightfully wrong. There was something here that called for the vengeance of heaven, the compassion of saints, the retribution of a whole world. Like Genghis Khan, the powerful had spread their banquet cloths upon the dying bodies of the helpless, and had feasted loudly above the groaning. But surely, there was a day of liberation approaching, and let those beware who stood in the path of the bloody deluge. He heard again, as in his dream, the shrieking of a multitude of voices, the rushing of millions of liberated feet. When that day came, there would be no mercy for the oppressors, for the smilers in ducal châteaus, for the mitred despoilers of the people, for thrones and kings.

The abbé saw the darkening and sparkling of the sick man's eyes as they were fixed unseeingly upon him. He exclaimed: "I have tired you. You must rest, my child."

He brought a bowl of cool water and washed Arsène's hot face and hands, drying them on a coarse clean rag.

"I have been thinking," said Arsène, with a smile. "And I assure you, mon abbé, that that is a peculiar thing for me to do."

But the abbé did not smile. He stood, with the bowl in his hand, and he looked down at the young man with a strange, grave face. His brown eyes were bright and stern. But he said nothing. He carried the bowl and cloth into the kitchen, returned. He sat on the bench and gazed at the candle as it burned, and he seemed to have forgotten Arsène. His wrinkled hands lay palm-up on his knees, in an attitude of weariness and desolation, his shoulders were bent and bony under his worn garments. There was infinite patience in his attitude, but bitter grief, also.

"What is your name, mon abbé?" asked Arsène, after a long while, and in a voice unusually gentle.

The old man started. He looked at Arsène, bemused.

"I am André Mourion, Monsieur," he said, at last, as from a dream. "And this is my parish. A poor one, a lost one, but I do what I can."

He sighed, deeply, and the sound was like the echo of weeping.

"The young girl, Cecile," said Arsène. "She is a maid-servant?"

At the mention of that name, the old priest smiled as though at the sight of a sudden sunbeam.

"Yes, Monsieur. Or, rather, she assists the seamstresses in the household of Madame de Tremblant. The lady has ten daughters, and there is constant sewing. Cecile has told me that one of them, the Mademoiselle Clarisse, is betrothed, and soon to marry."

He paused, in surprise, for Arsène's face had turned a deep crimson at the mention of these names.

"You know the family?" exclaimed the abbé.

Arsène's countenance increased in redness. "Slightly," he murmured. "But only slightly."

He turned his head aside, away from the scrutiny of the other. He was intensely confused. He had not thought of the pretty blond Clarisse since the night of his coming to this hovel—Clarisse, who was his betrothed. He saw her vividly in his mind's eyes, delicate and fastidious, with a dainty body like a graceful stem, and a mischievous and vivacious face all petulance and gaiety. He saw her flaxen curls and her brilliant blue eyes, her little white hands and smooth white shoulders. He heard her high flute of a voice, full of naughty laughter, and her capricious and endearingly imperious gestures. She was the third daughter of Madame de Tremblant, that vicious and corrupt dame, and the only one with great beauty, though the others, poor languishing creatures, were comely enough. It had been a fine occasion for Madame de Tremblant, to betroth Clarisse to the son of Armand de Richepin, Marquis de Vaubon, so lately restored to favor in the sight of King and Church.

An uneasy thought seized Arsène. He turned his head abruptly and stared at the abbé.

"Does Cecile know the name of the gentleman to whom Mademoiselle de Tremblant is betrothed?"

The abbé shook his head. "No, I think not." He was more

surprised than ever. Then he had a thought which made his worn face brighten.

He said: "The little Cecile, herself, is betrothed to my nephew, Henri Chalon. Madame de Tremblant has promised to engage him as one of her footmen very soon. Madame has been gracious enough to look upon Cecile with favor, and having learned of her coming marriage, has endeavored to soften the path of these poor children. Cecile, then, and Henri, will live at the residence of Madame, and the arrangement will be excellent."

"What an occupation for a poet!" murmured Arsène, with indifferent ridicule.

The abbé gazed at him with dignity. "François Villon was only a vagabond," he said, with gentle reproof.

Arsène thought of the young Cecile's noble and beautiful countenance, her distinguished bearing and sweet voice. And he thought of Madame de Tremblant, the foul old harridan, to whom nothing was sacred, and all things were evil. He was affronted, and angered, and then again, he wondered at himself. This was very strange! He had always been amused by Madame de Tremblant, the plotter, the gay and the shrewd, confidante and great friend of Her Majesty, the Queen, and arrogant mistress of ceremonies, full of intrigue and noisomeness. No Court affair had been complete without her shrill and ribald supervision, her fans and her attitudes, her scalding jokes and sly epigrams. Even the King's mistresses were afraid of her tongue, and the Cardinal, it was said, regarded her with amusement and appreciation. She knew everything, and also knew when to hold her tongue. To acquire her enmity was the nightmare of every ambitious courtier and corrupt lady. It was even rumored that she was feared in London, because of her influence, and that many costly and secret treasures found their way into her house as gifts from the British ambassador. Buckingham, himself, on those occasions when it was safe for him to appear in Paris, frequently was her guest.

She frankly prided herself on her greediness, her treachery, her power, and her viciousness. A widow, soon after the birth of her last daughter, she had inherited enormous wealth and estates from her father and her husband, the Comte de Tremblant, who had, in his time, also been the favorite of Church and Majesty. Though nearly fifty, she was still beautiful, still arrogant, still lewd and conscienceless, and her toilettes were the wonder and envy even of the Queen herself. But she kept her daughters as immured as nuns, while she

45

scrutinized, coldly and shrewdly, all the eligible young gentlemen of the Court. There were many who would gladly have married any of the girls, for reasons of dowry and influence. The three oldest, including whom was Clarisse, were already betrothed, and the betrothals reflected Madame de Tremblant's perspicacity and genius.

Arsène contemplated all these things with intensity. He had lost himself in his thoughts. When he glanced up, he saw that the abbé was watching him with some uneasiness. He did not know that he had been scowling blackly.

"There is some pain?" suggested the abbé.

"No," replied Arsène, impatiently. But he was exhausted. Thought was so rare with him that it wearied him, as flaccid and unused muscles are wearied by unaccustomed exertion. Then, as he saw the abbé's perplexed anxiety, he was reminded of his father, who often regarded him like this, perturbed, waiting for explanation.

The two men stared at each other in silence. But Arsène saw only his father's thin dark face.

In all his careless life, he had felt only aversion, disdain, amusement and ennui for his father. Given more easily to hatred than affection, he had yet not truly hated Armand de Richepin, for no one can really hate the creature who adores one. Now, recalling his father, he felt the old pure amusement, the old indifferent disdain, but with them, he felt new pity, new affection, and concern.

Now Arsène knew that his father's terror was less for himself than for his son. He felt shame for his past cruelty, remembering less his father's amusing weaknesses, greed, avarice and ambition, and remembering more his love and devotion. He had tormented this poor creature, without any more provocation than his own selfish contempt and callousness.

He studied the abbé, his dark eyes narrowing and brightening. Could he trust this old man, who wore the habit of a detested hierarchy, the tattered livery of a pestilence? At the last, would not superstition be stronger than pity, and the slavery of a soul more potent than human compassion?

"Can I trust you, mon abbé?" he asked, abruptly.

Surprised, the abbé could only gaze at him, bewildered. Then he inclined his head with a kind of humble pride.

"I am an old man of many sins," André Mourion murmured, sadly. "But never to my own knowledge have I betrayed a single soul."

Arsène still hesitated, his eyes fixed dourly on the other.

There were so many difficulties to be considered, even beyond the possibility of betrayal by the priest. He considered them. The abbé watched him, seeing the somber coldness and suspicion of the young man's face, the hard darkness of his eyes, the impatient twitching of his grim mouth. During all the nights of nursing, he had felt close to this human creature, who had been suffering with complete abandon. In the presence of torment, death, pain and compassion, they had been only two men. Now, the old priest felt the withdrawal, the coldness, the caste, of this stranger, and saw the glance of a haughty and aristocratic eye, brutal and contemptuous. He was familiar with this glance from gilded carriages, along dusty highways, on crowded thoroughfares, a glance that consigned him and all other poor humanity to the limbo beyond humanity. He felt nothing but his old heavy despair and sorrow.

"Old man," said Arsène, and now his voice was in accord with his look, "if you betray me, I promise you worse than death, even if the foul Pope himself interceded for you, or protected you."

He paused, abruptly, for the abbé had begun to smile, irresistibly, as at the empty threats of a conceited child, pampered and unfeeling. But there was sadness in his smile, also, and complete comprehension.

"Do not threaten me, Monsieur," he said, very gently. "I am afraid of no man, and fear nothing except man's wickedness and depravity and lack of heart."

There was such a simple sincerity in his voice, and such a weary rebuke, that Arsène was ashamed. Nevertheless, he said coldly: "Who can trust priests?"

He panted a little, in his exhaustion, but waved away the abbé's hand when it would seek to feel his forehead for fever.

"You must go on an errand for me, before the others return, and it must be a secret errand. You will go to the Hôtel du Vaubon, on the Champs-Élysees. There, you must ask for Pierre Brissons, a young footman. He will come to the gates. You will then tell him you come from me, and he will take you to my—to Monsieur le Marquis du Vaubon. To Monsieur le Marquis, you will say: 'I have come from one Arsène de Richepin—'"

He paused, and again fixed his penetrating and arrogant eyes on the abbé's face, and waited. The abbé stared at him, stepped back a pace or two. His mouth opened, and an expression of consternation and uncertainty grew momentarily deeper on the old man's face. But there was no fear upon it, no frightened awe. Once he glanced at the door, as if expecting the entrance of enemies. He moistened his dry and wrinkled lips, and looked directly at Arsène.

"You can clearly see," said Arsène, "that I need fear no one, not even your accursed Cardinal, himself."

There was boastfulness in his voice, but he was not certain of the truth of his own words. The Cardinal, the sinister and the subtle, the omnipotent and the never-sleeping, must surely know of the activities of Monsieur le Marquis du Vaubon's son, as he knew everything. There was hardly a man in Paris whose death he might desire more, but it would have to be an obscure and anonymous death for the sake of the great friend of the Cardinal, and the great friend of His Majesty.

Moreover, Arsène, despite the recent soul-moving revelations to which he had been subjected, could not so easily shake off the habits and the convictions of a lifetime. Consequently, he was annoyed by the abbé's lack of cringing, and his complete absence of fawning and eager adulation. He was too accustomed to the idea that the mission of the Church was to minister to and serve the powerful. He saw, to his irritation, that the abbé's sole concern was for the position of his poor friends, more precarious than ever.

"No one will be reproached," said Arsène, scowling. "How were you to know of my identity? You will tell that to Monsieur le Marquis, if he demands why he was not told before." He added, with impatience; "I need not tell you that Monsieur le Marquis, the close friend of the Cardinal, is my father."

"I know," said the abbé, in a low and trembling voice. He gazed at Arsène with mournful and intense eyes, the brownness in them like the shadow of bright sunlit water under bending ferns.

"You are not impressed," said Arsène, with a short laugh, and was immediately embarrassed.

The abbé was silent. He wrung his hands convulsively together.

"Speak briefly and quickly to Monsieur le Marquis," Arsène continued. "Tell him that it is to my interest that not even he know where I am hiding. Tell him I have commanded you not to speak of this. He is an impatient and nervous man, and you must not be cowed by his manner." He added: "And then, tell him I am recovering, that within a week I shall return home. He may be suspicious; he does not trust

48

priests more than I do, and you must impress on him your trustworthiness."

"You think he will believe me, Monsieur?"

"Most certainly." Arsène glanced at his sword, pointed to it. "Take this with you. My father will know, then, that you come from me. Ask him also for money for me." He laughed with sudden weak enjoyment. "Mademoiselle Cecile has made off with my money, and I am as destitute as a beggar—a very strange condition. You will also ask Monsieur the Marquis for a small bundle of garments for me, for I was forced to discard coat and cloak when I swam the Seine." He considered. "Tell my father that I was slightly wounded, but have now recovered." He touched the healing scar on his dark cheek, and ruefully glanced at his bandaged arm. "And that I must remain in hiding for some days longer. It will not be necessary to tell him that I have been ill, besides."

He looked at the abbé with vague astonishment. Never before had he sincerely considered his father's grief and anxiety. They had seemed foolish and petty emotions before, springing from a womanish nervousness and his father's chronic terror. He had even delighted, at times, in throwing his father into a frenzy of fear, for the mean pleasure of watching that contorted countenance and hunted eyes, and seeing the rippling shadows of apprehension on that pale and sweating face.

The abbé picked up the sword and held it in his hand. But he seemed not to see it, though he mechanically turned the hilt so that it caught fire from the candlelight. Arsène watched him curiously. Of what was the old man thinking? Then, as if the abbé had forgotten him, he left the room, walking with his enfeebled step.

Only when the abbé had gone did Arsène, cursing his carelessness, realize on what a dangerous errand he had sent his benefactor. Armand most probably would not trust him, out of his terror and cowardice. There was a strong possibility that he would order the priest seized. There was no predicting the hysterical reactions of this womanish man. And if he made his usual uproar in emergencies, there was no end to the hazardous possibilities. He might accuse the abbé of having murdered his son, of being an impostor, of endeavoring to rob him. He might scream denunciations, accusations, and the abbé might very well be dragged off to some prison den, there to die. All Paris might know within an hour, for Armand was not conspicuous for prudence and reticence. The only hope was that the abbé might find him in a mood of rare calmness, and that he might be convinced of his son's predicament. For there were others, in the Hôtel du Vaubon, who would easily believe, and dispatch a message to their diabolical master. In that event, murderers would be sent at once, quietly, to eliminate Arsène de Richepin, and throw his defaced body into the Seine, or bury it in some anonymous grave. Even in the event that the abbé was believed, he might be followed to this hovel, if the conversation were overheard.

"God!" muttered Arsène, "why did I have to have a fool and a woman for a father?"

His imagination, heightened by his recent illness, peopled the hovel with enemies within an hour, enemies coming secretly and silently, murdering him as he lay alone in his bed. The young girl, or her grandfather, might enter his chamber and find him weltering in his own blood, or worse, they might return during the sanguinary operations and be murdered in order to silence them forever.

It was strange, then, that this latter thought horrified the young man more than did the thought of his own death. It was frightful to contemplate that the only return he could give his benefactors was a swift and merciless death. He was intolerably alarmed, and started to his elbow, not even feeling the agony in his wounded arm. He did not have even his sword to protect him, and the old man and the girl, even if he had had the strength to rise and use it. He sweated, in the urgency of his vivid imaginings. He looked about like a frantic animal, for a place to hide. At that moment he heard a quiet sound. Someone was entering the hovel, softly.

Now the visitor was within the faint shaft of candlelight. It was François Grandjean, and behind him, Arsène could see the slender cloaked figure of Cecile.

CHAPTER VI

ON LEAVING HIS LABORS, François Grandjean would linger at the gates of the Hôtel de Tremblant for his granddaughter, Cecile. He was old and weary, but there was more safety in his presence for the girl, as they walked through the crowded dark streets at night, than had she taken her way home alone. Perfumed gallants in chairs, or, cloaked and masked, and accompanied by young reckless bloods like themselves, often waylaid helpless young girls out of pure deviltry. The least the unfortunate young damsel could expect would be a lustful mauling, a few boisterous kisses. During these episodes, for which young women had no redress, the police would indulgently turn their heads, perhaps being rewarded for their blindness with a few flung coins. Moreover, the police knew that no good ever came of righteous or indignant interference. More than one guard found his broken head in the gutter if he was so indiscreet. (It was said that the King, himself, until he took an incontinent interest in culinary matters, often entered into these nocturnal sports.)

During their walk home together, François would carry a stout staff, and Cecile would pull her hood down closely over her beautiful head and would imitate the walk of an old woman at the approach of danger. She remembered, with shiverings, that a young servant girl with whom she had been friendly at the Hôtel de Tremblant, had mysteriously disappeared one midnight, while returning to the home of her bed-ridden mother.

They had stopped briefly at the markets, where Cecile had competently purchased a good fat hen, some herbs, a bottle of decent wine, bread, a handful of onions, and a rabbit. François, though astonished, remained silent while she haggled, and gaped incredulously at the gold coin she offered in payment. Pausing at a stall, she purchased a nosegay of purple spring violets, which she tucked into her bodice. When they were in the streets again, he said:

"My child, where did you secure this money?"

"I took it from the purse of Monsieur Arsène, with his permission. In truth, I took the whole purse," the girl replied, coolly, from the depths of her hood. She paused at the door of a pastry shop, and while François, his head humming, remained outside, she purchased several dainty tarts. She placed these firmly in her grandfather's hands. All at once, she began to laugh, grimly.

"The gentleman intimated that he disliked our fare," she said.

"You asked him for money, Cecile?" questioned François, painfully.

"Most certainly. I have told you. He is a haughty wretch. We will be well rid of him, and good fare will hasten that day."

François' exhausted face flushed, and as they passed a watch carrying a torch, Cecile saw that he was deeply distressed.

"Grandfather," she said, in her chill young voice, "there must be no nonsense. He came unbidden; we gave him Christian charity. He is prepared to repay us with contempt, believing that it is our mission to minister unto such as he. There is no gratitude in him. In a day or two, I shall demand full payment for our care."

He could not see her face, but he felt the firmness of her step, and heard the uncompromising bitterness of her tone.

"I cannot permit this," said François.

She leaned against him, and laughed, indulgently. "My grandfather, I am only fifteen, but I know the world. In this, I cannot obey you."

"You are hard, ma petite," sighed the old man. But he could not refrain from smiling slightly. "You have told me," he added, "that our invalid is much better. That is excellent news. He has suffered greatly."

"But that is not our fault, nor our matter. He should be thankful we did not betray him to the Cardinal's guardsmen, or throw him into the gutter. We can expect nothing of such monsters, nothing of gratitude. At least, we can demand that we be recompensed. However, I hardly think he will respond to our demands."

They reached their miserable dwelling-place. The abbé was not to be seen, but Arsène had struggled to an elbow as they entered the chamber, and was regarding them with great and febrile excitement.

"My pistol!" he exclaimed, weakly. "I must have it at once!"

François hurried to the bedside, anxiously, gazing with experienced eyes at the flushed and sunken cheeks of the sick man, at his wildly inflamed eyes. But Cecile, without a glance, passed the bed and went into the kitchen with her purchases.

"My pistol!" shouted Arsène, flinging aside François' hand.

François, bewildered, turned his head, lifted the pistol from the bench, and silently gave it to the other. Arsène, struggling to sit up, cocked the pistol. Then he flung it from him with a groan.

"Empty!" he said. His eyes darted upon François feverishly.

"But yes," said François, with gentleness. "Did you not use this weapon before you came to us?"

Arsène's dry lips parted vehemently, then he was silent, panting on his pillow. François scrutinized him with concern, thinking that Cecile had been premature in her announcement of his recovery. Surely this man was in delirium, with his shouts for his pistol. Moreover, the absence of the abbé was puzzling. He had never failed them before.

However, François' first thought was to calm Arsène.

"There is no need for weapons in this house," he said, gently. He looked at the table, where stood a cup half-filled with water. He offered it to the sick man, but Arsène shook his head impatiently. His eyes dwelt on François with sparkling concentration. It was evident that he was losing control of himself.

"I have been a fool," he muttered, through clenched teeth. "I have sent that miserable old imbecile of an abbé on an errand—" He paused, then burst out, his control gone: "I have sent him to my father, who is a woman and an idiot, and who will not listen to his tale! At any moment, murderers will burst into this house, to destroy us all!"

François listened, bewildered and fearful. Now Arsène's eyes sharpened upon him.

"In some way, I must leave this house at once, for my sake, and your own."

Then François went to the door, barred and locked it. He came back to the bed.

"Tell me," he said, quietly.

He listened with intentness to Arsène's furious and panting story. He showed no perturbation. After Arsène had done,

53

he sat down wearily on the bench, and plunged himself into thought.

"Did you understand me, old man?" demanded Arsène, with wild impatience. "My father is Armand de Richepin, Marquis du Vaubon. And I have sent—"

"I have heard," said François, with great calm. "It is not necessary for you to excite yourself so, Monsieur du Richepin. Did you expect me to be impressed? If so, I assure you I am not.

"Let us consider this calmly. The abbé Mourion is no fool, no child. He has dealt with many men, and understands. You must trust his wisdom. There is nothing else to be done."

Cecile had built the fire on the kitchen hearth, and had put the fowl and the rabbit in a large pot. She returned to the bedchamber, her manner undisturbed, her young face cold. She regarded Arsène with contempt.

"This is one who trusts no man," she said. "But who can blame him, remembering that we can judge others only by ourselves?"

The candlelight glimmered in her beautiful blue eyes and on her light brown hair and white throat. She stood in the doorway, erect and still. Arsène stared at her, enraged.

"Go away, girl," he said.

But she entered the room, and laid Arsène's empty purse on the bed near his hand. Then she turned to her grandfather.

"I have heard his tale. Perhaps he is justified in his fears. But it is probable that the poor abbé will be discreet?"

"I have no fear of that, little one," replied François, sighing heavily.

He was profoundly concerned at Arsène's manner and agitation.

"Rest assured, Monsieur, there is no danger. None worse than we have already suffered. But you will sicken yourself more, if you allow your imagination to dwell too much on improbabilities."

His voice and his manner were so calm, so gentle, that Arsène was soothed in spite of his fears and his knowledge of his father. He permitted François to smooth his pillow, to bathe his face and hands. Cecile watched, coldly and remotely.

"How can we endure it, if the abbé is injured by this?" she murmured, looking at Arsène with bitter blue eyes.

"We must trust the discretion of the abbé," said François, with a reproving glance at the girl. "We know how wise he is. And we can be assured that no amount of coercion, or worse, will induce him to betray us."

Arsène was again alarmed, and not for himself. "I shall not forgive myself if harm comes to him," he said, and the words sounded strange even to his own ears.

François regarded him gently. "We must trust the abbé," he repeated.

They gazed at each other in a sudden and moved silence. The girl was impressed, in spite of her dislike and antagonism. She looked at Arsène with some softness, which recalled to Arsène the memory of fever-ridden nights when she had ministered to him.

Impulsive, rather than ardent, he exclaimed: "Mademoiselle, I have not thanked you for your kindness and your charity. I shall never forget it, and I swear this by all that is sacred."

"Sacred to us, or to you, Monsieur?" she asked, coolly, but her blue eyes twinkled a little. "But do not be afraid that I, at least, shall forget. We are poor and wretched. It is in your power to alleviate our condition in a measure."

He smiled, involuntarily. "Gold cannot repay you, Mademoiselle," he said, ceremoniously, and with some delicious mockery.

"But it will go a long way," she assured him. And they laughed together, though François pursed his lips wryly, and shook his head at his granddaughter's words.

"A thousand crowns," pursued Cecile, looking at Arsène with mingled laughter and calculation, "will purchase for us an excellent farm. Or, Monsieur, perhaps a thousand crowns is too high a price for your life?"

François rose, protesting. But Arsène replied gravely: "A thousand thousand crowns would not be too much in my opinion, Mademoiselle."

"That," said Cecile, consideringly, "is a matter of opinion, Monsieur." She added, with a smile: "It is not my opinion."

She went into the kitchen again, and, as she worked over the supper, she sang in a sweet clear voice. The sound was delightful to Arsène, and he listened with pleasure.

"It is a bold baggage," said François, with indulgent regret. "There is no softness in the wench." He sighed. "She is a one who looks at life with open eyes. As for myself, old as I am, I cannot bear the sight of it. I must retreat into philosophy, into a dream."

"And you think a dream, a philosophy, is protection against

the wounds of living?" asked Arsène. He was soothed, now, and a pleasant drowsiness was creeping over him.

"It is a drug," admitted François. "There are some who retreat to wine, to pleasure, to wars, to cloisters, to women, and to adventure, when life becomes intolerable. We must all have our anodyne. Adventure, Monsieur, was yours."

Arsène frowned. He could hardly admit this weakness, even if it were true. He lay back on his pillows and looked at François with his dark and vehement eyes, sparkling with renewed vitality in the candlelight.

"I have hated hypocrisy and lies," he said. "I have hated subtle machinations and fraud. If to fight against them is a mean adventure, an escape, then I am guilty."

"But why have you fought them?" asked François, quietly, with a piercing look. "To free the oppressed, to alleviate the torment of the helpless, to liberate the imprisoned? To burst the door of the cell so that all men can see the light?"

Arsène was silent, but the sparkle in his eye brightened, changed, was suffused, became fiery.

François shook his head. "No, you have not."

"I am a Huguenot," muttered Arsène, uneasily.

"But why?" pursued François.

Arsène became excited again. He flung out his hands. "Because I hate the priests, the plotters, the intriguers, the liars, the Jesuits—all the hierarchy of the devil."

"It is a personal hatred, then, springing from a personal loathing," said François, sadly. "This hatred comes not from a moral indignation, a universal compassion, a comprehension of the sufferings of the people."

Arsène was silent. He remembered his dream. The shadow of it dimmed his eyes as he looked at, but did not see, the old man. But François knew that something mysterious was taking place in the heart of the young nobleman.

"The evil men," murmured François, "pervert even the words of God and His saints into their wicked service. They use the torch of God to burn the houses of the people. They lift up the Cross as a stave to lacerate and wound the shoulders of the helpless. In fighting the destroyers of religion, we frequently destroy faith. That is wrong. André Mourion is a priest, yet you would hardly call him a liar, a hypocrite and a rogue." He added, with a catch in his breath: "No one suffers more than he—"

He rose and went to a wooden cupboard at the opposite wall. He brought from it three tattered volumes, and held them in his worn hands as he stood beside the bed.

"Here are the words of Erasmus, of Huss, of Luther. You are a Huguenot, Monsieur, but I would stake my life on it that you have not read these books."

Arsène regarded the volumes with humor. "I have not read these books in my life," he admitted. He stretched out his weak and trembling hand. "But I shall read them, if you will." He added, with surprise: "Are you a Huguenot, François Grandjean?"

François was silent a moment, then he said: "There is no name upon me, no mark or sign. Appellations are chosen by uncertain men, who are unsure of themselves, and must have a word to crystallize their vague emotions, a feeble light to guide their unsure feet."

He sat down again on the bench. He said: "Rome is no longer a City of Faith, a citadel of holy mysticism. It is a political organization, and its priests are statesmen and politicians, bent on the glories of temporal might and the subjugation of kings and governments, of fat lives of power for themselves. The Holy Roman Empire, through corruption and intrigue and avarice, has become the Black Roman Empire seeking the enslavement of all men for its own richness. What of the faith that once gave it radiance and verity? That has become a ruthless sword in their hands." He added: "Until the sword of their lust is broken, no man in any corner of the world is safe, no government is safe, and the dream of just men, a dream of liberty and enlightenment, must be dreamt in prison cells and in dark loneliness."

He sighed deeply. "The Church of God has become the Church of rogues and mountebanks, of actors and malefactors, of liars and enemies, of plotters in scarlet. The shadow of the mitred head is blotting out the sun of Christ."

Arsène had closed his tired eyes, but François' words were like words of fire written against blackness.

"But do not think," said François, sternly, "that the Reformation will bring universal enlightenment, freedom and justice to men, if it concerns itself only with material things. For faith must always be the first hunger of the soul, and the ceremony of faith the first delight of the eye." He added, after a little silence: "There can be no true liberation of the spirit without God. In a struggle against the Church, we must remember not to abandon faith."

His words drifted away from Arsène's ears, and the young man slept. His sleep was deep and profound, and refreshing.

He must have slept for some time, for his first impression on wakening, was that hours had passed. And his first sight was that of the abbé's face, bending over him, smiling sweetly.

An intense relief pervaded the young man's awakened mind, and he cried out.

"Hush," said the abbé, laying his hand on the other's forehead. "All is well."

"You have seen my father?" demanded Arsène, trying to raise himself.

"No," said the abbé. "They told me he was unwell, sickened by anxiety for his son, Arsène de Richepin, who had mysteriously disappeared."

Arsène stared up at him from the pillows. Then he turned away his eyes, as though ashamed. "Tell me," he muttered. He thought of his father, suffering that terrible grief and anxiety, unable to speak for fear of further jeopardizing his son. He felt a strange pang, which opened a wound in his careless heart.

"I spoke to the young man of whom you told me," said the abbé, in his gentle voice. "He took me then, to your brother, Louis de Richepin, whom they called to your father's bedside. Monseigneur de Richepin was very gracious, and very concerned."

Arsène turned to him, and gazed at him without speaking. He saw his brother clearly, with his pale and ascetic face and fair hair, and stern fanatic eyes. He had no real fear of this fraternal enemy, because of the unrequited love Louis bore for his father. Nevertheless, he experienced a qualm.

"You did not trust him, even as a priest?" he demanded at last. "My brother is one of the Cardinal's closest friends, and was ordained by him. He is my brother, but in some things I would rather trust the devil, himself."

"He asked me no dangerous questions," replied the abbé, with a faint smile. "Nor was he overly surprised when I told him my careful story, that you had been wounded, and were now being nursed by friends. He was satisfied with that, though he regarded me strangely and coldly, as though with suspicion. Then he said: 'I am content if he is in your hands, mon abbé. Take heed of his soul, also, as well as his flesh.'" He fumbled in his pocket, and brought forth a golden cross, which he laid in Arsène's hand. "He told me to tell you that he had blessed this, himself, and hoped that it would be a light to guide you home."

Arsène burst into such violent laughter that he tore his throat, and was thrown into a fit of coughing. He thrust the cross towards the abbé.

"Take it, from your youthful father in Christ!" he exclaimed.

The abbé lifted the beautiful, jewel-encrusted thing in his hands and regarded it with deep intensity. Then he gently laid it in Arsène's hand.

"It is not the cross which is polluted," he said, very gravely. "It will not harm you, Monsieur, and it may give you comfort. Take it, then, with my own blessing."

Arsène turned it over in his hot hands, then laid it carelessly on the table at his bedside. "With your blessing, mon abbé, it will have some potency," he said, with graciousness. "You see, then, that I am a trial to my family?"

The abbé ignored this. He pointed to a portmanteau on the table. "In there are some garments, as you requested. Also, one hundred golden crowns."

"My dear brother did not ask you for details about my condition?"

The abbé hesitated. He remembered the swift and unconcealed shadow of hope that had flashed into the young priest's eyes when he had told him that Arsène had been extremely ill, had almost died. He remembered, too, how the gleam had faded when he had assured Louis de Richepin that his brother would recover, and the severe accents which commented on this had convinced him, uneasily, that the younger priest was not too happy over this news, and that in some way he, the abbé, was to blame for a disappointing outcome. But he said: "I told him all I could, with discretion, and he was satisfied."

"He did not detain you overlong?"

"No," said the abbé, with more hesitation. "He seemed too concerned with his father's condition." He did not add that Louis de Richepin had been extremely uneasy during the interview, and that he kept glancing at the door of the private chamber as though he feared eavesdroppers, and that it was he, rather than the abbé, who had been hasty and hurried. Moreover, he appeared not overly anxious for details. When the abbé had offered a few, the young priest had visibly winced, and when the abbé had hinted at the circumstances which had brought Arsène to the hovel, Louis de Richepin had lifted his hand with a peremptory and haughty gesture.

"If my brother will engage in nocturnal, and, no doubt, disgracefully amorous adventures, I do not see the need why his family should be annoyed by the details," he had said, coldly, and had risen with an air of dismissal. "Arsène is imprudent and reckless. He must suffer his own consequences."

But Arsène, watching the abbé shrewdly, guessed at much of this. He remembered that Louis had been sedulous in spreading the rumor that Arsène was a lustful vagabond, with a penchant for other men's wives and mistresses. Fear of the truth prompted this rumor-mongering, as Arsène well knew. Arsène's life had been made considerably more gay and pleasant because of the rumors, and more than one beautiful lady had pursued him with ardor, because of his reputation.

Poor miserable Louis, thought Arsène, with indulgent contempt. How he must shake in his ascetic hotel, how he must be torn by his conscience, for the protecting of his hated brother for their father's sake. Arsène was pleased by the thought of the conflict between filial affection and holy duty. However, there was no predicting how close was the disastrous day when duty would gain the upper hand.

"You were not followed? You are sure of that?" he asked the abbé.

"I am sure of it," responded the other.

There came a soft knock upon the outer door, and the abbé rose to answer it, for François was busy with Cecile in the kitchen in the final preparations of the unusually savory and luxurious meal, purchased with Arsène's gold.

CHAPTER VII

ABBÉ MOURION GREETED the newcomer with tender exclamations of pleasure, and brought him to Arsène's bedside. "Here, Monsieur," he said, beaming, "is another of your nurses, my nephew, Henri."

Wearied by the new exertion of gratitude, Arsène smiled politely, as the stranger bowed diffidently, with a confused smirk. The vehement Arsène, given always to impatient extremes, decided instantly that he did not like Henri Chalon. The proud dignity of François, the gentle heroism of the abbé, the chill independence and gravity of the young Cecile, were all absent in this young man. His manner was sensitive, nervous, ingratiating, and overwhelmed, and almost servile.

There was something, also, in the pale clear pallor of his thin face that reminded Arsène of his brother, Louis. Henri was tall and slender, with bent rounded shoulders, and futile and uncertain gestures. His clothing, poor though it was, had a faintly dandified air. There was a flutter of poor lace at his throat and thin wrists, and he wore boots obviously cast-offs, though lacquered to a shining brilliance. His hair, dark and long, curled on his shoulders with an artificial grace. However, he had a kind of attenuated beauty, which Arsène vaguely remembered. His features were fine, even delicate, and there was a high-bred flare to the sensitive nostrils of his thin long nose. His eyes were extraordinarily large for a man, and were soft and deep, like brown velvet. His mouth was pretty, small and weak. It was his expression, however, which most annoyed Arsène, for it was too eager, too timid, too placating, and yet, given at moments, to a suspicious hauteur. In his hand he deferentially held a plumed hat. This, then, was the poet, the betrothed of the stern young Cecile, the aspirant to the position of footman in the household of Madame de Tremblant.

Arsène felt ridicule for this poor artificial gentleman. He

disliked his manner towards the adoring abbé, for it was petulant, imperious and arrogant, like the manner of a spoiled woman. But towards Arsène himself, he was all self-consciousness, all graceful attitudes, all deference.

"I trust, Monsieur, that you are recovering after our labors?" he said, in a high, too consciously musical voice.

"I am well," replied Arsène, with a curtness he could not restrain. "And I thank you."

"Oh, it was nothing, nothing at all," said Henri, with an eager gesture. He glanced haughtily and contemptuously about the miserable room. "Our only regret was that such a gentleman must be bedded in such a hovel. Had we known your identity—"

"I am Arsène de Richepin," said Arsène. He glanced at the abbé, who was gazing at Henri with fatuous adoration and pride. He felt angered at this, as though the abbé had degraded himself.

Henri bowed again, his long curled hair falling almost to his knees. He made a flourish with his plumed hat. Arsène bit his lip.

"And I, Monsieur de Richepin, am Henri Chalon, at your service." He turned imperiously to the abbé. "Uncle, has Monsieur de Richepin all that he desires tonight?"

"Yes, Henri. It will not be necessary for you to spend the night here any longer." One of the abbé's wrinkled hands touched his nephew's sleeve.

Henri Chalon seemed deeply disappointed. Then he said, pontifically: "I do not agree, my uncle. A night or two more will be necessary."

"On the contrary," said Arsène. "I am almost recovered. I shall not deprive you of your sleep another night."

"It will be no deprivation, Monsieur, I assure you," said Henri, with another bow. "It will be a pleasure to keep Monsieur company."

He became aware of the delicious odors coming from the kitchen, and looked at the abbé inquiringly.

"Yes, we feast tonight," said the abbé, with simple pleasure. Henri Chalon's pale and narrow face lit up with an extraordinary elation. A vague restlessness seized Arsène, and he turned his head and closed his eyes. His old fierceness and egotism returned, as the strength of his body returned. His sharp black brows drew together, knotted, over his shut eyelids, and his aquiline profile tightened. Reared in a tradition which regarded the people as less than vermin, and less potent, he could not restrain himself from a qualm of contempt for these creatures who found joy in the simple anticipation of a meal. Then he felt contempt for himself that he could descend so low as to honor this vermin with his disdain.

Thinking that he was drowsing in his weakness, the abbé and his nephew sat quietly in the candlelight near the bed and conversed in low voices. Arsène listened, his eyebrows twitching with impatience. He forgot everything, his new gratitude, new wonder, new gentleness, which he had experienced with François Grandjean and the Abbé Mourion. The old man and the young prattled of childish things. They discussed the people who lived about them, the weather, and other inconsequential things. The abbé's voice was low and soft, and Henri's pompous and querulous, filled with vanity and conceit. If they knew anything of the great world beyond their miserable borders, they did not speak of it. All at once, Arsène, who had despised the labyrinthine intrigues, the scandal and the debauchery of the nobles and the Court, found these things suddenly of importance, and amusing, exciting and significant. He amused himself by thinking of Clarisse, his betrothed, and he felt a deep yearning for her which he had never experienced before.

He forgot his strange dream of fury and liberation, and was conscious only of his straw bed, the fetid dusty odors of the room, the sickening smell of cooking rabbit and fowl. He moved restlessly on the bed, sighed deeply. He felt the abbé rising, bending over him, and he winced.

"He sleeps," said the abbé, softly. "He is young. He can still sleep."

Henri spoke, and his voice was patronizing, as though he felt indulgence for the simplicity of his uncle: "Why should he not sleep? He has been very ill, and is now recovering. What an extraordinary thing this is! I was despairing of any good thing coming to us, until Monsieur de Richepin entered this house so strangely. Now, it is a light in the darkness."

"I do not understand, Henri," said the abbé, anxiously, returning to his stool. "Of what significance is it, this coming, to us?"

Henri was silent a moment, then spoke with embarrassed impatience: "Surely he cannot be ungrateful!" He paused, then continued with a kind of anger in his impatience: "Only the powerful can patronize the arts. I have my hopes—"

The abbé was silent a moment, then in a tone of ashamed but deep distress, he said: "Henri, you have not considered

63

annoying him?" He stopped abruptly, as though his shame had become too intense for speech.

Henri burst out, with wild and effeminate vehemence: "Why not? Do you think I can be content forever with this miserable existence of ours, this degradation of mind and body? My uncle, if you are content, I am not. I would rather die than to live out my life like this! If you believe I must be content, why did you teach me? Why did you open my eyes? Why did you inspire me?"

The abbé interrupted in a trembling voice: "I gave you what I could, Henri, so that you might be wise, and understanding, and humble before God. Wisdom is its own glory. Must one desire to acquire wisdom in order to be rewarded with the things of this world?"

He was silent a moment, then continued with great sadness: "It is enough for a man to know God through learning of His glory, of His being. This is the beginning, the end, the purpose, of wisdom."

"I do not understand!" cried Henri, with febrile scorn. "But this life I can endure no longer. I must escape. I must escape!"

It was evident that this was an old subject between these two, for the abbé only sighed wearily, and was silent. Then, after a long silence, the abbé said:

"If you must concern yourself with the world, my nephew, then concern yourself with its miseries, its torments, its sufferings. Dedicate your life to the alleviation of grief and pain. Sing the songs of the people, so that the deaf ear of power may be touched, and the hard heart of majesty be moved. Sing of pity and justice and mercy. The artificial and dainty songs intended to please the decadent ears of the idle, the soft and the rich, die like tinkling notes in a hurricane." He added, with terrible solemnity: "For the hurricane is approaching, and only a strong and fearless voice shall ride upon it."

Arsène listened, and in spite of himself, he was stirred and amazed. Strange words in this wretched hovel, in the gutters of Paris! The dream came back to him again, and he felt a mysterious excitement. How many voices like this of the abbé's were there abroad in the world? How many were speaking of strange and revolutionary things in the vast sewers beneath the great screaming cities? Arsène seemed to hear again the rush of feet through the storm, but now they rushed up from the sewers into the thoroughfares of the world, and now they were the feet of an army.

He must have slept in the sudden exhaustion of illness, for

when he awoke again there were two candles upon the table, and there were laughing voices. Cecile had placed bowls, plates and pewter spoons upon the table, also, and there was a great savory dish of fowl and rabbit, seasoned with wine sauces and herbs. There was also a bottle of wine, and a plate of crusty white bread. Arsène became conscious that in the laughter there was some exclaiming, and François was demurring.

"But tobacco!" said François. "It is long since I have had a pipeful. My child, you ought not to have bought tobacco for me with Monsieur de Richepin's money."

"Why not?" demanded Cecile, coolly. "I have also bought you a new pipe, grandfather. Were you not saving for it, until you had to spend your money for unguents for Monsieur?"

She stood in the candlelight, and Arsène, as he awakened, saw her only. She was very pale, this tired child, and even her lips had no color in their soft fullness. But she held her head erect, and the light broke in golden shadows on her braids, which were coiled about her small head. The nobility which Arsène had first marked was stern and high upon her beautiful features, and her blue eyes, though ringed with mauve shadows, were deep, wide, and set nobly in patrician sockets. Her breasts were young and pointed under the tight black bodice, and he noticed the slender strength of her shoulders and her arms, the sure quiet movements of her calloused fingers, and the flexibility of her wrists. She was only fifteen years old, but a stern maturity was already upon her, a coldness and firmness, and, in the quick flash of her eyes, a peculiar recklessness. Arsène's interest quickened as it always did at the sight of a beautiful or unusual woman, and he felt a sudden compassion for this child.

She felt his regard, and paused abruptly in the midst of cutting bread to glance down at him. She had been smiling a little, but now, as her eyes met his the smile disappeared, and her fair brows drew together.

"You are awake, Monsieur," she said, and her voice was reserved and indifferent, for all its rich sweetness.

François came to him from around the table, and stood, smiling down at him. "We waited for you to awaken, Monsieur, so you could join in the feast. Bought with your money," he added, with a tilt of an eyebrow.

"Bought with the money we earned, grandfather," said Cecile, tartly, resuming the cutting of the bread.

"I thank you for the tobacco, and the consideration which prompted it," said François, gravely.

Arsène laughed. His teeth glittered white and youthful in the candlelight. His dark eyes danced, and he raised himself upon his elbow. Henri Chalon, murmuring with solicitous reproach, and glancing reprovingly at Cecile, rose from his stool and thrust the musty pillows behind Arsène, to support him. Cecile watched this, and a flicker of amusement sparkled deeply in her eyes. The abbé, on his stool, beamed sweetly. All at once, Arsène remembered the peasants on his father's estates, and the seething mobs in the streets of Paris, and he wondered at his simplicity. These people in this wretched room were no more a part of the peasants and the viper-faced mobs than he, himself, was. For some reason which he did not care to examine too minutely, his spirits lifted, his manner became genial and courteous, and he regarded even that vain poor creature, Henri Chalon, with interested and sympathetic eyes.

He looked at François, and said with mock gravity: "I specifically charged Mademoiselle this morning to purchase for you, Monsieur, the finest in tobacco and pipes. I hope you will accept both as a very small token of my regard and gratitude."

François smiled deeply, Cecile's lips curved irrepressibly, and Henri Chalon was bewildered. He stared from one face to another. When he encountered his uncle's face, he was more perplexed than ever. For the abbé was regarding Arsène with sudden consternation and somber distress. Smiling about the board at his elbow, Arsène, too, saw this peculiar long look, so grave, and so wise, and a blush seemed to start irritably at his heart and rise to his face. Damn the old priest! Was it possible he could actually read the thoughts of men?

"We are poor and miserable people," said the abbé, slowly. "We are grateful for small gifts, and the condescension of those who have power to oppress us."

François thought this a very odd remark, and Cecile tossed her head, her eyes flashing, and Henri gaped. But Arsène looked away, and the flush was deeper on his cheeks. His lower lip thrust out sullenly, and with hauteur.

Henri recovered himself, and he bent towards Arsène with a revolting mixture of eager servility, grovelling respect, and conciliation.

"It is true, Monsieur," he said, in his quick light voice

which seemed to have no resonance. "You must not think us ungrateful—"

"Ungrateful!" exclaimed Cecile, outraged. She held the long shining knife in her hand. She appeared genuinely shocked. "It is Monsieur who must not be ungrateful to us, he who is so indebted to us!"

Arsène smiled again. He inclined his head in Cecile's direction, but he looked at Henri with a disdainful twitch of his lips.

"I am indeed indebted to all of you," he said, graciously. "And do not think that I shall forget it." He added: "Mademoiselle is entirely right. A young lady of discernment." And now he flashed his dark laughing glance at her.

Henri's pale narrow cheek brightened with sudden hope. He looked about at his friends in delicate jubilation. But Cecile, frowning darkly, filled her betrothed's plate, and thrust it towards him with a gesture containing some viciousness. She filled the other plates, and Arsène observed that the best morsels were for the abbé and her grandfather. Then, casting Arsène a glance under her long lashes, she hesitated, and unwillingly removed some of the whitest meat from the others' plates, and put it upon his own. He watched her closely. He was delighted with her beauty, and his eye roved over her face and figure with open speculation and pleasure.

To his surprise, he discovered that Cecile was an excellent and subtle cook. Even his father's beloved Anton could do no better than this with the finest wine and most fastidious herbs. The wine was not too bad. The bread was sweet and fresh. His returning strength and health and youth took sustenance from the food. He felt an unfamiliar twinge at the sight of the ravenous appetites of the others. Even the abbé ate enormously. François drank copiously. The grave majesty of his expression lightened. His head was no longer the head of a weary and beaten old man, but a Roman Senator's head. He needed only a toga. Only Cecile preserved some aloofness, and ate with critical care, smiling just a little at the praises of her friends. Henri, soothed and flushed, regarded her with an open if diffident amorousness, which seemed hardly less to surprise Cecile than it did himself, for the girl flashed her eyes at him as if puzzled and vaguely affronted.

A heavy spring rain had begun to fall outside. It drummed on the roof, on the shuttered windows. The candlelight wavered, brightened, cast long shadows on the cracked wet walls. But there was warmth here, kindness, smiles and laughter about the board heaped with its food, and Arsène forgot that he was in a hovel. He felt that he was in the midst of old and delightful friends, and his heart was filled with good will towards them for the pleasure of their company.

CHAPTER VIII

ARSENE THOUGHT THAT he had slept but a moment, for the sound of conversation was still in his ears when he awoke. But when he came to full consciousness he saw that the two great candles were burned almost to their sockets, and their light was dim and yellow. Moreover, every vestige of the meal was gone, and the board scrubbed white and patched with dampness. Long thin shadows crawled over the walls and ceilings. The beating rain hummed outside, and the gutters rushed with water.

The voices he had heard upon awakening were hushed and grave. Arsène peered under his eyelids and saw that only the Abbé Mourion and François Grandjean were in the chamber, and they had removed themselves to a distance from the bed in order not to disturb the sleeper. Their heads were bent together. They were only two old men, beggarly and haggard and gray with years, but their faces were lofty with thought, and austere with wisdom. But the abbé's face was sorrowful and tender, and the face of François, though sad, was also possessed of a latent sternness and bitter patient calm. The candlelight flickered over their features, carving their cheekbones sharply in the withered flesh, lying in eye-socket and over wrinkled forehead.

There had come a pause in their conversation, which the abbé broke with a sigh.

"My friend, it is getting very late. I assure you again, that Monsieur is almost recovered, and within a few days there will be no sign of his illness but a certain emaciation, and that scar upon his cheek. He will cherish that!" And the abbé smiled tenderly, as he always smiled at the braggadocio of the young, and their vehemence. "So, you will please go to bed, for you are very weary."

François shook his head abstractedly. "There was a slight fever, when he first slept. Moreover, there are certain things which must be done for him. I shall not awaken him, for I have discovered that sleep does more than any unguent. But you, dear abbé—there is no reason for you to remain with me."

The abbé sighed again. "Have I not always remained with you, when I could? Too, there is some heaviness in me to-night, some malaise. In your presence, my friend, I find some alleviation—"

François was silent for a moment, then spoke with visible difficulty.

"I have told you nothing about me, though I have known it was only just. Perhaps, if you knew, you would not wish your nephew to marry Cecile, though Henri might find the story of pleasurable interest—"

The abbé laid his hand gently on his friend's arm. "I am not a priest with you, dear François! I am only your friend. You must tell me nothing. The opening of old wounds does no good. I know your soul. That is enough for me."

Arsène listened with intense interest and surprise, obscurely pleased at the significance of these revelations. He thought, with anticipation, that François would now unburden himself, but instead of that the old man sighed, again and again, as though his heart were overburdened.

But he only said, in a muffled voice: "There is no dowry, as you know, for Cecile."

"There is her heart; there is herself," said the abbé, his voice shaking a little.

"I have worried over the girl," said François, as if to himself. "What has life for these two? Nothing. I have given up everything, in one wild and passionate gesture. Now I am old, and I wonder. I have not feared hunger and terror, and now I ask myself: 'Would I wish Cecile to face this all her life?' What seemed heroic to me seems terrible for this child. We endure everything for ourselves; we cannot bear that our children shall endure this also."

"But Cecile has part of your own soul in her, François. She is brave and strong, far braver and stronger than Henri."

François burst into sudden virulent laughter, heavy with despair. He shook his head violently in his mirth, but he said nothing. His laughter seemed to be directed against himself. He passed his hands over his bearded face, and shook his head again. The abbé watched him, alarmed and moved.

Then François began to speak, at first in a low voice, then with increasing passion accompanied by the beating of his fists upon his tattered knees. He stared into space as he did so, and seemed to see nothing but of what he spoke:

"I have not feared men, or the things that men do. But now I see them in their full terror, revealed. I have felt myself equal to fate, even in the hours of the most frightful events. There was an illusion, a delirium in me. Now I see that my dream was sordidness, and folly. I am amazed at my earlier effrontery, that I thought I might set myself against the evil of the world. How could I have been so mad? Now I see that my life is nothing. Nothing, set against all other men who are evil and cruel and malignant. Only they are strong. Evil is stronger than good, mightier than God. At times I think that I would be young again, in these portentous days. I tell myself that never before in the world was there more need for a strong voice and a strong hand, when wickedness is more powerful than virtue."

He paused. There was silence in the chamber, with its guttering candles. Then François resumed, and his voice was hoarse as he tried to restrain its passion.

"This momentous hour, of war and intrigue, of dark and subterranean movements! This terrific day, when malefactors move in the huge darkness! Where is there good, or mercy? This is what I think, and I am old, and I have done nothing. And at times, I know it is all futile, even the longing."

His voice sank into a hopeless but echoing whisper, and his head fell on his breast. The abbé regarded him with deep compassion and sorrow.

"Only a noble soul can feel this," he said, gently. "Forgive me if I offend you, but this I must say: There are some who cry: 'Never were wicked men so ascendent as in this generation.' But I say this observation comes from an ignorance of history, and an unawareness of the perennial evil of a certain kind of human being. Every generation has its malefactors, its lusters, its soulless creatures and villains. We must deal with them as they eternally arise, as we deal with other violent natural phenomena of nature like plagues and pestilences, supplicating God."

François did not speak. His staring eyes regarded the floor in a kind of rigid horror.

"One must have faith, not in humanity," said the abbé mournfully, "but in what humanity may or can become."

Still François was silent. Now he was laughing silently to himself, and there was something more terrible than sound in that silent mirth.

The abbé spoke again, more loudly, and with urgency:

"Time, and the long topography of history shift, but man, and the eternal verities, which are the nature of man, remain forever the same. Man is the undying potential in the midst of chaotic flux. Even in the most despairing moments, I remember this. Even when I see the wallowing of men, and the ruin they create about them, I believe, I must believe, that in them are all potentialities of the angels, and that these potentialities, through the dark ages, must finally emerge."

Arsène thought he must be dreaming, that fever must be evoking these words out of the dreary silence of this hovel. He listened as a man listens to a language of which he does not know much, and strains his ears to catch a meaning. And then, faintly catching it, becomes dumbly incredulous. Surely such a meaning was not meant by the speaker! He must be mad with fever, still, and not truly hearing these strangenesses spoken at midnight by two old broken men clad in rags!

Yet, even while he told himself this, he felt a mysterious beating of his heart. He was like a blind man who feels the warmth of the sun on his shut eyelids. He has never seen nor known the orb of light, but he is conscious of its power and its hidden glory, and its enormous life.

Unaccustomed to thought as he was, unfamiliar with anything but the most superficial of emotions, and living only by his exuberant instincts and passion for laughter and adventure, he found his new sensations overwhelming, chaotic, and a little frightful. His whole mind, his whole being, were convulsed, blown upon by strange hot winds, dazzled by supernatural lights, thrown into disorientation. The skepticism of which he had always been more than a trifle proud was swept away like a leaf upon a whirlpool. Passionate and vehement, and possessed of a naïveté which could be dangerous in its strength, he was not given to questioning, to analysis, to judicious contemplation. Portals had burst open before his eyes. Emotional instinct made him stand before them, gasping at what was revealed. Later would come the disillusionment of the ardent man. In that was the danger.

His thoughts, his emotions, exhausted him by their very fire, though they were still formless, like nebulæ bearing in them the potentialities of new worlds. He closed his eyes for what seemed a moment or two. He opened them, and found himself alone. The old men were gone, with their sibyl words, which were old and forever new. The stub of candle wallowed, hissing, in its socket, blinked, wavered, prepared to go out.

There was a faint rustle near him, a soft breath, a movement. Cecile was approaching the bed. Thinking the sick man profoundly asleep, she approached him in her short shift, her long fair hair streaming over her shoulders and bosom. He instinctively half shut his eyes. But he could see the beam of last candlelight in her hair, the tendrils of spun gold at her white temples. He saw, as she bent over him, the blue veins in her young bosom, revealed by the gaping shift, the tender warm softness of her flesh between and below her breasts. She exhaled the humid sweetness of youth, which was like the spring air, and it was a perfume in nostrils which were accustomed only to artificial scents. Peering through his lashes, feeling the sudden hot pounding of his body, he could see only her parted pale lips, drooping with weariness, and the soft yet firm curve of her chin.

She hesitated, bending over him. He felt the touch of her hand, lightly, on his forehead, feeling for fever. Then, sighing, she blew out the candle. The cool dank air was permeated with the acrid odor of tallow and wick. There was complete darkness in the room, and it was filled by her breathing and the living emanations from her flesh.

She did not go at once. He heard her sigh again. Her bodily presence was more urgent, more exigent, in the darkness, than in the light. It was like some strong force, magnetic, innocent, compelling, full of passion and intoxication.

Then, he felt her lips on his forehead. It was like the touch of summer grasses, fragrant and warm from the sun.

She had gone. In the singing darkness he lay with dilated eyes, hearing only the roar of blood in his ears and an unknown surging in his heart.

It were as though for the first time in his life he had become aware of something ineffably sweet, ineffably lovely, too poignant even for the frailest thought, too exquisite for a touch, but so irresistible in its force, so powerful and tremendous, that man and God could not defy nor oppose it.

CHAPTER IX

"CERTES!" EXCLAIMED ARMAND, Marquis du Vaubon, irritably, to his son, Louis, "you have a low opinion of your brother!"

"It is not I who have been responsible for this opinion," replied Louis, with his accustomed icy hauteur, which was yet so humble. "Men create the opinions of others."

He sat in his father's lofty bed-chamber on a gilt chair, which his attitude reproved for its frivolity and insubstantiality. Arsène had often declared that Louis could display more disapproval, more cold displeasure, by the set of his broad thin shoulders, and the turn of his head, than other men could display by gestures or glances or words.

Louis de Richepin, Monseigneur du Vaubon, was still young, and extremely handsome in the manner in which a sexless statue is handsome. That is, his sexlessness was that of the great marble angels in the Cathedral, whose masculinity is revealed in an absence of female breasts and softnesses, and in a possession of stern large faces and soaring strength of contour. In truth, there was about Louis de Richepin the majesty of marble, the inexorability of stone, the largeness of a sculptor's heroic concept of an archangel. Tall, slender, spare, yet slow-moving, he had a hard and aristocratic grace of body, and a quality of quietness that was impressive and intimidating. Even the Cardinal had declared, with amused annoyance, that Louis frequently awed even him with his uncompromising silences, his noble reticence and severity, the cold impersonal rebuke of his pale and frosty eye. Louis was fair, almost colorless, resembling, at times, a statue of snow and ice, heroically clad in ecclesiastical black and white. His robes fell in beautiful folds about his graceful but somewhat stiff frame. His hands were white, slender, but exceedingly strong. He walked with august dignity. The unhuman grandeur of an iceberg was his posture.

The Cardinal, who secretly despised and feared true celibacy, had taken subtle pains to introduce Louis to irresistible women, had forced opportunities for luxurious dallying upon him. But all without success. There was another thing that also infuriated the Cardinal: Louis had none of the gusty appetite of the Frenchman, none of the exquisite love for the table. This inspired annoyance in the Cardinal. He often said: "I would never send a lover of food upon any mission involving ruthlessness. But neither would I trust the man who looks on wine and dainties with an unlusting eye." Nevertheless, he trusted his secretary, Louis de Richepin, as he did not trust even the Captain of his Musketeers or his familiar, Father Joseph, the Grey Eminence. In that unhuman passionlessness, in that stern majesty, was the quality that even so subtle and diabolical a man as Richelieu trusted as he never trusted his God. He was also vaguely ashamed before that quality, a shame that lurked deep in his labyrinthine and devious soul. He often accused himself of some naïveté in his trust of Louis, but never had he felt justified in his accusation.

But Louis' devotion to the Church, and to himself, could never be questioned. He was capable of the most extraordinary martyrdom and selflessness. He never considered himself at all. He lived only to serve Mother Church, and her servants. Sometimes the Cardinal, watching him slyly out of the corner of his cunning and subtle eye, wondered if Louis had heard any of the remarkable but only too true stories about him. But if Louis had heard, it was evident that he had not believed. Had he believed, the Cardinal was certain, the younger man would have stopped at nothing to expose his superior, or even to have destroyed him openly. So, with considerable impatience and irritation, the Cardinal concealed much of his irascible and voluptuous nature in Louis' presence, but yet, at times, could not resist in displaying some of his traits of character in an irresistible desire to prod, dismay or confuse him. He finally came to the conclusion that Louis was incapable of suspecting anyone so illustrious, so highly placed as the Cardinal, so brilliant, could possibly be venal, treacherous or wicked.

Many hated Louis, feared him for his enormous influence with the Cardinal, who was known to trust him above all other men. Many attempted to use that influence, without the slightest result, without, even, Louis suspecting that an attempt had been made. Once, the King himself had attempted to probe Louis for betraying details about the

Cardinal, but Louis had gazed so emptily, so icily, so uncomprehendingly, at His Majesty, that the King had felt both fury and shame and bewilderment.

"At the door of the Cardinal's house is a man of unmelting and transparent ice," the King had said, angrily, but with some secret admiration for his own metaphor.

Never, even in the wildest and most fanciful of moments, did Armand suspect that Louis had for him the only human love he ever gave to any living creature. He would have listened, astounded, gaping, blinking, if any one had ever told him, believing he was listening to the words of an idiot. Only Arséne knew this, and sometimes he wondered if he, himself, was mad, in his suspicions. What was there in this dark, restless, womanish man, this creature of facile emotions, querulous feminine voice, unpredictable but narrow passions, unreasoning caprices, and malicious vagaries, to inspire such horrifying and glacial devotion? For, indeed, there was something horrifying in it. It was as if an ice-covered mountain had conceived a terrible and voiceless and enormous love for a sparrow, a love that had in it nothing human, nothing of blood and warmth, but contained in it the wind of endless stark chasms under the earth, and the power of sunless rivers running through tortuous caverns, and the barren lightning that flashes over stony peaks unconquered by man. It was affrighting; it was frightful. And the poor little creature who was the victim, rather than the recipient of it, would have been crushed, annihilated, driven to screaming idiocy, had he understood even a part of it. So Arsène, knowing all this with an intensity strange in so unimaginative a young and lusty man, took care only to say humorously to his father, when pleading Louis' case: "But Louis has quite a little fondness for you, my father. Be, therefore, more compassionate, more gentle, with him."

"But Louis dislikes you with unnatural strength," Armand would return, petulantly. "How then, you miserable scoundrel, can I feel anything but annoyance with him? Besides, he oppresses me. He gives me the shivers. He always did. I should have strangled him when he was born." And he would laugh gleefully and childishly, and with malice, when he said this, as if he found some revenge in his words upon his younger son. "He is not human. He was born without the parts of a man."

Armand, as he lay in his invalid's posture by the sunny casement, this warm spring day, thought of this, looking at Louis sitting opposite him, so rigid, so tall, so straight, in his black robes. Louis seemed to have an unconscious aversion to sunlight; he sat in shadow. But reflected beams glimmered over his handsome face like lances of ice-struck radiance. He was a statue. Armand did not see how pathetic he was, how horribly alone. He never knew of the bitter cold despair, black and monstrous, which crouched in the nameless and subterranean caves of Louis' lonely soul. He never knew that the only other emotion, besides the love for his father, of which Louis was capable, was hatred. And even this hatred lacked the human quality of lesser men, though containing the potentialities of all cruelty, all ruthlessness, all inexorability, all monstrousness. Armand only knew that Louis alternately annoyed him, frightened him, made him uneasy and curiously breathless, as if the young priest brought with him that rarefied and smothering airlessness of great heights.

Armand was not really an invalid, but he was recovering at this time from the distress and apprehensions that had afflicted him upon Arsène's mysterious and complete disappearance. However, he was nervous enough to be the victim of frequent attacks of lassitude, vague pain, exhaustion and shallow melancholy. These induced a laziness paradoxical in one so spare, swift-moving and erratic. His body, his face, his nature, belonged to a man of restlessness and capriciousness, which he was indeed, in more sanguine moods. Hating all responsibility, vain, suspicious, sly, expedient and childishly treacherous, he had frequently to retire to his bed-chamber and refresh himself from the constant turmoil of his superficial but thronging emotions, which were like a swarm of gnats. During these periods, he gave himself up to luxurious pampering, calling upon his hairdresser and his valets to attend him constantly. He was as conceited as a silly woman. His long black hair, dank and straight and betraying a persistent tendency to grayness, was dyed, pomaded, polished and brushed, and loaded with fragrant pomades. It lay daintily on his narrow jerking shoulders with a false and oily lustre and in geometrical curls. His long lean nose, constantly twitching, was powdered whitely. The eyelashes on his small, too closely-spaced black eyes, were thick with oily dye, as were his sharp black brows, so like Arsène's. So sharp, so restless, so glittering were his eyes, so leaping about with suspicion, rolling, jerking, that they instantly inspired distrust and wariness in the beholder. There was more than a trace of rouge on his high and narrow cheekbones, and on his weak spasmodic mouth, with its protruding

77

and petulant lower lip. His face was dry, the skin coarse and flaking under its scented unguents, and furrowed with deep lines from nostril to mouth, and across the high but narrow forehead. His whole expression conveyed his chronic anxiety, his malice, his suspicion of all things, his slyness and his treachery. Even when he was alone, or not speaking, his hands jerked involuntarily, gestured without meaning, the thin dark fingers heavy with sparkling rings.

He thought himself irresistible to women, and if their attendance upon him was any proof, he was. He was too vain to consider that his position at Court, the affection the King had for him, and his wealth, might have something to do with this devotion. He loved rich garments, was a leader of fashion, designing many of his own coats and doublets and hats, and even sketching patterns for lace he had especially made for his collars and his cuffs. There was no doubt that he had considerable elegance and taste, and a natural eye for fashion, style and symmetry, for he was widely and enviously copied, and his word on the latest frippery was solemnly and slavishly accepted. He wore garments in dark intense colors, plum, deep fiery blue, crimson, and velvety black. He was inordinately proud of a really beautiful and feminine ankle, and slender legs and a tiny graceful foot. He was also a connoisseur of perfumes, having his own private chemists concocting them in a locked chamber in the Hôtel de Vaubon. Some of his latest, called Fleur d'Amour, stood in a beautiful gilt and crystal bottle on the baroque table at his chair-side, and this he sniffed in the uneasy intervals of his conversation with his son, Louis. His person was permeated with it, as was the lace and silken kerchief he flaunted delicately in his hand. Louis' nostrils distended painfully, as gusts of the musky odor assaulted his senses, and he would move his head backwards as if to escape asphyxiation. Armand noted this, and maliciously poured fresh scent on his kerchief, and gestured with it with even more elaborateness than usual.

Armand's taste extended to every room in his mansion. His bedchamber was baroque, but not oppressively so. There was grace in every gilt and marble and ebony table. Every surface sparkled with color. The walls were silk-hung in various shades of subtle gold, all melting into each other deliciously, so that the effect was of varying degrees of filtered sunlight. The Persian rug upon the polished floor was a subtle blend of poignant blues, gold, threads of scarlet, and tendrils of pure and delicate green. The canopied bed, with its soaring posts of scrolled gilt, had heavy curtains of the same material that draped the tall diamond-paned windows, and was covered, also, with this material. Upon the black and gilt chest of drawers near his bed stood a formidable array of scents, pomades, powders and golden brushes and combs, not to mention lotions for his feet and hands and cosmetics for his eyes and brows. An enormous crystal chandelier, like a series of icicles, hung from the plaster-scrolled and gilt ceiling. He had the best paintings upon his walls, all decadent, all warm and improper. As a concession, hasty perhaps, but necessary, a golden crucifix stood upon a small table, dressed like an altar with a snowy and lace-bordered cloth.

Armand irritably considered, and rightly so, that the crucifix was incongruous in that feminine room, and did nothing to enhance its delicate debauchery. But as a convert, or as one who had only lately returned to Mother Church, he must at all times display evidences of devout piety. Sometimes, when he had no dangerous visitors, he had a glittering Chinese screen placed about it. This was removed when Louis, or others like him, who could not be trusted, paid him a visit. But his restless eye came back to it at frequent intervals, with badly concealed impatience, for it annoyed him with its unfitness in the room. This increased his natural nervousness.

It was Louis who had given his father the golden crucifix, believing that its exquisite ivory figure and elaborate scroll-work would please the erratic and tasteful man, and might, while he contemplated it with pleasure, subtly imbue him with its deeper meaning. He could not know, in his large and mountainlike simplicity, that the very sight of it hugely annoyed Armand, and even infuriated him, for he had not forgotten his father and La Rochelle. The crucifix did more to disturb and torment Armand that did any other inanimate object, and sometimes he regarded it with a hatred singularly pure in so shallow a man. Once, in Arsène's presence, he had hurled it upon the floor, in a furious tantrum of mingled hatred and disgust, declaring he was ready to forswear everything rather than keep it in his room.

But Arsène had laughingly picked it up, and gently replaced it.

"Beauty, no matter if in a maudlin form, is always holy," he had said. Armand had become abruptly silent, in the midst of his hysterical tirade, and had stared unaffectedly at his son.

"It is not the object; it is the giver," he had mumbled, finally, rubbing his thin hands together, and shivering, and glancing uneasily at the door as if suspecting that some servant eavesdropped. But Arsène, with his rare flashes of insight, knew it was more than that.

Now, as Armand talked querulously and languidly with his younger son, his eye kept straying toward the crucifix. He held his scent bottle to his twitching nostrils. His fine jeweled hand kept up a constant faint trembling. Under his rouge, he was a little pale, and his heart was beating with that intolerable tremor which was the prelude to hysteria. The presence of Louis always had this effect upon him, but he was not subtle enough to understand it. He could not read the sad passion deep in those large pale blue eyes set so beautifully in their sockets. He saw no tragedy in the stiff yet graceful body in its black robes. He saw no somber grandeur and mournfulness in the folded white hands. He only knew that Louis stared at him heavily and constantly, and his malaise increased.

But he did know that Louis was anxious about him. Pardieu, if the wretch had not come today, he, Armand, would have been out in his carriage driving through the Bois and sniffing the fresh spring earth and reveling in the sunlight under the new trees! Louis' unspoken but visible solicitude oppressed him. He pretended great weariness and pain, in order to torment his son. This was instinctive. He never comprehended Louis' love for him.

"Mon Dieu!" he thought. "He has no more expression on his silly face than has a fish in a bowl!"

He said, aloud, moving restlessly on his pillows: "You never understood that rascal, Arsène. Perhaps you are incapable of such understanding, Louis. Arsène is gay, delightful. He has a heart of gold. He is amusing. He is elegant. He is liked by every one. Perhaps you are jealous."

A faint spasm touched Louis' wide and chiselled lips. But he said, quietly: "He is a dancer. He is frivolous, adventurous. He loves danger for its own sake. He is foolish and vivacious, and too carefree. He is not very intelligent."

There was now a faint tremor in his voice, as though some emotion had touched him, and he turned aside his head.

Armand laughed thinly, and with malevolence. He waved his saturated kerchief languidly in front of his nose, narrowing his eyes to peer at his son. He shrugged, stared pointedly.

"Nevertheless, His Majesty likes him. More than he does you, my dear Louis. Only yesterday he sent me a billet, in which he said: 'Where is that amusing blackguard, Arsène? We miss him sorely.'"

Again, the spasm touched Louis' smooth, marble-like lips.

"Once," continued Armand, with enjoyment, "His Majesty said to me: 'His Eminence would like Arsène to be Captain of his Guards. But I would prefer him under my own standard, if he would remain long enough in one spot to listen to the proposal.'"

A strange, faintly eager look flashed over Louis' eyes.

"His Eminence said precisely that to me, only yesterday. He would welcome Arsène as Captain of his Musketeers. But when did Arsène ever listen to anything but his own desires, for all he is such an excellent swordsman?"

Armand stared dreamily, with a pleasant smile, through the casement.

"He could be another M. de Bassompierre, if he willed. He is also a clever chess player. His Eminence mentioned this. But he cares nothing for all that. He is too independent—"

"Too intent upon his own ridiculous pleasures," interrupted Louis, with a darkening eye.

Armand was angered. "I repeat, you are prejudiced. Such a serious absurdity as Paul de Vitry is his devoted friend. De Vitry sees more in Arsène than you do, my surly priest."

Louis stood up abruptly. He moved, with his curiously slow but light tread, to the crucifix. He stood, looking down at it, his hands involuntarily clasped in an attitude of prayer. When he spoke, his voice was strange:

"My father, have you ever heard of Les Blanches?"

Armand jerked his head, and his eyes peered with sudden terror at Louis' tall and handsome back. He sat upright, clutching the arms of his chair. His knuckles turned white, the tendons strained torturously. His color became ghastly.

"Les Blanches," he repeated in a voice so dwindled that it squeaked. He moistened lips that had dried under the thick red rouge. "No. No! I have not heard. What is this Les Blanches?"

Louis, though he tried to prevent it, felt a suffering pang at the terror in his father's voice. He could not endure it. He came with unusual swiftness back to his chair. He leaned towards Armand, and his hand reached involuntarily to touch his father's hand. But he recovered himself almost instantly.

"Nothing," he murmured, soothingly. "Nothing at all. Except that M. de Vitry is suspected of being the organizer, the head, of Les Blanches. It is reputed to be a Huguenot society, bent on treachery, murder, the overthrow of His Majesty's Most Catholic government." He breathed, as if

81

with sudden difficulty, tried to smile. It was a painful and pathetic smile. Armand glared at him, with distended eyes of fear, like an animal.

"I was only thinking," Louis continued, "that such as M. de Vitry is no safe friend for Arsène, who is your son, and my brother."

Armand continued to sit upright in his chair, clutching the arms. Pale drops stood on his forehead.

"Nonsense," he whispered, for he could not speak aloud. He swallowed, convulsively, then, recovering his voice, he cried shrewishly, out of his fright: "It is a lie! One of your sanctimonious lies, Louis! I know M. de Vitry and his dead father. Besides, Arsène is too clever to have anything to do with this—this Les Blanches—"

"I did not say he had anything to do with this," said Louis, gently. He closed his eyes a moment, as if in pain. "I said, it was suspected that de Vitry has organized this. Arsène—probably knows nothing of it. De Vitry is too shrewd. But if de Vitry were apprehended, it would not look well for Arsène, who is his dear friend. We cannot bear suspicion, we who have so lately returned to Mother Church."

"I shall speak to Arsène, when he returns," said Armand. He fell back on his cushions. He held his kerchief to his nose, and then surreptitiously wiped his brow. His hand visibly shook. His face wrinkled. He simulated anger.

"That Arsène! When will he cease being embroiled in some brothel fracas! I have warned him. This must be serious, this time, or he would not be so long absent." He hesitated, then lied: "I have made inquiries. I know where he is. It was some woman, the mistress, it is alleged of—of—" His mind faltered as it sought for a name sufficiently impressive, yet convincing.

"It is disgraceful," agreed Louis, with severity.

Armand, at ease now, smiled roguishly. But the spasms continued about his lips and the corners of his eyes.

"Ah, what a dog he is! My grandfather was such another. No woman was safe, not even the nurse who attended my grandmother when her twelfth child was born." He began to babble, incoherently. His voice was like the vibrating wings of a mother bird, who flutters before a weasel, seeking to lead it away from its young. "You may not have heard, Louis, that I caught that wretch, Arsène, in a most compromising position with a housemaid when he was barely fourteen. Reprehensible! Unspeakably scandalous!"

"Disgusting," murmured Louis, looking away from his father.

Armand chuckled, and the sound was hoarse. "True, very true. But what can one do with a libertine like that? I whipped him soundly, and M. le Archbishop himself reprimanded him, imposed penances upon him. Nothing is efficacious. Ah, well, he is still young. Sobriety comes with age, wisdom with failing virility—"

Louis might have remarked that such was not the case with his own father, but he only regarded Armand with gentle compassion.

"Let us pray this is so," he said.

Armand chuckled again, stared delightedly at the ceiling. "Arsène is a rival in virility of His Unholy Eminence, himself!"

He recalled what Louis was too late. He brought back his eyes to his son's face in deep alarm, cursing himself. But Louis' countenance was only grave and remote, and his eyes were too piercing. The young priest said nothing.

Armand rang furiously for his valet. "The lout!" he exclaimed frantically. "It is time for my bath, and he delays in the scullery with the wenches! This is too much!"

The door opened, and Armand began a string of shrill foul curses. But it was not the valet who stood there, in response to the frenzied summons. It was Arsène, himself, smiling, pale and at ease.

CHAPTER X

ARMAND STARED, blinking and paling, at this apparition, unable to speak. Louis rose involuntarily, with a kind of convulsive haste, seizing the back of his gilt chair, his black robes falling about him, a dim spasm passing over his cold and stately face.

Then Armand, with a cry, burst into tears. He held out his arms to Arsène, the hands making frenzied and urgent movements, such as a mother makes to her child who is in danger, his features working and twisting.

"You hound of lubricity!" he cried, choking over his tears. "Where have you been hiding yourself, in what wicked boudoir? Come to me at once, and kiss me! Mon Dieu, how I have missed your foul face! I loathe you, I spurn you, I disown you! Kiss me at once!"

There was more than passionate love, more than passionate relief and joy, in his trembling voice. Arsène, laughing loudly, came to his father, suffered the convulsive embraces, the quivering kisses, which were too vehement even for Armand's fatuous adoration. In the midst of all this vehemence, Armand's painted lips touched Arsène's ear, and there was a smothered whisper: "Beware! Les Blanches! Louis!" Then the cries, the wild kisses, the embraces, were renewed.

Arsène's expression showed nothing of what he had heard. He finally freed himself from his father's clutches, stood up, and held his father's jerking hand tightly, his own warm and strong with affection and reassurance. He turned to Louis.

"Bon jour, Monsieur le Curé," he said, lightly, in a humorous but affectionate voice, which had in it, for Louis, a familiar touch of mockery and satire. "You are looking well, as usual."

The brothers regarded each other in a swift silence, Arsène smiling, Louis cold and remote, his large blue eyes fixed and gleaming. Then Louis said, in a controlled and dignified tone:

"It is well you have returned, Arsène. My father has been ill with anxiety. Do you not think you owe us an explanation for this long absence, and an accounting of this escapade?"

Armand exclaimed, with some incoherence: "Mais oui! Most certainly! But he is ashamed, the dog! Certes, he is ashamed, or he would not have sent that miserable old abbé to you, Louis, with a mealy explanation of some 'accident'! Ah," he said, shaking a lean dark finger at Arsène with a terrified archness: "That was a fine, hypocritical touch! An abbé, you libertine! Where did you find the innocent? In your lady's boudoir? Or had he come to shrive you when her husband discovered you in her arms?"

Arsène laughed again, loudly. But Louis merely gazed at him. Arsène touched his cheek, and winked.

"Regard this scar. Is it not becoming? But you must let me have my secrets, my father. It would be ungallant to tell, would it not? When there is a lady involved, one is silent. Is that not so?"

Armand became aware, for the first time, of the crimson and jagged line on his son's cheek, and he regarded it with dread, for he saw that it was no mean injury. He also saw that Arsène was much thinner, much paler, and that he appeared exhausted, even emaciated. His craven heart, his adoring heart, plunged, sickened, rose on a wing of terror and grief.

"Was there a lady?" asked Louis, coldly.

Arsène shrugged. "Why do you ask that, Louis? Have you not, yourself, given me a wanton reputation? It is strange how perspicacious you are, for a chaste priest. Or do priests usually expect and suspect the obscene? It is very odd, for such celibates."

For the first time a flush appeared on Louis' pale cheek, and it was like the icy flush of sunset on snow. Arsène, above all men, always had the power to disconcert and enrage him. He looked at his brother with a long stare, lifeless yet somehow virulent.

"Do you not think it time to take a more sober view of life, Arsène? Have you considered Mademoiselle de Tremblant, who took to her bed upon your prolonged disappearance? I have attended her frequently, consoling her."

Arsène grinned evilly. "Without a stir of those frigid pulses, Louis? How could you gaze on such beauty, such white sloping shoulders, such a neck, without a movement of your ice-bound heart?"

Louis said nothing. He continued to gaze steadfastly at his brother, but he became mortally pale, as if a violating hand had touched him.

"You are ill!" cried Armand. "You must go to your bed instantly. Reach for the bell-rope, you stinking blackguard, and call Pierre to assist you to your chamber."

Arsène negligently lifted the perfume bottle from the table at his father's elbow. He removed the stopper, and sniffed deeply, consideringly. He cocked his head, stared into space. He frowned, pursed his lips, smiled, shook his head a little. Even in the midst of his fright, anxiety and agitation, Armand was struck, and waited for an explanation of these antics.

"Marvelous," said Arsène. His hand trembled with weakness as he replaced the bottle. "I think this is the best you have concocted. But is there not a trifle too much musk? I believe it detracts from a really exquisite subtlety."

Armand wet his lips. He bridled. He followed Arsène's cue with a hysterical eagerness, not untouched by pride and annoyance. His glittering black eyes roved, jerked, could not keep still.

"You coarse reprobate! How can you appreciate delicacy? There is not too much musk! There is barely enough." He seized the bottle, sniffed it critically, adoringly, his eyes fixed restlessly on Arsène. "This is my best. I have sent a vial of it to His Majesty, and one to Monsieur le Cardinal. They are appreciative. They have no taste for the barnyard, such as you have, you miserable scoundrel. I call it Fleur d'Amour."

"Banal," said Arsène, shaking his head. "Unimaginative. Why not call it 'Her Majesty'? That will be a delicate hint, and might induce Her Most Illustrious Majesty, the queen mother, to take a bath more than once in six months."

Armand laughed with convulsive shrillness, but Louis' fair brows knotted together with disgust.

"You consider that pleasantry respectful?" he asked.

"I insist there is too much musk," said Arsène, to his father.

Louis moved slightly. He turned towards the door. "I shall wait in the Rose Room for you, Arsène. I must have a few words with you."

Armand was again seized with terror. He clutched Arsène's hand, and glared with distended hatred at Louis.

"You have no heart, Louis! Can you not easily discern that Arsène is weak, ill, and must rest? I insist he go to his chambers at once! There will be plenty of time for inconsequential chatter."

"Nevertheless," said Louis, standing in the distant doorway, "I will, and must, speak to Arsène."

"Go to hell!" screamed Armand, losing control of himself.

Arsène, smiling, laid his hand on his father's shoulder, and pressed it deeply. "I wish to speak to Louis, also," he said, in a peculiar voice.

Armand, panting, looked up at his son with dilated and burning eyes, full of fearful warning. Arsène shook his head slightly, still smiling. Armand was only a little relieved. He was trembling visibly.

The door closed behind Louis. There was a silence in the room. Then, moving as lightly as a cat, Arsène went to the door, opened it. The sunny corridor outside was empty. Arsène felt some embarrassment. He had known that Louis, the immaculate, the loftily proud, would never, even in the interests of all that he held holy, have eavesdropped.

Laughing to himself, Arsène came back to his father, who sat upright in his chair, rigid, the spots of rouge standing out on his withered dark cheeks. Fright had him again. He shook his head at his son, and lifted his glittering and attenuated hand.

"No," he whispered. "I wish to know nothing. You must tell me nothing."

Arsène sat down negligently in the chair which Louis had vacated. He pulled it into the sunlight.

"I have suffered," said Armand. And now, there was a moving dignity about his elegant frivolity. "But what I have suffered is nothing, now that you have returned safely." He clasped his hands together, as if enduring a spasm of pain. "No man, no woman, no torment of my own, have caused me such distress as you have caused me, Arsène. Perhaps it is because I have loved no one but you."

Tears rose to his eyes, and there was nothing maudlin in them, but only the most moving sincerity. Arsène was unbearably touched. He took his father's shaking hand and kissed it gently.

"I beg your forgiveness, my father," he said, and there was no lightness, no gaiety, in his voice. "I must always beg your forgiveness. I am not worthy of your love. But what I do I must do."

The tears fell from Armand's eyes, streaked the rouge. But he only looked at Arsène with despair. Finally, he said, with difficulty, and even with an imploring note:

"There was a woman, Arsène?"

Arsène hesitated. Then he lifted his head and gazed dreamily through the casement. The golden sun was heavy with warmth and dust. From the busy street came the movement of many feet, the sound of many voices, the rumble of many carriages on the rough stones.

"Yes," said Arsène softly, "there was a woman."

Armand sighed. He leaned back in his chair, his hand still held in his son's. He closed his wrinkled eyes, exhausted. The kohl was blackly visible in their wrinkles, and on the lashes.

"And Mademoiselle de Tremblant?" he asked, faintly.

"Clarisse has nothing to do with this," said Arsène. "She is my betrothed. We shall be married in June, as planned. This—this woman has no part in my life. She is very young, very sweet, very beautiful. She is my friend. And chaste as crystal. No, she has nothing to do with this. She is not for me. I would not dare to touch her."

His mobile face saddened; the scar on his cheek puckered angrily.

"Nevertheless," he continued, almost inaudibly, "I know, for the first time in my life, what love is, what love can be. I feel no regret, no desire. I doubt if I shall see her again."

"Ah, l'amour!" said Armand, without opening his eyes, and sighing sentimentally. But there was a mechanical quality in his voice as if he were indifferent. "You cannot make her your mistress? Who can resist you, you lewd reprobate?" Now he opened his eyes and smiled roguishly.

But Arsène, grave and quiet, stood up, and looked down at his father.

"You whispered something to me? What is the meaning?"

Stark, ghastly with increased fright, Armand whispered: "Louis—before you entered, he asked me if I knew of—of one Les Blanches." He seized Arsène's hand again, and his own was cold, rigorous. "He did not accuse you of belonging to such, Arsène! But he did say that your friend, Paul de Vitry, was the organizer—"

Arsène started. He compressed his lips, gazed at his father piercingly.

"Did Louis say how he knew this?"

"No. No! I would not listen. Arsène, I dare listen to nothing, nothing! Have I not told you that? Have I not implored you to take care, to cease, to—"

Arsène interrupted remorselessly: "You should have listened to him. You should have questioned him. This is most frightfully important."

"Why?" cried Armand, forgetting caution in the extremity of his fear. "Why should this matter to you? No, no, do not answer me! I cannot bear it! I shall not listen. I shall not ask you again to consider your father, his position, all that I have wanted, and gained, and intrigued for, and desired—"

Arsène's expression revealed that he heard nothing of this. It was hard and intent.

"Have you heard from Paul? Have you seen him? Has he disappeared? In the name of God, my father, you must answer this for me!"

Armand had never heard such a note in his son's voice before, stern, implacable, coldly agitated. He wrung his hands together, tried to shrink before those inexorable eyes.

"You will kill me!" he moaned. "Is there no peace on earth for me? Shall I have no pleasure in what I have—"

"Lied for, betrayed for, violated for!" said Arsène, in a low and bitter tone. He bent over his father, pressed his hands on the other's shoulders, forced him to look into his own eyes.

"You must answer me. Where is Paul? Was he—did he —where is Paul?"

Armand shuddered, whimpered. "How you torture me, Arsène. There is no compassion in you, no affection for me, no consideration. What is this Paul de Vitry to me? I loathe him, I hate him, for what he is doing to— I know nothing, Arsène! I only know that two days after you—disappeared —he came to this house and asked for you, and pretended amazement when I said you had not returned from one of your nocturnal excursions. His arm—it was in a sling under his cloak. He was very pale."

"Then," said Arsène, aloud, but to himself, "he got away, safely." He sighed; the stern paleness of his face lessened. He even smiled a little. And then because he was so weak, he staggered, caught himself by clutching the window draperies.

Armand continued, stammering in his extremity: "He came again, only recently. I told him that you had sent an abbé, a miserable creature, with a message that you were well, and would soon return. I—I cursed him for leading you into dangerous and amorous adventures at night."

Arsène thought of that fiery and dedicated friend, and smiled involuntarily. He could not resist asking:

"And what did Paul say?"

Armand's eyes glittered vindictively. He said: " 'It is wrong, most certainly, and foolish. But a young man must have amusement. I humbly crave your forgiveness, Monsieur le Marquis. But what is one to do when one's blood is hot, and life is short? Surely, you are not guiltless of such escapades, and are young, still, with an appreciation of them.' " Armand smiled, and so capricious were his emotions, so facile, that even in these stern and terrifying moments he could bridle, put his head on one side, and shake his oiled ringlets, simpering reminiscently.

"I told him," he continued, "that there must be discretion even in adventure, and love. Husbands are notoriously narrow-minded with regard to their wives. I told him that he was no fit companion for you, Arsène, and that I would thank him to terminate the friendship."

Arsène could see as clearly as if he had been there during that interview the vivid terror on his father's face, could hear his screaming vehemence and hysteria as he denounced Paul de Vitry, and none too subtly threatened him.

"You are too virtuous to have such a son as I, my father," he said, gravely.

Armand, the facile and womanish, was outraged. "Young sir, I have had adventure such as you milk-blooded puppies could not conceive of, with your clumsy intrigues and dallyings. But I was discreet; there was some elegance in me. You are only coarse, like the boorish Germans, or the blood-swilling Englishmen. Ah, but I suppose that coarseness comes from your mother. Her grandfather was a German. The boorish taint is there, the animal lack of delicacy, the absence of the manner."

He was more at ease now, and only the tremor about his painted lips revealed through what an ordeal he had been passing. He spoke loudly, for the benefit of possible secret listeners.

Arsène smiled. "There is much in what you say," he admitted. He played with a golden tassel that hung from the draperies. His heart was slowing to its normal pace. "I will try to emulate you more, my father."

He went towards the door. Armand cried out.

"That Louis!" he exclaimed, and the supreme terror was on his face again. "That cold white serpent! Beware, Arsène. Beware your tongue. There is an enemy to freeze a man's blood. You will take care?"

Arsène raised his hand, and inclined his head. "I will be discreet. Have no fear. It is I, now, who will do the questioning. Louis has no subtlety."

CHAPTER XI

ARSENE HAD NOT REALIZED how weakened by illness he was until he began to descend the white fluid ribbon of the gilt and marble staircase, which curved and swung exquisitely through the center of the hôtel of the Marquis de Vaubon. It appeared to the young man that the staircase had lost its moorings, that it flowed and rippled through space, rising and falling, fluttering and streaming. He had to grip the golden banisters, and close his eyes, in order to keep from falling headlong. When he opened his eyes, finally, he was bathed in sweat. He was halfway down the staircase now; its lower reaches were shining in golden sunlight. He was face to face, on this landing, with the portrait of his grandfather, Étienne de Richepin, Marquis de Vaubon, heroic, and long dead of a stern martyrdom.

The portrait hung in the shining silence against its background of rose-silk walls, recessed in its gilt frame. Arsène had often wondered, cynically, why his father had permitted this portrait to be displayed, for Étienne de Richepin had been one of the most ferocious enemies of Holy Mother Church. But finally he had come to the conclusion that vanity prompted this display, and not a secret fidelity and mournful conscience. For Étienne de Richepin, slender, dark and fiery, with eyes that glowed and pierced, was a compelling personage even in his portrait. There was both delicacy and strength in that aristocratic countenance, which a short pointed beard and black mustaches could not hide. Under his plumed hat his eyes were alive and vivid, and his brows were sharp and stern. Like most Huguenots, he had affected somber garb. His collar had no lace upon it, but was made of the stiffest white linen, as were the cuffs showing at his wrists. His coat, his doublet, were of dark crimson cloth, the buttons of plain gold. His white hand, slender and strong,

92

rested on the hilt of his jewelled sword, the same sword that hung at Arsène's hip.

Arsène had always admired that portrait, though later he had smiled at the vivacious fanaticism of his grandfather's eyes. Étienne de Richepin had believed ardently, and to the death, in something. Arsène believed in nothing. So he had smiled. Once, Armand, who spoke rarely of his father, had impulsively quoted him as saying: "Take from me all things, even life, but leave me faith in God and man and I shall still have everything." Only a few months ago, Arsène had found those passionate words pathetically amusing. How naïve had been Étienne de Richepin!

Now, as he paused, panting, beneath the portrait, it seemed to him that a clear loud voice had called him, and that the voice came from his grandfather's thin stern lips. He looked into those glowing and austere eyes, and a living soul commanded him to listen, to meditate, to understand. Visitors had often declared that Arsène resembled his grandfather to a disconcerting degree, but Arsène had not believed it. He believed it now. The face that gazed down upon him was his own face, older and bearded, but surely his own.

I am feverish, he thought, passing his hand over his wet forehead, and steadying himself by pressing his other hand on the wall beside the portrait. But he could not free himself from the eyes that both implored and imperiously demanded of him. The portrait took upon itself a third dimension. It was a living man, of flesh and blood and ardent spirit, who stood in that frame, and the breast under the white collar and crimson cloth stirred and breathed.

Arsène could hear the voice he had never heard in life. Its intonations were crisp and firm, arrogant yet patient, uncompromising yet oddly gentle. The words he did not hear. But the voice sank into his soul. He began to pant a little, in his agitation and weakness. He was caught up into swimming light and shifting shadow.

Then, at the bottom of the staircase, which appeared to descend into eternity, he saw his brother Louis, standing calmly and watching him. The sun lay on that chaste and inexorable face, in those forbidding pale blue eyes like bits of lifeless but gleaming porcelain. It shimmered on that pale flaxen head, revealed the marble-like contours of his still lips. He was a statue in black robes.

Surely, there was nothing forboding in that presence to the casual eye, yet Arsène suddenly found it sinister, inhuman. And, contrasted with the living portrait, strangely dead, significant and portentous. Dead, yes, but none the less potent and baleful. Arsène had the mysterious sensation that there was some intense spiritual meaning for him in the juxtaposition of the portrait and the priest, something revealed and tremendous. His breath stopped in his throat.

Then, recovering himself, he slowly descended the staircase. Louis watched every step. There was a peculiar glitter in his eyes, like sun on icicles. Without a word, then, he moved, with his tall and stately tread, into the rose and blue frivolity of the reception room, and stood there, waiting for his brother.

Arsène found him in the center of the room, incongruous against the white and gilt walls, his black robes harsh against the background of blue shimmering rug and dainty rose-damask chairs and love-seats. The hanging crystal chandelier hung over his head, splintering, in the sunlight, into thousands of brilliant and delicate colors. Some of those colors, thin and clear, ran over Louis' impassive countenance. In a distant corner was a large marble group, a nymph and a satyr, in a most astounding posture, calculated to bring a blush even to a sophisticated cheek. Arsène, his eye touching that group, and then Louis, smiled involuntarily.

"You are ill," said Louis, in that voice of his which was as cool as snow and as lifeless. His eyes dwelt upon his brother with a remote curiosity in which there was no affection or concern.

Arsène, dark and slender, and taller than average, yet was much shorter than Louis, and more spare of body. But there was vitality in every glance of his glittering and restive eyes under their sharp and tilted black brows. There was impatient animation in his mobile mouth, whose corners turned upwards more than they turned down. Even his nose, curved and slender, dilated of nostril, expressed unresting energy and zest. His movements were swift, ardent with life, full of grace and virility. He was fire in the presence of ice. Louis regarded him dispassionately, hating what his brother was, loathing him for that life-energy which he did not himself possess, and which he feared.

"I have been ill," said Arsène, indifferently. "But I am recovering. You wished to speak to me, Louis?"

But Louis only gazed at him with his long slow look, a painted look without motion.

Finally he said, coldly: "Yes. I must speak to you. It is extremely important. Important for our father, whose welfare and peace of mind are very close to my heart."

94

"Do you have a heart?" asked Arsène negligently. But the words were old and mechanical, for he had spoken them many times. Nevertheless, they brought a gleam to Louis' face, as they always did.

He said, calmly: "You have changed, Arsène. I cannot tell where the change is, but it is there. Is it too much to hope that this means more sobriety, more responsibility? Or, is it only the result of your illness?"

He studied Arsène, and assured himself again, with faint surprise, that there was indeed a change. Were those restless eyes more steady, the mouth graver, the brow slightly drawn? What did this portend? Surely, there was sternness in the older man's aspect, a sadness about his lips.

Arsène said nothing. He was surprised himself. He wondered.

"However," said Louis, "I have little time. What I say must be said quickly. I hope you will give me your full attention, for I doubt that I will have such an opportunity again."

"You are becoming tedious," said Arsène, sharply. Louis was putting himself into the ridiculous rôle of a schoolmaster chiding a recalcitrant student. It was intolerable, if amusing. Yet, Arsène felt danger about him. "Speak plainly, and have done. I wish to go to bed. As you can see for yourself, I am not yet completely recovered."

But Louis only stood in the center of the room, unmoved, in a long silence. Then he said:

"I have heard that your dear friend, Comte de Vitry, is organizer of a nefarious Huguenot conspiracy called Les Blanches. Doubtless he has told you of this?"

Arsène watched his brother closely. "I do not recall," he murmured, coolly. "But what has this to do with me?"

"You would lie, certainly," stated Louis, with calm dignity. "That is to be expected. You were always a liar. Too, you would lie unblushingly to protect the Comte de Vitry. That does not concern me overmuch. What does concern me is your possible connection with Les Blanches. Even more than this, I am alarmed for my father."

"You are making absurd and unfounded accusations!" exclaimed Arsène. "But that is the nature of filthy priests. You think that when you make preposterous accusations, and utter ferocious threats, your victims, in an effort to defend themselves, will blurt out the real truth you suspected. That is a game you cannot play with me, Louis! The tricks of priests are well known to me. You speak of Les Blanches,

95

and accuse Paul de Vitry of a connection with it. What is it? I know nothing about it, nor does Paul, I am certain. Where have you obtained your information? Who is your informant?"

Louis was silent, his face unchanged. Then he began to smile, and the smile was more a convulsion than a human grimace.

"I never underestimated your cleverness, Arsène," he said, tranquilly. "But in this, you are too obvious, too unsubtle. Did you actually think you could goad me into giving you important information?"

Arsène was both embarrassed and deeply alarmed. He had underestimated Louis, who had long been the butt of ribald jokes between himself and his father. Here was a deathly antagonist, it seemed, to be respected and feared. He assumed a nonchalant attitude, made himself frown in a puzzled way.

"I do not know what you are talking about," he said, artlessly, as if perplexed.

Louis sighed. He shrugged. Then his features became stern, inexorable, and full of menace.

"Let us have done with this nonsense. The Comte de Vitry will be dealt with at our leisure. That is nothing to me. As I have told you, my only concern is with my father. Should you be caught in de Vitry's presence, during a meeting of Les Blanches, my father would die of grief and shock. For," and he spoke slowly and balefully, "there would be no mercy given to any of de Vitry's accomplices. You see, I speak plainly. The Cardinal's Guards broke into a meeting some time ago near the Quai de Ferraile, and there was a fight to the death. Eight of the Guards were killed. Satan, himself, must have been protecting the members of Les Blanches—"

Arsène had paled excessively; his eyes had glittered as he had listened. Now, at Louis' last words, blood rushed into his cheeks, and he breathed deeply. Louis watched him, and that faint grim smile, so merciless, touched his mouth understandingly.

"But the next time, evil will not be triumphant," continued Louis. "We know more, for one thing. It is true that all the members escaped, though not without injury to many. They must be remarkable swordsmen," he mused. "Far superior to the picked men of the Guards. It is sad that they do not attach themselves to those powerful ones who would appreciate such dexterity and excellence.

"But that is beside the point. As I have said, they will not

96

be so lucky the next time. Plans will be laid too carefully. We have our spies, our informants. Of course," he said, quickly, "all this is of no interest to you at all?"

"Of course," murmured Arsène.

"Forgive me if I bore you," said Louis, and again, he smiled that merciless smile, which was now brightened with irony. "I thought, however, that as a friend of the Comte de Vitry you might be interested. You might warn him, for instance, to desist from his treason and his suspected crimes. I prefer to believe him puerile and childish, for he comes of a very illustrious family who have long given devoted service to France. The Comte, himself, has great gifts. He has been a visitor in this house, and his sister, as you know, is Mother Superior of the Convent of le Sacré Coeur in Marseilles. In the event he is captured with red hands, as he will be captured, not even I could help him, or would help him."

"I understand that," said Arsène, with bitter contempt.

Louis ignored this as a childish remark. He resumed, with tranquillity:

"We have the names of many of the members of Les Blanches, but not all. It is only a matter of time until we have them. And after that, we will catch them during one of their meetings. Then there will be no saving any of them, no matter what their names, or their family connections, or their positions. We intend to stamp out this foul conspiracy to the last man. We intend to save France and the Church, and wash them clean in a river of blood—" His face became contorted with a cold and vindictive fury.

"It is an old custom," said Arsène, with a shrug, but surprised at this unusual manifestation of emotion in his brother. "Fire and blood are the usual weapons of Holy Mother Church. And the rack. That is proof of her eternal affection and solicitude."

Louis ignored this also. He continued: "The obscene blasphemy of the German Luther shall never pollute France again. We are determined on this. The Church is in the veins and the souls of Frenchmen. No foreign poison shall enter into them."

All at once, he was filled with madness. He looked at his brother, smiling, nonchalant and watchful in his dark satire, and hatred convulsed him. This graceful jackanapes! This light and colorful and laughing fool! This drunkard and libertine and dancer! This creature without sternness and strength! This, then, was the thing that his father loved and adored, and which must be protected for his sake! Louis' fists clenched

97

in the depths of his black robe, and all the yearning, all the anguish and bitterness of a lifetime, all the frustration and grief and hunger, welled up in him like a stream of fire! Ah, he could kill now, God help him! He did not know that the roaring about him was the roaring of his own disturbed and riven heart.

Mist was before his eyes, and he could not see that Arsène was watching him, astounded. For his face was no longer human, but mad and black, and his eyes were full of flame. Arsène, alarmed by something he knew was not of living flesh, and of the emotions of men, stepped back involuntarily, stirred to swift uneasiness. His hand fumbled for the hilt of his sword, for he discerned that in some way he was the object of all this fury.

Louis' voice came from his lips, choked and strangling: "Beware!" he cried. He turned suddenly, and made for the door, moving with a kind of haste and disorder. But when he had reached the door, the monstrous madness suddenly abated, leaving him with frozen flesh and wildly beating heart and sanity. He pressed his hand against the door, and bent his head. He forced himself to breathe slowly. His forehead was wet, and felt as though fingers of ice had been laid upon it.

Arsène, his uneasiness ebbing, looked at Louis sharply. He had seen these enigmatic and unfathomable manifestations of Louis' too often, and if he had ever tried to understand them, indolently, he did so no longer. They were only a part of his brother's general peculiarity and and esoteric character, amusing but unimportant. But since his own illness, the world had sharpened in his sight, become many-dimensioned, lit with nuances of meaning never discerned by him before. He was like a man recovered from color blindness and dimness of vision, and he was filled with excitement and wonder, racked by sensations that were new and too poignant.

As Louis, with bent head and quivering back, struggled for composure, Arsène said to himself: I have seen these seizures all my life. What do they portend? What is the curse? Often, during the most casual conversations with him, he has been seized by a kind of fit while he looked into my eyes, or quarrelled with me. Am I so hateful to him that his composure cracks? But why should he hate me so, even though he is narrow of mind and brittle of temperament? What have I done to him to arouse such enmity, such loathing? What is there in me to create such madness, such wildness? It is incomprehensible!

An occult and dreamlike sensation came over him, as though he thought and conjectured in the midst of a smothering nightmare. And he was overwhelmed with compassion, for all his bewilderment. Even though I am different from him, he thought, he ought not to hate me so. Divergencies of temperament are no excuse, no cause, for such monstrous emotion, especially in so lofty a mind.

He wanted to speak to Louis, gently, to demand, with impetuousness, the explanation for this great upheaval. But he could not speak. He could only wait.

Louis lifted his head. A deep shudder ran through him. He prayed silently: My God, I have sinned against Thee again, as I have often sinned! I have desired to kill, as Cain desired! I am evil and unregenerate, and a lifetime of prayer and dedication and chastity has not changed me. Forgive me, if Thou canst.

A kind of numbed and frozen calm finally came to him, which was not peace. He turned a still smooth face to Arsène, though its color was mortal and his blue eyes were clouded over with mist and threaded red veins.

"I have said all that can be said. I have given you warning. This is today. Tomorrow, I shall be able to do nothing." His voice was weak, yet steadfast, and he looked at Arsène. But Arsène had the uncanny sensation that Louis did not really see him. Then, having said this, Louis opened the door and stepped across the threshold.

Arsène spoke in a voice very grave and hesitant for so careless a young man:

"Louis, I too have something to say, if you will spare me a moment."

Louis turned upon the threshold, and regarded him with the blind gaze of stone. He was the priest again, patient.

"Please. You will come into the room, Louis? It is important, at least to me."

Then Louis saw his brother's face, discerned its gravity and obscure distress. He slowly reentered the room, quietly closed the door behind him.

"Monsieur the Cardinal is waiting for me," he said. "However, if it is a matter of extreme importance, I am glad to listen."

So tranquil was his manner, so stately his voice, that Arsène could hardly believe that it was only a few moments ago that Louis had been contorted with obscure madness. His blue eyes had cleared, and there was the usual polished gleam in them, which seemed rather on the surface than rising from some source within.

Arsène, with his brother's face bent upon him, hesitated. He ran his hand through his long dark hair, as if embarrassed.

"Louis," he began, "I have been absent for some time. You have been generous enough not to ask me where I have been."

An inscrutable flash passed over Louis' face. He lifted his hand.

"I have not asked. I do not wish to know."

Arsène shook his head impatiently, but he said in a pleading tone:

"Hear me out. You have said I have changed. This is true. I have been thinking, and perhaps the change is due to this. How can I begin to tell you! I do not know. You are not helping me."

Interest quickened in Louis' eye. He approached a step towards his brother.

"You have a confession to make, to me, as a priest?" His voice was incredulous, but hopeful.

Arsène was silent. Then he said, averting his head: "Yes. In a manner of speaking. This is very hard for me, for I have always been careless, living on the surface of things, as a fly dances over a pool in the sunlight. You must bear with me, Louis. These words are strange and unfamiliar in my mouth. I find them hard to say. They are like clumsy boots being forced over feet that not do fit them."

He paused. Louis waited, majestical in his black robes, a strangely gentle expression on his features. He was also consumed with curiosity, tinged with malice. Was it possible that this silly courtier, this dancer, this haunter of boudoirs, had experienced a change of heart?

Arsène continued, and now he seemed to be thinking aloud, feeling his way, rather than speaking to his brother:

"I cannot express what has happened to me. The thoughts I think are peculiar, and strange. I am shaken to the soul. I am in a different world. I have seen and heard astounding things."

He looked at Louis, his mobile face darkening, shining:

"I may seem naïve to you, Louis. I speak to you now as to a priest. Surely you can explain these things to me, help me to understand them, for you must have heard of them, if not experienced them yourself."

Louis' large white hand played with the golden cross that hung about his neck. His expression was benign and smooth.

Arsène made a desperate motion with his hands. "You see!" he exclaimed. "I am saying nothing at all to you! The things I have been thinking cannot be put into words! Never before have I thought of religion, of faith, of the power they have in men's lives, and the miracles they can perform. I have had a glimpse of it—"

Louis was not too astonished. As a priest, he had heard many amazing things. He regarded his brother's working features with detached benevolence, in which there was still a little suspicion.

"I have often tried to tell you, Arsène, that in Mother Church is the only refuge, the only peace. You have not listened; you have laughed. Is it possible that my words did not fall on stony soil, after all?"

Arsène did not speak. The strangest look stood in his dark and restive eyes as he stared at his brother. Then he said: "I had hoped that you might help me understand the world, understand men, help to find the way to what I must do."

"The Church," said Louis gravely, with a quiver in his voice, "is the interpreter of the world, the mouth of God. Deliver yourself up to her, Arsène, with humility, and you will understand all things."

Arsène's lips moved. A brilliant point of light appeared in the pupils of his eyes. He said, almost inaudibly: "I feel that there is something I must do— Something I must understand. Something against which I must set my shoulder and my strength."

Again, he made that desperate gesture. He moved to the window, stared unseeingly down at the heaving and vivacious stream of humanity that poured down the Champs-Élysées. He forgot Louis, who had suddenly become a weariness to him. That obtuse but pathetic priest, who had only banal words to blow against fevered flesh! He felt no impatience with his brother, no animosity, but only a great tiredness.

He said, as if to himself: "The Church can survive only in two ways: by nobly serving the best interests of men, or by serving the powerful. These two ways are irreconcilable. From what I have seen, and heard, she is lackey to kings and oppressors. Can she have a change of heart? Must a man work for that change of heart, or must he work sternly for her destruction, dedicating himself to the service of the oppressed and the voiceless?"

Louis listened. He started. He gazed at his brother's slender back, disbelieving that he had heard these words. His face

101

moved; his lips worked. Stark anguish leapt into his eyes, and he clasped his hands together as a shudder passed over his flesh. Had Arsène seen these strange manifestations, he would have been amazed.

Louis cried out, and his voice was muffled, yet strong: "One must believe that the Church can do no wrong, that all her servants work only for the good of man and God, and that it is the will of God that she bring all men under her wing! How is it possible to live, if one cannot believe this?"

Arsène did not turn back to the room. It was as though a flash of blinding light had passed over his vision. His dark slender hands clenched, pressed themselves hard against the window-sill. He wished to look at his brother, but something stern and mysterious prevented him, like a pressure upon his shoulders from another who did not wish him to gaze upon a naked and tormented soul.

"One must believe!" cried Louis, his voice rising on the sound of a tempest. "Otherwise, one must die! Or go mad!"

There was a silence, and the air in the bright and frivolous room quivered as though something violent had passed through it.

Then Louis cried out again, and his voice was the voice of a man in the most dreadful of travail, crying out in the loneliness of a desert full of darkness and pain:

"Faith! One must always have the faith! One must refuse to see, knowing that the eyes can lie, the heart deceive. One must clasp the unseen garments of Christ in the blackness of the night, believing always. One must wrestle, always—"

His voice broke. There was a great sigh in the room, as if a heart were assaulted, breaking with a groan that could express itself only in that sigh.

Then Arsène slowly turned and gazed at his brother. He saw his face. He closed his eyes, and a sickening wave of profound compassion and understanding rolled over him. He thought: It is not Calvary which is the tragedy. It is Gethsemene.

When he opened his eyes, Louis had gone.

CHAPTER XII

IT IS NOT POSSIBLE! thought Arsène. I have dreamed this.

For it did not seem to him that he had really heard what he had heard, or had seen what he had seen. A few weeks ago, he would have been stupefied, confused. But now, as he considered his brother, he was both deeply moved and alarmed. He had touched the pillar of ice, and it had melted under his hot and urgent hand. Here, too, was a man distraught and frenzied. The unfamiliar pity which he had lately learned for all things was like iron in his own heart.

He returned to his father, who was waiting in a very dishevelled state of mind.

"Has he gone?" he cried. "Did he threaten you, Arsène? What did he say to you? I have been chewing my nails to the quick!"

But Arsène said gravely: "Louis is ill, father. Ill in mind and spirit. You must promise me something. You must treat him more gently, with more compassion."

Armand stared. He could not encompass this. Then he exclaimed: "Poof! What nonsense. He has no bowels. However, if it will benefit you," he added, shrewdly, "I will coddle the serpent. I will kiss and embrace him. I will listen to his pious stupidities. I will even make a novena! Will that satisfy you?"

Arsène smiled. "It will, indeed. Be gentle with him. And now, I am very tired, and will go to bed for a while."

He waved his hand affectionately, and climbed slowly and heavily to his own chambers. His father's favorite valet, Pierre, was waiting for him. A jug of hot chocolate had been prepared for his sustenance, and there was a silver platter of small rich cakes. Pierre had drawn the silken draperies across the window, and the shimmering covers had been turned down upon the bed. Arsène climbed upon the stool, sank down in the comforting softness, and allowed Pierre to undress him.

Pierre, a young lean native of Picardy, with a shrewd sharp face, did not speak until Arsène was under the sheets. Then he poured a cup of the steaming chocolate and handed it to the other man. Arsène held it in his hands. They exchanged a long and significant look.

"There were two, Monsieur, whom I cut down dexterously," Pierre said, in a low harsh voice. He chuckled under his breath. "When Monsieur raced from the house, there were twelve in pursuit. I engaged four. Two, I killed, the others I wounded. But since then, I have had many anxious moments. However, Monsieur le Comte later reassured me."

Arsène laughed weakly. "What would I do without you, Pierre! And your long sword."

"Monsieur had splendid legs. He ran like the wind. At the last, it is legs that are important."

He regarded the scar on Arsène's cheek with concern. "It was treated wrongly, that scar. Had I treated it, there would have remained hardly a line."

Arsène touched the scar. "It does not add to my beauty? No matter. Did the others fare worse than this?"

"Monsieur de Bouilliard is still at death's door, I regret to say, Monsieur. But he is too fat. His Antoine had a hard time rescuing him."

"There is a traitor, somewhere, Pierre. Have you any suggestion?"

Pierre frowned, shook his head. Then his eye sparkled. "Ah, Monsieur! Only let me guess, and there will be no more treachery." He sighed, gustily. "What a night that was! Never have I enjoyed myself so much."

"You are too ferocious, my Pierre." But Arsène spoke mechanically. He thought for a few moments. "Pierre, you will wake me shortly after sunset. It is very important."

"Monsieur le Marquis is entertaining a few friends at dinner tonight. Is it your intention to join them?"

"No. You will explain to Monsieur le Marquis that I am still sleeping, and that it is best that I be not disturbed. No one must know that I have left this house."

"You are not leaving tonight, Monsieur? That is impossible, in your condition!"

"I must see the Comte de Vitry, Pierre. Do not annoy me. I expect you to keep every one away from this door, so that it will appear I am still sleeping."

He fell, suddenly, into a profound and exhausted slumber. Pierre stood by the bedside, gloomily and affectionately studying that pale countenance with its red scar. He played with the buttons on his doublet, and shook his head. Then he drew the heavy curtains closer about the windows, tiptoed silently from the room. So disturbed was he, that he proceeded to the kitchens to bully the wenches. He was a favorite in that household, and he presumed on this favor to exercise a petty tyranny over the other servants.

Shortly after sunset he reentered the chamber where Arsène still slept. He laid out black coat, doubtlet and hose, and a cloak and wide plumed hat. The room was thick with twilight. Arsène was breathing uneasily on the bed. Pierre shook him gently.

Arsène woke sluggishly.

"I have brought water for Monsieur," whispered Pierre. "But it is evident that Monsieur is being indiscreet in leaving the hôtel tonight."

Arsène shook his head impatiently, and, softly groaning, sat up. He was dizzy with weakness. He said nothing as Pierre, frowning disapprovingly, helped him to dress. He could hardly stand without swaying. His hands shook as he fastened on his sword, and examined the pistol which Pierre handed him. He thrust it in its holster.

"Shall I order a chair?" asked Pierre.

"No. Certainly not. I wish no one to know I have left the house. Pardieu, but I am as weak as a babe!"

"Monsieur will at least let me accompany him?"

"What an idiot you are, Pierre! And have half a dozen people peering into this room? Did I not tell you that I am supposed to be resting, and you are to guard the door? Where are your wits?"

They tiptoed down the back stairway, Pierre going ahead to reconnoiter. They met no one. The distant kitchens were abuzz, and delicious odors wafted from them, and the laughter of scullery maids. They descended to the wine cellars. There was a strong and acrid odor here, mingled with dust. Cobwebs hung from the low damp ceilings. Pierre lit a candle. They crept through the crypts. Rows upon rows of bottles marched along the walls. Immense casks loomed in their way. The cellars were enormous, and it took some time to pass through them. Finally they reached an iron door set deeply in the stone walls. Pierre produced a large key and opened the door. Close cold air rushed in upon them. The door opened upon a long and tortuous stone corridor.

Arsène entered the corridor, and Pierre closed and locked the door behind him. As in a pain-filled dream, Arsène threaded his way in the darkness, touching the wet walls with his hands. At times the corridor was hardly wide enough for a man to pass, and Arsène had to wedge sideways in the complete and echoing darkness. The passageway seemed interminable. Arsène's shirt clung wetly to his back. He could hear his own panting, loud and hollow. His feet struck sharply on the stone floor.

Now the air was becoming warmer, and the floor was rising. There were rough steps cut in the stone. Arsène painfully climbed them, almost sobbing with exertion. There was another passageway. He could hear the gurgling of sewers behind the walls, and the dripping of moisture. Above him was the long rumble of traffic. He paused to wipe his face, to breathe deeply of the unclean air, which smelled of decay and corruption. Something scuttled across his foot in the darkness, and he shivered. He heard the squealing of fat rats, and the rattle of their feet as they fled by him. Here and there he saw twin glows of tiny phosphorescence, malignant and alive. He withdrew his sword and struck at them. They winked and disappeared. He quickened his step, and pressed upwards.

At length he reached the end of the corridor. He stretched up his hands and felt the roughness of rusty iron. He thrust with the last of his failing strength. The iron moved. He pushed upwards, and as the iron plate moved aside, he saw the brightness of warm stars. It took him several moments to heave himself up, and longer to replace the iron plate.

He was in a deserted alley, filled with refuse, the walls leaning inwards. He looked about him. He heard the distant voice of the city. Pulling the cloak closely about him, drawing down his hat, and keeping close to the crumbling walls, he hurried down the length of the alley. He emerged into a street near the Luxembourg.

It was a quiet street, empty, lined with small but dignified houses, whose diamond-paned windows were yellow with lamp and candlelight. No one was abroad here. A fresh spring wind blew through the street, and the stars overhead brightened. Over one roof the glowing argent crescent of the new moon peered. Arsène hurried down the cobbled road, keeping his head bent. He reached a small but stately gray house with balconied windows. The gray silk draperies were drawn, but he saw a line of light in one upper room. He crept to the rear, between green hedges odorous with new leaf and bud.

He knocked swiftly at the garden door, and waited. His breath was labored, and he felt nauseated. The crescent moon brightened. There was a sweet wind, whispering and mysterious. At the end of the garden there was a brick wall, covered with flowering vines. A bird twittered sleepily in one of the old thick trees. There was no other sound.

Then the door silently opened, and a woman stood on the threshold, holding high a flickering candle. The light trembled on her pale and pointed face, which was framed smoothly with black and shining hair. She was a young voluptuous woman, with a splendid figure and carriage, clad in rich dark silks. A chain of gold and diamonds glittered about her full white throat. Her eyes, in the candlelight, were cold and watchful, black as velvet, and inscrutable, and her mouth was a crimson plum.

This was Madame Antoinette duPres, the mistress of Paul de Vitry, and Arsène had always detested her when he had condescended to notice her. Her husband had been a small shopkeeper, one of Paul's most devoted followers. He had been killed in a street riot. Shortly after that, Paul had taken his wife as the mistress of both his bed and his house. Friendship and passion had both prompted this, and Madame duPres was apparently devoted to her lover, who could see no fault in her. But Arsène had noted the hard corners of her lips, the avaricious gleam in her eyes, the arrogance of her manner which was the arrogance of the plebeian. She also had impudence of the plebeian, and tried to conceal the coarseness of her blood with grand manners and exaggerated elegances. She intimidated the more gentle and naïve of Paul's friends, who vaguely believed her to be a grande dame, for she was haughty and impertinent.

For the rest, she managed Paul's household with a hard and parsimonious hand, bullying the two servants and keeping an undeceived eye upon the larder. She also managed Paul, who adored her, and was a trifle afraid of her. He acknowledged her flinty and practical intelligence with amusement, for his was a lavish and generous nature, and of great sweetness and compassion.

"Were it not for my little Netta, I would soon be begging on the streets of Paris," he would say, fondly, as he caressed her white neck or played with her plump white fingers.

Arsène usually ignored her. In his eyes, she was no more than a scullery wench. Her deep and dusky voice irritated him. It annoyed him that Paul fatuously insisted upon her presence during all conferences and little dinners. There she would sit haughtily and complacently at the foot of the table, attending to the wants of the guests, bridling her handsome head, throwing glances about with what she imagined was the grand manner of a great lady of the blood. She had an indulgent and patronizing way with Paul, and sometimes imperiously pouted when he devoted too much attention to his friends.

Now, as she threw the candlelight on Arsène's face, inimical fire leapt to her big black eyes, and her full mouth tightened. A flush rose over her cheeks. Her breast heaved. She had hoped he was dead. Yet, there was a quivering about her heart.

"Monsieur le Comte?" asked Arsène, abruptly.

Madame duPres inclined her head backwards, with an impudent look. Arsène brushed by her, and in the passageway he removed his cloak and hat. He flung them into her arms, as he would have thrown them to a servant. Flushing, she began to let them drop to the floor, then caught them back as Arsène's eye fixed her. He then went on, tightening his baldric, which had become too loose for him during his illness.

He found Paul de Vitry lying on a couch in the little drawing-room, before a low fire. The room was austere, but tastefully furnished, and on the walls hung the portraits of de Vitry's illustrious ancestors. A large silver candelabrum stood upon a gilt table, and by this light Paul was reading. Arsène stood in the doorway watching him for an instant, observing how pale and drawn was his friend's face, how listless his attitude. One arm hung in a sling across his breast, and the fingers were white and waxen.

Arsène's heart swelled with love as he stood, still unseen, in the doorway. Morbleu! he thought. He is in worse condition than I.

Paul de Vitry was a dark and slender young man, lean and vital, with quick gray eyes both humorous and tender, and more than a little naïve. He had good clear features, and an expression of mingled sadness and sweetness and humor. Unlike Arsène, he wore his dark curly hair cropped very short, in the manner of the English Puritans, or Roundheads. This gave him a youthful and fawnlike look, and revealed his small ears. His clothing, too, was severe and Puritanical, made of black wool. His shirt was white and plain, and open at the neck. His hose were woolen, also, his shoes of rough leather.

About him there was an air both gentle yet resolute, steadfast and kind. As he turned the pages of the book, he sighed a little. Then, feeling Arsène's gaze upon him, he glanced up quickly. He was startled. Then he smiled, and the smile was eager, alive with affection and delight.

"Arsène! You have returned!" His voice, very soft but clear, trembled. He stretched out his free arm, and Arsène took his hand. They looked at each other, smiling.

"Ah, but you have been ill, and hurt," said Paul, scrutinizing the scar on his friend's cheek, and still holding his hand.

"And you. You did not fare any better," replied Arsène. He sat on the edge of the couch. "The others: have they recovered, too?"

Paul nodded, still smiling. "Yes. All but poor Gaston de Bouilliard." His face saddened. "There was a wound in his right lung. It is not expected that he will recover."

He sat up on his cushions. "But tell me: where have you been? What happened to you, after that night?"

Madame duPres entered the room. She sat down in a nearby chair, took up some delicate embroidery. She seemed absorbed in it. But she listened, her head averted.

Arsène recounted his adventures and Paul listened with deep intensity, his features expressing all his various emotions.

"We have a traitor amongst us," said Arsène. His eyes darkened with ferocity. "We must discover him, and deal with him. At once. So long as he lives, we are not safe."

"I have thought and thought," said Paul, with distress. "But who can it be? We have been very discreet. Only your servant, Pierre, and the servant of de Bouilliard accompanied us, knew about our meeting place. Is it possible we were followed?"

"We could have been followed only by those who have been informed," remarked Arsène. "Moreover, it is now known that you are head of Les Blanches. Who could have disclosed this? Too, several other names are known."

Paul drew his brows together in alarmed perplexity. "This is bad news," he murmured. "It is evident that we must not hold a meeting for some time. But who is the traitor?" He repeated the names of all the members of Les Blanches, questioningly, and at each name Arsène shook his head with impatience.

"No. Not that one!" he said, over and over. "A man is a traitor for one of two reasons: greed or disaffection. All of our members are men of wealth and position. They all joined because of their convictions. The traitor is elsewhere. Gaston de Bouilliard has an easy tongue. Is it possible that he has babbled innocently? No, that cannot be. He is sly enough, when his own welfare is concerned."

He frowned, concentrating his thoughts. Madame duPres bent closer over her embroidery.

"If we begin to suspect each other, then we are lost," complained Paul. He shifted uneasily on his cushions. Madame duPres rose instantly, adjusted the cushions. He smiled up at her adoringly, and she passed her hand swiftly over his head before returning to her chair. He followed her for a moment with his eyes.

Arsène watched this little play, and scowled. He stood up and regarded the fire. He said, without looking up: "If you please, Paul, I should like to talk to you, in privacy."

There was a small but piercing silence in the room. Arsène felt, rather than saw, the apologetic glance Paul gave his mistress. She rose with a rustle and a flounce, gathered up her embroidery, and sailed from the room. Arsène waited a few moments, then went to the carved doors and drew them tightly together, with a bang. Paul watched him, smilingly uneasily, a flush on his pale cheek. But he said nothing.

Arsène sat down again at his friend's side, and regarded him with sparkling eyes and a grave countenance. Paul quickened. He saw, for the first time, some mysterious change in the other. Arsène began to speak quickly, in a low voice:

"Paul, once you accused me of joining Les Blanches because I loved adventure and had an aversion for priests, and not because of some passionate conviction."

"Yes, that is true," admitted Paul, wonderingly.

"You spoke truly," said Arsène. He hesitated. He looked away, and frowned.

"I have seen and heard some strange things," he muttered. "My mind is in an upheaval. I cannot think clearly. I have laughed at you in the past, not understanding you. I did not try to understand. Now, you can tell me."

Paul was silent. But he was much moved. Arsène turned to him, and saw his expression, delighted yet still incredulous. Instinctively, their hands met again.

Then Paul began to speak, softly, meditatively, and his gray eyes dilated in the firelight, so that they glowed and welled with an inner radiance:

"All my life, since my first thoughts, I have had a dream, and I have questioned in my heart. I have thought to myself: What sustains the people in their eternal unrelieved anguish, their hopelessness, and endless, repeated pain? Are they helpless, like sea-weed moved by dark and resistless tides, and thoughtless, capable only of dim suffering, and incapable of questioning and revolt? Do they endure, I asked myself, because they can do nothing else?"

His face reflected old pain and sadness as he gazed up at Arsène, who listened with intensity.

"Or," said Paul, "is there in the people some vast unconscious faith, some profound movement which comes partly from themselves and partly from some deep and mystic source? Is there some divine moon which raises the tide in human hearts, and sends it roaring over the stony shingle of the world, bringing with it strange treasures and strange creatures and the shapes of new life? Is this, then, the secret of the endurance, the primordial unthinking faith of the dumb people, that in them is eternity, the arching of the tidal wave, the source of all life, the promise of the future, and the outline of new continents of man's desire and man's hope?"

He could not contain himself. He rose, and stood beside Arsène, and the light increased in fervor in his eyes.

"Who can resist the people when they feel this immensity in themselves? No one, neither King nor priest, arms or fury or death. And then I knew that in this age the tumult in the people was beginning again, after sluggish centuries of oppression and despair. This was the age of enlightenment, of consciousness, of recognition of tyrants, of the understanding of the power of the people!"

He laid his shaking hand on Arsène's shoulder urgently.

"I am not a Huguenot by tradition, or by irritable revolt, like yours, Arsène! I am a Huguenot because I believe, and know, that in the Reformation sounds the voice of the people, stern and passionate, desirous of freedom, heavy with the future. The people are rising once more out of the ruck and mud of blind centuries, and they are looking about them. This age is clamorous with their voices, filled with the lightning of their eyes! The people everywhere, in England, France, Spain, Germany, Italy! This is the movement whose waves shall roll into the coming centuries, bearing upon them the sails of liberty, brotherhood, peace, knowledge and equality!"

Arsène was passionately moved. He heard a dim tumult in his ears, and he closed his eyes on a vivid remembrance of his dream.

"This is only the dawn," said Paul, in a trembling voice. "We shall not see the full noon in our lifetime, Arsène. But it is coming. Who can obscure the sun, cause it to hurtle down again beyond the black horizon? No one! The sound of the day is here, when there shall not be Frenchmen or Englishmen, Germans or Spaniards, Russians or Italians. There shall be only men. And all the foulness and plottings of evil men, of kings and priests and tyrants, can only darken the day a little with passing clouds. But they cannot halt the sun in his course."

Incredible words, words without meaning! thought Arsène. Yet he felt a movement in his heart below the incredulity of his mind. So must the Pagans have felt, at the first words of Christ.

Paul continued, and his voice was stronger: "The rivers of the world flow through every man's door. We are attached by an umbilical cord to the farthest star. This is a truth which wicked men have, through thousands of years, tried to deny, with lies and superstition, with treachery and greed. It was a truth which I did not always know. My mother was a devout Catholic; I was nurtured in the faith of Rome. Did it teach me the universality of all men? No, it taught me superstition and ignorance, oppression and bigotry. Who were the perpetrators of this montrous sin against all men? Christianity? No, the evil ones who served Christianity! Therefore, I have no quarrel with the Church. My quarrel is with her servants. It is they we must combat, destroy, if brotherhood and compassion are to come upon the world."

He paused, then went on: "And so it is that I have thought of de Buckingham, of Germany. I have thought to go to England, to the Germans, and enlist them in my crusade. There are some among them who think as I do—"

But Arsène was suddenly horrified, and alarmed.

"The English! Our hereditary enemies! And their brothers, the Germans, who are also our hereditary enemies! This is preposterous. It is treason, Paul. I loathe the English. I particularly despise the Germans. I have visited Prussia and Saxony. What boars! What indelicate beasts! The German soul is at once coarse and mystical, romantic and piggish, practical and illogical. It is also ghoulish, and full of nightmare, concerned with delicate fantasy and horrible cheeses." He laughed a little. "Once I heard the Duc de Richelieu say: 'A nation that concocts and eats such putrid cheeses is worthy of Luther.'"

Paul sighed, he smiled a little, and shook his head. He sat down again and contemplated the fire.

Arsène was sobered. He leaned over his friend. "Paul, I do not understand much of what you have said. But I have felt a little in my heart. But I cannot be allied with anything which is treacherous to France—"

"You do not understand!" cried Paul, with impetuous sadness. "I have not made you understand! I have not made

112

you see that there are no nations, but only men, and that our business is with men, and not kingdoms, not politics. I talk to you of men's souls and men's freedom, and you answer me with rubbish about cheeses! You are only a bravo, after all. There is no place for you at my side."

But Arsène was not offended. He stared sharply at Paul, and bit his lip.

"The Reformation," said Paul, clasping his hands and gazing at the fire, "is more than a religious movement. It is truly secular. It is the coming of a new world, a world of new boundaries, of new economics, of a new understanding of man's place in nature and before God, of new politics and new governments and new philosophies. What has the Church said: 'For the masters, piety, rule and charity. For the people, servitude, piety and obedience and ignorance.' But we say: 'For the masters, responsibility, justice and mercy. For the people, responsibility, brotherhood, enlightenment, and liberty.' This is the movement inherent in the Reformation, which is not only concerned with doctrines, but with men."

His face shone, became vivid with the violence of his faith and his passion. He seemed to forget Arsène. He struck his clenched fist slowly and heavily upon his knee. He took on himself a glowing beauty and fervor.

Arsène sighed, shook his head again. "I cannot encompass these things, Paul. Morbleu! With all my heart I wish I could understand! But though I do not understand, I know you speak truth. I will stand beside you, blindly, as a soldier stands, not comprehending the full extent of the orders he has been given, but wishing only to obey, trusting."

Paul smiled. He reached up and took Arsène's hand, pressing it warmly and firmly. "I have always trusted you, Arsène. I know I can still trust you."

"You are a saint!" exclaimed Arsène, impulsively, swelling with his love for his friend. "It is not given to men to understand saints, but only to adore them."

Paul laughed a little at this extravagance. He was still heavy-hearted. He had not made this exuberant, this headlong and foolhardy young man understand. But he knew his devotion, and though it was built only on personal affection, it was strong and ardent.

And then Paul knew that leaders must rely upon this form of adoration and service, even though it was blind and bewildered. It was not given to all men to understand.

But Arsène, as he painfully made his way home through the tunnel, felt that he was a little closer to the comprehension

113

of the things he had heard the Abbé Mourion say, and that though there was much that would forever remain closed to him, he was in the service of a dream that could not fail mankind.

CHAPTER XIII

It was Louis de Richepin's custom, after the early mass which he attended, and at which he sometimes officiated, to walk in the fresh morning in the Bois.

The hour would be so early that no one would be abroad but himself, under the spring trees struck deeply in their hearts by the new golden sun. The paths over which he would walk would still be tangled in moist dark shade, heavy with the perfume of the earth, and he would see snails lumbering before him, and the small writhing whiteness of worms. But the birds would be awake, trilling with unbearable sweetness in the boughs of the trees, and the slope of their wings, as they flew, would catch the shining brilliance of the sun, so that they carried a swift and momentary brightness into the bosky shadows. Here and there he saw small flowers in the new green grass, and sometimes, as the gentle wind blew, a scarf of perfume would be drawn invisibly across his face.

The peace and the silence would sink deeply into a heart that knew so little peace. He would pace slowly and majestically, and his features would become less rigid and more calm. Once or twice he would pause to observe, with strange tenderness, the scurryings of some small animal, or watch the wheeling curve of a wing against the pure sky. Here, he thought that he meditated, but in reality he did not think at all. His mind, always so filled with stern dark shapes, like images of frozen despair or grief, would empty itself, and he knew the blessed surcease from thought.

He often carried a prayer book with him, one finger in the midst of the pages. He would bend his eyes on the book at intervals, and his lips would move. But his mind and his heart did not absorb them, because, for a little while, he was happy. Along these silent paths, broken into sunlight or into darkness, he thought of nothing at all, not even of the God

115

who pursued him everywhere but here. For here was sanctuary and complete peace.

On this morning he had brought with him a book he had found in the Cardinal's library the evening before. His Eminence had watched him take the little book, whose leather cover, from which the gilt had long gone, was flaking away into brown dust.

"That is a strange book," said the Cardinal, in a peculiar voice. "I would not advise you to take it."

"Why?" asked Louis, with surprise. "It is well read, for the pages are worn and torn. Has Monsieur le Cardinal read it, himself?"

The Cardinal smiled. He bent his eyes upon the book in his secretary's hand. He was silent for several long moments.

"Yes," he said, at last, "I have read it. Many times. Nevertheless, I do not suggest that you read it, Louis. I do not forbid it." He paused, and his eyes, changeable and unfathomable like a cat's eyes, glinted with something very near to malevolence. He drew his brows together, and stared at Louis with a cold but smiling curiosity.

"Read it, then," he added. When Louis had left the great chamber, he had paused at the doorway, and had glanced back for some reason he could not understand. The Cardinal was watching him, and his smile had something evil and amused in it.

It was then, with profound shock, that Louis said to himself: He hates me!

That look, and that thought, had kept the young priest sleepless that night. He had placed the little thick book upon a table near his austere bed, and the low lamp had burned feebly upon it until dawn. And Louis had lain there, looking at it, and remembering the Cardinal's eyes.

He had gotten up, attended mass, and prepared for his morning's walk in the Bois. The book still lay on the table, and Louis had hesitated. Then, tightening his mouth, he had picked it up and carried it away with him.

He walked a considerable distance, with the book in his hand, vowing over and over that he would not read it. Now the weight in his hands seemed an evil weight, as if of some pollution, something deadly. But the morning was so peaceful, so brilliant, and so beautiful, that he thought that nothing could hurt him or distress him, no matter what it was.

He opened the book. It fell open at once to a certain page, as if some unseen hand had forcibly turned the pages. The characters were brown and faded. The title had long been obliterated from the cover, and the name of the author. Louis stood in a sun-washed break between two great trees, and read:

"The desolate heritages of the people! They are heirs to all sadnesses, all sorrows, all anguishes and agonies. They steal hope and faith, furtively, mournfully, as men search ruins for food. They set out with feeble lanterns through a dark land, turning their little lights despairingly over meaningless chaos through which deceitful paths run into nothingness, or into pits or chasms. They cry out in the night in response to echoes which mock them; they bivouack in stony mountains. They find nothing, not even a guidance, in the cold stars. They come upon empty temples whose fallen gods are nameless. They flee from the bellowing of unseen armies. In the shadows, they look for the faces of friends, but they find only bodiless ghosts. They wander in the mists, and cower beneath the storms. The earth is to them an unknown and a wild land, hating them as a far land hates the alien.

"And then men think in their hearts: We are strangers, and the earth looks at us with loathing. We have no home, neither in the darkness from which we came, nor in the darkness into which we go. We are lost in an eternity which heeds us not, and only our voices and our prayers return to us from the slope of the heavens. In the fugitive dawn there is no light for us. In our death we are alone, and we go into the bottomless abyss without hope, and only with one long last cry."

The book seemed to close by itself in Louis' hands. He stood in the sunlight, but all the tranquil peace had gone from his face. Suddenly, he shuddered, as if struck by an icy wind. He experienced a deep sickness, as though he had fallen a great distance, and he heard the painful beating of his own heart.

This is ridiculous, he thought to himself, but the thought echoed with a hollow sound all through the labyrinths of his brain. It is an evil thing, this book, he thought again. But I have read evil things before, and I have felt only contempt for them.

It seemed to him that a malignant laughing whisper blew into his ear: Ah, but never before have I read the things which have lain groaning in my own soul!

He looked at the book in his hand, and he said aloud, fiercely: "Satan, himself, has given this to me as a test of my faith!"

Satan! And then, as he stood in the sunlight, he seemed to see the Cardinal's faintly smiling face, and to hear his voice:

117

"My dear Louis, superstition is the realism of the simple, the allegory of the intelligent."

He had gazed at Louis with his ironical eyes, and had smiled again.

More and more sickened, Louis moved out of the sunlight into the cool dusky shadows under the trees. He felt extraordinarily weak and powerless. He sat down on the grass near the pathway. He looked again at the book. Then he shuddered again, and threw the book from him. He covered his face with his hands. He could not endure to look on all this beauty and brightness and peace, which appeared to have taken on itself the glare of anguish.

Again, the Cardinal's face rose up before him like a satirical apparition, and Louis said again to himself: He hates me. Now, with horror, he knew the extent of that hatred, which was impersonal yet none the less horrifying. Even he, whom I have served faithfully, hates me, he thought. There is none in all the world who loves me, or who has ever loved me.

He had another terrible thought, remembering the Cardinal, and remembering that peculiar smile and the last glance. He believes that I am a hypocrite, a liar, a man of weak faith and foolish lies, he said to himself, appalled. That is why he did not take that foul book from me. He wished me to read it, and see in its pages, as in a mirror, my own face.

An old black horror took hold upon him, deeper than despondency, nameless and cold and paralyzing. He felt all strength, all life, drain out of his body, and in its place was the dark ichor of dissolution, as though his heart was dying. A thousand, thousand times, he had beaten back this horror, this agony of the soul, and a thousand thousand times, he had believed he had triumphed. Now he knew that he had never won a single battle, in spite of all the tortured prayers, the passionate will to belief, the mystic affirmation like a cry in a whirlwind. He had tried to believe with the simplicities of a peasant, with the naïveté of a child, but he felt some dreadful sense of degradation after these agonized excursions into illiteracy. Litanies and paternosters, repetitions and chants: all these he had tried, in the depths of his torment. But his mind stood aloof, like a pillar of salt in the midst of surging ants, full of disgust.

Once the Cardinal had said to him: "There are some who believe with the heart, and others with the spirit, but only a few with the mind. Nevertheless, those who believe with the mind are the truly great, the rulers of men."

I have believed with my heart, and with my soul, he thought, wringing his hands together in his frightful desolation. But never have I believed with my mind.

He tried to conjure up a conviction of guilt, as a demented man will dash his head against a wall. But he felt no guilt. He felt only the old bottomless emptiness, the old shapeless horror, the old disintegrating despair.

It was this conflict between his mind and his will-to-believe, that had driven him into the Church. He had gone into the Church because he wished to believe, for in faith he believed he would find at last some peace, some consolation for a world that appeared to hate him, some love in response to the aching hunger of his heart. Many times, he convinced himself that he had found true faith, and he thought at those times that he was happy, because the pain had gone even if no ecstasy accompanied the going. But, most of all, he had found hatred, though he dared not peer down into his own soul to find the reason for this hatred. But his mind suspected it. It suspected that the hatred arose because he had no faith, and felt himself threatened, and so, he must hate others who felt no faith and threatened what little he sometimes had by their affirmation of faithlessness.

Now, this morning, he could not turn away his eyes from his hatred, and he remembered with what a strange gleaming smile the Cardinal had said to him one day:

"I have always suspected that the holy men of the Inquisition were atheists."

Louis' frightened mind had become confused then, but now he knew that the confusion was self-induced, in self-defense, for he dared not look deeply into himself.

"Do not become a fanatic, my dear Louis," the Cardinal had said on another occasion. "I distrust fanatics, for they are men who hate themselves, and thus hate other men."

This had been on the occasion when Louis, with one of his rare but savage bursts of vehemence, had forgotten the respect he owed the Cardinal and had cried out against His Eminence's policy of placating the Huguenot nobles "for the life and strength of France." What life and strength would France have, if heresy triumphed? Louis had cried out, his voice shaking with his passion and fury. What did it matter if France became the greatest among nations if the Huguenot pestilence became strong in her midst and her soul perished?

Better that France became the least and smallest, rather than the pestilence flourish.

But when the Cardinal had replied in his cool and serene voice, Louis had been silent. He had wanted to cry out again, but some inexplicable numbness had come over his tongue. Now he knew, and the numbness was no longer inexplicable.

He had gone back to the old conflict with a grim despair and determination. The Huguenots became an obsession with him. Heresy threatened not only the Church, but himself, his life, his peace. It became a sword at his own throat, held by a laughing and hating and jeering man. His natural severity increased to cruelty and ruthlessness, his natural melancholy to a brooding ferocity. Finally, at length, he deceived himself to the extent that he thought of himself as a passionate soldier of Christ, dedicated to God. His subordinates groaned under his severities, penalties and punishments, and the endless work he imposed upon them. They laughed at him. At length they hated him. He saw their hatred in their meek eyes. And never, even now, could he control the sudden sick plunging of his heart, the sudden frightful sadness, the sudden malaise and bitter hunger, at the sight of hatred for himself in another man's eyes.

Increasingly, now, he felt the emptiness of his heart. It was not a weariness of the flesh which oppressed him, though he slept little. It was a lack of feeling, as though part of his spirit were paralyzed. He could feel nothing but hatred and anger, and nameless yearning. But now, even the yearning had become dull, and only the hatred and anger remained, like madmen rioting in an empty house from which all others had fled.

Only in the Bois, as he walked alone in the morning, did he find even the shadow of peace. It was the peace of negation, when he had the strength to cease from thinking, when he could escape the God in which his mind did not believe in spite of all his struggles, and when the wild and enormous longing of all his life, nameless and formless, ceased to beat him with invisible but crushing wings.

But now the Bois was lost to him forever, too. He could never walk here again, for he would remember that foul book that looked up at him with his own silent words. He stood up, with a breath that was like a groan, and looked about him as a man looks for an avenue of escape from death.

And then, as always, when he passed through his private hells of despair and torture, he saw his brother's face, and his hatred flared up again with ghastly intensity, like the explosion of gunpowder. For his brother had become to him the symbol of the heresy which by its existence threatened the faith and life of Louis de Richepin. Arsène had become the visible sign of his own lovelessness and colossal if mysterious grief, that laughing buffoon, that maker-of-legs, that libertine and adventurer! Louis still did not know that it was his own personal hatred for Arsène which had driven him into a Church that brought him no consolation and no release, which had made him the enemy of all men, and had aroused in him a ruthlessness and inexorableness which was to destroy him. The Cardinal had long suspected this, and he derived much exhilaration in meditation upon the small but personal imponderabilities of individual men which finally shape world destinies. As a hater of mankind himself, but with amusement, the Cardinal never tired of these meditations, which gave him a pleasure beyond concupiscence.

Clenching his hands, groaning under his breath, Louis paced back and forth under the trees in his black robes, his face appalling in its expression as he contemplated the thought of his brother. Morning sunlight struck into his eyes, which flashed evilly. And so it was that he did not hear the soft thudding of a horse's approach until the animal actually stood before him, and the rider smiled down at him with timid pleasure and hidden ecstasy.

He glanced up, and started. A young woman, not more than seventeen years old, sat lightly and gracefully on the back of the great white animal. Her voluminous riding habit of black velvet heightened the translucence of her face and neck, in which all shades of rose and snow raced like delicate shadows. This fragile ebb and flow of soft color was strongest in her sweet curved lips. Under bronze brows as smooth and silken as a butterfly's wings, her shining eyes were golden and glowing and ardent with youth and life. Her small plumed black hat was tilted to show to best advantage the masses and riotious curls of dark but bright auburn hair, whose shadows burned with deep gold or rich red. She was slight of body, with a waist of astonishing fragility and a bosom arching and proud, yet tender, and her tiny foot rested firmly in the stirrup. Her gloved hand held the reins lightly, the other played lightly with the whip.

She was all grace, all delicacy, all dainty beauty, though the luminous quality of her coloring seemed more febrile than healthy. A light seemed to well through her flesh, an intense light which inspired those who loved her with the fear that

121

one day it might consume that small and lovely body.

She smiled down upon the young priest, and a wave of bright radiance passed over her face.

"Good morning, Monseigneur de Richepin!" she cried, softly, and her voice was like the pure trilling of a nightingale.

The glacial rigidity broke and vanished from Louis' countenance. He bowed and smiled, a nameless warmth beginning to radiate through him.

"Good morning, my dear Mademoiselle de Tremblant!" he exclaimed. He approached the horse, and laid his hand on the trembling neck. At a discreet distance, the groom, on his small brown horse, waited, and stared heavily at the trees. "Is it not early for you to be abroad?" continued Louis.

A curious breathlessness made him pant a little, and a tremor passed over his limbs. The girl let the reins drop upon the horse's neck, and though her smile had gone, the beautiful welling of tinted shadow increased in her cheeks and lips.

"I ride every morning," she answered.

There was a poignant moment of silence between the young priest and the girl, as they looked into each other's eyes. Then Louis said, in a voice that shook more than a little:

"And how is your sister, Mademoiselle Clarisse?"

"She is much improved, now that Arsène has returned, though he has sent only messages to her. However, he promises to visit her today."

At the sound of that hated name, Louis' features contracted. His hand fell from the horse's neck. He averted his head. Then, seeing that the girl had slipped her foot from the stirrup, he hastily offered her his hand. She sprang lightly from the animal's back, and stood beside him. The top of her bright plumed head hardly reached to Louis' shoulder. For a moment, as they faced each other, they remained unaware that their hands were still intertwined. The green light of the trees heightened the gold of the girl's eyes.

Too removed from the passions and the sensibilities of ordinary men except in his abnormal hatred, Louis did not understand the significance of the heat and trembling of his flesh. He was aware of the disturbed beating of his heart, of the sudden unbearable beauty of the light-struck brilliance of the glade. To his ears, the songs of the birds were distilled rapture, the wind a deep chant, the sky shaking with light. The ground under his feet appeared to move and tremble.

As he looked down at the girl, he was vaguely surprised

to see that she suddenly started, that her cheeks flushed a warm crimson. It was not until he felt the withdrawal of her little gloved fingers that he understood. With the withdrawal, he experienced a profound shock of deprivation and pain.

The girl moved gracefully down the path, and he followed her. She glanced back over her shoulder at the groom, but he had calmly ridden to the abandoned horse, had taken up the reins, and then had sat there, waiting in silence, as though at a silent signal. He watched his mistress and the priest until they disappeared through the trees, and then he winked, grinned, muttered a coarse word or two to the disinterested birds. He began to whistle shrilly.

Louis and Mademoiselle Marguerite de Tremblant continued their speechless passage through the green aisles. They came at last to a heap of sun-warmed rocks at a distance from the path. Louis helped the girl to climb upon the topmost rock, and then sat at her feet on a lower one. Marguerite, still without speaking, removed her hat, and shook her head until her loosened hair billowed about her cheeks and forehead and snowy neck. It seemed to have a vitality and life of its own, too powerful for her fragility, too heavy for her strength. But when she smiled, a dazzling light sprang from her lips and eyes. At the base of her white throat, a pulse beat and swelled as though her heart had risen from its accustomed place.

They did not speak. A dreamy ecstasy possessed Louis. He smiled dimly about him. He saw the girl's foot near his elbow, and one little white hand. She had removed her gloves. The hand shook more than a trifle.

He had seen Marguerite at the bedside of her petulant and pretty sister on each of his visits to his brother's betrothed. The girl had a quality of sustained devotion and selflessness that had impressed him most favorably. Not given much to speech, she had not conversed with him to any extent. He had innocently found it necessary to visit the distraught Clarisse frequently, to console her and minister to her spiritual needs. But even as he did this, he was not aware that his eyes dwelt long and deeply on her older sister, nor was he aware that she gazed back at him as intensely.

However, on one occasion she had timidly informed him that she believed she had a religious vocation. Then he had become eloquent. As he spoke, Clarisse's large pale blue eyes had wandered cynically from the young priest to Marguerite, and once or twice she had put her long white fingers irrepressibly to her lips. Neither of the two innocents had observed this worldly by-play. They had conversed eagerly with each other, each face brightening more and more.

Now, as they sat together in the lofty green peace of the Bois, Louis said:

"Mademoiselle, have you come to any conclusion about entering an order?"

Marquerite twined a silken curl about her fingers. She replied, in a low voice:

"I have consulted Mamma. She was horrified. She wishes me to consider the Comte de Ramboud." She hesitated. "Mamma spoke to my uncle, the Comte de Tremblant, my father's brother—"

"But he is a Huguenot!" cried Louis. A deep sickness at the mention of the Comte de Ramboud pervaded his heart, and his face paled. He was suddenly filled with an obscure but powerful rage, a bitter and enormous hunger.

Marguerite smiled, shrugged her pretty shoulders. "That is so. However, he gave me grave consideration, and urged Mamma to be patient and tolerant."

But Louis hardly heard. His eyes fixed themselves fully on the girl's face, and woman as she was, she saw all that was to be seen, and her heart bounded and leaped with an agony of joy.

"It is a sin to interfere with another's vocation," said Louis. His lips were white and dry. "Mademoiselle, if it is your heart, you must not disobey the call of God."

She was silent. A sudden and inexplicable sadness possessed her. She gazed down at him with a mute and passionate earnestness and yearning.

Again, neither spoke, but an irresistible force brought their hands together, and the fingers clung as if both were drowning in deep black seas.

A squirrel ran through last year's leaves, near their feet. A large bird pecked in the ground. The soft wind rose, parted the trees, so that shafts of long sunlight fell over them, was gone, leaving green translucence behind. The girl looked down at that still and marble countenance near her knee, and she drew a long and quivering breath that was almost a sob. The pulse quickened in her throat.

She said in a mournful whisper: "The world holds nothing for me. I am in such sorrow, Monseigneur de Richepin."

He did not ask the reason for this sorrow. For sorrow had, all at once, rolled over him, and they sat together, their hands intertwined. Yet, with the sorrow, was a formless but passionate rapture, like diffused light on turbulent dark waves.

They experienced it together; their souls ran to each other and clung, weeping wordlessly. They became aware of each other's flesh and warmth; their yearning mingled, but it was not a desperate yearning.

Their eyes grew dim and misted, seeing only the shattered and dazzling light of earth and sky. They heard each other's breath, uneven and shaken. The warmth of their hands mingled, and it seemed that the flesh dissolved and they were one flesh. The songs of the birds, and the deep shining silence, became part of them, part of their unspoken emotion and their rising anguish of joy.

Now, all at once, the invisible but crushing wings of Louis' old agony lifted, fled away into soundless space. A wild and unfathomable fulfilment flooded his soul, and with it came a feeling of power and ecstasy, and great release. It shook the bastions of his grim gray hatred. He was transported to some realm of flame, unbearably bright, and his spirit seemed to become incandescent. He shivered. His heart rolled and tugged. Nameless cries rang through his ears. His loneliness was consumed like a straw in a leaping fire. He thought: I am not alone! And as if the words were a spell, the pillar of salt that was his mind was shattered and destroyed and poured out.

Now, he could believe in the presence of God. He felt that presence all about him, like a pervading radiance. Everything was good, explained, full of bottomless peace. Tears rose to his eyes. He thought, humbly and with joy: I understand the visitation which is God.

But still, so innocent was he, that he did not know what had come to him.

He whispered: "Mademoiselle, the Comte de Rambaud—?"

She bent over him. Her dark bright curls touched his cheek.

"There is no one for me, but—" she whispered in return.

Their eyes were close together. They held their breath. Their lips came closer, met, clung. At that touch, they were both swept into a veritable agony, blinding, disintegrating, blown upon by winds of savage harmony. They felt nothing, saw nothing, but this. The universe swirled about them, filled with bursting stars and blazing nebulæ. They heard a roaring in and about them, and did not know that it was the beating of their hearts.

They drew apart. Like twin flames leaping together, their eyes held entranced. Then Marguerite's little white hands enclosed Louis' face. Tears ran down her cheeks. His face turned in her hold, and his lips pressed themselves against

125

one trembling palm, as if he were seized by a mortal hunger. Marguerite closed her eyes. She smiled through the tears that still fell from under the thick bronze lashes.

For long moments they sat like this, unable to move. The sun became brighter. The trees quickened.

Then, at last, shuddering violently, Louis sprang to his feet. A horrible coldness ran over him. He cried out. The girl rose, visibly shaking. She held out her hands to him.

"Do not leave me!" she moaned, and bent down towards him.

But he moved backwards from her, staring at her with horror and anguish. He had paled excessively. Turning, he fled from her.

He heard her call out to him, and he shook his head with numb and gasping violence. He stumbled, blinded. Once he lurched against a tree, and the impact stunned him. A bush tore his floating black cloak.

"Tomorrow!" came the girl's far voice, like an echo.

"Never, never tomorrow!" he groaned, pressing his hands over his eyes.

"Tomorrow!" sang the wind, and the sun smiled through the trees.

CHAPTER XIV

THOUGH HE WAS ONLY in his forty-first year, Armand-Jean du Plessis, Duc de Richelieu, was beginning to experience more and more that languid malaise of the body, those vague yet pungent pains of a chronically nervous and delicate constitution, those increasingly frightful headaches, which had, all his life, darkened occasions of the most intense joy and satisfaction in accomplishment.

There was many a time, when, remembering the tales of his mother about his sickly and precarious infanthood and childhood, he sincerely and gloomily wished that his physician had not been so skilful and so devoted, and had allowed him to sink, while still in a state of unconsciousness, into an early grave. And sometimes, meditating upon himself (a favorite occupation) he wondered if ambition did not always arise, like a strong and noxious flowering weed, from poisonous soil where gentler blossoms could find no roothold and no sustenance. Always, even deserts and wildernesses had their horrible blooms and plants, fatal and thorny, though never a violet and never a fragile rose. It seemed that the stronger vices and virtues, so ominous to men and nations, appeared only in stony or arid soil, in wild and dangerous places, or in deathly swamps, or in the crevices of mountains.

He had no illusions about himself, and of that disillusion had come his strength and his power. Only he knew the savage confusions and disorder of his own mind, from which came his passion for order in all things about him. The complexities of his devious spirit compelled a simplicity and implacable directness towards the world. The weakness of his frame and the instability of his constitution demanded a strength and inexorableness in policy and affairs. Hating hypocrisy in his heart, he employed it vigorously among men. Despising the ungrateful, he knew well the clever uses of ingratitude. Secretly, he detested exigent men, but knowing

127

that exigency was a sceptre of power, he cultivated it. He had a terror of weakness and gentleness, feeling these soft spots in himself, and so he displayed a ruthlessness and mercilessness and cynicism which made him the most hated man in Europe and in France. He had a vast and unremitting love and desire for peace. Therefore, masochist as he was, he created about himself an atmosphere of miasmic intrigue, turbulence and strife. To be himself, he felt, was to die. In all his suffering, he had an almost monstrous love and zest for life. Life was power. Afraid of death, he could not get enough of power. But at all times his soul and his body suffered from an eternal weariness, sickness and despair. Only his will forced him to seek power; only his intellectual love for life kept at a distance the dissolution that constantly threatened his flesh.

He knew he was hated, and in his heart he acknowledged that he deserved this hatred. But the knowledge of the hatred amused him vastly. He knew that his enemies called him the Red Death, the Cardinal of the Huguenots, the Black Pox. He was even more amused at these names, for in him was a mortal detestation for all men. Sometimes he half believed that it was this loathing, this detestation, that kept him alive. Morbidly self-analytical, he experienced moments of cynical wonder that his strongest motivation was his ambition for the unity and strength of France. Then he knew that this motivation was a form of escape, and that when under its influence he had no time to think, and felt no pain.

Ambition, he knew, was the great illusion, rising most powerfully in those in whose body or mind the seeds of death were the most deeply planted. It was the convulsion of desperate limbs, fleeing. Yet no one knew better than he the ghastly weariness and distaste and longing for death that took up their abode like dark specters in the house of the ambitious.

But, always, he was amused. In a lesser man, amusement enervated the will to strike and the will to seize. In him, it was wine and stimulation. He knew that desire for life springs the most passionately in those who are dying; he knew that amusement is the most delightful in those who know there is nothing amusing in consciousness.

"The only enemies I have are the enemies of the State," he was fond of saying. But he knew that his greatest enemy was himself. He loved to meditate upon himself, but indulged in this with increasing rarity, for when he so indulged, as in a secret and fatal vice, he was, for long days afterwards, so enervated, so exhausted, so prostrated and so benumbed, that he was only a ghost imitating the gestures and the sounds of the living. Yet never was he afflicted by so plebeian a thing as conscience, that haunter of the bourgeois soul, that puerile exercise of the feeble. Rather it was because he found in himself, in the moments of his vice, the futility and the horror, the illness and the despair, the soul-sickness, of all the universe, and perhaps of God.

Those who are genuinely enthusiastic and devoted are limited by their own passions. This, he knew. They were hampered by vehemences, by fervors, which rose from this enthusiasm. They were blinded by their own ecstasies. The man who attained real power was the intellectual man who had no enthusiasm, and so could operate only by will.

He surrounded himself with magnificence, as if to crush his secret love for austerity. His famous avarice was in reality the fevered terror of a man who builds barricades against an approaching enemy. Because he had no real desire for opulence and wealth, and knew that if he should allow these true characteristics to operate in his life he would be ruined and would perforce die, his hands were never satisfied in their grasping.

Sometimes, when experiencing the blackest moments of his immense disappointment in life, he indulged in a nostalgia for his early days at Pluvinal's Academy, where he had learned military arts. Economics, he would think, have the gravest influence over a man's life. It was the necessity for maintaining the endowment of Henry IV in his family that had made him a priest. In thinking of the military life he had abandoned at the request of his mother, and at the urging of the need for the continued endowment, he would be filled with pain and longing. He chose to forget, then, that he had abandoned the life of a soldier with promptness and without regret, seeing the larger possibilities of the priesthood. He forgot that a native conservatism and a shrewdness and immediacy had impelled his acquiescence. At these weaker times, he was sentimental, and liked to believe that in those early days he was a stern victim of circumstances. Later on, he would have moments of intense satisfaction that his decision had given him, in reality, a larger scope for his military accomplishments. His passion for militarism and his knowledge of strategy, his love for discipline, enforced order in his wild and disorderly mind and thus prolonged his life. Fearing death, therefore, he constantly cultivated his bent for militarism.

In short, he cultivated all those things which might tend

to keep him alive. Sometimes he became aware of his manœuvres, and tasted the dryness of death in his mouth. He would allow these moments to come rarely. However, his tormented soul, tormented almost from birth with a desire for extinction, revenged itself upon his body.

Sometimes he would think: I support tyrants because I despair of the people. But in the ruthlessness and inhumanity of tyrants he found strength for himself. A tenderness and compassion for the people would hasten his mortal disintegration. Compassion, he would meditate, is good, but it must not be indulged in promiscuously by those who desire to rule. (Or to live, would whisper his soul in reply.) And so, from one man's terror rose his detestable reputation for indifference to suffering, to injustice, to cruelty and to mercy. He was a man beset by death.

His fear had given his natural reserve a basilisk quality, his natural quietness of temperament an inscrutability, his native languor a specious tolerance, his French lucidity a contempt for abstract justice, his immense curiosity a genius for intrigue, his inherent firmness an indomitable immutability. There was a coldness of the quality of his temperament, and this had degenerated into an icy ferocity. His natural egotism had extended itself to an inordinate pride of family, in which even his sardonic self-analysis could find nothing ridiculous. Even his humor, with which he had been richly endowed at birth, had become a vicious irony and an obscene subtlety. His tendency to melancholy had become a constant black despair which had entered his very bones. Even his intellect had turned demoniacal.

It was rumored that there was a taint in his blood, which in some members of his family had become imbecility or madness. At all events, he was given, mostly in privacy, to moods of epileptic exaltation and causeless ecstasy, which left him ominously weakened in body while it enhanced the exaggerated vices and virtues of his temperament, and his fear.

In externals, only, was there safety for him. His genius for organization came from his inability to organize the thoughts that beset and besieged his rampant soul. He was keen and rapid in all things, because of the somber despair that lived always with him, threatening to destroy him at the last.

Once he said: "A passion for justice can so distract a man, can so confuse him, that he may become no more than a rag flapping in a dozen diverse winds. It imperils the

130

strength of the State, is a force for disunity." But in reality he meant that it was himself that might become a rag in the wind.

Always, he was terrified that he might discover that the mountain on which he had built his house was only a mole-hill, and the god he worshiped dwelt not in a far and momentous heaven, but in the habitations of earth-worms. From his earliest youth he had suffered from fits of inarticulate and gloomy depression. Now, as he was growing older, he suffered more and more that terrible paralysis of the spirit, that frightful absence of all emotional sensation, that suspension of the will like the suspension of the heart-beat. It was then, in stern terror, that he would rise from his bed and plunge into public and foreign affairs with an inhuman concentration and sleepless and ruthless ambition, and an extraordinary and supernatural intuition, all the stronger because behind them was nothing but the will to live.

His one unsleeping horror was that he might one day lose this will to live. Out of this frenzy came his devastating ambition for France, his dedication to the dream of bringing about her internal unity, his determination to confer power and splendor upon her, of vitalizing her and rendering her immune to disintegration and decay and ruin. She became, for him, a symbol of himself, of his own will to live, of his own indomitability. His soul believed that in the existence and strength and triumph of France was his own continued existence and strength and triumph. France must live, lest he die.

Death lived in his soul. This gave a kind of unearthly phosphorescence to his flesh, as if he were already dead. His mind operated through and over his dying and tortured body, with a grim and desperate defiance, shining incandescently through his large unfathomable eyes, which, at rare moments, were heavy and dim with melancholy. There was a fixity about them, like a cat's unwinking gaze, and their glance had a slowness of movement which intimidated, set as they were under commanding and extraordinary brows. They dominated his countenance, threw into insignificance his delicate slight face and extreme ascetic pallor, his arched, finely cut nose, the tight fragile lips between the soldierly mustaches and the pointed small beard. About that mouth were the graven lines of suffering and self-discipline, and between the eyes were the taut furrows which resulted from intense thought and frightful headaches. There was about him an inhuman assurance and steadfast quietness which gave him

131

the air of a man who suffered in silence. But this was not so. From himself came the stories of his headaches, and his complaints of them. In spite of his adult and lofty irony, his secret ridicule of superstition, his slightly smiling disgust of the simple folk who employed incantations and magic, he so descended, in the extremity of his pain, as to offer a Novena of Masses if public prayers would be instrumental in relieving his agony. He even devoted himself to Our Lady of Ardilles in those blind moments of fervor employed by the wisest and most disillusioned men when confronted by inexorable nature and calamity. Like the aristocratic Petronius, who believed nothing and sacrificed to the gods on the premise that it did no harm and might mystically do some good, he frequently implored the people to pray for him. Later, he had moments of amused and embarrassed shame, but these he did not betray even to his familiars.

He was a natural actor. His own artistry and love for drama made him sedulously study those aspects and attitudes needed to impress his people, those lovers of air and grace and rich color. He cultivated a presence, which his inherent dignity enhanced, though he was slender rather than tall. He radiated dominion, partly assumed, partly natural. He walked slowly and majestically, his thin dark hair clinging to the shape of his delicate skull, his red robes falling heavily about him in exquisite folds, as though he employed a toga-folder in the manner of the ancient Roman patricians. He had a secret admiration for the fineness and whiteness of his narrow hands, and even in the moments of deepest thought, and in audiences, had a mannerism of stroking them and holding them high to drain the discoloring blood from them and give them delicacy. Nothing in his slow and languid movements, his meditative manner, his quiet but resonant voice, gave a hint of the febrile vigor and passion of his mind. He was, even to himself, a character in a stately opera, neutral and silent and reserved, yet in these very things the more frightful and impelling, like an unbroken and violent storm approaching across serene heavens, always threatening to break into devastation and death while still silent and pent. This aspect of potential violence and disaster unnerved both friend and foe alike, and was partly the secret of his power.

Like all those great and terrible men who subdue and rule other men, he had a quality of mountebankery. But unlike his peers, he was not self-convinced by his own mountebankery, nor was he hypnotized by it into the belief that it was natural to him and not mountebankery at all. Never, save in rare instances, did he deceive himself. Strangely, this made him only the more powerful, and gave him flexibility, for he knew that mountebankery was a prime necessity of those who wish to impress and rule the masses, and even the intelligent. But he was never indelicate, never gross. This came partly from his real fastidiousness, and partly from his knowledge that the best of mountebanks cultivate elegance. So he cultivated this elegance, which was native to him, for he loathed the people and was nauseated by their sweat and their smells. He served two purposes, thus: he retained his own fastidiousness, and impressed the people.

Even his enemies admitted that Richelieu seemed inspired by but one ardor, one passion: the unity of France. Even his most hating foes acknowledged that he loved his country, that his most violent and ruthless machinations stemmed from his resolve to bring glory and strength upon her.

But Richelieu knew secretly that nationalism is the pretense of a man who finds some men who are not hateful—his own. Nationalism invariably springs from a hatred of all people; but egotism demands that one's own be at least thought tolerable. Richelieu, still not deceiving himself, knew that nationalism is the necessary illusion of the soldier, but a philosopher who espouses it has lost his logic, a statesman, his perspective, an artist, his creative sympathy, a wise man, his humor, a priest, his God. In serving France, Richelieu at least suspended his logic, his perspective, his sympathy, his humor, and, inevitably, his God. A man who did not suspend these was afflicted by hesitation and doubt, and so was lost.

When he was alone, as he was this beautiful morning in early summer, he was assaulted, beset and besieged, by himself, by his terror of death, by his illness, despair and melancholy. Believing that a man must first fight himself, he often forced himself to be alone, where he wrestled with that dual spirit of his as Jacob wrestled with the angel. But he himself was a dark angel, and not an angel of light. In these self-flagellations was the instinct of a masochist who despised himself.

Rigorously, in the morning, he officiated at Mass, or attended it. But afterwards, he retired to his chamber, to sink into bed in a veritable swoon of exhaustion. It was always well past noon before he rose again. About an hour before noon, he would arouse himself, and lie in his bed, feeling that he had just emerged from the tomb. He would lie supine, motionless, staring before him, his eyes idly following a ray of sunshine, a dust mote, a shadow. But behind that immobile countenance, his army of besieging thoughts would march and countermarch, however he might try to restrain and discipline them. Now he was vulnerable; now he had no defense. Nor, secretly, did he desire it.

His chamber was great and lofty, and very silent, though beyond the massive doors those called for the day's interviews waited in impatient masses. The white plaster ceiling, at which he frequently stared blindly, was carved chastely. The panelled walls glowed richly in the sun which poured through the tall windows, the polished glass of which was set in tiny leaded panes. His scarlet curtained bed, whose crimson velvet canopy, golden-fringed, extended almost to the ceiling, faced the window, and was covered by red silken coverlets embroidered with the arms of his family, and with an immense golden cross. To his right was the great carved fireplace, in which, even in the summer, burned a dull crimson fire, for Richelieu was eternally shaken by strong or feebler chills. The wall above the fireplace was carved intricately, and at the right was a tall gilt chair, covered by crimson velvet, in which he often sat during his midnight meditations. On the other side of the fireplace, near the wall in which the windows were set, was a carved chest of black wood, on which stood three golden bowls. A long black wooden table stood before the window, covered with some rare objets d'art, which he loved, collected and cherished. From his bed he could pick out the touches of red, blue, yellow and green which flecked them.

As he lay shivering in his bed, his slight body hardly lifting the silken crimson coverlets, he could hear, subdued, the murmuring and footsteps of passing throngs below. But these sounds only enhanced the breathless quiet of his room. He stared before him, and saw nothing but his life, and all he had done, and the things he must do. He could not decide which wearied him more: the past, or the future. His weariness was like a heavy stone on his body, crushing it.

The sockets of his extraordinary eyes burned dryly, aching with sleeplessness. He closed his lids; the light that poured through the windows lay on those lids and created dim red shadows before his shuttered vision. Though he did not drowse, dim tortured fragments floated before his eyes, like those which one perceives when falling asleep—a hand, an eye, a pale shadow of an unknown face, bloodless lips open upon a silent cry.

Suddenly, without any warning, without any premonition, the face of Anne of Austria, the Queen of France, rose up before his clouded vision, not faintly, not bloodless, but in its full young beauty and bewitching loveliness. A flood of intolerable heat pervaded his body, and he twitched violently, as a man afflicted with epilepsy twitches. "The vile Spaniard!" he murmured, involuntarily. But the heat of his body increased to a devastating fever. He saw those green large eyes under golden brows and lashes, the rose and pearl of those soft young cheeks, the arch of soft chestnut hair rising over the snowy forehead, the living moistness of that parted full red mouth with its Habsburg under-lip, pouting and protruding. He saw the slope of those famous white shoulders, and the curve of those beautiful arms, like marble come to life.

He writhed on his bed, overcome by agony. In his middle was a pit of aching emptiness and wild yearning. All the women he had known became only anonymous shadows, their wine emptied, the vessels of their bodies broken and forgotten. But this woman whom he had never known, whom his hand had never caressed, was like a disease in his flesh. Those emerald eyes had looked upon him only with fear, hatred and loathing. Even when his fingers had touched her own, he had felt their shrinking, and he had seen the averting of her gaze as if she had glanced at corruption. At the exact moment when his lips might touch her hand, she had withdrawn it with an almost imperceptible shudder. She had concealed her hatred under a calm and indifferent manner, but it had blazed in her eyes, trembled like the light of a sword on her parted lips. Though she was young, she had the imperious hauteur of the Habsburgs, the remote pride. But she had not been able to conceal her emotions at the sight of the Cardinal.

"I might be your friend," he had whispered once to her. But she had regarded him then with impassive coldness and immobile hatred. He had not added: "Or, I might be your most deadly enemy."

He had become her deadly enemy. There was nothing too mean, too base, for him to do to bring wretchedness and misery to this Habsburg princess. In tormenting her, there was surcease for his own pain. He had besmirched her in the eyes of her husband, that cold and capricious and violent man. He had poisoned the mind of her mother-in-law against her, that dull and repulsive woman, Marie de Medici. He had intrigued against her, in great things and in petty. He brought hell and purgatory to her life, sad enough as it was in that city of strangers and enemies. When he found nothing, he invented. It was a mystery, even to his familiars, how such a man, such a statesman and soldier, such a politician and prince of the Church, could gather all the forces of his nature, his genius, his intelligence and his subtlety, to annoy, frustrate, embitter and torture one defenseless young woman, hardly more than a girl. It was as if Lucifer himself might stoop to torment a poor frail little butterfly, or withdraw himself from the seduction of a world, from a frightful assault on heaven, to pluck apart a rose.

He set his spies about her, to report her slightest word to him, to watch her every movement. He had set a whisper about Paris about her debaucheries, which existed only in his imagination. She, in turn, quivering, fragile and helpless, watched him spin his black web about her. She struggled; had, in her own pay, spies of her own, but they were poor creatures compared with the diabolical cleverness of his. She felt the meshes of his lies about her, and could do nothing. She had no friends. She had learned the bitterest lesson of the defenseless: that every man's hand is against the helpless, every man's voice against the persecuted, every man's violence against the innocent. No wonder, then, that she drank gall in every cup, and ate poisoned bread.

Then came his most venomous opportunity.

He had attained a precarious peace with England. Charles the First had sent as his ambassador to France, the illustrious and handsome George Villiers, Duke of Buckingham. He became a great favorite at the French Court, for he was gay and subtle, ingenious and brilliant, charming and witty. From the first, it was evident that he pitied the beautiful young queen, moving in her pale isolation and misery among her remorseless enemies. From that pity had sprung his love. He was the more inclined to fix his attention upon her when he saw the dreadful enmity of Richelieu. At first, he had been amused, had said to himself: "The minions of that black and monstrous hierarchy find none too helpless, too obscure, too young or soft, for their vicious and fiendish attentions." But later, he saw that there was a personal element in all this, and he discovered the lust and passion of the Cardinal.

George Villiers found all men amusing, but it was an amusement without rancor, for he was, at heart, a young man much in love with life. He particularly found the Cardinal's mature passion amusing, though later he was impressed by its satanic violence and power. It had the grotesquerie of a giant's obsession for a delicate fairy. Still later, the young Duke began to frown uneasily.

He was, first of all, an Englishman. The peace between England and France, brought about by the subtlety of Richelieu who wished no ally for the German Protestants, was as tenuously balanced as a sword upon a pen-point. A breath would disturb it. Buckingham wished no breath to stir the thunderous air. So, when Richelieu began his whispers in Paris about an alleged and unclean love-affair between the Queen and the young Duke, Buckingham was inordinately dismayed. He returned to London with a precipitateness which cast no aspersion on his personal bravery, but was solely occasioned by alarm lest the peace be destroyed between the two peoples. The storm must inevitably break, but British caution, as always, advised that the breaking be postponed as long as possible. In that caution was the English maxim that all men, given enough time, must die. A postponed war might often become an indefinitely postponed war.

But the absence of Buckingham did nothing to abate the whispers. The Queen was snickeringly accused of corresponding with her lover, of meeting him in secret rendezvous on French soil.

And now, the incredible was occurring in the mind and soul of that strange and terrible man, Armand-Jean du Plessis, Cardinal de Richelieu. His hatred and venom against Buckingham aroused his sleeping animosity and loathing for all that was English. His caution was dissolved like a strand of silk in a fire. There is nothing like a war to unify a people, he said, with increasing frequency. Historian though he was, he refused to remember that wars destroy the victor as well as the vanquished. Madness had seized his mind.

He thought of all these things as he lay in his bed this summer morning. He allowed the destructive and drowning tide of his thoughts to inundate him. He remembered everything, and everything was colored by his fever, his passion, his frustration and despair.

And as he thought, his disgust for all men rose up in him like malignant black bile, and disgust for himself. In his own dishonor, he felt the dishonor of all other men; in his sickness for himself, was a sickness for the whole world. He felt in himself all the malevolence, all the viciousness, stupidity, shame, degradation, cruelty, obtuseness, bestiality and meanness of all his fellow creatures. There is not a beast, he thought, with that brutal clarity in which he regarded himself, that would not be ashamed of claiming kinship with us.

He remembered his youth, his single-heartedness, his

soldier's simplicity, his steadfast eyes and indomitable faith. He was incredulous, remembering. He looked at the far outline and faint lineaments of a stranger. And was wearily amused. But even in those days he had been instinctively disingenuous, otherwise he would never have abandoned his military career for the gown. He remembered a conversation he had had in those days with a devoted Jesuit, a friend of his father's. The Jesuit had maintained that the Church had solely for its object the spread of Christendom, and that all methods must serve that end, that the Church must oppose all those who first thought of temporal things, whether gownsman or soldier or king. The Jesuit, who had been a singularly simple and noble man for one belonging to a sinister and dangerous order, had considered that the Church must serve the welfare of men, and bring them into the fold with gentleness and mercy and saintliness, despising the means of power, and always opposing tyrants and oppressors.

But Richelieu, on the eve of renouncing his military career, had said:

"To survive, and grow stronger, the Church must always serve the powerful, ride in their train. To espouse the cause of the suffering and the oppressed is the first step to oblivion, to hunger, death and impotence. No sensible man, then, no hierarchy of vast aim and ambition, can afford a promiscuous Christianity or sentimental humanitarianism."

From the first, then, he had seen the Church, not as the server of God and the protector of the helpless, but as a world-organization bent on temporal power and mighty princes. He saw it, too, as the servant of himself, and France. Remembering the lonely, sweet-faced Jesuit, he smiled contemptuously. That man had been a crier in the wilderness, despised by his colleagues who were blood-brothers of Armand-Jean du Plessis, prince of the Church of Rome.

It served him well, that Church who was the inheritor of all the taboos and superstitions and paganisms of the centuries, and whose Christianity was the fog behind which it inexorably and fatally carried on its plottings against the enlightenment and freedom of men, against the souls of men. He used it, cleverly, and with enormous wisdom.

Yet, it sickened him. From some obscure ancestor he had inherited that deadly gift of never being able to deceive himself. The Church sickened him; it made him sick of his own soul.

By what falsehood, hypocrisy, cunning, craft, cruelty and indifference had he raised himself to be literally the King of

France, master of Europe! By what shamefulness and degradation had he exalted himself! He thought of the Queen Mother, Marie de Medici, who was a symbol to him of the debauchery of his own soul. That big gross woman, whose touch had been pollution, who had lain on his breast in fetid midnight hours! He felt corruption, prostitution, through all his flesh. Yet, strangely, it was the memory of himself sitting on a cushion at her feet, ogling her with amorous languor as he strummed the lute he had learned to please her, which revolted him the most. In that act was the summing up of his debauchery and his prostitution. The lute-strumming had been more shameful than the mere polluting of his body in his implacable search for power.

He was only forty-one years old, half-dead, obscenely stained and dishonored. He had attained the power to which he had dedicated himself. He lay today on his bed and looked at it, and his nausea of spirit communicated itself to his body.

He stopped at nothing. He plotted like a serpent in a jungle. He was sleepless. The spring of his lust and greed had been wound too tightly in him to be stopped. He dared not stop, lest he die. He betrayed wantonly, that he might live.

He encouraged the Protestant great nobles for the sake of the unity of France, and, secretly, the advance of his own power. But he also derived a bitter amusement in that encouragement.

As he lay thinking, he heard the great door open softly. He lifted his heavy lids, and his strange tigerish eyes fixed themselves upon the young priest entering.

"Ah, Louis," he murmured. He lifted himself slightly on his cushions and smiled. He loved Louis for the amusement he invariably offered him. He lifted his slender white hand in a languid blessing. Louis bowed silently. The Cardinal watched his secretary as the young man, with his stately step, approached the carved and gilded chair at the bedside, and sat down with his usual majestic grace.

The Cardinal surveyed him intently. With quickened interest, he perceived that Louis de Richepin was paler than usual, his countenance more rigid, more marblelike, and that there were purple stains under the large blue eyes. But directness was not one of the Cardinal's less subtle characteristics in dealing with individuals, and he held his peace. He would soon be able, by devious means, to ascertain the cause of the visible distress of the priest.

His manner toward Louis was both fond and ironical, and sometimes lightly teasing.

"The rabble outside is as thick as ever, eh?" he asked.

"There is a large audience waiting to consult your Eminence," replied Louis, stiffly.

"Ah, yes," murmured the Cardinal, smiling slightly. "Fetch me those papers upon the table, Louis, if you please."

Louis rose, his black garments rustling. He moved across the carpet and the polished floor like a noble ghost. He brought the papers to his master, and laid them on the crimson coverlet. He seated himself again. His silence had the quality of white stone.

The Cardinal, in a languid but firm voice, began to dictate messages to his secretary. He used Latin almost exclusively; he had a remarkably eloquent and smooth genius for that language. Louis wrote the dictation rapidly. The shadows of the golden sun became longer in the lofty chamber. The hum behind the doors increased in tempo. As he dictated, the Cardinal's eyes remained fixed on Louis' face, and the strange changing lights in them sharpened, grew more vivid. His heart beat with an anticipatory pleasure under his white silken nightshirt. Once or twice, he shivered involuntarily, for he was always cold, even in his warm bed.

There was a sudden pause. Louis waited, his head bent, his lips stern and cold.

"Yes," murmured the Cardinal, abstractedly. "Louis," he continued, "please request your brother, Monsieur de Richepin du Vaubon, to attend me tomorrow morning at this hour. He has returned, I hear, from some escapade?" He smiled. "Young blood," he murmured.

Louis started violently. He lifted his head, and across his pale and beautiful countenance a dim flush raced like a fever. Fear, stark and vivid, began to glitter in his eyes.

"Arsène," he faltered. His hands clenched on his knee.

"Yes, Arsène." The Cardinal's smile was friendly. "I enjoy his conversation. He has wit and charm, and is devilishly clever. Too, I wish to consult him about a certain matter." He paused, then added negligently: "He is a close friend of Paul de Vitry, is he not?"

Louis cried out: "That is true, but he is no plotter with de Vitry! I can assure your Eminence of that—"

The Cardinal raised his deep brows. "Did I allege he was? But perhaps he can give me some information which might be useful."

"We are not traitors, in our family," Louis said, out of his fear and agitation.

"Did I say so? But Arsène was never reconciled to the faith of his fathers, was he?" The Cardinal was enjoying the fright of his secretary. "But I suspect Arsène of nothing, except frivolity. I have always had a fondness for him. It is my intention to offer him the captaincy of my Guards, even though he is still a Huguenot, from what I have learned."

"It is a great honor," said Louis, in a stifled voice. "But, as your Eminence has so rightly said, he is frivolous and careless." He recalled the Cardinal's words, and a wild envy and hatred filled him, now that his fear had diminished. "Discipline is beyond him. He plays like a child, though he is no longer very young. He detests responsibility. Though my father is of delicate constitution, Arsène can hardly be induced to visit our estates and supervise them. He is careless and abandoned and immature. Your Eminence's offer will not impress him, I must confess. It will be a waste of your Eminence's time."

"Nevertheless, I intend to make him the offer."

The Cardinal, who knew the hatred Louis bore his brother, was delighted and stimulated at the sight of the young priest's visible jealousy and detestation.

He said: "I think you disparage Arsène too much, Louis. Because he has a lighter spirit than yours, and is concerned with amorous intrigues and swordplay, does not argue that he is worthless. I find him amusing. He is intrepid and fearless, and has a way with men. He is liked indiscriminately. He would make an excellent captain. M. de Cavois is becoming too stiff and rigid; he is no longer young, and I have a wish to retire him, for he antagonizes the Musketeers. He lacks the quality of adventure, and thinks only of discipline. Arsène would be a prime favorite with the men."

Louis was silent. He was affrighted. His imagination rioted. It was very possible that Arsène would accept, in order to be privy to the Cardinal's secrets, the better to betray him. Duty struggled with Louis' love for his father. To enlighten the Cardinal would be to betray Arsène, and through Arsène, his father. The flush on Louis' cheek deepened; dampness appeared on his marble forehead. His hands shook.

Then, in a dwindled voice, he said: "I must beg your Eminence to reconsider. I know my brother too well."

The Cardinal shrugged. "Arsène has not yet accepted," he replied, indifferently. "Shall we proceed with our correspondence?"

Half-fainting though he was with his agitation and terror, Louis could yet control himself, and attend to his duties.

There was no hesitation at any time in the Cardinal's smooth and quiet voice as it flowed between his frail, hardly moving lips. As he spoke, he drew his imperial thoughtfully through his white fingers. His melancholy eyes, opaque with reflection and concentration now, regarded Louis without seeing him. Power was in his voice, courteous but filled with potential violence, uncompromising and urbane. Once or twice he smiled to himself, reflectively.

He dictated a letter to the King, and now his hidden smile grew deeper.

"It is with the most intolerable regret, Sire, that your servant has been unable to attend the gaming tables as usual during the past week. I must crave your indulgence for my illness, which has afflicted my body with heavy rheumatic pains. Only the most disabling and painful agony could keep me from your Majesty's side, as you well know. But during this period my mind has not been inactive, and though I have apparently neglected your letter received two days ago, it is because I wished to give further study to the matter and clarify my thoughts."

He paused. Louis, writing swiftly, felt some grim excitement. He waited, his pen clenched between his fingers.

"I must beg your Majesty to reflect on the enormous difficulties inherent in any move against the great Protestant nobles and La Rochelle at this time. France is still divided, still weakened by war, still seething with tumult and disorder. One must move carefully in this regard, as you, Sire, with your enormous wisdom, are well aware. I remember, with humility, all your previous counsels in the matter."

He paused again. He raised himself on his pillows, smiling broadly, his eyes twinkling with enjoyment and malice.

"There are some, as your Majesty is aware, who would like nothing better than to see France torn asunder with religious dissension. I need not name their names, for fear of touching upon a most delicate situation in your Majesty's own household. As you so well know, Sire, I have at all times endeavored to reconcile your Majesty with those closest to you, believing that domestic bliss should not be denied kings. For my efforts I have received only disdain, calumny and hatred, as your Majesty can attest. Nevertheless, as a devoted servant of your Majesty, I shall never desist in my efforts to bring peace to your heart and happiness to your hearth."

The Cardinal's imperial had been pulled to a soft thin

string. He caressed it absently. His tigerish eyes gleamed. Louis did not look up, but there were blue lines about his lips, and his hand trembled visibly.

"Nevertheless, craving your Majesty's indulgence beforehand, I must, out of my devotion to you, be frank, however angered you might be after the perusal of this letter.

"Though your Majesty's most Catholic brother, Philip of Spain, is bound to you by the closest of ties through his sister, her Majesty, your Queen and mine, candor impels me to speak plainly. Investigation has proved to me without doubt, though with terrible anguish of mind, that Spain has been secretly negotiating with England for an alliance against France. Philip, in his hatred for France, is impelled to ally himself with our most formidable and heretical enemy. In refusing to be drawn into any premature conflict at this time, I humbly believe that we can restore tranquillity and strength to France, rendering her strong and invulnerable, better able to withstand battle abroad and confusion within. Let our enemies then beware!"

Louis' pen fell from his fingers. He lifted his head and gazed at the Cardinal with suppressed rage and disappointment. The Cardinal, perceiving this, was titillated. He arched his steep brows.

"Well, Louis," he said, indulgently. "Speak, or you will burst with spleen."

Louis stood up in his agitation, grasping the papers on which he had been writing.

"Your Eminence," he began, in a choked voice, "is, as always, very kind, very indulgent, to permit me to speak. You have never silenced me, claiming that I sometimes have flashes of wisdom. I crave your pardon in advance, but, as you are willing, I must say what I must say."

Crimson had flooded the white stone of his countenance; his blue eyes were passionate with anger and detestation. The Cardinal inclined his head, and smiling, waited.

"Her Majesty," continued Louis, pressing the palms of his hands rigidly together, "has frequently urged that we destroy that bastion of hellish heretics, La Rochelle, with immediate dispatch. So long as this bastion remains, a State within a State, we are undone, at the mercy of Spain and England, of the German Empire. It is the Achilles heel of our domestic and foreign policy, the unguarded breach in the wall through which our enemies can enter. Destroy La Rochelle, Monseigneur, and the English will have no port of entry into the heart of France. As it is now, the English can send

143

supplies to the Huguenots at La Rochelle, encourage them in their obstinacy and treason, fortify them with ships and German, Spanish and Italian malcontents, who love their Church less than they hate France."

He was forced to halt, his large pale features twisting with malignant passion. The Cardinal advanced his head slightly towards him, the better to observe these manifestations which could spring less from abstract indignation than personal hatred.

Louis continued, his voice trembling: "So long as the Edict of Nantes is in force, and La Rochelle unmolested in her effrontery and impudence, we are weakened, we are defenseless, we are open to attack by our hating enemies. I implore your Eminence to reflect upon this!"

"I have reflected," murmured the Cardinal. He passed his hand over his face in one of those sudden and frequent attacks of exhaustion which so afflicted him. "You are rash, Louis. You would spring into battle against the Rochellais without sufficient preparation. You would revoke the Edict of Nantes without meditating upon the strong possibility of devastating disunity in France. However brave the heart, bare hands are not sufficient to stop swords or deflect cannon balls. Every peaceful moment gained is an hour of strength and preparation for France. But do not consider even for an instant that I do not have my plans!"

He fixed his eyes upon Louis. "It is probably only a calumny, a libel, but I have heard rumors that your brother, Arsène, has many friends in La Rochelle, and that he visits them upon occasion."

Louis said nothing. He paled excessively. He sat down, abruptly. The Cardinal, smiling, indicated by an inclination of his head that the correspondence must proceed. Louis' fingers felt numb as they held the pen. Then suddenly he cried out in a strange voice, shaking with vehemence: "Your Eminence must destroy the serpent within the heart of France, the Huguenots, the plotters, the heretics! How shall we endure with this venom unchecked in our souls?"

The Cardinal, as if Louis had not spoken at all, continued his dictation, in the smoothest of tones:

"In your letter, your Majesty impatiently quotes the late lamented de Luynes, who had conceived the premature and short-sighted policy of re-establishing our Holy Faith in Béarn, and destroying the Calvinists there established. With sorrow, I must recall to you the events of Montauban, where de Luynes was so ignominiously defeated, and who died of a broken heart in consequence. The militancy of our faithful children is to be admired. But it cannot but be deplored after a study of the facts. We are not yet ready for a move against internal and external enemies.

"However," he resumed, in a firmer voice, "I promise, as always, to devote all my energy, and all the authority that it may please you to place in my hands, to destroying the Huguenots, abasing the pride of the great nobles, restoring all your subjects to their duty and in raising the name of your Majesty among foreign nations to its rightful place. I ask only faith in my prudence and in my devotion."

He paused, then said: "Louis, I must ask you to take that to his Majesty, in person. I can trust no other."

Louis bit his lip gloomily. His chest heaved under his black robes. He inclined his head. The Cardinal lay back against his cushions and regarded his secretary with malicious pleasure.

"Speak, Louis," he said, in fond tones.

Louis drew a deep breath, clasped his hands together. "Your Eminence speaks of national unity. Is not the unity of Christendom more important? It appears to me that this unity of Christendom, perforce, will automatically bring with it national unity." He continued: "The toleration of a State within a State can bring only ruin."

The Cardinal smiled mockingly, but his voice was gentle, if ironical: "If we are to subdue the Huguenots, return France to complete Catholic unity, we should do so by example, virtue, prayer and humility. Do you doubt the efficacy of prayer, Louis? Pray then!"

Louis grew paler than ever. He regarded the Cardinal with stark simplicity, yet with it was a white indignation.

"We must first prove to God that we are sincere in our determination that He shall not be blasphemed by heretics."

The Cardinal was silent a moment, then he said negligently: 'Ah, you fanatics! I have the conviction, Louis, that you would enjoy the reintroduction of the wheel, the gallows and the ax against the Huguenots. Essentially, the fanatic is uncivilized. And do we not boast that we are the most civilized of people, in comparison with the coarse English, the boorish Germans, the vicious Spaniards?"

"Civilized uses cannot be considered in dealing with heretics!" cried Louis, and again that convulsion passed over his face as from some secret spasm.

"The Holy Office missed a fine recruit by some centuries," observed the Cardinal, shaking his head. He thought to him-

145

self, with pleasure: How his brother torments him, afflicts his soul!

He regarded Louis with his long and melancholy gaze.

"My dear Louis, I am not your confessor, but I have thought that this morning you have been distrait. I hope that you consider me your friend, and allow me to assist you if you be in need of assistance."

Louis started perceptibly, and half rose from his chair. Then he was motionless. So uncomplex, so simple, was his essential nature, that he could find no duplicity in the Cardinal's words. Louis had not learned that Richelieu wasted no speech, and that every word was said with a purpose, if only a malicious one.

He put his hand to his eyes for a moment, and was silent.

Certain, now, that he had not been mistaken, the Cardinal forgot his malaise and stared at the young priest with increasing curiosity.

"Mon cher," he murmured, "it is evident that you are distressed. Again, I urge you to consider that I am your friend."

Louis began to speak in a pent, low voice: "I have never found it difficult to read my whole soul. Now, I find it impossible."

"You mean," said Richelieu gently, "that you dare not read your soul."

He was faintly excited. What could have stirred that blue-white glacier? The Cardinal knew that the movements of glaciers are never insignificant, that they bear in them the potentialities of death and enormous destruction, that their motion is irresistible and devastating. He sat up, and stared at Louis with avid interest.

"It may be true, what you say, Monseigneur," whispered Louis. He dropped his hand and looked at the Cardinal with complete anguish. "It may be I dare not delve too deeply in myself." He halted, and over him swept the avalanche of his emotions, confused, chaotic, and desperate. The pale smoothness of his countenance flushed feverishly.

"It began, this morning, with the book I borrowed from your Eminence."

"Ah," said the Cardinal, smoothing his imperial between his fingers with a sensuous slowness.

"I found a passage in that book which echoed the more undisciplined thoughts which sometimes assail me. I have told you, Monseigneur, of these thoughts, in the past. For some time I have believed that I had conquered them, driven

146

them out of my mind like demons. When I read that book this morning, they returned like dark and conquering armies."

"So!" exclaimed the Cardinal, more and more delighted. His strange eyes glowed with a molten light, and he leaned on his elbow towards Louis.

The young man clenched his hands together, and blue lines appeared deeply beside his pale lips.

"I wished to flee," said Louis, with desperate and simple majesty. "But where could I flee, except into death? I longed for death. A coldness came over me, and a sensation which assured me that my spirit was dying, my heart was expiring. After a moment or two I felt nothing except paralysis. I felt neither pain nor sorrow; I was no longer a man. This sensation has not passed. It is with me still. I am afraid," he added, in a lower tone, "that I have truly died."

The Cardinal murmured softly. Then, in the gentlest of voices, he said: "But this is not the symbol of death of the heart, my poor young friend. It is the mournful and unreconciled agony of a wounded soul that has temporarily lost all interest in men and all communication with God, from very exhaustion resulting from too strong a sensibility. You are too intense. Ah, I have read the strong emotions under that calm exterior of yours, Louis! Those who suffer and rejoice too strongly are vulnerable to all the disembodied storms and visitations which infest the universe. They are leaves in the wind. But, take heart. Men like yourself are beloved of God, for their consciousness of Him is tremendous. They can become saints, or devils, more easily than others."

Louis looked at him with an earnest passion, hanging on his words.

"How can Monseigneur understand this, for surely he has not felt this, himself!"

The Cardinal smiled in a peculiar way, and his eyes shifted. Louis' desperate passion mounted.

"Today," he cried, "I have felt that I want neither the love of men nor God! I do not want even death!"

The Cardinal was surprised. He had not suspected that Louis was capable of such extremities of emotion and misery. He had thought him inspired only by hatred. For a moment his unfathomable eyes softened in spite of himself. He felt a mysterious motion of his heart, such as a man feels in his amazement when recognizing a brother behind the face of a stranger. Pity took him by the throat. Such a man as this, he thought, had better be dead, for he lacks the implacability which is in myself. He is too single-hearted, and, paradoxically, too strong.

He began to speak, with a low and unaccustomed hesitation, watching Louis closely, meanwhile:

"I have often thought, Louis, that there is a hunger in you, a want, both of the spirit and the body. You lack a certain joyousness, though you are still young. But, alas, it is not age only that brings with it the dark void of weariness. I have seen old men laugh with joy at the morning, and young men hang themselves for very emptiness of heart. It is that which afflicts you: an emptiness of heart!"

Louis listened with an intensity that betrayed how closely the Cardinal had touched him. His large smooth lips shook; desperate hunger glittered in his eyes.

The Cardinal did not look directly at him now, but gazed at the shining windows reflectively.

"We are priests, Louis, dedicated to God. But we are also men. For the health of our souls, we ought not to deprive ourselves of female companionship."

Louis sprang to his feet, his face flaming. Breath came harshly through his clenched teeth. He tried to speak, but could not. The Cardinal, out of the corner of his eyes, observed these phenomena, with mingled surprise and amused cunning.

Richelieu placed the tips of his fingers delicately together, and allowed an expression of melancholy gentleness to pervade his features.

"Female society brings with it a soothing quality; the uses of a woman's mind are sweet as April rain. Purged of the purely sensual elements which afflict and burn the average man, a priest may find a lofty delight in association with women, especially if these women possess intelligence, wit, and sensibility. If temptation arises, the priest possesses a spiritual fortitude which enables him to resist in silence. Out of that inner conflict, the priest attains a greater strength."

Now he turned his eyes mildly upon Louis. The young man had been listening as though he had been attending the words of an archangel. His lips were trembling.

Ah ha! though the Cardinal. So, I have it!

"Reflect," he continued, tranquilly, and with a pure and steadfast look. "Do not deprive yourself of permitted and unsullied joys. Such was not the intention of God, except for those who feel called to the cloistered life. But you and I, Louis, live in a world of men. And women."

Louis spoke in a quivering voice, which would have given

148

a pang to a less venal and terrible man: "Your Eminence has rescued me—! He has given me hope, removed the blackness of guilt from my heart—!"

The Cardinal put his hand to his lips to conceal an irrepressible smile. But his eyes remained serious and gentle.

"Guilt, Louis? What imagination is yours! How you young devotees torture yourselves, when a moment's conversation with one who understands can relieve your self-flagellations!"

Louis sat down abruptly, for his legs were shaking too violently to sustain his weight. He leaned forward towards the Cardinal, and his face was living flesh and no longer marble.

"I have been guilty, then, of defiling myself in my thoughts, Monseigneur! I have sullied innocence with evil imaginings. What I thought was wickedness, then, is pure and natural. Alas, I can plainly see that my mind is vicious—" He paused, unable to continue.

The Cardinal raised his hand with a gesture of ineffable affection.

"You see, Louis, you run to extremes. Remember, at all times, priest though you are, you are only a man, with a man's self-deception. Partake of innocent joys and tender companionship. They will not debase you."

Louis was silent. He heaved deep and releasing breaths. Joy glimmered on his broad white brow. The Cardinal was flooded with revivifying and malignant amusement.

Near the fireplace was another door, smaller and not so massive as the door leading to the ante-chamber where those who desired an audience with the Cardinal waited. Now there came a short and peremptory knock on this door.

"Ah," said Richelieu, "it is our dear Père Joseph! He returned this morning. Bid him enter, Louis."

As in a bemused dream, the young priest rose and walked with a faltering step to the door. The Cardinal watched his passage, and a glittering pinpoint of light brightened in his eyes.

CHAPTER XV

THERE WAS A SAYING among the irreverent in Paris that Père Joseph was always preceded by a great stench.

To the Huguenot great magnates, the stench was more than physical, for it had in it that most dangerous of qualities: spiritual mysticism. A malefactor like his Eminence, le Duc de Richelieu, could be understood. There was the human element in him, and however colossal his crimes, however cunning and merciless his schemes, men found a common humanity in him, inflamed and swollen out of proportion though it was. They could, at times, laugh at him, seeing themselves in him become gigantic and grotesque. But they could not laugh at François le Clerc du Tremblay, the Capuchin mystic, the epileptic Père Joseph.

Even the Cardinal's madness was a human madness, occasioned by tainted blood and excess of ambition and excruciating sensibility. It could be understood, despised, feared and meditated upon. But the madness of Père Joseph transcended humanity, became one with those horrible mysteries dimly scented beyond the dark forest of reality. It was one with demons, with black angels, with subterranean monsters, with supernatural apparitions. The devout, though fearing him, believed that the Capuchin's madness was the result of an ecstasy-in-God. But others felt a real terror and frightfulness in him, as if he were not flesh but a being visiting briefly and terribly from some ghastly outer-place beyond the world. The Cardinal's cogency was familiar. It was the cogency of all the great conquerors and oppressors, and though hated, it could be comprehended. But there was a cogency in Père Joseph which suggested that behind him was an invisible and appalling host come from unfathomable places.

He could not be touched by a human hand. There were some who believed he was not flesh at all, but a spectre, this alter ego of Cardinal Richelieu, his closest intimate.

He was eight years older than the Cardinal, and at this time he was nearly fifty. Short, powerful, of a gorilla-like appearance, with long prehensile hands and long prehensile toes visible through his sandals, robed, cowled, lunging of gait, he inspired fright or repulsion at first glance. Under that robe, the Capuchin's habit, coarse and dirty, one caught the outline of strong gnarled limbs and a torso like the trunk of a tree. If he ever bathed, the matter was open to doubt, for he was surrounded by an aura of powerful and repelling smells which seemed less to come from his flesh than to emanate from his colossal vitality.

All this was enough to disgust the fastidious, but it was his face, his head, that were the most hypnotizing, powerful and fearful. He had an enormous furrowed forehead, continually wrinkling, like an ape's forehead. It was dark, almost russet in color, as was all the skin of his over-large countenance. His bulging eyes were enormous, burning, fierce, terrible, and of a fiery blueness, glittering with passion and inhuman mysticism. The nose was jagged, crooked, very acquiline, like the beak of a vulture, or an eagle. His beard was long and bushy, dark red and unkempt and dirty, streaked with gray, and it covered the lower half of his great face and fell on his ape's broad chest. Through this tangle of hair could be glimpsed a wide twisted mouth, sagacious and mobile.

Yet, he was no malefactor like the Cardinal. Had he been, he would have inspired less fear. There was no stain upon his private life, and even his enemies conceded that there was no personal lust for power in him. Had he had this lust, they could have understood him, could have felt the presence of his flesh. He was incapable of the silken intrigues of the Cardinal, the venality, the human viciousness. This lack in him appalled.

He had arrived from Rome and had reached the Palais-Cardinal only a few minutes ago. He had come directly to the Cardinal, who trusted him as he trusted no other man. Did he deceive Father Joseph? No one, not even the Cardinal, knew this.

It was difficult for the Cardinal, whose greatest weakness was a pride in blood, to be amiable to those of low birth or beginnings, however he might respect their intellect or admire their attainments (and he was lavish in this admiration). Father Joseph, therefore, pleased him because the uncouth Capuchin was of noble blood. He was the eldest son of one Jean le Clerc, Chancellor of the Duc d'Alençon, and Premier Président des Requêtes du Palais. His ancestors had been unusually brilliant administrators and lawyers, and his mother had sprung from the great landed nobility. Moreover, Father Joseph had inherited from his grandfather on his mother's side, Monsieur Claude de La Fayette, one of four baronies, and had been known at Court, in his earlier days, as the Baron de Maffliers. His father and mother had both been Calvinists.

Therefore, in his association with Father Joseph, the Cardinal felt no sensitive feeling of degradation. He was an equal in blood, and the Cardinal believed in blood as he did not believe in God. (He had an intense and unremitting hatred for the plebeian, and often said: "Where the people enter, they defile, not deliberately and with malice, but innocently, like a beast dropping ordure, out of the instinct of their natures." He believed that a deliberate defilement came from a superior comprehension of the enormity of the defilement, and so, could be forgiven. But the innocent defiling of the people he could not forgive, for it sprang from the very nature of them, and could never be cured, being intrinsic. When the Cardinal felt this truth most keenly, he was filled with an insane rage, and, like Nero, experienced a desire to burn Paris as Rome had been burned, to cure it of its stenches. Sometimes he felt that he could burn the whole world.)

When Père Joseph entered the chamber, the Cardinal sat upright in his bed, and stretched out his hands, which quivered. His impaling eyes softened, glowed. He smiled with love and delight.

"My dear friend!" he exclaimed. "My dear good friend!"

He had not seen the Capuchin for a long time, but they had corresponded frequently and regularly. Père Joseph smiled in return, his dark dour smile which yet had something singularly beautiful in it. He kissed the Cardinal's white extended hand, with sincere humility, and then pressed it between his brown and calloused hands. They did not speak for a few moments, but their eyes beamed at each other, filled with unspoken things. The Cardinal's mortal pallor brightened into evanescent health. His long pointed countenance, somber and melancholy, took on vivacity. He sighed deeply. Père Joseph, himself, was greatly moved. The austere yet passionate blue eyes became as gentle as summer skies. His enormous russet beard trembled.

He sat down in the tall gilt-and-crimson chair at the Cardinal's side. Louis had removed himself at a distance. A bitter jealousy filled him, the old chronic jealousy which had so afflicted all his life. He stood near the window, but in shadow, tall, black-robed, and faintly sinister. From out that shadow his eyes glinted watchfully, and with haughty disdain. There was a new hatred in his heart, joining with all the other hatreds.

He had seen Père Joseph only once, and then at a distance, and before he, himself, had been ordained. He had been very young, then, and his father had taken him and Arsène to visit his old Calvinist friend, the governor of the Huguenot walled city of Saumur, Monsieur du Plessis-Mornay. The governor was also a distant relative, and Armand sincerely liked him, as he liked few others. The visit had been more or less secret, and Armand, only lately a convert to Mother Church, had been furtive.

At that time, the Catholics, a bigoted minority, were allowed free religious worship in Saumur, and no one interfered with them. Du Plessis-Mornay was a true liberal, full of tolerance and humor. His friends had protested the presence of the Catholics, prophesying that they were the nucleus of disease, a nucleus which would fill the city eventually with pestilence. But du Plessis-Mornay was essentially a man of good-will, and could credit no others with malignance. He championed the Catholics against both real and fancied oppressions, and always lent an ear to their interminable and whining complaints against their Huguenot townsmen. Hating oppression of all kinds, he was tenderly sensitive to its slightest manifestation, bending backwards to be severe with his Huguenot fellows and refusing to listen to their justified anger and warnings against the Catholics. "These Catholics worm their way unobstrusively into the confidence and pity of their enemies," a friend had told him sternly. "They are meek and humble, while they are still impotent. They invoke the tolerance and indignation of worthy men in their own behalf, while they, in the meantime, plot to destroy these same men." But du Plessis-Mornay refused to credit this, having no slyness or viciousness in himself.

However, he had his own distrust of religious orders, and for a long while, though permitting the Catholics their churches, would allow no friars into the city. Father Joseph, in his indomitable determination, resolved to remedy this. He ingratiated himself with the abbess of Fontevrault, Madame de Bourbon, old aunt of the King, and asked her to intercede with his Majesty for the introduction of the Capuchins into Saumur. Du Plessis-Mornay, though an intrepid gentleman, dared not offend the King's relative when she placed her demands before him, and a Capuchin house had been founded.

Passionately elated with his success, Père Joseph had addressed an open meeting of the Catholics in one of the streets of Saumur. Armand, driving with his sons in his carriage, had been forced to halt because of the crowds. He and the two boys were, therefore, exposed to the wild and jubilant eloquence of Père Joseph. He had stood on a little elevation, wild, dark-robed, gesticulating against the quiet warm sky, inspiring his audience with his fervor and magnificent oratory. Arsène had amused his father with ribald comments and exaggerated mimickings, but Louis, still very young, had immediately decided to devote his life to God.

That had been the first and the last time, until today, that Louis had seen his Gray Eminence, the familiar of the Cardinal. But he never forgot that vehement and tremendous figure, nor the sound of that compelling voice. Père Joseph had become a semi-divine and limitless dream to him. But he forgot that dream today. He saw in Père Joseph, though still sensible to his tremendous personality and power, a man who was the Cardinal's only real friend. His egotism was so gigantic that he could not endure the spectacle of anyone whom he served, revered or liked, to be engrossed in another, to the forgetfulness of himself. In all his few relationships, he loomed as the most important element. To be debased to the stature of a mere secretary, a little man, to the Cardinal, poured venom into his veins. His pale and handsome countenance took on a greenish tinge. He literally trembled. Here was one before whom he was nothing at all. He saw the expression on the Cardinal's face, deep, strong, fond and tender, and remembered that never had his master looked at him in this manner. His old yearning for love and complete absorption (that old chronic sickness of his lonely soul) assailed him in full force once more, and made him physically ill. The look the two exchanged was eloquent with the memory of years of trust, affection and struggle, and with a thousand things not known to him. He was more jealous of the implications of those glances than he was of Père Joseph himself.

They had forgotten him. This was the supreme insult. He was no more than an earless and voiceless lackey in this lofty chamber, with its embossed gilt and white ceiling, its crimson curtains and soft green carpet. He clenched a fold of the window curtain in his hand and twisted it cruelly, as he might have twisted flesh.

The Cardinal and the Capuchin had plunged into rapid and breathless conversation. Their words tumbled over each other. At intervals they laughed, and then, pausing, exchanged that long deep look which so infuriated and tortured Louis. The Cardinal had become young again, potent, alive, passionate, and gay. His body vibrated with new life. His large reserved eyes sparkled without reticence. He continued to hold the Capuchin's hand, and to press it.

They talked of personal matters, sometimes bursting into laughter, and eyeing each other significantly remembering past events which gave a fillip to a conversation meaningless to the young priest. He saw for the first time the richness of old memory, which colored the present with shades and tints not possessed by itself, and perceived the hoarded treasures of old friendship. This increased his bitterness and jealousy. There were no memories between himself and the Cardinal.

Now the two, after another pause, plunged into more grave discussion. The Capuchin began to talk of his mission to Rome. He had covered that great distance, back and forth, on foot. His feet, in their rough sandals, were brown and enormous and sinewy. He had traversed the great dark forests of France, threatened by wolves, and even by bears, alone and unprotected, "save by God," he said, somberly. He had travelled over stony and muddy roads, infested by bandits and robbers, had slept in open fields or in haystacks, carrying his knapsack on his back. He had begged bread and milk and water at peasant huts. He did not speak of it, but his superhuman courage and quiet power were manifest in his every word. As he talked, his hand played with the wooden cross that hung from the cord about his middle, and he kept glancing at it with passionate reverence. As he did so, his capacity for orison betrayed itself in the mystical light which suddenly glowed on his bearded face and in his flaming eyes, and he seemed to lose consciousness of his surroundings, in a kind of catalepsy. He was very nearly blind, and the penetrating effort to see added to his countenance a rapt and piercing immobility.

And as Louis listened, the creeping black ice of his old desolation moved slowly and inexorably over his heart. He knew himself to be a forgotten dim shadow, a shallow image of glass, without substance.

"The Holy Father," said Père Joseph, with a bend of his head, "is deeply disturbed in his heart at the troubles ominously gathering in the Germanies. Ah, the Germanies! What a Pandora's box they are, filled with winged pestilences with which to afflict Europe! Who but the Germans could have begotten Luther? They are a seething pot constantly bubbling. That is because they are barbarians. His Holiness confided to me that he cannot sleep; he spends his days in distraction, his nights in prayer. He is impaled on two horns of the dilemma, the Protestants who threaten the Church by their very existence, and the Catholic Habsburgs. Between the two, who is our worst enemy? I do not know. But I know this: the Habsburgs are our most dangerous friends. They are the more sinister for wearing the livery which arrays ourselves. Philip of Spain and the Habsburgs, good Catholics all, are filled with venom against France, and, if to destroy France it were first necessary to destroy the Church, they would not hesitate."

"I know this," said the Cardinal sternly. The pale phantom at the window moved, advanced a step into the room. Neither of the older men observed him.

Père Joseph sighed, clasped his great brown hands together, and stared heavily at them.

"I feel," he said, in a low voice, "that if the Church is to live, France must be made strong. How can we bring this about, Monseigneur? You have done much. You have placated the Huguenots, persuaded them to join with you in the desperate struggle to create and preserve a unity, an integrity, in France. I told the Holy Father this. At first, he thought this a sophistry, a confusion, a bewilderment. Finally, I made it clear to him that if the Church is to live, France must first live. But sometimes he shook his head, sighing, wondering how the support of the French Protestants could possibly react to the welfare of the Church."

"You told him, my friend, that the Huguenots and the Catholics in France were first of all Frenchmen?"

The Capuchin smiled his dark and twisted smile. He raised his russet brows and looked humorously at the Cardinal.

"He had just heard how the Huguenots in La Rochelle were conspiring with de Buckingham, and how the Duc had promised them English aid in the event that we moved against them."

"Ah," said the Cardinal, smoothing his thin pointed beard delicately.

"I informed him," continued the Capuchin, fixing his eyes pointedly upon Richelieu, "that we would soon 'reconcile' the Rochellais."

"I trust you did not say that this reconciliation would take place by the gallows, the sword, the wheel and the dungeon?" asked the Cardinal sardonically.

Suddenly the two laughed together. Louis drew a hard and savage breath, and his heart burned with anger against this inexplicable laughter.

"But no," said the Capuchin, "I told him this would be accomplished by means always in the favor of the Roman Curia: prayer, love, persuasion and evangelism."

He smiled at this, only, but the Cardinal laughed again, deliciously.

"Nevertheless," said the Cardinal, "those are the means I would employ. The Rochellais are Frenchmen, and French blood must be preserved." He added:

"His Holiness is a vigorous man. No doubt he would prefer more strenuous methods?"

But Père Joseph only averted his eyes uneasily at this, as if the smell of ridicule had risen to his nostrils.

He said: "His Holiness was faintly annoyed that your Eminence is so absorbed in Frenchmen."

"Would he prefer the Habsburgs? Let him reflect on that. Once the slave of those barbarians, he, and the Church, would be lost. I hope you made him understand at last that France is the only true sword bared in the defense of the Church."

"His Holiness is not insensible to the menace of the Habsburgs. I have told your Eminence: he is confused. And vigorous men do not like to be confused."

He stood up. Though he was short, he seemed to fill the vast chamber like a wind of strength and vitality. He stared into space, while the Cardinal watched him closely.

"The Holy Father is not a Frenchman," said the Capuchin, musingly, and now his countenance was withdrawn and abstracted. "He cannot share yours and my devotion to France. Nevertheless, I must confess that I was in some sympathy with his complaints."

"Ah," murmured the Cardinal. Louis moved another step into the chamber, his nostrils dilated with his quickening breath.

The Capuchin sighed, compressed his lips, then resumed in his quiet and thrilling voice, which had in it always that hint of suppressed power:

"I have agreed with many things advanced by your Eminence. Nevertheless, I too, believe that there is much in the thought of a collaboration between the Catholic Habsburgs and the Catholic French for the suppression of the heretics. This would recreate a united Christendom."

The Cardinal had suddenly paled with wrath. He sat bolt upright, and there was an infernal lightening in his tiger eyes.

"You think, then, my dear friend, that Frenchmen, though Catholics, would endure to watch foreigners, though Catholics, murder other Frenchmen, though Huguenots? I thought you understood Frenchmen!"

The Capuchin returned to the bed, and now his own eyes were fiery.

"I am a Frenchman," he said, slowly and firmly. "But I am also a Capuchin. In the eyes of Almighty God, and Holy Mother Church, men are either the children of light, or the children of darkness. Racial and national boundaries melt away in the sun of this truth. If there is evil in our house, it must be destroyed, lest all the members within that house die of violence and plague." He added, and now his tone was both dignified and desperately pleading: "The integrity, the safety, of the Church, must always be our first consideration."

The Cardinal clenched his hand so that the nails entered his palm.

"And you think the Habsburgs would perserve her safety, and her integrity? Ah, you are silent, my dear Père Joseph! Your eye falters; you sigh."

He lifted himself on his cushions, and a thin red flame quivered in his narrow cheeks.

"Listen to me! The Habsburgs are diabolical, and extremely wise. They advance this argument of yours to His Holiness, knowing they will have a sympathetic ear. But it is the fiend's own argument. This hypocritical concern with the integrity of Church has, for its heart, the hatred for France. Madrid and Vienna brewed it in darkness, conspiring only for the destruction of our country and our King. No piety moves them. The Habsburgs desire only the hegemony of Europe, under themselves. If they can enlist the blessing of his Holiness, they will have accomplished much. But is Rome to be used as catspaw for politicians and conquerors and lusters for power? It is an old game. It was played before. It will be played countless times again. But, while I live, it shall not be played against France!"

The Capuchin was silent. The Cardinal's passion made the air vibrate. He was no longer a priest. He was a soldier, a Frenchman.

In moments of stress, the soldier returned with fury. He cried out:

"Sang de Dieu! It shall not be played against France! I have dedicated my life, my arms, my strength, my passion and all my being to her! I shall not stand idly by and see my heart's blood poured out in vain on sand. No, not if I have to oppose the world with my bare hands and face all hell alone!"

But the Capuchin looked at him gravely, and the mouth vaguely seen through the russet beard was tight and grim.

However, the Cardinal was beside himself. He had these moments of frenzy, when, discarding his ancient caution, his old craft and self-protectiveness, he flung out the red and bloody flag of his courage, his rage, his hatred and his pride, against black and ominous heavens. Then he forgot everything but that he was Armand-Jean du Plessis, swollen with passion, omniscient and powerful, manipulator of men and kings and priests, maddened with outrage that any dare oppose him for an instant, or say to him: "You shall!"

He sat on the edge of his bed, then sprang to his feet, standing before Père Joseph in his long white silken robe. And now all the dark evil, pride and unconquerable lust was out on that pale and narrow countenance so that it was transformed. The feline eyes were translucent, so that the savage fire of his soul leaped behind and through them. He lifted his clenched hands as if to utter imprecations. His sickly body seemed to shake in unearthly winds. So awful was his aspect that Père Joseph fell back, as at an apparition infernal and supernatural.

Now the Cardinal spoke, in a lower tone which was yet the more appalling:

"This is my France. What she is, what she shall be, is because of me. I have drawn and marked her boundaries with my blood. I have welded her flesh to mine. I have given her dead body my soul. I have built her fortresses with my hands. I have blown my breath into her lungs. This corpse that lay rotting in Europe has been made whole, as Lazarus was made whole again. It was my voice that called her out of her sepulchre, and my fingers which unloosed her grave-clothes. It was my sword that drove away the vultures that wished to devour her.

"Now, she is mine. She is no other man's. Neither king, nor Church, shall claim her. And not even God!"

Père Joseph stared, disbelieving, at these mad words which might have come from the lips of an inflamed and transported Lucifer. He crossed himself. His brown face became faintly blue with horror and affright. He was a strange and terrible man, but he was confronted by a stranger, and more terrible, one. He waited until the Cardinal had finished, until he had gotten back into his bed. And then he spoke, very quietly, but with menacing warning:

"This, then, is what His Holiness told me. But I believed him misinformed. He said that it was not France that your Eminence loved. He said it was not God you served. He said Monseigneur loved, and served, only himself. It was power that your Eminence desired, and power only, as Satan desired it."

The Cardinal, fallen on his pillows in complete exhaustion, yet smiled darkly, and his inexorable spirit gleamed in his eyes as he gazed at the Capuchin. To no one else in all the world would he have so stripped himself.

"This is my France," he repeated.

"It is the France of God!" cried the Capuchin.

The Cardinal regarded him derisively in silence.

The Capuchin began to pace the room like a russet bear, distracted, his head bent. His sandalled feet left mud stains upon the delicate carpet. The sunlight alternately bathed him in radiance as he passed before the windows, then allowed him to be plunged into darkness as he passed beyond them.

He began to speak in a quivering voice, as though communing aloud with himself:

"To love one's land is good, just as it is good to love one's home and family. Without this love a man is not completely a man, a prideful human being of dignity. To defend his land is good. —But to set about the business of conquest, of making one's land impregnable to the exclusion of all else, is not to love one's land, but to hate all other lands built by other men. His Holiness is not unaware of all this."

The Cardinal lifted his hand, and so profound was the effect of his spiritual power that the Capuchin paused as if stricken into stone, though he had not seen that gesture.

"Let His Holiness remember that he is an Italian, and that I am a Frenchman," he said, so softly that his voice was hardly more than a whisper.

Père Joseph slowly turned his eyes upon his friend, and he was mute with dread, aghast at this frightful arrogance, this diabolical pride. He could not speak. The pale phantom near the windows, still undiscovered, unobserved, felt that he was in some hellish dream without reality.

Père Joseph did not know that a man cannot approach God save through his own humanity. But he did know that man approached hell through his own pride, his own vanity, his own hunger for power. And it appeared to him, as he gazed steadfastly, and with dread, at the Cardinal, that his friend had taken on the very aspect of Lucifer. He felt an immense sorrow and grief, and an enormous fear. Never had he known such a man, though legend was full of these. More and more appalled, he cried out in himself that he had not heard the words he had heard.

He said: "Your Eminence is, first of all, a servant of the Church."

Again the Cardinal smiled. The flame receded from his eyes. His panting lessened. The pallor of exhaustion crept into his face again.

"I remember this," he said, softly.

Père Joseph passed his hands over his face with a gesture as if shutting out some horrific vision. Then, dropping his hands, he revealed a calm and rigid countenance. He approached the Cardinal's bed, sat down again, resting his hands stiffly on his knees. He sighed.

The Cardinal had for him a truly deep affection, and now he experienced compunction that he could so disturb and agitate and horrify his friend. He reached out and laid his cool and narrow fingers on that rigid hand. He felt its trembling, its coldness and rigor.

"Your sensibilities are too keen, too delicate, too raw," he said, in a tone of humor. "You attach impossible significance to words. You must forgive me for my extravagance."

Too willing to believe, Père Joseph smiled dimly.

"Your Eminence is famous for his extravagance," he said.

It was then that the Cardinal became aware of Louis, and he raised his eyebrows, his expression darkening. He lifted a finger and summoned the young priest to him. Père Joseph watched his approach abstractedly, and without curiosity.

The Cardinal had a fascinating and ingratiating smile. He regarded Louis with humorous affection.

"Père Joseph, this is my secretary, a brother in God. You know his family. His name is Monsieur le Marquis du Vaubon."

Père Joseph rose heavily, as if prostrated, and the two priests bowed deeply in silence.

"A young gentleman after your own heart, Père Joseph," said the Cardinal gaily. "His conversation is very edifying." He paused, and gazed at Louis inscrutably. "I thought I had only one friend I could trust. But in Louis I have discovered another."

Was there something threatening in the tone of this appalling man? Louis was certain of it. That marble countenance flushed with bitter pride, though he said nothing.

"Like his Holiness, Louis believes I should be rash and plot for the revocation of the Edict of Nantes," said the Cardinal, in his smiling voice.

But Père Joseph became excessively grave. He sat down again and stared at the Cardinal unflinchingly.

"I have not told Monseigneur, but his Holiness demands this revocation," he said.

The Cardinal shrugged. Behind his slight and fragile lips his teeth clenched together.

Père Joseph continued: "Her Majesty, the Queen of France, gave me an audience before I left for Rome. She urged upon his Holiness to demand the revocation."

He was taken aback by the sudden and inhuman fury which instantly charged the Cardinal's eyes with black lightning at the mention of Anne of Austria. The Cardinal's attenuated features became congested, as though with turgid and thickened blood. He sprang up on his pillows, and between his bearded lips his teeth were a wolf-like flash.

"She dared!" he exclaimed. "That weak and sluttish Spaniard, that whining and petulant trollop! She dared to go over my head, knowing my refusal—"

Père Joseph was hardly less horrified at these words than he had been at the others. A swift vision of the beautiful young queen passed before his eyes, and he felt, for the first time in many years, the anger of an upright man at the besmirching of a woman, who, though weak, was virtuous, gentle and simple, full of piety, and very helpless. He had a loathing and terror of all women, save those encased in the religious habit and immured behind cloistered walls, and those, who like Anne of Austria, were ablaze with the divine luster of kings.

"Your Eminence can speak so of Madame—!" he cried, and stopped, choking.

But the Cardinal was beside himself at the impudence of so frail a creature, who tortured all his senses waking or sleeping.

"So," he muttered, "she plots behind my back, this Spaniard, this enemy of France, this sly drab! It is the end. She must be destroyed."

"What are you saying!" exclaimed Père Joseph.

The Cardinal regarded him with eyes of fire.

"I have been patient," he said, through his clenched teeth. "I have been long-suffering. I have been merciful and understanding of this crafty enemy. I shall be so no longer. She is intriguing against France; she is in the employ of her brother, that black and dangerous Spaniard, who longs for nothing but the ruin of France! So, these rascals would have me revoke the Edict of Nantes, would they! Knowing only too well that such a revocation would result in the resumption of civil war within France. Thus, then, they would find her weakened and helpless, and could despoil and conquer her at their leisure."

He panted, glaring before him, seeing nothing but his hatred.

"The Edict of Nantes is the Edict of Satan," said Père Joseph, sternly. "It is an insult to Almighty God, this edict which accords to heretics equal rights with Catholic Frenchmen."

"Reflect!" said the Cardinal, with a menacing and flaming look. "This Edict was promulgated by the father of his Majesty, Henry of Navarre, for the protection of his Huguenot friends." He paused. "Henry declared that Paris was worth a mass, and so returned to the Church." His voice became lower, but more intense. "And I find Paris, I find France, worth the Edict of Nantes."

"His Holiness demands—" said Père Joseph, outraged.

"His Holiness," said the Cardinal again, "is not a Frenchman."

He lifted a finger and stared formidably at his friend.

"The wheel, the ax, the gallows, however beloved of his Holiness, shall defame France no more. I have said it."

Père Joseph turned away his eyes, helplessly, sickened, and encountered the eyes of Louis. Then Père Joseph was startled, for he saw the fanatical madness on the face of the young priest. His brows drew together, thoughtfully. He spoke to the Cardinal, but looked only at Louis.

"God is greater than France," he said. "Meditate upon that, Monseigneur. God can crush France by the lifting of an eyelash."

The Cardinal smiled somberly.

Then he said: "Can his Holiness find his sole concern in the Edict of Nantes? What of this war which is raging beyond France, which threatens the very heart of the Church? Does this not cause his Holiness the most acute anxiety?"

For the time being, Père Joseph forgot the Edict of Nantes, and immediately plunged into a discussion of the war, then mounting with slow fury toward the prolonged crisis. Then, remembering something with disquiet, Père Joseph fixed his fierce blue eyes upon the Cardinal.

"It is said that your Eminence is secretly supporting the Protestants which his Catholic Majesty, the Emperor of the Habsburgs, is seeking to overthrow. But this is not possible!"

"I have my defamers," said the Cardinal, tranquilly, with a gentle look.

Only partly reassured, Père Joseph resumed with excitation:

"The Germanies! Let the Emperor, from his throne in Vienna, crush them with ease! Let him destroy them utterly, those Protestant wolves! They are filled with greed, wishing to retain their nefarious grip upon the Church lands which they have blasphemously seized, and the Church revenues they have looted. Pray God and all His saints that the Emperor will annihilate them, join the Germanies once more in a Catholic brotherhood! Only then will Christendom be reestablished, Catholic culture revived, and France saved."

"Only then," said the Cardinal with soft inexorableness, "will France be ruined."

But Père Joseph was too transported to hear these words. However, Louis heard them, and the blue glacial eyes were filmed over with ice.

Père Joseph continued in his vehement denunciations of the Protestants, and his ecstatic adoration of the Habsburg Emperor, that most Catholic monarch. The Cardinal became wearied.

He said at last, ironically: "Philip of Spain, of a surety, is deeply interested in this holy crusade. He will, of course, drive out the infidel Moors from his Empire, upon completion of the war against the Protestants?"

"Most certainly!" cried Père Joseph. "And the Jews, also. They are conspiring, as of old, against Spain."

"I thought the torture chambers of the Inquisition, and the gallows, and the wheel, and the stake, were piously employed to good advantage against the Jews, and that they were now safe in the arms of Mother Church."

Père Joseph was suddenly silent.

The Cardinal delicately examined his pale oval finger nails.

"That was unfortunate, that converting by 'pious' means, of the Jews. That eliminated an eternal victim, an eternal means of preventing internal revolt and dissatisfaction with the government. A wise monarch allows the existence of a victim among his people, or even cultivates or invents one if

one does not exist. Thus he protects himself from the indignation of his people."

"His Spanish Majesty still has the Moors," said Père
Joseph, unguardedly.

At this, the Cardinal burst into loud and ribald laughter.

Père Joseph exclaimed: "The Protestant pretender to the
throne of Hungary allied himself without shame with the
Turks. The Moors are their brothers. They must be driven
out of Spain."

But the Cardinal's acrid laughter became only the more
ribald.

While Père Joseph continued his transported discussion of
the bloody war between the Catholics and the Protestant
Germans for the fate of Europe, the Cardinal lost himself
in virulent and delicious contemplation of mankind. What
a foul monster was man, filled with viciousness, stupidity
and evil, distracted by every slight wind, blood-thirsty and
voracious as only a mad beast could be, but without a
beast's innocent ferocity, a creature justifiably hated by all
more simple and honest animals, hating all things in return,
even himself! A thousand thousand generations of enlightenment, a hundred Christs, would not serve to elevate this perverted demon to even the elemental decencies which lower
animals understood instinctively. Where else in the universe
was such craft, such wickedness, such cruelty, such obtuseness and dirtiness? The evil of men was of such a degradation
that it could never aspire even to a kind of black grandeur.
Who could encompass the vileness of men, which was the
vileness of inconceivable filth, by comparison with which the
ordure of animals was sweet-scented?

The Cardinal was imbued again, with that implacable
hatred for his species which never failed to inspire and
revivify him. As some men are transported to superhuman
strength by love and religious ecstasy, he was so transported
by loathing. He felt the blood coursing through his veins like
an awakened river, irresistible.

I am what men have made me, he thought. And he
understood then that the tyrants, the oppressors, the mass-
murderers, the Genghis Khans and the Caesars, the engorged
monsters, were created by mankind out of its own substance,
its own desire, its own soul and infernal heart. The tyrant was
not guilty; the murderer had clean hands. They were the
helpless and fleshless emanations from the spirits of men.
At the end, the genii invoked from the abysses of men's souls

165

destroyed them. That was ironical justice. The Cardinal lost himself in pleased contemplation of this justice.

When he had been younger, and even now in flashes, he had endured awful anguishes of spiritual pain, so intense that it seemed his spirit became incandescent with tortured fires, when contemplating mankind. But now, after the first ectasy of his hatred passed, all suddenly became dark and formless before his eyes. All became tongueless as a silent bell, and all reality became to him an uttered sound without meaning.

It is hard to endure life, he thought out of the chasm of his sinking, but it is harder no longer to discern what must be endured.

The profound and disintegrating exhaustion had him again. He closed his eyes. Somewhere in outer space he heard an interminable and vehement voice continuing a senseless diatribe. But it no longer disturbed him. He was lost to all sensation, even to despair. At these moments, which became much more frequent as his flesh failed, he no longer desired even that which could not be attained. Nor could he remember what it was that he once desired.

He opened his eyes, opaque with weariness and dissolution. He saw the gray figure of Père Joseph, gesticulating, pacing. He saw the pale phantom of his secretary.

He dragged his voice up from the depths of his pain and deathly exhaustion.

"We shall discuss all this again," he said, and his voice had lost its resonance. "My dear friend, sit with me. I have others to interview. It should amuse you."

He lifted his hand as a signal to Louis to admit another visitor.

As he waited in silence, he wondered again, as he always wondered, if Père Joseph knew his thoughts, comprehended him. He wondered if he deceived him. He could not know. He only knew that Père Joseph was watching him gravely with that inhuman detachment. But he did not know that there was compassion and sadness in that regard, also.

CHAPTER XVI

A LACKEY, IN somber black, entered with a silver cup of hot milk mixed with spiced wine. The Cardinal drank slowly and gratefully. There was silence in the chamber. The golden shadows of the sun lengthened, struck the pale and subtle countenance on its silken pillows. Now it was imbued with an attenuated grandeur and delicacy, and it could now be seen that the Cardinal had in himself the quality of nobility and patrician melancholy. The soldier, the diplomat, the schemer, the liar and the hypocrite, the courtier and the politician and the murderer, were obscured by a frail envelope of transparent and luminous flesh. The face of the Jesuit, the priest, the dreamer and the poet arrested itself.

As the sunlight slowly mounted to his eyes, he recalled that visitors still waited in the antechamber. The light quenched itself from his features, and the old expression of intolerant malice returned.

Three gentlemen were then admitted, together, and at their appearance, the Cardinal's face narrowed, became closed and more subtle. But he smiled at them sweetly, and greeted them in the most affectionate terms.

The first gentleman was Raoul, the Duc de Tremblant, brother-in-law of Madame de Tremblant, who was the mother of Mademoiselle Clarisse, the betrothed of Arsène de Richepin. Monsieur le Duc was a Huguenot. Upon perceiving him, Louis turned paler than ever, and the most vindictive look appeared on his marble features. He hated almost all men; for de Tremblant he had a particularly virulent detestation.

De Tremblant did not appear to be a gentleman to inspire any one's animosity. It is true that he had little of the traditional Frenchman's elegance and urbanity and cynicism, and light grace of body and manner. He was a man of about fifty, tall, angular and somewhat ungainly of locomotion, his sober but rich garments hanging awkwardly on a lean but upright figure. His doublet, breeches and hose were of dark purple wool, his collar and cuffs of plain white linen, his shoes plain and simple with a silver buckle. The sword he wore had an unornamented silver hilt, and clanked against his hip and knee as if he were unaccustomed to wear it. However, he had the reputation of being a formidable swordsman, a reputation received incredulously by those who judged by superficial appearances. He might have been an obscure squire, a country gentlemen, a bourgeois of undistinguished ancestry, rather than a nobleman of an old and illustrious name beside which the family of the King himself was plebeian and coarse.

His face was long, gaunt, and much wrinkled, for it was a stranger to the perfumed unguents so sedulously affected by other gentlemen. Moreover, the skin was dark and parched by wind and sun. He spent much time on his country estates, sometimes, to the horror of his peers, working with his peasants in the fields and actually guiding a plow. As a result, his hands were calloused, the nails broken, his face so lined that when he smiled his gentle but disillusioned smile a whole deep web of wrinkles broke out about his large thin mouth, long bony nose and small contemplative brown eyes. He had shaggy grizzled eyebrows, and this gave him a quizzical expression, heightened by the one-sided twist of his mobile lips. Like many Huguenots who were Protestant in their souls as well as their politics, he affected no personal adornments, and his graying hair was closely cut about his long and narrow head. Some of his friends affectionately declared that he had the appearance of an elderly but patrician thoroughbred horse.

Even his enemies could find nothing venal or scandalous in any part of his life, for he had austerity and great simplicity and enormous kindness and understanding. When he smiled, his look was so sweet, so direct, so honest, that viciousness subsided in itself, growling. He was no innocent; he was never deceived. But he had acquired no bitterness in his association with men, though much sadness. As a consequence, he preferred the company of his ignorant peasants and the air of the unsullied country. "It is not possible to love men, nor to feel compassion for them, if one lives among them," he would often say.

He was one of the most powerful magnates in France, and his personal wealth was tremendous. Yet he never abused his power, never asserted it except in righting some injustice, and lived in the utmost simplicity. He needed no luxury about him, as did the Cardinal, to assure himself that he was adequately protected against others. He had too many inner fortitudes to be harassed by a constant fear of his fellows. Reticent, humorous, watchful and kind, hating no man and despising only the fearful and the ambitious, he was deeply loved by his few friends and appallingly hated by his enemies.

The Cardinal had a deep liking for him, wary though it was, and cynical. In de Tremblant's presence, as in the presence of Père Joseph, he relaxed to a great extent, knowing that there was no hypocrite, no creature of duplicity and self-seeking. He would have liked to see more of de Tremblant, but the latter rarely appeared in the Louvre or the Palais-Cardinal, except on grave missions concerning his friends or his religion. This explained the wariness of the Cardinal, and the arching of his eyebrows. The Duc de Bouillon, the Duc de Rohan, and the Duc de Tremblant were the three most formidable Huguenots in France. When they appeared in concert, as they did today, the Cardinal felt in himself the gathering of sly and formidable forces and uneasiness.

He greeted them with expressions of pleasure and friendship. If he liked de Tremblant, he hated the Duc de Rohan, and the Duc de Bouillon. He knew that de Tremblant would regard even his venalities and duplicities with humorous understanding. But the other nobles would have no such tolerance. He knew, too, that de Tremblant was a Protestant, not from desire to retain personal power and rich estates, but from deep conviction. The other two were Protestants less from conviction and devotion, than from hatred of the King and himself.

The Duc de Rohan was somewhat older than de Tremblant, but because of his colossal animal vitality and robustness appeared younger. He was not the son of his mother for nothing. His mother had been of the House of Parthenay, of Poitou, like the Cardinal, himself. Indomitable, arrogant, courageous and intrepid, she had bequeathed these qualities to her sons, and notably to the Duc de Rohan, though she was not responsible for his sly good-humor and loud infectious laugh. Her family was a branch of the famous Lusignans, who had never abandoned their dream of a union of France and England under one government.

Henri, Duc de Rohan, was tall but so broad that he appeared shorter than he was. His large strong body was full of power. Though dressing in soberer garments than those of his position affected, he yet loved elegance, and the darkness of his clothing was set off with rich lace collars, gold buttons and an elaborate sword. However, he was untidy, and not too clean. He had a broad coarse face, with the wide nostrils of those who loved life and lived gustily, and his hair and mustaches were bright red. This redness extended even to his skin, which was very florid, and even to his small quick and lively eyes, so that he seemed imbued with a vigorous hot fire. Though he laughed much, and always had great humor and a fund of obscene jokes rising from the less refined brothels and the gutters, the Cardinal knew him as a dangerous and remorseless man, obstinate, shrewd, brave and ruthless. He had the quick and irascible temper of those of his coloring, and his hand was almost always on the hilt of his sword.

The Duc was a powerful leader, the recipient of the complete devotion of his followers. The Protestants of the south and west of France adored him, trusted him as they did no other. They knew he would never betray them, even for reasons of overpowering self-gain. He was the best example of those who were Protestants by policy, and so was never bedeviled by those tolerant and thoughtful vacillations which afflicted de Tremblant, and made him too meditative, too hesitant, too reluctant to go to excess. Moreover, he was married to Sully's daughter, that dedicated woman.

Men like de Rohan find in their own hatred, and the hatred of others, their greatest stimulant. He knew that if the Catholics hated him, the powerful nobles of the Huguenot towns hated him also, fearing for their own power, and knowing that their own followers did not trust them overmuch. They knew that their followers adored de Rohan, especially the Presbyterian masses, who distrusted the Calvinists and the Lutherans. De Rohan had the ability to conciliate all these sects, weld them together in a strong Protestant bloc.

It had been the Cardinal's policy to conciliate the Huguenots for the sake of French unity against the enemies abroad. He had particularly conciliated de Rohan. But he knew that this conciliation was armed, that he was grasping a tiger by the tail, or holding a bull by the horns. No explanations could confuse de Rohan as they might confuse de Tremblant. De Rohan was uncomplex. He saw through all the Cardinal's magician's tricks.

The Duc de Bouillon was a Huguenot noble for whom the

Cardinal had the greatest respect and the utmost enmity. If he liked de Tremblant, and was wary of de Rohan, he feared de Bouillon. This scion of the mighty House of La Tour d'Auvergne was respected even by the King, and regarded with awe by the French people. Brilliant, lucid, cold and strong, he was too intellectual to be enamored of nationalism, and too sane to be enthusiastic and vehement over the beguilements of prejudice. An icy energy radiated from him, undeceived and cunning. He was a Frenchman, but had a great sympathy for the Germanies, and, indeed, there was something Teutonic about his calm, his method, his immovability and inflexibility. There was a balance in his character which no transport of others could shake. He was amoral rather than immoral, for he loved no one but himself, worked for nothing but himself. He loved power, not as the Cardinal loved it as a means to life, but for itself. His first wife had left him the principality of Sedan, and the Cardinal knew only too well that this principality on the north-eastern frontier was the vulnerable head of France, as La Rochelle was its Achilles heel. It was an ominous Huguenot stronghold, and of this stronghold de Bouillon was independent king. Henry IV, himself, had been more than a trifle afraid of de Bouillon, knowing that he was not inspired by any true Protestantism, and served it only because it was a barricade against the King, and the upholder of his own power.

He had been reared in the Catholic faith, and had abandoned that faith because he saw in the abandonment an opportunity for himself between the Germanies and Holland, and the King. He was a Calvinist, and did not hesitate to play the Calvinists and Lutherans against each other, for the advancement of himself.

So far, de Bouillon had operated with the Cardinal in the effort to prevent the House of Austria from succeeding in its plan of recovering all the Germanies for Rome. He had a loquacious tongue, and an open manner, but this hid a deviousness of temperament which the Cardinal only too well suspected. "A man who tells everything never tells anything," he would say, thinking of de Bouillon.

He had an extremely convincing manner, this Duc de Bouillon, Count of Turenne and Prince of Sedan, this cold and remorseless luster after power. He inspired trust in others, for he spoke with cool detachment and an air of logic. But never was trust less deserved, as many found to their bitterness. He served only himself, and so long as the desires and plans of others coincided with his own, he was sleepless in accomplishing them.

Slender, tall, graceful and yet compact of appearance, middle-aged yet vigorous, with short curling hair on a round skull, pale blue eyes full of strength and craft, a pointed beard which did not conceal his strong and rigid mouth, eloquent of glance and gesture, his was an imposing presence. The Cardinal feared him, with good reason. He had long suspected that here was no true Frenchman, devoted to his country and his people, but one of those creatures who have no race, no allegiance, no patriotism, and no love. He also suspected that the Duc de Bouillon's greatest ambition was the restoration of the old dream of Burgundy, in which a strong Rhenish principality took up its stronghold between France and Germany.

So, they came to him, these three, the first, a Protestant by devout conviction, the second, a political Protestant, the third, a Protestant by ambition. And the Cardinal, gazing courteously and smilingly at them, knew that in their hands and his own, was the fate of France.

"Messieurs!" he exclaimed, extending both his white and narrow hands to them, with the most open glances and air of pleasure. He reserved the longest smile, however, for de Bouillon, knowing him to be the head of the French Huguenots, the strongest enemy of the King, and himself, one of the greatest intellects in France.

They bowed, returning his smile. Père Joseph eyed the three with loathing suspicion. Louis regarded them with the wildest hatred.

The three were aware of the presence of Père Joseph. For an instant their eyes flickered at each other. But that was all. De Tremblant, who distrusted all great religious ardor, believing it the well from which flowed superstition, cruelty, oppression and hatred, felt aversion for the Capuchin. De Rohan was certain that Père Joseph was less a Capuchin than he was a politician, and, understanding politicians only too well, regarded Père Joseph with intense suspicion. De Bouillon, the renegade Catholic with a memory of the tremendous and mystic machinations of his former church, felt that here was his personal enemy. Each, then, out of his own reasons, ignored Père Joseph, who sat far back in shadow near the fireplace.

The Cardinal glanced swiftly at Louis, who colored, knowing that he was being imperiously called upon to act as lackey. However, the young priest, in silence, drew three chairs to the Cardinal's bedside, and the magnates seated themselves, de Tremblant with an awkward clanking of his sword, de Rohan with a spread of his stout thighs and an exhalation of strong animal smell, and de Bouillon with the cold and mechanical grace which was one of his characteristics. The Cardinal, still smiling, and sparkling of eye and gracious of tongue, let his rapier glance pass from one to the other.

Finally, after a long exchange of polite and amusing amenities, de Bouillon said coolly: "No doubt your Eminence is surprised at this visit in force?" And he elegantly waved his hand to indicate his two companions.

The Cardinal raised his eyebrows and smiled charmingly.

"Ought I to be surprised, Monsieur le Duc? Am I too egotistic in believing that I am being visited by friends who come to inquire with regard to my health?"

De Rohan laughed his loud and boisterous laugh. His reddish eyes danced. He winked at de Bouillon who gave him a cold and momentary stare.

"I for one," said de Rohan, with another wink directed at the Cardinal, "am no hypocrite. It is true that your Eminence's health is of momentous import to all of us. To France. But we have heard no rumors that Monseigneur's health is precarious. Therefore, this visit, though concerning a lesser matter than your Eminence's state of being, is of importance. Moreover, if Monseigneur had been seriously indisposed, I should have heard of it from Madame d'Aiguillon, herself." And the lusty Duc winked again, with an obscene smirk.

The Cardinal was not disturbed. He leaned back on his cushions and daintily held his hands high, stroking the thin fingers. He inclined his head, smiling again. He waited.

A furrow appeared for an instant between de Bouillon's cold blue eyes. He concentrated his formidable gaze upon the Cardinal. At that look, the Cardinal felt a queasy sensation at the pit of his stomach. Whenever he was engaged in treacherous activities, or contemplating them, nothing could be more open than his expression, more simple. So, he returned de Bouillon's penetrating regard with an air of gentle candor, which did not deceive de Bouillon in the slightest.

"I have no need to recount to Monseigneur the long and arduous campaign we three have been engaged in with your Eminence, for the welfare, glory and safety of France," said de Bouillon, in his smooth and emotionless voice. "Nor of our efforts in concert to frustrate and render impotent the

173

Habsburgs, who threaten the whole of France. I flatter all of us when I say I believe we have been increasingly successful. So long as France remains united, at peace within herself, she can come to no harm."

"Have I not always maintained this?" asked the Cardinal, with an air of puzzled surprise. "Have I been ungrateful to you gentlemen, or unaware of your services to France?"

"That is true," said de Tremblant. "None of us has doubted your Eminence's devotion to France." And he cast a glance at his two companions.

De Rohan pursed his thick, fleshy red lips and narrowed his mahogany-colored eyes. He thrust out his strong stout legs and stared boldly at the Cardinal. De Bouillon displayed no outward emotions. He sat as still as an apparition.

"Nevertheless," continued de Bouillon, imperturbably, "we have heard rumors. It was only courteous that we come to your Eminence to repeat them, and ask for reassurance."

"That is only just," said the Cardinal. He frowned faintly. "However, I cannot believe that Messieurs would lend attention to mere rumor. I confess I am bewildered."

Père Joseph, in his dim corner, leaned forward and listened intently. His fiery eyes gleamed and flashed in the dusk.

"Rumor," said de Bouillon, meditatively, "is sometimes the first flash of lightning before the storm. I am not given to lend credence to rumor, as a rule. Nevertheless, the air between all of us should not be clouded."

"If it become clouded, it must be clarified, immediately," assented the Cardinal, seemingly more and more puzzled, and assuming an air of patient dignity.

De Rohan laughed again, his loud hoarse laugh. De Tremblant drew his kind brows together reprovingly. But de Rohan could not be repressed. He pointed a derisive finger at the Cardinal.

"Your Eminence is noted for his genius for clarification," he said, boisterously. "That is why I insisted upon this visit."

De Bouillon ignored him. He regarded the Cardinal steadfastly with his passionless eyes. "It is said that almost irresistible persuasion is being brought upon your Eminence to revoke the Edict of Nantes," he said.

The Cardinal paled. His tiger's eyes flashed as he forced himself upright. "And there is a rumor, Monsieur le Duc, that you are conspiring with England for the advancement of your dream of another Burgundy, to the detriment of France," he said, almost in a whisper.

There was a sharp and thunderous silence, as the two men

174

stared fixedly at each other. De Rohan turned noisily in his chair and regarded de Bouillon with amazed suspicion. De Tremblant appeared incredulous, and the web of wrinkles on his face deepened.

"Which," said the Cardinal, very softly, "contains the most truth?"

But if he wished to nonplus de Bouillon, he failed. The Duc remained unmoved, even if his firm thin mouth tightened spasmodically.

"Rumor," said the Cardinal reflectively, and contemplating the ceiling, "is a hag who sits in a corner and spins lies. I have never given this most extravagant spinning of hers the least credence. No doubt Monsieur le Duc has been equally incredulous with rumors concerning myself."

"I hope," said de Bouillon, formally, "that the rumor concerning the Edict of Nantes is as equally without foundation as the accusation against me."

"I can assure Monsieur that it is," replied the Cardinal, as formally. Again, their eyes transfixed each other.

De Bouillon's countenance grew narrower, more intense. The Cardinal, with acrid amusement, knew that this antagonist was swiftly, in his mind, reviewing the list of his few confidants in an effort to determine who was the whispering traitor. The Cardinal waited, with a manner of sweet detachment, for the Duc to reach a conclusion.

De Rohan had been directing a scowling look from the Cardinal to de Bouillon. "This exchange of polite amenities is very edifying," he said, in a bellicose voice. "It is even more edifying to observe how trust is now completely restored between Monsieur le Duc and Monseigneur. However, I regret to say that I have a question of my own, and it is not edifying."

The Cardinal, having momentarily silenced his most dangerous antagonist, turned smilingly to de Rohan. Here was a red bear whom even the King and himself had not taught to dance, and whose apparent clumsiness concealed an explosive threat.

"It is said," exclaimed de Rohan, loudly, "that your Eminence is contemplating attacking La Rochelle, at the insistence of the Queen."

Again, the Cardinal paled, and a flame darted from his eyes. But his voice was cool and controlled when he answered: "And, Monsieur le Duc, it is said that you are in constant communication with de Buckingham, and are even now in possession of promises from him as to the number of English ships and English soldiers to aid in a new Rochellais rebellion. An unprovoked rebellion against the King."

De Rohan, less an artist in duplicity and in ability to conceal his emotions than was de Bouillon, stared blankly, his heavy mouth falling open. His florid countenance became slightly less ruddy.

The Cardinal continued tranquilly: "Rumor, as I have said, is a spinner of lies. She is also reputed to instill ideas where ideas never flourished before. I do not recommend lending an ear to her. For instance, I was only amused when it was reported to me that Monsieur le Duc's brother, Soubise, the captain of the La Rochelle Huguenots, is now very active in inciting his subordinates against the King." He smiled sweetly. "You will observe how ridiculous is rumor. It is even whispered that Monsieur le Duc, himself, has been in secret consultation with Prince Gaston, the King's brother, and even with the Queen Mother, when it was discussed if a rebellion from La Rochelle might not serve to destroy myself."

"Lies!" shouted de Rohan, turning a dark crimson. He panted. He glared at the Cardinal as if the latter were the fiend, himself.

The Cardinal inclined his head. "I have said this," he replied, soothingly.

De Bouillon and de Tremblant turned to de Rohan, who was becoming more and more congested of countenance, more and more infuriated. De Bouillon's gaze was thoughtful; on his lips hovered a grim faint smile of surprise that this coarse man might have the subtle intelligence to plot so astutely. He was also coldly annoyed. England could not so disperse herself as to aid, simultaneously, himself and de Rohan. England, apparently, was up to her old tricks of promising everything with great generosity, to every possible ally, to every possible enemy of the King. De Bouillon wanted all England's strength for himself, for his own ambitions. If she really intended to aid de Rohan, also, there would be less help for himself. I must immediately demand an explanation from de Buckingham, he thought with icy anger. The accursed Rochellais! He would not allow them to draw strength from his own fortresses, no, not even if he had to conspire with the Cardinal, himself, to destroy them!

As for de Tremblant, he was horrified. It seemed to him that stenches rose all about him, the stenches of treason and all duplicity arising from the wicked souls of these three men. He had the deepest conviction in himself that the Cardinal had struck at truth, just as he was certain that if the Cardinal had not yet decided upon attacking the Huguenots, he was contemplating the thought.

Disillusioned though he had long been at the acts and plottings of men, each fresh confirmation unnerved, saddened him, inspired him with despair. He, himself, wanted only that France be strong and unthreatened, his beloved France, whose every clod, every tree, every wind, blossom and blade of grass, was dearer to him than his own flesh. He had supported the Cardinal because he knew that the latter had for France a passionate devotion, tortured though it was, and dark and unfathomable. His abiding dream had been of an impregnable France, filled with tolerance, amity, unity, and peace, culture and tranquillity. Moreover, as a devout Protestant, the cause of Protestantism lived intensely in his heart, not a belligerent Protestantism, but a faith living in simplicity and affection with Catholicism, each drawing wisdom from the other as two brothers, differing in opinion, yet subsisting under the same roof in tolerance and love and understanding.

Now he saw that de Bouillon, out of his own ambition, would set England and France against each other, and France might fall, ruined forever. He saw that de Rohan, the intolerant political Protestant who hated political Catholicism, was conspiring against the unity of France out of his own hatred for the King. And he saw that the Cardinal, that obscure and vacillating man burning with frustration and lust, might very easily be impelled, against his own convictions and reasoning, to attack the Huguenots and so throw France into fatal civil conflict again. Which would win? The Cardinal's passion and devotion for France, or lust for a silly woman? With what frail and human threads were the garments of fate woven!

Yet, he thought, perhaps the Cardinal was less obsessed by a woman than determined that no foreign power should interfere with the internal affairs of France. If England's object was to destroy the unity of France by conspiring with the Huguenots, then the Cardinal had no choice but to attack and subdue the Huguenots. The reasonableness of de Tremblant, his unfortunate ability to see all sides of a controversy, bedevilled him again, left him exhausted, confused, depressed. His beloved France might soon again find her hands red with civil blood, thanks to de Bouillon, de Rohan and the Cardinal. He could not determine who was the most venal. He was only certain that he felt for the three of them the utmost anger, detestation and indignation. He never trusted the Protestantism of de Bouillon, knowing it rose from expediency and ambition. He did not trust the Protestantism of de Rohan, knowing it sprang less from faith than political faithlessness, hatred for the King and personal loathing for Catholicism. (Though what an excellent friar he would have made! thought de Tremblant bitterly.) And now, he did not know whether he could trust the Cardinal's love for France!

He sank deeply into his gloomy contemplations, sighing heavily. Then he became aware that the Cardinal had spoken to him, and he lifted his weary eyes.

He spoke slowly, ponderously, yet with such intensity that de Rohan, de Bouillon, the Cardinal, Père Joseph, and even the somber Louis, listened with intense and unwilling concentration:

"I have no personal ambitions," he said, casting a long and bitter look at de Bouillon, a contemptuous look at de Rohan, and a sad look at the Cardinal. "I have no desire for power, beyond that which God has seen fit to give me out of His own mysterious reasons. I wish only the strength and safety of France, in which she can renew herself, inspire herself, and live in rich and fruitful peace."

He paused. His long and unhandsome face, so thoughtful, so wise, so kind, was contorted by a spasm of sorrowful pain. He pressed his brown knotted hands to his temples, as if to subdue a pang. He sighed again.

"This only have I wanted, this, and the peace and tolerance which was promised my fellow believers by the Edict of Nantes. This only have I fought for, and dreamed." He dropped his hands and regarded the others with burning indignation, despair and anger.

"Why will you not let France live? Is there not in any of you a love for the land which gave you birth, no devotion to her? Must you be men first, and Frenchmen last? Is there no light in your souls, no dedication, no solemn determination that no enemy, internal or external, shall destroy our country? Who are any of you who is greater, more important, more significant, than France?"

He stood up, and because he was trembling so violently, he caught at the back of his chair. The luminous window behind him threw his long lean figure into heroic silhouette. No one stirred in the room. All stared at him fixedly.

He moistened his dry and shaking lips. "A few days ago, in examining my father's books, I came upon an old dusty prophecy.

178

" 'When Frenchmen are by Frenchmen foul betrayed,
  And hating brothers on invaders smiled.
  When Frenchmen's hands in Frenchmen's blood are laid,
  Then France is lost forever, and her fame defiled.' "

He paused again. The slow solemn words had rung like the sound of doom in the great, sun-filled chamber, and every man had listened, his heart beating rapidly. De Tremblant lifted his hand, and so stern, so warning, so terrible, was his aspect, that they could only gaze at him, fascinated.

"Reflect!" he cried. "I feel in my soul that this prophecy is true, that the day Frenchmen smile upon the invader, when they conspire with the invader and the enemy, when they defer to the invader, accept his proclamations out of hatred for their own brothers or their own ambition, when their love for France is less than their detestation of their brothers, when all courage, all honor, all dignity and pride have left France, when she is filled with venal and plotting little men who love their putrid small souls more than they love their country, then France will fall, crumbling in obscene fragments in the dust, never to rise again, never again to aspire, never again to light the torch of culture and faith in her temples. And never again shall peace come to her, save the peace of the grave!"

He flung his hands over his face, as if seized by intolerable anguish.

The Cardinal tried to smile, touching his mouth with his hand. A gleam of derision appeared on the cold bearded lips of de Bouillon. De Rohan's florid face thickened, and his red eyes flickered uneasily. Père Joseph leaned forward on his chair and gazed at de Tremblant as one gazes at a sibyl. But Louis smiled scornfully, thinking of the Habsburgs and the Spaniards, who, if they indeed wished to be "invaders" could yet save France from worse enemies: the French Protestants. The integrity of France was less, to Louis, than the integrity of Christendom.

The Cardinal indeed smiled, for a smile, to him, was a defense. But his subtle soul, always intrinsically mystic despite his cold reason, was disturbed and filled with dark clouds. He would have spoken, but de Tremblant, with a sudden wild gesture of despair, flung out his hands, glanced distractedly about him, and left the chamber, hurrying as from pestilence with his long awkward gait.

When the massive door had closed behind him, de Rohan

179

burst into a long raucous laugh. His full belly shook; he threw back his red bearded head, and his teeth glittered in the clear golden light. His big thick hands, overgrown with red curling hairs, slapped his huge thighs. De Bouillon sat in calm immobility, his classic and aristocratic countenance inscrutable. The Cardinal, though mechanically smiling, was yet absorbed in the chaotic visions in his own soul. But Père Joseph plucked at his russet beard, and his protruding blue eyes sparkled with vehement fire.

Then de Bouillon spoke in his monotonous and unmoved voice: "It is unfortunate that our dear de Tremblant is so passionate. I confess I never suspected such violence in him, and trusted him because I believed in its absence. Violent men, however, can never be trusted."

But the Cardinal, continuing his smile, regarded de Bouillon with the utmost candor.

"I believe only in violent men. Only these are no hypocrites, no plotters, no schemers, no liars."

De Bouillon returned his look with his frozen and formidable eyes. De Rohan, who had heard nothing of this exchange, laughed with increasing enjoyment.

Then de Bouillon raised his pale eyebrows. "It is said that his Eminence is never violent," he remarked, softly.

When de Rohan and de Bouillon had departed, and the Cardinal had completed his friendly reassurances, which de Rohan had received with truculence, and de Bouillon in polite silence, the Cardinal turned to Père Joseph.

"Well, my dear friend," he said, with a languid wave of his hand, "what do you think of these three?"

The Capuchin slowly approached the bed, and looked down at the Cardinal long and piercingly.

Then he spoke, with heavy significance:

"The Duc de Bouillon is a dangerous and unremittingly virulent man. Because he is ambitious, and has sacrificed himself for his ambition. The Duc de Rohan is dangerous, also, for he hates your Eminence, Catholicism, and the King. But he is not so menacing as de Bouillon, for he is not so ambitious."

He paused, then resumed solemnly: "But the Duc de Tremblant is the most dangerous of all. He is not ambitious. He does not hate. However, he has convictions, heretical though they are. And a man with convictions beyond his own welfare, his own ambition, is dangerous beyond imagining. Nothing will halt him. Nothing deter him. He is inspired by

180

his own private truth. And a man inspired by what he considers truth can not be silenced, not be turned aside."

He continued, after a moment: "De Bouillon can be bought. De Rohan can be made to pause, out of prudence. But you cannot buy de Tremblant. You cannot make him pause. He is of the stuff of the original Protestants; he is of the stuff of Luther. For him Rome has only one verdict—"

"Death," said the Cardinal.

The two friends looked intently at each other. It was the Cardinal, finally, who had to turn aside his eyes, and over whose face melancholy and sadness passed like a cloud.

CHAPTER XVII

THE PALAIS-CARDINAL lay in a pool of silence, as it slept under the moon. But in the Cardinal's chamber a light burned near the great red bed. His Eminence was one who loved the silent night, when petty minds and little souls had returned to that blank darkness from which they briefly emerge during the day, like worms creeping to the surface of the ground in the early morning. But at night he could forget his knowledge of mankind, could even forget his hatred, which was like a virus in his spiritual body, and which was so powerful that it infected his flesh. During the day, in his forced associations with his fellows, he was afflicted with a chronic inner trembling; he was nauseated with his loathing. At night, the tortured cramps left his body and his soul, and he would collapse among his pillows and breathe without that smothering constriction in his lungs. He would have all lights extinguished save that by his bed, and, lying there, he would read, meditate, drowse and muse, health precariously restored for a few blessed hours before the dawn. He would listen to the silence, and imagine, with deep consolation, that all but he were dead in the world, that the afflicting presence of man, by some divine and compassionate dispensation of God, had been forever removed from the miserable earth. No one dared enter his chamber. A new lackey had ventured to do so on one night, and was received with such desperate violence, such ravings, such cursings and hysteria, that the poor wretch had fled, not only from the Palais-Cardinal, but from Paris itself. For days, thereafter, the Cardinal could see no one, by orders of his physician, for he had become truly ill.

A profound stillness like velvet darkness would steal over the Cardinal. The cramps and rigors would leave his spirit. Slowly, throughout his body, would flow a blessedness of peace. Forgetting everything, even Anne of Austria, he would stare at the ceiling, at the shrouded windows, a book in his hand, a gentle smile on his lips. Sometimes he would glance at his bolted doors, and the expression of calm would deepen on his pale and haggard countenance. Now all craft and malice left his eyes, all bitterness his frail small mouth, all pain his tall sloping brow. Sometimes he thought it might be like this in the grave, a peaceful sleeping in a stone and narrow chamber, safe forever from the intrusions of a species he hated with justification and complete knowledge.

He could understand the God, then, that he had forsaken, or from whom the wall of human flesh had shut him. Had he ever truly believed, with simplicity, ardor and orison? If he had, he had forgotten. Now he was wafted towards the dark mystery of God, gently, as a shingle of wood is wafted on great flowing tides, unquestioningly, unresistingly. But he could not understand Jesus. Never, at any time in his life, had he understood the Christ. How was it possible for One who understood mankind to love it, to desire to die for it, to suffer for it? Once he had a faint, swift glimmering, a comprehension that it was mankind's very viciousness, stupidity, virulence, cruelty and madness which had inspired the pity of Jesus. But it was a comprehension mixed with wonder and contempt. He, the Cardinal, had a much better cure: a new flood, a new universal fire, a fiery comet out of space. He thought that much more sensible: to destroy the obscenity, rather than to pity it.

He thought that he alone was awake in the Palais-Cardinal. But Louis de Richepin was also awake. Where the Cardinal sought sleeplessness, for the healing of his body, Louis could not escape it. He suffered constantly from insomnia. In the night, all the devils of loneliness, sadness, bitterness and hopelessness, assailed him then, in the cold austerity of his chamber at the end of the long corridor. He would listen to the monotonous tramping of the guards, their dull challenges, until almost dawn. He would sit at his table, which was filled with books, his head in his hands, his dim slightless eyes fixed on the burning candelabrum before him. On the empty stone wall opposite him hung a huge wooden crucifix, crudely executed. Under it was the prie dieu, the low candle flickering as if about to die. Behind him was his hard severe cot. The high narrow window was open, admitting the cool night air. The floor was of stone, completely uncovered, and the two benches were innocent of cushions. It was a monk's room, an ascetic's room, a lonely and empty room, filled with vague candlelight and chill and dank smell of

183

stone. Even on the coldest day there was no brazier here, no cheerful fire. It was a chamber under the earth. The Cardinal, seeing it once, had shuddered and smiled, and raised his brows. But offers of luxurious furniture, of carpets, were politely refused by the young priest.

During the day, his constant duties enforced a suspension of thought in the mind of Louis. But at night, he had no defense against his melancholy and loneliness. If he meditated, it was a meditation filled with hopelessness and frigid despair. If he prayed, it was as if his lips were covered with choking ice. A great motionless emptiness filled him; all the outlines of a living world were dissolved into nothingness. Sometimes he thought: My body, which was once a cauldron, is now an ancient cracked vessel stained with dried tears whose origin I have forgotten.

So long had he been forced to crush hope, desire and passion in his heart that they had become like unborn children dead in their mother's womb—a memory of life, a murdered promise of fulfilment and joy, a weight of heaviness and stillness in his soul.

Once, when the dawn could not release him from the nameless agonies of the night before, he had broken down and incoherently confessed to the Cardinal, crying out like a man whose last defenses had gone. And the Cardinal had listened, hearing echoes in himself. But the echoes did not inspire him to compassion, though he understood. For some strange reason the understanding filled him only with anger. But he had said, gently enough:

"Louis, sharp pain and the capacity for suffering are the signs that the spirit is still fiery and eager. But when the ability to feel grief, rage, fear, agony and tumult is gone, the fool says: 'I have at last attained peace,' and the wise soul cries: 'I am dying!' Be thankful, therefore, that you still live. You suffer, therefore, you are alive."

But now, the night brought only deadness and emptiness to Louis, and the pain in his heart was muted though monstrous. He could not think; he could only endure. He could desire nothing, not even the death which would release him.

I have wanted love, he would say to himself. But the words were now only echoes, and mechanical. He was on fire, but the burning was like flames of ice, freezing his heart rather than imbuing it with incandescence.

The furies from the frozen pits of hell had him in unusual force tonight. They had a voice, a new voice, but he would not listen. He sat for hours, without moving, his eyes, from being fixed on the candles, having become dazed and almost blind. Therefore, when he heard a quiet knocking on his door, it was some long moments before the sound reached his consciousness. Then he was astonished.

He heard the tolling of the midnight bells of Notre Dame as he forced his cramped cold body to rise from the hard bench. He crept across the flickering floor like an old man, his shoulders stooped, his head thrust forward. He shot the bolt, and the door opened with a loud creaking. Père Joseph stood on the threshold, and the candlelight in the chamber struck on his russet beard and sprang back from his great hysterical blue eyes.

Louis, overcome with astonishment, fell back, and Père Joseph entered swiftly, closing the door behind him. The Capuchin glanced rapidly about the dismal room, then approaching a bench, he sat down upon it. Louis, without speaking, sat on the bench on the other side of the table, and the two regarded each other in a profound and speechless silence.

Uneasiness, awe, fear and suspicion filled Louis' cold spirit. He waited, while Père Joseph's rapid eye inspected every article in the chamber, then returned, strange and inscrutable, to the young priest. Evidently his inspection had pleased the Capuchin, for he smiled slightly.

"There is no luxury here, no corruption, no foolishness," he said, in his low resonant voice. "I was not mistaken in you, Louis."

Louis inclined his head. His egotism, never far below the surface, caused a warmer flush to infuse his glacial countenance. His weary heart lightened with an inexplicable thrill of conceit.

The bells of Notre Dame were still shaking the midnight air. Père Joseph briefly examined the volumes on the table. What he saw evidently satisfied him, for his great saturnine countenance softened. He laid his hand upon the cover of a book, tenderly. Then his expression changed again, became stern, fierce and inexorable. His eyes were pits of fiery blue, hypnotic and terrible.

He began to speak, so rapidly, and in so low a tone, that Louis had to listen with the greatest intensity in order to understand. The Capuchin's eyes held him immobile, like a charmer's eyes, so that he could not look away for an instant.

"When I saw you today, Monseigneur, I knew immediately that God had brought us together. Never have I been mistaken in these flashes of divine intuition. I knew you were the instrument God had placed in my hand. When the call comes, I do not delay. That is why I have come to you tonight. All slept in the palace, but I knew you were awake."

He paused. He leaned across the table towards Louis, and the young priest saw nothing but those pits of blue flame which were the Capuchin's eyes.

"I knew, also, that God would put understanding in your heart, and that I had only to speak.

"I need not recount to you the frightful forces which are abroad in the world today, and the ominous threat hanging like a falling wall over the Church. You know these things. You know that only the devotion of the dedicated and the faithful will save the Church. And I know you are one of these.

"The Church, at all costs, must regain spiritual omnipotence in the world as a prelude to the restored temporal omnipotence which must always be her dream, her aim, the purpose of God. Only when the Church has control over the political affairs of men, when she can command kings and emperors and princes and the machinery of all governments and be obeyed implicitly, can the plans of God be fulfilled. It is the duty of all of us to dedicate our lives, our thoughts, our prayers and our desires to the triumph of Christendom, to the extirpation of heretics and infidels by sword and by fire, by ruthlessness and strength. The forces of heresy must be destroyed. While one heretic remains alive in this world, the Church is threatened. While one independent government remains, defying the Church, the Church is unsafe. While one ruler retains power without the authority and the blessing of Rome, his presence is a menace to Catholicism. Wherever men make laws without consulting Rome, and deferring to her commands, there the forces of dissension, heresy and blasphemy are triumphant. The Church, as God intended, must rule all the world, must make all laws, must appoint all rulers, must have the first and the final word, if the divine purposes of God are to be accomplished.

"The Holy Father knows this. All the Popes, from the instant of receiving the Crown and the Keys of Saint Peter, are dedicated to this. In the hearts of all true servants of the Church is the vow that Protestant, Jewish, Mohammedan and Buddhist heresy must die, and their supporters with it. This is the command of God. We can only obey, with joy, pain, service, devotion and martyrdom."

Slowly, as the Capuchin spoke in a low but vehement voice,

filled with passion and fanaticism, a fire had been rising in Louis. The dullness vanished from his eyes. Winds of exaltation, of fury, madness, hysteria and transport flung themselves up in his soul, like flaming coronas. They lifted themselves, roaring, out of the black and fathomless caverns of the hatred that dwelt eternally in him.

The Capuchin saw the sudden leaping of these fiery winds behind the young priest's face, which became whitely hot. Those glacial eyes glittered like mountain ice struck by wild moonlight. And Père Joseph said to himself: I have not been mistaken in the quality of this savage virgin soul, remorseless and dedicated.

His voice was like urgent hands seizing Louis. The young priest sprang to his feet in a transport, trembling, quivering like a tree struck by lightning. He cried out: "What shall I do? For there is something I must do!"

The Capuchin was too astute and intuitive a man to be deceived that Louis' transports rose from religious rapture and devotion. The true devotee was as one divinely inspired, glowing and radiant, caught up in ecstasy, almost angelic in aspect. But Father Joseph saw that something evil, something dangerous and uncontrolled flamed behind the face, the words and the gestures of the young priest, something which made his flesh incandescent with an infernal blaze.

Père Joseph said, fixing the shafts of blue fury which were his eyes upon Louis' face, holding him by his hypnotic power:

"Yes, my son, there is something you can do, something you must do. And, you must listen carefully to me, for the fate of Christendom might depend upon your integrity, your strength and your wisdom."

Slowly, shaking violently, Louis reseated himself, leaning forward across the table, clutching its edge as though about to spring, his eyes glittering, his teeth bared.

Père Joseph lifted his hand solemnly, and spoke in an even lower voice:

"I am the friend, and the confessor, of Madame the Queen. Nevertheless, she has some distrust for me. I cannot, therefore, impel her to listen to me without suspicion." He paused. "You are regarded favorably by Madame?"

Louis hesitated. There were beads of moisture on his broad white brow. He touched them with his trembling hand.

"I am his Eminence's secretary, father, as you are his friend. Therefore, the same distrust had formerly been extended to me by Madame. However, I have thought this distrust has subsided, for I have had many conversations with her, and she has been convinced of my sincerity, and my desire that the Huguenots be destroyed. Though I have sometimes accused myself of disloyalty, I have disagreed, in her presence, with the policies of his Eminence. But that is not secret to Monseigneur!"

Aroused, the Capuchin leaned forward towards Louis.

"This is extremely significant, far better than I hoped! Repeat, if you please, some of your conversations with Madame."

Flattered by the concentrated attention of the Capuchin, Louis obeyed. The Capuchin listened. He hardly breathed. His extraordinary eyes blazed, welled, glowed. He smiled, gripping the edge of the table. He weighed every word. Occasionally, he nodded, with intense pleasure. Once, he ran his hand through the tangled russet beard, as though unbearably excited.

"That is most excellent!" he cried, when Louis had finished. "Most amazingly excellent! I am certain you have convinced Madame of your sincerity." He paused, and now his eyes narrowed cunningly and sharply upon Louis. "It has always been a great sadness to me that her Majesty suspected, and disliked, his Eminence. No doubt without reason."

He waited, wondering how much Louis had heard of the Cardinal's lust for Anne of Austria. And then he saw that Louis would never have believed anything obscene about his master, for there was no obscenity in that egotistic and glacial soul.

Louis shook his head, frowning and sighing. "I regret that there is a reason, father. Madame has always desired that the Edict of Nantes be revoked, that the Huguenots be exiled and suppressed and destroyed, for the sake of Holy Mother Church. She has pleaded so, with the King. But Madame has very little influence with his Majesty, who listens only to his Eminence. And his Eminence has always believed that the strength of France depended on an inner integrity, and for the sake of that integrity, he has placated and conciliated the murderous and rebellious Huguenots." He hesitated again, looked at the Capuchin imploringly. "I have not agreed with his Eminence. I have agreed only with Madame."

The Capuchin nodded. He smiled darkly in his beard.

"Madame has not received his Eminence lately?"

"No. She leaves the room when he enters the chambers of

the King. I know that he has sought audiences with her, to no avail."

"Ah," murmured the Capuchin, well aware of the reasons for the young queen's aversion for the Cardinal.

There was a sudden and portentous silence in the room, in which the Capuchin kept his eyes fixed unmovingly on Louis' face. And Louis waited, his very spirit sweating.

Then Capuchin said, as if meditating aloud: "I have thought that if her Majesty could be induced to receive his Eminence, many things might be accomplished. Once I urged this, before going on my mission to Rome. She refused, with great agitation, suspecting me. Therefore, my pleadings would be of no service. However, if one she trusted, like yourself, pleaded for this interview, it might possibly be granted."

He paused. Louis' eyes widened, but a frown wrinkled his forehead. Then he was excited.

"You believe that my pleas might have some effect, father?"

The Capuchin was relieved. He smiled affectionately. "I know this! And that is why I have arranged an interview for you, and you alone, within the hour, with her Majesty!"

Louis was astounded. He half rose from his chair, staring. "Now?" he cried. "At this hour, when all of Paris is asleep, and the Louvre sleeps also, and Madame?"

The Capuchin smiled sadly. "Her Majesty has few friends, and those friends are suspect. The spies of his Majesty, and—er—his Eminence, are ever watchful. Therefore, she receives her friends in secrecy, after midnight."

Louis, astonished and bewildered, shook his head numbly. The Capuchin reached across the table with a sudden and violent movement, and seized Louis' cold and rigid hand. He impaled the young priest with the rapier of his eye.

"You must go at once, alone, in secrecy, my son! Wrapped in your cloak, your face hidden. Madame will receive you! I have sent a messenger in your name, seeking this appointment, and it has been granted!"

He waited for some exclamation following this amazing revelation. But Louis only stared, incredulously.

"Now, at once!" cried Père Joseph. "Without an instant's further delay. Upon this interview, my son, depends the fate of the Church in Europe!"

"But what reason shall I advance to her Majesty in pleading for her to receive his Eminence?" asked Louis, in a hoarse voice.

The Capuchin was silent a moment, while the flame became intensified in his eyes. Then he said:

"You will say to her that you are certain his Eminence can be persuaded to abandon his present·policy with regard to the Huguenots upon her pleading." He paused, then said, very slowly, very portentously:

"And you will say to Madame that the sacrifice of a single woman's delicacy, aversions, modesty and hesitations are nothing, if the Church is to be saved. You must say to her that it is the command of God that she sacrifice herself."

He wondered if he had gone too far, if Louis had indeed heard of the Cardinal's lust for the Queen, for the young priest's face became very pale, and a cold hauteur spread over it, in spite of the perspiration that gleamed on his brow.

But he was reassured when Louis said: "But that is impertinence, father."

The Capuchin, in his relief, struck the table with his clenched fist.

"A priest is never impertinent, in serving his Church and his God! Your words are absurd, worldly, my son! In the name of the Lord, a priest can speak with all frankness, all imperiousness. Have no fear. Her Majesty will listen with all consideration to you, as a true daughter of the Church."

Without another word, Louis rose. He wrapped himself in a voluminous black cloak. He pulled the hood far over his features. Then, he glanced at the wall, upon which hung his sword. He went to it, removed it, buckled it to his waist. Then he turned to the Capuchin.

"I am ready," he said, simply.

Père Joseph put his arm about him, after blessing him solemnly. They left the Palais-Cardinal through great corridors. They passed the guards, who saluted. They emerged into the dark and gloomy streets. Père Joseph watched Louis until he was swallowed in the midnight darkness.

He shook his head a little. But it was not the first time, he reflected, that a priest had acted as a panderer.

CHAPTER XVIII

LOUIS FOLLOWED THE Capuchin's last instructions. The Louvre slept in complete and gloomy silence. Louis approached the rear, where he discovered the Captain of the Guards standing motionless, cloaked and silent, near the gate, his plumed hat pulled down closely over his face. His sword was in his hand. No other guard was visible, though, at a distance, the monotonous fall of their footsteps could be heard. Over the Louvre, a white moon sailed through ragged black clouds, plunging the city into alternate wan light and darkness.

Louis, his pulses hammering violently, approached the Captain, who knew him well. He drew aside his hood and revealed his pale face. His large blue eyes glittered feverishly in the moonlight.

"It is a quiet night," he said, softly, giving the password.

The Captain was silent a moment; he scrutinized Louis' features. Then he saluted, without speaking. They entered the court; the moon had failed again, and they felt their way in complete blackness. Louis heard a door creak open, and found himself in a lightless corridor. His arm was taken firmly by the Captain, and he traversed numerous narrow corridors, which Louis knew were passageways in the servants' quarters. Doors opened and closed behind him. There was no sound at all but their whispering footsteps. Louis felt a balustrade under his hand. They climbed innumerable stairs. There was another flight, and another. Finally, the Captain stopped at a narrow door, and rapped three times, waited, rapped twice, then three times again. The door opened, and Louis found himself in a tiny dim chamber, lit only by a feeble lamp on a far table. The windows were shrouded in rich tapestry; the narrow pointed ceiling was lost in flickering shadows. At one side of the chamber was a purple velvet divan.

He turned to the Captain, who scrutinized him piercingly.

The soldier was as pale as the young priest, and his expression was stern. He spoke in a whisper:

"Monseigneur, there is only one punishment for treachery."

Louis grew even whiter. He drew himself up haughtily, without answering. The Captain was apparently satisfied, but, after going to a distant door, he paused a moment and shot the priest a long and ferocious look. Then he unlocked the door and disappeared. There was a long and waiting emptiness.

When he was alone, Louis was filled with a great disquiet. He paced slowly up and down the room, his footsteps muffled by the thick golden carpet. His was not a nature attuned to intrigue, to passwords, to furtive approaches. Now he had his moments of apprehension and doubt. Was he being treacherous to the Cardinal? Was he violating his trust? But surely Père Joseph, the Cardinal's dearest friend, would not urge him into a situation where he would do treachery to the Cardinal. Nevertheless, Louis' aversion for the task forced upon him in moments of transport did not lessen. He was no adventurer. He was not excited by secrecy and tension and danger. All his life, he had fled from anomalous positions, and had felt that there was something ridiculous and childish in intrigue. There was something in the nature of men, he had reflected, which impelled them to silly excitements, torturous deviousness, elaborate precautions and signals, when the best approach was the simplest and most uncomplex. But that latter approach held no adventure, no gaiety, no breathlessness, and so, was despised.

Sighing impatiently, and frowning, he removed his cloak and flung it irritably upon the divan. He stood in his somber black, his sword about his strong and slender waist. All the singular beauty of his large white countenance was revealed in the lamplight. His fair curling hair, his handsome blue eyes and perfect features gave him the aspect of a militant angel, so full of proud dignity was he, so quiet and of statuesque proportions. He was no churchman, now, but a young military officer, and only the silver cross that hung from his neck on a black cord betrayed his calling.

Though he heard no sound, the narrow door opened soundlessly, and the Captain appeared. He glanced swiftly at Louis, momentarily withdrew. A female form appeared, small, delicate, graceful, and Louis recognized the young queen.

She was dressed in a simple robe of blue velvet, pearls about her famous white throat and in her tiny ears. Upon one finger of her perfect right hand blazed a single diamond. Her hair was loose, and clung about her smooth white forehead and cheeks and neck in a profusion of gleaming chestnut curls. Her green and sparkling eyes were full of reserve and sweetness, and only the protruding red underlip of the Habsburgs marred a face that otherwise was exquisite and bewitching. All her movements were perfect in their simple and haughty beauty, and she seemed to float rather than walk. Following her was her only female friend, donna Estefania, a Spanish noblewoman, the last of those driven from the Queen by her suspicious husband. Then the Captain entered the chamber on the heels of the Spaniard.

Louis gazed at the beautiful young queen, and a strange agitation seized him. In the light and shape of her eyes, in the brightened radiance of her flowing hair, in her manner and sweetness and reserve, she resembled Marguerite de Tremblant. The Queen, to Louis, had always been a remote and exalted personage, to be treated with distant reverence, and hardly to be regarded as human. But now she was a woman to him, formed of the same dear and lustrous flesh of one of whom he hardly dared think. It was her femaleness, her resemblance to that other, which made his heart beat suffocatingly, made a pervading warmness creep through his body, made a dimness blind his eyes. He felt deep love for her, and adoration. He bowed deeply. When she extended her hand graciously to him he could hardly take it, and when he pressed his cold lips to it, he felt that a fire had burst within him.

When he looked up, the Spanish woman and the Captain had gone. He was alone with the Queen. She seated herself on the velvet divan. She was pale and agitated, and her hands were clasped convulsively together. She regarded Louis with dignity and remoteness, but there was fear and urgency in her emerald eyes.

"Monseigneur," she murmured, "it was against the promptings of discretion that I granted your plea for an interview at this hour."

Bemused though he was, Louis experienced a pang of anger. Haughty and egotistic as he was, he resented the subtle hand which had impudently manipulated him into this dangerous situation, and had thrust him forward to flounder or succeed according to his unprepared wits. He could not speak. His anger gave a white flame to his face, and his eyes glowed. The Queen could not know the reason for all this, and it appeared to her that Louis was inspired. Moreover, she was not immune to manly beauty, and she had always secretly admired the young priest. For some reason which she could never explain, but which arose from her intuition, she had trusted him. She trusted him now, though she was plainly terrified.

He drew a deep breath. He approached the queen and stood before her. All his bemusement had gone. He remembered, with rapidity, what the Capuchin had told him, and his natural caution assisted him in his efforts.

"I shall be brief," he said, in a low voice, "and not detain your Majesty a moment longer than necessary."

The queen sighed. Her rigidity relaxed. But she gazed at him with anxious penetration.

"Your Majesty and I have had frequent conversations about the Huguenots, the Edict of Nantes, and the infamous promises of the heretical English to the rebels in La Rochelle. We have discussed the danger to France, to the Church, and to all Christendom, in this nefarious situation. Forgive my impudence, Madame, if I recall these conversations to you at this time."

The eyes of the queen became full of lightning and passion. She leaned towards the priest, and clenched her dainty little hands on her knees.

"It is not necessary to recall them to me, Monseigneur!" she cried, vehemently. "I think of nothing else but this most frightful condition, and spend all my hours in prayer, and in despair! I can think of nothing but the insult to the Holy Father, to my brother, his Majesty of Spain, to the Habsburgs, to all those faithful to God, in the present policy of France, which conciliates our deadly enemies and the foul heretics!"

She sprang to her feet. She was filled with wild indignation and grief. She regarded Louis with a passionate look.

She exclaimed, bitterly: "But of what avail are my prayers, my tears, when, seated in the power of France, is my most vicious enemy, and the enemy of the Church—your master, Monseigneur!"

Louis said coldly: "Madame, I crave your forgiveness, but the Cardinal is no enemy of the Church. The thought is preposterous, insulting." He was carried away by his indignation, and forgot that this was his queen and not a presumptuous and hysterical woman. His eyes fixed themselves upon her reprovingly, and even with disdain. She was not familiar with such a look and such a manner, and while they aroused her anger and astonishment, they also reassured her and convinced her afresh of the young priest's integrity and sincerity.

Nevertheless, she regarded him with outrage, breathing swiftly.

He continued: "His Eminence has been impelled at all times with a profound devotion to France. One must not question his devotion, which springs from his heart. At the worst, one can only question his wisdom. I have disputed with him often upon this matter."

He paused, then continued in a firm tone: "I am not betraying his Eminence when I speak of this to Madame. He is well aware of my sentiments. I am convinced, however, that he is wrong in his policies, in conciliating and placating the Huguenots. I have told him often that his policy is giving strength to these vile heretics, and that, if the Church is to be saved, and France, also, they must be forever destroyed, and Catholic culture and authority restored to supreme power in Europe. He has asked me: 'Would you have another slaughter of St. Bartholomew?' And I have answered him: 'Yes!' "

At these words, the fire of hatred and fury rose to his eyes, and he was like one possessed. He communicated his emotion to the queen, and between her red lips her little white teeth flashed hungrily.

"Yes!" she cried, striking her hands together. "Let all the gutters of Europe flow with Protestant blood!"

They regarded each other in a transport of hysteria. Louis' hand had flashed to his sword. He trembled visibly. The queen was so shaken that she put her fingers convulsively to her throat, and sank again on the divan. There was a terrible silence in the chamber, while they gazed at each other, panting.

Then Louis whispered: "There is a way, Madame, in which we can accomplish the will of God, and destroy the heretics. I have been assured of this. And that way is to receive his Eminence in secret audience, and plead with him."

He was astounded at the effect of his words. For the queen was propelled upwards, as though forced to her feet in a violent convulsion. Her face turned ghastly; it became a mask of plaster in which were set fiery green eyes. Even her lips whitened. She pressed her clenched hand fiercely against her breast, and her chestnut hair appeared to rise about her head. She regarded Louis with wild fury.

"How dare you?" she said, in a stifled voice. "How dare you come to me with this proposal, you lackey of an infamous scoundrel?"

Louis fell back a step. His hand half lifted. He could hardly

195

control himself from striking that small and frightful face. His efforts at automatic control unnerved him. He shivered. He forced sound to his lips, which felt like hard stone:

"Madame. Though you are the queen, I cannot forgive these words!"

She stared at him, disbelieving, and the fury increased on her features.

"You! You cannot forgive! You, knowing how this man has hounded me, persecuted me, spied upon me, defamed me to all the world—you dare to say this to me! Begone, before I call the guards and have you thrown into the Bastille!"

At this deadly insult, Louis felt his control disintegrate. Could he have summoned strength, he would have struck her down. But he could do nothing but regard her with such a face, such appalling eyes, that she retreated involuntarily, grasping the edge of the table to keep herself from falling. She pressed her fingers to her lips, and gazed at him with open terror, her white breast visibly heaving.

Louis heard his own voice speaking, strange, distorted, muffled: "This is an insult that cannot be overlooked, Madame, even when it is you who have uttered it. I came to you in faith and sincerity, to ask you to receive the Cardinal, and plead with him for the restoration of Christendom, believing that you would have some influence with him; in return I receive unpardonable abuse and coarse threats. I cannot remain any longer in Madame's presence. I beg you to dismiss me."

Now astonishment filled the frightened queen. Her hand dropped from her lips. Incredulously, she gazed at him. Wonder appeared in her eyes, for she clearly saw that the young priest was entirely unaware of the lascivious designs the Cardinal had had upon her. How was it possible for him to serve such a man, and live in Paris, and not have heard the snickering tales? But that was apparently true. There was no duplicity in that marble countenance, that infuriated and distended eye. She moistened her lips. She stood upright, and regarded him with deep sadness. She tried to speak, to enlighten him, but at the thought of repeating the details of the Cardinal's pursuit of her, her cheeks turned scarlet. Now, her expression became gentle, almost compassionate.

"Wait, Monseigneur," she said, sighing. She put her hands for a moment over her face, and the diamond flashed like a tear. She struggled to compose herself. Louis watched her, bewildered, but still enormously enraged. Then she dropped her hands, and gazed at him, sadly.

"Monseigneur, speak to me frankly. Who sent you on this mission to me? Was it that—man?"

Louis' uncontrolled anger returned. "Madame!" he exclaimed. "Reflect! The very thought is absurd, and upon a moment's thought, your Majesty will perceive this."

He could not understand her long and mournful look. She had caught the corner of her red lip between her teeth. Her eyes flickered with her profound thoughts. Then she fell upon the divan, and her head dropped forward upon her breast.

"Wait," she murmured. "Let me think, Monseigneur."

He waited, still shaking with the violence of his past emotions. Then, after a long silence, he said, in a more controlled but still urgent voice:

"I am well aware that Madame has an aversion for his Eminence, because of his foreign policies. This can be understood. And I believe that the Cardinal has some element of malice in him, which helps to force him to pursue a policy repugnant to Madame, because of Madame's aversion. I have heard that his Eminence has a dislike for Madame, which is completely returned. I know that to receive his Eminence would be to your Majesty a great ordeal. Nevertheless, I beseech Madame to receive him, forgetting all personal considerations, and remembering only that the sacrifice of one personage's aversion, instincts and reserve are little enough to pay for the accomplishment of our deepest desire."

The queen flung up her head, and again her eyes glittered with fury. Then, seeing how grave, how solemn, was Louis, she bit her lip and was silent. She rose, slowly, approached the shrouded window, then halted there, not speaking. He saw that her small and fragile figure was trembling, and that she had dropped her face into her hands. Something inexplicable was transpiring here, and it filled him with a perplexed but powerful pity.

He said, gently: "Madame must reflect on the grave issues involved in her decision. Madame will understand that not even herself must stand in the way of these issues."

She returned to him, very slowly. He saw that her eyes were full of tears, and that they were running over her cheeks. So might a victim about to be immolated appear. Louis thought: How great an emotion, how much despair, what extravagant transports, seem involved in the mere granting of an audience! And he felt some amazed contempt for the young queen.

She said, in a voice trembling with tears: "I have reflected. I see my way clearly. But only God knows with what misery I have made my decision, what loathing, what terror and sickness! How can I endure—" She paused, and again her cheeks flushed to a shameful crimson. Then she lifted her small head imperiously, with terrible courage.

"I shall ask his Eminence to present himself to me tomorrow."

When he returned to the Palais-Cardinal, Louis found the Capuchin waiting for him in his chamber. He related what had transpired, and his voice and manner expressed his astonishment and contempt for the extreme emotions of the queen. The Capuchin listened with the utmost breathless intensity. Then, when Louis had done, he sank onto the wooden bench and shaded his eyes with his gnarled hand.

Finally, he dropped his hand and gazed in silence at Louis. His mystical eyes were somber, and there was a mysterious red mist in them, as though filled with tears of blood.

CHAPTER XIX

THE YOUNG QUEEN, Anne of Austria, had chosen the hour, when the King went hunting, to receive the Cardinal.

She dismissed her women, and waited, with rigors of trembling, in the little chamber where she had received Louis de Richepin. Clad in voluminous blue, with a silver bodice, with pale and glowing pearls about her girlish throat, her hair sparkling with golden lights, her aspect was that of a young and defenseless girl. Her face was very white, and in it her full red Habsburg mouth bloomed like a flower. At moments, while she waited, she was seized with uncontrollable agitation, and she would rise from the divan, clasp her hands convulsively together, and pace up and down the chamber feverishly, moaning under her breath, biting her lips hysterically. She shivered at intervals, at the thought of the Cardinal, who had not only inspired her with hatred because of his foreign policy, but with a powerful physical aversion. She was well aware of the truth of the gallant stories about him, and had heard whispered and scandalous tales of his association with her mother-in-law, Marie de Medici. Despising the King's mother, and influenced by her husband's loathing stories of her, she could not but be further revolted by the Cardinal.

As she waited, she was periodically stricken by such horror, such detestation and fear, that she would spring at the door leading to her apartments, in an involuntary effort at flight. Then, as at a loud word of command, she would halt stiffly, her hand on the door, shivering so violently that she would almost fall. More than once, she sank, moaning, to her knees, praying desperately for divine help in the ordeal facing her, praying that in some manner the Cardinal would be prevented from coming. Then, less comforted than rendered numb, she would force herself to her feet, wiping away her bitter tears.

When she actually heard his soft knocking on the door, she could not speak for a long moment. Her lips parted, turning pale as death, but no sound would come from them. Her heart seemed to burst her bodice. She was certain that she was about to swoon. She was not aware that she had uttered a word, but, as in a horrific nightmare, she saw the door open noiselessly, and the Cardinal appeared on the threshold. Her eyes dilated at the sight of him, as a doe's eyes regard the merciless hunter, and all her flesh became encased in ice.

The Cardinal had faced a delicate and excited quandary that morning. Amazed, transported and incredulous at the summons of the Queen, he had wondered how he should array himself for that interview. If he dressed in his majestic ecclesiastical garments, she would be impressed too much with his office, and be horrified at any amorous approaches, and filled with dread and repugnance. If he dressed as a soldier, his favorite apparel, she would receive him as a particularly disliked man. However, if he came as a priest, she would reluctantly defer to his authority with proud submission. He would have more power over her in his gown, but no power as a man. He saw that he must be clothed in authority, but an authority that, while it subdued, did not inhibit.

As much of his physical sufferings were due to the abnormal and sleepless vitality of his mind, events had the power to prostrate or invigorate him. He had awakened that morning with an unusually profound sensation of exhaustion and illness, so that he again was haunted with the belief that death was imminent. He had lain, sunken in his pillows, staring sightlessly at the window, hardly breathing. When Louis de Richepin entered, the Cardinal closed his eyes, wincing. He lifted a feeble hand, and spoke in a failing voice:

"No audiences today, Louis. You must so inform those who wait."

Louis hesitated. In his hand was a small letter, pale blue and heavily scented, and sealed with a coat of arms. He said, quietly, "I shall inform them. However, there is a letter for Monseigneur and it bears the royal coat of arms."

The Cardinal's eyelids tightened over his eyes so fiercely that the delicate skin wrinkled. He groaned. "Another summons to his abominable slaughter, which he calls hunting! Open it, Louis. I am in no condition to read."

"I do not believe it is from the King," said Louis.

"What!" The Cardinal's eyes flew open, revealing their

inexhaustible and glittering power. He lifted himself on his pillows. Faint color rushed through his haggard face. He held out his hand for the letter.

His fingers shook so violently that he could hardly open the dainty missive. His eyes devoured the few words with voracious and incredulous hunger. Then, suddenly, he laughed aloud, exultantly, and with discordance.

Immediately, an unbelievable metamorphosis took place in him. His exhaustion was burned away in an uprush of vitality and delight. His pallor was replaced by vivacious color, and the lines about his fragile mouth and in his sloping forehead disappeared. An immense aura of life and potency radiated about him. Years dropped from his flesh. He sprang up from his bed, laughing uncontrollably, with an evil sparkling in his eyes.

"At last!" he cried, and looked at Louis with such powerful exuberance that the young priest was amazed and taken aback.

"The hour, Louis?" demanded the Cardinal with tremendous impatience.

"It is almost ten, your Eminence."

"Ten! And the audience is at eleven! Call my infernal valet and lackeys! I have not a moment to waste."

Louis was more and more amazed. He could not understand this excitement, this fury of vitality, this discordant laughter at the receiving of the Queen's letter. He tried to find exultant triumph and malice in the Cardinal's manner, or grimness, all of which a spurned diplomat might reveal at the summoning of a disdainful royal personage. But the Cardinal betrayed none of these. There was something personal, something violently uncontrollable and wicked, something privately joyous. Why did the Cardinal display all this, when it was common knowledge that he despised "the Spaniard," and joked indecently about her? Louis had had a moment's apprehension, earlier that morning, that the Cardinal might disdain to answer the summons at all, knowing the young Queen's impotence to enforce a command.

The Cardinal, forgetting Louis, was plunged into concerned meditation about his dress. He cursed the valets who assisted him, shouting down their suggestions. He was no longer the supple and crafty churchman, the power of France, but a querulous and excited man. Louis, more puzzled than ever, could not understand these nervous doubts, hesitations and passionate discussions with the valets. But something obscure and uneasy stirred in him, as he sat in shadow near

201

the window and watched the vehement proceedings. For the first time, he felt no awe, no reverence, for the Cardinal, but a kind of superior impatience. The Cardinal was revealing himself in all his humanity, scornful of the revelation, absorbed only in his rapturous thoughts.

Finally, the costume, after exhaustive discussion, was decided upon. It was to be of severe but rich black velvet, redolent both of the churchman and the aristocratic nobleman. The collar and cuffs were of the finest lace, delicate as a silver web. The Cardinal buckled on his gemmed sword. Resplendent in his cloak, his sweeping plumed hat, his glittering boots, gemmed fingers and sword, inflamed with his febrile vitality and his eyes flashing lightnings of power, he was an imposing presence. No one, gazing at him, could believe that here was a dying man, sick unto death of himself and life, who, only an hour ago, had lain in a coma of approaching dissolution forgetting everything.

A last flickering of perfume over his shoulders, a touch of perfumed unguent on his thin and noble imperial, a last tucking away of a lace-bordered kerchief, and the Cardinal was ready for his audience with the Queen. Never had he appeared so compelling, so handsome, so virile, and so young. The potency and almost superhuman strength which radiated from him were dazzling. He studied himself closely in the mirror held up for him, and smiled with satisfaction.

When the chamber was at last empty of that passionate man, it yet seemed to ring for a long time afterwards with the electric vibrations of his flesh. The vibrations affected Louis disturbingly. He felt exhausted, himself. Suddenly, he started. He forgot the Cardinal. He glanced through the window at the golden morning, soft in its light and invitation, and crimson color raced over his cold face. He stood up, trembling. He walked to the door, hesitated, breathing deeply. Then, he departed.

In the meantime, the Cardinal arrived at the Louvre in his elaborate coach, and was taken to the chambers of the Queen. He had allowed himself no conjectures on the short journey, thinking only of the young woman who had at last summoned him. That was enough.

The young Queen was so paralyzed with her fear, loathing and hatred at the appearance of that inexorable enemy, that she could only sit upon her divan and stare at him with the fixed gaze of a beautiful image. Never had he seemed so gigantic to her, so appalling, so remorseless and evil, as he did at this moment. He was a man, not a priest, and this further affrighted her. She had need to remember, with the utmost frenzy, that she had summoned him for a grave and momentous purpose, otherwise she would have sprung to her feet involuntarily and fled.

His swift glance assured him that she was alone. He had seen her rarely except by lamplight, in ball rooms, at masquerades, and in great drawing rooms. Now, in the morning light, unpowdered, unrouged, girlish, she was more bewitching than ever in her natural fairness and sweetness. He knew that she was a fool, hysterical, superstitious, shallow and unpredictable. He was not a man who preferred foolishness in women, having too deep a regard for rare human intelligence, and had the Queen been less lovely, less young, less unattainable, he would have despised her for herself, and been her enemy because of her inferior intellect. Even in the moments when he was less lustful for her, he detested her for her sparrow-like mind and silliness. But so fresh, so young, so untouched and charming did she appear this morning, trembling in her agitation, that he forgot his detestation of her mental parts, and felt himself that flaming hunger which came with increasing rarity as time passed. He was grateful to her, then, that she possessed the power to arouse him, to reaffirm in him his hope that he was not poised on the edge of dissolution.

He had the amazing ability to fill a room with the aura of his presence. It appeared to the terrified woman that he had the aspect of a huge bird of prey, the walls and ceiling quivering with the vibrations of his dark wings, his eyes devouring her, the very sunlight lessening as at the interference of a great shadow.

He bowed deeply, and advanced towards her. It was not until he stood before her that she extended her cold little hand. When he pressed his lips to its white softness, she felt a rigor stiffen her flesh, and she closed her eyes with repugnant nausea. He had thrown aside his cloak and his hat, and, divested now of his churchly robes, she saw that he was more dangerous than ever.

He spoke quietly, but his feline eyes burned incontrollably. "Madame, I could hardly believe, this morning, that you had sent for me. I have long languished for this opportunity."

Remembering her mission, she forced herself to smile, but it was a painful and pathetic grimace. She compelled herself to gaze up at him, and the green brilliance of her eyes was feverish.

"One does not send for another, whom one is convinced

203

is an enemy," she murmured through dry lips, praying that the wild beating of her heart would subside.

"An enemy, Madame!" he exclaimed, with simulated and passionate disbelief. "I, Madame? I, who have striven at all times to render your Majesty's life tranquil and secure, to plead your Majesty's cause against enemies?"

At this hypocrisy, this grandiloquent lie, the young Queen could not restrain herself. She sprang to her feet, clasping her hands to her breast, her face flaming. She panted audibly.

"Monsieur le Duc, I ask you to spare me this dissimulation! I am only a young and foolish woman, but even I am not unaware of your persecution of me, of your enmity, your tales, your laughter! When have you been my friend? You have influenced my husband against me, induced him to regard me with the most shameful of suspicions. You have driven my friends from me, as you caused the assassinations of the Concinis, the servants of his Majesty's mother! You have made me friendless in an unfriendly land, so that I dare hardly to whisper my prayers for fear that one of your spies is at hand to report my tears and supplications to you! I tremble at shadows; I flee at the rustle of a curtain. On every hand you have set your agents, so that I suspect every smile, every gesture of friendship, every sigh of compassion. *Why* have you done this to me?" she demanded, bursting into tears. "What is there in me that has inspired such hatred and vengefulness in a priest of the Church we both serve? In what way have I offended you, set my feeble strength against you?"

The Cardinal was not taken aback at these manifestations of grief and hysteria and indignation. He was never more in possession of himself as when others lost self-control. He, therefore, assumed an expression of amazement and cold dignity.

"Madame, it is evident that my enemies surround you, defame me to you. At all times, I serve the Throne. I serve France. Even my enemies cannot deny this."

He was delighted at the passion which enflamed the young Queen, and enhanced her beauty. He fixed his eye for a moment on her soft white breast, which appeared, in its swelling and panting upheaval, about to burst the confines of her low bodice. Never had she appeared so desirable to him, so voluptuous, and the veins in his thin and delicate temples swelled with lust.

She cried out, striking her palms together: "Yes, Monseigneur, you have served France! But what is France to me?"

She had hardly uttered these dangerous and impetuous

words when she realized the enormity of them, and her fingers flew to her paling mouth in a gesture of complete terror. Over those fingers, her green eyes regarded him with a distended and affrighted expression.

But he was evidently not disturbed by them. He gazed at her gravely, inclining his head as though he was considering her words. Then he said: "Your Majesty is distraught, for some mysterious reason, and not responsible for her unguarded words, which do not come from her heart. Remembering this, I have forgotten them. In the same spirit of forbearance, I receive Madame's accusations."

But the young Queen was completely undone by her terror. She sank upon the divan. She shivered, pressing her fingers against each other. She was paler than her pearls. The Cardinal studied her with pleasure and satisfaction. Let her, then, fear him completely, understanding how deeply she was in his power. She would then be more amenable.

It was only by a supreme effort that Anne was finally able to control her shiverings, her deathly fright. Praying silently and desperately, she forced herself to look upon the Cardinal with an assumption of her usual imperiousness and pride, though her lips were stiff and numb.

"Your persecutions of me, Monseigneur, are forgiven, forgotten, for I am defenseless. I leave it to Monsieur's conscience to punish him. However, Monsieur's disregard of his Holiness' desires cannot be forgiven. Monsieur's conciliating of the vile Huguenots, his friendship for the enemies of our Church, is an offense in the face of God. Duty impelled me to ask you to this audience, in order to plead with you to consider, to reflect, before all is ruined."

Ah, thought the Cardinal, with contempt and cold anger, now it can be perceived.

The young Queen's own words had inspired her with courage. She lost her terror. She looked at him with bitter contempt and indignation.

He seated himself calmly, without permission, and resting so, in his languid posture, one narrow white hand dangling negligently beside his knee, he was more formidable than when standing. He said, as one speaks to a child:

"Madame must be well aware that all I do is for the good of France. The Huguenots are no less repugnant to me than they are to Madame. Nevertheless, the welfare, the unity and peace of France, depend upon a policy of—temporary—conciliation." He paused, then added indulgently:

"What has your Majesty to suggest?"

When he spoke of France, a grimace of disgust and scorn, even hatred, had passed over the Queen's lips, and she had raised her head with haughty disdain. She exclaimed: "What heed will Monsiegneur pay to my suggestions? What will he say when I urge him to ally himself with the Habsburgs, to avail himself of their pious assistance, and destroy, annihilate, exile and burn all Protestants, which must always be the desire of a true servant of the Church? Surely," she added, with a disdainful smile, "Monseigneur is not unaware that the policy of Rome must always be the complete destruction and extirpation of the Protestant heresy, to the last day and the last hour of the world, forever and forever, whenever or wherever it arises in the world?"

"I am well aware of that, Madame," he answered, gravely.

She became increasingly excited. "How, then, can Monseigneur persist in his policy?" She smiled again, with acid scorn: "Surely Monseigneur knows that the welfare of his beloved France is jeopardized by the existence within it of this foul heresy?"

The Cardinal was silent. His attitude, as he surveyed the Queen intently, was languid and negligent. But in those mysterious tigerish eyes a baleful glare was mounting. The Queen, caught up in her raptures of hatred and venom, did not see this.

He thought to himself: In the hands of such dangerous fools, such weak soft creatures, such meddlers and haters, is the fate of the world often laid.

All at once he despised himself. He, the uncrowned ruler of France, the most feared and hated man in Europe, beguiled his time in the perfumed chamber of a stupid and foolish woman, listening to her imbecilities, her treacherous, her malevolent plottings—a god pausing in his concerns in the affairs of men to listen to the shrewish chatterings of a sparrow! Yet, with an interested detachment, despite his self-detestations, he observed the light of fury and cruelty in those beautiful green eyes. He experienced that old thrill of mingled pain and loathing which always assailed him when discovering the meannesses and malices and foul hatreds of mankind.

Then he said to himself: I must forget that she is a plotter, a tool of the Habsburgs. I am here because she is a woman, and I desire her, and dream of her naked in my arms.

He smiled. "Madame's concern for France touches a heart that has dedicated itself to the life of its country."

Her fierce look wavered, fell. She moistened lips suddenly dry. He remembered a letter he had intercepted, a letter she had written to her brother, that Catholic monster, Philip of Spain, in which she had urged him, in concert with the Habsburgs, to attack France, in order to exterminate the Protestants therein. And he knew that she was remembering, also.

He spoke gently: "I am not yet convinced that the extirpation of the Protestants in France is necessary to the consolidation of Europe, to the safety of Holy Mother Church. I think, on the contrary, that an attack on the Huguenots at this time would precipitate an attack on France, by England. That must be avoided. Consider what would happen if we attacked La Rochelle: de Buckingham would send the promised aid to the rebels, and would precipitate civil war again."

As he said this, in the mildest of all voices, he watched her with rapier sharpness. She looked up eagerly, her eyes flashing with malicious triumph. She laughed aloud, and leaned towards him.

"But Monsieur le Duc de Buckingham has promised me that no English aid shall go to the Rochellais in the event the heretics are attacked!"

The blood rushed into the Cardinal's head. So! the wanton was in truth in communication with her English lover, as he, the Cardinal, suspected! He was caught up in sheets of frustrated and jealous fire, in which he felt an impulse to seize her by the throat and strangle her. And then, in the midst of his almost insane fury, his diabolic jealousy, he felt an impulse to laugh aloud, derisively. This miserable woman, with the weapons of her shoulders, arms, hands, white breast and red lips, could seduce so easily a powerful Protestant Englishman, and make him forget his racial and religious allegiances! More worlds have been lost in a woman's body than historians dream of, thought the Cardinal, and again experienced that pang of contempt and hatred which followed every fresh discovery of the venality and littleness of mankind.

Nevertheless, through his cold politician's mind ran an exultation. He had no longer to fear de Buckingham, and his English men-of-war. This Spanish harlot had rendered France a mighty service, unknown to herself, and one which would have filled her with wild grief and rage. At every time he had moved cautiously, because of de Buckingham, fearing the icy English eyes across the channel. Now, the Queen had rendered the English impotent, kept the fleet immobile in

207

their harbors. And all this because her flesh was warm and snowy, and her lips sweet as a morning rose.

He, the Cardinal, would move now, boldly, knowing that England would not interfere, as usual, in the affairs of Europe. His terrible eye flamed with his exultation.

But the Queen was again overcome by the most abysmal terror. She had again betrayed herself. She knew that the Cardinal had accused her, throughout all of France, of being the mistress of de Buckingham. For months she had defended herself desperately and valiantly, maintaining that she had never communicated with de Buckingham since his flight from France, that the relationship between them was only that of a courteous ambassador and a royal personage. Now, in her rashness, she had openly confessed her associations with the Englishman. She started to her feet with a faint cry, and her visage was that of one who is dying of terror.

The Cardinal saw this. He rose, and approached the Queen. He took her cold and trembling hand. The hand twitched involuntarily in instinctive repulsion.

"Madame," he murmured, his eye falling to the swelling whiteness of her breast, "I cannot express my gratitude to you in adequate words. By your Majesty's faith and devotion, by her dedication to the cause of France and the Church, she has paralyzed our greatest enemy. I am humble before this confidence; I cannot give word to my joy. I can only stand amazed before such sacrifice, such wisdom, such noble immolation."

She listened to these amazing words, her golden lashes lifting and falling rapidly, her senses swimming. Her heart was beating with agonized fear. She could hardly comprehend what she was hearing. But slowly, she perceived the fact that the Cardinal was not threatening her, not exulting over her, but was expressing gratitude, joy and triumph, and drawing her, with him, into a conspiracy. And she was assured, in her foolishness, that the conspiracy was against all Protestantism.

The faintest smile of vanity, of uncertainty, of pride, crept across her pallid lips, which began to resume their usual bloom. She tilted her head, pursed her mouth, gave him a knowing and smirking glance. He watched these manifestations with inward derision.

His lust for her increased. He knew that in his pleasure with her there would be an acrid mental satisfaction. There would be his triumph over a plotting fool. In conquering her, he would conquer, in symbolism, all those miserable creatures he hated and despised, all his intriguing enemies, all the squawling impotent wretches whom he detested, and who threatened France.

He pressed closer to her, and now his senses became heated. He forgot everything in the nearness of her body, in the fragrance of her breath, in the warmness of her mouth. Still engrossed with her piteous conceit, she did not recoil from him. Her eyes were bemused in a reflective and triumphant mist.

"Madame's lightest wish is sacred to me," he murmured. Between her breasts, he observed, was a small area of warm white satin, glistening tenderly. In the hollow of her throat was a delicate translucence, like mother-of-pearl. Her mouth was so near his own that their breath mingled.

Some awareness of all this finally permeated the silly and helpless consciousness of that foolish woman. She became aware of his look, of the sweat upon his pale brow, of his closeness. She tried to recoil, paling again. But he held her by his eye and his hand.

"Madame has only to command," he whispered.

She cried out, through trembling lips, her eyes dilating: "His Eminence is well aware of my desires!" But the cry was mechanical. She twisted her hand in his in a desperate effort to escape.

"Madame's desires shall be accomplished," he said, with the utmost solemnity.

At these words, she was still. She ceased her strugglings. She gazed at him in disbelief, as though she had not heard aright.

"God will reward you, Monsieur," she murmured.

He sighed, deeply, still gazing into her flickering eyes.

"And Madame?" he whispered.

There was a silence in the room. The hand he held grew cold again. The lovely young cheeks paled, and blue lines sprang about the lips.

For the first time, then, the poor indiscreet creature became aware of the enormity of the circumstances in which she was caught, into which she had been forced by her own shrill hatreds, unhappiness, frustrations, and despairs, and the machinations of priests who ignored the fragile sensibilities of a woman for the bloody end for which they indefatigably lived and worked.

But she had been too long the feeble slave of an implacable organization, which sacrificed the heart's blood of its victims with cold precision whenever those victims advanced its long and sinister designs. She could not revolt. In the very thought was mortal sin, and even while she quaked before the Cardinal, sought to escape from him, she was conscious of her guilt.

Nevertheless, she made one final effort at pathetic escape. "The reward of God is not enough for Monsieur le Duc?" she said, in a dying voice, piteous in its fright and dread.

He sighed again, profoundly.

"Alas, Madame," he said.

He watched her inner struggles with a grave countenance but inward amusement. He saw how she quaked, how her white lids fell over her fluttering eyes.

Her voice was fainting, hardly audible.

"Monsieur will find I am not ungrateful."

He lifted her hand to his lips. It was like dead flesh, stony cold and rigid. Still bent over her hand, he whispered:

"Madame will give the humblest of her servants some token, some remembrance?"

"What do you wish?" she muttered.

On her silver bodice, between her breasts, was a knot of blue ribbon, sewed with pearls. When she saw his fixed gaze upon this, she unfastened it with fingers that felt stiff and numb. She gave it to him. He pressed it ardently to his lips. Over its gleaming substance his eyes transfixed her with an evil and smiling look. "Tonight?" he breathed.

When he had gone at last, she stood in the center of the chamber, too filled with horror to move. Finally, with a cry, she threw herself upon her divan and burst into the most dreadful sobs and tears.

After a long while, her face drenched and discolored, she fell upon her knees, her lips moving in a soundless incantation of terror and despair. But slowly, as she prayed, her agony lessened. She began to smile, whitely. Before her dim eyes a vision opened: the streets of Paris, of every city in the world, running red with Protestant blood, and over these cities the shadowy figure of an avenging archangel, holding high a glittering and gigantic Cross.

CHAPTER XX

IT SEEMED TO LOUIS DE RICHEPIN, upon entering the Bois de Boulogne, that he had descended into a luminous world floating soundlessly under green still seas. Here the sunlight entered only as a circumambient emerald light, and the aisles formed by the trees were caverns brimming with dim translucent water. It was a hushed world, unreal, profoundly motionless, where strange creatures might be expected to swim out with long graceful movements from hidden caves, posturing a moment in half-unseen attitudes, then gliding away with a flash of a fin, a sparkle of gleaming scales, or only a faint movement that melted into the all-pervading green silence. The thick vegetation resembled undersea growths, so heavily weighted was it with cool watery immobility. Even the birds were still. No warm breath came from the earth, and when a sound did penetrate the smothering silence, it came as a muffled murmur like that made by a swimmer, who moved in a dream.

As Louis penetrated deeper through the ocean-like caverns and passageways of the Bois, he slowly and completely lost his sense of identity. The coolness and heaviness, the radiant but subdued greenish light, the mysterious stillness, engulfed him. He did not feel the moist and spongy earth under his feet. He lost the imminence of his flesh, the pressure of his weariness, the lonely ache which haunted his every thought. The pathway he traversed descended deeper and deeper into the jade gloom, and the shadows blended into one dusky sanctuary of trance-like peace. His thoughts became diffused, formless, so that they floated away from him as upon the breast of a breathing pool, and he felt them go with a dreaming sense of release, as a drowning man releases his last feverish hold on a straw, and struggles no more.

Now, in the green mist, he saw a mermaid's figure, whose flowing and voluminous garments were the same tint as the

211

pervading light, poised lightly on a heap of black wide rocks. Her hair was golden in the floating gloom, streaming upon her delicate shoulders, and her face, neck and arms were white marble wavering in water, struck with feathers of drowned sunlight.

A hundred times, since he had left the noisy and turbulent purlieus of the Palais-Cardinal, he had anticipated this moment when he would see Marguerite de Tremblant again, and pain, ecstasy, fear and dread had halted him as though he had been struck in the breast. A dozen times he had actually turned and retreated, before proceeding on his way. When he had gone on, he had been like a man, drugged and helpless, forced to move his body under the compulsion of a stronger force. He had even dumbly prayed that she would not be there, that in these long days she had become weary of waiting for him, that he would find nothing but emptiness and loneliness waiting for him on the great flat rocks. So, at last, it was with the passionate hope that she had not come that he had finally allowed himself to enter the Bois.

But when he saw her upon those rocks, motionless, glimmering in the green and watery light of a world beneath the sea, he felt no shock of joy or dread. He moved towards her on an irresistible current, and there was nothing in him but the sweetest peace and the most exquisite rapture. Something whispered in his ear, hot and exigent, but he closed his hearing against it.

She did not smile when he stood at the foot of the rocks and gazed up at her. She swayed towards him, bending her neck, the copper curls streaming over it, and she gave him her hand. It was cool and soft in his own, and at its touch a stream of fire seemed to burst through his flesh in a very agony of expanding joy. Her eyes bent down into his, flecked with light, so that their brown hue was invaded with sparkles of vivid gold. Her soft rosy lips parted and she sighed.

She had become so frail that her flesh appeared to be translucent, and the febrile glow of her spirit pervaded it. With the sharp and searing prescience of passionate love, Louis felt a pang of sudden dread and anguish, of impending loss which filled him with black terror, with violent denial, with a soundless and howling cry. He pressed her hand to his lips, wildly kissing the palm, each finger, and finally, the fragile white wrist in which the veins pulsed with a desperate life. He felt the leaflike touch of her other hand as she laid it upon his bent head. And then, in a moment, she had drawn that head convulsively to her breast, and held it there in one supreme gesture of pure love.

And so they stood there, clasped together like flesh fused into one being, and Louis heard the soaring tremor of her heart. One by one, warm drops fell from her eyes upon his cheek. He felt infinite pity and gentleness in her, the most delicate of passions, the most tender of understanding. The terror had him still, but in her arms it was part of the ecstasy of his love.

They did not speak. They sat down together, still embracing, and now her head rested on his shoulder. They looked into the far green distances, darker now, for the sun had fallen behind a cloud. The shade was duskier, more unfathomable, more withdrawn under the earth, more motionless. His spirit was part of it, still throbbing with suffering, but so pervaded with peace and rapture that it was like a pain felt under opiates. There was nothing else in all eternity but those strange immobile shadows and silences, drawn up like impenetrable cloudy barriers between them and the world, shutting them off forever from weariness and loneliness.

He played with one of her shining curls. Its substance clung lovingly to his fingers. He kissed its perfumed length, until he approached her lips. Their mouths met simply, inevitably, with purity and sweetness.

At last, he tried to speak, but she laid her trembling fingers on his lips. She smiled through the tears that filled her eyes.

"No," she whispered, "let us say nothing."

Moments glided into an hour, and into another, and they sat there, not moving except for gentle caresses. Everything else had fallen into nothingness, had ceased to exist.

CHAPTER XXI

MONSIEUR LE MARQUIS DU VAUBON slid deeper and deeper under his silken coverlets until only his tiny malicious eyes peered over the edges. He was acutely uncomfortable; a sharp cleft appeared between his dyed brows. But there was vitriolic and uneasy reflection in the glances he kept darting his son, Louis, who sat near windows whose silken curtains kept out the hot morning sun.

It was one of the marquis' most sacred beliefs that the morning hours were inviolate, sacrosanct, and no person of delicacy and discretion would presume to invade them. During these hours the exhausted constitution could refresh itself, hidden away under bed-draperies and curtains, with perhaps a cool damp cloth upon a feverish and aching brow. Then, a man desired only a lackey shod with silence, who ministered with downcast eyes and voiceless tongue. Later, perhaps, a massage, a hot potion, a spraying with refreshing cologne, another period of relaxation, and a man was ready once more to face the world.

The marquis' indignation mounted. It was bad enough to experience pangs of acute nausea, and to have a taste in the mouth like the underside of a cow's hoof; it was worse to have this period invaded by one who, at the best of times, did nothing to exhilarate a man or raise his spirits. Louis had known for years that his father never received any one before the sun was well on its way towards sunset. Yet, this morning, he had come here with cold imperturbability, and had insisted on seeing his father. Now he sat near the windows, silent, his calm chaste hands folded on the knee of his black robe, his large quiet eyes meeting those of the marquis with absolutely no expression at all in them!

However, the speculation increased in the marquis' aching mind. There was something strange in this abominable Louis this morning. Something less rigid, less marble-like, less implacable. At moments there was a softness, a gentleness, almost imploring, in his glances, a timid questioning. He even gave indications of a desire to speak shyly and impulsively, but these indications were silenced under the marquis' irate and irritable looks. More surprising than all else, however, that pale and immobile countenance appeared almost human, and there were times when the faintest and most irresolute smiles touched those large smooth lips which actually seemed formed of flesh for the first time.

"There was no necessity to force yourself upon me so early in the day!" exclaimed the marquis, peevishly, for the second time. "There is no comprehension in you, Louis, no subtlety. Arsène has not yet returned from the hunt, but you might easily have waited for him in his apartments without disturbing me."

"It is nearly three o'clock," replied Louis, in that gentle voice he always reserved for his father. The marquis was amazed to hear the note of apology in that voice, a rare thing for Louis. "You usually rise long before this hour."

"But not today," said the marquis, wincing as Louis' arm disturbed a drapery at the window, and thus admitted a brief hot dagger of sunlight. "I am not well," continued the marquis, with rising petulance and irritability. "You were told this."

A shadow of alarm touched Louis' face. He rose and approached the bed, his black garments falling heavily about him. Armand slid an inch or two lower under his coverlets; his eyes glared reproachfully over their edge at his son. He felt some angry embarrassment. His vanity was so intense that he could not endure his son to observe how raddled and debauched he appeared even in this dim light. He was further outraged and astounded when Louis dared to lay his cool firm hand on the older man's brow to test its feverishness.

Armand angrily struck aside that hand. But Louis was not offended. He was too concerned. He said, in a very measured and thoughtful voice: "A man of your years, my father, should exercise more discretion. One does not ask you to become a monk, but an earlier retirement a few nights a week, a little less dancing and exertion—"

But this was too much for Armand. He sat up in bed, the ruffled white silk of his nightshirt revealing too starkly his dark and withered flesh and the cadaver-like hue and substance of his face, still heavily caked with rouge and powder from the night before. Though the gloom in the chamber was very thick, Louis could see what was to be seen, and he was horrified, and sickened.

"'A man of my years!'" screamed the marquis, for a moment apparently about to rise from his bed and fall upon Louis with murderous intent. His black eyes were malignantly alive, like leaping beetles darting about. "How dare you, you eunuch of a priest, you piece of misbegotten stone, you white-faced Jesuit!"

Louis was accustomed to abuse from his father, but for some reason this morning it affected him visibly. He retired to his chair and sat down. But he kept his face turned to the screaming man on the bed, and there was a strange and melancholy look upon it. He listened in silence to the screams of obscene and hating words that gushed like jets of vitriol from those writhing lips, upon which spots of paint still lingered like bleeding scabs. And for the first time, he seemed to hear those words, and they seemed to burn into his heart, for at last he averted his head and allowed it to drop upon his breast.

Even Armand, in his transports of embarrassed and outraged fury, became aware, after some moments, of Louis' inexplicable attitude. Nevertheless, he hated the sight of his son, and even his curiosity could not quiet that hatred. He cried out, before subsiding under the coverlets: "Begone! Morbleu, if I were not ill before, I am of a certainty ill now!"

Louis rose, in all his majesty and handsome dignity. He was even paler than before. "I shall await Arsène in his apartments," he said, quietly. "I ought to have done that in the beginning, without disturbing you."

He traversed the long shining expanse of the floor, and Armand watched his passage, glittering-eyed, panting. Then curiosity, and apprehension, made him exclaim: "Why, then did you annoy me, you fool?"

Louis, his hand on the handle of the door, paused without turning. He said: "I have a message of importance for Arsène. I thought you might be interested. Too, peculiar as it may seem, I wished to have a few moments' conversation with you, alone."

But Armand had heard only the first words, and his hidden and chronic fear rose up in him, clamoring. He had long believed that in Louis lived an implicit danger to his beloved Arsène. He wrenched himself up once more in his bed.

"Stay," he said, sharply. Louis slowly turned, but did not

advance again into the chamber. Cold dignity had fallen like a stony mask over his features again.

Armand surveyed him with active uneasiness, his head thrust forward the better to aid his vision in that sultry and perfumed gloom. He licked his dry and scabrous lips. "Give me the message, and I shall relay it to Arsène." He smiled evilly, his countenance wrinkling. "Then you can return to those mysterious pursuits which absorb the attention of priests."

"The message is for Arsène," answered Louis, with quietness. "His Eminence wishes to see him in an audience tomorrow morning."

A pange of hysterical fright pierced Armand. But he made himself smile derisively. "'A matter of importance!' A letter would have been sufficient. But it is your way, and the ways of all the rascals of your calling, to attach weighty significance to everything." His voice was goading, his manner contemptuous, but the fear in his piercing regard did not lessen.

"The message is harmless, and courteous enough," assented Louis. "But I wished to speak to Arsène at some length about it. His Eminence gave me some hint about the purpose of the audience, and I desired to impart my conclusions to my brother, for his own good."

"Do not stand there like a cursed spectre!" shrilled Armand. "Mon Dieu, my blood is cold enough!"

Louis returned to his chair. The faintest of cold and bitter smiles curved his lips, which once more seemed formed of marble.

Armand wet his lips, his darting eyes fixed on Louis. "What is the purpose of this audience?" he asked, scornfully.

Louis shrugged almost imperceptibly. "It would be too exhausting to impart it to you, my father, and then to Arsène. But perhaps, after I have seen Arsène, and have gone, he will repeat it to you." He smiled again, with subtle comprehension.

This did nothing to alleviate Armand's womanish alarm. He was certain that something sinister was inherent in Louis' remarks. He plucked feverishly at the ruffles of his throat with his thin veined hand, and tried to penetrate the icy layer that covered Louis' face.

Knowing his son's detestation for Arsène, Armand concluded that safety for Arsène lay in placating this formidable and terrible young priest. Now he recalled Louis' words before he had attempted to leave the chamber. He forced a languid and exhausted expression upon his countenance, lay back upon his pillows, whimpered, and sighed, closing his eyes.

"You are annoying, Louis," he murmured. "Nevertheless, I apologize for my hasty—remarks, a moment or two ago. I am distrait. I have suffered some mysterious but miserable malaise for the past few days. My physician finds nothing alarming in my condition, however," he added, hastily, cringing at a movement from Louis which indicated that the young priest might arise again and approach the bed. "But I have thought that a few days' rest, perhaps, or a month or two, on the estates, might have a salutary effect upon me. This has been an unusually arduous season at Court, for one of my delicate constitution."

"I cannot urge you too strongly to visit the estates," agreed Louis, gravely. "Arsène has shown no overpowering interest in them, though they are his inheritance."

At the note of contempt in Louis' words, Armand's eyes flew open with a virulent glare. However, he choked back the words hastily. With hypocrisy, he inclined his head, and replied: "Certes, you are correct, Louis! Arsène is somewhat too frivolous. I shall have a conversation with him very soon. I shall insist that he accompany me."

Louis was greatly surprised. He could not remember when his father had shown him such consideration, and had listened with such interest. He moved upon his chair and directed a long and even eager look upon Armand. Armand, from his cushions, smiled amiably, though his eyelids contracted with the pain in his head.

"I seem to recall that you mentioned wishing to have a conversation with me, Louis," he said, tentatively.

At this, Louis' expression changed again with a sort of agitation. He did not flush, but the opaque quality of his face lightened, and became intangibly softened. He rose, abruptly, and glanced about him as if confused. Then, as if there was no conscious effort in the gesture, he unloosened his black outer robe and laid it aside, standing before his father in his black doublet and white shirt. Now he had the aspect, not of a gownsman, but one of those Puritan Englishmen whose soberness of garment gave them an appearance of lofty dignity and austerity. This was heightened by his fair coloring, the large and impassive outlines of his features, and the mountain blue of his eyes.

There was no rigidity in Louis' manner as he stood at the foot of his father's bed, gazing at him with shy eagerness, unable to find words to express the faint stirring within him.

Unnerved at this, the older man fumbled on the table at his bedside for his snuffbox. He helped himself to a pinch of snuff, and, to escape his son's hopeful regard, he pretended to examine with interest the cover of the box, as if he had never seen it before. He smiled maliciously, and with enjoyment, for there was portrayed on the box, in brilliant enamel and gold, the most audaciously debauched duo. The figures of man and woman were exquisite in their minute naked beauty, the colors delightful and true, the attitudes, though intimate, full of grace. Arsène had given this as a gift to his father on his last birthday, and Armand had enjoyed it, received it with delight. For a moment, Armand forgot Louis, standing in mute and eager supplication at the foot of the bed. He found the female figure especially entrancing, and he remembered how the Cardinal, always the lover of the exquisite and the unusual, had admired it, with laughter. Remembering the Cardinal, he remembered Louis, and furtively replaced the box on the table in an inconspicuous position.

But Louis, the innocent, had seen the gesture. There was something infinitely pathetic in his look when he approached the table and picked up the box. The act was instinctive. He had seen how his father had smiled, and he wanted to share in the happy secret of this smile, believing that this would draw them closer together. Armand, seeing Louis' purpose, thrust out his hand to conceal the box, then, grinning malevolently, he withdrew his hand and allowed Louis to pick up the object.

Louis held the glittering box in his hands, and stared silently at what was depicted upon it. Armand waited, regarding his son with that venomous grin. He was prepared for a freezing start, for an exclamation of cold disgust and shame. But Louis, though flushing, did not recoil, and if there was, for an instant, the beginnings of a gesture of revulsion, it passed without being perceptible.

"Arsène gave this to me," murmured Armand, wickedly.

Louis turned it about in his fingers. He was silent for a moment. Then he said, actually with a smile: "My brother has a strange sense of humor."

His color had increased to a bright red. He seemed to forget Armand. He gazed at the tiny and brilliant picture on the cover. A moistness crept over his cheeks and brow. When he laid down the box, his hand was trembling. He tried to speak again, and could not. Armand, astonished and gaping, looked at him.

At last Louis spoke, in a low trembling voice, his eyes fixed eagerly on his father's face, as if he were imploring him.

"All my life," he said, "I have been unable to approach another human being. Perhaps it was a certain difficulty in my own temperament. Perhaps it was a certain inclination in me to withdraw from other men. I do not know. But now I realize what has been so miserably lacking in my existence. I have not desired to withdraw, to flee, to draw aside. No!" he exclaimed, on a rising and vehement note. "I have always desired to approach and to be approached, to be understood, to be part of life and laughter. I can see that I was always afraid, that it was my fear that kept me mute and isolated. I do not know why. I only know it is so. But now I know that my fear is the cause of my misery, my loneliness."

He paused. Armand was staring at him incredulously. Louis lifted his hands, then dropped them to his sides.

"I have not wished to be isolated," he said, almost inaudibly, but with a beseeching and despairing look.

Had one of the stone images in his garden opened its mouth and spoken to him in these strange accents and stranger words, Armand could not have been more astonished, more taken aback. Possessed of a certain perverse subtlety, he understood much of the new turmoil in his son. And slowly, as he regarded him, his malevolent cruelty awakened afresh, laughed in diabolical silence.

Ah, if only Arsène were here! he thought, deliciously. How he would laugh with me at this pious and pretentious fool! His mind rapidly formulated the words with which he would inform Arsène of this delightful scene, and his dry and painted lips writhed.

"Morbleu! You are not becoming sentimental, my Louis?" he murmured, with a long and evil look.

"Sentimental?" faltered Louis. The light in his eyes dwindled. He seemed to shrink.

Armand lifted a thin forefinger, and shook it archly.

"There are twinges in your soul, my dear Louis! I know these twinges! They arise from a desire to bed with a luscious woman, or from indigestion. Were you a less dedicated man, I would advise either a new mistress, or a new chef. But," he continued with enjoyment, intoxicated by the strange stark expression on Louis' face, "as you are a chaste priest, I cannot advise the first, and as I know your lack of palate, it would be useless to advise the last. You are in a bad way, Louis!"

He continued, with mounting delight: "The liver or the genitals, Louis! I advise you to commune with yourself, in silence, or with your noble master, as to which, in your situation, is the cause of this languishing. No doubt his Eminence, who is well qualified to assist you, will render you good service."

Louis was silent. His figure seemed to melt into the gloom of the chamber, so that only his eyes remained, fixed and still and luminous in the semi-darkness. And those eyes did not move from Armand; they were like the last despairing gaze of a dying man.

Armand paused. He saw that look. A cold chill seized him, and a sensation of inexplicable fright. He shrank in his bed. He darted a swift look about the chamber, for it seemed to him that something terrible was transpiring here.

He cried out, virulently: "Why do you annoy me with your drivelings, you disgusting creature? Is this why you invaded my apartments in the early day? To listen to the rumblings of your belly, to the complaints of your bad digestion?"

He pulled the coverlets to his chin and glared over them at his son. His victory had vanished. He was filled only with fear, which arose from his vague comprehension that he had done a murder.

Then he heard a deep and trembling sigh. Louis' head fell on his breast. He moved back to his chair. He sank upon it, and covered his face with his hands. The fear passed from Armand, but a vast and icy uneasiness replaced it.

There was a soft knock on the door of the cabinet. It opened silently, and Arsène's dark smiling face appeared. Armand experienced sudden sharp relief, followed by hysterical anger and resentment against Arsène for so long delaying his appearance. He pulled himself up in his bed.

"Ah, there you are, my frivolous gentleman, my cavorter with the falcons and the horses, my pursuer of wanton petticoats! What is it to you that your father lies prostrated in his bed, attended by filthy lackeys who lurk behind kitchen doors with chambermaids? I could die alone and neglected, for all of my fine son!"

Arsène arched his brows with good humor, and advanced into the room. He did not see Louis immediately, though the priest had started to his feet with a violent movement at his brother's entry.

"What extravagance!" exclaimed Arsène, sauvely. "You know very well that you sleep almost to sunset. Moreover, I was not cavorting. I was reading in my own apartments."

"Reading!" screamed Armand, beside himself with nervous rage. "What sons have I! A priest and a reader behind

221

locked doors! What degeneracy has come to you, Arsène? You who never touched a book except to admire its bindings?" He was incredulous, fiery with suspicion. "Have you lost your manhood? Are you contemplating entering a monastery?"

"I was reading," repeated Arsène, with a wider smile. "Erasmus, Socrates, Plato, Aristotle, Luther. Calm yourself, my father. Your eyes are starting from your head, and they are badly blood-shot as it is."

Armand's mouth felt open on his astonishment. But Arsène had become aware of Louis, and though he hardly saw his brother's face in the duskiness of the chamber, he sensed the hideous hatred that flared whitely upon it. He had never been alarmed nor disturbed by any previous manifestations of aversion on Louis' part, but today it was either more malignant than usual, or his sensibilities were more acute. He was silent, frowning, experiencing a new sadness.

Then he said, in the gentlest of voices: "Louis."

Louis did not move, but Arsène had the sensation that the priest had advanced upon him with deadly menace, wild with savagery. He was immeasurably startled. From that looming presence, fraught with danger, came a low and heavy voice:

"I have come to warn you, for our father's sake. His Eminence has requested that you attend him in the morning, at eleven. He is about to extend to you a magnanimous offer. I warn you not to refuse it. Guard your tongue! For I tell you that the direst consequences will result from any levity or impudence. Monseigneur is well aware of your activities, your treason. Nevertheless, he has looked benignly upon you, out of his generosity and mercy. Beware that you do not exceed his patience!"

"What is this offer, you black Jesuit?" cried Armand, terrified.

But Arsène was both astounded and angered at his brother's manner more than his words.

"I am no lackey, Louis. I take orders from no priest, whether that priest is Monsieur le Duc, or yourself. I take exception to your address, which is neither courteous nor fraternal."

"This offer?" shrieked Armand, making a motion as if to leap from the bed. He grasped Arsène's arm in a tight and trembling grip, as if to defend him.

But Arsène and Louis stood in silence, regarding each other. Frightful things passed between them. Then Louis flung his cloak upon his shoulders, and without a glance at his father or his brother, left the room like a foreboding doom, walking, not rapidly, but with his usual hard and stately tread.

Arsène, with an impatient yet abstracted gesture, approached the window, flung back the draperies. The sun entered like a gold shout, filling the chamber with a blinding light. Armand covered his eyes for a moment with his arm, cursing.

"Why am I afflicted with such sons?" he whimpered. "A monster and a studious fool? Mon Dieu, there is a fate upon me!"

Arsène returned to the bed, and looked down upon his father dispassionately, and with some sternness.

"What have you done to Louis?" he asked.

Armand dropped his arm, and stared, affronted and outraged. "I? What is this language, these words? How dare you, you buffoon?"

But Arsène was not intimidated. He could not restrain a smile.

"You defend him? You reproach your father?" exclaimed Armand, with excitement. "You assault him with your impudence, you rascal, you scoundrel?"

Arsène, still smiling slightly, arranged his father's cushions. He poured a small glass of amber wine from the decanter upon the table. He placed it in Armand's hand. Armand, still simmering with rage, drank mechanically, his glittering eyes fixed upon his son. Armand found his father's lace kerchief, and touched the scabrous lips gently. At this gesture of tenderness and affection, tears rushed into Armand's eyes. He seized Arsène's hand, and whimpered again.

"Arsène, what is this white fiend contemplating? There is danger in him." He rubbed his mouth with the back of his other hand, and the terror quickened on his raddled face. "What is this offer? Be sure he has had his hand in some deviltry."

"There is no deviltry in Louis," said Arsène, gravely. "But there is in you, my father. What have you done to Louis?"

Armand uttered a foul expletive, then he began to smile maliciously.

"Ah, that Louis!" he cried. He laughed with thin delight. Finally, it was uncontrollable. He rocked on his cushions. He related the conversation he had had with Louis, omitting nothing. He had the faculty of vivid narrative. Arsène seated himself slowly, listening intently. His face slowly grew dark and somber. His eye began to glow with pity and indignation, and a mournful wonder.

"Ah, that countenance!" cried Armand, overcome with his delight. "It was a revelation! It was a sheep's face. It was delicious to contemplate. Who would have thought that he could mewl so pathetically? I must relate this tonight! Madame Doumerque, who is the wittiest woman in Paris, will be entertained beyond imagining. Tomorrow, it will be all over Paris. Louis has long been the game of the Court."

Arsène rose. He stood over his father with so strange and fierce an expression that Armand uttered a single muffled exclamation of astonishment: "Awk!"

"You will say nothing," said Arsène, in a penetrating voice. "Nothing. What you have done is a cruel and shameless thing. But how could you understand this? But I warn you now: if the story becomes the gaiety of Paris, I shall leave this house and never return to it, or to you."

His face kindled, changed. "A cruel and shameless thing! Nom de Dieu! There is no heart in you, no compassion." He paused. He realized the impotence of speech, of the inability to inspire in another man the sentiments foreign to his nature. He gave a futile and despairing gesture.

Armand was speechless. He lay on his cushions, panting, incredulous, blinking. He watched Arsène pass over the floor to the door. He watched him open that door, saw it close behind him.

Then he began to shriek madly. He seized objects on the table beside his bed and hurled them across the chamber. First was the decanter of wine, then the glass, various crystal boxes and bottles, a decadent novel of thin fluttering sheets. Finally he grasped Arsène's little snuff-box, raised it in his wild hand to hurl it also. But that hand stopped in mid-air. It fell, sweating, upon the bed, clutching the box.

He burst into painful and whimpering tears.

CHAPTER XXII

ARSENE WAS AMAZED at his own sadness and indignation. He
had never disliked his brother. He had felt only indifference
for him, and amusement, and, at the worst, annoyance. Never
had he considered that Louis possessed uncertainties. Fear
had been a thing apart from that cold and somber spirit. Now
that he perceived that Louis was vulnerable, bewildered and
mournfully lonely, he was overcome with compassion. Impulsive and ardent, his first impulse was to seek out his
brother and offer consolation, plea for a rapprochement. This
further amazed him. He could not understand his own emotions, or the reason for the new acuteness of his sensibilities
with regard to others.

His pristine awareness of a world that had seemed only
a brightly colored dream of gaiety and adventure were now
so sharp that at moments it was painful. Men were no longer
either friends or enemies, the one to be loved, the other to be
hated and exterminated. They were creatures whose sensibilities and spiritual personalities impinged upon his own,
invading him with their individual despairs and anguishes.
There were new perceptions in him, new subtleties, like small
and aching wounds, threatening to open in impersonal agony
for others. He was filled with an immense excitement, a
troubling restlessness, which a more sophisticated or intelligent
man would have recognized, or with which he would have
been familiar, as some men are familiar with old pain.

The circumstances of his private life had become dusty with
ennui for him. Though he was to marry Clarisse de Tremblant
within the week, his betrothed seemed only a beautiful in-
consequence in his thoughts. He delighted in her bewitching
face and exquisite figure, but she did not touch his thoughts.
There were days when he forgot her entirely.

Forgetfulness assailed him frequently in these days, and
offended friends eyed him coldly or pointedly ignored him

upon meeting. He would say to himself: What dinner or fête did I forget? At first, this distressed him, and he tried to struggle through the overpowering dreaminess of his new thoughts, which had invaded him like a strange and soundless army. But later, he was indifferent. The only thing of importance was to understand.

On the eve of the day he had encountered Louis in his father's chamber, he went again to the house of Paul de Vitry. Paul received him with affectionate delight, grasped his hand warmly, and looked at him with his radiant gray eyes in which there was only love and tenderness. But Arsène was annoyed. Paul was entertaining a stranger, a middle-aged man of tall and portly appearance, somberly clad, gray of imperial and mustaches and cropped hair. The man's broad face was thick and ruddy, and he had small brilliant blue eyes like the points of swords, and red fleshy lips. When he courteously acknowledged the introduction to Arsène, he spoke in a gutteral voice, though his French was perfect. The sword-points which were his eyes penetrated Arsène with simplicity and no deviousness.

He was the Comte Derek Van Tets, Arsène learned, a Dutch Protestant living in Paris temporarily. Within a day or two he was to flee to England, with a message for the British Parliament. A Dutch gentleman of large estates, his lands had been in the path of the invading Spaniards under Philip. He told this simply, but, as he spoke so sparsely, he paled, and his eyes filled with a baleful light.

"I loved my people," he said, very quietly. "I have seen what the Catholics have done to them. But Dutchmen are Dutchmen. There will come a day."

And as he said this, he clenched his heavy hands and looked at Arsène with a bottomless and frightful meaning.

Paul laid his hand on the Comte's shoulder, and said to Arsène:

"We were about to depart for the Hôtel de Rohan. Monsieur le Comte Van Tets has a message for de Rohan. We understood that the Duc de Bouillon and the Duc de Tremblant await us also. Perhaps you would like to accompany us?"

Arsène consented with eagerness, for he perceived that something of importance was transpiring. Too, there was something in the profound simplicity and ominous strength of the Dutchman which had inspired his respect and sympathy. Formerly, he had disliked all foreigners, regarding them either with detestation or amused contempt. Now he understood that men are of one substance.

They proceeded on foot to the Paris residence of de Rohan at Number 8 on the Place Royale. The Hôtel de Rohan was well guarded, for de Rohan trusted no one. It was evident that Paul was recognized by the captain, who, however, pretended ignorance and suspicion to show his authority. Arsène impatiently grasped his sword, but Paul was smilingly patient, addressing the captain repeatedly by his first name. This captain had once served the Marquis de Vaubon also, and had known Arsène since that young man had been hardly more than a lad. Yet he pretended to regard Arsène with suspiciously beetling brows and much lip-biting. Arsène could not restrain his laughter at this.

"Ah!" he exclaimed, "you need not pretend not to recognize me, Grimaud! That will not absolve you from owing me fifty livres!"

The captain colored mightily, and bowed to the ground. "Pardon me if I seem to err too much in my duty, Monsieur de Richepin!" he cried.

"That is an improvement," replied Arsène, good-humoredly. "I remember that you and your men became so drunk on a certain Christmas Eve that thieves entered the Hôtel de Vaubon and made away with everything portable."

They found the Duc de Rohan and his friends awaiting them in the great library, which was filled with books which the Duc's father had assiduously collected for many years. The Duc, however, was robustly indifferent to books, and seated there, surrounded by them, his red grossness was the more exaggerated. The subdued light of great bronze-footed candelabra was shed into every far corner, and mingled with the mighty red logs which smoldered, in this damp twilight, in the huge black marble fireplace. The portraits of the Duc's ancestors lined the panelled walls, their severe faces pale and spectral in the shifting light. The crimson draperies had been drawn across the windows, and there was a tenseness in the atmosphere which the three newcomers discerned immediately. However, the Duc de Bouillon sat with graceful negligence in his tall gilt chair near the fireplace, distinguished as always in this distinguished hall, slowly sipping a golden goblet of wine. The Duc de Tremblant had been pacing through the length of the room, and as Paul and his friends entered, he turned and smiled at them with a kind and troubled look. He laid his goblet on a long vast table of carved oak, and advanced towards them. He shook hands with Arsène, his smile a little lighter, as if he was surprised at the young man's presence. His glance at Paul was deep

227

and affectionate, and that at Van Tets was thoughtfully courteous.

De Rohan, as always, greeted the three with boisterous nonchalance. "And how is our dear Marquis?" he asked of Arsène, one red eyebrow cocked whimsically. "He took five hundred crowns from me last night at the gaming tables."

"And a thousand from me," remarked de Bouillon, with his chilly smile. He turned his head slightly in Paul's direction, and bowed formally. "I knew your father well, Monsieur. If his son is half as dexterous a swordsman, and half as noble a gentleman, he will still be extraordinary."

Paul's presence had immediately lightened the atmosphere in that room. His address was so gentle, his manner so frank and simple, his smile so open and without duplicity, that he could not fail to sweeten any air into which he ventured. De Tremblant, who loved him as dearly as a son, could hardly glance away from him, and the trouble on his countenance continued to lighten until it had almost disappeared.

"Messieurs," said Paul, looking from one gentleman to another, "when I requested that I bring the Comte Van Tets with me this evening, it was with the desire that you hear from his own lips what has transpired in Holland, and what we may expect in the event of another Huguenot persecution in France, from the same source."

"It was reported to me," interrupted de Rohan, with a sour and ribald grin, "that his scarlet Eminence had recently visited a certain lady on numerous occasions, in the greatest privacy. He is alleged to have left her presence at dawn two days ago, and that he cherishes in his bosom a peculiar pearl-sewn token which once nestled in a beautifully intimate spot on that lady's person."

Paul's lips tightened with distaste, and though he was alarmed, he averted his eyes. "I have never believed evil gossip," he said.

De Rohan nodded his head grimly. "Rest assured, Monsieur, I am no gossiper. I have this on unimpeachable authority."

"Hired with your own money," added de Bouillon.

But de Rohan was not embarrassed. "It is so," he answered. "You perceive, gentlemen, that the delicious seduction of his Eminence now places us in the gravest jeopardy. He has stood between us and the Habsburgs and the Spaniard. Immured, now, in a certain lady's bed, he is deaf to all danger threatening France. And ourselves."

De Bouillon turned the stem of his goblet in his elegant fingers, thinking of the Sedan, and his ambitions. His cold hard lips set in a secret and implacable curve. Not given to conversation except when he had something to conceal, he listened to the others intently.

De Tremblant spoke in a reflective and disturbed voice: "If this is true, and I am assured that Monsieur le Duc would not so inform us if there was the slightest doubt of it," and he bowed to de Rohan, "then the possibilities of what confronts us is menacing in the extreme. We know the sleepless hatred of this—certain lady—and we know that if the Duc de Richelieu is won by her, we are lost. There is no end to the probabilities. La Rochelle will be attacked. The Edict of Nantes will be revoked. The Huguenots will be destroyed, or exiled, in every corner of France. Civil war will come again amongst us. We shall then be open to assault by England, by the Germanies, and we shall be invaded by the Habsburgs under the pretense of a holy alliance with us against the 'heretics.' This is the end of France."

De Bouillon gazed at him with his cold and watchful eyes. "If La Rochelle is attacked, and falls, it does not follow that all of us are lost," he said, meditatively. He thought of Sedan again, and the Rhenish state always in his thoughts, and he said to himself that at the worst he could come to an understanding with the Cardinal.

De Tremblant, always acutely aware of the thoughts passing in the minds of others, turned to de Bouillon, and in a trembling voice, exclaimed: "Monsieur, do not believe for an instant that any corner of France will be safe if La Rochelle falls. There is no amnesty for traitors, either from the enemy or from former friends."

De Bouillon regarded him with his cold masked expression which betrayed nothing. De Tremblant continued:

"There are some, for the sake of expediency, for personal ambition and devious and selfish designs, who would betray France. These are not Frenchmen. They are only evil men. Inexorable fate invariably overtakes them. This is the evidence of history. Unfortunately, before they are punished, the innocent are lost. We know, now, that the traitor must always be the first the patriot must destroy. Be assured, Messieurs," and he turned to the others with a moved countenance, "I have always been a man of peace, but I shall consider it my duty as a Frenchman to kill the traitor with my own hand."

De Rohan laughed loudly, and clapped the other on the shoulder. "What extravagance! There are no traitors here, my friend. Or, do you suspect one of us?"

But de Tremblant did not smile. He was too shaken. "I

suspect no man by repute of others, but only when I have discovered him myself."

The faintest flicker of contempt glimmered in de Bouillon's chilly eyes, but he did not move even a finger. The Comte Van Tets had listened to this with profound attention, and his glance dwelt on each man separately.

Paul, who had sensed some menace in the room, was greatly disturbed. He looked about at the company, appealingly. "I am certain that none of us has a deeper love or a deeper allegiance than France. I trust, Messieurs, that you will hear me, and, after me, our distinguished visitor. It is necessary that I speak first," he added, with an apologetic glance at the Dutchman, "for what I will say he will confirm."

Arsène had been wandering about the room, surveying the books critically, with his new-found interest. Now he returned to the group seated about the fireplace.

Paul was silent for a few moments before speaking. As he gathered his words in his mind, he looked at the assembled gentlemen with desperate pleading in his eyes, as if he implored them to comprehend his sincerity, his passionate conviction. There was none in all of Paris, who, entering into the circle of the young Comte's personality, could hate him, for one knew instantly that here was a spirit without cruelty or malice, and filled only with good will and gentleness and compassion. Even de Bouillon could not despise him. He reverenced men of power, and though Paul's power was strange to him, and suspect, he still admired it. Moreover, that inhuman heart was mysteriously touched.

He began to speak, urgently yet softly, his voice filled with the potentialities of passion; his hands half lifted as his burning eyes engaged each gentleman separately:

"It has been said that Protestantism is the heir of all the good men of the ages. The men of heart and sensibility and pity, the men who formulated the revolutionary doctrine that all men are brothers, and that each soul is equal before God. On this premise, they have declared that men should rightfully be equal before other men, not oppressed, not unjustly punished, not regarded without mercy, not destroyed wantonly by tyrants. They have declared that a man's thoughts and his honest words should be respected, that no hindrance be placed upon a man's coming and going, and that his home is inviolate, and that the fruits of the earth shall not be withheld from him when he has earned them by labor and courage.

"These are simple things. These are simple verities. They were said by noble men in Egypt, in Israel, in Greece and in

Rome. They were said by Erasmus, by Luther, and their followers. But only a few have believed them."

He paused. De Tremblant's long ugly face was deeply moved. De Rohan stared with open mouth and blinking russet eyes. The Dutchman, seated near the fire, had bent his head and his hand partially concealed his face. Arsène, standing near his friend, felt a mysterious swelling of his heart, a mounting excitement. But de Bouillon listened with an expression of restrained but amazed contempt, his fingertips feeling his rigid mouth.

Paul resumed, in a quickened and rising voice: "The Roman Church has professed to espouse these principles of brotherhood, justice, mercy and compassion. It has professed to believe in that equality of man propounded by Jesus.

"Nevertheless, without mercy, and only with oppression, cruelty, persecution and hatred, its actions have denied all this. It has done so since its accession to power. Power has corrupted it. While its voices utter the noblest of truths, its priestly agents have set themselves against the oppressed and the defenseness, against the thinkers and the liberators. For it knows that should mankind universally awaken, it will be robbed of the power it has obtained through its service to tyrants and murderers, the rich and the noble.

"The Church has set its face against the enlightenment of the people. Once the Duc de Richelieu said to me: 'I would say the greatest calamity Europe suffered in the past five hundred years, is not Luther, but the printing press. For that, we cannot forgive the Germans.' This frankness is not only his own. The Church has frequently expressed its opposition to the universal enlightenment of men. For it understands that access to the thoughts of the great ages will make man think. It has always set its face against the thinker, for the thinker arouses other men to a realization of their dignity before God and man, and has given them strange and angry thoughts, full of indignation against the oppressor.

"The Church has declared that God has decreed the situation and the state of every man, that if he is born humble and hopeless, he must remain in that condition, nor revolt against his masters. This is excellent for the masters, whom the Church so slavishly serves! The Church has decreed poverty and ignorance, obedience and humility for the huge mass of the miserable people, and charity, piety and power for the rich and the fortunate. In this way it has mortally offended the greater portion of the world, by relegating it to the level of lower beasts, and has exalted those who by the accident

231

of birth have inherited power and privilege. By this doctrine, by its service to the great, it has obtained power for itself."

His voice, urgent and passionate, held his listeners, though to three, at least, his words were revolutionary and astounding. But de Tremblant, smiling tremulously, leaned forward a little the better to hear. The young Comte's face was radiant with fervor, with the light of his dedicated and unselfish spirit. His eyes burned and flashed in the mingled firelight and candlelight, as if illuminated by an inner conflagration.

"In the beginning," he continued, "Protestantism set itself against the injustice and the oppression of the Church and those it served. It set itself against the dark ignorance which that Church had advocated for all those multitudes of the nameless and the despairing. Erasmus wrote of these things. Luther, with his great and powerful voice, projected them into the world of all men. In the beginning, Protestantism was liberation for mankind from the chains and the whips of centuries of domination by the Church. It lit a lamp which had been unlighted for hundreds of years, and showed the misery and the torment which the Church had inflicted upon the mute and the disinherited of the ages.

"God had placed His blessing on the spiritual revolution of Protestantism. For the first time in centuries the people lifted themselves from all fours and gazed, blinded, on the light of liberation. A new dawn seemed heralded. Protestantism, for the first time in human history, had universally and actually projected into reality the ideals of fraternity, liberty and equality. It promised to sustain these ideals, to project them into history as a revivifying and powerful force, free and life-giving. The Church feared and hated it, for it knew that Protestantism was the drums which would awaken men everywhere from the sloth and the inertia of oppression and despair."

No man moved as he spoke. De Bouillon's countenance had seemed to recede into shadowy pallor and narrowness, so it was less a countenance than a spectral outline. But strange to say, the face of de Rohan, gross, strong and brutal, had changed, become refined and eager, as if that earthy soul had felt the touch of a new and mystical spring. Strange, too, there was a kind of shame in his vivid eyes. He thought to himself: So my father spoke, and I have forgotten!

But Paul's face had darkened, become attenuated with suffering and anguish. His hands lifted, dropped to his sides.

"But in these last hundred years, the dawn has fallen back into the night. The shout of liberation is silent. For Protestantism was seized upon by the great princes to throw off the grasp of the Church on large areas of land, and immense wealth which they coveted for themselves. It must be admitted that to a certain extent the Church had restrained the princes from too much seeking after personal power. Now, the princes would be revenged. They cared nothing for the liberation of their people, for the enlightenment of the souls of men, for the principles of liberty, equality and fraternity. Protestantism was the trumpet that called them to revolt against the restrictions of the Church which denied them complete power, which it jealously wished to retain in its own hands. The dream was lost. Man has been compelled again to wait for another day of liberation. Between the upper stone of the Church, and the nether stone of the Protestant princes, the multitudes were ground and crushed. But the cold and sterile Protestantism of the princes held no warmth, no hope, no vitality for the people."

He lifted his hand again, and cried out in a strong and impetuous voice:

"Against the lust for power of the Church, against its betrayal of the oppressed and the helpless, and against the rapacity, treachery, cynicism and political expediency of the powerful Protestant nobles, we equally set our hearts and our hands! Both are enemies of the freedom, justice, peace and dignity of men. Neither has in it a true and compassionate religion, an awareness of the relationship between God and man. For Rome desires only the slavery and the blindness of the people, in order that it may grow stronger on their ignorance and submission, and Protestantism desires only to keep the people in hating ferment, in order to blackmail the Church for political advantage!

"Against these infamous two we must rise with sternness and passion. Otherwise the cause of man against his oppressor is lost forever. That is why I have come tonight, to ask for your help, your hearts, and your hands. You must forget your political expediencies, your love for your own privilege. You must revive in yourself the old holy Protestantism, for the sake of all mankind. You must dedicate yourselves to the liberation of the world, to freedom and justice and mercy!"

He fell abruptly into silence, but his face, his eyes, his shaking lips and outstretched hands were more eloquent than words. De Tremblant came to him, and put his arm about his shoulders, and faced the others.

"Unless we do this, with dedication and courage," he said, "France is lost."

233

"But not only France," pleaded Paul. "The cause of Protestantism is lost to the world if we are remiss, if we succumb to the treachery in our own hearts. Protestantism had pursued a winding course in England, but because of the labors of a few of her noblest men, it is beginning to blossom in some of its potential fruits. A conscience has awakened in England."

De Bouillon stirred at this, and gazed at Paul with his hooded and receding eyes. There was speculation in them, a curious reflectiveness.

"You believe, Monsieur, that England is generously concerned with the safety of Protestantism in France?"

"Yes, I believe this," replied Paul. "I believe that de Buckingham will aid us, if we are attacked by the Cardinal or the Habsburgs."

"Nevertheless," said de Bouillon, thoughtfully, "I have heard that a certain lady has prevailed on de Buckingham not to send succor to the Rochellais in the event of a rebellion." He leaned forward a little towards Paul as he said this.

Paul lost much of his color. His eyes became brilliant with alarm.

"You are certain of this, Monsieur le Duc?"

De Bouillon shrugged. "I am not accustomed to repeat mere rumors."

Paul was silent. He looked desperately from one face to the other.

Then de Rohan spoke hoarsely and slowly: "But there is a way, Messieurs. For instance, if it should appear that that—certain lady—is in reality false to her new admirer, de Buckingham might not survive long enough to keep his infamous promise."

There was a profound silence in the great room. De Rohan looked at them all blandly, his reddish eyes baleful yet smiling.

Paul was still pale. "I do not advocate murder, even of a traitor," he murmured.

De Rohan exchanged an amused look with de Bouillon. "Ah, what a saint this is, and so young a man! Monsieur, have you not learned that violent men must be dealt with violently?"

"It is a visionary," said de Bouillon, favoring Paul with a cynical smile. "Monsieur, is it true that you have liberated your peasants, set them as free men on your estates, sharers in your property and your incomes, accountable to you only for a small portion?"

"It is true," said Paul.

"And you advocate this extraordinary procedure for all of us?"

"Most assuredly," said Paul, with a steadfast look at them all. "I have more than enough for one man. My people labor on my estates, and the greater portion of the fruits are rightfully theirs, before God. I need no more than I have. No man should have more than he needs."

"Most revolutionary," muttered de Bouillon, and he laughed a little, with amazed derision. "But I assure you, Monsieur, that your astounding generosity will not be repeated universally."

"Yet, this has been advocated by the noblest Protestant leaders," said Paul.

De Bouillon shrugged. He still smiled, but he gazed at Paul with that sinister reflectiveness which his enemies knew only too well. "I have never heard such madness!" he exclaimed. "What will proceed from this? Does Monsieur believe he can teach cattle to walk like men, and converse in human language?"

De Tremblant interrupted, with a sad smile: "Monsieur de Vitry believes that men can be educated above their instincts. I do not believe this, entirely. How can one impose reason upon natural emotion, or the prejudice that springs from emotion? In a final crisis, instinct and emotion will destroy education and reason.

"Nevertheless, I believe something of Monsieur's conviction. I do not believe that freedom and enlightenment will raise all men above their inherent stature. But I do believe that the air of freedom and enlightenment will cause to flower and flourish a rare and occasional soul, of value to the world, and which in these days is inevitably lost. That rare soul must be saved, sought out, nurtured, for the sake of all of us, for the sake of France. The price we must pay is small contrasted with the great end."

"I do not understand all this subtlety," said de Rohan, with impatience. "I know only that Protestantism must not be lost in France, that I shall protect my people to the death. That is all I can promise. I am a direct man. I am no Jesuit, with fine phrases and obscurantism."

"It is enough," Paul assured him, with his gentle smile.

"But surely Monsieur le Comte is not truly serious?" exclaimed de Bouillon. "Let us be realistic. Though I am a Huguenot, I am not blind to the results in England. The Reformation has, in England, resulted in the rise of a coarse and rascal species, who are creating a despicable intermediary class of shopkeepers, tradesmen and petty artisans. In the noxious atmosphere they exude, the aristocratic tradition must die, the tradition of nobility which maintains an unassailable bastion between the benighted and inferior multitudes and majesty."

He included the others in a humorous look. "Let us reflect. We are of the aristocratic tradition. We cannot allow the transports of visionaries to jeopardize our ancient privilege, the ancient right of our blood and birth. It is unfortunate that Protestantism seems to give rise to a degraded middle class wherever it flourishes. We must not allow this, however fervent are our Huguenot convictions."

De Tremblant gazed at him steadily, his long kind ugly face convulsed with anger and contempt.

"Monsieur le Duc," he said, coldly and deliberately, "appears to care less for Protestantism than he does for his own ambition. If this be offense to the Duc, he is aware of the proper redress, and is privileged to demand it." He touched the hilt of his sword. "But I warn Monsieur now that I care nothing for the privileges conferred by the accident of birth, nor those who boast them. All that I have, in my person, in my estates, in my power, is at the demand of Monsieur le Comte de Vitry. And I say also, that I am no mean adversary, and am never turned from the course I wish to pursue."

He added, laying his hand on Paul's arm, but looking at de Bouillon:

"There are extremes in this young gentleman's idealism. But battles are not fought and won temperately. If everything of what we consider our rights and our noble privilege must be destroyed to save Protestantism in France, in the world, then we must abandon them."

De Bouillon had turned as white as death at these courageous and candid words. He was silent. But he gazed at de Tremblant with a hidden and dangerous light in his eyes. The others had listened with great excitement, fully anticipating that de Bouillon would take offense with the inevitable result. But the Duc sat motionless in his chair and only gazed at de Tremblant with the immobility of a serpent.

Paul broke the silence. He was still pale, and now he began to tremble.

"I implore you all to believe that I covet no extreme power for Protestantism. No disproportionately great and arbitrary power, whether secular or religious, can exist in the world without endangering the liberty and the lives of all men. But I do believe that in Protestantism is the hope of the modern world, of the present and the future, if it retains its original nobility and disinterestedness. It was the proclamation of freedom for all mankind. Let us remember this, and not be diverted into selfish desires and political expediency."

The dangerous air in the room had lightened somewhat, but de Bouillon still gazed at de Tremblant with that reflective and hidden menace. Paul nervously turned to the Comte Van Tets, with an imploring gesture.

"Speak, Monsieur le Comte. Tell these gentlemen what has happened in Holland."

They had forgotten the Dutchman, but as he rose awkwardly and heavily, they turned to him courteously. He stood before them, embarrassed yet simple, and moving in his attitude of pleading.

"Messieurs, le Comte de Vitry has expressed what is in my heart, in the heart of all Hollanders. I know that he does not speak intemperately. That is why I have come to you to implore your generous aid for my countrymen, for your sympathy, for your indignation and anger.

"My words cannot express to you the full measure of the horror, death and agony which now afflicts my country under the sword and the fire of the Catholic Spaniard, who seems inspired by all the evil of his Church, all the mercilessness and cruelty of his priests.

"There is, in the nature of my countrymen, a passion for liberty, for independence of thought and action, which is peculiar to them. The Romish Church detests this nature, for it is a challenge and a menace to that condition of servitude and docility which that Church has always recommended as a virtue in the people. Always, and forever, the Church, in its service to the powerful and the oppressor, must oppose the thoughts and the actions of free proud men, must always set its face against the liberation of the multitude. In no other country in Europe has she encountered such noble resistance and selfless pride as she has encountered in the Netherlands. Therefore, she has determined to destroy us, believing that in our destruction she will have exterminated the passionate heart of an awakening Europe."

Suddenly that phlegmatic Dutch face was enkindled, and grief, wildness and pleading blazed upon it. He extended his trembling hands to each man in turn.

"Messieurs! In the history of every people there comes an hour when brothers cry out to brothers across borders and across seas: 'Help us, lest we perish, and you die in our perishing!' And this hour has come to England, to France!

237

We of Holland implore you, you who have felt the sun of the Reformation on your faces and have turned your eyes to the liberated morrow! Will you turn from us? Will you, from your expediency, your greed, your internal hatreds, your lusts and your cowardice, close your ears to us?"

He gazed at them with fiery eyes. "If you do, you are lost, Messieurs. You and your people. Think not that you shall save yourselves. You shall die with us.

"Let me tell you, noble lords, what has come to Holland, in those parts which the Church, with the aid of her evil son, has conquered."

He could not speak for a moment, but his eyes, more fiery than ever, gleamed, sparkled and flamed in the candlelit dusk. His sincere passion, his agony, held them, and one or two at least felt shame and fear.

He continued in a lower voice, but it had in it such vibrant power, such awfulness, that it seemed stronger and more impelling than before:

"I beseech you to contemplate my poor country." His voice broke for a moment, then continued, shaking yet inexorable.

"We lived in peace. Our burghers, our mayors, our government, scoffed at the terrified warnings of those who were not blinded by complacency and a false safety. We know the unremitting hatred of the Church for all who have freed themselves from her. We saw her gleaming and macabre eye across our borders, watching endlessly through the nights of our easy slumber and our quiet harmless days. But we could not arouse those in whose hands lay the safety of Holland. It is a sad peculiarity of men that they prefer to believe the pleasant, and hate those who attempt to arouse them to the imminent awareness of unpleasantness.

"But Rome has struck at us, after long years of silence and treachery."

He clenched his hands together, and a look of horror spread over his broad ruddy features, and he stared into space as if what he saw convulsed his soul.

"Messieurs, I have seen the auto de fe with these eyes, in Southern Holland. I have seen the revival of the Unholy Office. I have seen men, women, little children, maidens and helpless youth, dragged to the stake, there to perish while black priests with monstrous faces sang.

"I have seen the shut windows of those who awaited the terror in the night. I have smelled the ghastly odor of burning flesh, as the innocent perished. I have seen the peasant seized

238

in his hut, the lord in his castle. I have seen the wasted land, the starvation of children, the last anguish of the faithful."

He paused again, and now he wept, wiping his tears away with the back of his great hand, with simplicity and despair.

"Messieurs, you have said to yourself: 'It shall not come again to France.' I have heard Englishmen say, with stern pale lips: 'It shall not come again to England.' I have heard the voices of liberated men all over the breadth of Europe, crying: 'It shall not come again to us!' But Messieurs, I tell you in this most solemn hour, that it shall come again to all men, if they awaken not to their danger, to the horror of the Crimson Pestilence which resides on the Seven Hills of Rome, ever watchful, ever fuming with evil.

"For wherever a tyrant shall arise, a madman who hates other men, a despoiler, a ravager, a destroyer, a luster after power, a fiend risen from the pits of hell, there shall the Church stand behind him with all her tentacles of strength and hatred, all the resources of her blind and miserable people, all the arms of her suborned princes, her blackmailed kings, all her limitless wealth."

He looked at the listening faces in the candlelight. And he saw the stern countenance of de Rohan, the moved eyes of de Tremblant, the tears of Paul de Vitry, the enraged lips of his friend, Arsène de Richepin. But more than all, with a failing heart, he saw the cold smile of de Bouillon. And so it was that he turned to de Bouillon with a passionate cry.

"Monsieur le Duc! You have listened to me with scepticism and with chill withdrawal. You have said in your heart: 'This man speaks with extravagance and fever, with ridiculous vehemence. We are civilized men. The spectre of Rome which this Dutchman would fain conjure up before us is the hysterical scream of an overwrought and intemperate nature.'

"But let me remind Monsieur that it is the Church's own boast that she never changes, that she is the same yesterday, today and tomorrow. The same, Monsieur, in all her ravishing hunger and cruelty, her lust and her insatiable greed for wealth and power. Do you believe she lies, Monsieur? Ah, she lies only to gain men's confidence, in order to invade their countries under the guise of meekness and godliness!"

He flung out his hands to all of them.

"Aid us, Messieurs! Give help and comfort to your brothers, whether they be in Holland, in England, in Spain or in the Germanies! Reflect that you are Protestants, not only Frenchmen. Reflect that should the sun of the Reformation be quenched in Europe, a thousand years of darkness will settle again over all men. Reflect upon your children, your faith, your manhood, your freedom. All these things are in jeopardy in this hour!"

A profound silence fell over the great library, while Van Tets' burning and imploring gaze importuned each gentleman in turn. Each eye met his steadfastly, but de Bouillon's stare was both tranquil and oblique. Finally every man came to the Dutchman and grasped his hands with deep feeling.

De Tremblant spoke earnestly: "Monsieur, my heart, my hand, my sword, all that I have, is yours to command. I shall go with you to England on your mission. De Buckingham is my friend. Rest assured you shall not speak to deaf ears."

"The thanks of my countrymen, Monsieur," said Van Tets. "And France?"

"I speak for the Rochellais," said de Rohan, firmly, his eyes sparkling with vivid red lights. "Be assured we shall not betray Protestantism, even at the cost of our lives." And he regarded de Bouillon with a dangerous look.

De Bouillon removed his snuff box from his pocket. He was smiling reflectively to himself. He used the snuff elegantly, flourished his lace kerchief, which he used to brush away flecks of the substance from his imperial. His eyes were pale agates, shining coldly. He gazed at de Tremblant, who waited for him to speak with a hard stern countenance.

"Surely, my dear Raoul, you have reflected on your impulsive promise to accompany Monsieur le Comte to England? Our relations with England at the present are, to speak very euphemistically, not at the most cordial."

De Tremblant's seamed and unhandsome face changed, became ominous. He spoke deliberately: "Monsieur le Duc is not apprehensive that England's aid to Holland might disperse her strength, in the event that certain gentlemen might desire that aid in the furthering of their own interests?"

De Bouillon tugged his imperial thoughtfully. Then he shrugged.

"Let me speak openly, mon amis. Monsieur le Comte must bear with me if what I say shall offend him. The people of Holland are harborers of strange doctrines. Exceedingly dangerous doctrines for the people of France, should they hear of them. Even more dangerous doctrines than those of the violent English."

"The doctrines, Monsieur?" urged de Tremblant, smiling bitterly, as de Bouillon paused.

"Ah, yes. These doctrines are dangerous to established order and privilege. They would incite the people to rebellion against

240

authority, inspire strange desires in them, dangerous doctrines of 'freedom.' What will become of us, born to privilege and power? We would perish in a holocaust of braying asses. Our culture would be lost in an upheaval of swine. Culture is, and always will be, the possession of the superior, and culture can exist only in narrow and tended gardens, like rare flowers. How shall we control the people, if they are indoctrinated by revolutionary ideals? How shall we retain our power, our traditions, our established authority?"

"With the help of God, we shall not retain them," said de Tremblant, quietly.

"He speaks like the Cardinal, this de Bouillon," said Arsène, to Paul.

De Bouillon made an elegant gesture. "Monsieur de Tremblant, I take issue with you. I cannot agree to anything which will jeopardize my position. Therefore, I cannot aid Monsieur le Comte, even in his countryman's struggle against Philip of Spain. Let him set his hand to subduing the revolutionary doctrines of his people, before he seeks the aid of those who would be endangered by those doctrines. What! Does he actually believe that such as I would aid him?"

"These people of the Comte's are Protestants, as we are," said de Tremblant, in a soft and menacing tone.

De Bouillon shrugged again, deprecatingly.

"They are revolutionary, Monsieur. I repeat: let the Hollanders restore authority and respect for the superior among themselves, and subdue those who rant of universal freedom and equality, and I shall reconsider."

De Tremblant exchanged a glowing look with the others. He turned again to de Bouillon, who was smiling slightly.

"Monsieur le Duc has spoken plainly. Let me, also, speak plainly. The cause of Protestantism, the cause of humanity which Protestantism serves, is endangered by such as Monsieur. If Monsieur le Duc has taken offense at this, let him demand redress."

De Bouillon shook his head indulgently. "I quarrel only with Monsieur de Tremblant's ideas, not with himself. I trust," and he glanced blandly at the others, "that these gentlemen will not consider these the words of a coward."

The others eyed him with furious hostility. Still smiling, he bowed elaborately.

"I am no longer welcome, because of my candor. Therefore, I shall withdraw."

They watched him in silence as he traversed the room to

241

the door. On the threshold he paused, and bowed again, with deep and ironic courtesy.

"Reflect, Messieurs. A man must first consider his own country."

When he had gone, de Rohan burst into obscene roars. "There is a serpent, that de Bouillon! But take heart, Monsieur Van Tets: all Frenchmen are not such as he!"

He turned to de Tremblant. "While you two gentlemen are in England, I shall recruit my Rochellais."

They shook hands with fervor.

CHAPTER XXIII

THE CARDINAL, lying supine in his bed, thoughtfully stroked his fingers, held them a moment to a shaft of thin sunlight to admire their transparency. But throughout all these delicate manoeuvres, he eyed the Duc de Bouillon with piercing intensity. It was very early in the morning, but so urgent had been the Duc's message, that he had been admitted through the Cardinal's private cabinet into the bedchamber. At the Duc's haughty demand, Louis de Richepin had been dismissed, but he knew what he had to do. He retired behind the door of the cabinet, and there sat on his stool, listening not without a pang of shame at this enforced eavesdropping.

There had been a prolonged silence. Finally the Cardinal sighed. "Ah," he murmured, and lifting his eyes, regarded the ceiling with languid fixity. The Duc, quietly garbed, sat near the bed, his pale long face, inscrutable, in shadow.

"I congratulate Monsieur le Duc on both his loyalty and perspicacity," continued the Cardinal at last. "This is a grave matter. I agree with Monsieur that should Frenchmen, recruited by two of the most powerful magnates in France, be sent to the aid of Holland, this would present the Habsburgs and the Spaniard with the perfect reason to attack us. Ah," he murmured again, "what individualistic rebels are these Frenchmen of mine! One has to admire the Germans for their dogged racial solidarity, whatever else one rightfully despises in them."

He continued, smiling wanly at de Bouillon: "Too, Monsieur's point that the introduction of astounding ideas of freedom and enlightenment for the canaille would be catastrophic. I am astonished. I have long been aware of de Tremblant's extraordinary idealism, but I believed it tempered with wit and intelligence. Men, as they age, have not been unknown to espouse strange and amazing causes. But I cannot understand de Rohan, who is a realist."

"I have said," remarked de Bouillon, impatiently, "that this Dutchman hypnotized him. Had I not heard it myself, I should not have believed it." He smiled acridly. "I swear to Monseigneur that de Rohan was literally incandescent."

"I should have enjoyed seeing that," said the Cardinal, with a light laugh. "A red incandescence. Yes, that would have been edifying to see." He daintily shaped a nail between two pinching fingers. "However, I cannot help but believe that de Rohan's incandescence came less from a selfless fervor of soul than his own bottomless love of power. I have perceived, in my long dealings with my kind, that all ideals and revolutions which convulse mankind have their origin in one man's fear, avarice or despair. De Rohan is without fear; he has not the intellect to experience despair. Therefore, it must be avarice. Yes, it must be avarice."

He mused, as de Bouillon listened with a tight and evil contraction of his lips: "I have gathered from your conversation, Monsieur le Duc, that our Dutchman has inspired in his audience a veritable lust to kill, even in our gentle de Tremblant. Now, when a man believes he kills for a noble ideal, he is in reality only trying to destroy his neighbor because that neighbor infuriates him by his racial or political differences. This perplexes me. Our de Tremblant has shown no ferocity heretofore towards those who differ from him. He has often played chess with me, and is an excellent player. We have discussed many controversial things with the utmost amiability, enjoying each other's conversation. Is it possible that in reality he has hated me, and that his passion to kill is inspired by that hatred? It must be so."

De Bouillon lifted his elegant hand impatiently, let it drop upon his knee with a sharp sound.

"It pleases Monseigneur to be philosophical," he said. "But I did not come to your Eminence to converse of subtleties. The fact remains that de Tremblant and the Dutchman must be prevented from going to England."

"Ah, yes," sighed the Cardinal, gazing at him through hooded eyes. "That, certes, must be prevented. Has Monsieur any suggestions? Remember, we are not dealing with rabble or petty lords. We are dealing with a powerful magnate."

A look of frozen contempt stood in de Bouillon's merciless eyes. "Monseigneur is reluctant to accomplish the inevitable?" he said.

"On what charges can we seize de Tremblant and throw him into the Bastille, Monsieur? Ah, it annoys you that I speak so plainly. De Tremblant, it must also be remembered,

244

is much beloved of the people of Paris. There is unrest abroad in France, ominous and strange and terrible things, and, should a cataclysm occur, those things would be precipitated. A de Tremblant in the Bastille is not a de Tremblant silenced. Monsieur must remember this. Even the King admires and loves him."

De Bouillon rose. He began to pace up and down the bed-chamber with silent and graceful steps, feline and swift. The Cardinal watched him, smiling covertly. Finally the Duc paused abruptly by the Cardinal's bed, and gazed down at him with cold and virulent eyes.

"Monseigneur, then, out of his reluctance and necessity, is willing to leave this matter in my hands? Even if de Tremblant is a most excellent chess-player?"

Slowly, inch by inch, the Cardinal raised himself on his cushions. The two men gazed at each other with sudden grimness and fatality.

Then the Cardinal said, very softly: "A de Tremblant imprisoned, even in a remote spot, is not a de Tremblant silenced. Moreover, there would be a hue and cry."

"There will be no hue and cry," whispered de Bouillon, and his smile was dark and wicked.

The Cardinal sighed deeply. He slipped down into his bed. He contemplated the windows through which the early sun was climbing. His expression was inscrutable, ruthless, yet tinged with a sad regret.

"Monseigneur is willing to leave this matter in my hands?" repeated de Bouillon. "And Monseigneur will not, himself, raise a hue and cry?"

"Is Monsieur accusing me of duplicity?" murmured the Cardinal, still contemplating the window.

De Bouillon smiled. He stood near the Cardinal's head, and the priest was aware of the deadly exhalations which came from this man's cold and perfumed flesh. The most malignant hatred filled him. But this did not deter him from his ruthlessness.

"I must have Monseigneur's admission that he is aware of the necessity," said de Bouillon.

"You have it," said the Cardinal.

They gazed at each other again, then de Bouillon bowed very low and mockingly.

"As for de Rohan, his Rochellais must be subdued," said the Cardinal. "A red incandescence can easily become a conflagration which could consume France." He looked blandly at de Bouillon. "Monsieur has no objection to the subduing of his brother Huguenots?"

De Bouillon's cold and shining gaze did not shift. He assumed an expression of stern dignity.

"I have no desire to see France plunged again into civil war. Monseigneur must remember that I, too, am a Frenchman. If the Rochellais rebel against the King, and Monseigneur," and he bowed again, very deeply, "then their treason must be punished."

"I believe," said the Cardinal, thoughtfully, after a little silence, "that Monsieur and I understand each other completely. It is unfortunate that Monsieur is not a Catholic."

They stared at each other steadfastly. Then, without speaking again, the Duc took his leave. The Cardinal gazed at the door through which the Duc had left, and began to laugh silently. After a few moments Louis appeared, and the Cardinal's laughter became audible.

"There is a contemptible man!" exclaimed Louis, pale with disgust.

He sat down near the Cardinal, and a white shade of trouble passed over his large handsome face. "It is easy to perceive that he intends to murder the Duc de Tremblant. That is a foul thing. I detest de Tremblant, but that does not prevent me from understanding that, according to his own convictions, he is a good man."

The Cardinal was astonished, and raised himself in the bed. "What! Louis! Is it possible that I have heard these noble and tolerant words from you, with regard to a Huguenot?"

Louis colored, duskily. He rose and with a trembling hand drew the draperies across the window. The Cardinal watched him acutely.

"When necessity arises, nobility, and regret, must be laid aside," he said. "I shall miss an excellent chess-player. But France is above chess."

"Can nothing else deter him?" said Louis, in so low a tone that it was barely audible.

"Nothing, Louis. I know this. I know my dear de Tremblant."

He sighed, over and over, and there was no hypocrisy in those sighs.

At last he said: "Our dear Arsène has arrived? Admit him, Louis. I do not care to see any one else until two o'clock. I am very indisposed this morning."

Louis turned from the window, and once more his face was glacial and full of hatred. He hesitated.

"Your Eminence is aware of the frivolity of my brother?"

The Cardinal smiled, though his frail lips still retained their bluish appearance.

"May I suggest, Louis, that I am no fool? Go at once and admit Arsène. I have recently heard curious rumors about him. Do not look so alarmed. I have remembered that young men are reckless from their youth, and not from evil. They would conspire against God, Himself, out of pure exuberance of spirit."

Louis did not answer this, and with amusement, the Cardinal followed him with his eyes as he moved with his stately tread to the massive doors and opened them. A babel of voices invaded the chamber, and the Cardinal winced. "Morbleu!" he muttered, massaging his brow. Louis stepped aside, and Arsène entered. The Cardinal looked at him with pleasure, for the adventurer that lived in his heart recognized a brother. He admired that restless vivid face, with its dark glow, the vital dark eyes which were never still, the black hair which sprang up and back from the nervous brow. Arsène brought into the chamber with him an air of gaiety and zest, of insouciance and daring, of fearlessness and pride, and arrogance and hauteur, which reminded the Cardinal of the youthful officers whom he had loved in the days of Pluvenal's Academy. "I must have this young scoundrel," he said to himself, and so determined that Arsène should be his next Captain of the Guards.

The Cardinal experienced a thrill of returning life and interest as Arsène bowed before him, smiling. The Cardinal graciously extended his hand, which Arsène kissed lightly. Then the Cardinal grasped that hand and held it tightly.

"Ah, the bridegroom!" he exclaimed. "Yet I have not yet been importuned to perform the ceremony."

"Is it possible?" asked Arsène, raising his sharp black brows. "I understood Madame de Tremblant was to ask you, Monseigneur."

Louis advanced towards the bed, white with jealousy and detestation. He fixed his cold pale eyes upon his brother.

"Monseigneur has many weighty duties on his mind," he said. "He has, certainly, forgotten such an insignificant matter. But I have recorded Madame de Tremblant's request, and if his Eminence is not too burdened or too indisposed on that date, he will perform the ceremony."

"Forgive me," said the Cardinal to Arsène, who was regarding his brother with a faint smile. "I recall the request at last. It will be an excessive pleasure. When you are finally married, Monsieur, to a devoted daughter of the Church, you will remember your duties and obligations to that Church, which you assumed upon Catholic baptism." He pressed Arsène's hand, which he had retained. "You have not forgotten that you are a Catholic, my son?"

A pale convulsion passed over Louis' lip, but Arsène courteously inclined his head in reply, his dark eyes twinkling.

"Now, sit beside me," continued the Cardinal, with affectionate animation. "It is so seldom that you deign to visit me, Arsène. I have not forgotten that you defeated me in our last game of chess."

"Are we to play chess?" asked Arsène, assuming surprise as he seated himself.

"In a way, yes," said the Cardinal.

If he expected a flash of caution and apprehension to appear on Arsène's face he was disappointed. Arsène merely waited, with an open and candid air. The Cardinal smiled internally. He was well acquainted with Arsène's character. He, too, assumed the friendliest of manners, full of paternal affection. His tigerish eyes lingered on Arsène's countenance with a softness which was partly genuine.

"I see you no longer at the gaming tables," he observed. "Your father, the Marquis, is a robber. Perhaps you believe that one highwayman is enough for one family?"

Arsène laughed, but did not reply.

The Cardinal delicately fitted the tips of his fingers together, and over the slender framework regarded the young man benignly.

"Nor do we see much of you at the Court," he added.

Arsène merely smiled. But the corners of his eyelids narrowed.

"One must remember, certes, that a young man on the eve of marriage to a delightful and noble young lady has much to occupy him," continued the Cardinal. "Nevertheless, your friends regret your absences, Arsène."

"That is excessively courteous and magnanimous of Monseigneur," said Arsène.

Again, the Cardinal smiled internally. He liked this adroit by-play.

"May I inquire as to the health of Mademoiselle de Tremblant?" he asked, with a fatherly interest.

Ah, thought Arsène, he knows that I have not seen Clarisse

for some days, that I am rarely at the Hôtel de Tremblant. He said aloud: "Mademoiselle sends Monseigneur expressions of her deepest devotion and respect."

"I saw her at Vespers last night," observed the Cardinal, in a dreamy voice.

Arsène still smiled, but his teeth clenched behind his lips.

"She complained," added the Cardinal.

"Women always complain," said Arsène, carelessly, meeting the Cardinal's eyes boldly.

"Ah, yes," sighed the Cardinal. "It is a failure of the sex."

"If Monseigneur conversed with Mademoiselle de Tremblant last night, then he is well informed as to the condition of her health," said Arsène, with a sweet look.

"But is Monsieur so well informed?" asked the Cardinal, smiling angelically.

"My heart is at ease with regard to Mademoiselle's condition," replied Arsène, tranquilly.

Louis had seated himself on the other side of the Cardinal's bed. He had not looked away from his brother during all this light conversation, but his face expressed all his irrepressible hatred and suspicion.

The Cardinal reached out and patted Arsène's hand indulgently.

"I have heard that there is a pretty soubrette near the Rue des Fossojeurs," he said. "Ah, young blood!"

But Arsène was no longer smiling. He thought of the soubrette, one Mademoiselle Annette Benet, whom he thought he had hidden with excellent discretion. Not even the Marquis, his father, had known of the affair with that young person, though he had remarked on her regretted disappearance from the gayest of the Paris theatres. To no one, not even his friend, Paul, had Arsène confided his connection with his mistress. The Cardinal, it seemed, had eyes everywhere. The remark, then, had dangerous implications, a subtle warning in it that Arsène had concealed nothing from that terrible man. Arsène had a moment of fear, which he hid under a bold smile.

"Monsieur le Duc appears to know everything about me, though he is not my confessor," he said.

But if he thought to goad the Cardinal into revealing, even obscurely, how much he knew, he failed. The Cardinal only smiled gently.

"I am prostrated with humility before Monseigneur's interest in my affairs," continued the young man.

Still smiling, the Cardinal turned to Louis, who had been

listening with wrinkled brows. "Louis, will you bring us a bottle of wine?"

Louis, flushing, rose obediently, hating the Cardinal for this humiliation. He brought the wine, and with it, two goblets. The Cardinal arched his brows. "And you, Louis?"

"I thank you, no, Monseigneur," replied Louis, stiffly. He looked up to discover his brother regarding him with a curious expression. He, unacquainted with compassion, did not recognize that look, and thought it contemptuous.

The Cardinal and Arsène drank with slow amiability. But their thoughts were neither slow nor amiable.

"As your priest, and the friend of your father, Arsène," said the Cardinal, "it is incumbent upon me to advise you on the eve of holy matrimony. Therefore, with all true concern, I must beg of you to reflect upon your duties and your obligations, which are serious ones."

"Monseigneur would advise?" said Arsène, delicately.

"I would advise you, Arsène, to engage in nothing which might bring distress to a young demoiselle whose happiness must always be my concern," replied the Cardinal, in a gentle tone.

"I assure Monseigneur that Mademoiselle will find me a satisfactory huband," said Arsène. "I am well acquainted with female vagaries, and the delicacies of female nature."

The Cardinal held out his glass to Arsène, and the young man filled it with great and filial care. As he did so, the Cardinal regarded him piercingly, and once more he smiled.

"I love you, my son," he said, with engaging frankness. "That is why I must secure you. There are so few whose presence I enjoy."

Arsène bowed, sipped his wine, and appeared agreeably impressed.

The Cardinal also sipped his wine, leaning back upon his cusions with a relaxed manner and utmost amiability.

"Let me be candid, Arsène. One gains nothing by obscurity. Moreover, I can rely upon your discretion that no word of our conversation will leave this chamber.

"When the Edict of Nantes was promulgated, and full rights granted to the Huguenots, the Protestant nobles were reconciled to the Crown. Many of them have become my most devoted friends. We have the greatest thing in common. France."

He paused a moment, then continued in a meditative voice: "Wherever Protestantism has become significant, or dominant, in a nation, that nation becomes nationalistic. Catholic culture, by its very nature, cannot be nationalistic. It embraces all men, considering them as one, no matter the artificial boundaries of border, language or race."

Arsène smiled darkly, and the Cardinal, after a moment, returned that smile. "In theory, at least," amended the subtle Cardinal, with an arch of his brows, "so far as Catholics are concerned.

"But Protestantism is less—shall we say, universal? Protestantism is the religion of the State. I find myself in peculiar sympathy with that idea. I may make a prophesy now that the Germanies will become powerful in Europe because of their Protestantism—their State idea. England, too, shall be dominant in the world. I have long perceived that a nation, to become powerful, must be embued with a secular religion of State. So, understanding the nationalistic character of Protestantism, I have been tolerant of it. But you are aware of all this?"

Arsène reflected uneasily to himself that the Cardinal would not be so frank with him, so candid, had he not possessed information that would destroy him, Arsène, at a moment's lift of a hand. However, he nodded gravely.

The Cardinal's amiability increased. He leaned towards Arsène, and again patted his hand.

"I have been called the Cardinal of the Huguenots, because I have shown sympathy for the Germanies and Sweden, in their founding of nationalism. I must confess that I understand them. I would wish, for France, a birth of the nationalistic idea, lest she perish."

Again he contemplated the carved ceiling. "But there are those who mistake my inclination to nationalism as a tolerance of heresy. They are seriously mistaken.

"The future, the immortality of the Church, in France, in Europe, must always be my first passion," he mused.

Louis, who had been listening with the wildest anger, half rose from his chair. The hands that grasped the gilded arms shook violently.

But Arsène merely listened, his head inclined, his dark eyes fastened on the Cardinal's placid and aristocratic face.

"There are those who misinterpret me," said the Cardinal, softly.

He suddenly rose upon his pillows and gazed at Arsène with a steadfast but strangely terrible look, but his voice remained soft when he spoke:

"I have been lenient, understanding, with the Huguenots. I will be frank, my Arsène, as I have not been frank with others! To the Huguenot, sincerely convinced of his religion, however it appeared to jeopardize Catholic culture and authority, I have shown tolerance, understanding that nothing can truly injure the Church. But to the Huguenot who would not be reconciled to the Crown, to the welfare of France, I have been ruthless, and shall continue to be ruthless, to the death. For this kind of Huguenot desires, not the peace and security of France, but a state within a state, operating antagonistically and apart from France, conniving with her enemies, thus endangering her very existence. He does not love France; he merely hates the Catholics. To the Huguenot magnate, who, in his conceit believes that he is king over his own lands, and who will not bow to the mandates of the Crown, I have been merciless. There can be only one power in France, and that is the Throne."

He paused; the flame in his eyes increased, and Arsène felt a thrill of dread all through his body.

The Cardinal's smile was now demoniacal.

"The Huguenot rebel against the final authority of France, which is the Church and the Throne, shall die wherever he is found. He seeks to destroy this authority; he seeks only blackmail for his own gain. I shall hunt him out, wherever he hides, and nothing shall save him. He conspires with our enemies; he seeks power for himself; he drives a schism between the unity of France, and her peace."

He fell back upon his cushions, and the baleful light subsided on his face. It was again calm, and very serious.

"Your grandfather, Arsène, was such a gentleman. I do not deny his deep religious convictions. But with them, he nurtured rebellion against the final authority of the State. He professed to believe, and he did not keep his opinion to himself, that Navarre had betrayed France in returning to the bosom of the Church. He sedulously importuned his friends to refuse to be reconciled to what he declared was the 'treachery' of the father of His Majesty. But one by one, his friends and rebellious associates were reconciled, and these, in the majority, gave all their strength to the restoration of peace in France, and the establishment of unity. Not so your grandfather, who was gallant and obdurate, stiff-necked and proud, fanatical and passionate."

Arsène listened, and deep within his dark eyes a slow spark grew to a flame. He saw again his grandfather's face, and his own took upon itself the aspect of those vehement yet austere features. The Cardinal had paused, and now he gazed at Arsène, startled and bemused.

Now, if he could only reconcile this fanatic! There was something in himself that was powerful and passionate, and, recognizing the same fire in Arsène, he felt a pang of nostalgia, of paternal affection, and strong determination that he must bind this young man to him.

"The estates which had been confiscated were restored to the Huguenots. Under the Edict of Nantes, generous tolerance was extended to them. They were received, no longer as rebels, but as Frenchmen, devoted to France. But your grandfather refused to be received. He and his son, your estimable and admirable father, retired to the Gascon estates of your mother, where they lived in deep modesty and obscurity. I might even say, in poverty. Though he was foolish, and ill-advised by his own fervid conscience, one could not help but admire him! It was he who nicknamed me 'the Buffoon,'" and the Cardinal smiled in wry appreciation; "it was he who called me the Priest of the Devils. Nevertheless, I continued to esteem him. Honorable men, rigid men, however mistaken, command our respect.

"After his death," continued the Cardinal, "from old wounds received at La Rochelle, your father and his lady, and his two sons, remained in Gascony. But your father, though less a fanatic than his own father, revealed unexpected realism. He was finally reconciled to the State. Moreover, he was reconciled to the Church."

At this, Arsène could not restrain an irrepressible smile, which he conquered immediately. The Cardinal also smiled. But Louis, hovering in the shadows, the light and shade trembling over his tall black figure and white fixed face, did not smile.

"I am not a man to question the degrees of reconciliation," said the Cardinal. "It is enough for me if a man professes reconciliation, and behaves himself as if from intense inner conviction. Conformity is the law of princes, but they do not demand that a man carry the conformity in his heart, so long as his actions are in accordance with the law. As for myself, the return of the du Vaubons was very gratifying. I have found much pleasure in the present Marquis' conversation, sprightliness and person, though I confess that I do not enjoy the frequent losing of large sums to him."

"My father," said Arsène, looking into the Cardinal's smiling eyes, "is a gambling realist."

"Ah, yes," murmured the Cardinal, in appreciation. He was becoming more fond of Arsène each moment.

"His perfumes," he continued, in a meditative voice, "have done an excellent service in scenting Paris, which long needed scenting. For that alone I admire him. Moreover, his performances—and you must admit, my dear Arsène, that they are indeed performances—have done much to enliven a Court which threatened to increase in dullness. Even more, they have distracted discontented minds. Circuses are still the best method of quelling exercises of the mind, which might be dangerous to the State."

Arsène was silent. His premonition of danger was returning.

The Cardinal glanced affectionately at the pale Louis. "The Marquis brought his sons to the Church. Again, I am grateful. Louis is the most excellent secretary I have ever had. As for yourself, my dear Arsène, I have long determined that I must find a way to bind you to myself."

"That is most generous of your Eminence," said Arsène, whose color was disappearing. "But I dislike responsibility. I dislike discipline. I prefer the gay and carefree life, where I alone am master."

"A happy life, this of yours," said the Cardinal, fondly. "But you must remember, my son, that you are no longer very young. Nor do I believe I am mistaken when I suspect that there is in your nature no real love of irresponsible gamboling and continued heedlessness. I am convinced that you are not so reckless and frivolous as you would like us to believe. Men wear many masks, and the mask of carelessness and frivolity is the most profound of all.

"Yes," mused the Cardinal, "you have begun to think, my dear Arsène. And there is a freshness and vitality in the thoughts of mature men who begin to think for the first time. They are done with the folly and incoherence of youth. A vital and living brain in the head of a man past his first youth is a valuable asset to the State. Or a dangerous one," he added, softly.

"Monsieur le Duc is very astute," said Arsène, ironically. "Or, rather, he flatters me."

"Flattery," reflected the Cardinal, "is the largesse of the prince. Nevertheless, I am not flattering you, Arsène. I am merely appreciating you."

Arsène bowed. He caught a glimpse of his brother's face, and it sickened him with melancholy and foreboding.

The Cardinal suddenly laughed aloud. "My dear Arsène,

I love you! But, we are wasting time, even though the waste is delightful. I have asked you to come in order to make an offer. I am retiring my Captain of the Musketeers. I am offering you his post."

Now all the color left Arsène's thin dark cheeks. His black eyes glittered under his drawn brows. He saw now, completely, in what danger he stood.

The Cardinal gently contemplated him. "You can perceive that I have the most utter faith in you, Arsène. You are a man of gallantry, of exhilaration, fearless, one of the best swordsmen in Paris. You are a natural leader, and the men will adore you. Moreover, I suspect you are a disciplinarian. That reveals itself in your face. Two months or more ago, I should not have made you this offer. But, as I have said, there is a wonderful change in you. I admire and appreciate this change."

Arsène remained silent. He rose. "Monseigneur will allow me to consider?" He was trembling, and bit his lip hard to quell its shaking. "It would not be an easy thing to abandon my carefree life. I must consider."

The Cardinal waved his hand indulgently. "I beg you to consider, Arsène."

"Monseigneur has my profoundest gratitude, both for the offer, and the consideration."

The Cardinal's teeth glimmered for an instant between his bearded lips. He inclined his head. "Gratitude is the first emotion of the noble man," he observed. "I must ask you to give me your answer soon, Arsène. For I have decided upon a certain campaign—" He turned his bland face fully upon Arsène.

Then, it is true, thought the young man. The Spanish woman has seduced him. He will attack La Rochelle.

"I have a fancy for activity again," resumed the Cardinal. "First of all, I was a soldier. I shall lead the campaign, myself." And he glanced at a mailed vest which lay on a chair near the fireplace.

We are lost, thought Arsène. But the thought did not paralyze him. A grim core of iron grew in his heart.

Then Louis spoke for the first time, in a hoarse voice: "Rest assured, your Eminence, that my brother will finally accept the offer you have so graciously extended to him. He could not refuse."

Now he looked fully at Arsène, with all the hatred of a lifetime ablaze on his large white face, and all the danger, and all the fatal warning.

At this, in spite of his alarm and anxiety, Arsène could not restrain his amusement.

The Cardinal extended his hand to Arsène, who kissed it briefly. Then, after assurances of his gratitude, Arsène departed. Louis opened a door for him upon the quiet secret passage which led to the chamber, and Arsène passed through. He was surprised to see that his brother had followed him, closed the door behind him.

"You dare not refuse," said the young priest, through clenched teeth. "You dare not refuse, for my father's sake."

"I dare anything," replied Arsène, coldly. "But I have not yet refused. Be assured, Louis, that no threats or coercion on your part will change my ultimate decision."

Louis breathed deeply. Deep red blotches appeared on his face. His hand groped instinctively at his side for a sword which was not there.

But Arsène forgot everything in his pity, and his remembrance of his father's derision. He reached out and laid his hand on Louis' arm. The young priest recoiled as at the touch of something indescribably unclean and loathsome. But Arsène, trying to find words, retained his grip.

"You think too much of our father, Louis. I love him. But I am not unaware of his worthlessness."

"You dare to speak of him so!" cried Louis, beside himself. "To me!"

Arsène shrugged. He sighed, and withdrew his hand. He regarded Louis with compassion, but searchingly.

"You are changed, Louis. I have been much encouraged. There is some gentleness in you, some softness, perhaps. I thought this might presage that we could become friends."

"I cannot be a friend of one who is the enemy of the Church!" Nevertheless, the young priest colored, and his eyes faltered as if in confusion.

"I am not your enemy, Louis," said Arsène, gently.

Louis was silent. Yes, thought Arsène, he has changed. He is thinner, and seems consumed by a fever. A woman? That is incredible! A dawn of more understanding, more tolerance? That, too, is incredible. He has an effort in whipping up rage even against me. That is because his heart has been touched in some manner. What is it that touches a man's heart most profoundly? A woman.

He was astonished at the conclusions of his own logic. However, he remained incredulous. What woman could finally possess that austere and glacial soul, that frigid blood, that mind which could feel only arctic tempests?

Again, he pressed Louis' arm, and moved away, bewildered. He had gone several paces when Louis called after him. His voice was baleful, but Arsène again had the impression of conscious effort.

"You must not refuse, Arsène!"

CHAPTER XXIV

THE CARDINAL'S MOOD of exhilaration after Arsène's departure remained in a kind of febrile and excited glow. When Père Joseph returned, after a discreet knock on the cabinet's door, he was pleased to see his eminent friend so animated. Ever careful to observe the august amenities due to one of the Cardinal's exalted position, his pleasure was so great, however, that he exclaimed fondly: "Ah, Armand-Jeanne, you seem exceedingly vital this morning!"

"My dear Joseph," returned the Cardinal, stretching out his hands in affectionate greeting, "you came too late to hear an edifying conversation. That young Arsène de Richepin! I have put a flea in his ear. But I shall have him. I am sure of that. Then we shall have a little excitement in this dull Paris."

Père Joseph smiled. His autumn-colored beard parted at the lips to reveal his excellent white teeth.

He turned to the Cardinal again, and now he no longer smiled. "I crave your Eminence's pardon, but I have brought with me this morning the Bishop of the diocese of Chantilly."

The Cardinal's excited humor was quenched. He regarded Père Joseph with annoyance, and closed his eyes with an exaggeratedly weary expression.

"Why should I be annoyed with this rustic Bishop?" he said. "Dispose of him, Joseph, dispose of him. I confess that I am amazed at you."

Père Joseph set his lips grimly. "I must crave, again, your indulgence, Monsieur le Cardinal. It is a matter of great importance. In truth, I requested the Bishop to come to Paris to consult with you."

The Cardinal's eyelids flew open with angered astonishment. "Have I nothing else to occupy my mind but the troubles and tribulations of a yokel Bishop? Is some wealthy lady of his diocese recalcitrant? Does a parishioner demand a place for his son? What is this nonsense?"

258

But Père Joseph was unmoved by this show of irascibility. He waited until the Cardinal further relieved himself of heavy sarcasm, then said somberly:

"Has your Eminence forgotten that the diocese of Chantilly contains the estates of the late Comte Renaud de Vitry, and are now in the possession of his son, Paul?"

The Cardinal, though still exasperated, was a little curious. "I never forget anything, Joseph, so it is not necessary to assume surprise, nor to instruct me. I remember the Comte well. A devoted if eccentric Catholic. You have not come to tell me that Paul de Vitry is a Huguenot?"

Père Joseph's somewhat wild and protruding eyes flickered with annoyance. He said, with deep and ironic courtesy: "Your Eminence is well aware of the activities of Paul de Vitry. We need not review this. But if his secret activities in Paris are reprehensible, his conduct on his estates near Chantilly are dangerous. But your Eminence must have heard rumors of this."

"I have heard that he does not gouge his peasants," replied the Cardinal, who wished to exasperate his friend, out of his perversity. "I have heard that he pays their taxes to the Crown, in order to keep them from starving. I have heard he mends the roofs of their huts, opens his grounds to them for hunting, settles grievances and crimes with justice, mercy and understanding. I have heard that he keeps their Church in repair, does not interfere with their religion though he no longer can be counted a devout Catholic, is gentle and generous to their priest, the old Père Lovelle, himself appointed by the Bishop. I have heard that he allows them to keep the major portion of their crops, their cattle and their fowl. No doubt, all this is reprehensible. Is this what you have come to tell me?"

Père Joseph rose. "I believe it is best for your Eminence to hear the Bishop himself," he said, coldly. He nodded to Louis, who had been listening with a pale grim smile, and the young priest opened the massive door and directed the guards there to conduct the Bishop of Chantilly into the Cardinal's presence.

The Bishop was an enormously fat man, sleek in his black robes, very short of stature so that he was almost as wide as tall. His robes, stretched over his great belly and chest, glittered and shimmered. He waddled from side to side as he sidled obsequiously into the chamber, and so ponderous was his weight that the hewn floor vibrated with his tread. He had a huge, egg-shaped head, almost completely bald, with large outstanding ears like reddish-purple wings. His face, mottled and greasy with good living, glistened, the flesh tinted with all shades of ruddy red. Tufts of thick wiry hair, black and coarse, stood above little black eyes like hard beads, and his heavy mouth, set in an urbane and servile smile, was both sensual and cruel, and full of sly humor and false good temper. He had a short flat nose, set so deeply in the swelling flesh about it that the flaring nostrils were like holes in his face, a thing which made the Cardinal momentarily close his eyes in aristocratic nausea.

The Bishop wheezed, his breath was short and hoarse. The golden cross lay on the mound of his quivering belly, and so it blinked and winked as it caught the morning light. He bowed deeply before the Cardinal, who impatiently extended his delicate narrow hand. The Bishop reverently kissed that hand, and the Cardinal winced. He exclaimed: "Well now, my Bishop, what is this nonsense?"

But the Bishop was temporarily overcome with awe at being in the presence of this great and terrible prince of the Church. His eyes walled themselves at Père Joseph in trepidation and speechlessness. Even when Louis presented him with a chair, he stared at it helplessly, as though it were an object not familiar to him, and it was only when the Cardinal shortly commanded him to sit, that he fell into it. He had begun to tremble. He clasped his fat white hands across his belly as if to control its agitated quiverings. Beads of sweat burst out all over his great red countenance.

Père Joseph, perceiving that nothing would be accomplished in the light of the Bishop's demoralization, and also perceiving that the Cardinal was fast losing what little patience he possessed, laid his hand encouragingly on the Bishop's heaving shoulder. He smiled down at him reassuringly, and the Bishop regarded him with the importunate despair of a miserable human who appeals to a super-being for protection and help.

"Monsieur le Bishop," he said, in his voice which resembled the soothing chords of an organ, "I pray that you speak briefly and quickly to His Eminence, who is anxious to hear what you have to say."

The Cardinal snorted delicately, and regarded the ceiling with exaggerated patience. Then, his irascible humor returning with twinges of the vague pains that afflict the nervous, he directed his knitted brows and contemptuous eyes again upon the Bishop.

"Speak, man," he commanded. "Speak, or begone."

The Bishop sweated still more. His mouth fell open, but no

sound came from it. Groaning internally, the Cardinal made his irritable voice quiet:

"I believe you have something of importance to communicate with me regarding your diocese. You have observed the crowds of those outside in the ante-chambers who await an audience with me. Therefore, you will be concise and rapid as possible." He added: "If it is a matter of money, I will recall to you the fact that Madame de Collioure is a member of your diocese, and while not noted for her generosity, I am certain that it will take only coercion on your part to make her disgorge. What is a priest for? It is useless for you to come to me for assistance. Père Joseph administers these affairs, not I."

"It is not a matter of old Madame de Collioure," whispered the Bishop, hoarsely, more and more agitated. Then, remembering this obstinate old grand dame, he forgot his own fright in a measure. "Though I must confess that she is a harridan, and makes my life miserable with her inordinate demands and humors, and forces me to pay with blood for every centime. Moreover, she has the abbess and the nuns with her. It is a petticoat rebellion, and one which I will not endure much longer with good temper and saintliness. But your Eminence will pardon me for the impudence of wearying him with my troubles," he added, with returning fright at his audaciousness.

The Cardinal smiled. He recalled his own former troubles with high-tempered and obnoxious old ladies when he had been a young Bishop. But, he reflected, he had indeed been young and handsome, with an air, and the most vicious old dame had not been able to resist him. He had always had a way with women, he meditated.

He said, with more kindliness: "All this is very bad, and you have my sympathy, my dear Bishop. But this is not why you have come to consult me? Père Joseph assures me it is a matter of the most enormous importance," and he shot his friend a truly malevolent glance.

"It was Madame de Collioure who insisted that I communicate with Père Joseph," said the Bishop, faintly, wringing his hands.

"Ah," said the Cardinal, with a still heavier glance at his friend.

"Her estates adjoin those of the Comte de Vitry," continued the Bishop. He added, beseechingly, seeing the darkening look on the Cardinal's face: "She declares she is in constant fear of her life, because of the impudence and arrogance of the Comte's peasants. She asserts that she cannot sleep, for fear they will overcome the guards about her house, and rob and murder her in her bed."

The Cardinal was amused. "This Comte de Vitry, then, feeds his peasants so well that they are bursting with high spirits?"

The Bishop gained courage from this levity. Forgetting his terror of this fabled man, he exclaimed, indignantly: "Madame de Collioure has justification for her apprehensions, Monsieur le Duc! I must confess that I have long been desirous of seeking help against this most deplorable and dangerous state of affairs on the estates of the young Comte de Vitry."

"Please continue," sighed the Cardinal. But he was interested. He leaned on his elbow and fixed his unfathomable eyes upon the quivering Bishop.

"I have no quarrel with Monsieur le Comte's treatment of his people," said the Bishop, with a brief, sanctimonious lifting of his eyes. "He has my blessing on the good he has brought to them. Would I be a priest if I objected to huts that do not leak, to wooden tables amply supplied, to fatness on the faces of children, to dancing and singing which are the result of peace and plenty and kindness? It is not these things which trouble me. Too, I must confess that the Comte has been very generous to the Church, and that he urges his people to their religious duties, and that he treats old Père Lovelle as a friend, deeply respected and beloved. Père Lovelle has nothing but the most enthusiastic and enchanted reports of Monsieur le Comte."

"Well then," insisted the Cardinal, with returning impatience.

The Bishop sighed. His face took upon itself an expression of malignance.

"The Comte has taken upon himself the task of instructing his people," he said, with heavy significance.

"He hopes to convert the Abbé Lovelle and his people to Protestantism?" suggested the Cardinal, with incredulous amusement.

The Bishop's malignance increased. He leaned towards the Cardinal, exhaling with vicious agitation. "It pleases your Eminence to make light of my misery," he said, almost in tears. "No, there has been no subversive attitude on the part of the Comte. He, himself, when he is on his estates, punctiliously attends Mass, followed by his people, and his attitude is reverent in the extreme, though I have heard that he is no true Catholic as was his sainted father. The Abbé Lovelle informs me that the Comte has reverence for all religion.

"My quarrel with the Comte is not because of any irreligiousness on his part. It is, in a way, deeper than that. Perhaps your Eminence is not aware of his dangerous interference with the life of his peasants, beyond mere benevolence? Your Eminence does not know that the Comte has imported teachers for his people, and that he urges, not only the children to attend classes of instruction—reprehensible enough—but also full-grown men. And women!" he exclaimed, his eyes dilating in expectation of the Cardinal's astonishment.

The Cardinal was indeed surprised, but he did not reveal this. He merely waited, with fixed attention.

The Bishop was fully aroused. The chair creaked under his agitated movements. He flung out his hands. "I informed the Comte that the convent was only too willing to instruct the village girls, and he replied, smiling: 'In needle-work and household pursuits and farming toil, in order to make them meeker and better servants for those who are in the sight of God vastly their inferiors?' Your Eminence must fully understand, now, how dangerous is this man!"

He could hardly breathe, in his rage. "I see his peasants under their trees and about their tables, laboriously spelling out their letters or reading strange books! It has been reported to me that they discuss heretical things in their taverns, and that they question, argue, cogitate about matters not fitted to their stations, and better left in the hands of priests. It has been reported to me that they question the decrees of his Majesty, that they speak disrespectfully and treasonably about your Eminence, that they accept nothing, argue always, and deliver themselves indignantly!"

He wrung his hands, implored the Cardinal with tear-filled eyes. Then his face took on an expression of horror:

"It is further reported to me that they say among themselves: 'Are we not men? Have we not, in the sight of God, equal rights to this France of ours, and her fruits and her wealth and her privileges? Are we not possessed of divine souls, beloved of God as are the souls of magnates and kings, and is not the earth ours as well as theirs, and have we no right to freedom, justice and fraternity? Has God decreed misery, or is this the decree of the Church? And if the latter is true, as the light of reason reveals it to be, why should we then countenance wretchedness and hunger, ignorance and unquestioning obedience, meekness and poverty and humility?' "

He paused, abruptly, for his breath was choked off. He was beside himself.

The Cardinal was no longer supercilious or amused. "The Abbé Lovelle has made these reports to you?"

In spite of his agitation, the Bishop appeared suddenly embarrassed.

"No, your Eminence. It was a lady."

"Madame de Collioure, who fears for her life?"

"No, your Eminence. I must confess it is another. A lady who lives in an unholy condition with the Comte, a true daughter of the Church, lately converted to Mother Church." The Bishop dropped his eyes discreetly, a blush bursting over his fat cheeks.

"Ah," murmured the Cardinal, leaning back upon his pillows. "The Comte has lately discarded this lady, and she wishes to do him a mischief?"

"On the contrary, your Eminence. He is still devoted to her. She came to me, weeping, begging for indulgence because of her betrayal of him, and avowing that it was only after long prayer and meditation and searching of her soul that she was induced by her conscience to come to me."

"She has probably found another lover," suggested the Cardinal.

"Indeed, not, your Eminence! She has every wish to marry the Comte, but, as she is of lowly blood, he will not do this."

"But she believes if he is reconciled to the Church, in obedience and meekness, he can be induced, by you, to reward her with his hand?"

The Bishop's little pig eyes shifted. He cleared his throat. Then he said with meek defiance: "It would only be just, as your Eminence can perceive."

The Cardinal looked at Père Joseph with a faint smile. But the Capuchin's countenance remained firm.

"All this is very reprehensible," mused the Cardinal. He added, drily: "Nevertheless, though it has been done, and frequently, I do not see at this time how a man can be sent to the Bastille for practicing Christian charity among those dependent upon him."

"The Bastille—for the Comte de Vitry?" cried the Bishop, paling with horror, and clasping his hands together. "I knew the late Comte well! He was my dearest friend!"

"Then, Monsieur le Bishop, what would you suggest?"

The Bishop swallowed, but gazed appealingly at the Capuchin.

"Monsieur le Bishop is in a delicate situation," said Père Joseph, angered by the Cardinal's indifferent calm. "He has thought of removing Père Lovelle, who is sadly in need of discipline, as he obdurately upholds de Vitry in his dangerous work. He is fatuous. But, after all, a de Vitry is a de Vitry, and Monsieur le Bishop hesitates to offend him. The de Vitrys remain the most powerful lords in that locality."

"And we are dependent on the support of the de Vitrys," mused the Cardinal.

"If Madame de Collioure were but more generous!" said the Bishop.

"But she is not. Therefore, the chief support of the diocese emanates from Monsieur le Comte, who must be a dexterous young man."

"A paradox," said the Capuchin, with a significant raise of his brows.

The Cardinal leaned back on his cushions and fitted his fingers together. The Capuchin knew the signs. The Cardinal was preparing to enjoy himself in his usual pleasure of discussing human vagaries.

"Here we have a young and powerful magnate who is under our suspicion," said the Cardinal. "His activities in Paris are fully covered in his dossier. He was born and nutured a Catholic. Yet, he is no longer a Catholic, though not yet excommunicated. He is one of the most energetic enemies of the Church. Nevertheless, a Huguenot in practice if not in open avowal, he is devoted to old Père Lovelle, who adores him, and he leads his peasants into their Church with an ardor and dedication which our more vociferous Catholic lords might emulate. A paradox, you say, my dear Joseph. No, not a paradox. It is not our religion which he despises and wishes to destroy. It is Us." He smiled thoughtfully. "There are among Us who cannot see the distinction, but it is clear to me. Nor is there confusion in the young Comte's activities. It is apparent that he believes in faith, in tolerance of all faiths, but is the passionate enemy of any servant of a faith that engages in the pursuit of power, and in the acquisition of temporal authority."

"The distinction is plain sophistry," said the Capuchin.

The Cardinal inclined his head quizzically, but said nothing. However, after a moment, he made a sign to the Capuchin, who thereupon turned courteously to the bewildered Bishop.

"Monsieur le Cardinal requests that you retire, Monsieur, into the ante-chamber, for a few moments."

The Bishop, affronted and puzzled, left the chamber.

The Capuchin returned to the bedside. He was so angered that he forgot his usual respect. "Armand-Jeanne! This is no laughing matter. Surely you can perceive that if this man's dangerous theories and methods spread among other dioceses France itself, the Church, is ominously endangered. The education and liberation of the masses can result only in impudent defiance of all authority, in atheism and heresy, in constant clamoring and questioning, in confusion, chaos, and the loss of authority in Government and Church. The next step will be demands on the part of the people in their own right, and our ancient system will be demolished.

"You know, as well as I do, that authority must remain vested in the hands of those ordained by God to retain it—those who by birth and position have inherited this authority. You know that the Church has always upheld the rights of those who have inherited position, or those who have obtained it by her sanction and assistance. To allow even the smallest measure of power to fall into the hands of the anonymous people is contrary to the will of God, and the Church, and will make only for bloody revolutions, heresy and wretchedness."

Louis, impelled involuntarily by his own passion, moved to the foot of the bed and looked first at the Capuchin and then at the Cardinal with glowing eyes. The Cardinal gazed absently at the young priest, and again speculated as to the reason for the dark wild hatred on his face.

"Your imagination, my dear Louis, is running rampant," observed the Cardinal.

Père Joseph leaned over the bed and fixed the nonchalant Cardinal with his vehement and terrible eyes.

"Has Protestantism brought happiness to the people! No! It has brought confusion, doubt and faithlessness. The Church believes in the inherent right of men to happiness, and she knows, in her wisdom, that property and wealth are not necessary to the people's happiness. The ordinary man can only be bewildered by possessions, for his wants are as simple as his nature. It is the desire of Mother Church, then, to prevent the humble man from obtaining sufficient goods to complicate his life, render him anxious about their security, swell his vanity and greed, and increase his lust for more. She knows that if he obtains all these, he will be a threat to his natural masters, that he will confer final authority and

266

decision and conscience in himself, and not in the Church, and in the State. Anarchy, the death of religious authority, will be the inevitable result."

"Do not be so passionate," said the Cardinal. "Have I disagreed with you, my dear Joseph?"

The Capuchin vehemently beat the bed with his clenched fist.

"No! But your Eminence assumes an air of indifference and tolerance which is dangerous! Surely your Eminence perceives that de Vitry is more dangerous in France than a pestilence?"

The Cardinal was not agitated by all this passion and anger.

"Let us consider, and cogitate. I am no advocate of the young Comte. But I cannot believe that de Vitry is truly a menace to France. What he advocates has, in a measure, come to pass in England, and from the reports of my agents England is betraying no immediate signs of disintegration and collapse—"

"But Frenchmen are not Englishmen!" said the Capuchin, with contempt. "The Englishman has icicles for bowels. He is incapable of excesses and passions. Even what small frozen soul he has is held in check by his native caution, his native expediency, his native greed. He is incapable of dedicating his whole heart to any cause; always, he holds back, remembering his precious skin before anything else. 'How will this affect my shop, my draperies establishment, my tavern, my plot of land, my beer, my fireplace?' he asks himself. And this question gives him pause. He can devote himself to nothing with burning fervor and selflessness.

"But the Frenchman is capable of burning up his whole soul in the incandescence of his convictions. He can immolate himself on spits and swords, with a cry of joy. There is frenzy in the Frenchman, a frightful abandon. Let him, therefore, be introduced to strange and catastrophic theories—let him then be convinced—and all that is France, all that is the Church, will be consumed like a feather in a flame. That is our danger. So far, France has been spared a complete conversion to Protestantism, because of the coldness and sterility of that heresy, because it has no drama, no color, no blaze of glory, no passion, no call for sacrifice to the death. But in the theories of de Vitry there is the nucleus of all of these. Men will not sacrifice themselves for a scholarly thesis, but they will sacrifice themselves for other men."

"You do not think this noble?" murmured the Cardinal, satirically.

"I think it dangerous. For France."

The Cardinal meditated in silence for several long moments. Then slowly his narrow and aristocratic countenance became even more narrow, tighter, pale with evil.

"I agree with all you have said," he remarked at last. The Capuchin drew a deep breath. A relaxation, as of exhaustion, pervaded him. He looked at Louis, who returned that look with satisfaction.

"Nevertheless, we are, ourselves, in a dangerous and delicate situation," resumed the Cardinal. "Let us review the facts. The simplest cure for the folly of the Comte de Vitry is to remove old Père Lovelle, who is no doubt a dodderer, and replace him with a sound priest, who will control de Vitry's people. He will do this with subtlety. But should we remove Père Lovell, this will anger de Vitry, and arouse his suspicions. We must have an adequate excuse.

"Moreover, de Vitry is a close, if not an intimate friend, of the brother of his Majesty, Prince Gaston. And this Gaston is beloved of the Queen Mother, who would not regard an opportunity to annoy me without joy. Too, de Vitry has other powerful, if lesser, friends. If he is dangerous in quietness, on his estates, he will be the more dangerous if we force him to come out into the open. He might even go to His Majesty, who does not particularly love me at this moment. When personal issues are involved, reason takes a holiday."

He meditated deeply, stroking his fingers, turning his left hand so that the magnificent ring upon it sparkled in the golden dusk.

"If a blow is struck, it must be struck deeply, to the heart. In the event we can remove Père Lovelle and his fatuous influence over de Vitry's people, who would you suggest? He must be a priest, of necessity, who can be ruthless, merciless, even terrible, under an exterior that is all sweetness and piety."

In spite of his triumph, the Capuchin paled a trifle, and in consequence his russet beard seemed to catch fire. The Cardinal gazed at him with a bland half smile, and at last Père Joseph averted his eyes.

"You think that—such a man—might influence the people against de Vitry? Considering all that the Comte has done for his people?" The Capuchin shook his head with doubt, and his troubled breath was audible.

The Cardinal patted his friend's hand lightly. "At the last, my dear Joseph, you are defeated by your conscience."

He stared reflectively at the ceiling.

"It is plain that you do not understand the people. Good

is an unnatural condition for them. Evil is their natural state. A man would rather, out of his instincts, be vicious, cruel, wicked and murderous, than gentle, compassionate, just and tolerant. Man is born evil. The good which generations of priests and wise men have tried to impose upon him sits like a precarious crown of flowers on an ape's head. A prince who wishes to rule unthreatened must remember this. He has only to deliver a victim into his people's hands to live in peace himself. We have discovered that with the Jews.

A malignant expression appeared on his frail but malevolent lips.

"One of these days," he murmured, inaudibly, "the people will revenge themselves upon Jesus because He has urged them to rise from all fours and walk erect—a most uncomfortable position."

He turned to Père Joseph again. "I repeat—who would you suggest for our campaign against de Vitry? There is a more direct method of course—the complete elimination of de Vitry, a method to which I have given considerable thought. But this would not destroy the influence he has established over his people. He would be canonized as a martyr. No, it must go deeper, to the heart of the people themselves. If there is destroying to be done, they must do it."

The Capuchin was silent. His pallor was extreme. The Cardinal watched him, with cynical amusement. It was always his way, when violence and terror were urged upon him, to delegate the final act to the urger. This was frequently demoralizing. It always relieved him, the Cardinal, of responsibility.

Finally the Capuchin spoke in a low but firm voice: "I have the man. Your Eminence knows him well. Monseigneur Antoine de Pacilli."

They gazed at each other intently. Then the Cardinal made a wry face. "Italians have never appealed to me," he said.

The Capuchin gestured with angry impatience. "Only his paternal grandfather was an Italian. Your Eminence is well aware of his fanatical devotion, his fervor, his passion—"

"He was born too late. The Holy Office missed a splendid Inquisitor," said the Cardinal, provokingly.

"Moreover, he is practically unknown in Paris," continued the Capuchin, ignoring this irrelevant comment. "That gives him an advantage. He is a man of brilliance, of learning, of subtlety. He can assume any rôle he desires. Since he arrived in Paris from Rome, he has immured himself, lived a life of the utmost austerity and obscurity among the Franciscan monks. He delivers his life up to prayer, only, and though he has frequently importuned your Eminence for an audience, you have refused this."

"I repeat, Italians have never appealed to me."

The Capuchin compressed his lips. "It pleases you, Armand-Jeanne, to attempt to annoy me. Monseigneur de Pacilli has waited almost a year for an audience, for a position, yet you have perversely refused to see him, though he came here after the request which you sent to his Holiness."

"I have only been meditating as to where we can use him to the best advantage."

"This, then, is the advantage. He is not too young; he is not too old," added the Capuchin, with an ironic intonation. "Let Monsieur le Bishop sympathically urge upon de Vitry the necessity of a holiday for old Père Lovelle, who has two nieces and a nephew near Rouen. Pacilli, then, will take his place, ostensibly for the period, only. We have only to explain what we wish to him. He will do the rest."

Within less than two hours, Monseigneur Antoine de Pacilli was admitted to the presence of the Cardinal through devious and secret passageways. No one saw him come. He was filled with delight and satisfaction at finally being called into the august and terrible presence.

CHAPTER XXV

THERE WAS, in Paul de Vitry, the mysterious and indefinable element of greatness, which has nothing to do with fame, or her handmaiden, acclaim, or her false buffoon notoriety. He spoke simply, yet gently; he had a smile of singular sweetness. When he laughed, he laughed with his eyes as well as his lips, and a glow, clear and translucent, would light up in them. His manner was soft and deprecating, as if he felt a deep humility. If his opinions were vehement, they were nevertheless not dogmatic or arrogant; he lived in apprehension that they might offend unintentionally, and he would frequently apologize for them. He was generous, sympathetic, subtle and sensitive. He was a devoted friend, and felt no enmity for any one. There was no bitterness or hatred in him. Above all, he was compassionate and merciful, loathing nothing but injustice and cruelty and oppression.

Perhaps it was the sum of all these things that made him great. He possessed them all, whereas other men possessed one or a few. Perhaps he lacked reserve in his virtue: he had no reticences in mercy, love, tenderness and honor. There was no moderation in his goodness. His heart was as wide as infinity. He was like a spring that gushes inexhaustibly, not confined by the stones of caution, or selfishness, not made brackish by constant consideration of his own good, not restrained or thickened by the mud of judiciousness or self-restraint. He gave all of his heart and did not ask if by doing so he exhibited wisdom, prudence, or moderation.

The greatness of great men is in the complete abandon and openness of their souls. Too, Paul's greatness was in his infinite passion, the boundless horizon of his spirit. Where there is artifice there is reserve, and where there is reserve, there is no greatness. Some of his greatness lay in his lack of artifice, and in his noble disregard of the disapproval, incredulity or contempt of others. He had a lofty and fervid innocence,

271

which, however, was not unconscious of evil. But in his recognition of it, and his invariable and outraged astonishment at it, was that pristine affirmation of his own majesty. There was in him the quality of exaggeration, which is the mark of all greatness, good or evil.

For all this, he was adored by a few, and violently hated by the majority, for it is a sad fact that greatness in a man is the unpardonable sin.

Arsène had always loved him, but it was not until his own still confused awakening that he realized the full stature of his friend. He would not have said: "I would trust Paul with my life," for in that admission is the element of simpering self-consciousness. He never thought of this, for it was an empirical fact to him.

He went to Paul immediately with the report of his audience with the Cardinal. Paul listened with the deepest concentration.

"I have thought that I must accept," said Arsène, "for many reasons. Among them is the plan that in such a position I would be privy to any plots of that man."

At this, Paul burst into an involuntary laugh. "Arsène, I adore you!" he exclaimed. Then at Arsène's offended frown, he quickly threw his arm around his friend's shoulder. "Ah, now, I have annoyed you! But you must perceive how this is not feasible. The mere acceptance of this post would not remove you from suspicion. It would only expose you to easier spying. What a gallant, but innocent soul you have, Arsène! You are too passionate, too angry of temperament, to play a subtle rôle. Too, you would be excessively unhappy. Treachery is not easy for you. I could not advise you to entangle yourself in such a situation. Moreover, the idea, itself, is immoral. One does not accept benefits, nor take a solemn oath, with the inner determination to betray all of them."

"It is you who are the innocent," said Arsène, mortified.

"No," said Paul, with sudden seriousness, "it is not that. I would have you do no injury to yourself, not even for me, or our friends."

"But, if I do not, you are in danger."

"Not in more danger than I am. Too, all this is in God's hands." He added: "I do not fear overmuch for you, Arsène. You are the son of the Marquis du Vaubon."

"Nevertheless," said Arsène, wryly, "that would not prevent the Cardinal from hiring an assassin to despatch me."

"Your best recourse, then, is to inform a large circle of

friends and acquaintances of the Cardinal's offer, and your own refusal, with regrets. I suspect that even the Cardinal would hesitate to do a deed that would put him under the foulest suspicion."

He sighed. He began to speak of the Duc de Tremblant and the Dutchman. "They leave tonight, inconspicuously, with only a small number of guards. A large retinue would inspire curiosity and suspicion. They will travel modestly, on horseback, arousing no conjecture. Gentlemen of small means taking a quiet and unheralded journey."

"The road is infested," said Arsène, gloomily. "Moreover, do not think that the Cardinal will not learn something of it."

"That is not possible. Only de Bouillon, de Rohan, I and yourself know of this. Where, then, can enter the treachery? Besides, who would dare molest the Duc de Tremblant, even if it were known?"

"You do not know the Cardinal."

Paul then asked Arsène if he would like to accompany him on a visit to his estates. He had recognized that the bravo, on the search for adventure, was beginning to think. He had eagerly taken it upon himself to direct that thinking. Arsène expressed himself as delighted.

"I must return within five days," he said, "for my marriage."

He said this calmly, with no lighting of his eyes, no smile of tenderness. Paul studied him with quick penetration. When Arsène spoke thus of his wedding, a shade darkened his eye and a gloomy shadow appeared about his mouth. Paul did not speak of this, but he felt some sadness. "Tomorrow, then, we shall go," he said.

Arsène sent a letter to the Cardinal, filled with the most exaggerated expressions of regret, declining the honor of the post offered him. He told his father of the offer and the refusal, and the Marquis was filled with excitable wrath and disappointment. "I have dreamt of this, you fool, you scoundrel!" he exclaimed.

"How could I be false to my convictions?" urged Arsène, amused.

"Bah, convictions! Only women and eunuchs can afford convictions! There is no room in an ambitious man for such folly."

"I am not ambitious, my father," replied Arsène.

"You are only a rascal!" cried the Marquis. "Have you never realized that this is your only chance to escape murder? Have you never thought what the Cardinal might know of

273

you, you and your Les Blanches?" When the Marquis had said this, he turned excessively pale, and Arsène fully understood in what terror his father lived perpetually.

He set himself to soothe the Marquis. "He will not murder me. I shall tell every one of the offer, and my regret, and my inability to accept the disciplinarian life. That will tie the Cardinal's hands."

The Marquis clasped his own hands, and even Arsène could not smile at the theatrical gesture. "I beseech you!" said the Marquis. "Do you not owe this to me, your father? Have you ever contemplated in what misery and fear I live, because of your recklessness? How long do you think it will be before you are ruined?"

"I have thought much of my grandfather," replied Arsène, quietly.

At this, the Marquis was silent, his lips twitching, his eyes darting away. A strange look appeared on his face, and then, after a moment, he regarded Arsène as he would regard a fearful stranger. He said, at last, in a dwindled voice: "You must do, then, what you must."

Arsène was amazed. With a burst of love and tenderness, he tried to console the Marquis. Never had he felt such affection, such gratitude, for him, and his heart troubled him. But though the Marquis accepted these gestures of consolation, of appreciation and understanding, he would not be comforted. He allowed Arsène to kiss his cheek and hold his hand. When Arsène tried to withdraw his hand eventually, the Marquis clung to it. His eyes were full of tears which rose from his heart.

Arsène mused much on this strange scene later. Was it possible that after all there was some nobility, some noblesse oblige, in the frivolous and shallow Marquis, who lived only for intrigue, women, perfumes and the Court? He was incredulous.

He had neglected Mademoiselle Clarisse de Tremblant lately, and that night he called upon his betrothed, going to the Hôtel de Tremblant in his sober doublet, cloak and hose. The cavalier, the gallant, no longer appeared to care for gay raiment. Heretofore, Arsène de Richepin had been known for his dashing elegance and excellent tailors, and admirable figure. But lately his wardrobe had been neglected; his valet, Pierre, would shake his head dolefully as he brushed the unworn garments and polished the fine boots, which were rarely used in these days. "Monsieur has become an English puritan," he would complain, with disgust. Even the jeweled rapiers hung dustily in far corners. Arsène carried with him always the sword of his grandfather, like a talisman.

Now, as he approached the Hôtel de Tremblant, he saw that all the tall glittering windows were blazing with lights, that music issued softly from the gardens in the rear, which were illuminated by myriads of lamps strung from the tall dark trees. Carriages turned and wheeled through the narrow streets, which were crowded with curious ragged Parisians, staring blankly, or discussing, with inimitable French obscenity, the personalities of the various scented and beautiful women and elegant gentlemen who were alighting. However, they were kept at a respectful distance by detachments of the King's and the Cardinal's Musketeers, who swaggered and glowered and pulled plumed hatbrims incessantly. Hubbub resounded all through the neighborhood. When servants opened the massive oak and brazen doors, gushes of hot yellow light spewed out into the dark and fetid street, and the ribald and sardonic populace jeered and cheered. In the seething and anonymous mass, Parisians were not respectful, and even the Musketeers curled their mustaches and smiled under them at some of the shouted witticisms. In the distance, the towers of Notre Dame floated against a pure dark blue sky swarming with trembling stars.

Arsène halted in the press of the crowd, astonished. Apprehensively, he searched his mind. What had he forgotten now? The crowds buffeted him, for he was not to be distinguished, in his plain and sober garments, from any other man, except for his sword. He was assailed by the foul odors of sweat and dirt which emanated from the mobs, and he winced. He looked about him at the faces splashed by torches, and all at once a cold hand of terror gripped his heart. For in these dark and dirty faces, lighted by black and glittering eyes and the glisten of wet exposed teeth, he discerned a formless but frightful danger. They laughed and shouted as each carriage expelled its fragrant and magnificent freight, but under the laughter there was a sound as of caged and savage beasts, hungry and powerful.

He perceived the Captain of the King's Guard at a little distance, and struggled to reach him. Arms, shoulders, bodies blocked his passage. Finally, in desperation, as a man who is drowning calls, he shouted to the Captain, who turned in astonishment in the direction of his voice. Then, he moved towards that voice, and the crowds sullenly separated. When he saw who had hailed him, his mouth fell open in imbecile astonishment. "Monsieur de Richepin!" he exclaimed, unbelievingly, and he glanced over his shoulder as if he expected to see a duplicate of Arsène alighting from some carriage near the entrance. He could hardly persuade himself that this young disheveled man fighting among the mob was in truth Arsène de Richepin.

Persuaded at last, that this was indeed Arsène, he pulled him from the press, and stared in still greater astonishment at the young nobleman's plain and disordered dress.

"Ma foi!" exclaimed Arsène, fastidiously brushing his cloak with his hand, and removing his hat that he might shake loose the bent dark plume. "What is this that is afoot?"

Now the Captain seemed overcome with the extremity of his amazement. He gaped; his eyes goggled. He had the aspect of a fish that is removed from water. Two or three of his men joined him, and when they recognized Arsène, they, too, gulped and goggled. Arsène experienced some uneasiness, and said irritably: "Can no one speak? What is all this?"

The Captain finally found his voice. "Is it possible that Monsieur has forgotten that a fete has been given in honor of himself and Mademoiselle de Tremblant, and that Monsieur le Duc de Richelieu and his Majesty are momentarily expected?"

Cold dismay made blank Arsène's countenance. "Ah, yes," he muttered. "I had forgotten."

At this, the Captain appeared about to swoon. He literally trembled. "The Marquis du Vaubon and Monseigneur de Richepin have already arrived," he said, weakly. "No doubt they are wondering at Monsieur's absence."

Arsène was full of consternation. Not to be on hand to greet their Majesties would be unpardonable. Madame de Tremblant would never forgive him for this affront, nor would the King. Yet, how dared he enter that magnificent, laced and silken assemblage in these garments, dusty, worn and fit only for the street? Nor did he have the time to return to the Hôtel du Vaubon for a change of costume. At any moment august personages would be arriving.

"Clear a way for me to the servants' entrances," he said desperately to the Captain, cursing himself. When he was conducted to those entrances by a gloomy and astounded Captain, he was greeted with further astonishment by the men on guard there. The servants were overcome. He demanded to be led to the apartments of the Duc de Tremblant. When he entered those apartments, he discovered the Duc suffering, indifferently, the ministrations of his valets. His curled wig was being dangled before his eyes and he was regarding it with distaste. When he saw the figure of Arsène in the mirror, he stared, incredulously. Then he turned, stared again, and burst into laughter. For indeed, the young man's desperate face, disordered hair, wrinkled and bourgeois clothing, were a strange and unexpected vision.

"There is no time for laughter or explanation other than I forgot, and have no time to return to the Hôtel du Vaubon," said Arsène hurriedly, and with offense. His dark thin face was flushed with mortification and anger at himself. He could not bear laughter at his own expense. "I must beg your indulgence, Monsieur le Duc, and ask if it is possible for me to wear one of your own costumes."

The Duc no longer laughed, but his grave brown eyes danced irrepressibly. "What a bridegroom this is!" he murmured. Then even the laughter died from his eyes, and he regarded Arsène with sudden searching gravity. He turned to his gaping valets. "See if it is possible for us to oblige Monsieur."

He stood up. He was some two inches taller than Arsène. He circled him slowly and thoughtfully, while the color increased in the young man's face. The valets circled also, fingers at dubious lips. Even at this distance, through muted doors, sounds of revelry and music penetrated. Sweat appeared on Arsène's brow, and his eyes began to glitter at this absurd scene. He was like a strange animal being carefully and wonderingly studied. He was humiliatingly conscious of his body.

At last one of the valets scurried to the wardrobes, and returned with a gorgeous costume of plum colored velvet laced and decorated with gold. Another valet produced a white silken shirt, foaming with lace at the neck and cuffs. Still another burrowed in a chest and triumphantly brought to light an elaborate curled wig, and silken stockings and slippers with golden buckles.

"Ah, yes," exclaimed the Duc, with relief. "That is a costume I meant to return to my tailor, for the imbecile made it much too small for me. Hasten, rascals, hasten!"

Confusion fell upon the mirror-lined chamber. Basins of perfumed water and white towels were brought. The valets assaulted Arsène feverishly, while the Duc, smiling again, attended to his own toilette, and watched. Buffeted, swung about, splashed, disrobed, Arsène, with increasing mortification, allowed them to do what they would with him. Suddenly he caught a glimpse of the absorbed Duc, whose wig hung over one ear rakishly, and he laughed reluctantly.

The doublet, however, was too long for him, and he surveyed it with dismay. But there was nothing to be done. The slippers were too large, and one of the inspired and sweating valets stuffed the toes with a torn handkerchief. The wig showed an alarming tendency to fall over his eyes. Inspiration again came to his rescue, and another kerchief was folded upon his head and the wig lowered with trepidation. "If Monsieur will be careful, and keep his head erect, there will not be much danger," stammered one of the valets.

There was a louder burst of music from the gardens and the hotel. One of the valets darted to the Duc for the final touches. By this time, Arsène was in a bad temper. He appreciated jokes, but not on himself. He felt himself offended, robbed of dignity. With much majesty, he buckled on his sword, himself. The Duc was encrimsoned in his efforts to preserve his gravity. He saw that Arsène moved cautiously, for the breeches were a tight fit. The Duc's long shanks were notorious for their leanness. Arsène tried to hitch the skirt of his coat about his shimmering thighs. He noticed, wretchedly, that his borrowed garments were tight or loose in too strategic spots.

Nevertheless, he was a suitably magnificent figure. Pretending to ignore the Duc's silent but visible mirth, he carefully leaned forward and peered in a mirror, rubbing one rouged cheek which was a shade too heavily tinted. Suddenly, they heard a distant fanfare, and the accelerated roar of the crowds outside. Simultaneously, he and the Duc leaped for the door, the valets in pursuit, desperately spraying them with perfume from huge flagons. The valets chased them down the entire length of the corridor outside, waving forgotten kerchiefs, brandishing the flagons. Servants appeared in doorways, open-mouthed and gasping, and watched incredulously the strange running figures of Arsène and the Duc, pursued by the leaping valets.

The valets left them at the top of the great gold and marble staircase, and they flung themselves down, pushing through the streaming magnificence of the guests who were elegantly disporting themselves on the steps. The Duc seized Arsène's arm, and rushed him to the spot where Madame de Tremblant, surrounded by her eight lovely daughters, was waiting. Even at a distance, it was evident that Madame was infuriated. Her large coarse face under the massive coiffure was flushed, the eyes gleaming dangerously. She was fanning herself with rapid fury, and her glance kept darting through the crowds with a speed that augured very badly for some one.

The Duc touched her arm, and she swung about, breathing stertoriously. Her pale gray eye fell upon Arsène, and a vicious expression passed over her big plebeian features. "Ah, so our less important guest has finally condescended to arrive!" she shouted, in her hoarse and booming voice. She curtsied deeply, with much exaggeration. Her daughters, with the exception of Marguerite and Clarisse, tittered behind their lace fans. The guests within ear-shot, and they were many, tittered also, or smiled broadly.

Arsène's face was dark red, and he bowed speechlessly in return. The Duc leaned towards his sister-in-law and said: "Lucille, it is I who am to blame. I detained Arsène with some discussion—"

But Madame de Tremblant was not to be placated. She surveyed Arsène minutely. "And the discussion evidently necessitated the wearing of one of your costumes," she observed. The girls tittered again, as did the guests. Arsène's hand clutched the hilt of his sword, and he glared about, helplessly.

"I implore you, Lucille," said the Duc, with sudden sternness, and his eye engaged the eyes of the listening others, so that each countenance became grave again.

Madame de Tremblant tossed her head, and her wide thick mouth, heavily rouged, tightened ominously. Nevertheless, she said nothing more.

She was a big buxom woman, of heroic stature and proportions, better fitted to the hunting saddle, to which she was enslaved, than to the drawing room. Her mauve velvet costume heightened her natural florid coloring to a purple tinge under the orange-red rouge, and her low bodice, foaming with lace, hardly concealed her full and enormous breasts. Her towering hair, elaborately arranged, was incongruous above her bold light eyes, thick broad nose and heavy mouth. She was a stout dragoon in delicate costume. She disdained and disliked elegant costumes, and her neck was browned by sun to a leathery texture, as were her large masculine hands, now heavily loaded with gems. The lustrous pearls about her throat contrasted alarmingly with its tint and texture. When she walked, she strode. Her character was compounded of honesty and guile, of obscenity and brusqueness, of lascivious stable laughter and brutality, of rude good nature and cruelty, of generosity and avarice. She was one of the most powerful and feared women in Paris. The King liked her, enjoyed her voice, however distant. As for the Cardinal, he was always

279

refreshed by her, and would repeat her witticisms inexhaustibly.

Her daughters surrounded her like graceful flowers about the huge statue of a peasant which was arrayed in incongruous frippery. Annette, Yvonne, Bernadette, Louise, Antoinette and Marie were there with their elegant and patrician young husbands. Clarisse stood at her right hand, and near her, standing with bent and gentle head and air of sweet humility, stood Marguerite. Clarisse was the most beautiful of the Tremblant demoiselles, taller, more graceful, more exquisite of figure and manner, more artful and languishing. Her flesh was like luminous alabaster; the roses in her cheeks needed no artifice to enhance them. Her arms were rivals of those famous appendages of the queen, herself, and her shoulders gleamed as though polished by some loving hand. A man could span her delicate waist with his hands; her bosom was perfect. Her costume of shimmering white satin and cascades of the finest convent lace attracted every envious female eye. She had a profusion of silky flaxen curls which fell over her white neck and shoulders like a faery drift. Her oval face was daintily pointed; her eyes were wide and blue, set apart and shining with points of light. Her mouth was a smiling rosy flower. Nothing could have been sweeter than her expression, or more fascinating in its changes, which were at once demure and malicious, full of vivacity and bewitching merriment. The gestures of her entrancing hands were accompanied by the flashing of jewels on the fingers. If her beauty was not artificial, her soul was. Her mother, her confessor, her betrothed, knew no more about her than she chose to allow. This was part of her enchanting charm. She had a thousand moods, each more graceful, more magical, more magnetic and lovely than the others. She was her mother's favorite. Even that hoarse and bellicose grande dame could not resist the girl's fascinations, though, unlike others, Madame de Tremblant suspected that under that beauty and exquisiteness lived a small and greedy soul, without charity, love, tenderness or mind. Nevertheless, she remained enslaved, consumed with pride.

Arsène, who in her absence forgot her completely, could not resist her presence. She dazzled his sight, threw him into worshipping confusion. She had only to flash the blue lucidity of her eyes upon him to make him forget all else. She had only to smile to make him grovel. When he kissed her hand, he was utterly lost.

She pouted her full and vivid lips upon him, and inclined

her head capriciously as he whispered his apologies. When his breath was too ardent upon her cheek, she daintily covered her face with her fan and her curls fell over her neck and brow. But tonight, for some reason, he soon tired of all this play. He turned from her to Marguerite, whom he loved tenderly.

Clad in blue velvet and pale lace, Marguerite was hardly less lovely than her sister, but so shy and humble was she that her beauty was not so evident to the careless eye. The bright pure vapor of her soul illuminated her face and deep innocent eyes. Smaller, more fragile than Clarisse, she was yet all perfection. Arsène kissed her hand with gentleness. When he looked up into her face he saw that it was shining and blushing. Nevertheless, his acute sensibilities felt a strange sadness. The girl seemed more ethereal than usual, more frail. The blue veins in her temples throbbed feverishly. The hand he held was hot and trembling. He knew how her rude mother constantly upbraided her for her steadfast refusal of innumerable suitors. He had heard that she contemplated entering a convent, something which outraged Madame de Tremblant, who was considerable of a pagan. Yet, in spite of her trials, no one had ever heard a word of complaint, anger or impatience from this poor child. She was seventeen years old, a year older than Clarisse. This was a dangerous age for an unmarried woman, and young noblemen had already begun to woo younger ladies.

Arsène, never too subtle in the past, tonight felt a vague alarm for the girl, and a deeper tenderness such as one feels in the presence of a child upon whom an early doom appears to portend. The light in her eyes was too bright, too febrile, her color too hot and vagrant, her flesh too tenuous. Now he saw that her lids were swollen and discolored, as though she wept too much. Even as he spoke to her gently, her gaze left him, searched feverishly through the surging crowds about her, and her trembling was more evident. He followed her glances, wonderingly. For whom was she waiting? Was that virginal heart touched at last?

The great drawing rooms were flooded with the light of the enormous crystal chandeliers that glittered overhead. The silken-shrouded walls were almost hid by tall flowers and branches of blossoming trees. The floors, polished to a mirrored brilliance, reflected back the colorful figures of the guests and their vivacious movements, so that they appeared to be a myriad tall flowers imaged in a bright lake. The air was permeated with thousands of languorous scents and the

281

murmurs and laughter of hundreds of gay voices, and the distant strains of sweet music. The senses soon became confused by the light, the heat, the dazzling colors and costumes, the restless and rapid gestures, the swaying of tinted garments, the turning and bending of hundreds of curled heads and the flashing of a thousand jeweled hands. The vision became confused by the gleaming of countless white arms and the glittering of many eyes, and the blaze of innumerable gems. It was a magnificent assemblage. Madame de Tremblant was bored excessively. She loathed courtiers, though they, themselves, adored her, thronged about her to hear her latest indecent witticism, which they repeated to those behind them, who carried it to the farthest walls on tides of increasing laughter. There was much snuff-taking, much flourishing of lace kerchiefs, much leg-making. The ladies affected to blush, but in spite of the coquetting, not a cheek was honestly dyed.

The fanfare which Arsène and the Duc de Tremblant had heard in the latter's apartments had heralded the approach of the Cardinal. Now, the mighty brazen doors were flung open, the Captain of the Cardinal's Musketeers appeared, followed by his men, who formed passage and lifted swords to create an arch.

Now the Cardinal entered. Clad in black velvet, with severe white linen at his throat and sleeves, he was, as always, an impelling and majestic sight. His cloak had been removed to reveal his frail and slender figure, upright and graceful. Nothing could have been more aristocratic than that narrow countenance with its pointed imperial. Nothing could have been more haughty yet benign than that arrowed glance from those tiger eyes, which saw everything with one rapier flash. The slow and noble movements of that small and royal head compelled reverence and awe. The smile, sardonic and subtle, inspired apprehension and respect. Increasing illness had increased his pallor, so that he had the aspect of a specter; the delicate bones of his face were outlined under the pale and transparent flesh. Power radiated from him, and a lofty and amused condescension. Not an eye touched him without fear, hatred, dislike or servility. Not a heart but beat quicker at the sight of him. Every smile was artificial and nervous. A cool psychic dampness blew over the gay faces, hushed the frivolous voices.

He was too great, too powerful a man, to feel much satisfaction at the effect he created. Moreover, he had too much contempt for his fellows to experience any gratification, other than that which a man might feel upon entering a jungle and seeing the eyes of lower animals fixed fearfully upon him. Yet, he was all graciousness, inclining his head gravely and smilingly as he approached his hostess.

Madame de Tremblant extended her red hand to him and winked fully and coarsely, grinning lecherously. "How, now, Monsieur le Duc," she boomed. "I had heard your Eminence was too indisposed to grace our assemblage this evening."

"A summons from Madame de Tremblant is a royal command," replied the Cardinal. At this, the woman laughed outright. She tapped him impudently on the shoulder with her fan. "Ah, what a courtier it is!" she exclaimed. "One might almost believe Monseigneur, and be deceived that it was not a priest with such addresses!"

The Cardinal took no offense. A smile of genuine amusement touched those pale and delicate lips, and the cold and baleful light in his eyes warmed.

She leaned towards him and whispered hoarsely: "The piece of iron flies to the magnet: is it not so? But the magnet has not yet arrived."

"But soon," replied the Cardinal, with a cool stare. Madame de Tremblant was disappointed. She had expected some flush, some start, some angry glance, some attempt at intimidation. She had bearded the Cardinal, and in return he gazed at her emptily.

She tapped him again, and essayed a grotesque archness. "Ah, what is man? Even a priest?" she murmured. "Nevertheless, women can forgive, and understand, and feel gratitude."

The Cardinal smiled faintly, and turned his attention to the beautiful daughters of Madame. Now an ardent warmth crept over his transparent features. He accepted the flurry of curtsies with the utmost majesty and benevolence. When he gave his attention to Marguerite, there was a long and inscrutable reflection in his eye, and a little sadness.

"May I inquire as to Mademoiselle's health?" he asked, gently. "She seems to be melting before the eye."

The girl blushed violently, and moisture appeared in her golden eyes. Madame de Tremblant interposed: "Ah, what it is to be a mother! This girl is not yet betrothed, and still speaks of the convent. Can Monseigneur not dissuade her, and receive a mother's gratitude?"

But the Cardinal was gazing at the girl intently. He held her hand strongly, and felt its instinctive and trembling efforts at withdrawal. Now his expression was stern. He said nothing.

He became aware of Arsène, who was watching him with

caution and uncertainty. He smiled, laid his hand on the young man's shoulder. He shook his head. "Ah, I little expected such a disappointment!" he exclaimed. "Nevertheless, I am not resigned, not without hope. I have not accepted the final word."

He paused, absently marked Arsène's nervous smile, and vague shaking of the head. He spoke in a slightly louder voice, and now his eye, rapid and brilliant, touched, without seeming to do so, the lovely countenance of Marguerite de Tremblant.

"I had hoped that your brother Louis might accompany me this evening," he said, "but unfortunately he pleaded indisposition and the press of duty."

He felt, rather than saw fully, the girl's start, her sudden whiteness, the faint dropping of her eyelids, and her shrinking. But this was not evident to any one else but the Cardinal. Even as he smiled, the sternness increased about his mouth, and he sighed. He observed that the girl retreated until she melted into the throng, and that her head had fallen on her breast as she drifted away.

The Marquis du Vaubon had finally forced a passage through the multitude of guests, bowing, swaying, smirking, arching his brows, flourishing his scented kerchief. He was followed by scores of envious and scrutinizing manly eyes, which marked every item of his costume, which was of golden velvet with black touches. His curled black wig was enormous; there was an unusual wide flare to his jewelled cuffs, and the excessively full skirts of his coat were embroidered and glittering with jewelled embroidery. The lace at his throat was a fountain of airy foam, sparkling with diamonds. Gratified and smug at the sensation he created, he remarked to himself that tomorrow would be an unusually busy day for tailors and jewelers and lace-and-wig-makers in Paris. What it was to be the creator of fashion! Ladies sniffed avariciously at his new scents, and openly admired his costume, and his excellent slender legs which gleamed and shone in their golden silk stockings. He bestowed amorous glances upon them in his passage, and his arching brows were implicit with indulgent promise. The debauchery and fatigue of his thin malicious face was hidden under skillful layers of rouge and powder. There were black patches cut in the intriguing shapes of stars, flowers, hearts and squares on his bony cheeks, and, daringly! on his chin and forehead.

"Ah," murmured the Cardinal, "the arbitor of elegance and the glass of fashion approaches in his exaggerated splendor!"

The Marquis invariably amused him. He thought him a fool, but a fool who was malevolently witty, which excused his folly.

He bowed deeply. "Hail, Phoebus!" he said. "But where is your chariot?"

A spray of titters burst from the avid guests nearby. Arsène's hand tightened on his sword at this gibe at his foolish father. But the Marquis was well able to defend himself. For a moment his little black eyes darted, gleamed and rolled malignantly, though his painted lips remained fixed in a grimace of a smile.

Then he returned the bow, even more elaborately, and said: "Hail Pluto! But where is Proserpine?"

Bravo! thought Arsène, delighted by his father's wit. He looked about him for approving and astonished smiles. What he saw alarmed him. For the Cardinal had become deadly pale at this enormous and foolhardy insult, and its wider implications. The guests, horrified and uneasy, began to retreat like the edges of a wave, leaving the insulted priest and the Marquis facing each other in a little empty space. The Marquis wore a satisfied smirk and looked the Cardinal full in the eyes. His small brain had not yet encompassed the enormity of his folly.

Then, thought the Cardinal, it is common knowledge.

Madame de Tremblant was an astute woman. She burst into a loud hoarse laugh. "What classicists are these!" she exclaimed. "You must pardon us, Messieurs, if we are too ignorant to comprehend these subtle allusions." She glanced about her with a hard look, and as at a command, the edges of the wave advanced once more and surrounded the Cardinal and the foolish Marquis, who was still pluming himself on his dangerous witticism and trying to gather admiring eyes as one gathers flowers.

A diversion came in the person of a great lady whom no one but Madame de Tremblant had known was in Paris at this time, believing that she was still secluded at her home in La Rochelle. So seldom did she appear in Paris, that only the older guests were immediately aware of her identity. But Huguenot and Catholic alike regarded her with admiration and deep respect. For the lady was the old Duchesse de Rohan, a life-long friend of Madame de Tremblant, and a very old friend indeed of Monseigneur.

A hush followed as she made her way tranquilly through the crushing and glittering assembly, which parted instinctively before her as though she were royalty. And most certainly, there was something most royal in her walk and her manner. She glided towards her hostess with an imperious and magnificent air, for her blood was nobler than the blood of those who sat on the thrones of France. Her dainty and diminutive figure was exquisite in its perfection. Authority and pride, hauteur and aristocracy, were inherent in her slightest gesture, her slightest word, the briefest sentence which she uttered in a voice singularly strong and calm for such a small person. The flash of her eye was imperious, intimidating.

She was dressed with a stately magnificance, her white hair piled high upon her small and quietly arrogant head. Great diamonds sparkled in her ears, about her erect if withered throat, and upon hands hardly larger than those of a child. Her little face was thin, somewhat long, with a high arching nose implicit with royal dignity. Her full blue eyes under white lids were steadfast and haughty, shrewd and cynical, heavy with sadness one moment, sparkling with dry amusement the next, and coldly disingenuous at still another moment. Her long pale mouth, unpainted, and crooked and mobile, expressed a thousand restrained thoughts, but could, in an instant, take on the hard lines of courage, contempt, and uncompromising fortitude. She was a woman of brilliant intellect and sternness, and her sons respected her opinion above the opinion of any one else in France. Sometimes, when they were alone, they called her "our adorable, obstinate old harridan," but they said this with love and reverence.

Madame de Tremblant greeted her with deep affection, and the ladies embraced. Others crowded close to pay their respects, and listen to the conversation of the Duchesse which was famed for its pungency and bitter humor. She spoke with devastating candor, touched with delicate ribaldry, and was not above calling a man a fool to his face if his folly offended her, or if he appeared stupid. Above all else, she loathed a fool, and would have none about her, even if he were endowed with the noblest of other virtues. Disillusioned, but strangely idealistic, she did not utter an opinion until she had investigated all facets of it first, and then she delivered it with authority and quiet inflexibility. Nevertheless, those few whom she honored with her friendship knew her great kindness, her sensibility, her selfless devotion, and her enormous tact.

The Cardinal, whose haggard face had taken on life and vivacity at the appearance of his old and valued friend, greeted her with only a trifle less affection than had Madame de Tremblant. Her eyes twinkled upon him as he took her hand and lifted it gallantly to his lips. She smiled at his compliments, and she assured him, with a wry but affectionate smile, that apparently the last unguents she had sent him from La Rochelle had done him much good. They understood each other very well. Both were inspired with the same passionate love for France, and desire for French unity against her enemies. They were of the same cynical and disingenuous spirit, the same profound intellect. Though the Duchesse had no personal desire for power, she comprehended it in the Cardinal, and did not think less of him for harboring it. Nevertheless, she pitied him for it, as she pitied the other diseases which afflicted his body. Only to this aristocratic old grande dame had he ever confided the whole extent of his physical sufferings, and when she came to Paris she never failed to bring him pots and vials of strange but efficacious remedies concocted, brewed and mixed by her own hands. If he expressed extravagant claims for them, there was much sincerity in his protestations.

But Madame de Tremblant had no desire to allow the Cardinal to monopolize her old friend, whom she had not seen for a long time. She wished the Duchesse to admire her daughters, and led her away.

"Ah, that Cardinal," she said, to the Duchesse. "What a rascal it is! But one must admit he is a charming man, with excellent manners."

The Duchesse smiled. "And manners in a man are not to be condemned. I must admit, too, that we have much in common." Her face became somewhat anxious and secret. "Have you seen my Henri? I have been in Paris a week, but though I have received messages from him, he remains invisible."

Madame de Tremblant glanced cautiously about her, and her own face darkened with anxiety. "Henri has been to this house, to discuss certain matters with the Duc de Tremblant. I know nothing about these matters," she added, hastily. "I do not care to know about them. They are dangerous, perhaps."

The Duchesse glanced at her inscrutably. "When one has marriageable daughters, it is unwise to have dangerous knowledge."

The Cardinal looked long and thoughtfully after the two ladies when they retreated from him. He promised himself that he would call upon the Duchesse very soon. He adored her conversation. He loved her presence. Too, there might be something to be learned, quite accidentally, though he doubted this, knowing the cleverness of his old friend. It was more likely that she would learn something from him.

287

He felt some one approach him, and turned with that feline swiftness of his which never failed to disconcert others. The Duc de Tremblant, who had retreated a little distance at the advent of the Cardinal, now came forward and bowed gravely. A curious change came over the Cardinal's features. He seemed dimly concerned and suddenly heavy of heart. He laid his hand on the Duc's shoulder and looked into his eyes with sad affection.

"You have neglected me, Monsieur," he said. "We have not had our customary game of chess. Tomorrow, perhaps? You will dine with me at the Palais Cardinal at nine?"

"Your Eminence flatters me upon my prowess as a chess-player," replied the Duc. "Tomorrow? Perhaps."

The Cardinal pressed the other's shoulder with his hand. He did not remove it. But the shadow on his face lightened a little. However, he continued to gaze searchingly into the Duc's eyes. The others had become engrossed in some new witticism of the Marquis', and the Duc and the Cardinal were isolated except for Arsène, who had manœuvred quietly into a position behind the priest.

"It is a promise?" urged the Cardinal.

The Duc hesitated. His eye met Arsène's. Then he said in a low voice: "It is a promise."

The Cardinal sighed. His arm dropped from the Duc's shoulder. A somber shade appeared in his restless and incandescent eyes.

"There are few in Paris whom I dare call my friends," he said, and there was all sincerity in his voice, and the hint of a plea. "You are one of these, Monsieur le Duc." He paused, then said in a penetrating tone: "Should you leave Paris, I should be desolate, fearing that you might not return."

The Duc's glance involuntarily and swiftly rose to meet Arsène's alarmed stare. Then he bowed again. "Be assured, your Eminence, that I should return."

The Cardinal suddenly grasped the Duc by the arms, urgently, and compelled his gaze. "These are dangerous times," he said, softly. "I fear there would be no return, Monsieur. Reflect upon this."

The alarm in Arsène's eyes had quickened to terror. His lips moved almost soundlessly, but the Duc caught his words: "We are betrayed!"

However, the Duc smiled very quietly. He truly liked the Cardinal, as he liked all that was subtle and brilliant. He had spent many enjoyable hours in his company. He said: "Should

I decide to leave Paris, my deepest regret would be my separation from your Eminence."

The Cardinal was silent. He seemed the prey of a thousand sad, grievous and anxious thoughts. His eyes remained fixed upon the Duc as though he were trying to read the other's soul, trying to impart to him some ominous and desperate warning. There was an obvious struggle within him, like one who wrestles with caution and wisdom in an access of generous and natural feeling.

"Monsieur," he said, finally, very slowly and emphatically, "is of a naïve and trusting and noble nature. Such natures tend to repose confidence in the unworthy. Let Monsieur be warned in time."

"I trust none of my friends are unworthy. I cannot believe this," replied the Duc, very gravely and sadly.

"That is not noble innocence," said the Cardinal, with sudden and irascible impatience. "It is only egotism."

He took the Duc's arm. "Remain with me," he added. "I am fatigued. I loathe the conversation of fools. Do not leave my side, I pray of you."

They moved away together. Arsène looked after them, consumed with anxiety. He was about to follow them, when he felt the tap of a fan upon his arm. It was his betrothed, and she was in a pet, which added enchantment to her beauty.

"You are neglecting me, Monsieur," she said, arching her head upon her slender white neck. "But I have grown accustomed to neglect, I am grieved to say."

Arsène moved restlessly. The Cardinal and the Duc had been swallowed up in the moving throngs. He was about to make some hasty excuse, but the limpid blue light in Clarisse's eyes suddenly fascinated him. He kissed her hand.

"Forgive me, Mademoiselle, for being distrait."

She pouted, but she was secretly mollified. Her countenance became radiant. She tossed her flaxen curls. "It is two days to our wedding," she remarked. "Does that render Monsieur distrait?"

"What else?" he murmured, gallantly, his eyes upon her pearly bosom, which immediately flushed a delicate pink under that bold gaze.

She exclaimed: "I trust that Monsieur will not continue his neglect after the nuptials! I have not been nurtured on neglect."

"Believe me, Mademoiselle will have no reason to complain."

He accompanied these words with so meaningful and amor-

ous a look that she blushed even brighter, and tittered helplessly, covering her face with her fan. Virginal though she was,
her thoughts had not been virginal for years, and her mind
was as corrupt as her body still inviolate.

A great weariness suddenly descended upon Arsène.
Whence had gone his former delight in all this gaiety, this
music, this colorful movement of debauched courtiers, this
lovely girl and brilliant light? There was a suffocating heat
in his nostrils, a sickness in his heart. All at once he was
filled with a terrible longing, a hunger and deep nameless
anguish. He looked down into the blue eyes of Mademoiselle
de Tremblant, and he saw a pair of other eyes, no less blue,
but grave and steadfast and sweet. Where had he seen such
eyes? How had he suppressed the knowledge, the memory?

A dark shadow passed across his vision. He saw wet dank
walls, the flickering of a candle, the strench of mold and
poverty and dust. And in the flame of the uncertain candles
he saw a pale young face, stern and quiet, lighted by those
forgotten azure eyes.

It is not possible! he thought, wretchedly. I have truly forgotten.

His misery increased. Mademoiselle was alarmed. Arsène
had one of those vivid and restless countenances which concealed nothing, however he strove to conceal it. She saw that
her betrothed was miserable, heated, agitated and undone. It
is some woman, some wanton! she said to herself, with a
vicious pang of anger and jealousy. Acute of sensibility, a
malicious student of human nature, she now observed that a
deep change had come over Arsène which she had sub-
consciously noted for some time. He appeared older, worn,
preoccupied and leaner, as though bedeviled by thoughts that
would not let him rest. In her small category of life, which
admitted only sensuality and intrigue as important, she could
never dream that men might have thoughts beyond these
trivialities. When an acquaintance appeared distraught or saddened, she believed that some affair of the heart disturbed
him. She had heard of spiritual conflicts, of passionate upheavals of the soul. But when she had heard of them she
had smiled incredulously and knowingly. She recalled the
witticism of some decadent fool, which she had enjoyed: "All
the torments of the spirit begin in the pelvis."

Arsène's intense restlessness communicated itself to her.
She felt him straining away from her side. Helplessly, and
with anger, she turned to the Marquis, who was smirkingly
receiving the plaudits of a group of admirers on his latest

witticism. He turned impatiently at her touch, then revealed his pleasure at the sight of her beauty. He bowed, kissed her hand.

"Mademoiselle!" he exclaimed, exhilarated by his successes.

She beamed upon him, inclined her head, inundating him in the blue wash of her eyes.

"I have been complaining to Arsène," she said, thrusting out her rosy lips. "He has been neglecting me. He is distrait. He seems absorbed in mysterious things."

The smile remained fixed on the Marquis' lips as he glanced at the uncomfortable Arsène, but there was a virulence in it now. Moreover, his eyes blinked with apprehension and anger.

But he said: "That is not possible, Mademoiselle. He speaks of nothing but you, and your coming wedding. Is that not so, Arsène?" he demanded in a louder voice, imperious and sharp.

Arsène replied listlessly: "It is so, father. But Mademoiselle will not believe me." Again his glance tried to pierce through the moving guests to catch a glimpse of the Duc and the Cardinal. He felt his father take his arm in a fierce grip. The Marquis was still smiling.

"Women," he said, "prefer acts to words, my son."

Arsène slowly returned his gaze to his father, and he was touched by the fear and pleading in those malevolent black eyes. Therefore, he smiled ardently, lifted Mademoiselle's hand again to his lips with every gesture of amorous devotion. But the girl, though she coquetted, was not in the least reassured, and her rage and jealousy increased.

There was a sudden fanfare and commotion outside, and again the doors opened. The ensign of the King's Guards entered, the Sieur de la Coste, followed by a coterie of guards, musketeers and archers. These latter distributed themselves swiftly near the doorways of the Hôtel de Tremblant, moving as if oblivious of the suddenly excited guests. Two more companies of guards now entered, Swiss and French, and moved to positions about the walls of the drawing-rooms. Acclamations and shouts now sounded in the streets. It was midnight, but the crowds had increased rather than diminished.

Now, there was a louder, more insistent fanfare. The King, accompanied by his beauteous young queen, was entering the Hôtel de Tremblant. The assemblage, with one accord, bent in curtsey and deep bow. The King acknowledged this obeisance with a slight inclination of his head. The music clamored louder. A wind of excitement and adoration passed over the great drawing-rooms. The coterie of nobles and magnates who accompanied the royal pair filled these rooms with new colors and costumes and scents.

Now the festivities could proceed, and the gaiety become unrestrained.

CHAPTER XXVI

THE KING, LOUIS XIII, was still in the prime of his young manhood, and though as yet bitterly disappointed that his queen had not presented him with an heir, still could hope. Had not his favorite astrologer assured him that in good time a son would be born to him who would be the greatest king who ever sat upon the throne of France? Superstitious and duly mystical, he believed this, and later events bore out his earlier faith.

Oppressed, beaten, despised and ignored by his terrible mother in his youth, ridiculed and neglected by the courtiers who had surrounded her, always the game of his younger and gayer and whistling brother, Gaston, who was a favorite of Marie de Medicis and her slavish Court, overlooked by ministers and statesmen, ignored and relegated to silent musty corners as he had been before his access to the throne of France, it was to be expected that he would now have a timid and deprecating air, a humility and embarrassment, an eagerness to please, a fearfulness of temperament.

Nevertheless, he had none of these characteristics which usually beset those upon whom oppression, ridicule and neglect have sat for all the formative years of a man's life. His manner, though quiet and reserved and cold, was yet simply arrogant. He had none of the frail physique of the persecuted. His body was strong and supple, giving an impression of full activity. He loved sports and the military life, and was impressive in them both. His temperament was hard and fixed, narrow and capricious, obstinate and silent, always jealous and suspicious and inexorable. In all, he exhibited an astonishing metier de roi. His was truly a triumph of man over circumstance, reticent yet proud, sullen yet imperious, commanding respect and filling the beholder with uncertainty.

He was dressed so soberly, but so regally, that he was conspicuous in that dazzling assemblage. His toilette was conservative, for he had no eye or care for color or elegance, preferring a soldiery aspect. He was not handsome, but he was impressive. His complexion was yellowish, revealing his Italian blood, as did his cold yet luminous dark eyes. His face was long, somewhat cavernous, and had an air of gloom and abstraction, heightened by long dank locks of black hair, which he disdained to cover with a wig. His mouth, with its heavy underlip, usually was apart, but this, strangely, did not detract from its firmness and stubbornness. When he spoke, his voice was low, carefully controlled, for he was afflicted at times with a stammer. Cold and disdainful, there were none who could claim intimacy with him, except the Cardinal, whom he passionately disliked and feared. (Nevertheless, being an astute man, he was never unconscious of the fact that it was the Cardinal who had restored the dignity of the throne, and its power, and that it was the Cardinal who served him with unremitting implacability and devotion. Perhaps it was this, and his own jealousy, that impelled his dislike.)

Overpowered as he was by the Cardinal's personality and genius, he could yet be grateful as a king, if not as a man, for all that the Cardinal had bestowed upon him. In every fresh success presented to him by the Cardinal, he could say ceremoniously yet coldly: "France is grateful to you, Monseigneur." Nor was there hypocrisy or duplicity in this statement. However, in his private life and thoughts, he was consumed by detestation, fear and hatred, suspecting always the Cardinal's words and motives.

His queen, who moved modestly a pace in his rear, was a vision of beauty and bewitching charm, dressed in a pale rose petticoat flounced with lace, with a bodice of silver fabric. The pearls she wore about her neck were no more lustrous than those famous bared shoulders and graceful arms. The perfume that scented her seemed the emanations from her own fair body. Her chestnut hair, loosened, curled in a cascade from the crown of her head, and glittered with diamonds. Lovely though she was, it was noted that her face was paler and sadder than usual, and deeply abstracted, as though she had recently suffered overmuch. Her smile dazzled, but it was the smile of a mannequin, and her eyes darted before her in a kind of dull terror, as if seeking an enemy.

The Cardinal materialized, as it were, from the air itself, still keeping the Duc de Tremblant at his insistent side. He greeted the King with the deepest reverence, but that young man's eyes regarded his master with dislike and ill nature, tempered with gloom and resentment.

"How, now," said the King, "I had heard your Eminence was too indisposed to attend such a gay event."

"I could not resist, Sire, having been given to understand that your Majesty would be present," replied the Cardinal, gravely.

"Ah!" exclaimed the other, with bad humor. "I have been present at the tables almost every night, but your Eminence has not been there!"

During this exchange, the sly and gloating eyes of the guests noted with what loathing and fear the young Queen regarded the Cardinal, with what a tremor she shrank from his touch when he lingeringly kissed her hand, with what horror and despair her green eyes blazed. She appeared to dwindle before him, as if her very flesh melted. When he murmured a greeting to her, her pale lips fell open, then did not stir again, as if no effort of her will could compel her to speak.

A collation had been prepared for the King, who had a voracious appetite. Even though the orchestra and all the fiddlers set up the gay lifting strains of his favorite ballet, La Merlaison, he would not be detained, but repaired to the waiting chamber and the delicacies. The Queen kept to his side, like a frightened dog, fleeing with him away from the presence of the loathsome Cardinal. He watched her flight with a peculiar smile, and his breath was quickened.

The guests began to dance. They were well acquainted with the appetite of the King. But the orchestra had changed its tune, on the disappearance of the King, who would wish to lead the first measure of the ballet. Back and forth, round and round, in long graceful circles, the dancers flew over the polished floors which reflected back the color of their costumes and the motions of their bodies. The air became suffocating.

The Cardinal had led the Duc de Tremblant near a quieter corner behind pots of flowering shrubs. He seemed determined not to leave the Duc for an instant. They sat on little gilded chairs and thoughtfully watched the dancing for a moment or two. The Duc hid his anxious impatience. He knew the hour. And within that hour, he must leave on his secret mission. Concealed in his apartments, waited the Comte van Tets. Nevertheless, he strove for an appearance of ease and tranquillity.

The Cardinal began to speak languidly of inconsequential things. Then he remarked that he was excessively weary, that he had been urging the King to allow him to retire from affairs of State, because of the condition of his health. The

Duc hid a faint smile at this hypocrisy. But the Cardinal must have discerned it, with his subtlety, for he smiled slightly, himself.

"What did his Majesty say to this?" asked the Duc.

"He implored me not to desert him," replied the Cardinal, meditatively.

What grave concession did you force from him, then? thought the Duc, and some cold premonition moved in his heart.

"But even kings are not insensible to the illnesses of their servants," he said, watching the Cardinal with a penetrating look.

The Cardinal sighed, lifted one shoulder. "Who am I, compared to the State?" he murmured. "I live only to serve France." Suddenly his pale and narrow countenance quickened, and his eyes became incandescent. "You do not believe that, Monsieur le Duc?"

"I do believe it," said the Duc, sincerely. "But what is truly the welfare of France—your hopes, or mine—I do not really know."

The Cardinal seemed pleased by this honest answer. He laid his thin white hand affectionately on the Duc's arm. "You are no liar, and I love you for that, Raoul. What it is to find a man who is not a liar! You speak of your hopes. But you are a Huguenot. Your design for France cannot be truly salubrious. Would you reduce France to the arid sterility of Protestantism? That creed of the shopkeeper and the petty land-owner and the yeoman? The Church has always been the patron of aristocratic art, understanding that the common man can never truly appreciate the arts, nor comprehend them. It is sacrilege to expose them to him."

"Art is universal," replied the Duc. "When it becomes aristocratic, it is no longer art. That is a contradiction in terms. In Art, there is only a democracy, an equality; it is like sunshine."

The Cardinal pondered these words, during which the orchestra became louder and gayer. Then he shook his head. "Do not think that I am not acquainted with the words of those who preceded and followed Luther. I have followed all their weighty arguments. I consider Erasmus, for instance, a dangerous and stupid man, as are all visionaries.

"When men consider themselves the equal of all other men, then there will be no heroes. Heroes are vitally necessary to inspire the people. Hero worship is the most powerful, the most noble, instinct of man. In the dead level of Protestant

296

equality there shall rise no heroes, no saints, no lofty statues to stand against the sky. The Church knows this. Therefore, she encourages aristocracy of birth and privilege, and an aristocracy of mind. She comprehends that men are not created equal."

He continued: "Do not misunderstand me. The Church knows that in the sight of God every soul is equal to another. But there are those who are called upon to serve in humility and poverty and pain, and those who are born to rule, in this world. She does not fly in the face of God.

"When every man is literate—and, please God, this shall never happen—when every man is given opportunity equally with that of all other men, the ultimate result can only be a dread uniformity, a dull sameness and colorlessness imposed upon the rich variety and colorful exuberance of human life. Would you wish this, Monsieur?"

"I admit that there is in inequality an inherent capacity," said the Duc, slowly. "But I affirm the doctrine that every man shall be given freedom to develop what capacity he possesses, for his own joy, and the welfare of the nation. I believe in the right of every man to peace, to personal dignity and freedom, to a measure of security upon the secure and fixed earth."

"Nonsense," smiled the Cardinal. "The very stuff of life is alarms, uncertainties and dangers. The seeker after peace is the seeker after death, the weary man, the impotent man, who can no longer deal with the emergencies of the day. Does your faith promise such security?"

The Duc was silent. Now his brow was wet. Even at this moment he ought to be in his apartments. But the tenacious Cardinal would not let him go, and now the Duc felt a stirring of fear. Was it truly possible that the Cardinal knew of this mission? The Duc was still incredulous, though he was well aware of the enormous spy system of this frightful man.

The Cardinal was speaking again, indulgently. "Raoul, if you had a moment's absolute power in this world, what would be your first and only act?"

The Duc turned to him, and his long unhandsome face was kindled with a sort of passionate beauty.

"I would eliminate from the minds of all the peoples all memory of history," he said.

The Cardinal meditated upon this, with deep somberness. At last, he smiled. "I see!" he exclaimed. "Yes, I see all the possibilities!"

In the meantime, the King had returned to the drawing-rooms. Arsène, who was wandering through the guests like an apprehensive ghost, sought out a friend of his, a courtier close to the King, the Comte d'Harcourt. He drew the Comte aside, and said:

"What is this between his Majesty and his Eminence? Did you note the Cardinal's abashed countenance?"

The Comte d'Harcourt, a simple and devout Catholic, nodded in anxious agreement. "His Majesty has only ill-natured things to say lately of his Eminence. It seems that the King wishes an instant attack upon England, which the Cardinal will not countenance, in his wisdom." At this, he allowed his voice to drop cautiously.

Arsène affected to laugh lightly. "Ah, so that is it! I was conversing with his Eminence, and he hinted that he had about arrived at much of the King's opinion. But you know how devilishly proud he is. He will not approach his Majesty unless summoned. How trivial matters can decide the fate of nations! Now, if his Majesty should summon him, speak graciously to him, who can tell what might transpire?"

The Comte was all eagerness. "Are you sure of this, Arsène? Then, not a moment must be lost. The King has slept little lately, and the Cardinal has avoided him. I shall speak to his Majesty instantly!"

When the Comte had pushed his way into the press to the King's side, Arsène, moving swiftly, approached his betrothed, who was infuriated the while she smiled and coquetted with two gallants. She watched Arsène's approach with blazing eyes, and tapped her little foot. But he spoke boldly: "Mademoiselle, your uncle is in yonder corner conversing with the Cardinal, who bores him. Will you not rescue him? I would do so myself, but I see Madame beckoning to me imperiously."

Clarisse was fond of her uncle. Moreover, she was deeply mortified at Arsène's latest neglect, and wished to escape from her cavaliers. Arsène followed her at a discreet distance. He dared not let the Cardinal see him, whose suspicions were always supersensitive. He saw Clarisse engage the two gentlemen in conversation, and now he saw the approach of the eager Comte d'Harcourt. The Comte whispered something to the Cardinal, who showed every indication of annoyance and uncertainty. Then he turned to the Duc. But the Duc had requested his nece to dance with him, and the Cardinal had apparently exacted some promise from the Duc, for the latter had bowed and smiled before sweeping his niece into the intricacies of a new ballet.

Arsène slipped along the outskirts of the dancing guests, keeping the Duc and Clarisse within view. At last he saw the Duc lead the girl to a group of friends, where she began to fan herself, laughing at her uncle's strenuous activity. The Duc began to search the crowds, and Arsène deftly inserted himself within range of his glance, but discreetly retired again. He moved to a quiet and isolated spot, and within a few moments the Duc joined him with an anxious face.

"There is no time to waste!" he said. "I thank you, Arsène. Let us go!"

They made their way to the rear of the mansion, and fled silently up the winding servants' entrance, for they had avoided the crowded stairway of the drawing rooms. They reached the Duc's apartments, unseen. On the journey there, the Duc had already begun to unfasten his garments and remove his wig, which he carried under his arm. No one was in the apartments. The servants were having festivities of their own. Here all was silence, except for a burning taper. The Duc unlocked his cabinet, whispered a word, and the Comte van Tets, perspiring and crimson, emerged, dressed in dark garments and a voluminous cloak. They all conversed in whispers as the Duc changed his clothing, fastened on his sword belt.

"I beseech you again to allow me to accompany you," said Arsène.

"Impossible! Have you forgotten, too, that you are to be married within two days, you impatient bridegroom?" The Duc, even in his haste, paused to laugh soundlessly.

Arsène said nothing more, but his expression became more and more apprehensive. Then, at last he said:

"I regret your decision to take only four guards with you, Monsieur. I fully recognize your argument that a larger coterie would attract attention. But it would also give would-be attackers pause."

"We must not attract attention," replied the Duc, pulling his plumed hat far over his face, and then examining the holsters of his pistols. "So, we must face some danger in order to keep our mission secret. However, I anticipate no trouble. Who knows of our going? Now, Arsène, I beg you to return to the dance. Our absence may already be noted."

He hesitated, then suddenly embraced the gloomy young man with unusual warmth and affection, kissing him heartily on both cheeks. Then he held his arms in his strong kind grasp, looking deeply into his eyes.

"God bless you, Arsène," he said. "You are young. Whatever occurs, you must not forget. You must not turn aside."

This seemed ominous to Arsène, who paled. He laid his hands on the Duc's shoulders, and felt tears rising to his eyes. But before he could speak, the Duc and the Comte van Tets had left him.

He was left alone in the dim chamber. Through open doors he could see the other rooms, flickering wanly in the single taper. A coldness gathered about his heart. It appeared to him that death and danger had lurked here, that they had gone in the wake of his friend. He did not have the faith of a Paul de Vitry. He really believed nothing. He could not pray. Now, he passionately wished that he had faith, that he could fall simply on his knees and beg the protection of heaven upon the Duc. But he had no words, in spite of the long years of his training under priests, which had served only to bestow ridicule and skepticism in his heart. He had more faith in his sword. That cursed wedding of his! But for that he would be cantering at the Duc's side at this very moment. In the strength of his youth and his egotism, he believed that his presence would be sufficient to ward off all danger and protect his friend invincibly.

At last he had a thought: I must keep the Cardinal in sight. I must allay any of his suspicions.

He returned to the festivities. He found the Cardinal conversing languidly with a group of gentlemen and smirking ladies. He discerned that the Cardinal looked frightfully ill. His face was drawn and blue with fatigue; his terrible eyes were sunken and haunted. He stroked his imperial, and his hand shook, in spite of his smiles and his courteous air of attention.

Arsène inconspicuously made his way to the Cardinal's rear, so that it appeared that he had been standing there for some time. So it was that when the Cardinal turned and glanced about him, he saw a young man who had the aspect of one who was filled with ennui. His eye lighted until it was blazing with a baleful light. But he smiled amiably.

He took Arsène by the arm and led him away.

"Have you seen Monsieur le Duc, Arsène? He promised to wait for me in order that we might finish our conversation."

"The Duc?" replied Arsène, with a look of artless surprise. "Certes, I saw him but five minutes ago!" He turned and searched the crowd with an excellent imitation of concentration. He knew that the Cardinal was afflicted with poorness of vision. "Ah, there he is, Monseigneur. I believe he is dancing with Madame Deauville, yonder."

The Cardinal squinted in the direction Arsène indicated. His bearded lips parted as though he drew a breath through them.

"Good. Arsène, I am retiring to the spot where I last conversed with the Duc. Will you ask him to come to me there?"

Obediently, Arsène moved away. He found Madame de Tremblant the center of a hilarious group. He drew her aside. Her pale and protuberant eyes regarded him with annoyance, yet affection.

"Madame," he whispered, "I have a message for you from the Duc."

Her expression immediately became concerned and secret, and full of anxiety.

"He has had to leave inconspicuously, upon an urgent call. He will return within a week. He begged me to tell you that you must suffer no apprehension."

She played with her fan, and wet her thick painted lips. She darted a glance about her of furtive fear. Then she said: "But your wedding, Arsène. He was to give Clarisse to you! Who can take his place?"

But she spoke absently. She was pallid under her rouge. She regarded the young man with grave fright. She loved her husband's brother with a deep intensity. She had loved him before her marriage to his younger brother, but he had not returned her love. She understood many things about him. Now her rude heart was filled with a hideous premonition that she would never see him again.

She suddenly caught Arsène by the arm, and her fingers were the fingers of a stableboy in their iron strength.

"No! Tell me nothing! I have not asked! My God, what is to become of him? He is in no danger, Arsène? No, do not tell me. I cannot bear to know."

Her bosom heaved. Drops of sweat appeared on her upper lip. They burst through the powder on her brow.

Arsène was silent. His heart was heavy and dark. Madame covered her mouth with her fan, and over it her eyes regarded him with savage terror.

Finally he whispered: "I must return to the Cardinal. He is waiting for the Duc. I must delay him—"

"It is as bad as that?" she murmured.

"It is as bad," he replied, somberly.

"My God!" she moaned.

He left her and sought out the Cardinal, who was leaning back against a white plaster pillar in an attitude of extreme exhaustion. He opened his eyes as he heard Arsène approach, and when he saw that he was alone a white shadow passed over his countenance like the shadow of dissolution.

Arsène bowed before him. "The Duc begs that you will excuse him for a few moments longer," he said. "He will return shortly."

The Cardinal was silent. His hand fumbled for the golden cross that hung from his neck. He played with it for a moment, then he lifted his fingers high and let the cross drop heavily. During all this, his sunken and gleaming eyes did not leave Arsène's face.

He said, in a strange and sinking voice: "I await his return."

CHAPTER XXVII

THE DUC DE TREMBLANT and the Comte van Tets left by the servants' entrance of the Hôtel de Tremblant. They clung to the silent walls of houses, fled in the deep black shadows of the trees, not speaking, scarcely breathing. They leapt from shadow to shadow in the moonlight, as if from ambush to ambush. They sped through winding alleys, crept along the edges of gutters, avoiding all patches of illumination. Once they saw a gendarme carrying a lantern, and flattened themselves in an embrasure until he had passed. Once he had been within touching distance, yawning and swinging his lantern in the darkness. They finally arrived at the Bois de Boulogne, disappeared into its leafy silence and black shadows.

The Duc paused, and whistled softly. Within a moment or two Paul de Vitry and four silent cloaked men emerged. They brought with them six powerful and saddled horses. It was two o'clock. The deep tones of the bells in the towers of Notre Dame struck with long and thundering clamor.

"I ought to accompany you, Monsieur," whispered Paul.

"No. The fewer who leave the less the danger, my dear Paul." As he had embraced Arsène, but now with an even deeper love, the Duc embraced the young Comte, who was in tears.

The four silent guards who were to accompany the Duc and the Comte van Tets were all faithful and devoted Huguenots, friends of Paul, himself. Intrepid and powerful swordsmen, their eyes gleamed in the vagrant beams of moonlight that fell from the trees. The Duc, who was studying them critically, was satisfied. Two of them were slightly known to him.

"Ah, my dear de Longueville, and my dear de Condé! We have a hard journey before us."

The men drew their swords, and silently kissed them before returning them to their scabbards.

303

Taking final leave of Paul de Vitry, the six horsemen left the city by the Barriere St. Denis. They did not speak, but crouched in their saddles wrapped in their cloaks, their hats pulled far over their faces. No one accosted them. The streets were silent and deserted, washed in alternate silver moonlight and intense black shadow.

They maintained silence as they galloped swiftly through the hushed countryside, not feeling safe until Paris was a lost dream behind them. The guards glanced warily at every copse of trees, fearing ambush. De Longueville and de Condé rode ahead, the Duc and the Comte came next, and the other two guardsmen followed. Every hand held a pistol. Wrapped in their cloaks, fleeing like shadows under the moon, the horses' hoofs padding through the warm summer dust, they were spectral horsemen, their faces hidden under their hats. They passed hamlets sunken in sleep; the roofs of small churches were silver in the moonlight. Crickets murmured incessantly in the tall waving grass.

Once they dismounted to drink of the cool waters of a little running stream, and here the Duc lit his pipe for a brief moment. The curling smoke turned white as moonbeams touched it. The horses panted and bent their heads to the water. Even yet they dared speak hardly above whispers.

They rode on like the wind. At length the sky paled, and birds broke into passionate choruses of song, and the air became cool as water. Now along the distant low horizon a pale flickering fire began to run, and from the earth rose a poignant scent. The wind quickened; the trees murmured hoarsely before it. At length the eastern sky became like an opal conflagration, and the zenith was as white as milk. They heard the lowing of distant cattle, and the crowing of cocks. The breeze in their tired faces was filled with a thousand fresh cool odors.

At seven in the morning they saw the distant spires of Chantilly, the crosses and the pointed steeples bright red in the brightening morning. But they avoided the town itself, skirting by it. They were to pause briefly at de Vitry's estates, where fresh horses were waiting for them. At half-past seven they arrived at these estates. It was a small village set in green meadows and fields, the low hills beyond them mauve and pink in the morning. The Duc glanced about him with deep satisfaction. Here there were no wattled huts, but strong low stone houses surrounded by gardens and white fences. The small church, exquisite, seemed formed of the very stone of the earth itself, small but sturdy and simple. The cross glittered in the new sun, and from the church came the deep slow voice of the priest.

They arrived at a small neat tavern with a painted goat swinging in the fresh sweet wind. The cobbled yard was empty, except for a servant girl drawing water from a well by a creaking chain. She lifted a round rosy face alertly as the six horsemen rode into the yard, then, bending her head, she ran into the quiet tavern. A moment later a huge fat giant of a man emerged. He had an enormous bald head and his face was fierce and taciturn. When he saw the horsemen, he came himself, but slowly and insolently, and helped them . dismount. He had small bright brown eyes which sparkled with a choleric humor, thick pouting lips, a snout of a nose, and a deeply wrinkled forehead. He did not appear pleased at these guests, but he said nothing, merely jerking his head towards the tavern. Then he grasped the bridles of the horses in each hand, and so tremendous was his strength that the exhausted animals did not resist him, did not throw up their heads in protest at a strange touch. He headed them to the stables nearby, removed their saddles, gave them food, locked the stable doors carefully, and proceeded to the tavern. As he walked, he swung his bare arms like a gorilla, and the muscles in his arms and thighs bulged and swelled.

The Duc was in no wise prepossessed by this surly and taciturn man, but Paul de Vitry, with a smile, had described him as an unreconciled, violent but honest man, whom all his own blandishments had not conquered or softened.

"You are Crequy?" asked the Duc, abruptly, his sunken eyes sparkling with weariness.

The man muttered an affirmative. He eyed the Duc and his companions with visible aversion and ill-nature.

"We will have our breakfast, and our fresh horses," said the Duc, wondering if Paul had not been mistaken, and they might be betrayed by this knave.

The host said nothing. He retired behind his counter, hoisted himself upon his stool, and sat glaring at them unblinkingly like a huge wrinkled statue. The serving girl entered with a tray of food, which she laid on the table before the six gentlemen. They ate in nervous silence, for they did not like the unwinking stare of mine host. He did not move even an eyelash as he contemplated them with open savagery.

"Zounds!" muttered de Longueville, "the rascal destroys my appetite." The food was simple and good. They had fresh eggs and ham, milk and newly baked bread. The small mullioned windows of the inn turned bright gold, and hot gusts of wind blew in through the opened door.

Then Crequy, still silent, led them out into the courtyard and up an outside staircase to the floor above. He showed them into bare but spotless chambers, containing only clean beds and rough blankets. Here they threw themselves prone. They heard mine host locking the doors behind them. Then they heard his rough harsh voice speaking to the serving girl.

"There is no one in these rooms, Roselle. No one came this morning. You understand? If you speak, I shall strangle you."

He must have made a threatening gesture with his vast hands, for the girl uttered a squeak, a cry, and they heard her running footsteps.

Reassured, the Duc turned on his side and fell into a deep sleep. But Longueville took turns with the others on keeping guard.

It was gray twilight when the Duc and the Comte awoke. A key turned in the lock, and the host entered with a gigantic pitcher of water and some towels. These he laid on the single bare table in the room, and disappeared again. Stiff and sore, they all washed. They waited. It was not until night had actually fallen that the man reappeared, and beckoned to them. They found a sturdy repast waiting for them, and fresh horses.

The Duc opened his purse to pay the host, but the man gestured aside the golden crowns with a contemptuous motion. He looked the Duc fully in the eyes, and grimaced.

"Monsieur the Comte de Vitry is a fool. But he is a good man. I take no money from his guests, even if they, too, are fools," he said. And now he scowled at them with ferocity.

"I shall not forget your kindness," said the Duc, nonplussed, glancing at his wary companions.

The man snorted, and gestured them to the door. He followed them. Fresh, fine horses awaited them, and they mounted. The host watched until they had disappeared in the darkness.

"I like not that Crequy," remarked young de Condé. "I should have spit him upon my sword for his insolence. De Vitry has been remiss in the training of his peasants."

"I suspect him," agreed de Longueville.

"We must not look for enemies ambushed in shadows," the Duc rebuked them. He turned to the Comte van Tets, who rode at his side. "Monsieur, you are enduring the journey well."

The Dutchman, who had spoken rarely during all the hours he had spent with his companions, smiled heavily. "There is nothing too arduous to endure in this cause, Monsieur le Duc," he answered. He caught his breath in something that was between a sob and a sigh, and bestowed a deep glance upon the Duc.

"Monsieur, my country is eternally grateful to you. I can say no more."

The Duc reached over and laid his gloved hand for an instant on the other's. He saw that the Dutchman had sunken again into his mournful reveries.

The moon sailed over the massed treetops which lined the rutted road. Once they heard the distant howl of a wolf as the country became wilder, more desolate, more formless and menacing. They could see great moors spread about them, and never a comforting light shining through a window. The sound of rushing water filled the chill air. Very often they lost the road, and came back to it over sharp half-concealed rocks, twisting roots of trees and through broken forests.

Now a floating mist rose from the moors, twisting into a thousand ghostly shapes under the mysterious moon. De Condé, who was superstitious, crossed himself frequently, forgetting that long ago he had abandoned the Church. The Duc smiled to himself at these nervous gestures. But the profound silence, the drifting misty forms illuminated by moonlight, the black forest all about them, which they dared not abandon for more open places, the immensity of the stricken plains in the distance, all weighed heavily upon him, and filled him with crushing foreboding. He came to believe that in some fashion they had left the world of men, light, laughter and city, and had been transplanted to some wild uninhabited planet full of danger, death and drifting apparitions.

"We shall reach Beauvais at dawn," he said. No one answered him.

He comforted himself with the thought that that night they would reach St. Omer, and a little later, Calais. That would be sixty leagues in all, a prodigious feat of riding.

But in spite of his efforts, his forebodings increased. Soon they would reach the edge of the forest, and in the most dangerous hours, be forced to ride in the open as they neared St. Omer. He ridiculed himself, in an effort to raise his courage. Who knew of their going? It was true that the Cardinal had his spies, but if the Cardinal had heard of their mysterious journey he would not know their mission. At the worst, he would have them followed to Calais, itself. But they would be on shipboard and still the spies would know no more except that the Duc and his companions had sailed for England. Certainly, that was dangerous knowledge for the Cardinal to possess, in itself. But upon the Duc's return, not even the Cardinal would dare question him. In spite of the strained relations between England and France, hundreds of Frenchmen and Englishmen crossed the Channel every day on diplomatic or private business.

Yet, though he reassured himself, he would frequently strain his ears for the sound of pursuers or ambushes.

Now he was eager for the towns. The silence, the moonlight, the moors and the drifting darkness began to chill him to the very soul. He wished that the young men, de Longueville and de Condé, were more gay, might sing or chaff each other in the manner of youth. But they, too, were silent, bending over their saddles, their gleaming eyes searching the night.

The moon disappeared, and now there was a deep roll of thunder, and a mutter of rising wind. Suddenly Van Tets reined in his horse and spoke quickly and quietly to the Duc: "Monsieur, I have the strangest premonition that if you do not abandon me now, and turn back, we shall die. I am not given to fancies. Abandon me, I beseech you!"

His voice became more urgent, and the Duc could hear his hard breath in the black of the night.

"Abandon you, my dear friend? That is absurd. Within two hours we shall be in St. Omer, and safe. It is only the night that has unnerved you."

The others heard this conversation, and drew in their horses. They stood, huddled together, hardly able to distinguish each other in the gathering darkness. The Duc felt their fear and their irresolution. He knew how to appeal to these.

He laughed a little. "Monsieur, you are impugning the courage and the gallantry of these Frenchmen! Under more favorable circumstances every one of these gentlemen would demand satisfaction for an affront which only your weariness and past suffering can pardon. Is it not so, Messieurs?"

There was a moment's hesitation, then the young men answered emphatically: "Assuredly, Monsieur le Duc!" And they heard the swift movement of swords in scabbards.

Van Tets said nothing more, and they rode on in renewed silence.

The storm was rising. The moon, at intervals, burst wildly from ambuscades of black ragged clouds, fleeing into other ambuscades. During these moments her light was vivid and desolate, shining on the white faces of the horsemen, before plunging them again into the thick obscurity. Now drops of cold rain lashed their faces, and the horses, frightened, whinnied and increased their exhausted pace.

The moon emerged again, with a light resembling steel upon which the sun glitters. It was then that de Longueville, who had the keenest eyes of all, saw a glint in the thick shrubbery to the right, down the twisting road.

He uttered a faint low warning, and they drew in their horses.

Though they could barely see him, they discerned that he was pointing ahead. He whispered: "I saw a glint, as of a musket, Monsieur le Duc!"

They drew their horses together. Every heart thundered. Every hand reached for sword and pistol. But it was too late.

The shrubbery suddenly blazed. The wet dark air was torn asunder by volleys of sound. The terrified horses reared and plunged, striking each other with their hoofs. There was another blaze, another crash of sound. Confusion burst all about them, the singing of bullets, the screaming of the horses, the shouts and cries of the ambushed and the ambushers. The horsemen were trapped. On each side of the road high stony banks enclosed them, prevented their escape. They could not wheel and flee. The Duc heard a sharp groan near him, and felt, rather than saw, Van Tets slide ponderously to the ground under his slain horse.

"Highwaymen!" thought the Duc. But he knew in his heart that these were not highwaymen.

There was another cry, and de Longueville and de Condé seemed to leap from their horses. They crashed into the bushes, and lay still. The moon shone more vividly now, escaping from her clouds. The Duc saw that the shrubbery was alive with at least a dozen crouching and armed men. It was the end.

He glanced about him, in pure terror and despair. And as he did so, the other two frantic horsemen fell from their horses and rolled under the plunging hoofs.

"Halt!" he cried. "It is I, the Duc de Tremblant! Touch me, at your peril!"

Now, all was darkness and confusion again. The Duc saw a flash of scarlet light, and felt a sudden burning in his breast. A whirlpool of blackness shot with flame engulfed him. He threw up his arms and fell to the ground, silent and motionless.

Lightning darted across the sky, penetrated into the broken roof of the forest. Twelve men cautiously emerged from the thickets and stood near the heap of dead men and horses. One of them, the leader, turned the dead Duc on his back and peered down at his face.

"The Huguenot swine!" he muttered, and kicked the helpless face brutally with his booted foot.

He gestured, and his men bent over the dead men and rifled their pockets of purses and papers, which they thrust into their own pockets. They worked swiftly and in silence. They dragged the slain companions into the thickets where pits had already been dug in grisly readiness. They threw the bodies into the pits. Rain and wind and lightning mingled as they hurried about their tasks. The gale caught their cloaks and whirled about them, so that they resembled huge bats. They shoveled earth over the bodies, strewed branches and stones over the hasty flat graves. Then, mounting horses which they had tethered at a distance, they dragged away the dead horses of the Duc and his companions until they came to a great crooked ravine. Down this crevice they tumbled the bleeding animals. Then, bending over their horses they rode away into the night.

The storm broke in all its madness.

CHAPTER XXVIII

THE FRIGHTFUL STORM had passed at dawn. Now the earth was sweet and fresh in the glittering morning. Arsène de Richepin and the Comte de Vitry rode out towards Chantilly just as all the bells of Paris were ringing in happy exuberance.

Arsène's nature was so volatile that he had rid himself of the doubts and fears of the previous night. He began to sing, slapping the reins on the neck of his horse and cavorting about the wide smooth road in an ecstasy of light-heartedness and gaiety. Even the dull and hopeless laborers repairing the roads looked up with a smile after his passage. He galloped and cavorted; he waved his hat in the air. Then he would rein in his horse, impatient and laughing, for the more sedate Paul to reach him.

"You jog like a curé on an ass!" he exclaimed.

Paul, who was younger than he by at least two years, smiled. "What it is to be young in heart!" he replied. He did not speak of the Duc de Tremblant, for he did not wish to shadow that radiant vitality which emanated from his friend.

He had his own thoughts, which seemed to bestow a secret pleasure upon his tired and thoughtful face. Arsène at length became conscious that Paul was giving him furtive but delighted glances, as though in possession of some information that gave him affectionate joy. As time passed, this expression became more marked, and once or twice Paul laughed softly as if at some personal jest, which was without malice, and only with disinterested love.

"You are smug, Paul," remarked Arsène, at last.

Paul inclined his head and gazed at his friend with such a light in his eyes that it quite startled the young man. "You are about to give joy to two old friends of yours," he said, after a moment's hesitation. "Ah, do not press me. But I shall be sorely disappointed if you are not as delighted as they."

311

Then, as he spoke, a faint dimness as though a sad thought had occurred to him, passed over the light in his luminous gray eyes. He sighed, spurred his horse, and now he, instead of Arsène, rode a little ahead.

Arsène was devoured by curiosity. But the early morning was so fair that he could not be piqued at all this mystery. He had the happy faculty of being able to forget all distressing thoughts at will. He had already forgotten that tomorrow was his wedding day. He would not allow himself to think of the Duc de Tremblant. When the thought did occur to him, he repeated to himself all the reassurances of Paul de Vitry.

He gazed about the green countryside with great satisfaction. He sniffed deeply of the warm fresh air, permeated with hundreds of scents. His eye was keener than ever before. When they passed through village hamlets and saw the wattled huts of the miserable peasantry, the dead stupefied faces of the people, the misery and dirt in which they lived even among these vineyards and fields, the lightness of his heart passed away and he was filled with a vague and guilty distress. He had seen these sights for many years. His father's own estates were similar. Yet, never had they affected him as they did now. He perceived that Paul was gazing also, and that his face was both angry and sad. It appeared to him that Paul lingered unnecessarily long in these localities, as if he silently wished Arsène to see all that was to be seen.

At noon, they arrived at Chantilly. They left the town, plunged again into the bright countryside. At length they arrived at Paul's estates.

Immediately Arsène perceived the contrast between these estates and those others with which he was familiar. Here he saw no wattled huts, but only good small stone houses set in private and blazing gardens. The cobbled paths were clean and bare, free of rubbish. There was a fountain in a small open square, where men and horses could refresh themselves in the heat of the sun. Pigeons flew over the statue of a little naked boy who poured the water from a large stone jug into the granite basin. Children and geese mingled in happy confusion together around the fountain, and the children caught handfuls of the water and threw it into the air and watched its sparkling with cries of pleasure.

Women stood in doorways with infants in their arms. At the sight of Paul, they curtsied, following him with faces bright with adoration. Children trailed respectfully in their rear, as they might trail a saint. When he threw them handfuls of coppers, and small silver pieces, they scrambled about, screaming, like agitated pigeons. There was no condescension in his gestures or his smiles, no contempt. He regarded them all with a beaming face of affection and understanding.

Arsène saw that they were approaching a tavern with the sign of a goat swinging in the breeze against the vivid blue sky. A groom came to take their horses, and when the man saw Paul, he bowed almost to the ground and gazed at his lord with passionate devotion. They entered the cool dimness of the little tavern and perceived a huge bald giant squatting behind his counter. He did not rise nor come forward when they entered, but his great fleshy underlip thrust itself outwards as if in profound contempt, and his great gleaming forehead wrinkled above his protruding brown eyes.

"Ah, Crequy," said Paul, affectionately.

The man did not move or answer. Arsène was filled with rage at this insolence, and regarded the man with incredulous anger. As if feeling that eye upon him, the giant turned his enormous face in Arsène's direction, and he stared, without a change of expression.

Paul sat down at a little bare table where the Duc de Tremblant and his companions had sat only a few hours ago. He knew that they were sleeping upstairs, but he gave no sign. The giant detached himself, muttering, from his stool, and with a slow and heavy step, approached the table. Then, only, for an instant, his eyes met Paul's and some secret message passed between them. Paul smiled, appeared satisfied, and in a voice of much good nature ordered wine.

The two friends drank. Paul considered. Should he tell Arsène that his beloved Duc was sleeping upstairs, and allow a few moments' happy reunion and exchange of greetings? It would give Arsène pleasure, but it would also weary the Duc who must resume his journey at nightfall, for he dared travel only by night. Paul decided to say nothing.

After serving a very good wine, the giant retired behind his counter again and resumed his ferocious scowling. His brow wrinkled with his contemptuous thoughts as he stared at Paul. But now Arsène perceived that in spite of all this frightful grimacing, there was some reflective sadness and softness in those piglike brown eyes, which Crequy tried to conceal with even more formidable scowlings and pursing of lips.

The cleanness and quiet of the little tavern raised Arsène's spirits even higher. Through the open door he could see the distant fountain and the children, and could hear the laughing

313

voices of women. For some strange reason content filled him, as if all his friends were gathered together under this one roof.

"All are well, Crequy?" asked Paul, turning again to the host, who was still staring at him as if hypnotized.

The man stirred, threw up an enormous hand scornfully, and grunted. At last he spoke, in a rumbling and rusty voice:

"Feed canaille, pamper them, regard them as human beings, and they will be well enough," he said, with deliberate contempt.

Paul took no offense. He appeared accustomed to this insolence. He laughed. He turned to Arsène.

"Here is no lover of his species, mine host," he said. "Crequy would prefer I appoint him steward and whip the poor wretches to the fields. It is an old quarrel between us."

The man struck the counter so violently, yet so ponderously, with his great fist, that all the pewter cups danced upon it. His eyes blazed with malevolence and rage.

He shouted: "An old quarrel, yes, Monsieur le Comte! And a just one! Do I not know these swine! Do I not know how they will repay Monsieur? Ah, have I not warned, until I am sick of the warning? But it is not enough for Monsieur. He will not listen, will not hearken to the voice of understanding!"

He snorted. He deliberately leaned across the counter and spat. Arsène stared, actually popeyed at this display of incredible insolence and freedom. He could not believe that Paul would endure it. But Paul only threw back his head and laughed. The laughter infuriated Crequy, who came from behind his counter, breathing flame. He pointed an enormous and shaking finger at Paul.

"I have warned Monsieur! I shall warn no more!"

Arsène was dumfounded. A red anger against Paul filled him. Had he no pride? Why did he not draw his sword and murder this vile wretch instantly? He could not believe his ears; he could not believe that the great lord of these estates might permit, even for an instant, this astounding insolence and threatening attitude from one who was only a serf, a wretch, a rascal and a vagabond.

But Paul, it seemed, was only amused. He caught the gigantic finger pointing almost in his face, and shook it back and forth with gentle affection, as a child might shake the paw of a growling mastiff, whom it trusts and loves.

And then Arsène saw an astonishing thing. The man no longer shouted or growled. He was silent. He still scowled

314

with more ferocity than ever, and his huge bald forehead was frightfully wrinkled. But those starting eyes were filled with tears. He stood there, while Paul slowly and gently shook his finger, and he gazed down at the young Comte with such yearning, such sadness, that Arsène was more amazed than ever. He saw that the immense thick mouth was trembling.

Paul still held that finger, but he spoke to the blinking Arsène:

"Crequy had a tavern in Paris. He came to Chantilly at my own request, and opened this tavern, which was formerly in a filthy condition. I knew him in Paris. I thought that here he would come to a better understanding of his fellows, whom he frankly hates. I shall not always be disappointed!"

The man tore his finger away, and lumbered back to his counter. His great face had resumed its expression of evil and unremitting hatred.

"I have told Monsieur that there is no changing the hearts of men!" he shouted. "I have told him how they will repay him, with betrayal, hatred and wickedness! But now I say no more! But let Monsieur not believe for an instant that I will receive him with grief and consolations when he has discovered that I am right, and he is wrong!"

Now he looked at Arsène, and his brows drew down over his eyes. He addressed the gaping young man, pointing at him:

"If Monsieur is a true friend of the Comte's, let him add his warning to mine, before it is too late! Let him tell Monsieur le Comte in what danger he stands from this unspeakable filth, which flatters him now with its fawning. But some day it will show him its teeth, and that will be the end of Monsieur le Comte! Hah!" and he grinned malignantly. "I await the day!"

In spite of his anger and astonishment, Arsène felt a faint stirring of embarrassed sympathy for the giant, for he had seen those brief tears and the trembling lips. He felt himself, however, in a mad world, where servants address masters with contempt and insolence, and masters only laugh. He still could not believe it.

Paul was laughing again, with unaffected good nature, throwing back his cropped head with its dark curling hair.

"Crequy believes my peasants should cringe and cower before me, that they should never dare look me in the face, that they should be beaten and enslaved, that I should use my power of life and death over them," he said. "In short, he heartily approves of the measures of my colleagues. And this, in spite of the misery, starvation and despair which he saw in Paris. I have long discovered that it is the miserable who most despises the miserable, the man of the gutters who hates the inhabitants of the gutters, the slave who once felt the whip on his own shoulders who advocates the whips on the shoulders of his fellows. Is it not a paradox?"

"Not a paradox!" screamed the giant, striking the counter again, in a transport of fury. Arsène saw that he had no little intelligence of his own. "What can Monsieur le Comte know of these beasts? Only a hog who grunted and snuffed with them can comprehend them. Do I not know them? Have I not slept with them, and wallowed with them? Who can know them better than I?"

Paul shook his head, smiling. "Ah, but you have a good heart, my poor Crequy. I have not lost faith in you, yet. Are not my people happy and content, sharing in the fruits of their labors? Do they not sing, rather than weep, at their work? Is that not enough for you?"

"I know their black hearts!" screamed Crequy.

They went out again into the sunlight. The host did not accompany them to the door. But a young rosy girl eyed them shyly from a doorway in the yard, and Paul beckoned to her with a sweet smile. Blushing, and with bowed head, she curtsied deeply before him. He laid his hand on her head and turned to Arsène.

"This is the bear's little niece," he said. He touched her pink cheek with his finger. "Everything is well with you, my little Roselle?"

Again she curtsied, and gazed timidly at him with adoration. Paul thought, for a brief instant, of the first moment he had seen her, a filthy starveling in her uncle's arm. Now she was all rosiness and sweetness, in her white apron and white cap. He sighed a little. When he and Arsène had mounted their horses again, the girl stared after them. Then she threw her apron over her face and burst into silent tears and sobs.

Crequy saw this from his counter. Groaning under his breath, he heaved his immense bulk from behind the counter, and waddled to the yard. He gathered the girl in his mighty arms with the tenderness of a mother, and pressed her head to his breast.

"Alas," he murmured. "Do not weep, ma cherie. There may come a day when it will be necessary for thee to comfort him."

Paul and Arsène proceeded to the beautiful white château

316

which lay at a distance in a veritable forest of roses and brilliant blooms and great plane trees. Here in the garden was a dark blue pool spanned by a white marble bridge. Silvery swans floated on the surface of the water, which was spangled with jeweled water-lilies. Birds brightened the air with the passage of their wings, and filled its warmth with their songs. Youths and old men worked lovingly in these gardens. When they saw Paul their faces lighted as though by beams of light, and they crept about him as though longing to touch him. He spoke to them with interest and affection, inquiring about the family of each.

Arsène could see the distant emerald fields of grain, the vineyards, the rosy hills and the passionate blue sky of France. Here there was nothing but peace, good will and love. He saw the small white stone houses in the valley, and nestling at the foot of the hills, and even as he breathed of the scents of earth and flower he could hear the sweet chiming of the bells in the little but exquisite chapel in the left near distance. The cross glittered in the sunlight. He saw two black figures near the portals, one old and one fairly young, and they appeared to be in grave conversation. At moments, the old priest lifted his head with a slow and tranquil movement, and surveyed the peasants working in field and vineyard, driving their horses with vigor, and singing in the fresh and shining silence.

Arsène had never visited Paul's estates before. Again, he was filled with guilt. How different was this place to his father's estates, where the peasants dared not lift their heads, where they pursued their endless work with hopeless faces and ragged bodies! It shall be different, he vowed to himself. Ah, how easy it was to live in love and tranquillity, not surrounded by hatred, but knowing only the devotion of humble folk.

The interior of the château was simple but beautiful, and filled with a cool green light. Arsène saw stately rooms, gracefully furnished in the best of austere taste. He saw the gleam of polished silver candelabra, the glisten of mirrored floors, the lustrous folds of rich draperies at the tall windows. Every table, every mantelpiece, every tabouret, held vases of glowing flowers. The same peace and content dwelt here.

"We shall dine," said Paul, as an old lackey divested them of their cloaks and hats. He smiled at Arsène, and it seemed to the latter that a light broke from that gentle countenance. After they had bathed, they entered the dim and lofty dining room. A lady was waiting for them, in a flowing gown of

317

white silk, the bodice caught with a nosegay of crimson roses, which were no more colorful than her lips.

It was Madame duPres, and Arsène was conscious again of his old contemptuous dislike for this beautiful young woman with the large dark eyes and secret expression. After Paul had kissed her hand, she extended it to Arsène, with a lowering of her long black lashes and a swift gleam between them. He bowed over the hand, but did not touch it to his lips. He was extremely annoyed and ill-at-ease. He had thought the woman immured in Paul's small hôtel in Paris, and had not expected to find her here.

He became silent. Paul was dismayed at this, not knowing the cause in his innocence. But Madame duPres was not so naïve. Her mouth, so like a rich dark plum, smiled secretly. She was more gracious than ever to her lover's guest, more affectionate and attentive to Paul. Her smile grew more irrepressible.

If Paul was not entirely enslaved by her, he was kind and thoughtful. She began to complain of the insolence of the servants, which seemed to distress him.

"Ah, they cannot be insolent!" he exclaimed, with an imploring glance at her bewitching face. "But they are free men now, and give their services voluntarily, without compulsion and without fear. The attitude of slaves must necessarily not be that of liberated men, my love."

She tossed her head and pouted. "They answer my calls when it pleases them, Monsieur. When I reprimand them, they reply to me with impudent spirit. Is it possible that they believe I am nothing, and that I must suffer their insults in silence?"

He was increasingly distressed. "My dear Antoinette, you are overly sensitive. Morbleu! It cannot be so bad as you say. But if it will please you, I shall discuss the matter with them."

She gazed at him with open disdain, and bridled her head with so cavalier a manner that Arsène felt his heart burn with hatred for her.

"Monsieur, I truly believe you are afraid of this cattle!" she exclaimed, with a musical laugh, and a light mocking gesture.

Paul bit his lip. He seemed more sorrowful than exasperated. They pursued the rest of the meal in a pained silence. At length Arsène was so sorry for his host that he forced himself to converse inconsequentially, for which Paul appeared touchingly grateful.

Madame pleaded indisposition after the dinner, and retired to her apartments, after casting Arsène a provocative and artful glance full of merriment and seduction. He appraised her in his mind with no complimentary epithets, and left the château with his host. Here their horses awaited them, and they rode down to the fields and the vineyards in a sunlit air that was like spiced and heated wine.

As if the love which Paul felt for all living things had extended itself to the very earth, everything bloomed and flourished here beyond belief. He saw the welcoming affection on the faces of the laborers. They sat under the thick purple shade of a tree and drank water cold and sparkling from a well. Delight shone in Paul's eyes, and a bottomless peace and satisfaction. His short dark curls stirred in the warm breeze. He gazed about him as though at a spectacle forever new and fresh to him.

"I must soon return," said Arsène, reluctantly. "You have not forgotten that tomorrow is my wedding day? Moreover, I am still wounded that you are not to attend, Paul."

"Forgive me," implored Paul, taking his friend's hand, and pleading with all his sweet expression. "You know my love for you, and my devotion. But it is not possible. I must remain here until the Duc returns, as you know. Too, there are many things that need my attention."

Arsène laughed. "You mean that you cannot endure Paris, you hypocrite! Ah, do not distress yourself, mon cher. I forgive you. Remain with your charming lady, and your beloved estates. I am not offended."

They rose and moved slowly down to the chapel near the mouth of the valley. Two old women knelt at their prayers in the twilit gloom, lightened only by the glowing brilliance of the exquisite stained windows, and the ruby light at the altar.

Arsène thought that not even Notre Dame was so incredibly beautiful as this small church. Paul had poured treasures into it, so that it lacked nothing. The cloths on the side altars were of the purest white linen, dripping with delicate lace. The statues were wrought by a master hand, the floor paved with blocks of alternate white and black marble. The pillars that soared to the groined roof were also of the snowiest marble, as was the little pulpit. Immense vases of flowers stood at the altar, filling the cool dim air with an overpowering scent. All the concentrated peace of the countryside seemed gathered here in this white and jeweled loveliness, this sacred silence.

Paul genuflected with stately simplicity, and after a moment's hesitation, Arsène followed his example. They knelt side by side before the altar. Paul lifted his face, and it was exalted and pure with emotion. He prayed simply and openly, clasping his hands. All at once his expression was filled with an austere beauty, like that of an angel's. Arsène was moved to the heart. He could not pray, but all his being was pervaded with reverence, and an adoration for this gentle young man.

When they left the church, Paul did not speak. But he smiled and pressed his friend's hand, as though words were beyond him. At the door, they were met by the old priest and a tall younger priest.

The Abbé Lovelle seized Paul's hands and gazed at him with passionate love.

"Ah, Monsieur!" he exclaimed, "we did not expect you today! What inexpressible pleasure you have bestowed upon us!"

Paul embraced the old man, who appeared to Arsène to possess many of the physical and spiritual attributes of the Abbé Mourion. The old priest's eyes dwelt on Paul's countenance as on that of a worshiped saint. He could not relinquish Paul's hand, but clung to it fervently.

Paul glanced inquiringly at the other priest, who remained discreetly in the background, and seeing this, the old abbé contritely apologized, and turned to the other man.

"This is Père de Pacilli, Monsieur le Comte!" He pressed Paul's hand beseechingly, as the other priest bowed deeply and respectfully. "The bishop believes that I must rest for two months, Monsieur. Nay, he has insisted upon it. So, if I have your permission, I shall visit my niece and nephew in Rouen, and return refreshed."

"How inconsiderate I have been!" ejaculated Paul, placing his arm about the old priest. "I have not thought that you needed refreshment and rest. Call at the château tonight, my dear abbé, and take with you a purse to insure your safe and comfortable journey, and to purchase gifts for your relatives. Ah, how selfish I have been, never thinking of your comfort and your weariness!"

"Monsieur is a saint!" replied the abbé, with tears. "There is only one of whom he never thinks, and that is himself."

He choked in his emotion, but his face was eloquent. Finally, he faltered: "The bishop has sent Père de Pacilli to take my place while I am gone, and after a long conversation with him I am assured that he will care adequately for our little flock until my return."

Paul greeted the younger priest cordially, gazing into his eyes frankly and simply.

But Arsène was uneasy. Where had he seen this long dark countenance before, these black almond-shaped eyes and long delicate skull? Where had he seen that mouth, wide, thin and crafty, and that spade-like pale chin? It was the expression that puzzled him, for he could not remember that, alone of all the other characteristics. For it was meek and subdued, silent and respectful, with lowered glance, and deprecating. The other expression he vaguely remembered was crafty and arrogant, amused and keenly intellectual.

He was consumed with an astonishing dislike. He surveyed the tall spare figure in its black habit, the narrow white hands which were not brown and calloused as were the broad hands of the Abbé Lovelle. Here was a man of aristocratic breeding, a noble, and whatever his blood, it was foreign, unfathomable and too refined for this disguise. And Arsène was certain that all this was a disguise. Surely this priest was not a one to substitute for an old country curé on an obscure estate! The priest turned his profile for a brief instant to Arsène, as he conversed respectfully with Paul in a low and mellifluous voice, and Arsène saw the long and delicate nose, aquiline and large, with the nostrils so thin and chiseled that the red membrane was visible. There was an accent in that voice, aristocratic and assured, with an undertone of hauteur which he could not conceal.

Engrossed in his thoughts, he had not listened to the gracious and amiable conversation between Paul and the priest. So he broke in harshly and abruptly:

"Where have I seen you before, Monsieur le curé? For certes, I have seen you!"

Paul was surprised at his friend's tone and short manner. But the priest gazed at Arsène respectfully, and with every appearance of genuine surprise. But Arsène had seen the wary flicker in those brilliant and narrowed black eyes.

"I do not know where I have had the honor of being in Monsieur's presence before," he answered, bowing. "I was formerly in Chartres, and then in Amiens. I have never been in Paris."

Arsène glowered. He plucked at the ribbons on his doublet, and bit his lips. He felt himself a fool, for Paul and the old abbé were regarding him with bewildered smiles.

"Are you a Jesuit?" he demanded in a still harsher voice.

The priest was apparently amazed. He smiled humbly. "No, Monsieur, I have not that honor. I am only a poor abbé, whose inconsiderable talents have not merited a permanent parish."

The old abbé felt the hostility in Arsène, and he placed his hand on his confrere's arm, and pressed it.

"Père de Pacilli deprecates himself," he said, tenderly, pleading with Arsène and Paul with his faded yet luminous old eyes. "He has many talents, but the bishop has hinted to me that he is of a restless nature, and prefers to travel from diocese to diocese, assisting where he can." Père Pacilli returned this affection with a slow sad smile, and an inclination of his head.

But Arsène was even more suspicious, though for the life of him he could not understand his own suspicions. However, he was increasingly certain that he had glimpsed that secret and subtle countenance in some assemblage in Paris, and that the priest had not been there what he pretended to be now. If this were so, what was he doing here in this quiet and isolated spot, substituting for an old and obscure priest?

He stared penetratingly at de Pacilli. Paul had flushed with discomfort. But Arsène saw no one but this priest, who stood before him humbly, with downcast eyes and a perplexed and meek expression. Arsène was seeing more and more each instant. He saw despite the simple attitude, the man had the bearing of a prince, the voice of an aristocrat, the gestures of a man of noble birth.

And suddenly he was certain that there was a danger in this man, like a concealed poniard. But, to whom? What danger was there in him for Paul, and these quiet estates near the town of Chantilly? Yet, all at once, he knew that the danger was for Paul.

He turned to his friend. "Pardon me if I am too insistent," he said. "But I am positive that I have seen Père de Pacilli before, I cannot remember where."

"Does it matter?" asked Paul, gently, with an apologetic glance at the two priests.

"Disguises always matter," replied Arsène, shortly. "One asks: why does a man disguise himself? What does that disguise portend? And for whom?"

He turned again to the priest. "Monsieur le curé has not deceived me. He is no son of a peasant, or an artisan. He is a man of birth and nobility."

The priest raised his downcast eyes and looked fully at Arsène. He could not conceal the uneasiness in them, nor the subtle amusement, nor the disdain. But he said softly: "Monsieur flatters me. My father had a small tavern in Chartres. But Monsieur is astute. My mother came of the petty nobility."

"Ah, that explains it," said Paul, with his kind smile. He glanced hopefully at his friend. However, Arsène betrayed only new suspicions.

"Why have you come here? What are you to do here, my curé?"

"I do not understand Monsieur," said the priest, assuming a stammer and increased bewilderment. "I was requested by the bishop of this diocese to substitute for the Abbé Lovelle during his absence. As I am of a fragile constitution, it was thought by my superiors that country air and a quiet period might restore my health."

"Who are your superiors?" asked Arsène, menacingly.

But the priest could only gaze at him, as though completely astounded.

Paul was embarrassed. He took his friend's arm. "Your friends," he murmured. "If we do not make haste, you will have no time to greet them."

They walked away together. Arsène's cheek was flushed, and his eye was bright with ire. "I tell you, Paul, I have seen that serpent before! He is not what he seems!"

"And if he is not, what portends?" asked Paul, lightly. "What can he do to me? Within eight weeks, he will have gone."

"A priest is bad enough, but a disguised priest is ominous!" exclaimed Arsène. Now that he was removed from the presence of de Pacilli, all his doubts and suspicions appeared absurd to him.

Paul laughed. He shook his head, but said nothing.

Now they were approaching a snug white stone house set in pretty gardens. The house was larger than those Arsène had previously seen on these estates, and it had an air of dignity. Paul appeared excited. He began to laugh softly to himself, and to glance at Arsène with tender merriment. He opened the gate.

He could not contain himself. "Steward!" he called, eagerly. "My good steward, I have brought a guest to see you!"

A tall gray old man appeared in the open doorway. He held a pen in his hand. He bowed before Paul. But Arsène stared at him in profound amazement.

"François! François Grandjean!" he cried. "It is not possible!"

CHAPTER XXIX

FRANCOIS GRANDJEAN was no less astonished than Arsène, who came leaping towards him with outstretched hands. He took the young man's hands numbly in his own, but continued to gaze at him incredulously.

Arsène was delighted. He embraced the old man with fervor. François' blue eyes became misted; he smiled tremulously. His classical Roman head was like that of a senator receiving the embraces of a son. Then he looked beyond Arsène at Paul, who was smiling, much moved.

Paul inclined his head and said: "When you told me, François, that a certain Monsieur de Richepin had presented you with money to secure land, I held my counsel, for immediately I foresaw the pleasure I would experience in this meeting. You spoke with such affection of Monsieur de Richepin that I suspected some deep attachment between you, and I guessed many other things by the implication of your tones and the expression of your face. Remembering, too, the tale of Monsieur, that he had been succored by one like you in his extremity, I knew, then, the whole story." He came to them, and took a hand of each simply, gazing first at one and then the other with the clear candor of his gentle look.

"My dear friends," he said, with emotion in his voice, "I rejoice in your rejoicing."

A faint flush appeared on Arsène's cheek, and he said with a frankness that did not deceive François, but did deceive Paul: "I went to the Rue du Vieux-Colombier but no one could tell me where you had gone."

François replied gravely: "I left no word among my neighbors, for I doubted that Monsieur would return at all. It was not to be expected."

A wry but indulgent glint appeared in his eye. Arsène was embarrassed and silent, enraged at himself for his childish lie, and more enraged that François had detected it at once. Even François' kind if somewhat sad smile, contained no malice, only increased his irritability; for an instant the aristocrat's old hauteur and contempt for the canaille flashed in his look and revealed itself in his bearing.

They entered the stone house, and were plunged into cool shadow. Here the small windows were thrown open upon the country scene of tall golden grain crested with the first fire of sunset, dark sapphire hills mantled in the green lace of the vineyards, a distant stream of glittering quicksilver, and, to the right, the massed somberness of an ancient forest. The blue of the sky had become fervid, and pulsed like a passionate heart. Plumes of rosy flame floated over the hills. From afar, peasants were singing at their work, and their voices were sweet and gay as they came over the fields. Some one was bringing in the cattle, and their lowing came clearly through the hot and fragrant air. Pigeons, as they fluttered over the roof of the house and the stables, caught dazzling sunshine on their wings. Bees, heavy with loot, hummed drowsily over the flowers in the garden. Now a radiant mist crept over the valley, so that the tops of the forest floated in a shining vapor.

Upon the red stone floor of the cottage were set simple but sturdy pieces of furniture, settles, tables, cabinets and stools. Flowers stood in earthenware pots on every surface.

As he entered the cottage reluctantly, the disdainful and confused anger still in his heart, Arsène felt a beating, strange and shaking, throughout his body. But the cottage was empty. He breathed deeply and cautiously, glancing at a curtained doorway. However, no one emerged.

François, with grave dignity, bid his guests seat themselves, and brought forth a jug of wine and some small excellent cakes. But Paul shook his head, smiling.

"Ah, no, my dear friend," he said. "I shall leave you two together. Too, I think I hear the approach of Mademoiselle, and shall go to meet her and the cattle."

At this, Arsène lifted his head alertly, a thousand questions on his tongue, and a brighter flush upon his cheek. Paul left the cottage, and he and François were alone. Arsène could say nothing. He sipped the wine which François silently presented to him in a pewter cup.

The old man was no longer shabby, and his emaciation was less. He wore the rough sturdy garments of the comfortable peasant, and his wooden clogs clacked on the stone floor. His pallor had disappeared, and his face was ruddy under the whiteness of his hair. But his dignity, his austerity and loftiness of expression had increased, and when Arsène involuntarily met his gaze, he smiled gently, but with simple majesty.

"This surprises you, does it not, Monsieur?" he asked, in a low voice.

Arsène did not answer. He was beginning to feel ashamed.

François, without asking permission, seated himself near the table also. The clear blue sharpness of his eyes fixed themselves on Arsène, and now his face darkened as though some despondency had seized him.

"I came here to Chantilly, with the money you had given me, Monsieur. I not only leased a small portion of land from Monsieur le Comte, but was offered the position as his steward. I accepted, with joy. It was a retreat, and a peace, for me and my granddaughter."

"You need not apologize to me, nor explain!" said Arsène, with irritation.

The old man's brows drew together with some sternness.

"Monsieur does not understand. I am not apologizing."

Arsène compressed his lips. The beating in his body was augmented. He strove for a natural tone, and looked at François with an assumption of benevolence such as one bestows upon a servant whom one wishes to patronize.

"You speak of your granddaughter. Has she not already wed that young poet to whom she was betrothed?"

François shook his head. He replied with reserve: "No. He did not wish to immure himself in this spot."

Arsène forgot everything and inquired: "Mademoiselle is reconciled? She is not inconsolable?"

François' seamed face broke into a deep smile. "Mademoiselle," he replied, "is not only consoled, but relieved. I suspect that she did not hold overmuch affection for young Henri in her heart. She is self-contained, that one, and happy in her new life. The blood of land-owners is in her veins, as well as the blood of sailors."

He refilled Arsène's pewter cup once more. The wine was pure and rich, filled with the breath of the countryside. Arsène watched the old man as though absorbed in his gestures. But this was merely affectation.

He was astonished to discover that his limbs were trembling, that the beating of his heart was causing the ribbons on his doublet to vibrate.

"Monsieur has completely recovered, I perceive," said François, softly.

326

Arsène touched the long scar on his cheek. He looked up, with warm frankness and a curious breathlessness.

"It is true, François, and all thanks must be given to you. Do not believe that I am ungrateful."

François said nothing, but the shadow of a smile lingered on his lips.

Arsène, seized by a nameless restlessness, rose and began to pace the stone floor. François rose also, respectfully, leaning with one gnarled hand upon the bare table.

"You are happy here, François?" asked Arsène, as he paced back and forth before the windows, and glanced through them feverishly. "You are content? This is so different from your habitation in Paris."

"I am content. I am happy," replied the old man, in a deep and shaking voice.

Arsène came back to the table, and flung himself in his chair. Silent question after question formed themselves on his lips, but he did not speak.

"There is no man like Monsieur le Comte," said François, and his tone was passionate with love. He gestured widely. "Monsieur sees here an experiment in humanity. Monsieur is not offended at my freedom in speaking so of Monsieur le Comte?"

"Speak," said Arsène, urgently. "There is much that must be explained to me. In Monsieur le Comte's presence one is only dazzled and confused, as if in the presence of the sun. But you are living on this land as steward. You can tell me many things."

François was silent for a long time. He traced an invisible design upon the table with one of his long and tremulous fingers. But he gazed before him with a far and lofty expression, touched with uncertain sorrow.

"The dreamer's dreams are impossible. But without a dream, and a star, no man can chart his course over the black waters of despair, and through the darkness of an awareness of reality, which is the source of despair—"

"You believe that my friend is a dreamer?" asked Arsène, with an obscure sensation of annoyance and disappointment. "A most impractical dreamer?"

François hesitated. He covered his eyes suddenly with his hand. There was dejection in his attitude.

"I have said, Monsieur, that Monsieur le Comte de Vitry has a dream, and a star."

Now he pressed both hands over his eyes, as if they burned with weariness and pain.

"I should believe that you, of all men, François, would be most worshipful of the Comte!"

François dropped his hands, and now the eyes turned upon Arsène blazed with a blue and fervent light.

"Believe me, Monsieur, that is true! Who can know Monsieur le Comte without adoring him, without an impulse to adoration such as one would feel in the presence of a saint?" He paused, then added with a sad smile: "But saints do not always understand men."

"You speak of an experiment in humanity!" said Arsène, with growing impatience. "I am interested in this experiment. Surely, you, François, cannot dissent from it? My memories of you speak in contradiction."

"It is hard to explain," replied François, in a low and uncertain voice.

He pressed his hands again to his eyes, and began to speak as if to himself:

"This is so new and strange a thing, in France, and perhaps in the world. After so many centuries of an avowed Christianity, it is still so new and strange! Mercy, justice, tenderness, love, compassion and generosity: all these things have we heard from our priests. Yet, except in far instances, they have not appeared. They have appeared here. You have discerned the health and the content of these peasants, and their apparent love for Monsieur le Comte? You have seen their habitations, their fields, their comfort? You have seen freedom in their voices and their manners, dignity in their attitudes? You have seen all these things, Monsieur, and have understood that they have been wrought by Monsieur le Comte?"

"I have seen," said Arsène, with even more impatience.

François dropped his hands and stared at Arsène with mournful steadfastness.

"Then perhaps Monsieur can explain why so many of these formerly miserable peasants love Monsieur le Comte yet so few respect him? And so few honor his words?"

Arsène was aghast.

"I cannot believe this!" Rage rose in his volatile spirit. "I cannot believe this, François!" He sprang to his feet, fiery indignation consuming him. "But, if you have perceived this, why have you not spoken of it to Monsieur le Comte?"

François did not rise. He said, quietly: "I have done so."

"And he replies?"

"That I am mistaken, or he laughs, and asks: 'Who am I, a creature of the same flesh and earth as these, to demand a slavish respect? It is enough for me that they are content, and happy, and fear no hunger or pain.' "

"Ah, he would say that!" exclaimed Arsène, moved, but still enraged.

"I have said to Monsieur le Comte, who has pardoned my insolence, that reforms such as these must come slowly, or spontaneously, like a conflagration, over all the world. Small revolutions are dangerous, grotesque, out of joint. But Monsieur le Comte asked me in return: 'A man must begin somewhere, and he must begin in his own garden.' "

"That is sensible!" said Arsène. But his eyes sharpened eagerly upon François.

The old man shook his head, slowly. "Too much freedom, suddenly, is like too much wine on an unaccustomed stomach. It deranges; it confuses; it enflames; it finally destroys. God moves slowly. Yet men persist in moving with rapid ardor, as if they wished to hasten the ages and compress the whole world in the hollow of their hands. Such is Monsieur le Comte."

He flung out his hands in simple despair. "I do not know! I, too, am confused. I only know that there are many among the peasants, who owe their lives and their peace to Monsieur le Comte, who neither respect, admire, nor love him. I have heard murmurs of ridicule from them—"

"But why?" cried Arsène, in bewilderment.

François shook his head again. "I do not know, Monsieur. I have lived many years, but I still do not comprehend humanity. Once, when I was younger, I believed I had this comprehension. That was my insolence. But this I have discovered: common clay respects the master. If he is a harsh and cruel master, respect is darkened with hatred and memories of suffering. If he is a kind master, then he is regarded with contempt. Who can explain the dark deviousness of the evil human heart? Who can explain why a man kisses the hand that flays him, and bites the hand that succors him?"

He paused, and continued in sinking tones: "Once the Abbé Mourion said to me: 'Believe it, François, that evil is more powerful than good, that it is a distinct entity, pure and unsullied, like a devouring flame, that the hearts of men are steeped in natural wickedness.' I laughed, then, believing this to be the cant of priests. But now I know it is no cant. It is a reality, like a holocaust, like a storm, like a tidal wave."

Strangely sickened at all this, Arsène ran his hands with a gesture of distraction through his hair. His eyes implored the old man.

"You do not know what you are saying to me, François! You do not know what poison you are instilling in my heart, what confusion you have placed there, what wretchedness! What is a man to believe? What must he strive to do?"

François pondered on this, while his long brown face grew more despondent.

"There is a belief, Monsieur, that kindness and gentleness indicate weakness of temperament, and timidity. The human beast, so lately civilized, bears in itself all the ferocity and the temperament of its primitive beasthood. It still cannot believe that kindness and gentleness are the strength of the noble and steadfast heart, and not the softness of the coward." He hesitated, pleaded for understanding and forgiveness with his eyes: "I have suggested to Monsieur le Comte that reserve and dignity in a master do not prohibit kindness and mercy, compassion and justice. But he only laughs at me gently. He goes among his people with brotherly freedom and simplicity, implying to them in every word and gesture, that they are his equals and, in some instances, probably better than himself. There is the fatality, I truly believe. If nothing else, his own great heart is superior to the hearts of the mean and the humble. He cannot condescend, and condescension, mixed with benevolence, is the only wise procedure for a man who would reform the world." He continued after another hesitation: "Always, there must be dignity in the ways of the superior man, and the knowledge that a confessed equality is the first step to anarchy."

"You believe that Monsieur le Comte is too Christlike, François?"

François lifted his eyes and looked sternly at the young man.

"I do not wish to see him crucified, Monsieur."

There was a profound silence in the cottage, while Arsène, his brows drawn together, bit his lip and pondered confusedly on the old man's words. He heard him speak again:

"The man who has always gently despised mankind is often consistently merciful, in contradiction to the man who has idealized it and is later disillusioned. Hell has no greater hatred, then, than his."

"You believe, my friend, that Monsieur le Comte will some day hate those who have been succored by him?" asked Arsène, incredulously.

François shook his head. "No, there will never be any hatred in that lofty heart. But he may be destroyed."

"That is fantastic!"

François was silent. Then, again, he flung out his hands.

"Monsieur! I do not know! Who can know?" He added, after a moment: "When one strains after a star, one can never hope to reach it. The best one can do is to chart one's course by it. I may be foully wrong. Monsieur le Comte may be right. In my insolence, I have said too much. Without faith, a man is nothing. My faith is weak and confused. The faith of Monsieur le Comte is as lofty as heaven."

He bowed his head, and murmured: "It may take many centuries before men realize that those who love and raise them are neither fools nor cowards, nor deserving of a contemptuous martyrdom."

Arsène pondered all this in the gravest disquiet, feeling that the high and precarious ground he had lately attained was being rocked in earthquakes.

François, seeing this, exclaimed: "Monsieur! Even if one is not convinced of the value of humanity, that does not free him from the necessity for compassion and justice. In truth, the obligation is greater."

They heard the thudding of cattle entering the stables, and their somber sustained lowing. Through the small opened windows Arsène saw that Cecile and Paul were shepherding the beasts with dexterity. The strange heavy pulsing of his body began again. He saw the girl once more, slender and strong in her blue petticoat over which her black peasant skirt was drawn high and knotted behind. He saw her wooden clogs, her tight black bodice, and the folded white of her kerchief and the snowy stiffness of the cap that hid her shining light brown hair. Her bare arms were nut brown and strong as they wielded the stave. She walked swiftly and with vigor. Arsène saw that her face as no longer pale and pinched. It had become carved and full of noble strength, shining with a steadfast and serene peace. As the declining sunlight struck them, her eyes glittered blue and vivacious, full of reserved laughter. He saw the white nape of her young neck, across which fluttered a ribbon of her bright hair, blowing in the early evening breeze.

He could hardly believe this vigorous young peasant woman was the pale girl in her shift who had kissed him one dank midnight by the light of a guttering taper. As she drove in the last of the cattle, he saw her glance, laughing, over her shoulder at Paul, who was having difficulty with an obstinate calf. The glance was tender and indulgent. Paul, having succeeded in his task, came to her and took her hand, laughing gayly.

331

Arsène perceived the expression of the young Comte's face, tender and concentrated, for all its laughter. Now a shyness had come over the girl, and a blush, like a shadow, ran over her cheeks and brow. But she did not withdraw her hand.

All at once, a veritable dark fury swept over Arsène, accompanied by a sensation of intense sickness and desolation. He had seen what there was to be seen in Paul's gentle eyes, in the expression of his smiling lips. The two stood there in the blue shadow of the stables, the roof above them red in the last sunlight, the heaving bodies of the cattle behind them, the wind blowing the girl's skirt and that one gleaming lock of hair. Beyond the stables lay the green countryside and the violet hills and the fervid sky.

It is not possible! thought Arsène, biting his lip. And then he added to himself, tasting gall and vitriol on his tongue: Is he contemplating replacing Madame duPres with this buxom peasant girl?

It was quite customary for a lord to take whom he might choose from among the comely wenches on his estates. Arsène was not guiltless of this himself, to fill an idle summer hour during the ennui of a country excursion. Even to himself, at this moment, therefore, he could not understand the black and furious pain that assailed his heart, the smoking tides of hatred that boiled up from his soul. He found something obscene and fatuous in Paul's frank and innocent smiles, in the girl's blushes and laughter. The hand that pressed weightily on the stone window ledge trembled. It seemed that his breath came with painful gasps. He is no better than another! he said to himself.

Lost in the paroxysms of his obscure hatred and rage, he was not aware that the two were now entering the cottage, and when he heard the girl's voice close at hand he started as though awakened from some dark and smothering nightmare. She was standing near him, regarding him gravely and soberly, though the laughter still gleamed in her blue eyes. Meeting his glance, bemused and opaque, she curtsied to the stone floor, then rose with dignity and awaited what he might say. And now the laughter had gone.

"Well, Mademoiselle, it seems that we meet again," he stammered, lamely. Now he saw nothing else but those blue eyes fixed so gravely and quietly upon his. Was it only the dimness in this cottage that appeared to drain the girl's cheeks of color, make sharper her nostrils and paler and more severe her firm lips? Was it only the uncertain light that impelled her brow to appear like cold marble, the outlines of her head and throat to be cut cleanly out of rigid stone?

He did not know that both François and Paul, caught in some nameless fascination and warning apprehension, were staring at him and Cecile as at some astonishing spectacle which perplexed and vaguely alarmed them.

Arsène's senses whirled in confusion and chaos; the aching pain in his heart extended so that it seemed to him that all the universe throbbed with it. Now he understood the bottomless depression that had frequently seized him lately, to which he had refused to give a name, the sense of futility and weariness that had assailed him in the most light and frivolous hour.

"You are happy here, Mademoiselle?" he asked, faintly, drawing a pace nearer to her.

"I am very happy, thanks to Monsieur, and to God," she replied, quietly. Now her straight glance seemed to be accusing him coldly and with obscure scorn.

The soft ringing of the Angelus blew gently over the shining fields and the gilded hills, and the little windows were frames enclosing a scene of bright and supernal peace. The radiant mist that enfolded the distant forest crept over the whole countryside. There was a murmur of dove wings, and a flash of light as they fluttered over the red roofs of the stables.

In his sudden effort to escape her eyes, Arsène turned to Paul. The young Comte was very pale, and his expression was like one who has been struck fully in the face, by a murderous fist. He was leaning against the back of a settle, and one of his hands hung heavily over it. In his new sharpness of vision, there was something poignant and eloquent in the heavy hanging of that hand to Arsène. It was more expressive than a thousand words, a thousand cries. That gentle and compassionate hand, which had never struck a rude blow or dealt harshly with a single soul! All at once Arsène was flooded with renewed love for his friend, and a great suffering.

I shall go, he thought, and aroused himself from the numbness that weighted him down. What was this humble peasant maiden to him, who was to be married the next day to the daughter of the illustrious house of de Tremblant? Clarisse's bewitching face rose before him. And then that face seemed to him to be as brittle as a painted and jeweled mask of plaster, and he was sickened by his revulsion from it.

He was aware of the sweet scent that came from Cecile to him, the scent of pasture and field and sun. Again, his senses

333

were assailed by an emotion of profound loss and desolation, and his lips became cold as ice.

"I must go at once," he faltered, in the profound silence that engulfed the cottage. He attempted to smile. "Tomorrow is my wedding day."

"Monsieur is to be felicitated, then?" said the girl, in her clear strong voice. The blueness of her eyes appeared to enlarge and blaze, but her face was calm and composed.

"I thank you, Mademoiselle," he said. The girl was silent.

He forced himself to turn to François. "I thank you for your hospitality, François," he said, striving for a note of grand patronage. "It is a great pleasure to me to see your improved situation, for I have not forgotten that I owe you much gratitude."

François did not answer. The classic Roman head was imbued with some mysterious and haughty dignity, some sad and indignant melancholy.

The girl curtsied again, and this time did not rise. Her head fell on her breast. She remained on the floor in an attitude of frozen stillness, her hands fallen to her sides.

Arsène found himself alone with Paul under the darkening skies and the celestial peace of the country. He walked rapidly to the spot where they had tethered their horses. They did not speak. Arsène mounted his horse, but Paul did not do so, as yet. He stood at his friend's side and gazed up at him with bottomless pain and sadness.

"It is not possible to withdraw from this wedding, with honor?" he asked.

"It is not possible," replied Arsène, in a stifled voice. Later, he wondered why he had not been amazed at Paul's words.

Paul mounted his horse in silence. They proceeded towards the château. Arsène refused Paul's urgent invitation to enter for a last refreshment. His one desire now, was to be alone with his desolation and suffering. He would have begone instantly, but became aware that for some time Paul had been mutely extending his hand to him. Pain was alive and glowing in the young Comte's eyes.

Arsène took that hand. Suddenly, he felt such a rush of emotion and torment that he could hardly restrain himself from weeping. He rode away, furiously, and Paul watched him until he had disappeared in a copse of darkening trees.

Arsène continued his headlong flight for some moments, then, his heart thundering so that he could hardly breathe, he drew in his horse in the thick purple shadow of a tree. He dismounted, flung the reins over the neck of his panting horse. He let himself fall prone on the thick wet grass, dimly aware of the somber evening chorus of frogs in a distant pond. The horse wandered away a few paces to graze. The light steadily decreased, and now fireflies pierced the thickening gloom with points of shifting brilliance. The wind blew steadily from some far hay-field, and its breath was sweet and pure. Again, the bells were ringing softly in the church steeple, their voices shaking the perfumed air. The fragile curve of the moon rose with silent and stately movement from the west, which fumed faintly with gold and crimson light. The calm and fulfilled dark peace of the night spread itself over all the world like soundless water tinted mauve and blue. The trunks of the trees about the reclining young man became black, and motionless, like clusters of giant spectators.

He heard the shrilling of awakened crickets, mingling with the deepening melody of the frogs. The grass was warm and fresh against his aching cheek.

He did not think. He only endured. But as his heart pressed against the earth he felt that the poisoned pain of it seeped healingly away into the boundless heart of the mother of all things. He felt strength rising in him, and a strange numbed comfort.

"Peace!" whispered the trees, bending their heads in the evening wind. "Peace!" sang the crickets, and the frogs.

It was not for some time until he became aware that he was hearing hushed and cautious voices deeper in the forest. It was a woman's voice, low and tinkling, and a man's, heavier, sonorous and reflective. Lovers, he thought, and once more the pang divided him.

Now he heard their words, and at the clearer sound of the woman's voice, he lifted his head alertly, for it was familiar. Its tone was impatient and pettish.

"I do not know how long he will remain this time, Monseigneur. I have told you this!"

"But it is necessary, Madame, most urgently necessary, that he leave at once. I cannot impress this upon you too profoundly. Is it possible he will remain over a week?"

"It is possible that he will remain for years!" Her voice rose on a vicious and hating pitch.

"Then, you must urge him, on some excuse, to return with you to Paris, Madame." The man's tone was cold and virulent, full of authority.

Arsène sat up, now, the better to listen. But they did not speak again. Hearing the rustle of footsteps, he flattened himself to the ground. Two forms emerged from the gloom. By turning his head cautiously, Arsène saw that these forms were those of Madame duPres and the mysterious priest, Père de Pacilli. They floated away together, their voices low. Now they were lost to sight.

Arsène rose. What he had heard was insignificant, but he was certain that something ominous and dangerous had been in those words. Engrossed now, in his conjectures, he pursued his journey to Paris, feeling his own personal sufferings diminished in the awakening of his apprehensions for his friend.

A few days later a messenger brought a letter from Arsène to Paul. Paul was in his fields and vineyards. Madame duPres received the message. Some prescience warned that cunning woman that in this message was a threat to herself. How she knew this, she could not explain. Perhaps the heightened intuitiveness of those engaged in nefarious and treacherous undertakings impelled her to her suspicions.

The missive was sealed with Arsène's signet, but Madame duPres was dexterous. After prolonged and delicate effort, the letter was opened. It was brief and appeared to have been written in haste, and as if the writer was in the grip of some restraining emotion.

"When you receive this, my dear friend, I shall have gone on my wedding journey. I thank you excessively for the gifts which you had conveyed to Madame and myself, and I trust, upon our return, that you will not wait an instant to visit us.

"I am compelled to write you this letter because of a disturbing event to which I was an unsuspected witness. But first of all, I must recall to your mind my first suspicions of that saturnine priest, de Pacilli, which embarrassed you upon my open expression of them. I could not believe he is innocuous. Now I am certain that he is even worse than I suspected, and more unfathomable.

"Upon leaving you after my visit to Chantilly, I paused to rest at the edge of the forest, in the twilight. I heard voices, which I later recognized as those of Madame duPres and that ominous priest. He was urging her to plead with you to return with her to Paris. He appeared most insistent and commanding, and no longer spoke in that mawkish voice of feigned meekness which he directed at you and me. They spoke no more that I could hear, but all my sensibilities were aroused to an appreciation of some danger to you. I cannot urge you too strongly to insist that his bishop replace him immediately. Even in this event, be warned: there is some evil afoot against you.

"I conclude this hasty missive with the hope that we shall meet again within a brief period. Because of the disturbed conditions now prevailing throughout Europe, our wedding journey is not to be extensive. I intend to spend some time on the estates of my mother in Gascony. Please accept my expressions of love and devotion, eternally."

Cold terror seized the woman upon reading this message. She hastened at once to Monseigneur Antoine de Pacilli, who was now all alone in the humble house of the old priest. He read the letter in chill black silence. Then he fixed his glittering almond eyes upon her with malignant resolution.

"We must work with all speed," he said.

And then he tore the letter to shreds with precise and vicious and delicate movements, as though it were a living thing with nerves and muscles to endure agony.

CHAPTER XXX

MADAME DE RICHEPIN wrote to her mother, Madame de Tremblant from Gascony:

"Dearest Mama, it is with deep anxiety that I beseech you to inform me if there has been news of my dear uncle, who disappeared so alarmingly before my wedding. You know how I love him, not only because he is my godfather, but for the excessive kindness he has always bestowed upon you, dear Mama, and me and my sisters. Arsène joins me in this message, as he appears sorely apprehensive about Uncle Raoul, though he persists in his refusal to divulge to me wherein lies his anxiety.

"I received your missive upon our arrival in Gascony, in which you affectionately inquire as to my health and my state of happiness. My health is excellent, as always. But I cannot speak so about my happiness.

"I was innocently under the impression that Arsène and I were to have a gay visit to his father's estates, where our neighbors would be amiable and agreeable people. It is true we visited these estates, where for a brief time, we were regaled with banquets and balls and hunting and riding. The toilettes of the ladies, however, left much to be desired, and it was evident that few of them had been to Paris recently. My gowns were greatly admired and envied, and there is quite a flurry among the local dressmakers to copy them for the ladies. All this was very agreeable. The gentlemen, though tinged with the manners of the country, were excessively gallant, and Arsène pretended to be green with jealousy. But this was only pretense, for, to my distress, he appeared preoccupied, and had the alarming habit of disappearing for long intervals to inspect the estates. Alas, this was not all. He engaged our hosts in long arguments about which I still remain in ignorance, though I believe they referred to what he called the 'condition' of the peasants about the estates. The gentle-

338

men, though always polite, appeared astounded and bewildered, and, in some cases, very angry. I feared at every instant that he would be challenged. In truth, some of the replies of the gentlemen would hardly have been borne by a man of spirit. And Arsène was always ready with a challenge and a sword, and formerly appeared to take umbrage at the mildest remark. However, he appeared to be unaware of hardly veiled insults, and only sank deeper in his preoccupation.

"This, too, might have been endurable. I am a bride, chosen by him, and always he appeared to regard me with the deepest interest and affection. Yet, while we remained on his father's estates, he would disappear unaccountably for hours at a time, and even overnight. My natural pique and tears passed unnoticed by him. He developed a permanent frown, and an irascible tongue. I might have been an old and wearisome wife of many years.

"He scarcely danced with me at balls, though he was once most expert at ballets and minuets. I frequently discovered him hidden in distant corners engaging hosts and other gentlemen in long obscure arguments, during which much heat was displayed, and voices were not amiable.

"I do not know what has happened to my husband, though I perceived a change in him since the dolorous time when he disappeared for a long interval in Paris, and I was made ill in consequence. He has become progressively paler and thinner, and I hardly recognize his expressions, so grim are they, so concentrated and alarming. He was always quarrelsome, but it was a light-hearted quarrelsomeness. Now, it is actually gloomy and somber, and quite menacing.

"Very abruptly, and without allowing me the opportunity to take polite leave of our former gracious hosts and hostesses, he bore me away to Gascony. Dearest Mama, do you know Gascony? I assure you it is the vilest and most desolate spot.

"The heat is intolerable. The country is a glare of white light. The faces of the people are strange to me, and their dialect grates upon my sensitive ear. Nevertheless, I was prepared to be amiable to them. But from the first they were suspicious of me. The ladies covertly sneered at my toilettes. They dress coarsely and simply, and appeared amused at my manners and my gowns. There is much hunting, but of a gross sort. Moreover, the château here is most uncomfortable, and the servants boorish. The few dinners to which we were invited were conspicuous for their disgusting dishes and strong bad wine. It is very dull and tedious. I believed that Arsène, who had always adored gaiety and dancing and the light life of Paris, would soon become weary of this abominable and ugly place. But, alas, here his peculiar new preoccupations only manifested themselves more threateningly.

"Dearest Mama, I am conscious that this is a most astonishing and mournful letter for one who is only lately a bride to pen to her mother. But I am so distraught that the words pour from my heart. Is it not possible for you to write an urgent missive to me implying that it is most necessary for us to return to Paris at once? I close with the most passionate expressions of devotion for you and my dearest sisters. Clarisse."

After completing this affecting letter, Madame de Richepin wiped her great blue eyes daintily with her lace kerchief, and folded the paper with angry and exaggerated gestures which testified to her distrait condition of mind. She glanced about her austerely furnished boudoir with a shudder, recalling, with grief, the luxurious chamber of her maidenhood. The open swinging window framed the bronzed bare fields simmering under a sun that was almost as brazen in a sky white and molten with summer heat. Young Madame de Richepin regarded all this, flinging out her soft and delicate hands in a gesture of complete and bewildered despair. It was only the wildest dream! She had married the gayest and most dashing gallant in Paris, a gentleman famous for his quickness and dexterity with the sword, a dancer par excellence, a wit that could convulse a marble statue, a graceful maker of legs far surpassing any other courtier. And by some sinister legerdemain, he had become a somber and irascible man, preoccupied with strange and incomprehensible thoughts, a scowler and a curser, given to mysterious humors and to comings and goings without preamble or excuse. This was surely not her Arsène! The tears flowed again, and she wiped them away carefully, so as not to deface or blotch the soft rose of her cheek. She shook out the shimmering white silk of her morning robe, and patted the profuse flaxen curls that fell over her brow and ears and long white neck. She caught a glimpse of her beauty in an opposite mirror, and the vision both saddened and soothed her.

Ah! if she had followed her heart and married her real love! But he was a Huguenot, and though dear Uncle Raoul was one, also, Mama had not countenanced such a match, which would jeopardize her position at court. How tedious were these men with their passionate adherence to one religion or another! All that was important was love, balls, dazzling toilettes, gaiety, laughter, and flirtatious intrigues. In such a delightful world, why did gentlemen conspire to destroy all delight for some vague doctrine or another? Was it not wiser, and simpler, merely to be gay and happy?

She felt a consuming anger and indignation at all this folly, which had left her, a young and blooming bride, quite alone in a bare chamber in an inexecrable country château, while her bridegroom tramped about his burned and barren acres with lowering brow, quarrelling fiercely with that honest Monsieur Dariot, and raising his voice in abominable language every hour of the day. Who would have believed that Arsène would have been transformed into a fanatic, especially into that brand of fanaticism that was totally incomprehensible to the female mind?

She was overcome with her longing for her beloved Paris, for her coarse mother and pretty sisters, for the Bois and the balls, the laughter and the candlelight shining on rouged faces and jeweled toilettes, for polished floors and beautiful restrained gardens and fountains sparkling under the moon. She listened to the bitter burning silence of the Gascon countryside, broken only by the strident shrieking of hot insects. The blinding light quickened when the fiery wind blew, a parching wind like the dazzle of sun on brass, increasing that light.

The she heard Arsène's footsteps on the stone corridor, and a moment later he flung open the door and entered the chamber. His boots, once so polished and elegant, were crusted with red clay. His britches and his doublet had been donned hastily, and they, too, were gritty with dust. His dark hair was disordered; there were smudges on his cheeks and chin. His sharp black brows were drawn together over his glittering dark eyes, and his mouth was gloomy and heavy. Worse than all this, to young Clarisse, was the startled and sullen glance he gave her, as though her presence was unexpected and none too welcome.

She rose automatically at his entry, and her knee bent politely. He was not wearing his sword, but he was carrying a whip, which he stared at for a moment before hurling it pettishly into a distant corner. She did not love him, but he had the power to render her faint and palpitating. She hoped that he perceived how bewitching she was this morning. But there was no lightening of his countenance. He looked at the small commode upon which she had been writing, and asked quickly:

"You have written the letter, then?"

"But certainly, Monsieur," she answered, tossing her head so that the silken curls flowed backward upon her shoulders in a delicious flurry.

He stared at her blindly for a long moment or two. Then he said: "I cannot rest until I know he has returned safely."

He flung himself, sprawling, on the wooden settle near the bare window and gazed over his simmering land.

"That Dariot!" he muttered. "A piggish imbecile! What would Paul do with such a creature? He has a skin as thick as leather, and a mind closed to all argument! How is one to endure him?"

"I have always considered that gentleman to be completely incomprehensible and impossible!" exclaimed Clarisse, eagerly.

Arsène stared at her blankly. "When have you entered into conversation with him, Madame?"

She was perplexed. "But many times, Arsène. However, he was not a frequent visitor at the Hôtel de Tremblant. But it is well known that he is tiresome and dull, a poor wit and a worse dancer."

Arsène stared again, then laughed abruptly. "Ah, we talk, at cross purposes. I was speaking of Dariot, not the Comte de Vitry." Now he was both annoyed and impatient. "The Comte is my friend, and worth all the rest of Paris, Madame. It is your loss that you do not realize this."

She tossed her head once more. "Arsène, you are droll, and tedious. The Comte inspires nothing but ennui in the discerning. His conversation excites yawns. He is gauche and careless, and a discredit to his father. So says my mother—"

"Your mother, Madame," interrupted Arsène, with a rude and kindled violence, "is a fool. Like the rest of Paris. But what else is to be expected from a city of jackdaws and screeching peacocks?"

Clarisse was so stricken at this, that she burst into tears so sincere, so bewildered and wretched, that she did nothing to halt them, and forgot entirely about her petal complexion. The crystal drops flowed over her cheeks and ran into the corners of her trembling mouth. There was something so touching in this pretty spectacle, something so helpless, that Arsène, with an impatient mutter, rose and took her in his arms. She sank against his breast and would not be comforted.

"Ah, Monsieur, it were better that we had never married!" she lamented. "It is not hard to discern that I am nothing to you. Why, then, did you seek my hand?"

For one brief instant, Arsène, the headlong and selfish and fiercely impulsive, had a glimmering of the incongruous situation into which he had forced his young bride, and an understanding of her bewilderment and his own heedless confusion. In that instant, he experienced an angry shame and embarrassment in the clarified light of his understanding, and a peculiar humiliation as though he had allowed himself to be trapped in some profound and ridiculous foolishness. He stood apart from himself, stupified. Less than a year ago, dazzled with this young girl's beauty and charm, he had become betrothed to her. She was a part of his frivolous and light-hearted world, a world that might bore him occasionally, but was almost always exciting and delightful, and excessively amusing. More and more stupefied in retrospect, he recalled that until very recently he had never had a serious nor disturbing thought, that his mind had been occupied with adventure and intrigue, with quick flaming hatred and amorous episodes, alike evanescent and trivial. Had he ever had a serious thought? Not since his schooldays. And he remembered little of them, except in swift and disordered flashes. "To philosophize is to learn how to die," Montaigne had said, and though he had quoted that with an air on occasion, he had never understood it. Until now.

It was not Arsène de Richepin who had married Mademoiselle de Tremblant. It was a changeling in his body which had considered that in honor he had been bound to a promise given by a stranger.

Now as the girl wept, there was a terrible anguish in him. He had an impulse to exclaim to her, in pity and self-hatred: "I have wronged you! I am not he to whom you became betrothed!"

But who he was, he did not know. Complete confusion fell over him like a black and swirling cloud. All things upon which he tried to fix his despairing vision lost outline and substance, became gyrating apparitions without meaning or coherence. He only knew that for some time he had been the victim of aching spiritual pain, formless, huge and distracting. He had listened to Paul de Vitry, to the Duc de Tremblant, to the Abbé Mourion, to François Grandjean, and these voices, once tedious and repetitious, like the oft repeated and tiresome phrases of a disliked and stuffy teacher, had suddenly impinged on his inner ear with the impact of impassioned significance and urgent summons roaring into the ear-drum of an only half-awakened man.

He was still half-blind in a new, gigantic world, whose

infinite dimensions filled him with vague terror and affright. He had only been able to follow the voices of his friends, relying, in the darkness, on the touch of their fevered hands.

And into that terrible and enormous world of reality, he had brought this poor pretty child.

Now, in his new capacity to see circumstance through the eye of another, he saw through her eye, beheld her perplexity and terror, her grief and suffering. He saw that she gazed at him, through her tears, as one gazes at a threatening stranger, fearfully trying to trace, in his lineaments, some reassuring familiarity.

He sighed, profoundly, and with weariness. He owed her the debt, at the very least, of attempting to gain her understanding.

He sat down, drawing her upon his knee gently, her arms still clinging about his neck in childish fear and despair. She laid her head upon his shoulder, the fair flaxen curls falling over his breast. And then, like a knife dividing his heart and exposing its inmost nerves and pulsing arteries, a pain convulsed him, a frightful longing and sorrow. He forgot the girl in his arms. He saw another face, another pair of stern blue eyes and a young and quiet mouth restrained in endurance and fortitude. This is she, my heart, my soul, he thought, with the devastating simplicity of appalling and inexorable truth.

He began to speak, almost inaudibly, and so strange and hoarse was his faltering voice that she had to listen to every word, with fear and increasing bewilderment:

"What can I say to you, ma cherie? How can I put my thoughts into comprehensible form? It is not possible, for I do not know myself, of a certainty."

"It is true that you have changed, Arséne," she whimpered, clinging to him.

"I have changed," he repeated, looking down at her with sunken and darkened eyes. "To what have I changed? I do not know. I only know that I am tormented and unhappy. I am stung with gadflies I cannot see. Where are there words to express myself, so you can understand? There are no words, for I do not know, myself."

He gazed beyond her, mournfully. "I only know that there are things I must strive to understand. I am borne away on a current I resist at every moment. I only know that I must understand, that there is nothing else of substance in all the world for me."

She was seized with terror. She took his face in her soft

344

and trembling hands and forced him to look at her. There was a tearing pain in her heart as love was born in her for him for the first time.

"Arsène!" she cried, incoherently, "Arsène, return to me, my darling! Let us leave this horrible place, and go home, to Paris! If we do not, what calamity shall not fall upon us? I know this, in my soul!"

All at once he was stricken with a hungry and despairing passion for Paris, for the Paris of his youth, for the Paris he had known, light-hearted and careless, gay and amusing, full of music and laughter and candlelight and pleasure. He gazed upon that vision with the agony of an exile. And in the frivolous and thoughtless heart of that young girl came a dark and comprehending intuition of loss and desolation. She did not understand what disease had fallen upon Arsène. She only felt its presence. She clutched him as one clutches a beloved sinking into quicksand, in a nightmare.

He gazed at her with dull eyes, empty of all but pain and weariness.

"I cannot return, Madame," he said.

He cried out, pushing her away from him: "Return to your mother! There is no hope for you in me, Clarisse!"

He left her as she wept, and rushed through the bare and echoing château with its sullen and listless servants. He sought out his steward, Dariot, who was gloomily watching the peasants as they cut the hay with long scythes that glittered in the burning sunlight. When Dariot perceived his headlong approach, his long brown face darkened, but he saluted his master with respect enough, and then was silent.

"I have done with arguments, Dariot," said Arsène, abruptly, not shrinking now from the cold gray of his steward's watchful eye. "The wattled huts of my people must be destroyed. Good small cottages of stone must be built. I have said my final word."

Dariot sardonically indicated the meadows of uncut hay, and the distant fields of shimmering wheat.

"Monsieur would have the men abandon the harvests for this salubrious purpose?"

Arsène hesitated. A dark flush rose on his cheek at his servant's tone and calm gesture.

"No," he said, at last, while the nearby peasants, gaped, disbelieving. "Let the harvests be gathered. You know what I have commanded, Dariot. When the accounting is made, the revenue is to be divided, as I have instructed. Then the cottages are to be built by these men. I have said enough. That is all."

Dariot was silent. He gazed sternly before him, flicking his whip against his dusty boots. Then he said, slowly: "You think—these—will be grateful, Monsieur?"

"Of what significance is gratitude?" cried Arsène, impatiently. "We have conversed about this, tediously. I say again: gratitude is nothing to me. I wish to do only what is just."

Dariot was silent again. But he stared at Arsène with a long and thoughtful look, in which there was a gleam of derision. Under that gaze Arséne felt embarrassment, as though caught in a childish and ridiculous act.

He spoke stiffly: "I am delighted that you have reconsidered, Dariot, and that you will remain as my steward."

Dariot bowed ironically. His former respect for his master had gone forever. "Monsieur has made the conditions too tempting," he said.

Arséne gazed over his parched and fuming acres and thought sadly: "It is strange that men can comprehend harshness and cruelty, and adore the hand that wields the whip, but have naught but contempt for justice and mercy."

Perchance there was something in his dark and saddened look which touched the cynical heart of Monsieur Dariot, for the steward's expression changed to one of curious meditation.

"Monsieur," he said, gloomily, "I pray that you will not regret this. I pray that this will bring you no misery."

CHAPTER XXXI

A LONG THIN SHADOW fell across the open doorway of the tavern, and Crequy, glowering and dozing behind his wooden counter, looked up to see the new priest, Père de Pacilli, standing before him, smiling a thin, but sweet and deprecating smile.

Crequy's face became ferocious with his distaste. He sat and blinked at the priest, and the long fleshly underlip became a crimson shelf as it protruded beyond his thick and enormous countenance.

The priest wiped his damp pale brow with a white kerchief, then seated himself, still smiling at a small bare table. "Ah, Monsieur," he murmured, "the day is exceedingly hot. May I request some of your excellent wine, for a refreshment?"

Crequy, for several moments, appeared not to have heard. His face became more lowering. Then, muttering a curse, he produced a dusty bottle and a cup and brought them to the table. These he thumped down with an insolent whack.

"Twenty sous," he growled.

The priest merely arched an eyebrow to indicate his humorous surprise.

"It is customary for the curé to pay for his wine?" he asked, with a pleasant but humble smile.

"I give alms to no man, whether he be priest or other beggar," replied Crequy, with a dangerous and baleful glare in his piggish eye.

The priest laughed lightly, as though Crequy had enunciated a clever jest. He produced his purse, which was a humble one, and slowly counted out twenty sous. "You will drink with me?" he pleaded, in his soft and musical voice, which tantalized even Crequy's dull ear with the hint of a foreign tone.

Crequy contemptuously ignored this amiable request, and

retired behind his counter. From that point he continued to regard the priest balefully.

The priest drank a glass of the wine, and with admirable self-control, he controlled the wry repulsion he felt as its acrid taste stung a tongue accustomed only to the most delicate bouquets and delicious aromas. "Ah, excellent," he murmured, gratefully. Crequy did not deign, even by a flickering of his lashless lid, to acknowledge this compliment.

The priest wiped his lips daintily after one experiment with the wine. For the life of him, he could not continue to drink. He touched the bottle gently, and glanced at Crequy. "Please give the rest of the wine to the next weary wayfarer who ventures to chance by," he said. "It will give me a small pleasure to know that some poor man has been refreshed by it, as I have been."

Crequy heaved himself from behind his counter, deliberately and ponderously approached the table, seized the bottle in his great hand, approached the door, and poured the wine out into the dust of the cobbled yard. He returned to his counter, seated himself, and stared at the priest expressionlessly, like a malignant Buddha.

The priest approved this act heartily; he thought it very sensible, and discerning in Crequy. He said, in a soft sweet tone, melodious with sadness: "I did not poison it, my friend."

Crequy was silent. His enormous red face glowed like a molten moon in the dusky warmth of the tavern.

"You do not like priests?" suggested de Pacilli, with a sigh.

Crequy ignored this. The priest began to feel uneasy at that unwinking and unhuman stare, in which no thought was reflected.

"The good Comte de Vitry has no such aversions," continued de Pacilli.

At the sound of that name, a strange change came over Crequy's countenance.

"The Comte is a fool," he rumbled, and the piglike eyes flashed viciously.

It was not to be expected that the priest be any wiser than the peasants on these estates. He had heard that Crequy had for the Comte only the greatest contempt and animosity, that he loaded the Comte with insults which would have earned him the noose from any less merciful and foolish master. In the flash of the porcine, opaque brown eye, the white of which was yellowish and veined with red, in the outburst of the huge and glistening lip, in the brutish gesture, he read

348

hatred and scorn. Was it possible that this animal was the receptacle for some dangerous knowledge against the Comte?

He lifted his thin white hand in pious protest, and assumed an expression of gentle shock and sorrow on his long and subtle face.

"Ah!" he exclaimed, in a reproachful and amazed voice. "How is it possible that Monsieur can so misunderstand so noble a nature as that of the Comte de Vitry? Does not Monsieur perceive that the Comte's magnanimity is proved by Monsieur's invulnerability to punishment for these rash words?"

A gust of fury agitated Crequy's eyes, so that they rolled like small fuming balls in his great face.

" 'So noble a nature!' " he ejaculated, mimicking the priest's controlled voice virulently. "What does Monsieur le Curé know of nobility?"

The priest sighed, and shook his head. He covered his eyes with one hand, and appeared to fall into a melancholy revery. When he finally removed his hand, nothing could have been more humbly sweet and gentle than his look.

"What do I know of nobility?" he murmured. "Ah, I admit I have seen little of it in this depraved and sorrowful world. But I have seen it in the Comte de Vitry. Who could observe that gracious man and not be touched to the heart, however hard that heart might be?"

Crequy was a shrewd man, and he hated priests, for his own good reasons. However, he had reluctantly come to love Père Lovelle, in his savage and grudging soul. He had been prepared to hate and suspect the new temporary priest, being unshakably convinced that priests and goodness were natural enemies. Now, as he gazed at de Pacilli, an uncertain expression clouded his face, and he chewed his lip in sultry silence.

"Who can observe the good works with which he surrounds himself, and not bow the knee in reverence before the Comte de Vitry?" sighed the priest, and touched his forehead as though about to cross himself. "He is a saint. Ah, what I could tell you, my friend, of the conditions upon other estates, where the lords did not possess Monsieur le Comte's greatness of heart, sweetness of soul, and generosity of temperament!"

"The Comte is a fool!" shouted Crequy, and smote the counter resoundingly with his meaty fist.

The priest smiled subtly to himself. All was proceeding well.

"In what way, my friend?" he asked, mildly.

349

Crequy spat, then sat and rubbed his bristling chin with his fist. He growled: "Monsieur le Comte presumes to know more than God, and be wiser."

The priest puzzled over this remark uncertainly for a few moments. He approved the sentiment, however. He sighed deeply.

"I presume you are jesting?" he said, with a meek smile.

"Jesting!" roared Crequy, pounding the counter again. "Monsieur le Comte does not comprehend that some are born to crawl, some to walk on all fours, but few to stand upright! He would have the serpent and the swine stand on their tails and call themselves men!" He added viciously, his lips twisting and a glisten of saliva appearing on them: "Let Monsieur le Comte beware that the serpent and the swine do not strike him from the vantage point upon which he has placed them!"

The priest was surprised and inordinately pleased at this remark. It convinced him that here was an ally after his own heart. He regarded Crequy with that intent and respectful attention so flattering even to the most disillusioned of men.

"Ah!" he exclaimed, fervently, "it is said that so few are so perspicacious as Monsieur. I would wager that Monsieur is the only man in this village who has arrived at this intelligent conclusion, and that he is the only one who disagrees with Monsieur le Comte de Vitry."

Crequy growled again, like a ferocious bear. But he was not impervious to this flattery. He came heavily from behind his counter, approached the table and sat down near the priest. His eyes bored into those of de Pacilli; his great face was swollen and scarlet with his brutish emotions.

"There are a few who agree with me, in some manner," he said, roughly. "There is Dubonnet, who was the former steward, and an excellent one, though not to Monsieur le Comte's delicate taste, for he had a hard hand for the peasants. There is Brisset, the malcontent, but a man of sensibility. He was overseer in the fields. There is La Farge, who had charge of the vineyards. All these has Monsieur le Comte replaced, and reduced, and why? They were careful managers of his own property! But this Monsieur le Comte could not endure."

"They were stern with the peasants, then?"

Crequy nodded with grim malevolence. "Ah, were they not!" he gloated.

Now his face swelled and darkened even more, and his eyes shot sparks.

"Monsieur le Comte does not know these animals! No

matter what benefits he bestows upon them, their voices become louder and more discontented. Do you know why, Monsieur le Curé? It is impossible to fill the cup of human greed. Give a starving man a crust, and he will ask for two. Give him a sou, and he will return for a pistole. Dress him in a whole garment, and he will hate you if you withhold another. Sit him at your table, and he will be your enemy if you fill your own plate with more than his. Call him your friend, and he will demand to be your master. This is what has come to pass in this village, once so orderly and peaceful. Now, it is full of contention and resentment."

De Pacilli recorded these remarks in the cold Jesuit brain that lay behind that long and narrow skull. He tapped the table thoughtfully with his pale and transparent fingers.

"There are none, who are grateful to Monsieur le Comte de Vitry?" he asked, with a sigh.

Crequy grunted, shifted his mighty weight on the stool.

"A few there are, who profess to adore him. But even these are being contaminated by that noisy rascal, Dumont, who would demand the Comte's last sou at the bottom of his purse and then insist upon examining the Comte's pockets. Should he then discover that the Comte had no further revenue, he would kick him violently. Such is Dumont, who believes he argues learnedly to the other peasants from the ill-advised books which the Comte has distributed to these thieves and murderers. They read, now, these pigs!"

The priest rose. He appeared to be weighted down with his sorrow over human bestiality and ingratitude. He shook his head mournfully.

"Ah, how sad this is, Monsieur! But still, one dares not censure Monsieur le Comte de Vitry for presuming to walk, however, humbly, in the footsteps of Our Lord. If there is an error, it is not his. It lies in those who do not understand." He smiled at Crequy with a humble pleading: "Do not despise me too much, Monsieur, for discovering in Monsieur le Comte virtues beyond our more sinful comprehension."

Crequy grunted again. He watched, in silence, as the priest soundlessly glided across the stone floor, casting a black and writhing shadow in his passage through the sunlight.

He is a priest, thought the tavern-keeper surlily, but with some uncertainty now. And all priests are serpents, with the possible exception of the Abbé Lovelle.

Nevertheless, he experienced a sullen relief. He could not understand, however, why some deep nagging uneasiness remained in his scarred heart.

Monseigneur Antoine de Pacilli pursued his thoughtful way through the cobbled street of the little village, walking without a sound, his long thin body in its black garments swaying a little with the grace of his aristocratic movements.

He had felt some cold affront when the Cardinal had informed him of this new mission to Chantilly. He, the Baron Antoine de Pacilli, to be sent to suborn brutish peasants in an obscure village! For this had he spent long bitter years in the great universities of Italy, Spain and France! However, he was a man of brilliant and subtle intellect. The Cardinal had hardly begun to explain the character of Paul de Vitry and the conditions upon his estates, than he comprehended the larger implications. He had bowed respectfully to the Cardinal.

"One plague spot in a nation may become endemic, nay, even pandemic," he had said.

A gleaming look had appeared on his countenance, which was reflected in those narrow almond eyes. The Cardinal had regarded him with distaste. For he had recognized that look, with humiliation and haughty egotism. It did not please him that another human being might be impelled by the same degree of emotion as himself. He had recognized that look, indeed, and he knew it for hatred of all other men. He, himself, hated mankind, but that was because once he had loved it. He knew that the Baron de Pacilli had never loved it, that he hated it from the beginning, without passion or the virulence which comes from an abscessed and wounded heart. He had hated it because there was in him no virtue, no humanity.

Though the Cardinal was now almost forty-two, there had lingered in him a naïveté which he sometimes acknowledged with frustrated and angry mortification. He still had not been able to rid himself of a secret belief that men were what the world had made them, that the world was a catalyst operating on the varied chemicals which composed each man in differing degrees. How, then, had the world affected the Baron de Pacilli? By discreet and kind questioning, de Pacilli had divulged to him that always he had lived a quiet and scholarly life, especially dedicated to Greek and Latin and the classics, that he was much attached to the colder and more abstract of the philosophies, that he was a mathematician of astounding ability. Discreet probing by the Cardinal elicitated the fact that the baron's father had died in his childhood, that his mother was a gracious aristocrat with great pride in her son. Nothing but the most amiable relationships had ever existed between them. He had had no frustrations, no struggles, no humiliations, no disillusions.

Where, then, had he acquired that pure distilled malignance, that hatred? For the Cardinal knew that it was the very essence of poison and refined cruelty. For a long time the Cardinal, who still licked old and aching wounds in secret, refused to believe that some men are born like this, silent, brilliant-eyed, malignant, learned and endowed with gifts of the mind, without human emotions but appallingly aware of all human storms and darkness, spectators of mankind without cynicism. Had the Baron de Pacilli been cynical, the Cardinal might have felt some mysterious relief. But he was not. He had no bitter comments to make about the viciousness and dangerousness and stupidity of other men. He accepted them, without revulsion or detestation. In that, the Cardinal realized, he was the most dangerous of evil things.

He was a natural enemy of mankind; he was soulless. He had no cause for enmity, either imagined or real. It lived in him like a foul and glittering joy, cold as death and as detached.

The Cardinal did not like puzzles. When he had finally reached the conclusion that this man was a natural evil, he was filled with wonder. Never had he known a man who was naturally evil, as some men are naturally passionate or bellicose, tender or weak.

There is a reason for everything, the Cardinal had protested, before his surrender. But now he knew that the reason for some things in some men was only that they were. Another fatuity of the Cardinal's had been that he believed that only in the measure of a man's own experience and passions could he understand other men. Now he knew he had been humiliatingly mistaken. De Pacilli understood men as even the Cardinal did not understand them, for the Cardinal was often astonished.

In all things he had served the Church faithfully and with that dazzling cold brilliance which distinguished him. Had he become an adherent of any other organization, government or prince, he would have served it as well, not out of loyalty, but only if it contained large possibilities for his evil temperament. And all this, without animosity, without even human ruthlessness, but only with deadly inimical purpose.

In his mission to Chantilly, he was once again fully satisfied, for his temperament was delighted over the possibilities extended to it in this field. He had no enmity or dislike for Paul de Vitry. He hardly remembered his actual features, since Madame duPres had induced Paul to return to Paris with her. Not for a single moment did he remember Paul with hatred or vengefulness or anticipated triumph. Paul was not even a symbol for him of the grave and portentous winds of thought which were now sweeping over a tormented Europe. He cared, in truth, for none of these. His joy lay in the accomplishment of an evil thing only.

At the present time, during isolated midnight hours in the little house of Père Lovelle, he was writing a large book on the Inquisition. It was exceedingly learned, precise, icily and brilliantly written, and full of that lifeless abstract philosophy to which his mind was naturally bent.

He proceeded now, in the early evening, to a large copse of trees that gave shelter from the sun, standing as they were, at the border of the grain fields. Paul had placed long tables here, stools and benches, where the men could gather and refresh themselves with big pitchers of milk or wine, and bread and cheese. Though it was not yet time for vespers, the men were already seated at the tables, or standing in the cool purple shade, wiping sun-dark faces and looking with idle contentment over the glittering golden sea of the grain. They watched the approach of the priest with that wide open look one sees in the eyes of serene cattle. But some were not serene. These, seated about the table, drinking and chewing voraciously, were in the midst of heated argument. Worn books were scattered on the bare board, and one young man in particular kept beating an open book with his fists and haranguing his audience with much fierceness. When he perceived the priest, he thrust the book aside with an angry gesture, and glowered. His companions rose respectfully, but he sat still, impudently, scowling.

This was Jean Dumont, of whom Crequy had spoken with such ferocity and hating contempt. The priest saw everything about the young man, without appearing to do so. Though he had seen him often, though not in the Church, he was familiar with that short and muscular form in white cotton shirt and woolen britches, and the brown corded throat which rose from the broad and twitching shoulders. The square and bellicose face was almost black from the sun, and the large nervous hands were stained with the juices from the grapevines, which he tended. In that face were set glistening and active black eyes, humorless yet fiercely shining, a broad distended nose and full red lips, always pouting, rarely smiling, and broad peasant cheekbones, glistening with sweat. Over his brown brow thin black locks of hair fell in disordered tongues, and longer tongues lay on his neck and reached to his shoulders.

It was a wild, disorderly but intelligent face, that of Jean Dumont, who was the bastard son of a kitchen wench and an unknown father. It betrayed his vehement and quarrelsome temperament, savage and impatient, astute and intolerant. Paul had not needed to educate him. Jean had shown such quickness of mind that Père Lovelle had long ago undertaken his education, and the young peasant had absorbed much disjointed knowledge. From the first, he had been skeptical and ribald, much to the old priest's sorrow. Nothing had gentled him. In that undisciplined mind lived only suspicion, ambition and a strange uncontrolled passion for justice.

Monseigneur de Pacilli greeted the peasants with much sweetness and softness. They were shy of him, and wary, missing their old priest exceedingly. But they had the uncouth politeness of their class, and they made a place for him opposite Jean Dumont at the table. Some one poured a mug of milk for him. Milk was no less distasteful to him than Crequy's wine, but he drank it with every appearance of humble and simple pleasure. As he drank, he was aware that Jean Dumont was watching him with suspicious sullenness and dark open derision, for the young man instinctively hated priests, and despised them. He affected to ignore the priest, and when he glanced at him fleetingly, his eyes gleamed with contempt and elaborate derision.

The priest questioned the men gently about their day's work, and listened to their replies with gentle absorption, indicating his affection for them, and his interest in their hard pursuits. This flattered them. He was no simple Père Lovelle, of peasant stock, himself. Instinctively, they had recognized the aristocrat, for all the deprecating manner, the soft voice, the tender glance. They were not entirely at ease with him, and their voices were boisterous and rough, though uneasily polite. They laughed too much, and poked each other with embarrassed elbows, chuckling hoarsely as they did so. They were like rude schoolboys in the presence of an attentive teacher who appeared to like them, but of whose character they were none too sure. One of them ventured some obscenity, and a score of watchful and furtive eyes fixed themselves on the priest to study his reaction to this. But he merely smiled serenely, as though thoughtfully and indulgently amused.

He spoke of Père Lovelle, and suggested that they were eagerly awaiting his return. They were silent at this, only nodding briefly. But their expressions became surlily fond. He remarked that he, himself, was so enjoying his sojourn in this pleasant and tranquil spot that he would regret leaving. They were pleased at this, and glanced over the fields and behind the trees towards the château with important looks, as though they agreed with the priest that this was an excellent place and they were entirely responsible for it, and that he had reason for his regret. Their manner became somewhat condescending, and less uneasy.

During all this amiable conversation, Jean Dumont had sat, a derisive half smile upon his saturnine but wild countenance. His eyes had narrowed; they glittered watchfully. Sometimes he tried to catch the eyes of his companions, to communicate his ill-tempered opinion of the priest to them, but they were too intent on de Pacilli's soft words and beaming fragile smiles. The priest appeared still unaware of his pointed animosity, and when his eye touched the young man its tranquillity and fondness did not decrease.

"It was not until I came to these lovely estates that I understood completely how some men can bear within themselves nobility and true Christian generosity," said the priest, sighing a little. "How blessed are you all, my children, in possessing a lord such as the Comte de Vitry."

The others murmured awkwardly, but the priest, his watchful ear cocked, heard the contemptuous snort of Jean Dumont, and saw his rude movement on the bench.

"I must correct myself. I have seen another such a spot," continued the priest.

The peasants were vaguely interested. Some of them recalled poignantly the former conditions under which they had dwelt. One of them shyly asked the priest the location of this spot and the name of the lord. But he shook his head.

"It would be presumptuous and insolent of me to tell you this," he said, pleading with them for their indulgence. "It is a long way from this spot, however. One would not have expected such behavior from the lord. I knew him personally. A somewhat brutal and greedy man in all other things. At one time, not so long ago, his people cringed under the lashes of his stewards and his overseers, and knew starvation and misery and disease and suffering. But now, this has recently, and most spectacularly, changed—"

"A priest prevailed upon him," suggested Jean Dumont, speaking for the first time, and in a tone supremely insolent and mocking.

Monseigneur de Pacilli looked at him with bland gentleness,

and with a slightly startled air. Then he smiled, subtly, but not so obscurely that the young peasant's attention was not immediately caught.

"No, that was not the reason," said the priest, in a hesitating voice, as though faintly saddened.

He began to speak of something else, but Jean Dumont struck the table with his pewter mug, and broke in on the gentle conversation.

"What was the reason?" he shouted. "What changed this animal lord of yours, Monsieur le Curé?

Again the priest hesitated. He seemed distressed. He murmured, imploringly: "It would be ungenerous of me, and most impudent, if I ventured an opinion, my dear son. I beg of you not to press me, my son, for it might instil erroneous thoughts about your own dear lord, the Comte de Vitry. And that would be unpardonable. There was no resemblance between Monsieur le Comte and the Marquis—" he stopped abruptly, apparently more distressed than ever.

"I insist!" bellowed Dumont, and furiously caught the eyes of the others, for he was a stronger character than they, and was their leader even when they argued with him, and disagreed with him violently. The others, who were not too interested, finally felt deep curiosity stirring in them, for there was something portentous and peremptory in Dumont's fierce glances at them, as though he commanded them to listen.

The priest sighed and bent his head. He imparted to them all, including Dumont, that he was a somewhat feeble and complaisant character, though harmless.

"My opinions are nothing, less than nothing," murmured the priest. "I am only a humble curé, with no great learning, and no ambitions. How, then, can such as I dare to form conclusions, or presume to question the reasons behind the acts of great and powerful magnates?"

"We forgive you, Monsieur le Curé," said Jean Dumont, with ferocious humor, and still holding his companions' eyes. They laughed uneasily at this rude jest, and scratched their heads. Many were bewildered at this strange conversation.

The priest closed his eyes as though unable to contemplate the iniquity of others without pain. He seemed to become exceedingly weary.

"It has been rumored to me—for who am I that any one of importance should convey direct facts to me?—that our most benevolent and gracious King has, for a long time, contemplated great changes affecting the powerful lords of France. It has been told him that conditions upon the large estates are untenable and most dreadful, and his heart has been moved in consequence."

"Excessively noble!" exclaimed Dumont derisively. "This touches our hearts to hear that his Majesty has turned his attention from tin soldiers and the intrigues of Madame long enough to perceive the general misery of the people!"

At this audacious remark, the others muttered in fear, and half turned away. But the younger men were fascinated, and grinned uneasily. They had heard these remarks often from Dumont, and were much intrigued by his daring. As for the priest, he was not shocked, angered or outraged. He merely regarded the young man with grave and eager earnestness.

"I assure you, my son, that the King is not insensible to the misery of the people. But until recently, he has been impotent. But only a few years ago he began to give much thought and study to this dolorous question. I have it on the highest authority that he has repeatedly discussed this with the Duc de Richelieu and hinted that he would soon bring about vast changes."

He paused a moment, as though hesitatingly choosing his words, and then continued: "The magnates have begun to see the writing on the wall. Again, I have it on the highest authority that at the next meeting of the States General, His Majesty is to demand a revocation of the supreme rights of the magnates, and that their power shall be taken out of their hands and relegated to the Throne."

"The King, then, or rather, his mind and soul and master, Richelieu, is fearful of the power of the princes and the magnates," said Dumont, with an exaggerated wink at his companions. "They would seize it for themselves."

The priest shut his eyes for a moment, once again, and a look of tired sadness passed over his features. "You are wrong, my son," he said, wanly. "I am not a cardinalist, myself," and now he smiled with faint and confidential humor, "and, therefore, am not influenced by his Eminence's plausibility. While it is true that the Duc de Richelieu might harbor motives of personal expediency, this is not the case with His Majesty, who is sincerely distressed over the vast multitudes of the French people who are helpless in the power of their lords. He remembers, only too well, his own oppression under those who wielded limitless power, and now his heart beats in sympathy for his people.

"You must reflect how true this is from the following: The magnates are greatly alarmed, and the most ominous rumors fly among them. Many of them have scrutinized their immense estates, and have callously admitted to themselves that the King has much logic on his side. They have come to the conclusion that they must, to retain their power, change conditions on their estates beyond reproach. In this, they believe that they can avert the seizing of their power by the King."

Jean Dumont did not, now, exclaim impudently and mockingly. He leaned across the table and regarded the priest with breathless and savage interest, lifting his hand to attract the attention of his companions. But he did not speak. His black eyes glittered intensely.

The priest smiled darkly to himself. He gazed at Dumont with limpid eyes and a tender, abashed smile. "And now, my son, you can perceive what has changed that brutal lord of whom I spoke. It is expediency."

The face of Dumont became black and vicious, and his nostrils distended. His fists clenched on the table. He turned to his companions with a triumphant and portentous expression.

De Pacilli then appeared distressed and alarmed. "But, my dear sons, you must not deduce from this that your own dear lord is moved by ulterior motives, and that he, too, hastens to improve your condition in order to avert the seizing of his power by the Throne!"

A horrible and guttural sound rose like a snarl from the throat of Dumont. Now the other peasants were no longer indifferent, vague or bored. They understood all that the priest had said, and their slow minds turned it over and over, as dull tongues turn over and over a strange but pungent morsel. They gazed at each other uneasily; their brows darkened sullenly and unwillingly.

The priest raised his pale and aristocratic hand, and his mouth and eyes were stern. "But, his Majesty is not deceived! That is what I hope, and pray. However, who can be certain of this? Who can be certain that this hypocritical behavior will not have its destined effect, that when the King is reassured and lulled, and has turned to more momentous things, that the lords will not revert to their old horror, seize once more the power of life and death over their peasants, and plunge them into worse slavery?

"I have it on excellent authority that the King had planned to dissolve the great estates, to divide them among the hapless people, lower their disastrous taxes, and guarantee to every man individual dignity, peace, plenty and comfort. This is what the lords fear. Therefore, it does not take the mind of a Jesuit to understand that to avert this disaster, the lords will make an appearance of magnanimity until the King is placated, and his plans forgotten."

Dumont rose from his seat as if propelled by an explosive force. He flung wide his arms and turned to his companions. His face was wild and terrible, and his eyes glittered upon them like the eyes of a madman.

"Have I not whispered this to you, myself, you cattle, you obstinate, dull-witted fools? Have I not told you to examine the tender 'mercy' of Monsieur le Comte, and endeavor to discover for yourselves what nefarious plot lay behind that benign countenance and soft words? Have I not said to you: 'When a great and powerful lord stoops to shine upon the helpless and distressed and the exploited, that he has only greedy evil in his heart?' Have I not said that no man is merciful and benevolent except from evil and avaricious motives? But you have not listened, you fools and cattle! You have fawned on Monsieur le Comte and allowed him to lull your wits, without a single question in your minds!"

He flung up his arms and shook his clenched fists in the air.

The men, startled and dazed and stricken, only gaped at him, blinking. But many drew nearer, with the noiseless and slinking step of aroused tigers.

"You have taken crumbs and watered milk with fatuous adoration!" he shouted. "You have licked the boot that refrained from kicking you, for its own reasons! You have sunken into lathargy and sleep, sung into unconsciousness by sly lullabies! And never have you said to yourselves: 'All this is being done for us because of a lord's fear that much more shall be given us, honorably and with dignity, as free men!' "

He approached them from behind the table, his head bent and thrust forward like the head of an enraged bull. They gaped at him, fascinated, trembling, their dull faces wrinkling and darkening as his eloquence stirred their simple souls.

"The King has planned that the land upon which you work shall belong to you, as free Frenchmen! That your labors shall be for yourselves, that the harvests shall be your own! Have you reflected upon this? No! Only I have perceived, only I have known. And you have laughed at me, cackling in your foolish voices!"

The priest rose soundlessly and slipped away, smiling to himself. No one noticed his departure. Even when he had left the copse of trees and its infuriated haranguer, he could hear Dumont's voice and the dull faint roar of an awakening audience.

CHAPTER XXXII

THE MOON ROSE that night with singular argent beauty, frosting every tree with quivering silver light, liquid and cool. The valleys were lustrous and brilliant in it, like valleys in the moon, itself, and the dark forests shook with the songs of countless nightingales. The roof of the château was plated with silver, the walls trembling with black leafy shadows. The hills ran with silver cataracts, and the flashing of the distant river was like the flashing of thousands of bared swords. From the vineyards rose the sweet strong smell of ripening grapes, and from the east came a wind heavy with fragrances and faint mysterious sounds. Where was the heart that was not shaken by the songs of the nightingales, and the long white shadows of the moon, and the dark murmurous peace?

There was one heart, and that was the heart of Monseigneur Antoine de Pacilli, reading and writing in Père Lovelle's little humble house. He studied and wrote by the light of a taper, never once consciously gazing through the open window at the scene of unearthly loveliness and silence which lay outside. The candlelight carved his pale and sinister countenance and cavernous cheeks, so that it was the sharp hard sketch of an artist done in charcoal. Those narrow almond eyes under winged brows had no human warmth in them, no gentle human meditation.

He was writing his essay on Reason:

"There are those who expound the principle of reason in the realm of spiritual and physical humanity. But history is her own plagiarist, and repeats old truths persistently throughout the ages.

"When one searches the physical universe for Reason, one is confounded. The sentimentalist will discern benevolent reason in rain and wind, snow and sun, the wheeling of the seasons and the tides of the moon. He will ascribe an anthro-

361

pomorphic and anthropocentric pattern in this. But in reality, all these things have transpired for many ages, long before there was a man to appreciate them and ascribe them as agencies to minister to his own egotiscal perfection and importance. When he listens to the singing of a bird in the moonlight, he says to himself: 'Lo, what beauty God hath created for me!' When trees lift themselves in the radiant mist of morning, he cries: 'How lovely that God hath made this for mine eyes!'—But the bird will sing, and the mist will brighten when the last man has removed his afflicting presence from the earth.

"Therefore, in the universe there is no Reason, and where there is no reason, there is no anthropomorphic or anthropocentric pattern of ordered events.

"Man creates Reason for himself, for it is his necessity that there must be order in the universe. Reason, and order, therefore, are artificial concepts, existing only in the imaginations of men. However, these are necessary imaginations. Civilization could not exist, or existing, would be destroyed without them.

"But man's invention of reason does not postulate that he is a creature of reason. He remains elemental, primordial, in all his relations. Reason is his poesy, apart from life. It does not extend into his own reality. Therefore, those who advocate reason in manipulating and guiding mankind, are operating in a fantastic realm, doomed to destruction. One cannot 'appeal to the reason' of men, for it is an element he does not possess as relating to himself.

"Princes, per se, are strong in proportion to the lack of reason with which they rule. Understanding the nature of man, the prince will only command. He will not hesitate to use the lash and the gallows, the torture and the wheel, in enforcing his decrees. Let him be merciful, and his people will argue: 'Why?' Let him use force only, and they will obey. The Church has long known this. It says: 'Thou shalt,' and not 'Wilt thou, for this good and sufficient and intelligent Reason?'

Tomorrow, he reflected, as he laid down his pen and precisely wiped it clean, he would refine, pare down, and sharpen this essay, over and over, until it was a sharp and glittering gem. He opened a drawer in the table, and regarded a heap of manuscript with cold pleasure. His "Essays on Man and the Nature of the Universe" would soon be finished, and ready for the printer. He contemplated dedicating the book to the Cardinal, who would appreciate it; however, many would be the wry mouths he would make over it. For the Cardinal, whose emotions would disagree violently, would feel the reason implicit in the essays. For a moment or two, de Pacilli contemplated the thought that these essays were far superior to anything written by Machiavelli, who hated mankind because he had once loved it.

The priest was always cold, even on the warmest day or night. The core of black ice which was his heart was never touched by rays of sunlight or the effulgence of any moon. He wrapped his cloak about him, drew the hood far over his face, and proceeded on his mission.

His thin black shadow writhed behind him on the cobbled stones of the village street as he made his way in the moonlight to the small home of Guy La Farge, the overseer once in charge of the vineyards, and now only one of the workers in them under the supervision of François Grandjean. Long and careful study had brought to the priest the information that this thin, sullen and silent man, in his forties, had a passion for Cecile. He was a childless widower, and was of a saturnine and sour temperament.

When he answered the priest's timid knock upon the door, he scowled at the sight of his visitor. But he was surlily polite enough to step aside and invite him to enter. He was a thin man, with graying hair, but with a lean and alert countenance, always suspicious and sultry. He sat down on the opposite side of the table, and awaited what the priest would say.

De Pacilli glanced about the bare and shining order of the little room with open pleasure. "Ah, it is a monk's cell!" he murmured. "In cluttered surroundings, one's thoughts are muddled and confused. I see in this chamber the evidence that you are a man of thought, my dear Monsieur La Farge!"

La Farge had this conceit, himself, which was the mother of the contempt and detestation he felt for the simple peasants. He smiled darkly, and gazed with an air of secret but mournful self-knowledge. He gazed into space gloomily, tapping his brown fingers against his lips and chin.

"There are some," continued the priest, with a regretful sigh, "who affect to discover danger in men who think. I cannot ascribe to this sophistry. I see, however, that those who might be endangered by men of thought might set themselves furiously to destroy them, for their own evil ends."

He began to speak of other things. He expressed himself as the humble son of humble cultivators of vineyards. With his knowledge of men, he had discovered in La Farge a passion and dedication to vineyards, warm and spicy under

363

the sun. The former overseer began to listen with great intentness, and his dour countenance appeared much moved. There was a moisture, now, at the corner of his eyes, such as appears in the eyes of those who think suddenly of a lost beloved.

There was no doubt that de Pacilli had a great fund of information about vineyards and wine-making. As a connoisseur of wine, he could give expert opinion as to the various flavors and aromas. Within a few moments, La Farge plunged into a heated discussion with him on this subject. The priest prodded him, but never to the point of animosity. He appeared to be overcome in each instance by the logic of La Farge, and would nod his head finally with reluctant agreement. He would allow a gleam of admiration to show furtively in his eye. As for La Farge, he was now very warm, his dark saturnine countenance glowing and vehement.

"Why do you, my dear Monsieur La Farge, remain in this quiet village, when you would be enormously appreciated by greater lords who would find in your discrimination an invaluable assistant? Or, in Paris, for instance, your delicate talent would bring fortune to you!"

He said this, with such open wonder and candor and appearance of bewilderment, that La Farge felt a well of warm exhilaration leap up in his lonely heart. He bridled. He curled his thin gray mustachios. He simpered a little. Then a darkness clouded his eyes, and he looked away.

The priest noted all this. "Ah," he said, smiling, and shaking an arch finger at the man, "it is I who am wrong! It is loyalty to your good and excellent lord which keeps you in this lovely but isolated spot!"

As this statement appeared to excite the approbation of this amiable and unexpectedly discerning priest, La Farge merely simpered again, bashfully. But his eyelids flickered with a sudden balefulness and hatred.

"It is fortunate," continued the priest, in a tone of fond meditation, "that the good Comte de Vitry is a gentleman of rural and simple habits, with no grand aspirations and no love for the courtier's life. It has been whispered to me—and I hope this is true—that he even has the thought of espousing a daughter of his people, a simple maid of health and comeliness. This is an excellent thought, if true. It will bind him closer to his land and his people."

La Farge uttered a savage and guttural sound. His light blue eyes blazed in the candlelight. He regarded the priest with the infuriated gaze of an elemental animal, and his fists clenched on the table.

The priest affected not to see this demonstration. He contemplated space with a benign and very sweet smile, as if seeing a vision that touched a tender heart. Then suddenly he sighed, dropped his head mournfully, shook it, covered his eyes with his hand. Even La Farge, in his passion, observed this, and cried out: "Pardieu, Monsieur le Curé, what ails you?"

"Nothing," murmured the priest, in a broken voice. "Forgive me. I was only remembering another story, and this was an evil one. I must forget it."

"Tell me!" exclaimed La Farge, rising.

"It has nothing to do with your good lord!" cried the priest, with an affectation of great distress. "I was only remembering a story I had heard on another estate! Please forgive me, my dear Monsieur La Farge.—It was a sordid story. The lord of these estates became enamored of a virtuous and beautiful young maiden, the daughter of the tavern-keeper. The girl believed he intended to marry her, in spite of her low birth, for she was of much gentleness, and had been well educated by the dear nuns. However, he only seduced her, and the poor child drowned herself. You can see, then, why this should sadden me, for I was her god-father."

He continued, in a tone of great passion: "Even this heinous act might have been forgiven, had it not been that the lord had affected to be concerned with his people's welfare, in order to seduce the girl more easily. For she had the tenderest heart, and loved her people. She believed that in yielding to the importunities of her lord she would make permanent the reforms he had begun. But, alas. After her dolorous death, he was more savage than ever in his treatment of his hapless peasants—" He paused. "He was assassinated. None was brought to justice, for the culprits could never be found. The opinion of the judges, however, was that he had richly deserved his fate."

La Farge began to pace up and down the room, muttering to himself, striking his breast with his fists. His face was contorted. Sweat rolled down from his brow. He was a man in agony and uncontrolled rage. The priest smiled to himself. He knew that La Farge, in spite of his past sternness, was highly regarded by the peasants as a man of integrity and truth. Whatever he might say would be hearkened to.

The priest rose. He reached out and took La Farge by

the arm. But the former overseer's eyes were blind and dazzling with madness and fury.

"You are a man of sensibility," said the priest. "And it touches my heart that my sad story had reached to your soul. Praise God, Monsieur, that your own dear lord is not guilty of any such evil plotting."

He continued on his way, this man who could find equal joy in seducing and disordering the wits of the humble as well as the wits of the great.

He approached the cottage of Pietre Dubonnet, the former steward, also a man of integrity, if renowned for his sternness. He was also a prideful man, of limited imagination and much energy. Best of all, he was a devout Catholic, fanatical and passionate. One of his daughters was a nun. He had some education, and some shrewd intelligence.

He lived with his devout and sly wife in the largest of the cottages, which François Grandjean, upon replacing him, had refused to occupy. Conscious of the man's honesty and uprightness, Paul de Vitry had continued to pay him generously, though he was now only a laborer in the fields with the other peasants. The injury to the man's pride was permanent. He smoldered constantly. This, the priest knew.

He was received by Dubonnet and his wife with deep reverence. Their plain dull faces glowed with wonder and pleasure at this visit from the priest in the night. They knelt before him as he blessed them with great solemnity. Then Dubonnet escorted the priest to the table and lit another candle. De Pacilli glanced about the warm clean chamber with real approval, admiring the red tiles of the floor, the dark wooden walls and rafters, the gleaming pewter hanging near the fireplace, the simple but polished settles, chests and commodes. The large crucifix hanging over the bed in the nearby room was a gift from Paul de Vitry to his former overseer, and the priest was surprised at its delicate excellence and workmanship as he observed it from his stool.

Dubonnet brought a dusty bottle of wine and a thin crimson glass to the table, and poured it slowly and carefully. Sighing to himself, acridly, the priest lifted the glass. He was amazed when the wine touched his tongue and pervaded the dry narrow cavity of his mouth. Never had he tasted better bouquet, more wonderful flavor.

"It is from the cellar of Monsieur le Comte, himself," said Dubonnet, with pleasure, observing the amazement and delight of the priest. "Three of these bottles were given me at Christmastide by our lord."

The priest glanced at Madame Dubonnet. She was a short fat woman, shapeless with flesh, but giving an impression of great activity and stolid peasant endurance. Her black hair was neatly combed back from a broad dull face, the color of a plum, and in this ruddy flesh her black eyes were small and restless like the eyes of some sly animal. Astute in his reading of human countenances, the priest knew that Madame Dubonnet was everything that was suspicious and greedy, cruel and rapacious, cunning and stupid, yet possessing a virulent shrewdness. He decided that it was to her that most of his insinuations must be expressed, for in Dubonnet, himself, he had discerned an obstinate integrity, a forthrightness and simplicity which even the cleverest seduction might find hard to overcome.

"I have noted the comforting devoutness of you, Monsieur, and Madame," said the priest, turning a face full of love and sweetness upon them and smiling in a paternal fashion. Then his eyelids drooped, and he appeared to be overcome by melancholy. "How delightful is this devoutness, my dear children! It is like coming upon a brilliant flower in a desert."

Dubonnet flushed, averted his gaze, but said, stubbornly: "This is no desert, Monsieur le Curé."

But Madame had become excited. Her full breast heaved. "Hold your tongue, Pietre, you old fool!" she cried, shrilly. "How dare you speak so insolently to Monsieur le Curé?"

"Oh, forgive me!" exclaimed the priest, with soft distress. "My choice of words, my dear Madame, was unfortunate! It is an extravagance of mine. When I spoke of your piety, and mentioned the desert, I really meant the desert of the world, and not Chantilly——"

Madame was more excited. She approached the priest, bent sideways so she could stare inflexibly into his face. He felt her hot breath, flavored with garlic, upon his cheek, and winced.

"Monsieur le Curé spoke in truth! This place is a desert! There is no piety here. And why? Who knows? Perhaps it is because Monsieur le Comte is too lenient with these rascals. He forces them to do nothing. He suggests. He leads them into Church: Hah! Some will go, others not. He declares that no man should do what he does not desire to do, in the matter of God! I have heard him say this, himself!"

The priest allowed his expression to become grave and somber, and somewhat grief-stricken. He spread out his hands helplessly, and implored them with bewilderment in his eyes:

"But how is the humble child, the simple child, to know

what is just and right, if he goes not into the schoolroom? No child by choice would subject himself to discipline and learning. Madame, I am afraid that you impugn strange things to your dear lord, who is all justice and mercy, and exercises these things among his people—"

Madame flung herself upright, put her hands on her hips, tossed her head and regarded the priest with malevolently glittering eyes:

"So! Monsieur le Curé, in his good simplicity and out of the greatness of his heart believes that our dear lord is all justice? Hark, Pietre, I will finish! Monsieur le Curé perhaps does not know that my husband, here, was removed from his position because he was stern with the peasants, and served Monsieur le Comte with devotion, regarding only his interests? Is that justice, Monsieur le Curé? Is that mercy and understanding, and gratitude? Is it good that my husband is reduced to a worker in the fields? Does Monsieur le Curé know what our dear good lord said in doing this: 'Pietre, it will give you understanding of the sufferings of others, and their labor, if you work with them.' I ask you, Monsieur le Curé, if this is sensible, if it is intelligent, is it just?"

The priest assumed a look of complete astonishment and perplexity. "I did not know," he said, in a trembling voice. "But, I am certain there is some explanation."

Dubonnet's dull but honest countenance had flushed darkly and uneasily. He was enraged with his wife, it was evident. But it was also evident that in some things he agreed with her outburst. His pride made him breathe stormily.

"My husband!" cried Madame Dubonnet, with rising rage, "is a man of some learning. He could read and write long before Monsieur le Comte insisted that this cattle learn their letters and their books, also. He was a man of industry, and knew the people. Selflessly, he devoted himself to the interest of Monsieur le Comte, and enforced order and discipline upon these creatures. Yet, now, he must see them idling under the trees at noonday, their books before them, arguing with passion about matters which do not concern them, but which are treasonable, heretical and dangerous."

She became more and more enraged. "I know whereof I speak, and this dull fool of mine acknowledges it with his blushes and his silence! We have a wayside shrine, as you know, Monsieur le Curé. With these own eyes of mine I saw a group of the peasants returning to their houses from the tavern. They were drunk. One of them discerned the shrine, and shouted: 'Here is the image of the slavery of France!'

And Monsieur le Curé, may God strike me dead this moment if they did not spit, laughing and blaspheming, in the very face of the Holy Mother, Herself!"

The priest appeared horror-stricken, overcome. His eyes started from their hooded sockets. He crossed himself, with every appearance of terror and disbelief. Dubonnet and his wife followed suit, immediately. The air of the cottage ran with dread.

Then the priest spoke in a shaking voice: "You dare not tell me, Madame, that Monsieur le Comte de Vitry encourages this, advises this? You dare not tell me that he is instilling heresy in his people?"

Now Dubonnet found his tongue. He looked wrathfully at his wife, and exclaimed: "We tell you nothing of this, Monsieur le Curé. My good wife is loose with her tongue, out of her resentment and anger. Our lord encourages all pious observances, and has shown only friendliness to priests. He restored our Church, paid for the opening of the abbey, and is a close friend of the abbess. He has wronged me, it is true, and I am heart-broken. But in all justice it must be said that he has done all these things out of goodness of heart, and a belief that he accomplishes the welfare of his people—"

"Such as not punishing the blasphemers who spat in the face of the Holy Mother?" exclaimed Madame Dubonnet, with ferocious humor, and a glance at the priest.

Dubonnet subsided a moment, then muttered: "It is true that Monsieur le Comte declared that it was disrespectful, and childish, and intolerant of the beliefs of others. However, he pointed out that no one in that group was offended, that it was not done in the presence of those whose sensibilities might have been wounded. He has also declared that those blasphemers were free men on his estates, and so long as no one else was offended, and no rights of others injured, they acted in accordance with their convictions."

"I was offended!" shrieked Madame, turning like a tigress upon her husband. "I was there!"

"Then, you were idling, woman," said Dubonnet, sternly. "You were presumed to be in your own garden, attending to your vegetables. Why were you there?"

Madame was nonplussed. She bit her swollen lips. Then she said, lamely and with defiance: "Had I not a right to visit that shrine?"

"There is one in the garden," her husband pointed out.

The priest smiled internally. But none of this appeared on his pale and shaken countenance.

He said, slowly and thoughtfully: "I have observed much, in my days in this glorious and contented spot. I have seen the happy condition of the people, the soundness and comfort of their good houses, the beauty of the little chapel, the health on the faces of the children. All this is very good. All thanks are due to the noble Comte de Vitry. If he has erred in some matters, he has accomplished much that is salubrious. I am afraid, my dear Madame, that personal pique regulates your ill opinion of your lord."

"That is true," said Dubonnet, eagerly, before his enflamed wife could answer.

"One must not harbor evil thoughts, however much provoked them," urged the priest, beaming gently upon the woman.

"You are a saint, like all priests, Monsieur le Curé!" cried Madame. "But you are not fully aware of the wickedness which transpires in this 'glorious and contented' spot of yours! But I know," she added, with a vicious and triumphant look.

The priest sank into a reverie. At intervals he shook his head, as though in distress. "No, no," he muttered once or twice, and his distress appeared to increase. The man and his wife watched him with disturbed intentness.

Finally the priest looked up. He was pale. He smiled at them with the saintliness and the saddest of smiles.

"Be happy, my dear friends, that your beloved lord is not like another I have known. He, too, instituted reforms, such as these good things. But he had an evil motive. His thought was to pervert the souls of his people against Holy Mother Church, to seduce them into Protestantism. By his good works, he secured their confidence and their trust, and when this had been accomplished, he led them into heresy."

Madame snorted with triumphant joy, jerked her head. But Dubonnet regarded the priest with horror and terror, wetting lips suddenly dry. Now all the narrow fanaticism of his inherent nature appeared in his eyes. He clenched his fists. He suddenly trembled.

"Not that!" he whispered, in a voice of dread and anguish. "Oh, not that! It is incredible! It is not to be believed!"

The priest rose. He laid his hand tenderly on the man's shoulder, and gazed down into his stricken eyes.

"Praise God, Monsieur, that such is not the case, apparently, with your own dear master. Do not let suspicion enter your thoughts, even with such evidence as Madame has produced, before you. There are many pious and humble people on these estates. Guard your tongue, for it would be ingratitude to raise dark suspicions in their simple minds."

He went on his way. He looked upon the moon, the white château, the lustrous valleys and the dark forests. A nightingale sang on a branch above him. The moonlight illuminated his face. He smiled in satisfaction.

CHAPTER XXXIII

IT WAS A PALE and lamenting bride whom Arsène brought home to the Hôtel de Vaubon. The Marquis had not been remiss in the decorating of the apartments the bridal couple were to occupy, and Clarisse found temporary alleviation for her distress in the gaiety and exquisite taste of her father-in-law, who adored her. Her boudoir of rose, blue and fairy gold aroused her listless spirits. It looked out, not on the teeming Champs-Elysées, but on a graceful garden, all green grottoes, white marble seats, bending willows, gleaming dark pools floating with jeweled water lilies, and beautiful graceful statues. A staircase led down from her balcony into these gardens, and at its foot were two great Chinese vases filled with the most beautiful flowers and ferns. She glided eagerly from room to room, exclaiming in her sweet flute of a voice, while the haggard Arsène followed, smiling faintly, pleased that his father, who was keeping pace with the delighted girl, had surpassed himself to give her pleasure. He pitied her, sadly, and felt for her the first tenderness of their association, a tenderness such as one feels for a bewildered child whom one has had to offend reluctantly.

As for the Marquis, he bridled excessively, curling one strand of hair over and over on his jeweled index finger, and avidly listening to the girl's exclamations. He delighted himself in the joy of her flushed and pretty face, in the flow of her flaxen curls in the warm Paris breeze, in the panting of her fair and snowy bosom. She was lovingly appreciative. She squeezed his arm, and thanked him lavishly. With his understanding of the feminine taste, he had spared nothing to add beauty and delicacy in all the appointments. He had had a bed made for her, in the shape of a silver swan, and as she flung herself upon it with little cries, he glanced with envy at his son, who was not looking at his bride, but was gazing with lassitude out upon the gardens.

372

The Marquis frowned, pulled his lip, but not so strongly that it marred the rouge upon it. The dog was, certes, not too appreciative of all the effort and thought which his father had expended for his happiness. Then the Marquis was suddenly and selflessly alarmed. For Arsène appeared ill of some obscure but lingering disease, his cheek gray, his lip colorless, his dark eyes ringed with mauve.

He waited until Clarisse had gone to give orders to her women, whose apartments adjoined hers. Then he took Arsène by the arm and forced his son to look at him. He saw grief and passionate anxiety in Arsène's eyes.

"Forgive me," said the young man. "I am not indifferent to all this finery, and this pleasantness, my father. But I have heard, from Madame de Tremblant, that the Duc has not returned. He is four weeks past his time."

The Marquis frowned. He glanced about him cautiously, closed every door. Then, returning to Arsène, he whispered:

"'Past his time?' Where did he go? It is true he has been absent, but we believed he had visited his estates."

Arsène hesitated. He grew even paler. Seeing this, the Marquis cried:

"No! You must not tell me! Have I said I shall not be discommoded by plots and counterplots?"

He was in real terror. He rubbed a dry patch of rouge on his lower lip feverishly. Then he glanced in the mirror, and carefully repaired the damage. But his hand shook. He said, gazing at Arsène in the mirror:

"Are you involved in this?"

Arsène nodded, in silence.

The Marquis swung about. His eyes were alive with fear.

"Is there nothing I can do to induce you to desist? Have you not outgrown foolish adventure, now that you have a bride, and are of some consequence at Court, and looked upon benignly by the Cardinal?"

Arsène said nothing. He fingered a fold of the drapery about Clarisse's bed. He grew more haggard. Then at last he said: "I must go at once to Paul. He may have heard something."

"That de Vitry! Cursed be the day you first knew him! He has brought only fear and anxiety to this house."

He began to pace the room with disordered but dainty steps.

"Is it not enough that Europe is teeming, rife with threats? Who knows but you will soon be called to engage in war?

373

Is there not trouble enough, but you must sally forth to engage it in odd places?"

He paused beside Arsène. He seized him by both arms and forced the young man to give him full attention. His eyes were full of tears, and the paint upon them began to drip blackly upon his seamed and painted cheeks. Arsène felt a pang divide his heart. The Marquis spoke in a trembling voice:

"Look you, my son, I am an old man. I say this now, for the first time. I looked in my mirror this morning, and knew the truth. What is there left for me, in the world? I have suffered in my life; I have endured exile and humiliation, discontent and apprehension. I have never possessed what I have desired, for I have not known what I have desired. My life has been frivolous and superficial. Have I been happy in these latter years? Even I cannot say yes. I have plotted and intrigued, for I have a love for these things. But, now I am old, and it has been profitless. The women I have known sicken me with their memory. I rise more weary than I retired the night before. There is a dry and revolting taste upon my tongue, and it does not come entirely from a bad stomach."

His jeweled hands tightened on Arsène's arms, and his voice shook with wild sincerity:

"No man is responsible for another's futility and sickness of heart. This I know. I have done much folly, and I blame no one but myself. But, does that decrease my weariness, my emptiness? At the last, what brings joy to a man's soul? His good children, and his children's children. He longs only for peace, in his family. I have been guilty of absurdities and foolishness, and now I am tired. Must you punish me, Arsène? Is there no pity for me, in your heart? Why will you not let me look upon you without fear, and rejoice in my grandchildren?"

He paused. His expression became full of vague wonderment. "My grandchildren! I have loathed the thought. But now it brings me a sense of exhilaration, and hope. Arsène, you will not deprive me of my son, and his sons?"

Out of his silly, vain, malicious and effeminate spirit, the old roué spoke with moving passion, with tears, with hands that held and trembled, with eyes that implored humbly. Arsène turned aside his head. He could not look upon his father's tears without anguish. He put his hand over one of the hands that clutched him. Then he lifted it to his lips and kissed it with true and fervent love.

But he spoke resolutely, looking at his father with unfaltering gravity:

"You say there is a sickness in your heart and soul, my father. You declare you do not know its cause. But I do."

The Marquis started. He tried to recoil, but it was Arsène who now held him.

"Would you have me, at your age, know the same sickness? Would you not spare me that, for the sake of your own father?"

The Marquis tore his arms from Arsène's grasp. He retreated, looking at Arsène with wild terror, feeling himself naked. Arsène pursued him, with loving relentlessness.

"I was following behind you, my father, on the path that was leading to the same cul-de-sac, and futility, and self-disgust. Now, I have left you. Do you wish me to return?"

The Marquis put his dark and sparkling hands to his lips. Over them his eyes glittered. Arsène waited.

"They will kill you!" whispered the Marquis, livid. "Do you not know that within a fortnight La Rochelle is to be attacked? Do you not know that they have already assassinated de Buckingham, who, for all his promises to a certain lady, had finally decided to give aid to the Rochellais?"

This was horrifying to Arsène. He forgot everything else. A faint scene began to form before his inner vision, and he saw the red face and beard of de Rohan.

"Who assassinated him?" he whispered, fiercely.

"It is said it was done by order of the Cardinal! After secret news had come that de Buckingham had repudiated his promise, and was preparing his navy to sail to la Rochelle." The Marquis' voice dwindled in fright, at the expression of Arsène's face.

Arsène stared blindly before him, with a strange and evil smile.

"He did not repudiate his promise," he whispered, almost inaudibly. "And so, he was removed, in order that the English might fulfill that promise against his desire."

"What are you saying?" moaned the Marquis.

But Arsène was walking up and down the chamber, striking the palms of his hands together, with fierce exultation.

"It is war, then," he said, unable to control himself. "To the death! It has come. Let it, then, come. We are ready."

The door opened on a light laugh and Clarisse reentered. Color had returned to her pretty face, and vivacity. She ran to the distraught Marquis, stood on tiptoe, and kissed him with ardor. He looked down at her unseeingly, trying to

375

smile. He placed his arm about her, but it was without true feeling.

She looked about her, laughing, for Arsène. But he had disappeared. She exclaimed aloud, pettishly, withdrew from the circle of the Marquis' arm.

"He has disappeared again, that amiable husband of mine!" she exclaimed, bursting into tears. "Oh, my dear Marquis, I believed that when we should return to Paris that strange malaise of his would disappear, and he would again be my husband! But there is nothing but misery for me!"

The Marquis drew her to a seat. His face was gray and drawn under the rouge. He began to question the lamenting girl closely. He listened with grave attention, without malice, without smiles. And as he listened, he grew more despondent, more hopeless.

Arsène made his way with running steps down the gilt and marble steps of the circular staircase. His grandfather's portrait gazed down at him with sudden and thrilling significance. He paused to contemplate it. Now it had a new message for him, urgent and stern. While he gazed into those painted eyes, now so alive and portentous, his lackey, Pierre, following behind, adjusted his cloak.

"Pierre," asked Arsène, suddenly, "do I resemble my grandfather? Look closely, and tell me truly."

Pierre obediently scrutinized the portrait, and then his master. "There is not so much impatience, Monsieur, in this portrait. But, then, he was an older man when this was painted, and impatience dwindles with youth, 'tis said. Then wisdom comes."

Arsène, laughing slightly, proceeded to the bottom of the staircase. He had hardly reached the lower floor when the Comte de Vitry was admitted.

The young Comte was as pale as death. When he saw Arsène, he smiled stiffly and feebly. The two young men embraced. "I received your message that you had returned, and would see me tonight," whispered Paul. "Though I gathered that you hardly believed that I was in Paris." He was breathing like a man heavily burdened. Arsène knew that he had come to announce calamity. He led his friend into the great empty drawing-rooms, where gilt mirrors lining the walls sent back to them countless ghostly replicas. Now that the Court season was in a state of suspension, all the multitude of golden chairs and marble tables and exquisite statuary in scattered niches were shrouded in linen cloths, and the draperies across the tall windows plunged the room into hot twilight.

Arsène began to realize how grave was this occasion, which had sent the dangerously suspect young Comte to him in broad daylight. It would not wait then, this terrible news. Arsène believed that he knew the ill tidings borne by his friend, and he said quickly, in a low voice: "I know, Paul. It is de Buckingham. My father has told me."

Paul's face changed. He shook his head slightly. "That is bad enough, pardieu! I heard it a day or two ago. But, this is worse." And now Arsène perceived that his friend's eyes were rimmed red with weeping.

Before Arsène could speak again, Paul whispered: "There is one with me, near the servants' entrance. Send for him."

Arsène beckoned across the long shining floors to his lackey, who was poised on the threshold. Pierre came immediately, but his anxious peasant's eyes fixed themselves upon Paul, whom he adored, and from whom he was also accustomed to take orders as the leader of Les Blanches.

Paul whispered a word in his ear, and Pierre fled like a bullet in obedience. Then Paul turned to Arsène, and, in spite of his grief, he tried to smile. "Ah, it is excellent to see you once more, mon cher," he said, in his kind and gentle voice, but mechanically, now.

Arsène, dreading the divulgence of the news for some reason, asked: "You received my message, Paul? Then, why are you here?"

Paul was surprised. "What message? I received no message."

Arsène took him by the arm, urgently, his eyes glittering. "Then, it is true, what I suspected! The message was destroyed! And you have returned to Paris!"

Before Paul could reply, Pierre appeared with a tall middle-aged man, wrapped closely in a cloak despite the heat of the day, his dusty hat pulled over his brows. He had a pale lean countenance, its pallor heightened by fierce black mustaches and black restless eyes. He appeared like a man who had ridden long, pursued by furies of despair. Arsène had never seen him before. He stared at him, frowning, even when Paul took his hand and led him aside, urgently. Now the tears ran down Paul's cheeks, and Arsène, unable to contain himself, exclaimed: "It is the Duc—!"

"Hush!" whispered Paul. He glanced at Pierre, and then at the stranger. "It is true. It is the Duc. His body, and the bodies of his companions, have been discovered. In a pit. Near St. Omer."

After a moment of horrible and spinning shock, Arsène cried out, despairingly: "It is impossible! I do not believe it! Who would dare assault the Duc de Tremblant!"

He seized Paul by the shoulders, shook him in agony. "It is not true! If he had been found—so—I should have heard. Madame de Tremblant informed me only this morning that there has been no news!"

"Listen to me," said Paul, quietly, holding his friend with his wet but stern eyes. "It is true. Madame has not yet been informed, for the news has only now reached Paris. But I heard it last night, by special messenger. Moreover, this gentleman has brought me a full account," and he indicated the stranger.

The stranger bowed his head. He clasped his hands together in a paroxysm of anguish.

"The news which has now reached Paris is that the Duc and his companions were attacked by highwaymen. Their pockets and pouches were rifled, to give credence to this rumor. This is the news which will be accepted by every one. But it is not true, Arsène." Paul spoke in a dull and stricken voice.

He turned to the stranger. "Speak, Monsieur," he said.

Arsène, in his torment of sorrow and bewilderment, regarded the stranger fiercely. The latter began to speak, somberly, yet faintly:

"I am Eduard de Brisson, of Sedan, Monsieur. I am second in command of the guards of Monsieur le Duc de Bouillon."

Arsène's dry lips parted, but no sound came from them. He did not feel Paul's restraining hand on his arm.

De Brisson sighed, and passed his hand over his eyes.

"Monsieur le Duc called me to him. I must diverse, Messieurs, at this point, to explain that I frequently accompanied the Duc upon his excursions, such as that which occurred upon the evening when you two gentlemen were present at the home of Monsieur le Duc de Rohan for a certain discussion. So it was that I knew Monsieur le Comte de Vitry, and you, Monsieur de Richepin."

He paused. Arsène advanced upon him. "Proceed!" he cried out, menacingly. But the stranger did not retreat. He regarded the young man with a haggard look.

"Monsieur le Duc trusted me, as he trusted few others. I was his orderly at Pluvenal's Academy. I rode with him on every adventure. I, too, am a Huguenot. I am not playing the

378

traitor because I came to Monsieur le Comte. It is the Duc who has betrayed all of us."

"Fool! Go on!" exclaimed Arsène, his face darkening and becoming contorted.

"Patience," urged Paul.

De Brisson sighed again, from his heart, and he wept openly.

"On a certain recent night, the Duc called me to him and said: 'De Brisson, I have a mission for you. La Rochelle is to be attacked; Sedan is to be attacked. Our hope lies in our English Protestant friends, in the Duc de Buckingham. Messengers have gone to implore his immediate aid, lest we all perish at the hands of the bloody Church of Rome. But in a night or two messengers are to ride to Amiens, and thence to take passage to England. These messengers are from a certain lady—' " he paused, his voice dwindling in his throat. " 'These messengers,' " he resumed, after a moment, " 'carry importunities from this lady to de Buckingham, commanding him not to aid us. He is a weak and amorous man, and will obey her, for she promises everything. They must not reach their destination. If they do, we shall all die, and Protestantism is lost in France forever.' "

He clasped his hands feverishly together, and his eyes were wild. "The Duc spoke to eager ears when he spoke to me, Messieurs. For my father and my mother were killed in La Rochelle, murdered in their helplessness, by the demonic servants of Rome. Comprehend, then, how deep is my hatred, and my desire for vengeance. When the Duc spoke so to me, he knew how willingly I would obey. I gathered a few chosen men about me, and the Duc gave me full instructions on a certain night. He had taken us, himself, to St. Omer, and we were to ride out—"

"No! No! It is madness! I do not believe it!" cried Arsène, turning wildly to his friend. But Paul regarded him with desperate sternness, and indicated by a motion of his head that he must listen to de Brisson, who was weeping without restraint.

"At St. Omer," continued de Brisson, in stifled and trembling tones, "we were joined by a dozen strange men. The Duc indicated they were hired assassins. He urged upon me that we must not speak to these men more than necessary, in order that our identity be hidden. I was to lead them."

Arsène listened like one in a dream to the dread story of waylaying and murdering. De Brisson's voice came to him as from a far and hideous distance. He shuddered, felt himself about to swoon, at the relentless account. Cold paralysis held his body.

"I did not see the faces of the Duc de Tremblant and his companions," said de Brisson, and now his voice was a hoarse whisper. "It was not until they were dead, and one of the assassins kicked him in the face and exclaimed: 'Huguenot swine!' that the first frightful premonition struck me. Then, by the light of the torch which I held close to the face of the Duc, I recognized him."

He could not continue for a moment, then went on almost inaudibly: "None of my friends had heard that exclamation but me. I, too, could hardly believe it, Messieurs. But, after the Duc and his companions had been thrown into a pit and buried, I questioned the man who had so revealingly exclaimed aloud, hoping and praying in my heart that what I had heard had been a delusion of my own ears."

Now he stopped completely, and wrung his hands in agony.

"I seized a moment, Messieurs, to question the speaker, a rough and ferocious adventurer, who had begun to speak to his own companions about the lavish reward they were to receive for this night's evil work. He was free in his answer. He did not know the identity of the Duc de Bouillon, to whom he had been sent by one whom he would not name. However, he believed the Duc to be a Catholic noble, sent on the King's and Cardinal's business. He had been told that the Duc de Tremblant and his companions were Huguenot plotters against the King and the Cardinal, and that it was their wish that they be destroyed."

He implored the two young men with his streaming eyes: "You cannot comprehend, Messieurs, how stricken I was at this news. I dared not tell my friends, lest they fall upon these wicked men and murder them at once. I feared for their lives. I had led them on this frightful adventure, and they had come in stern Huguenot faith. And now they had killed their best friend, and his innocent entourage. My task was hard enough to restrain their indignation and astonishment when they saw the brigands rifle the pockets and pouches of the slain gentlemen."

Arsène groaned, and covered his face with his hands. He hardly felt Paul lead him to a shrouded chair and gently help him to sit down. Anguish, rage, grief and despair tore at his heart. He groaned over and over, not hearing Paul's urgent murmuring in his ear. When he finally looked up, he saw that Paul and he were alone. Paul was kneeling beside him, overcome with compassion and his own sorrow. Arsène allowed his head to drop on his friend's shoulder, and he wept aloud.

At last he cried out in a desperate and changed voice: "We must have vengeance! The Duc must be avenged!"

"Yes," said Paul, in a strange but quiet tone: "He must be avenged. That is what we must consider. But more than that, we must consider what we, ourselves, must do. The hour is late. The enemies are dread and determined. La Rochelle is to be attacked almost immediately. I have already dispatched a messenger to the Duc de Rohan in La Rochelle, acquainting him with these facts, and the death of our dear Duc de Tremblant. Within a few days, we, ourselves, must go to La Rochelle, to aid our friends."

He stood up. His gentle face was grim, and very still. He looked into space and spoke as if to himself:

"I do not understand. I thought in every man was loyalty to one single unselfish thing. I thought that in every man, no matter how base, there lingers some pure decency, some devotion, some integrity. But in the Duc de Bouillon there exists none of these things. If he is one like this, how many more are there in the world?"

He sighed, over and over, as though his heart were breaking with grief.

"If he, a Huguenot, powerful and determined, can be a traitor, who is there to trust? If he can murder a friend, out of inexplicable reasons, how dare a man go forth freely, unsuspecting treachery?"

But Arsène thought all this mere maunderings. His more volatile and fierce nature saw things more clearly and sharply. It was enough for him that the Duc de Tremblant had been done to death by the Duc de Bouillon. That was a simple fact. He cared nothing for obscure reasons. The fact remained, and must be avenged.

He forgot his grief in his lust for vengeance. His thoughts crowded close together, as the tears dried on his cheeks. His face became narrow and cunning with his plottings. He spoke half aloud:

"The Cardinal hates de Bouillon. He loved de Tremblant. Remembering many things, I recall that he must have known that de Tremblant was to take this journey, and wished to save him from it. I recall his importunities, his clinging to de Tremblant on the night of the ball. He will have a double opportunity now, to avenge his friend's death, and destroy de Bouillon. I shall go to him immediately."

Paul had listened to this in silence. He seemed preoccupied with his own mournful thoughts.

Arsène rose. He was imbued with inexorable determination. There was a fierce smile on his lips.

"Wait," said Paul, placing his hand on his friend's arm.

He moved away from Arsène, and put his hands over his face. Arsène began to speak impatiently, imbued as he was with his single-hearted desire for blood and vengeance, but something in his friend's attitude arrested him. When Paul removed his hands, after a long interval, his countenance was sick and stricken, and tragedy was dark in his eyes.

"Am I a fool?" he asked, with sudden and singular passion. "Have I dreamt a dream of the inherent goodness and decency of men? Am I mistaken? Have I lived in roseate mists that have no substance? And if so, how can I endure living? How can I exist, if I finally believe that all men are evil, scoundrels, murderers, traitors, avaricious?" He seized Arsène by the arms and shook him in a kind of tragic hysteria. "Arsène, I tell you I cannot live in such a world of men!"

Alarmed, Arsène sought to find words, but none came to his mind that were not cynical. He could not endure the imploring wildness of his poor friend's expression. He said at last: "Why are you so extreme, Paul? Why cannot you realize that most men are neither good nor evil? That is your tragedy, that you believe in pure goodness."

"You are killing my heart," whispered Paul, through dry white lips, and his eyes were the eyes of the dying, pleading for one last hope.

Mingled with his grief for Paul, and his love, was a thrill of impatience in Arsène. "Paul, you are unwise! At this moment I can assure you that I know nothing that would induce me to betray you. But how can I foresee the future? Before his foul murder of Tremblant, perhaps de Bouillon might have believed that treachery was beyond him. Man must always be the victim of circumstances. But you, my dear visionary, would have men superior to circumstance. You are one of the few who have this inexplicable capacity. Perhaps. But who knows? Reconcile yourself to the modifying aspects of reality—"

"I cannot live," repeated Paul, and passed his hand over his face as if to wipe away webs of agony.

"Jesus did not expect too much of men," urged Arsène, marvelling at the strange inspirations which came to his mind, which he knew contained little subtlety. "Are you not egotistic in expecting more than He demanded?"

382

"Is this new world I see in truth reality?" asked Paul, faintly.

"Let us work within the framework of this reality," replied Arsène, even more urgently, dismayed at the pallor of his friend. "Let us do what we can. Who knows but what we shall help bring into being a greater and a better world? Would you change it overnight, you impatient man?"

"Who can I trust?" said Paul, in dying tones.

"Trust me, to the extent of the frailties of which I am made," said Arsène, almost weeping. "Do not expect too much of me. I shall do what I can. Make allowances for my humanity, and for the humanity of others. I am no angel, but neither, please God, am I a devil. But perhaps the hour will come that I shall be a devil. Remember then, that I have shown the capacities, in the past, of a man."

At this, Paul smiled with pale sadness. Arsène knew that never again would his friend be happy, and what he did henceforth he would do with his mind and not with his heart. Some pure and exalted virtue had left him. Some desperate weariness had come to live with him forever.

At this moment Arsène perceived a figure on the distant threshold. It was Louis, majestic in his black robes, the faint light throwing a nimbus about his bright high head.

CHAPTER XXXIV

BECAUSE OF THE dimness of the light in the shrouded drawing-rooms, and his own somewhat defective sight, Louis de Richepin was momentarily unaware of the identity of Paul de Vitry, and advanced into the room with his stately tread, looking piercingly at his brother.

"I have heard of your return, Arsène," he said, in his cold voice, "and I have come to welcome you and Madame to your home."

But he had now become aware that the figure near his brother was not female in the least, and certainly not Madame de Richepin. Moreover, he now recognized the young Comte, for whom he had the greatest hatred and enmity. They met but rarely in Paris, and on these occasions Louis demonstrated his aversion and his fanatical detestation for his brother's friend without subtlety or the faintest politeness, much to the amusement of spectators. Paul, on his part, betrayed only a faint distress, uneasiness or embarrassment, and usually withdrew gracefully from the proximity of one who was so inimical to him.

Louis paused abruptly in his advance into the room, and there was something ludicrous in his start of recognition, his paleness, the baleful gleam in his eye as it fixed itself upon Paul. The latter might have been a gargoyle, a malefactor, a traitor, a murderer, and would have elicited from Louis no greater manifestation of loathing, rage and hatred.

Arsène, overwhelmed with his own emotions, could only regard his brother with the wildest impatience because of the interruption of his unwelcome presence. He replied hastily and impatiently to Louis' remark, and indicated in every way that he wished his brother to withdraw again. But Louis, breathing harshly through distended nostrils, had no such intention. He ignored Arsène, and seemed aware only of the Comte.

"Is it necessary for you to invade this house on the day of my brother's return to his family, Monsieur?" he asked.

"Go away, and leave us!" exclaimed Arsène, too excited to take offense. "Can you not perceive that we are engaged in matters of importance?"

But Louis ignored him. He said, in a stifled voice: "I must ask you to withdraw at once from my father's house, Monsieur le Comte."

Paul, for all his kindness and gentleness of nature, was not entirely saintly. The quick and haughty blood of his forebears suddenly flamed in his face, and it became stern and forbidding at these enormous insults. His hand, slow to the sword, more accustomed to stretching forth in friendship, reached for the hilt at his thigh, and grasped it.

"Monseigneur," he replied, slowly and quietly, "I have not asked your permission to visit my friend, nor shall I heed your discourtesy nor your vulgar words and manners. Arsène has requested that you withdraw. I pray that you will honor his request, for we have matters of import to discuss."

For all the quietness of his voice, there was an undertone of cold contempt in it, and a sparkle began to grow in his gray eyes.

Arsène, of the mind which could heed only one thing at a time, suddenly became aware of what was transpiring between Paul and Louis, and he became enraged. While he fumbled for words appropriately devastating, Louis, still ignoring him, regarded the Comte with growing fury.

"The matters of import to which you refer, Monsieur le Comte, are matters of treason, disorder, blasphemy and revolt. You have brought nothing but ill, disunity, quarrelsomeness and danger to this house. You have divided a family, placed one of its members in peril, and created unhappiness and uneasiness between a father and his son. I am a priest, but beware that I do not forget my orders and take summary action against you."

Arsène listened to this incredulously, with a stupefied expression upon his face. But Paul smiled grimly, and still grasping the hilt of his sword, replied: "I disdain to answer Monseigneur's foolish accusations, but if Monseigneur prefers to discuss this some morning, at dawn, in a more peremptory fashion, I am at his service."

Finding his voice at last, Arsène shouted at his brother: "Morbleu, you incredible fool! Why have you come here with your babblings and your folly? How dare you intrude upon us? I ask you again, withdraw, lest I force you to do so with my own hands!"

Louis gazed at him with long and malignant bitterness. "Appeals to you have entered deaf ears. You persist in your criminal stupidity. You are proceeding to the ultimate consequences of your acts, which can bring nothing but death and ruin to yourself, and anguish of mind to our father, and suffering to your wife. You have associated yourself with traitors like this, not from any ardent conviction of mind, which might be understood, but from pure adventurousness and a love of confusion and violence." He pointed directly at Paul, and continued to address his brother: "This man has seduced what poor intelligence you possess, and would lead you to only one end: the gallows or the ax. He is imbued with the evil of Satan, and would guide foolish victims like yourself to one foreordained end. I protest his presence in this house, and I have means to make more peremptory my protest. I ask you now to send him from under this roof, and do not mistake my feebleness of intention."

His voice, as he spoke to his brother, was full of the scorn and hatred he felt for him, the jealousy and burning poison of his own nature. In Louis' worst moments, Arsène had never seen such a look upon his face, nor had heard such a voice. For an instant he was daunted, as all sane men must be daunted at the aspect of madness. Then his rage gathered itself together again, and he advanced menacingly upon his brother; for he was stung unbearably at the comments upon his intelligence:

"Unless you apologize to my friend, and withdraw immediately, I shall take it upon myself to rectify your insults at whatever cost!" He forgot his former compassion for Louis, and his new understanding, and obscene words burst from his lips:

"You are filled with poison because you do not possess a woman, because you have fixed your perverted love upon one who rightfully despises you, and has despised you from your birth! You do not like these remarks, Monseigneur? I perceive that you pale, that you start. You did not think I knew your secret? You will now reflect that I do, you venomous priest! Return to your cloister, your master, and your itching, and leave honest men to their thoughts and their affairs. Intrude again, and by the wounds of God, I shall do you a mischief!"

Filled with a sudden sickness and aversion for these savage

remarks, Paul caught Arsène's arm, but Arsène, in his transports of rage, shook him off violently. He stretched out his hands toward his brother's throat, but Louis did not flinch nor recoil. He seemed to grow in stature, in menace and ominousness, for all the blue lines about his lips and his sunken eyes.

"No sword shall soil itself with your polluted blood!" screamed Arsène, beside himself because of the fear for his friend in his heart. "I shall do what is to be done with these hands, as I have longed to do for many years!"

He was truly enraged, but he was also afraid. He well knew that Louis had been one of the most gifted swordsmen at Pluvenal's Academy, and understood instinctively that it is not the vehement or violent man who is the most deadly, but the man of cold and austere temperament, who can proceed and calculate every thrust without passion. Louis had defeated him on more than one occasion during fencing lessons, and in moments of sport, and Arsène did not deceive himself that Louis, for all his calling, had lost his skill. Paul, for all his cleverness with the rapier, had not the brutal heart and callousness necessary for deadly duelling, and, again, Arsène knew that Louis comprehended this, in his icy and vitriolic mind. To fight successfully, Paul would have to be imbued with burning ardor and indignation. He would not have these in any contest with the brother of his friend. For one distressed instant, Arsène contemplated the impotence of the civilized man. Therefore, he sought to turn Louis' adamant intention upon himself.

But Louis smiled at him with deadly scorn, and brushed aside those hands so near to his throat. Now he was truly dangerous, because of his brother's violently indiscreet remarks.

"You fool!" he said, in low and crushing tones. "Do you think for a moment that I would engage you? Do you think for an instant that you would dare lay a finger upon me?"

He seemed to increase even more enormously in stature, to fill the dim and lambent air with lightning and storm. His eyes blazed upon Arsène balefully. Then he turned to Paul de Vitry.

"You perceive what division, what danger, you have brought to this household. I am prepared to engage you whenever you desire, Monsieur le Comte. But I am also prepared to destroy you by more impersonal means. Do not deceive yourself that your activities and treason have been undetected. The trap is drawing closer about you. Your days are numbered."

Paul was silent. He looked at his friend, and there was a great sadness and weariness in his expression.

Truly beside himself now, Arsène seized the hilt of his sword. The weapon was half withdrawn, when Louis caught his wrist easily. His fingers of cold steel crushed Arsène's flesh. He smiled down into his brother's eyes with savage bitterness. Then he flung aside that wrist in a gesture of complete contempt. He lifted his hand and struck Arsène fully in the face, with slow and calculated brutality, as a master strikes an impudent servant or a loutish child.

"You would play Cain with me, you imbecile?" he asked, with that strange and glittering smile.

A darkness, filled with swirling sparks, fell over Arsène's eyes. He heard an immense thunder in his ears. He felt a supporting hand on his arm, which he tried to throw off. It tightened. When the mist cleared, he discovered that he was alone with Paul, who was speaking to him urgently.

But he could not listen. He was overwhelmed with shame. An almost voluptuous paralysis held him. He writhed physically and spiritually. He felt that he was dying. He had hated before, lusted before, but never with this complete and flaming madness. He began to sob, with nauseated dryness and agony.

"Some day, I shall kill him!" he cried aloud. He raised his clenched fist, and regarded Paul with madness. "I swear by all that is holy to me, that I shall kill him!"

Paul was too wise a man to find bravado in these cries. He was horrified. He caught that upraised hand, held it tightly in his own, tried to control Arsène by the quiet fire in his own eyes.

"Arsène, I implore you to control yourself. You have been unbearably insulted, as I have. This man seeks a quarrel with us, to destroy us. Would you play into his hands? Control yourself, I beseech you. We have work to do. Am I to be disappointed again, in my last friend? From no other man but this would I endure the infamy which has been put upon me. But there are matters beyond our mere satisfaction. I beg of you to remember them." His voice broke, sternly, and after a moment he resumed: "Do not betray me. Do not desert me. You have promised me this, and I hold you to your promise."

The madness retreated like a fiery wave from Arsène, but

a cold deadliness replaced it. When Paul released his hand, he let it fall heavily to his side.

"Until I kill him, I shall know no peace," he said, and his voice was as quiet as Paul's. "I swear this. I cannot endure with this shame poisoning me. I have endured a lifetime of insults and provocation from that foul and inhuman priest. Now is the time for retribution. But I shall withhold my hand until I have served you, Paul. That is my word to you."

Paul sighed. He said nothing. He seemed overwhelmed with sudden and tragic thoughts, sick and disintegrating. When Arsène, frightened at the aspect of his friend, put his arm about him, Paul replied to that gesture with a heart-broken smile.

CHAPTER XXXV

THE CARDINAL SAT in his chair near the window of his chamber. His black garments enhanced the yellowness and mortal texture of his delicate and narrow face. He was an unbreathing effigy of wax, his aristocratic head thrown back against the crimson cushions, which were fringed with gold, his frail eyelids, full and large, purple as if bruised, his pale and fragile lips parted in his beard. The golden shadow of the muted sun chased itself vagrantly over his rigid still features, increasing his deathly aspect. His hands lay motionless on the arms of the chair, relaxed, drooping, exquisite in their slender colorless beauty. Never had he appeared so close to the edge of dissolution, so exhausted, so undone, and yet, strangely, never had he appeared so unearthly, so inexorable, so full of power. It was as if the approach of death, closer than ever, only enhanced the terrible potentialities of this man, threw them into more implacable relief against its black shadow. He might be prostrated in the flesh, but his spirit gained in potency by the dwindling of its body. That body, toxic and overwhelmed by its own poisons, might sicken by the weight of its own soul, and the weariness and agony of that soul, but through its disintegrating sheath the mind that had terrorized all of Europe glittered like an immortal sword.

Père Joseph had done speaking, and sat near his friend and beloved master. His russet brows were knitted as he contemplated this stricken and frightful man, and he felt a pang of grief and fear, and that great reverence for the Cardinal which pervaded him in moments of such contemplation.

Now the dim shadow of a voice proceeded from the Cardinal's lips, though he made no movement, and did not open his eyes:

"So, de Buckingham has been done to death so that the conspiracy against France can proceed in all its enormous implications." He mused on this thought, then the strangest and most sinister smile touched his mouth, and Père Joseph knew that he was thinking of the young queen, and her agony at the death of her lover.

For a terrible instant, Père Joseph suspected that the Cardinal had, himself, ordered the death of de Buckingham. It is not possible! whispered the Capuchin to himself, in swimming horror. Yet, how much did he truly know of this basilisk of a man? Was it possible that he had even jeopardized the very existence of France in order to remove a man beloved by a foolish and inane woman whom he, himself, coveted? Could such as the Cardinal forget himself for such a woman?

The Cardinal was speaking again, and the waxen aspect of his countenance deepened:

"But more appalling to me is this news you bring me of the murder of the Duc de Tremblant by—highwaymen. He was my friend. I cannot endure this news."

The Capuchin's unearthly blue eyes bent themselves piercingly on that shut and austere face before him. Were these words hypocrisy? Never had the Cardinal played the hypocrite with him before. Was there irony in these words, a deadly satisfaction and amusement? The expression of the Cardinal had not changed except to become more deathly and prostrated, and now there was a sunken look about him as if he had already died. Not a breath stirred the gray hairs of his thin and pointed beard. The full hooded lids lifted and the Cardinal's eyes were revealed, and they were clouded and moist as though a hemorrhage had occurred behind them, and he was blind to all except the horror of some secret anguish.

"It was unfortunate, but the man was an enemy of France," said the Capuchin, in quiet and steadfast tones. "We must comprehend the hand of God in this. He was dangerous. If, by the muskets and the swords of robbers he has died, then we must see that God uses strange and mysterious instruments."

Now the Cardinal fixed his eyes upon some distant spot and smiled. It was a most dreadful smile. The limp hands on the arms of the chair flexed like frail but cogent claws. He was like a corpse animated by some sudden and evil life.

"I have been thinking," said the Cardinal, in his mist of a voice. "I have been wondering if the death of one such as de Tremblant is not too much to pay for France."

Appalled, the Capuchin listened with turmoil in his heart. He clenched his teeth on his lips. The dreadfulness of the Cardinal's smile deepened; he seemed to be staring at some

391

frightful and leering vision from out of the ghastly limbo of the universe.

"I am tired," said the Cardinal. "I am weary of living. I would that I were dead."

The Capuchin rose abruptly. He began to pace up and down the chamber with disordered steps, running his hands through his thatch of russet hair and through his great russet beard. There was an element of fierce flight and fury in his manner. The Cardinal did not appear to see him.

The Capuchin spoke in a loud but muffled voice: "God has disposed of one of the most formidable enemies of the Church. We must not shrink from that solemn fact. We must remember that the Huguenots hold fortressed cities and embattled towns, that France is in the most awful danger. We must remember that the dangerous hour approaches, and must forget everything else. France is to be split asunder again, to be inundated by a river of civil blood. Everything else must be forgotten, while we gird up our loins."

He paused before the Cardinal, whose fixed smile had something spectral and dead in it, like the grimace of a corpse.

"Can nothing avert the shedding of the blood of Frenchmen?" cried the Capuchin, in real anguish, stretching forth his hands as if he would literally seize the Cardinal's attention. "Is there nothing we can do to weld Frenchmen together, Huguenot and Catholic, and avert this bloody dream which is settling over France? Can we find no external enemy, no scapegoat, real or imagined, to wed together these opposing forces, and bring peace to France?"

The Cardinal did not speak. He still stared into space. The Capuchin spoke with even more passion:

"We cannot say to all Frenchmen: 'England is our enemy. She upholds our French Huguenots in order to divide and destroy France.' It is true, this plot of England's, but the Huguenots will not listen. Above France, they adhere to their heresy. They do not hate their hereditary enemy, who has promised to assist them against other Frenchmen, and the Church. No, it must be a nearer enemy, a faction that is hated by both Huguenot and Catholic. It must be a more helpless enemy, that will cost little if any French blood, but will serve to divert the people from the civil war they contemplate."

"An enemy," whispered the Cardinal, "who by exhausting the blood lust of both Catholic and Huguenot, will bring tranquillity to France, and the peaceful end of Protestantism. Yes, I can see that."

The Capuchin was silent. The Cardinal stirred in his great chair, and smiled again. Now he gazed directly at Père Joseph, and the latter could not read the expression in the Cardinal's eyes.

"But, we have no Moors," said the Cardinal, with a delicate and exhausted gesture of his hand.

The Capuchin approached nearer to his master, and waited.

"It must be an innocent and defenseless enemy," continued the Cardinal, and now he laughed, a faint and most frightful laugh, full of dreariness.

The Capuchin bent over the Cardinal, and whispered: "But we have Jews."

The Cardinal laughed louder this time, throwing back his head as if seized by a convulsion of torment. "A mere handful of Jews! Thousands of Frenchmen exist who have never seen a Jew! Oh, I do not doubt the ingenuity of the Church to dress up a miserable Jew in the most sinister of garbs in order to render impotent a large and dangerous body of Huguenots; even those who have never seen a Jew! But, are there enough Jews to go around, my dear Joseph? Are there enough Jews in France to satisfy every Frenchman's love for murder? Or, would you suggest importing some from the Germanies, from Spain, for this salubrious purpose?"

The Capuchin's face darkened, and the Cardinal's laughter became thin and mad.

After a moment, the Cardinal said in a changed and normal tone: "I have ordered a mole built across the harbor at La Rochelle. The aid of the English is delayed; by the time that bungling monolith of a nation moves to assist her fellow Protestants (and how strange it is that English aid is always reasonably delayed to her allies!) the mole will be completed and no English ship will be able to enter the harbor. I, myself, intend to lead the campaign against the Rochellais, and we shall destroy that nest of pollution forever."

He seemed suddenly invigorated and sat up in his chair with his old aspect of vital power. The Capuchin, relieved, but not yet placated, said: "But what of de Bouillon, and his principality of Sedan? What if he remains intransigent, and decides to assist a Huguenot uprising all over France? There is a most formidable man! Would he, rather than de Tremblant, have been murdered!"

"He awaits an audience at this moment," said the Cardinal. Louis, entering at this moment with his cold and gloomy face, was requested to admit the Duc de Bouillon.

The Duc entered, formal, alert and calm as ever. His eye

393

met the eye of the Cardinal with full but calculating frankness as he bowed before the priest. The Cardinal extended a languid hand, which the Duc kissed with an air of deep respect. His chilly and handsome face was replete with confidence and virility.

"De Buckingham is dead, as you know," said the Cardinal.

"An unfortunate calamity," replied the Duc, assuming an air of regret.

"He will not, then, either betray or assist your fellow Huguenots," remarked the Cardinal. The Duc inclined his head with a thoughtful but noncommittal look.

"I sometimes forget," continued the Cardinal, with a sweet smile. "You were once a Catholic, Monsieur le Duc, were you not? Have you thought of returning to the bosom of the Church, or, do you prefer to hold to your power in Sedan?"

The Duc was alarmed. He distrusted the smile and the piercing and sardonic glance of the Cardinal. He seated himself with grace and formality, and said nothing.

"Your return might be worth considering, Monsieur le Duc," said the Cardinal. "It is true that you would have to submit to the Throne and to the Church. Thus you would relinquish your autocratic hold upon Sedan, where you are king. On the other hand, returning to the Church as you might, and bringing your people with you, might make more secure the power of Sedan. You would have the authority of the Church to uphold you."

The Duc knitted his thin brows, and from under them his remorseless blue eyes regarded the Cardinal unflinchingly. His heart was beating with great rapidity. But he was a brave and courageous man, haughty in his own strength and egotism. At last he smiled.

"You would seduce my religious convictions, Monseigneur?" he asked, softly.

There was a moment's silence, then the Cardinal returned that smile, and shrugged.

"I assume, then, that you prefer the unlimited power you wield over the Sedan, to a limited power granted by the Church, Monsieur. I am not unsympathetic. I admire men of power. Nevertheless, I do not allow them to stand in my way."

Now his smile had gone. It was replaced by a look of much candor and blandness. The Duc's heart began again its rapid beating, and he paled excessively. His eyes were calm but fierce as he stared at the Cardinal.

The Cardinal lifted his hands and let them drop onto the arms of the chair again.

"The Duc de Tremblant, as you have no doubt heard, has been assassinated by—brigands," said the Cardinal, in a voice of mournful regret.

There was a little singing silence in the chamber. The Duc shifted in his chair, but a more formidable and steely look settled upon his countenance. It became secret and inflexible.

"That, too, is extremely unfortunate," said the Duc, in his calm and musical voice. A tenseness pervaded his body. He pressed his hands upon his knees. Père Joseph waited in the background, like a hovering and russet wrath.

The Cardinal regarded space thoughtfully. "I loved de Tremblant. His death leaves a wound in my heart. I would avenge him."

"A man of power who 'stood in Monseigneur's way,'" said the Duc, very softly.

The Cardinal delicately laced his fingers together and studied them.

"Ah, yes," sighed the Cardinal. He appeared to be plunged in thought.

At length he aroused himself. He gazed at de Bouillon with terrible but smiling directness.

"No help can come to the Rochellais," he said.

"Thus," remarked de Bouillon, "the Rochellais can be overcome with a minimum of trouble, and peace will be restored."

"You do not regret their conquest, you, Monsieur, a Huguenot?"

The Duc was silent. He was not certain to what destination this conversation was leading, but he experienced a cold stab of fear. He said, at last: "I am, first of all, a Frenchman. I do not desire civil war at any time."

The Cardinal leaned towards him, his eyes brilliant and full of menace. "You think, perhaps, you can now solicit the complete aid of the English without its being diverted by the Rochellais?"

The Duc, hearing these words, half rose from his chair, grasping the arms. Dizziness seized him. He fell back into the chair, slowly, and said through white lips: "I have said, I do not desire civil war."

There was a bursting pain in his head. Nevertheless, he stared at the Cardinal with hating grimness and threat.

The Cardinal inclined his head, and smiled gently. "It has been rumored that Monsieur le Duc is no true Frenchman, that he has no passion for France, and only for himself. That is a libel, Monsieur?"

"A libel," said the Duc, steadfastly, the grim threat increasing in his eyes.

"Ah," murmured the Cardinal, "that removes a weight from my mind."

The Duc said nothing, but his hand instinctively reached for his sword. The Cardinal saw the gesture. His smile broadened. Now he was excited, thrilling with hatred and power.

"I have a suggestion to make. Monsieur," he said, still in a thoughtful and murmurous voice. "I would suggest that Monsieur leave Paris at once, and return to the Sedan. I would suggest that Monsieur despatch those English emissaries who await him in his château in Sedan, and tell them that he does not desire their aid, that he has decided to lift no hand against France."

The dark and choking blood rushed to de Bouillon's face. He struggled for breath. He was like a man in extremis. He gazed at the Cardinal like a cold python which has been aroused to murderous life. But the Cardinal appeared unaffected by the extraordinary change which had come over the great noble. He appeared only to reflect murmurously.

"I suggest that Monsieur, upon retiring to Sedan, cease his plottings, that he administer his province in peace and obscurity, that he refrain from all acts, open, overt or hidden, against the State. I suggest that he forego his ambitions, which have taken possession of him like a league of devils."

He raised his voice a little: "In other words, I suggest that Monsieur exile himself at once, and have no further dealings with the English."

The Duc sprang to his feet with a black brow and blazing eyes. Distraction was evident in his every movement.

"And," he said, in loud and penetrating tones, "if I do not follow Monseigneur's suggestions—?"

The Cardinal reached out to the table nearby and lifted a sheet of paper. He regarded it with visible pleasure, nodding and murmuring to himself. Finally he looked at de Bouillon blandly.

"I have here a double warrant. One is for the murder of the Duc de Tremblant, much beloved of the people of France, and another is for conspiracy against the State. The latter charge you may defeat, after a long sojourn in the Bastille, which I assure you is an unpleasant place, Monsieur. But the first you cannot defeat."

The Duc was beside himself with fury. He struggled for speech. The congested blood had empurpled his fastidious and haughty countenance. He lifted his hand and pointed it at the Cardinal.

"Monseigneur, this a moment for plain speaking. You consented to the—removal—of de Tremblant. Without your consent, it would not have been done!"

The Cardinal was undisturbed. His bland smile was deadly.

"Monsieur le Duc will need to prove that. He will find that impossible. But I have nearby a witness who can prove my assertion that the Duc was murdered by Monsieur. This witness was brought to me yesterday."

The Duc caught the back of his chair to keep himself from falling.

"There was no witness!" he cried.

"Unfortunately for you, Monsieur, there was. Monsieur has shown himself without cleverness in his seductions, or his selections of assassins. Even assassins are wont to be free with their tongues. Perhaps these assassins talked too openly to one who was devoted to Monsieur."

With a truly frightful countenance, the Duc recalled names to his mind. All at once he started, remembering that for some days he had not seen de Brisson, his most trusted aide. He had not been unduly disturbed, believing that de Brisson was engaging himself with the soubrettes of Paris. But now he recalled the man's changed face, his silences, his pallor. He clenched his fists. "It is not possible," he muttered.

"The witness," said the Cardinal, gently, "is in a safe spot. Do not attempt to discover, and murder him, my dear Duc. He has made a deposition. He has told his story to unimpeachable gentlemen. He has told it to me, in the presence of witnesses, also. The dossier is in a place beyond your reaching. It makes strange reading."

The Duc contemplated the ruin of his ambitions. Cunning narrowed his suffused eyes, as he stared at the Cardinal.

"I have no true conviction that Monsieur will faithfully follow my suggestions. I should regret it, however, if he did not. In the meantime, circumspect delay on Monsieur's part will be of great assistance to us." He paused, leaned back in his chair and closed his eyes. "Good day, Monsieur."

The Duc, almost reeling in spite of his struggle to control himself, left that chamber. It was not until he was in his hôtel that he gave way to his enraged frustration, hatred, murderous wrath, and despair.

CHAPTER XXXVI

A TRULY APPALLING malaise had taken possession of Louis de Richepin like a black pestilence of the mind. Always, that cold and phlegmatic exterior had been the glacial shell over turbulent and disordered passions. Always, he had been the screaming prisoner behind ice-covered and silent walls. There are men who are born to solitude, and there are men who have it forced upon them, either by evil circumstance or by their own natures. Louis de Richepin was a curious victim of both these alternatives. Vain, proud and haughty, he suffered the consequences of these defects in the curse of an inordinately sensitive and suspicious temperament. He was repellent in manner and speech, enraging when he did not intimidate. The casual observer did not hear the groan behind the measured and indifferent words, or see the extended hand behind the stony and glancing eye. None suspected that anticipation of rebuff, a bewildered lack of comprehension of other men, and an abysmal fear, were the stones of the wall that enclosed him away from humanity.

He pursued his duties with his old methodical care, spoke as usual, moved as usual. But nothing stirred in him, in that black and empty grave which daily grew deeper and wider as the molten core cooled and turned to blowing ashes. Never having sought the company of others with true eagerness, for all his constant yearning, he now avoided contacts with other men as much as possible. He had once delighted in learned discussions with the Cardinal, and with other scholarly Jesuits. Now, in the midst of such discussions, the sickness would well up into his throat so that he retched, would be obliged to flee. He went no longer to the Bois de Boulogne to see Marguerite de Tremblant. For on the last innocuous occasion, the sickness had fastened upon him so that his agony had been too great for endurance and he had left her suddenly.

No one had ever suspected, or cared, that there had lived

in him at one time a pure delight in the simplest manifestations of nature, that a breeze filled with perfume had had the power to plunge him into shy ecstasy, that often the mere passing of a silver cloud across the face of the moon had brought trembling tears to his eyes. And none knew now that he could look on all beauty with the glazed eyes of a dead man, with no response in his heart. The prisoner under the glacial shell was dying; he no longer implored and shrieked for help. Nor did he care, at last, whether help came or not. Sometimes, for hours, he would sit with his swimming head in his hands, conscious only of a dim and boundless pain as vast as eternity.

The siege of La Rochelle, his dearest wish, was about to begin, his dearest hatreds were about to be fulfilled. Yet he could not arouse himself to interest in them. In him was the final suffering instinct of the dying animal: to creep away into some solitary blackness of obscurity and expire soundlessly. On the few occasions when he was aroused to fury, it was the mechanical fury of an impersonal storm, or the lashing-out of a man tormented beyond endurance and striking blindly as a wounded dog bites in his extremity.

He spent hours on his knees, not praying, only enduring, his empty eyes fixed upon his crucifix, and from out his soul drifted the thin mist of the ashes that blew about in him. He received no comfort, expected none. The emptiness increased. He forgot everything.

At times, terror seized him briefly, and he would force himself to external acts, to speech, for there was an instinctive knowledge in him that his flesh would soon lose its limits of endurance and he would go mad or die. But these efforts to climb up the long and agonizing slope towards the light exhausted him. At last, he did not care whether he reached the light again or not.

All Paris was now aroused by the tragic and mysterious death of the Duc de Tremblant. His body was returned to his home, and he was buried with his illustrious forebears. Madame de Tremblant was prostrated, but she did not weep. Her daughters knelt about her, sobbing, in the cool blue twilight of Notre Dame, but she stared before her, drily. The great cathedral was filled to bursting. Louis de Richepin did not attend any of the masses for the dead man.

But several weeks later, he was overcome by an unfathomable impulse, and wrote a missive to Marguerite de Tremblant, whom he had not seen for a long time. It was a cold, but incoherent missive, in which he expressed his commiseration for her sorrow, and urged her to seek comfort in spiritual consolations. As he proceeded to write, his incoherence grew, his writing became illegible. When he had done, had forgotten he had written to her, and only gazed dully at the letter, he was trembling throughout his body, and was forced to fling himself upon his bed, to lie for sightless hours staring at the opposite wall.

The next day a messenger brought him a reply from the girl. He turned it over and over in his hands. Finally, he opened it. It was not for long moments that her words became coherent in his mind.

She began the letter without salutation, and ended without signature:

"Words of comfort and sympathy from a friend are received with gratitude. If this kind friend will appear at a certain spot known to him, at midnight, tonight, he will hear words of this gratitude in person, and a last farewell."

After some dazed minutes, the import and strangeness of this missive finally pierced to the dulled consciousness of Louis de Richepin. He felt a slow but rising beat deep within the empty chaos of his being. A mysterious terror began to pervade him, and another emotion he felt had died forever. The word "farewell" began to imprint itself on his inner eye in letters of fire.

The spectral terror increased as the day passed. Now, he was no longer empty. An enormous restlessness, a prescience of agony, swept upon him. Everything darkened and changed before his eyes. The long interval of soundlessness and emptiness in which he had struggled in diffused torment, fell behind him like a black tunnel as he emerged into gathering storm. He felt no presence but the presence of Marguerite de Tremblant, and he exclaimed to himself: "How was it that I had forgotten her, that I could not think of her?"

As sunset approached, his anguish increased. Remembering the horrible agony of the last weeks, he dimly suspected that in some manner the girl had been involved in this, that his withdrawal from her had been the withdrawal of fear, that in his absenting himself lay the secret of his suffering. At intervals, as he waited for the night, he was caught up in a rapture which he dared not name. But the rapture increased, alternating with despair and anguish. Never having in all his life confronted himself fully, understanding and confessing in himself, he closed his eyes before the dazzling mirror remorselessly set up before him, fearing, as always, the truth. Now as his flesh burned, became heated, as the pounding of his heart communicated itself to all his veins and his arteries, he still would not understand, or confess.

Would the torturous hours never pass? The empty days had gone by like clouds, featureless and formless, but now they were endless corridors through which he rushed impatiently, sweating in his extremity. Life roared in on him like a fresh and virgin flood, tempestuous and violent. He could not endure its onslaughts.

At eleven o'clock that night, he was waiting at the spot where so often he had met Marguerite de Tremblant. He heard the melancholy booming of the bell in the belfry of St. Cloud, and every tree in the Bois seemed to vibrate with the sonorous tones. There was only a faint moon. It made ghostly and stygian caves in the woods; the tips of the trees were silvered in the most spectral light against the black heavens. There were strange rustlings, faint breaths and murmurs in the underbrush, and formless shadows swept down upon the earth, from which a dank and ominous smell arose in heavy gusts. Louis de Richepin, chilled and weighted in spite of his fever, felt himself alone in an abandoned universe.

He tried to calm himself by seating himself upon the stones on which he and Marguerite had sat for so many warm summer mornings. But the stones were stones of fire. He would leap to his feet, striding back and forth in the black hollow formed by the surrounding trees, dried leaves crumbling and crackling under his foot, the cool wetness of the air blowing on his hot and tormented face. Sometimes he groaned softly to himself, striking his hands together at intervals. Now the trees had a leathery and slapping sound in the wind, and from the depths of the forest came the long wild notes of a melancholy bird, restless and sleepless. Once or twice he saw the phosphorescent eyes of small animals gleaming at him from the darkness, and they seemed to him full of malignancy and evil. Pale forms like apparitions drifted through distant aisles of black shadow, and he shuddered with superstitious fear. Paris slept behind him; not even the rumble of a carriage on cobbled streets, or the sound of a horse, disturbed that deathly silence.

As the hour wheeled towards midnight, his nameless agony of mind and soul increased. Blood pounded in his brain, leapt from his heart, made his knees tremble and sweat to burst from every pore. He felt himself drawing to some appalling climax, a climax still veiled and voiceless, but all the more terrible. The stillness and blackness about him did not calm or soothe him. He was the bursting and flaming heart of the forest, and it seemed to him that at length he must ignite those weighted and ominous trees.

There was no approaching sound of Marguerite de Tremblant as St. Cloud boomed out the midnight hour from its grating and iron throats, but Louis at length became aware that he was not alone. He saw a pale and floating oval before him, and halted in his tracks. The moon slid from behind a cloud, shot down long pallid beams into the enclosure, and he saw the slight form of the girl advancing towards him, clad in black, with a black mourning veil floating from her head. She stopped a pace or two from him, her hands clasped before her, and those hands gleamed like cold marble. He could not see her expression, but he felt that his own torment was on her face and in her heart, and when he seized her with a strangled sound of violence and clasped her in his arms, it was more a gesture of frightful compassion and despair than a gesture of love. Her heart beat against his own, in the same language of pain and grief, and the soft white arms about his neck were arms that pleaded for help.

One in suffering, they clung together in that silence and darkness, torn and distraught, voiceless and desperate. They sought to find refuge in each other, a hiding place from the enormity of life. Louis bent his head and pressed his lips against the girl's quivering mouth, and she responded with feverish passion. Her hands clutched his body under his arms; she dropped her head to his breast, and, finding relief, sobbed aloud.

He lifted her in his arms and carried her to the stones. They sat together, as closely as possible, her head upon his shoulder, his arms about her.

The hot anguish began to recede, and with it came a heavy lassitude in which they sat without speaking. The night closed in upon them. They heard their own disordered breathing in the black silence.

"Ah, Louis, Louis!" murmured the girl, in a faint and mournful voice. "It is farewell. Why do I weep? I do not know. But tomorrow I leave for the convent in Amiens, where my aunt is abbess. Kiss me, Louis. Hold me. Let me forget for this night."

When he kissed her again, he tasted the tears that fell from her eyes. He held her as he might have held a sinking child. Some bleeding wound opened in his heart, like a gaping flame.

"No," he said, at last, "you cannot leave me, Marguerite."

He listened to his own words, and a cold horror seized upon

him. He repeated them in his mind. He said aloud: "I am a priest."

She lifted one of his icy hands to her lips and pressed it there, and her cries were stifled against it. He kissed her hair through her veil, caught her to him. Now he sobbed aloud, without tears, but as a man sobs who cannot endure his mortal pain.

All at once the endless and empty torment of his days seemed to rise before him in visions lighted by infernal fire. All at once all the terrible hours of doubt, hatred, fury, madness, loneliness and yearning welded together in one upsurge like a devouring conflagration. He felt himself dying. He fell on his knees before the girl; he dropped his head in her silken lap, feeling the warmth of her young thighs under his cheek. His arms embraced her despairingly. For an instant her hands took his head as though to lift it away from her, and then she dropped it. She sat motionless and silent, staring blindly into the darkness.

He began to speak in a hoarse and tearing voice, and his head rolled upon her lap in torture:

"Have pity on me, Marguerite. Do you know I love you, my child? We have met here, often—it has been a dream, a nothingness. What has it been to you, also? A nothingness. But it has given me happiness. Do you know I have never been happy, Marguerite? Do you know there has been nothing for me in all the world, in all these years, but longing and pain, loneliness and sadness, doubt and fear? Who has cared for me, but you?

"Do you know why I entered the Church, my little one? Never have I had the courage to know until now! I sought peace in the Church, a stifling, a thoughtless tranquillity, because I found nothing in the world, in living. For me, there has been only repudiation, only scorn and disdain. Who has known me, or cared to know me, but you?"

He paused a moment. His voice came back to the girl in doleful echoes from the forest. It was a voice from the very depths of the hell of a man's soul. She shuddered. She looked down upon him, and her hands pressed themselves to his cheeks in compassion and understanding.

Now his voice rose on the wave of his mounting agony, as at last the iron walls went down and the flood burst forth:

"What has the Church been to me? I see so clearly, now! Why did I not see before? I found no peace in it, for there is no God, Marguerite! There is only a devil, an Evil in the world! I found only malevolent faces in the Church, the malevolent faces of a universe of men. I listened to the plottings, and I told myself they were the plottings in the service of God. But there is no God, my little one, my darling. There is only nothingness, an eternal darkness. We are lost in a wilderness."

His strange and incoherent words, bursting from his lips, filled all the forest with dread murmurings and cries, incomprehensible. The girl shuddered more and more. Wild terror possessed her. She caught his head to her breast and held it there, crying aloud. But, in spite of her youth and innocence, she knew that he was hardly aware of her except as a channel through which his torture roared, finding expression at last for a lifetime of confusion and appalling suffering. And some deep eternal awareness came to her, a lofty understanding and tenderness, for all her inexperience. She felt that terrible forms and faces were gathering breathless about them in that forest, listening dangerously to these revelations, and that they were waiting for revenge on one who dared to speak from out his soul at last:

"O Marguerite!" he cried. "Where can a man fly? Where is there hope, light and refuge in all this universe of horror? We look upon each other and ask ourselves: Does there live in this man, under his calm face and his lying words, the frightfulness that is in me? The same knowledge of nothingness and evil, of blackness and death, of pain and despair? Who can tell of the hatred which inspires one against the other, because of the silence of the secret, because we dare not speak? Marguerite, do you know how I have hated all other men, because of my agony? And now I know that we hate each other because of our mutual agony, because of our knowledge that there is no God, and we are lost in a pit from which we cannot escape!"

The warmth of her innocent breast beneath her black bodice at last heated his cold flesh. He felt her hands, such little tender hands, pressed against his cheeks, as a mother presses a wounded and suffering child.

"There is love," she whispered. "Oh, my dearest one, there is always love. And who knows but what that love is God?"

She felt in herself the passionate nobility of suffering for another, the strength of that suffering. She desired nothing but to give this writhing man a moment's peace, a moment's alleviation. She could find no words that were not worn thin and featureless by the lips of shallow men, as coins are worn by thousands of anonymous hands. Where were there words that had not become hollow and shameful, maudlin and foolish? Her heart was opening in a wide wound of compassion and love, and no words but empty ones could rise to her lips. Incoherent whisperings rose from her throat. Her eyes overflowed with her tears. She sobbed in her helplessness.

But he had heard her. His rigidity did not relax, but he was silent, drawing her closer and closer to him. And now a golden wave flowed from her to him, as though she was a spring rising from the depths of life. The bright wave engulfed her in radiance, caught him in its fringes, drew him nearer to her beyond the barriers of flesh. She felt that their souls embraced in that dazzling light. She was overcome with joy.

"No," she said, and now her voice was pure and soft and steadfast, "there is no death, my dear one. There is no darkness, but the darkness in our own eyes. There is God, beyond our knowing, but always waiting."

She wondered if he had heard her. He said at last: "I am weary. I wish to die, to rest. I wish not to know, or feel, or be. I am tired of God. As He is tired of us."

"Rest," she murmured. "Rest, for a little while."

She cradled him in her young arms, rocking back and forth, murmuring words against his forehead, his hair. A faint crooning sound came from her lips; her eyes were shining in the dark. She smiled a little, with infinite mercy and tenderness. She felt the mortal exhaustion in his flesh, but it could not hurt her now. She was stronger than it. Her joy increased.

Now he stirred. "Have pity on me, Marguerite," he said, hoarsely. "I love you, as I never loved a thing before."

"I love you," she said.

She sat in silence as his hands rose to her breasts and moved over her body. Now the soundlessness and the darkness of the forest was thrilling with life. She could not move. She was a glowing and ecstatic image of fire, love, desire and compassion. Moons wheeled before her staring eyes; she heard strange harmonious crashings in her ears. Now the soft earth and grass was beneath her, and she saw Louis' eyes bent over her, burning and filled with light stronger than the enveloping darkness. She reached up to him, encompassed him in arms filled with the strength of all life. All at once she knew that the price of such life, such rapture and joy, was death. But she knew also that this death would pass as the night passes, and there was the renewal of the morning.

She was not the seduced, the helpless. Some wild and passionate ecstasy welled up from her, some solemn knowledge

405

and enormous surrender which was in itself strength and heavy with eternity. In giving herself up to him, she redeemed him, and granted him peace.

There was less of lust in that frenzied and convulsive embrace in which the wretched man grasped the girl than a wild and piteous hunger for human contact, for human warmth; the mad passion which had seized him was the primordial desire to escape from isolation and imprisonment into light and freedom. His spirit was obsessed with his hunger, and his desire, and thus his frenzy. He could not press himself close enough to her; he buried his lips in her bosom, in her neck, and arms and hair. He sobbed aloud in his ravening starvation. She felt his hot breath in her ear, against her soft flesh, and she smiled in the darkness.

When at last he was exhausted, he fell at once into a deep and profound slumber. The moon's faint long beams penetrated the forest and lay upon his face. It was quiet and still, almost deathlike in its expression of peace.

The forest was weighted under the approaching dawn. Now the trees hung in cool silence over the little glade. The moon had sunken beyond the horizon of the world. The eastern sky turned to a faint and pulsating opal. The voices of awakening birds called from branch to branch. Not a wind stirred, but from the earth rose the sweetest and most poignant of scents, and the pale air turned to crystal.

Marguerite slept on her lover's breast, her little hands still holding one of his. As the air brightened, she smiled in her sleep and turned to him. He lifted himself on his elbow to gaze down on her, to fill all his eyes and soul with the sight of her. The black veil had gone, was lost. Her copper curls were disheveled about her face, which was too bright, too luminous. Her parted lips glowed, and the fringes of her lashes were golden shadows on her cheeks. Her disordered bodice revealed the soft whiteness of her bosom and one shoulder, which was like a translucent pearl.

"My sweet love," he whispered. Now the agony was gone from him; it had been replaced by a vast but strangely comforting sorrow and peace. He experienced no shameful and petty guilt, no regret, and no remorse. He had risen beyond these things. There was a sad joy in him, a speechless but all-pervading tenderness.

And now as he looked down at the frail body of this girl, he had some mysterious prescience that death was upon her. But there was no despair in him. He felt that a strange covenant, a promise, was granted to him. For the first time in his life he was aware of God, of life, of radiance and eternal rapture.

He looked about him at the forest, and his eyes were heavy with dreams, too vast for the narrow confines and patterns of thoughts and words.

She stirred, and her eyelids lifted. She smiled at him, and turned to him. He held her in his arms. "Do not leave me," he whispered. "Oh, never leave me!"

"Never," she said. "Never."

CHAPTER XXXVII

A SHORT TIME before, Paul de Vitry would have smiled gently at the story which Arsène told him of Madame duPres and the priest, de Pacilli, believing it some exaggeration of his friend's vehement and colorful brain. But now he listened with incredulous dismay, still half-doubting. His last experience with the perfidy of man was still heavy upon him, and he was almost prepared to believe anything.

"I shall return at once to Chantilly," he said. The loss of that bright virtue which had distinguished him was more obvious than ever. He sighed with weariness. "However, there may be some explanation. It might not have been Madame, nor the priest. The world is full of plotting—. It is strange, though, that I did not receive your message."

"The woman is still at your château?"

"Yes."

"Pardieu! Then there is no time to waste!"

Force of habit made Paul part his lips to calm Arsène's extravagance, but they closed again without a sound, and the new drawn lines on his pale face sprang into strong visibility. He appeared overcome with lassitude, a lassitude of the spirit rather than the flesh. Arsène scowled with suppressed impatience. He could not conceive, in his vigor, that any one should be permanently distressed at the discovery of human meanness and treachery. He, Arsène, had known of it all his life, and morbleu! it had never robbed him of an hour's sleep or a relish for a good meal! In truth, it added a piquancy to life. One then could match wits with rats and weasels and small monkeys, and see who was the better! There seemed something a little contemptible in Paul's crushing wretchedness and ingenuousness.

They sat in the small drawing room of Paul's Paris hôtel, warming their feet at the fire, for the evening had turned cool. Paul had already ordered his lackey to prepare for the journey to Chantilly. Paul gazed at the fire, and his thin and delicate features were etched with scarlet. His hands lay on the arms of his carved chair, and there was a disarmed appearance about them, more than a trifle touching. He began to speak in a low voice, without looking at Arsène:

"We meet next, then, at La Rochelle, in two weeks?"

"Yes. Certes! We shall have trouble enough there. I do not flinch from it. I anticipate it."

Paul, despite his misery, could not restrain a smile. Still, he did not look at his friend.

"Is there a message you desire to give me for your old friend, Grandjean? And Mademoiselle Cecile?"

Arsène was abruptly silent. Then he spoke in a strained voice: "Give them both my remembrance."

Paul said, as if Arsène had not spoken: "It is a strange history which Grandjean has told me, of himself. No doubt he communicated this to you?"

"I was too ill. Moreover, I was not interested."

Paul shifted in his seat. "Nevertheless, it is very strange, and might intrigue you."

Arsène was about to say curtly that he could not imagine himself intrigued, but something peculiar in his friend's persistence aroused his curiosity. He felt that all this was pertinent to himself, and he was not a young man who would overlook such pertinence.

Paul spoke half aloud, still gazing at the fire:

"The family is very respectable, of good Breton sailor stock. Grandjean was captain of his own small merchant vessel, plying between France and England. Moreover, he possessed a large grant of land, which had been the home of his forebears for generations. He had a young daughter, who was the core of his heart, and whom he had brought to girlhood himself, as her mother had died at her birth."

Paul was silent a moment. His hands moved listlessly on the arms of his chair.

"He had frequently taken Eloise, his daughter, on his sea journeys. But now, as she was almost a woman, he left her at home, to manage his house. He emphasized that she was gently bred, of much beauty and charm. She had been educated unusually well at the local convent, and was much loved by the abbess and all the nuns."

It was a dull enough history, and only the peculiar tone of Paul's voice kept Arsène from yawning and moving restlessly, for his quick mind lacked the ability to focus with concentration on much of anything that did not concern himself.

"Mademoiselle Eloise finally became betrothed to the first mate on Grandjean's vessel. They were to be married in a certain June. Unfortunately, the vessel, out on a journey which they anticipated would be concluded within five weeks, was lost in a storm. They did not return to France for nearly four months. They had been given up for lost. But the most tragic thing was that the young mate had been swept overboard at sea, and was never found."

Now Paul was silent for a long time. But Arsène's attention was now caught with a premonition of dread excitement.

"It seems," Paul almost whispered as he proceeded, "that the priest of the parish was a man in full vigor of life. He had long before observed the young Eloise and her growing beauty, and her innocence. He had seduced her a short time before her father and her betrothed had gone on their ill-fated journey. The results were already known. However, he had persuaded the distracted girl that her marriage, which was to have taken place in the near future, would hide their guilty secret, and the girl, who dearly loved her betrothed and dared not think of the possible effect upon him, could do nothing else but listen to the priest, in her despair."

Arsène listened to that sordid story with wrinkled brows and angry disgust. He leaned towards Paul, who still did not look at him.

Paul continued: "Imagine that home-coming of the devoted father, with his tragic news of the death of his daughter's betrothed! Imagine what took place between him and the poor distracted girl, when all was revealed and confessed! Grandjean was beside himself. That night, he sought out the priest and killed him."

Arsène uttered a short ejaculation. Now he was truly absorbed in the story.

"He returned to his daughter, who had attempted to kill herself. He rescued her, in his great compassion and despair. But they had to flee at once, after that murder. Think what it meant to that man, to have to abandon his land and his vessel, and flee in the night with a girl almost in extremis. He had little time to prepare himself. There was one small bag of gold in the house, and this he took with a few garments of his own and the girl's, and a single horse, on which they both rode. After exhausting journeys, they arrived in Paris, and lost themselves in the gutters and the anonymity of the masses. It was in Paris that the young Cecile was born, at the moment that her heart-broken young mother died."

There was silence in the room after Paul had finished his

story. Arsène had risen. He stood near the fire and looked down fully at his friend, whose eyes were averted. Then Arsène said in a changed voice:

"Why have you told me this?" But his heart was beating in a very strange manner, and he was more than a little disgusted.

Paul finally lifted his eyes and looked fully at Arsène, and now there was a stern expression upon his face.

"Grandjean told this to me when I asked him for Cecile's hand."

"You!" exclaimed Arsène, incredulously. "You, the Comte de Vitry!"

Paul rose abruptly to his feet. He regarded Arsène with scorn and hauteur. "I thought you would say this, Arsène! But I hoped that there had been a change in you. I thought you had become a man, a reasonable, understanding being, at last. It seems that I was mistaken."

Arsène flushed darkly. His thoughts were all disordered and angry. He said thickly: "But that does not eliminate the fact that you are the Comte de Vitry." And felt an inexplicable shame which only further angered him.

Paul turned aside as if he could not endure the sight of his friend.

"What can finally be the fate of a world which persists in its silly little vanities, its illusions of birth and position, of nobility and privilege? Its isolation from its fellows, all built on falseness, pride and stupidity?"

Arsène, biting his lip, and still darkly flushed, said nothing.

Paul continued: "Grandjean did not tell me this in order to set aside my desire. He believed that Cecile might look favorably upon me. He wished me to know that he came of a strong and decent family, that Cecile might, in the light of this, be no low bride for me." He smiled drearily. "It appears that our Grandjean, himself, is not guiltless of pride."

"You have forgotten the priest!" said Arsène, stung with overwhelming and obscure emotions, in which the desire to taunt his friend, and his own fiery jealousy, had no small portion.

Paul turned to him, with increasing sternness. "I did not forget the priest. I remembered his crime. But it might interest you to know that he was the bishop of that diocese, and the bastard son of the Duc d'Ormond."

"The Duc d'Ormond!" exclaimed Arsène, before he could restrain himself. He colored more than ever.

A bitter smile appeared on Paul's lips, and he said nothing.

Arsène clenched his fists. His mind was whirling. He dared not confess to himself the shameful thoughts that were stirring in him.

Then Paul seemed to lose control of himself. He whirled upon his friend, and his face was alive with his scorn and passion, and his eyes were glittering.

"Let us be done with pretenses, Arsène! Let us speak frankly, as men, and not fools or mountebanks! I have seen what there was to be seen, in the cottage of my steward. This girl loves you, and you love her. Is that not true?"

Arsène did not answer. He averted his head.

"Loving this girl, you married Mademoiselle de Tremblant. I confess that I, myself, could see no way of withdrawal from that marriage, with honor, for a man like you. Had I been in the same position, I might have been more ruthless. You are a bravo, with attitudes, and I am perhaps a sentimentalist."

He waited, but Arsène did not speak. Paul then said, more temperately: "What will you do now?"

Arsène stirred, and asked brutally: "What would you have me do? Seduce this girl?"

Paul suddenly put his hands on his shoulders and spoke earnestly:

"This is a foul and dreadful world. What light lives in it is the light of love. You are going to La Rochelle. Take Cecile with you. For, in some mysterious way, I know that you shall not return to Paris again. When you leave this city, you leave it forever. Are you to die in La Rochelle? I do not know. But it will be farewell."

A cold thrill of superstitious premonition passed over Arsène.

"Consider," said Paul. "This is to be no mere skirmish. Those who fight for La Rochelle will be forever proscribed in France, if we are defeated. You will be compelled to flee —all of us will be hunted to the death. There will be no mercy. If we are defeated. And something most solemn tells me that we shall be defeated. Is that the end of the growing struggle for Protestant freedom and liberal dreams in France? I do not think so. A dream once dreamt is a dream remembered in the hearts of men. But the fulfillment may not come for many years. In the meantime, we who participated in this struggle are lost. It is exile or death for us.

"Therefore, I urge you to forget everything else, and seize happiness while you may. Why do I urge this upon you? Because you are my friend; because I love you. Because I love Cecile."

Arsène sat down slowly in his chair. He covered his face with his hands, and said, in a muffled voice: "You would have me take this girl into such a precarious and dangerous future?"

"A moment's happiness is better than a lifetime of unhappy security," said Paul, with moving eagerness. "And, who knows, you may find peace at last, together, in exile."

Arsène looked up. Paul was smiling; his gray eyes were moist and shining with tenderness, renunciation and compassion.

"In a few days, come to Chantilly. I shall be there. Arsène, you will come?"

"I will come," answered the young man. And he breathed deeply. After a moment his dark face was suffused with joy and exhilaration.

CHAPTER XXXVIII

BUT THE MOOD passed, after Arsène had bidden farewell to his friend. Reality inexorably invaded his thoughts, as he remembered Paul's solemn words of prophecy. Arsène had never given much reflection to the possibility that doom might lower over him. He had assaulted the fortresses of danger in moods of exaltation, vigor and joy in the act of combat. If he had been motivated by anything, it had been personal hatred or disgust or the sheer pleasure in opposition. When others had prophesied that he was inserting his neck in the hangman's noose, he had laughed, not with bravado, but with humorous incredulity. Such a possibility could never occur to the ebullient Arsène de Richepin, who had no real personal enemies, and whose wit, charm and audacity caused smiles of welcome and appreciation to appear on the faces of even remote acquaintances and potential enemies. He had mouthed such words as "danger," "ruin" and "death," but never for a lucid instant had he truly connected them with himself. The darling of his father and the Court was removed from such uncomfortable and disagreeable contingencies.

Part of the confusion which had assaulted him after his wound and his illness was due to the struggle between his inner conviction of his natural invulnerability, and reality, and the realization that for the first time he had been catapulted into the tempestuous world of adult men and adult problems. He had clung to boyhood in the manner of all men who naturally hate responsibility and the necessity to think. Consequently he had played at all things. In that, in a measure, had been the secret of his invulnerability, though he did not know this. Serious men of consequence had simply not taken his disaffections with any solemnity. They had not believed that one such as Arsène de Richepin could have the true sternness and fortitude to engage in anything of a for-

414

midable nature. And deep in his reckless and vehement heart, Arsène had agreed with them.

But now, to his secret dismay, Arsène discovered that he stood in the raw and blinding lightning of a dangerous country, into which he had strayed out of sheer light-heartedness and restless exuberance. Until Paul had spoken to him the night before, in those words of doom and prophecy, he had still felt himself invulnerable, a player in an exciting melodrama. But now he saw death, exile or ruin before him, in ruthless and violent colors. His father had spoken of them to him, on innumerable occasions, but he had listened impatiently, as to the drivelings of senility and stupidity, loftily declaiming that such contingencies could never induce him to turn back. Now, in horror, he saw that Arsène de Richepin was not invulnerable.

It was not that he was afraid. But all his life he had revolted from anything disagreeable, or final. He was confronted by both.

He went to his bed-chamber and locked the door, and sat and thought fully and deeply for the first time in his life. It was a painful process. He blinked as the inexorable light dawned blindingly before him. He was dismayed at the realization that he could not withdraw. All noble reflections vanished, as they always do in the final awakening of a man to maturity. Only grim resolve and duty remained. He could not withdraw because, in his twenty-eighth year, he had at last become a man. He had broken through the bright and vari-colored brittle crust of delusion, and stood at last on the black and iron ground of reality. It was a dreary awakening, and the wind was chill. His life of gaiety and irresponsibility was forever behind him. He had often dallied with the thought of returning. Now he knew he could never return.

He stood up. He looked about him. Everything had changed, because he had changed. He sat down at his commode and made a long list of the things he must do before leaving Paris. He wrote a letter to his father, and it was a moving and simple one, not sentimental. It was full of consolation and gentleness. He wrote a letter to Clarisse. Beginning this letter, he started. He had actually forgotten the existence of his young and bewitching wife! Now he wrote her passionately, imploring her forgiveness, leaving to her the greater part of his riches and his treasures.

Now he felt a strange emotion as he suddenly remembered Louis. His hatred was gone. He felt nothing but compassion. He implored Louis' forgiveness for any heartlessness or mockery or callousness he had displayed. He left their father in his brother's care.

When he had done, he felt like a man who is about to embark upon a journey from which he will never return, or like one who is stricken by a fatal illness. He was a little sick. He discovered that he was shaking. But his courage and determination were like a rock in him. He locked the letters in his commode, and held the key in his hand for a long and motionless time.

He heard a timid knock on the door of the chamber, and he opened the door. Clarisse, dazzling attired, smiled at him with uncertainty. He drew her within the chamber and embraced her with much sad ardor and sincerity. She clung to him, smiling through grateful tears. Then he put her from him, but held her hands tightly.

"My love," he said, gravely, gazing down into those large blue eyes which regarded him adoringly, "I shall soon be compelled to go upon a journey. In my commode yonder are certain papers. Three weeks after my departure, you will open that commode and give those letters to those to whom they are addressed."

Terror blanched her pretty face. She flung herself into his arms and clung to him for all his gentle efforts to disengage himself.

"No!" she cried. "You must not go, Arsène! Or, if you go, you must take me with you!"

He could not help smiling drearily to himself at these words. The frivolous and selfish Clarisse, absorbed only in her toilettes and silly artificial intrigues and fripperies, in the embattled La Rochelle, with its shadow of death and destruction! Yet, when he looked down into her face, he was truly startled. For he saw there self-abnegation, love and stern resolution. She did not know where he was going, but her loving heart warned her that he would not return.

He was freshly dismayed. He had not at any time believed that she loved him, or was capable of love. It had been a betrothal of convenience on her part, a betrothal begun in lust on his. Both of them had been superficial dancers and pleasure-lovers, contemplating marriage with light indifference, knowing themselves strangers. But intense and boundless love had had nothing to do with it. Arsène was profoundly moved, but also exasperated. This girl must not love him, who did not love her! It was no part of his plan that she love him. She was interfering, shaking his heart when he could least endure it. From his inherent egotism and impatience rose his vehement denial and annoyance.

Yet, he could not summon his old ruthlessness, which had served him well when dealing with irritating and unexpected contingencies. He could feel sorrow, as well as exasperation.

He drew her again into his arms, faintly wondering why he felt no response but sadness. He spoke soothingly:

"These letters of which I speak, my dearest, are only certain directions. I cannot take you with me, for you have already evinced an unflattering opinion of our estates."

He thought to distract her with this implied lie, but she answered eagerly: "Ah, but I have changed, Arsène! No matter the spot, or its dreariness, it will be delightful if only I am with you!"

He was incredulous. He took her face in his hands and stared down piercingly into her eyes. But their luminous and swimming light at length convinced him, much to his wretchedness. When, in their brief and turbulent married life, so ludicrous and disastrous, had love come to this shallowhearted and pretty child? God knew that he had done nothing to arouse it!

How he had complicated his life! Again, he felt resentment and exasperation, but now, for the first time in his selfish existence, these were directed against himself. Paul had spoken contemptuously of "a man, with honor," but now he realized that he ought to have withdrawn from this marriage before it had taken place. He had lacked ruthlessness, when ruthlessness would have been justice. He despised himself.

He spoke urgently: "Clarisse, believe me when I tell you it is impossible to take you. You must be patient. I leave you as mistress of this house, and I leave you the care of my father. Surely you must have perceived how distrait he is, since our return, and how a certain mysterious malaise has overtaken him. Would you willingly desert him, you who are now his daughter? I leave you this responsibility. Am I to be disappointed in you?"

He spoke with inspired artfulness. He had appealed to this girl's own egotism and desire for authority and importance. The tears dried in her eyes. She listened earnestly. Then she said with much formality: "You will need never reproach me again, Monsieur, with neglecting my duties as a wife."

She said this, with such pretty dignity, smoothing her disheveled gown and touching her disordered flaxen curls. She looked straightly in his eyes, and lifted her head. He admired her, much touched. He lifted her hand to his lips, and she endured this with wifely majesty.

"Too," she continued, "my poor sister, Marguerite, is ill. She was to have left for the convent of our aunt, the abbess, but now the journey is indefinitely delayed. My mother is distracted. She has need of my comfort."

Arsène was saddened at this news of Marguerite, but relieved that his own problem was solved. He embraced his wife again, an act she suffered without her previous distraught passion, but only with that new and imperious dignity.

He gave her the keys of the commode, assured that she would not trespass upon his secrets until the prescribed period had passed. She held the keys in her hand, with a cool expression, and listened intently to his final instructions. When she left him, he looked after her, smiling sadly to himself. Would he ever see this lovely child again? He could not know. He felt regret, as one always feels regret at this last appearance of anything that is gracious and desirable.

He remembered that he had one last commission, and it annoyed him. But he had given his word. Dressing himself as inconspicuously as possible, he left on foot for the Rue du Vieux-Columbier, in which obscure and miserable quarter the Abbé Mourion lived.

The warm sun lay on the dark and red chaotic roofs of Paris. The Seine glittered in blue and distracting brilliance. As he made his way through progressively meaner streets, filled with the stench of the cobbled gutters and alleys, Arsène could partially forget the wretchedness and noise which increasingly surrounded him, and feel a mournful regret that he was soon to leave this congested and turbulent city, and that he might never return to it. In his mind, he was already an exile. He stepped in putrid muck and filth; he was jostled by impudent mendicants, beggars, peddlers and vagabonds. He side-stepped brawling, half-naked children, carts, gossiping women, the edges of market-places, and he found all this infinitely lovable and nostalgic. Even when a woman hurled the contents of an unmentionable receptacle through a leaning upper window into the gutter below, and they splashed foully not five paces ahead of him, he could laugh a little, as he paused. The woman, hearing that laughter, peered down impudently at him, and grinned. She was a comely, if a dirty wench, with wild black curls and dancing black eyes. She shouted some indecency down at him, but with high good-humor, and he replied in kind, to her delighted and pretended horror.

For the first time in his life, he felt a whole-hearted brotherhood for these anonymous and teeming masses of humanity. They were his own; he was of them. He loved them, knowing he might never see them again.

The miasma of stench and heat and dust enfolded him. He passed through narrow alleys, whose opposite walls he could touch with both hands. He stumbled in gutters, running with foul water, and crowded with filthy children. He saw the dull blank faces of half-starved women staring at him blindly from thresholds and little windows. Now there was a feeling of evil in the sickening air, a destitution and hopelessness, of hidden violence, crime, hunger and bestiality. It was no longer amusing. Under his cloak, his hand held itself close to his sword. He could hardly breathe. He drew in his nostrils, and inhaled as little as possible, for the stench was becoming overpowering. Now he was conscious of hidden and wicked eyes, in which there was no humanity left, and only awareness of ferocity, pain and starvation. The fog of oppression and hopelessness closed more deeply about him. There was a spiritual roaring in the atmosphere, unheard by indifferent ears, but clearly heard by Arsène. His spine began to prickle. He glanced about him warily.

The alleys became more littered with refuse. The children here no longer played. They sat like grimy animals in the gutters, fishing hopelessly and mechanically in the trickles of black water for morsels of food. When one found such a morsel, his companions, electrified, fell upon him with hoarse screams of savage hunger, and tried to wrest it from him. They rolled together in the unspeakable filth. Arsène shuddered. He turned away his eyes. His heart was beating in a suffocating manner.

The Abbé Mourion lived in one of the worst of such quarters. Arsène had difficulty in finding his house, which he had never entered. He had to question, to shout, at the sullen faces which peered at him, before one man pointed silently to a mean little house set in a starving garden. When he approached this house, he was alarmed to discover that nearly a score of wretched, sore-laden and half-naked men was following him, their dirty faces lowering, their red-rimmed eyes glittering. There was something ominous in their silent pertinency, their closing-in about him. About him were the leaning and crowded walls, the gutters, the stench and the heat. He looked at the eyes approaching him, and they were not the eyes of human beings, but the eyes of ferocious animals, wary, hating, suspicious and murderous. Though he

419

was so shabbily dressed, his manner, his walk, his glance, had marked him.

He tried to cow them with an imperious look, but their evil aspect only quickened, and they moved more closely about him. Am I to be murdered, robbed? he thought, with real fright. Was he, Arsène de Richepin, to be torn to pieces in a Paris gutter, and disappear forever from sight?

Standing there, his heart pounding, he withdrew his purse, opened it, and tossed the golden and silver coins with one instinctive movement towards the men. There were women, now, among them, ragged, with black disheveled locks streaming about their shoulders, their dirty hands clenched into ominous fists.

The coins rose in the air, fell in the dangerous silence with loud tinkles into the gutter. The men followed the passage of the gleaming bits of money with empty and smoldering eyes. One or two of the women darted upon them, gathering them up with loud exultant screams. But to Arsène's astonishment, none of the men made a movement. They merely stared at the women for an instant, then returned their savage regard to Arsène.

Precipitously now, and with confused amazement, he seized the knocker on the abbé's door, and pounded it furiously. The sound echoed through the silent and crooked alley, into whose dusty and cavernous depths a few rays of the hot sun penetrated. The thickening throng moved closer; Arsène could smell the effluvia of their dirty bodies, and hear their snarling breath through their pale lips and broken teeth. Then he heard a mutter: "This is no gendarme." The glittering circle of eyes moved nearer, to peer at him.

The door opened a crack, and the Abbé Mourion peeped through the aperture. Arsène, with great haste, exclaimed: "It is I, Monsieur l'abbé!"

Now the door was flung open. The abbé exclaimed with joy: "Monsieur! How thankful to God am I that you have come at last!"

He stretched out his arms to Arsène and embraced him feverishly. Arsène glanced back over his shoulder, with apprehension. The crowd, however, had relaxed. A few of the men had begun to smile sheepishly, and to scratch their heads. Others, however, deprived of prey, glowered with uncertain disappointment.

The abbé drew Arsène into his miserable little house. Then, looking at the throng, he said, gently: "It is well, my children. This is my dear friend."

He closed the door. Darkness plunged over Arsène, and he blinked, trying to accustom himself to the gloom and dry dust of the little corridor in which he stood. The abbé took him by the arm, and led him into a small and barren chamber, and Arsène found himself in a hovel hardly less luxurious than that in which François Grandjean had lived. But this chamber was dominated by a great and noble crucifix which hung on the cracked and dripping wall.

Dim daylight crept through small barred windows near the ceiling. By this light Arsène perceived that the abbé had aged excessively, that he appeared smaller and more wizened than he remembered, that anguish and sorrow had withered his countenance. But his large soft eyes, brown and luminous, were more tender than before.

He smiled at Arsène. He indicated the wooden bench near a trestle table, and Arsène sat down upon it, gingerly. He was still shaken from his encounter in the streets.

"This flock of yours, Monsieur l'abbé, are somewhat noisome and dangerous. I feared for my life. I am certain that had you not so opportunely opened your door, I should have been torn to pieces."

He spoke with hauteur, to hide the evidences of his past alarm. But the abbé, whose hands were tremulous, did not hasten to apologize. He sat down near Arsène and gazed at him with visible suffering. At length he said: "Monsieur, they are guarding me."

Astonished, Arsène asked: "Why?"

The abbé was silent. He passed his veined hands over his face, as though inexpressibly weary. He shrank in his habit.

"I have been unfrocked; I have been excommunicated," he whispered, dryly.

"Excommunicated!"

The abbé dropped his hands and regarded Arsène with simple and lofty anguish. "Monsieur, I have prayed constantly for deliverance. God has sent you to me. In a moment, I will tell you what you wish to know."

He drew his shallow breath feebly, as if his heart was laboring. Arsène waited; then, in an effort to bring composure to the old man, he said:

"I have not forgotten the great debt I owe you, Monsieur l'abbé."

Now a deeper shade passed over the old man's face. He said: "He is living with me still, my poor Henri. We subsist on his earnings, which he acquires in cleaning the gutters of the more fortunate streets of Paris. Too, we have not been

421

forgotten by my dear friend, François. Once a month, a packet of money is sent to us."

Arsène was embarrassed. He cursed himself that he had not remembered the abbé in a substantial manner. So he said: "All this shall be changed. I regret that I tossed your guardians my purse, Monsieur l'abbé. But as much as you desire shall be sent to you upon my return to the Hôtel du Vaubon. Why did you send no message to me, if you were in such dire misery?"

"You owed me nothing, Monsieur de Richepin," replied the old man, with quiet dignity. A faint flush crept through his weary and withered flesh. "However, I knew that some day you would come. I urged this upon Henri, who believed you had forgotten him."

"I did not forget," said Arsène, with irritation, remembering how well he had forgotten. "But there were matters—. Moreover, I have just been married."

"I understand," said the old man, softly, gazing at him with a pleading look.

"You shall leave this deplorable spot at once. Tonight at the latest. I shall give you an address of a friend, who will undertake to establish you in more comfortable quarters—"

Now the joy disappeared from the abbé's eyes. He appeared more agonized than ever. He regarded Arsène with piercing attention, as if he were attempting to judge him. "That is impossible," he said.

"But why?"

But the old man's penetrating regard intensified. He seemed seized by an extremity of wretched uncertainty and indecision.

"You have not told me why you have been excommunicated, driven from the Church," continued Arsène, impatiently. "Is this a secret? Or do you wish to confide in me? I assure you of my interest, and my sympathy."

The abbé lifted his head, as though listening with enormous concentration. Arsène repeated his last words, but the priest had the expression of one who was not aware of his immediate surroundings. He lifted a hand slowly, in a gesture commanding silence. Arsène listened also, with frowning alertness. From somewhere, in the depths of this hovel, came a faint moaning sound.

The priest rose. He appeared to increase in stature, his emaciated form rigid as iron. He spoke solemnly, and his eyes gleamed at Arsène in the dusk: "Monsieur, I must trust you. I have prayed for help; I believe God has sent you to me. Perhaps I am mistaken. But I must trust you. If you betray me, and others, I promise you that there will be no peace for you henceforth in your life."

Arsène, inclined at first to be affronted at this audacious remark, rose and stood before the old man, his brows drawn together sharply over his aquiline nose. "Be assured, Monsieur l'abbé, that I shall not betray you," he said coldly.

The old man beckoned, then, and Arsène followed him into another corridor, whose door was locked. He unlocked and opened the door of another chamber, in which there was no window. A sickly yellow taper stood on a table. On the floor was a straw pallet, and on this pallet, in the circle of ghostly light, lay a huddled and moaning young man.

Astonished, Arsène did not at first see the two villainous creatures who guarded this chamber and this man. Seeing them at last, he started, for their aspect was so ferocious, so menacing, that they would have intimidated the strongest heart. Ragged, bent but tall, with dank black locks streaming on their shoulders, daggers in their belts, and with bared wolfish teeth, they had less the appearance of men than of wolfish animals. Their black eyes glittered savagely upon Arsène. Now the young noble saw that on the table near the candle was laid a musket, primed and ready.

The abbé locked the door behind him. He said softly to the guardians: "It is well, my dear sons. This is a friend, sent by God to rescue our poor Alphonse."

The men growled deep in their throats. They withdrew. They sat on the bench near the table, without removing their appalling regard from Arsène. The latter turned to the abbé with considerable apprehension:

"Explain!"

But the abbé had approached the pallet, and was now kneeling beside it. Arsène, peering over his shoulder, saw that the invalid was very young, hardly more than nineteen, and that he was horribly wounded. His dark bare right arm was lacerated in a dozen places, covered with thin white rags stained with blood. An open and oozing gash lay across his forehead, over which the tangled black hair fell in ragged points. His chest had been bared; it was covered with bloody bruises, and appeared crushed. His face was pathetically young, in its groaning unconsciousness, the eyes half open, and his bleeding lips twisted with torture.

The abbé lifted the taper from the table and held it in his hand as he gently examined the youth. He touched the hot and wounded brow. He sighed deeply. But he said with quiet-

423

ness: "There seems less fever. God is good. This poor child will recover." He made the sign of the cross over the sufferer, who appeared to feel the presence of this gentleman, for his groanings slackened, and he seemed to listen intently from the depths of the crimson hell in which he writhed. A faint smile appeared on those broken lips; he sighed as a child sighs, and instinctively moved closer to the priest, who had begun to weep, the tears running down his face. The guardians, forgetting Arsène, crept near; they gazed over the shoulder of the abbé. One of them sobbed aloud, and now Arsène discovered a faint resemblance between this older man and the youth.

Hearing that sob, the priest looked up and smiled tenderly at the man.

"You have done well, Jacques. Your son will live, by the grace of God."

He rose, beckoned to Arsène, and together they left the chamber, returning to the other. The abbé moved with increasing feebleness, as though he bore a great weight on his frail shoulders. He looked at Arsène with anguish:

"For two weeks, this child has lain at the point of death in this house. He will recover. But he must be moved at once."

He sat down. His trembling hands sank on the knees of his worn habit. The faint daylight rimmed his white head like a halo. He spoke in a low voice:

"Two weeks ago, the landlord of this quarter rode through in his carriage, attended by his grooms and lackeys. You have seen the misery of this quarter, Monsieur. At times, such misery arouses the jaded amusement of the powerful, the oppressors, and they visit their tenants in their wretchedness, from some perverted desire to gloat, to laugh, to despise."

He paused, then lifting his head he regarded Arsène with such powerful and blazing wrath, such strong white fury, that the young man involuntarily recoiled:

"Monsieur, what thought have you, and others like you, given to the people of Paris? You have considered that the world consists only of your nobility, your privileges, your narrow circle of parasites, gilded scoundrels, fools and plotters, the corrupt circle of sycophants, robbers and oppressors about the Court. Have you thought of the teeming millions beyond that circle? Have you reflected that these are men also, not beasts, not animals, but creatures in your own image, with hearts and blood and souls like your own, with the same capacity for suffering and grief and hunger and longing?

These are your brothers, flesh of your flesh, and you have thought them less than your dogs, meaner than your horses, because they have neither name, nor title nor estates nor power! What influence have the doctrines of the humble Christ had upon you, this Christ who declared that all men are brothers, that the least are no less worthy than the greatest? What have the abjurations of charity, mercy, justice and compassion had upon you? None! They were only cant spoken by fat priests, bought with your gold, arrayed in the silks and the velvets and the laces you have bestowed upon them, for the promise that they would protect you from the hot and steaming bodies of your brothers, for the promise that these would not disturb your soft beds and your privileges and your power! For the promise that they would seduce these millions upon millions, and threaten them with mystical horrors if they dared to revolt and demand their place as men in the sun of God!"

He pointed a trembling finger at Arsène, and his wrath grew:

"It is you, Monsieur de Richepin, who have destroyed the Church and its servants, you who have traduced its name and prostituted its glory and its strength. You who have made it a charnal house and a stench in the nostrils of men. Was there no last bulwark for the wretched whom you oppressed, that you must take from them their last hope and force them to believe that the crucifix was no refuge for them, but a sign of their slavery, their starvation and their hopelessness? It is you who have made the Christ their oppressor, and for this there is no forgiveness in all of heaven!"

He clenched his hands before him, and shook them in his access of frenzied agony:

"It is you who have ordained that the keys of St. Peter lie in a dead and jeweled hand, that the man, crowned with the three crowns shall be no servant of God, humble and poor and compassionate, but a golden and lifeless image in a carved chair from whose hollowness shall come your rapacious and cruel voices! You have bought the vicar of Christ, Monsieur de Richepin! And with that purchase, you have bought your own damnation."

The little chamber resounded with his strong and passionate voice. Arsène listened, unable to move, caught in a nightmare, in which his heart pounded and his limbs were dead. He could not look away from this little old priest, embued now with power and dread authority and mighty anger.

The old priest flung out his arms and stood like one await-

425

ing crucifixion, his agonized eyes lifted as if imploring help from a blind and hidden heaven.

"Monsieur, I tell you now that out of this muck, this chaos, this suffering, this evil and this torment, this starvation and hopelessness, this oppression and wickedness and tears, this violence and bitterness, this ignorance and cruelty, will come a frightful revolt, a death and a fury! And when this revolt comes, it will sweep away, as in a burning and dreadful flood, thrones, kings, nobles, privileges, power and priests! It will destroy the oppressors of the people in a cauldron of blood. How long do you believe the people will endure, Monsieur? They have endured so long, these nameless children, these suffering men and women, these lightless and diseased and starving masses! They have endured so long that God must be deafened with their cries, and must at last stir in His remoteness and take revenge."

The abbé groped for his bench, as though his limbs would no longer sustain him. He fell upon it. His head dropped upon his breast. He wept aloud, rocking back and forth, as if his grief were too great for endurance. Arsène took a step towards him, his own thoughts in chaos, his compassion choking him.

The abbé spoke again at last, in a lower, and more hoarse voice:

"Such a one, the landlord, came to this quarter, Monsieur. His carriage, winding through these narrow streets, struck down a child, in the gutter. The wheels rode over the child, mangling it. The horses struck at it. The landlord and his entourage laughed, as at some delicious joke. This was only the spawn of the canaille, whom the wheels and the horses had crushed!

"This youth, this poor Alphonse, seeing this, was maddened. In him had begun to burn the fire that will sweep like a conflagration through Paris, through France, through the world. He leapt upon the step of the carriage, in his excess of madness. He tore the fat landlord from his seat. He dragged him into the gutter. Before a soul could interfere, he had throttled him, he had ground him into the streaming gutters, he had kicked his face to a pulp, he had killed him.

"I have known this Alphonse from birth, Monsieur. A youth of intelligence, of fire, of thought. He trusted me. He ran to me for a hiding-place. But not before the lackeys and the grooms had fallen upon him, seeking to tear him to shreds. He shook them off, and covered with blood, made his way to me. I have hidden him here.

426

"We have been well guarded, as you have seen, Monsieur. The gendarmes have come for Alphonse, on many occasions. But they dared not carry this house by assault. The masters are becoming wise. They prefer to temporize, to threaten, to promise, to bribe, in an attempt to secure Alphonse. But their patience will soon be exhausted. Hourly, I expect a formidable force to arrive, which we shall not be able to resist. I expect that much blood shall flow in these gutters. But at the last we shall not be able to protect Alphonse any longer. The death of scores will not serve to save him.

"My own superiors have come to me, demanding that I deliver Alphonse to the tender mercy of his oppressors. I have refused. I have been threatened, and cajoled. Still, I have refused. And so, because of my crime of 'interfering with the proper justice of the law, and persisting in my defiance of those placed by God above me,' I have been divested of my religious authority, I have been excommunicated."

He rose, approached Arsène, seized him by the arm. Now he pleaded, urgently, in wild words:

"Monsieur, I believe God has sent you to me. You have spoken of a debt you owe me. You owe me nothing. I have done nothing. But in the name of this imagined debt, I implore you to help me, to help this wretched and hunted youth!"

Most enormously moved, Arsène laid his hand on the withered hand that held him.

"Monsieur l'abbé, you have no need to plead with me. I have already thought of a way. Tonight, I shall return with a force of comrades, at midnight. We shall take Alphonse from this house. We shall carry him to a place which no one will dare assail, a hidden place. There he shall be restored to health. After that, perhaps we shall smuggle him from France. The final plans will be perfected after his recovery."

He held the old and weeping man in his arms, and spoke strongly:

"Be of good cheer, my poor friend. Nothing is hopeless, nothing is lost. At midnight, then. In the meantime, I must go at once, and seek out my comrades, for this work."

Clinging to him, the priest brokenly pronounced an extravagance of blessings.

The abbé, exhausted but shining with hope and peace, accompanied him some distance through the fetid alleys. When Arsène took leave of him, he glanced back. The abbé, framed by the walls of the narrow alley, lifted his hand in silent blessing.

At midnight, Arsène returned with several members of Les Blanches. He had appealed to them artfully. They, like himself, were members of the powerful aristocracy, and he was none too sure that he could enlist their sympathies in aiding one who had murdered another member, however noxious. So, he had told them that this was a youth, a Huguenot, who was hunted for his convictions, and his attempts to arouse the inhabitants of his quarters against the priests.

But when he arrived, he was paralyzed with horror. The whole quarter was ablaze with fire. The abbé's house was destroyed, a gutted ruin with the walls agape to the stars. The alleys were crowded and jostling with gaping and stunned men and women, gasping and blinking and weeping in the thick smoke of their burning dwelling-places. Gendarmes, on horses, with bared swords and with pistols in hand, had herded the people against the walls, and had commandeered a number of men to put out the fires. Their horses reared and trampled and screamed in the red and flickering light.

It was a long time before Arsène could find his voice to question the officer in charge of the gendarmes, who touched his hat respectfully, and showed his wonder at this invasion of a large and armed group of gentlemen. Then Arsène learned that only two hours before his own arrival, a body of the gendarmery had been given orders to take the house of the renegade priest by assault, to demand the deliverance of a certain murderer and brigand into the hands of the police. The priest, barricaded with his nephew in that house, guarded by seething masses of men and women armed with clubs and stones, had refused to give up the murderer peaceably. The gendarmes had attacked. They had been assaulted by the miserable wretches of the quarter. Five gendarmes had been killed. Scores of the wretches had died. In despair, the gendarmes had set fire to the house, believing that the smoke and flames would force the priest, the wounded man, the nephew and the two guardians, into the alleys. But, it seemed they preferred to die in the fire.

They had died. In the meantime, the fire had spread in that crowded quarter. The animals had been subdued. That was all, Monsieur. A deplorable incident, but what could one do with such cattle?

Arsène looked speechlessly at the flames, at the wild black faces of the people. A slow sick dread, enormous and overpowering, filled him, overcoming even his grief for the heroic abbé.

"It was a renegade and evil priest," continued the officer.

428

"He had been unfrocked, for just reasons. However, he had a nephew, a young man of intelligence, who well understood the wickedness of his uncle. He had come to us, today, telling us of an hour when the house was least guarded. There was a large reward offered, and he sensibly chose to take advantage of it. He was to give us a signal, when we might attack. But first, he was to enter the house, leaving the doors unlocked behind him, which he could easily do, the priest trusting him. He appeared at the window, and gave the signal. Unfortunately, a crowd had already gathered, from the walls and the gutters. When we attacked the house, they attacked us, with the sad results you see, Monsieur. We were forced to fire the house.

"There was a horrible incident. The nephew appeared at the door, seeking to escape the fire. But on the threshold, the priest, like a demon, appeared behind him. He had discovered, certainly, his nephew's part in this. He seized the young man with his fiendish arms. He pulled him back into the flames, closed the door behind him, and locked it. We saw his face for an instant—" The officer shuddered. "It was a devil's face, Monsieur. It was a mad face."

"My God!" cried Arsène. His comrades, puzzled and watchful, closed in about him on their horses, and glowered down at the captain, who was intimidated.

But Arsène looked at the funeral pyre of the Abbé Mourion, who had given up his life, the life of his beloved nephew, in one last act of despairing and heroic defiance against an evil life, an evil world, and an evil fate. It was a piteous defiance, which had wrought nothing of good, had been useless.

But all at once, Arsène's heart paused momentarily in its beating. Was it indeed useless? Or did fires like this, rising from the lives of such men, have portent in them for the world?

CHAPTER XXXIX

MONSEIGNEUR DE PACILLI knew well that the most powerful impulses in the human heart are evil, that men are naturally turned to lust, hatred, avarice, cruelty and revenge. Once, by meticulous mathematical calculation, drawn from the evidences of history, he had proved unimpeachably that it would take a thousand pious and virtuous priests a thousand indefatigable days to impress a single man with gentleness, mercy, justice and love, and to impress him so strongly that it would require exactly twelve hours before an equally indefatigable group of seducers could turn him from his former teaching. "But by the end of that twelve hours, the man, fortified by his natural evil impulses and emotions, would be forever immune to the teachings of the thousand pious and virtuous priests," the priest had sagaciously concluded. "The Prince, therefore, mindful that in a millennium and a half the human race has been exposed to Christianity for short and fitful periods, and never at any time sedulously wooed by my hypothetical thousand pious and virtuous priests during the thousand hypothetical days, comprehends that it needs only one hour of exhortation to evil to cause a man to forget his Christian teachings and become as he was: a furious and pestilential beast, moreover a beast operating fully and completely in his evil, which is his natural spiritual state."

Imbued as he was with the irrefutable strength of his knowledge of the foulness which is mankind, he had no doubts of the ultimate outcome of the seduction which he practiced among the peasants of the estates of the Comte de Vitry. But his cool and logical mind studied the effects of the seduction he had sowed with detachment and scientific interest. Would it take an hour of active seduction, a day, a week or a month? Calculating that the average peasant was about thirty years of age, that he had, since childhood, been taught Christian precepts on an average of one hour a day, the priest speculated that one week was sufficient to cause that peasant to revert to his normal temperament. But, as astronomers calculate deviations in the movements of planets caused by the influence of other planets, so de Pacilli was forced to calculate deviations in the normal conduct of these peasants, caused by the benign and noble influence of the Comte de Vitry. Moreover, proceeding on astronomical theories, he was further compelled to realize that as planets differ in deviations in proportion to their inherent weights, so men deviate in speeds in returning to their normal natures in exact proportion to the effect absorbed by them individually from their teachers. Some, he perceived, would return with great acceleration; others would be slower. Carefully calculating then, with icy and logical figures, he came to the conclusion that ten days would suffice, thus bringing into his sphere of influence those who would return to normal evil in two days, and those within twelve days.

He concluded his calculations without cynicism, without acrid comment in himself. These were mathematical facts, demanding no bitter reflections.

But, at the end of ten days, he was forced to realize that it would take fourteen days. He toiled over his figures; they totalled ten days. But fourteen days, despite the figures, were inexorably indicated.

At the end of fourteen days, he had completely seduced even those most devoted to the Comte, most grateful to him, and most dependent upon him. Even those, the older ones, with long memories of previous oppression and suffering, succumbed in two weeks. De Pacilli, however, was irritated. Figures, after long application, inevitably revealed irrevocable conclusions, which neither God nor Satan could refute. Therefore, his own figures were wrong. After two endless nights of new calculations, he came to the conclusion that it would need a thousand and four days on the part of the thousand tireless and devoted priests to impress a single man, instead of the original thousand days. Ah, that was it! Calculating on this revised basis, the figures led to the fourteen-day conclusions. He was satisfied. He slept peacefully.

He allowed the fourteen days of complete seduction to pass. After all, furies, like wines, must age suitably, to gather depth, flavor, and potency. At the end of thirty days, allowing for those unamiable deviations, he knew the peasants were ready. He rose on the proper morning, knowing that his task was done.

That night, the Comte de Vitry and his mistress, Madame duPres, arrived at the château. Paul was never a suspicious examiner of the countenances of others, seeking for evidences of disaffection, treachery, or wickedness. Had he done so, he would have noticed that the servants in the château were surrounded by an atmosphere of suspense, that their eyes shifted evilly before his candid gaze and smile, that there were whisperings, imprecations and shaken fists in the corridors, that several spat upon his passing, that a spirit of wickedness, portentous danger, and brooding violence hovered over the château.

Madame duPres felt all these things, however. Uneasily, she locked the doors of her chamber, and lay in her bed, listening for hours. Was it her imagination, or did she hear shufflings and mutterings in the corridor outside her door? Was there a flare of a torch in the garden below? She rose, and crept to the window. Then she uttered a wild and terrible cry.

The gardens, the grounds, were filled with a frightful horde of men and women, armed with clubs and stones. Torchlights glimmered on their faces. Even as the woman screamed aloud, the nearer ones hurled their torches through open windows, and advanced upon the château, shrieking foul and infuriated curses.

The doors went down before them.

CHAPTER XL

MONSIGNEUR KNEW THAT there were only two kinds of men who could not be easily shaken in a profound conviction: a fool and a wise man. The fool had no wit to combat argument, and no reason with which to reflect upon it. The wise man was usually too egotistic to admit any logic in an argument which challenged the final result of his own previous and exhaustive researches.

As he was such a sagacious and astute and subtle man, his conclusions about Crequy and François Grandjean would have been startling to any one less brilliant. For he had concluded that Grandjean was a fool, and Crequy a wise man. He had attempted, on numerous occasions, to seduce both, but all his artfulness was in vain. Grandjean, like so many dignified men of integrity and honor, unfortunately silenced the priest immediately, when he suspected that the latter was coming to him with implied contempt of the Comte de Vitry. The old man had been indignant. Had he been wise, he would have listened, and so perhaps might have helped to avert a terrible tragedy. So, like all men of rigid integrity, he demonstrated his immense folly, his lack of foresight, and subtlety. Had he been wise enough to have in his character a touch of dishonor and deviousness, he would have written to the Comte in warning. But, in his folly, he forebore to do this.

Crequy, the wise man, was not approached by the priest again after that one interview in the tavern. For, after long meditation, de Pacilli had come to the shrewd conclusion that here was no man who hated the Comte, but a man who loved him, and wished to protect him. Therefore, he warned the leaders of the growing disaffection not to speak of the Comte in the tavern, and to urge those who had begun to listen to them to refrain, also. But he did not explain why.

Thus it was that Crequy, the wise man, and Grandjean,

the fool, were almost completely unaware of the vicious fury which was growing among the peasants. But towards the last, Crequy, with his peasant's sensitiveness to other peasants, began to sniff an evil stench in the winds that blew from field and vineyard. He began to investigate, with great caution. But he found nothing. Nevertheless, his suspicions grew, and now they embraced the priest.

He decided to speak to the Comte when the latter returned to the château. "But," he exclaimed in ferocious despair to his niece, Roselle, "that saintly imbecile will not listen to me! He will remember that I have often urged upon him the foulness of this cattle, and will laugh gently in my face."

As the Comte and his mistress arrived late at night, the village was unaware that they had come. But, after they had dined, Madame duPres had called a servant to her, and sent him with a missive to de Pacilli. The priest, then, rising from the table where he had been writing, wrapped himself in his cloak and sped in shadowy darkness from door to door. He knew that men's wits and men's consciences are at the lowest ebb at midnight, especially if they had been summarily aroused from bed.

He returned to his house. It was no part of his plan that he be on hand to witness the results of his seduction. That part was done. He had finished the fifth of his voluminous books; the final pages were before him. The others were already in the hands of his superiors in Paris. He began to gather up his few belongings, to place them in a portmanteau. His work was complete. Now his agile and profound mind, dismissing Chantilly, went on to other matters.

Once or twice, as he glanced through his narrow windows, he saw the furtive and distant flare of torches, the hoarse humming of the awakening village. He shrugged. He was not interested. But all at once, an animal prescience caused his spine to prickle. He crept out of his house, and made his way through back alleys to his little church. The doors were always open. But that prescience warned him again. He shot the bolts, slipped like a black shadow in the moonlight, which fell through the high pointed windows, to the altar.

He stood before the altar, and gazed at its flickering, eternal red light. He did not light a candle. He stared at the altar, his face pale and masklike in the spectral moonlight. What did he think, as he meditated there before the crucifix? None could know. But momentarily the mask became more inscrutable, more marblelike in texture and expression.

After a long time, he went behind the altar, and examined a small thick door set in the wall. He opened that door with the rusty key which was in the lock and peered down into the thick and stygian darkness. A flight of stone steps led down into an unused crypt. The priest heard the trickle of water from far below, and smelled the dank and fetid odor of all underground and hidden places. The stench came up like a miasma, poisonous and stifling. He covered his nose hastily with his fine linen kerchief, and closed the door. Nevertheless, he did not lock it. Moreover, with satisfaction, he examined the door. It was of heavy wood, reinforced with iron, and set closely in its aperture. He sat down near it, his hands motionless on his knees, and stared imperviously, and like a stone image, at the crucifix. No one could have seen him in that pattern of black and silver which laced and fretted the little church. He was one with the blackness; his pale marble face was one with the moonlight.

Paul de Vitry, mentally and physically exhausted, retired early. Madame did not, as usual, annoy him with her perpetual poutings and importunities. He was weary of her, and she knew this. He avoided her as much as possible on all occasions. But he was too kind-hearted to dismiss her, with a stipend, as other men did. He had the cowardice of the gentle-souled: he could not endure wounding any creature, however foolish, tedious or repellent. He consoled himself with the hope that she might weary of him in turn, and abandon him. So far, the hope had not been justified. She clung to him with stubborn tenacity. But he knew that in that tenacity there was no real affection, and only avarice and resentment. However, he hoped that she might eventually tire of his gentle remoteness and indifference, and seek warmer pastures. In that event, he intended to dower her handsomely. In the meantime, she was to him an old woman of the sea, clinging stubbornly to his weary back and weighing him down.

He said good night to her with his accustomed thoughtfulness and gentleness, and urged her to retire early in order to recover from their tiresome journey. But for some reason, she seemed reluctant to leave him. Her beautiful face was unusually pale; her manner uneasy and restless. She invented excuses to keep him with her. At last, worn down by his own chronic sadness and weariness, he tore himself away with more curtness than ordinary.

He lay in his bed a long time, gazing blindly before him,

his eyes fixed unseeingly on the shadows of silver moonlight which spangled the molded ceiling. He followed, mechanically, the movements of the draperies at his windows, stirring in the soft and scented night wind. He listened, without real awareness, to the clamor of crickets in the damp grass outside those windows. Once a nightingale sang with piercing and bitter sweetness to the moon, and Paul's heart contracted on a spasm of poignant anguish. But there was no other sound in the moonlight darkness.

The moon wheeled eastward. The trees began to rustle uneasily. Now Paul, through his window, saw the sudden brilliant flashing of the cross on the steeple of the church, as it caught the moon's argent rays. The wind became heavier with the odors of earth, grass, flower and tree. Yet, strangely, the profound silence seemed to increase.

Tears suddenly rose to Paul's tired eyes, and he closed them, sighing. The weight on his heart became too terrible for endurance. His whole being was engulfed in tides of suffering, despair, weariness and nameless grief. Existence had become for him a dry and windless desert, in which he wandered, parched and lost and full of exhaustion. All hope had gone from him; all his innocent joy in living had forever departed. He had lost faith in his fellows, that faith conceived in his own ingenuousness and purity of spirit, and like others of his kind, there was no consolation for him, no cynical philosophy, no shrug of fatalistic and humorous acceptance. Out of that lost faith, in many men, came hatred. But there was no seed of hatred in his heart. He could feel only sorrow and complete deathly despair. To him, all men had become treacherous beasts, prowling lustfully.

He had lost love. He had loved the young Cecile Grandjean with a passion unknown to most men. Others might say to themselves: "This is but an obscure peasant wench, and there are thousands more of her pattern." But to one so innocent, so single-hearted, so ingenuous as Paul de Vitry, there was no other woman. He had never heard of the aphorism that all women are the same in the dark. The lusts of the flesh had never been overly strong in him. The thin strata in him, which was almost womanish in its character, was capable only of devotion and eternal fidelity.

He was filled with the impulse to flee, blindly. But where could he flee? There was no refuge, no quiet and shadowless spot for him.

Overcome at last by his exhaustion of mind and body, he

fell into a brief and uneasy slumber. Once he stirred, restlessly, and opened his eyes. Had he heard a scream? But that was only a nightmare. He turned in his bed and tried to sleep again.

Then all at once, he heard a faint roaring. The wind. He opened his eyes again. Now all his senses came fearfully awake. The roaring had increased. And above it was a prolonged screaming. There were several thunderous crashes. Now the moonlight was gone. Long streamers of red light devoured the ceiling of the chamber, and he smelled the sudden choking stench of smoke. He heard shouts and running in the corridor, the shrieking of oaths.

He sprang out of bed, fully aroused, pulling on his dressing gown over his nightshirt. He ran to the door, and wrenched it open. The corridor was empty now. The arches were full of red light and drifting smoke. Now the lower floor of the château was filled to bursting with teeming and twisting men and women, brandishing their fists, their sweating faces black and red in the flames that licked the frescoed walls, like faces out of hell. Out of their mouths poured screams and imprecations and mad howls. Many, in their excess of maddened rage, were hurling articles of delicate furniture and porcelain against the walls, smashing them, crushing the fragments under their feet. Others were tearing the draperies from the windows. Dozens of others, attempting to rush up the narrow stairway, had been caught in the crush, and they struggled and fought each other, and howled.

This was the sight that burst upon Paul's incredulous and smarting eyes as he approached the head of the stairway. He stood, frozen, and gazed down upon the writhing, red-faced mob reeling and struggling in the smoke. When they saw him, a famished and demoniacal roar burst from their throats.

"There is the pig, the oppressor, the murderer, the liar and the heretic!" shrieked the women. They stretched up their hands to him, curved like claws, as if to seize and rend him.

Paul stood, unmoving, gazing down. His mind was reeling. He saw those familiar faces, now transformed into the faces of devils. He fell against the wall, gasping. The scene below swam before his vision: the flame-streaked walls, the billowing smoke, the scarlet faces, the clenched and flourishing fists. Heat choked him. The noise deafened him. It was a nightmare! It was a horror! He was dreaming! He heard the shouts and the howls, the snarling sounds from bursting and savage throats. He could not believe. His mind refused to accept this.

Some one brushed his elbow. He shook his dazed head and saw that Madame duPres stood at his elbow, her black hair streaming wildly over her shoulders. She was clad only in her long white silken shift, which glistened in the red and streaming light. Through its diaphanous substance her white and shapely flesh gleamed like marble through mist.

Distraught, beside herself with terror, she did not see Paul, or, if seeing him, she was hardly aware of him. She stood on the top step of the staircase and extended her arms imploring to the mob below, who, upon her appearance, momentarily halted, lifting their contorted and transformed faces up to her.

"No!" she screamed, incoherently. "It was not to be so! It was not promised me like this! Where is the priest? Where is Père de Pacilli! Why is he not here?"

She moved down a step or two, then, as the mob roared in regained fury and madness, she shrank back, precipitately sprang up the steps to Paul's side. Her face was ghastly; her eyes glittered as she rolled them from side to side. She pressed her hands to her bosom.

"Where is the priest!" she shrieked. "Cattle, step aside, I must descend, escape! I was to be given time, you fiends! It was not to be so! Were you not told? It was I who assisted in this; it is I who am your friend, the friend of the priest! Let me descend, in the name of God, lest I perish!"

She extended her hands to them. Her black hair flew about her. Her white and twisted face glimmered in the red light. Paul fell back from her, pressing himself against the wall. He stared at her, as at a horrible apparition.

Now from the mob below came a prolonged howl of hideous laughter. The mouths of the women opened, like black and gaping caverns.

"It is the harlot!" they shrieked. "It is the mistress of the heretic! Kill the whore! Tear her to shreds!"

Foul epithets assaulted her. She shrank back, whimpering, covering her ears with her shaking hands. Her eyes rolled about, feverishly, desperately, seeking escape. At length they fell on Paul. Her hands dropped to her sides. The whimpering became a moan in her throat. "Save me!" she groaned, and groped her way to him with her hands extended.

He looked at her, and shuddered. Then he looked again at the faces he had loved, at the men and women he had succored, at the people to whom he had devoted himself in love

438

and tenderness and mercy. Who could know his thoughts as he gazed down at them in such unmoving silence?

The woman clutched him, her hands gripping him feverishly, seizing his shoulders, his arms, his lifeless cold hands. He did not see or feel her. He only stood there and looked down the staircase. And now, there was no horror, no fear, no dread on his face. There was only a stony sadness, a long profound meditation.

Something in his aspect halted the plunging and maddened throng. They looked up at him, and fell silent. And in that silence the flames crackled and roared, leaping at the windows, stealing more hungrily along the walls, nibbling at the pillars.

Lord and peasants gazed at each other in that red and flickering light. The men, lowering, scratched themselves uneasily. The women snarled deeply in their throats. A restless and fetid stench rose from them, mingling with the acrid smoke. The men looked at the motionless and silent man above them. They saw his pale and glistening face. They saw his eyes.

It was those eyes, striking down into their mean and animal souls, which completely maddened them. Horror, remorse, frenzy and agony seized them, inspired them with sadistic murder. They knew only one thing: they must strike down that man. They must destroy those quiet eyes. They must stamp into obliteration that still face. They must do these things, for their own sakes. If they did not, that face, and those eyes, would haunt them forever, into the very depths of hell.

Maddened, terrified, they struggled again to ascend that staircase. Many shut their eyes. The women sobbed and groaned; the men cursed and panted. Now the clutching hands were less than two feet away. Paul could see the scarlet light glinting on staring and insane eyeballs.

Madame duPres had fallen to his feet. She was clutching his knees, pressing her head against his body. He looked down upon her. Then he stooped, swept her up into his arms and fled down the corridor. He reached his chamber. He dropped the woman, who fell in a heap on the floor. He locked the chamber door. Now, feverishly, he seized a chest, a cabinet, and thrust them in front of the door. He ran to the window. But there was no escape there, either. The grounds of the château glowed with torchlight.

The distant cross on the steeple glittered tranquilly in the moonlight. The dark trees nearby were rosy with fire. Then, on the fringe of the teeming and running men, Paul saw a face. It was the face of Crequy.

Paul was standing on the balcony, his figure outlined clearly against the white walls. He was bathed in flame. He looked at Crequy, standing motionless in the background, staring up at him. The eyes of the men met.

Crequy did not move. Gigantic, stolid, awkward and fat as always, the tavern-keeper stood motionless. But across the heads of the surging and shouting men, their eyes spoke to each other. One of Crequy's hands rose, fell again to his side. But for a long moment they communed with each in the midst of that fire and death and violence.

Suddenly, Crequy was no longer there. Paul gazed over his estates. He saw a distant fire. A faint groan escaped him. He knew that that fire came from the home of François Grandjean.

He returned to the chamber. Madame duPres had lifted herself to her hands and knees. Her hair streamed over her. She raised her face to Paul. And now these two stared at each other in silence.

Then, inch by inch, the woman crept on her knees to Paul. She dropped her head on his feet. "Forgive me," she whispered.

He looked down upon her. And then, in the depths of his ingenuous and noble heart a human impulse stirred. His foot moved instinctively. But, in its very motion, savage and unrestrained towards that bent head and defenseless body, he arrested it. The woman had felt that lifted foot, that motion. She shrank for an instant, gathering her endurance together. Then she felt the impulse wane. She lifted her head; tears were streaming down her face. She rose to her knees, clasping her hands as though praying.

"I have betrayed you, Monsieur," she whispered. "Kick me, strike me, kill me; it will not be too much."

He gazed down at her in silence. Then he asked, quietly: "Why did you do this, Antoinette?"

"It was the priest," she moaned.

Paul passed his hand over his face. When he dropped it, his expression had not changed. "It was so easy?" he said to himself. "So very easy? After all these years, it was so easy for a black priest to undo all that I have done?"

She clutched him about the knees, straining her body against him, weeping terribly. "So easy, Monsieur! It was nothing to do it!"

Wonder dawned like a frozen light in his staring eyes. His

lips moved, but no sound came from them. He turned his head from side to side, in a motion of strangulation. Then he sighed, over and over. He looked down at the woman, and pity passed like a bright light over his face.

He lifted her to her feet. He held her to him. She wound her arms about his neck, her tears running down his shoulder, wetting his shirt. But he looked beyond her, sighing heavily. The sound pierced her to her vain, hard heart.

Now the mob had roared into the corridor, full of blood lust, screaming and howling. They assaulted the door of the chamber. It trembled and shook under their blows. The vilest epithets and threats could be heard, coming muffled through the wood. Paul looked at the door. It would not be long before it would go down before that furious assault, and then the ferocious mob would pour into this room, to do unspeakable things.

Paul gently lifted Madame duPres' head from his shoulder. He took her wet face in his hands, and looked down into it penetratingly.

"In a moment they will break in, Antoinette. Shall they find us alive?"

She groaned; she shuddered. Then, she was silent. She looked back at him, and into those beautiful shallow eyes, streaming with tears, came a still and desperate light, but a light of supreme courage.

He put her aside, very gently. She did not move; she watched him as he went quietly to the table and lifted his sword. She saw its flash as he unsheathed it. Then, he picked up his pistol. He returned to her.

"There is only one bullet in this weapon, Antoinette. It must be for me. Have you courage? It will be a pang of but a moment."

His voice was almost drowned out in the deafening roar that came from the corridor. The door was squealing on its hinges. In a moment it would burst open.

Paul lifted the sword, and pressed its point against the woman's half naked breast. A drop of blood sprang up about that point. He looked into her eyes. She had not winced. But now she smiled, and half extended her hands to him, whispering one last request.

He leaned towards her slowly, his sword pressing forward. As it plunged into her heart, their lips met.

The door burst from its hinges. But as it did so, there was one loud report in the room.

When the sun rose in a scarlet dawn, it looked down upon the château de Vitry. It was completely gutted. Here and there a chimney, a fragment of smoke-stained white wall, gaped emptily at the sky, wisps of curling gray smoke still rising from them.

CHAPTER XLI

CREQUY HAD NEVER been known to have an intimate, or even the most casual of friends. The peasants had known always that he hated them. They hated him in return, but respected him. His tavern was popular, for he never cheated, and at times he was seized with a strange generosity which made him produce hams, sausages and other delicacies, and, with growls and curses, would invite his guests to partake of them without charge. No one had ever fathomed why he did this. On these rare occasions, the peasants would feel quite an affection for him.

No one had ever suspected that he loved the Comte de Vitry. The legend existed that he loathed him. The peasants, then under the guidance of the Abbé Lovelle, felt great wrath and indignation over this matter. Their anger was no way decreased by the fact that he drove away all young men who came to woo his pretty niece, Roselle. "One would believe he is preserving her for the Comte, if the Comte were a man such as his father," they would grumble.

But the priest, de Pacilli, had guessed Crequy's sullen secret. However, he did not consider it of importance enough to mention this to those whom he was seducing. In that, he made his cardinal error.

Another matter which Crequy kept secret was his slow and reluctant friendship for old François Grandjean. The friendship had not grown steadily. But it had grown. Cecile and Roselle became friends, also.

In order to conceal his "softness" in the matter of taking a friend, Crequy would visit Grandjean late at night, and they would sit for hours over a bottle of wine, Crequy arguing ferociously, Grandjean smiling gently, but persisting in his point of view. The friendship was a consolation to both. Grandjean had acquired no popularity with the peasants, in spite of his efforts. His simplicity of manner had not deceived them that he was one of them. However, they were inclined to look kindly upon him, because of the friendship the young Comte evidently had for him. But they were jealous.

The priest had done his work well with regard to François Grandjean. He had come to share in the suspicion and hatred heaped upon Paul de Vitry.

On this certain night, the young Cecile had been visiting at the home of her friend, Roselle, who had been suffering an indisposition for a few days. The young girls had been so engaged in pretty and vivacious conversation and laughter, and Crequy had so enjoyed this innocent diversion, scowling and grinning in his corner, that the hour was late before they all realized it. With great haste, therefore, just as the sonorous bell in the church tower was ringing eleven o'clock, Cecile had snatched up her cloak and caught up the empty basket which she had brought to this house filled with delicacies.

Crequy announced his intention of accompanying her to her home. The girl protested, declaring there was no danger. But Crequy obstinately insisted. "There are no animals in the street and the woods," Cecile declared. "No, not four-legged ones," said Crequy, grimly.

The cottage of the Grandjeans was a considerable distance from the tavern, a walk of at least half an hour. The evening was fair and brilliant, and the shadows of the two, the great lowering giant and the slender young girl, writhed before them. The village apparently slept. The moon struck the high white walls of the distant château on its eminence in its gardens. The night had a holiness and a sweetness, and the two walked in silence.

But Crequy was not a peasant for nothing. As they approached the silent dark cottage of the Grandjeans, he suddenly caught the arm of the girl and halted her roughly, lifting his nose to sniff the air. "There is something strange," he muttered.

Frightened, the girl paused, and looked about her. Before her, at the end of the cobbled street, her grandfather's house slept in moonstriped silence. On each side, the square and solid stone houses slept also. Not a light was visible. A nightingale was singing in the massed trees that sheltered the houses.

"There is nothing," she whispered, sniffing also, fearing fire. But the air was fresh and cool, heavy with sweet scents. Crequy shrugged, listened again. "Was that a sound, a voice?" he asked. His hand felt at his belt for the strong club he always carried there.

444

"And if it was, is that strange?" asked the girl, impatiently. "A child stirring, wakefully, a mother, a sick man—"

Crequy turned his head from side to side, like a great bull, muttering to himself. Then, with an irritable grumble, he took the girl's arm and led her to her grandfather's cottage. Near the door, he stopped again. Had that been a rustle in the garden, among the bushes and the trees, a stealthy rustle like the sound of several men creeping? He left the girl at the gate and investigated. The garden slept in the moonlight; the tops of the trees were silver, the paths were rimmed with silver, the roof of the house was plated with silver, the tree trunks were outlined with ghostly silver. And here and there a leaf, stirring darkly in the faint wind, suddenly turned to an ovoid of silver.

Shaking his head uneasily, Crequy returned to the gate, where Cecile, her lips compressed in an impatient smile, waited, tapping one foot.

"Go in," he ordered her. "I shall wait here until the door has closed."

She laughed a little, gently. "My grandfather sleeps; we must not disturb him." She rose on tiptoe and kissed his scarred cheek affectionately. He was touched at this, sheepishly. But he remained at the gate until she had opened the door, and had waved to him archly. The door closed behind her.

He stood there a moment or two in the moonlight, then returned the way he had come. But he could not rid himself of the sensation that he was being watched by many stealthy eyes.

He walked swiftly, with his sidling lumbering gait, for some five minutes. Then he paused suddenly, lifting his head again. There was a thin acrid stench in the air. He swung about swiftly. A dim rosy glow was leaping towards the sky. He began to run quickly back to the Grandjean cottage. It was a nightmare journey, his shadow leaping about him on the cobbled street. Nothing stirred or moved, but that rosy glow deepened.

It was indeed the Grandjean cottage, as he now observed, groaning. But why was no one else disturbed? Why did nothing move on the earth or in the houses? He told himself that there had been an accident, a careless flame on the hearth, a fallen candle as the girl had climbed upstairs to bed. But his peasant's prescience and awareness denied this. He knew something frightful was afoot.

He reached the cottage. It stood far apart from the others,

445

in its large gardens and trees. Now those trees were a cave of crimson light, in which the cottage was burning fiercely. The distant houses were still shrouded in ominous darkness. He heard a roaring. This roaring came from the flames, but there was another and indefinable sound with it, as from a kindred roaring at a considerable distance—a human sound.

He leapt over the gate, not waiting to unfasten it. The windows of the cottage were scarlet with the shadow of the flames inside. He burst open the door, shouting loudly. The smoke and heat stung his eyes; water ran from them. For some moments he could not see.

Then, as he stumbled about in that inferno, he fell over something. The flames flared up. He saw that the old man, François, and Cecile lay at his feet, huddled together in one heap.

His mind tottered with his horror. With his great strength, he seized both of them, dragged them from the fiery pit which momentarily appeared about to engulf them. He carried them far from the house, deposited them on the grass, whose dew sparkled like quivering rubies in the reflection of the flames. He shouted, again and again, looking backwards desperately at the silent houses at a little distance. But no one answered his shouts.

The girl was moaning. Crequy saw that a wound had been dealt her on the head, and that it was bleeding profusely. He bent over the old man. François' gaping empty eyes stared upwards at the moon. His mouth had dropped open, and no breath came from it. A terrible wound oozed on his forehead, which appeared crushed in deeply. Crequy knew that the old man was dead.

Loud tearing sobs came from Crequy's throat. He shouted frantically, over and over. Still, no one came. Then, seeing the serious condition of the girl, he lifted her in his arms and started back to his own home. Her blood dripped on his hands. She had ceased to moan; she lay in his arms like one already dead.

He had almost reached his tavern, weaving and running desperately, when he became conscious of a prolonged and savage roaring. He looked towards the château.

And then, he halted in his tracks, gaping idiotically, the girl sagging in his arms. For the walls of the château were leaping with rosy flames. And around the grounds Crequy could see the black dancing shadows of a countless number of men. He could hear a far distant screaming.

And then it was that he knew. He did not think, as a

more civilized and urban man might have done, that this was all an accident, that the men leaping about the château were endeavoring to save it. He did not deceive himself frenziedly as would have done that more civilized and urban man. Aware, naturally, of the vileness and ferocity of the human mind, he understood at once.

He flung himself in the shadows along the trees and the houses. Now he raced towards his tavern with numbed legs. His groaning breath tore at his throat. He dashed into his house, closed the door after him, and bolted it. Roselle, hearing that precipitous entry, appeared at the doorway of her chamber, in her shift. She had a candle in her hand. When she saw her uncle, and his burden, she swayed and cried aloud. But he brushed by her, carrying the unconscious girl to his niece's bed, and laying her upon it with trembling arms. Then he turned to Roselle, and spoke hoarsely:

"See you, my child, listen closely. Old Grandjean has been murdered by these foul animals. They thought they had murdered this little one, also. They then set fire to their cottage, thinking to hide their murder. Do not swoon, or I shall thrash you violently! Take care of this child, hide her. Let no one enter this house. See, there is my pistol on the fireplace, Keep it with you. I shall return in a short time."

The girl did not scream. Crequy, with one last longing look at the pistol, ran from the house, hastened towards the château. He had but one thought: to rescue the Comte de Vitry. As he rushed headlong, his slow peasant mind was red with his fury. He understood it all. Like a foul phantom face, the countenance of the priest flickered before him, smiling darkly and subtly.

But when he arrived at the château, he saw it was useless. He would only be murdered, if he attempted to reach the Comte, and then what would happen to his little cabbage, Roselle, and Cecile? Nevertheless, he slunk about the burning château, seeking, like a wild animal, for some means of carrying out his desperate hope. Some one shouted in his ear, and he paused, dazed:

"Ha, now, Crequy, you have your revenge on this monster, this heretic! Have you not always hated him? Behold him, then, on his balcony. Laugh you in his face, Crequy!"

Crequy lifted his streaming eyes. He saw Paul de Vitry on his balcony, looking down at his seething, red-stained gardens.

Crequy gazed at the Comte, and the Comte gazed at him,

over the sea of writhing and leaping heads. For a long time, they gazed like this, in the light of the devouring fire.

Then Crequy raised his hand, slowly, terribly, as though taking an oath. The Comte did not move. But in his eyes there appeared a strange and mournful pleading. Crequy shook his head, with a frightful expression.

Crequy turned away. He slipped stealthily from the throng of maddened faces.

He made his way to the priest's house. He knocked, softly. There was no answer. Crequy pushed open the door. The house was in darkness. Softly, moving on the balls of his feet, Crequy searched the house. Then a howl broke from him. The priest had escaped! He was gone.

Crequy rushed from the house. He glanced about him, like a wild thwarted beast. On what road had the priest fled? The road to Paris was beyond the house of Grandjean. He, Crequy, had seen no horse, no carriage, no man on foot. His glittering eyes plunged about him in the dark. He saw the gleaming cross on the church.

He began to run towards the church, his club in his hand. Now he knew that in that sanctuary the priest was hidden. But he was not entirely sure of it until he attempted to open the ancient doors. They were locked. A deep savage shout burst from him, primitive and full of blood-lust.

His strength was great, heightened by his insane fury. He broke down the doors in a few moments, and plunged into the deep black vault of the church. Nothing stirred under the curved arches. The tops of the old pillars were silver with moonlight, but all below was in profound silence and darkness.

Silent now, like a stalking animal, Crequy crept towards the altar. The flickering red light was like a malignant eye. He fumbled on the altar for a candle, found the short thick stub of one. He reached up and lit that candle from the eternal flame of the altar.

Then, inch by inch, holding the wavering taper high, he searched the little church. But he did not find the priest.

Now that long savage howl, frustrated, burst from him again. It rang back in dreadful echoes from the groined roof and the crowding pillars. The light of the taper glanced back from the ancient walls like the dancing shadows of demons.

Again, he searched the church, peering behind the altar. And so it was that he found the small sunken door.

He stopped there, glaring at it, smiling evilly. He examined the lock. The key was not in it. He pushed against the door. It did not stir under his hand.

Then he spoke softly, his mouth near the wooden door, and his voice was wheedling and horrible:

"Ah, now, father, there is a suppliant here, a sinner, who would confess to you, dear father! Will you not come out and listen to him? Will you not join him in confession, good father in Christ? While he tells you of his sins, will you not tell him how you murdered a poor old man, and the Comte de Vitry? Ah, father, do not be deaf to this miserable suppliant! Come forth and confess to him, before you descend into hell and meet your master face to face."

His dreadfully soft voice came back to him in muffled echoes from the walls and the ceiling. The altar flame leapt up once, then seemed to cower. The darkness crept nearer, seemed filled with unseen but terrible faces.

Crequy knocked gently on the door. His wheedling voice was frightful to hear. "Ah, now, sweet father, you cannot be asleep? Not while the Comte is being murdered? Not while a suppliant pleads with you?"

Grinning madly, he pressed his ear to the door. Was that a faint gasping stir behind its wooden panels? Was that a caught breath, a shuffling, a descending, a creeping away?

Crequy began to laugh, at first gently, then with rising power, until all the church echoed back in broken and thunderous sounds that inhuman laughter. The pillars seemed to tremble in it. The walls appeared to groan and quiver.

Crequy set down his candle carefully. Then he applied his shoulder to the door. But, set in its aperture, it did not move. Again and again streaming with sweat, he assaulted it. Now his flesh was broken and bleeding. His great brow and bald skull were wrinkled like an ape's. His lips were drawn back over his teeth. He bent his head, straining at the door. All his life, his heart, his spirit, were concentrated in that assault. He appeared to be leaning against it, like an exhausted man. But that was deceptive. For now a faint splintering and squealing sound came from the tortured wood.

Moment after moment passed away, and Crequy did not appear to move. But the muscles of his neck and arm and back turned purple, became black with the congested blood. Veins sprang out over his brow and mighty crimson cheeks. His legs bent forward, and the muscles sprang out like huge rocks under the straining cloth of his britches and his hose. And now there was no sound at all in the church, except that dim groaning of the strong door.

Then, all at once, the hinges gave way. The door fell inward with a deafening crash. It thudded down the wet and stony steps leading into the crypt. Crequy, having picked up his candle again, stood on the threshold, peering into the gloom. He was gasping aloud, his lungs laboring. His body shook like a tree in a storm.

Now he was smiling again. With slow dainty steps he descended holding the candle high.

He found himself in a tiny crypt. The old stone walls ran with moisture. A lizard, and other noisome small creatures, sprang across his feet, disappeared in the darkness. The floor of the crypt was slimy, running with thin snakes of black water. And, in a far corner, huddling on his knees, was the priest.

Now, never before in his life, had the thought of personal death occurred vitally to Monseigneur Antoine de Pacilli. Like all men, of powerful good or evil, death had appeared to him to be a swamp which sucked under others, but could never engulf himself. It had been an academic idea to this priest, but not one of such importance as to demand pondering or reflection. It was something which stealthily attacked lesser men, but none such as those of supreme intellect, cold egotism and superhuman endowments. In fact, it had something vulgar in it, and shameful and humiliating. This calamity which destroyed rats and canaille had naught to do with such as Monseigneur Antoine de Pacilli.

Now, he was face to face with this detestable, this degrading, this contemptible, but all-powerful enemy.

So it was that Crequy, when directing the full candle-light on the white face of the staring priest, saw no fear upon it, no whimpering dread, but an all-pervading horror and repudiation. That delicate carved countenance, those almond eyes, that sleek dark head, seemed to vibrate before him in an aura of its own. Even in that dread moment, the aristocrat was there, fallen to his knees from exhaustion, and not from fright.

Crequy laughed aloud, rocking on his heels. The candle-light leapt upon the walls, the low ceiling, the floor. But de Pacilli did not move. His face became narrower and whiter than ever, as if in cold and intellectual denial.

"Ah, now, sweet father, why so silent, so pale?" cried Crequy. "Why have you ignored a suppliant? Or have you been so engrossed in your foul prayers that you did not hear my voice? Or have you been listening to the murdered soul of the Comte de Vitry, whispering its last confession in your ears?"

The priest was silent. His tilted black eyes glittered like the eyes of some evil serpent, watchful, unmoving, expressionless.

Crequy carefully laid his candle on the floor. He stretched out his hands; he grinned; he carefully examined, then curved, his great murderous fingers. He looked at the priest again, and licked his lips. Now an obscene and inhuman light danced, flickered, blazed in his little starting eyes. Slowly, inch by inch, he crept across the cracked streaming floor towards the priest, his hands extended, his lips uttering strange gibberish.

The priest did not move. He watched the approach of death with no change of expression. He might have been a dead man, waiting.

Crequy reached him. He paused for a moment, and executioner and victim stared at each other in the uncertain candlelight.

Then Crequy howled again, and it was a wolfish, a tigerish, sound. He reached down. He seized the priest by the throat, dragged him to his feet. De Pacilli did not resist. He hung from Crequy's hands like a narrow black sheath topped by a white fixed face.

Crequy drew that face so close to his own that they almost touched.

"Pray now, dog, pray now, sweet father, for in five instants you shall see the face of Satan," he whispered. He shook the limp body by the throat, so that it swayed in his grip.

Then, his hands closed tighter about that slender throat. He felt his hands sink through the flesh to the bone. He felt muscle and vein crush and dissolve under his grasp. The priest did not struggle; his arms hung slackly at his side.

Slowly, that white narrow face turned red, purple, then black. The eyes had fixed themselves, even in their rolling upwards, upon Crequy's fiendish countenance. Now, they fastened there, as he died.

But, to the last, those eyes did not flicker or close. The horror only increased, as if transfixed by a most frightful and appalling vision.

CHAPTER XLII

THERE WAS ONE man at the Court of Louis the Thirteenth to whom the powerful Catholic reaction and the liberal Protestant drive towards liberty, enlightenment and justice meant little or nothing. At the most strenuous, he was vaguely amused; at the least, he found it all excessively tedious. He was a very young man at this time, vivacious, heedless, irresponsible and gay, full of light malice and high humor. He found every one ridiculous to a lesser or greater degree, and it was not unusual for him to burst out laughing even in the face of the Cardinal.

Once, with the most imperturbable gravity, he had addressed the ambitious Cardinal, in the very midst of an illustrious assemblage, as "your Majesty." Then, as the Cardinal paled, and his tiger eyes glittered ominously, and those about caught their breath and glanced at each other, the young man had hastily amended with a mockery of a confused bow: "I implore your pardon, your Eminence: I meant—lèse majesté."

This appalling witticism had gone the whole length and breadth of France, and had aroused fury, laughter, applause and admiration, depending upon the audience and its political or religious affiliations.

The witticism rose from the fact that the Cardinal, by his pressure on the Queen Mother, had induced her to arrange a marriage between this young man and Mademoiselle de Montpensier, a young lady of great family and enormous wealth, whom the youth loathed. By his insistence and arrangement of this marriage, the Cardinal had usurped truly royal privilege. Hence, the witticism. It had been a personal and narrow jest of the young man's, and he was too light-hearted and superficial to have meant any larger implication. But the larger implication was applied to it by all Frenchman, and the young man received the reputation of being exceedingly subtle and sinister, a conclusion which would have astonished and amused him.

Nevertheless, in his whistling, careless, jesting way, he had no mean intelligence. He never lost an opportunity to bait the Cardinal. To the casual observer, this young man was only an amusing and powerless nonentity, for all his royal birth. Only the few who were his intimates knew of his true ruthlessness, vindictiveness, and sleepless hatred for the Cardinal.

This young man was Gaston, younger brother of the young King. He was in high contrast to his brother, for he had gifts of tongue, person and personality which humiliatingly dwarfed the sullen, morose and silent Louis. Gaston was also the darling of the Queen Mother, who had personal reasons for hating the Cardinal. There was nothing which the wheedling Gaston could not accomplish when appealing to Marie de Medici, especially if it had something to do with disconcerting either the Cardinal or the King.

As if the projected marriage was not sufficient to annoy young Gaston, another and more serious matter had arisen, which had turned him from light malice against the Cardinal to iron hatred.

He had had, as his tutor, one old and aristocratic Corsican, Marshal Ornano, who was devoted to his pupil, and to the Queen Mother. Seeing the young man's repugnance to the marriage to Mademoiselle de Montpensier, he had urged him to refuse the young lady. The matter became not only a skirmish in the royal household, but an affair of national, and international importance, to those who wished to break the power of the Cardinal and the King. Mesdames de Conde and de Chevreuse joined in the conspiracy. Conde, Soissons, and Nevers came surging with secret offers of help. The young man's powerful and illegitimate brothers, Vendome Governor of Brittany, and Vendome the Grand Prior, enthusiastically joined the tumult. England, Savoy and Spain hastened eagerly forward to observe the proceedings and join in the plotting. All the disaffected magnates of France gathered together in secret session. At length, it was decided that Gaston was to conquer and hold some frontier province. In the meantime, his adherents were to murder the Cardinal, and rid France forever of that gigantic and looming shadow of power.

However, the Cardinal's spies were only too efficient. Ornano, the devoted and ancient Corsican, was seized and thrown into the prison of Vincennes, where he was later poisoned at the command of the Cardinal. Gaston, broken-hearted, thrown at last out of his light-hearted and indifferent malice into a fury of hatred, grief and lust for vengeance, appealed to his brother, who refused to see him. He rushed to the Cardinal, broke through his advisers and intimidated guards, forced his way to the bed-chamber of his Eminence, and, leaning over the gold and scarlet bed, struck the priest violently in the face, over and over. When he had done this, he raised his fist, uttered slow and dreadful imprecations, and vowed that he would never sleep until he had avenged the death of his beloved tutor.

The Cardinal did not forget that insult. He went at once to the King, and offered his resignation. Louis, who had no love for him, but only fear, nevertheless was terrified, understanding only too well who upheld his own power and his throne. He offered the Cardinal anything he desired, if he would remain. The Cardinal, then, in a low and hesitating voice, declared that he had no devotion except to the throne, and that he found it impossible to devote himself to the King if, in the King's own household, there lived one who had vowed to continue his plottings against that royal authority. "Therefore," said the Cardinal, sadly, "if I am to remain to serve your Majesty, I must ask, out of my love for you, Sire, that Prince Gaston be forced to swear the oath of loyalty."

The Cardinal knew only too well the inherent pride and hauteur under the superficial mannerisms and laughter of the humming and singing Gaston. This was a petty revenge he had asked. But the King did not observe the pettiness. He was all aglow, touched, at this evidence of the Cardinal's single-hearted devotion to him. He commanded that Gaston appear before him, in the presence of the Cardinal, and humbly swear that oath of loyalty to the Throne.

Gaston, still prostrated with sorrow over the death of his adored tutor, at first decided to refuse, let the heavens fall if they wished. But the Queen Mother, terrified at the danger about to fall upon her darling, implored him on her knees to humiliate himself, for her sake. "And," she added slyly, through her tears, "wait your time, my sweetest boy. Wait your time! Is not your mother still beside you? We will find some way to circumvent this fiend of a Cardinal!"

Upon reflection on this, and also having a high regard for his own personal safety, Gaston consented to swear the oath. But in his burning heart, he added another score to settle with the Cardinal.

The Italian Queen Mother had the blood of vendettas in

her veins. She, too, had her private, and shameful, reasons for hating the Cardinal. Had she not raised him from nothing, worked endlessly for his elevation to power, glory and influence? Yet, in the end, he had visited only remorselessness, cold indifference, and humiliation upon her, after he no longer needed her. A passionate and vicious Catholic, a Habsburg, she was now forced to watch him check the Habsburg power—that supreme and Catholic power!—and temporize with the Huguenot magnates (those vile heretics!). All in the name of France, the traitor had declared! What cared she, the Habsburg, the Italian, for France? What had she, the Catholic, the vindictive hater of Protestant England, the Netherlands, and the Huguenots of France, to do with the "tolerance" the Cardinal was continually urging?

Moreover, in her love for her younger son, Gaston, she had been imploring the King, whom she hated, to grant Gaston the governorship of Champagne or Burgundy. But this plan the Cardinal defeated with his usual subtlety and dexterity. This scarlet upstart had again frustrated her, flaunting the power she had given him in her own outraged face! In her own chamber, she wept, beat her pillows with her hands, cursed the Cardinal, sobbed, groaned, vowed vengeance, and drowned herself in floods of aching and burning tears. For still, in that coarse, violent and brutal heart lived a passion for the elegant Armand-Jean de Plessis, a passion she could never obliterate, and which was stung only to fresh excesses, voluptuously, at every new humiliation and frustration he inflicted upon her.

She had never had much fondness for Anne of Austria, though she had arranged the wedding between Anne and the King. But now, in this lovely and frightened, suffering and seduced girl, she found an ally against the Cardinal. Thus, these three, Marie de Medici, Gaston, and Anne, formed a nucleus of hatred and plotting, in the heart of the royal household. All three, now, having originally had only dislike, indifference, ridicule or aversion for the King, were aroused to the most fiery hatred against him, only slightly less than the mutual hatred they felt for the Cardinal.

Young Prince Gaston had just finished his breakfast, and was playing with his dogs in his bed-chamber, when his gentleman-of-the-chamber entered respectfully to announce the arrival of Monsieur Arsène de Richepin.

Gaston had a fondness for Arsène, as he had a fondness for all young men like himself: gay, irresponsible, reckless, brave and amusing. Arsène had written him yesterday, imploring him for this audience. So the prince put aside his dogs, and requested that Monsieur be admitted at once.

As he waited for Arsène, Gaston frowned. From the urgency of Arsène's message, he had come to the conclusion that this was to be no light request made of him. Gaston, under his lightness, had true devotion for his few friends, and it irked him that he was now so powerless, watched constantly by the Cardinal's spies, hated and suspected by his brother, Louis, the King. Nevertheless, he decided that if he could assist Arsène, he would do so.

He stood in his dressing-gown of red satin, by his window in the palace, glowering and biting his lip. This expression did not sit easily on an open and handsome countenance, already lined, despite his youth, with the thin furrows of natural laughter and vivacity. He was rather tall, well-made, and of a fair complexion, with dancing blue eyes and large quantities of thick, curling brown hair, which fell on broad, straight and soldierly shoulders. His every movement was quick and supple, full of grace and power and strength. Though he was dissipated, amorous, given to violent excesses in all things, his native and abundant health had not suffered, and his vitality was still enormous and bubbling. In the lines about his eyes, in his quick, lilting glance, in the curve of his humorous and mobile mouth, were the evidences of a nature which loved plotting for its own sake.

Arsène entered. He was dressed in somber black. His face was gaunt and haggard, his eyes sunken. He greeted the prince with deep reverence, but when he would have kissed Gaston's hand, the young prince raised him with a gay laugh, and kissed him lightly on the cheek. He was indeed delighted to see his old friend, in whom he knew there was no superficial treason, slyness or meanness. He led him to a love-seat near the bed, and they sat down on it together, looking into each other's eyes.

In his exuberance, the prince burst gayly into a stream of witticisms, malicious light stories, laughter, and questions which he did not wait for Arsène to answer. As he did so, he kept his hand fondly on the other's shoulder, pressing it heavily as he threw back his handsome head to laugh deliciously. Then, becoming aware at last, even in his selfishness, of Arsène's dark pallor, of his heavy and reluctant smiles, and sick silence, he exclaimed:

"What ails you, Arsène?"

He no longer laughed. His own face became sober, and

somewhat uneasy, and he was conscious again of his power-lessness in a pending emergency.

Arsène drew a deep breath; it quivered, like a suppressed moan. He looked for a long and piercing moment into Gaston's eyes; then asked, in a low voice: "You have not yet heard, your Highness, about the Comte de Vitry?"

Gaston started. He drew back a little. "Paul?" Then after a moment, he said in a quicker and more disturbed voice: "Paul? What is wrong with Paul?"

He was not indifferent now. Among his very few friends, Paul had loomed as the kindest, the most loyal, the most devoted. Their encounters were rare, but when in contact with that gentle and noble nature, Gaston had felt some strong and simple virtue enter even himself. He seized Arsène's wrists, and forced that sunken face to turn fully to him.

Arsène was silent a moment, then he whispered: "Paul has been murdered."

Gaston sprang to his feet with a great muffled cry. "Murdered! It is not possible! Who would murder him?" Now his face turned ghastly; the blue eyes were full of fire.

"If your Highness will be seated, I will tell you everything," said Arsène, gripping the back of the seat with straining hands.

Trembling, Gaston slowly sank back on the seat. His countenance, now, had become an evil white mask, and his very lips were colorless.

"It was by instigation of the Cardinal," said Arsène.

"The Cardinal!" Gaston half-rose from the seat, and his nostrils flared. Then he was quiet. He waited.

"Paul was murdered by his peasants, for whom he had done so much, to whom he had devoted his fortune and his life," whispered Arsène. He swallowed, as though his dry throat threatened to choke him.

"Go on," said Gaston, in a whisper, also. His face, if possible, grew even whiter.

Arsène passed his hands over his face. He gasped. His agony was visible even to those careless eyes.

After a long moment, during which he struggled to speak through parched and shaking lips, he said: "You will remember, your Highness, that Paul lived only to enlighten, free and comfort his people. You have disapproved, I remember. I recall your arguments with Paul.—Nevertheless, you know his goodness of heart, his purity of motive, his visionary zeal.

"Some one, some fiend, convinced the Cardinal that all

this was only a prelude to a plot, that our poor friend was intriguing, in some inexplicable way, for the destruction of France. Moreover, he had enemies, who hated him for his gentleness and tolerance and mercy. They affected to believe that should Paul's methods gain new adherence, France was in danger—!"

"To hell with France!" said Gaston, quietly.

"So," continued Arsène, "these enemies came to the Cardinal. He appointed a priest, one de Pacilli, to seduce the people, cause them to rise against the Comte. He did his work well! Paul was murdered, two nights ago, in his château. The priest's body was found in the church. Some devoted soul accomplished that just execution."

His voice trailed away. He could speak no more. He dropped his head on the back of the seat, and wept in appalling silence.

There was no sound in the chamber. Gaston stared blindly before him. His voice was hardly audible when he finally spoke:

"You are certain of all this? Who was this de Pacilli?"

Arsène struggled to control himself. "I met this priest some time ago. I did not recognize him at first. But I was plagued by some memory. It was only after I heard of Paul's murder that I remembered seeing him once in the Cardinal's entourage. Then, I knew the whole plot. I did not even need the explanations of the messenger who came to me."

"The Cardinal!" whispered Gaston, still staring before him. And now a malignant smile touched his mouth.

"This morning," continued Arsène, in that dry and fluttering whisper, "a young woman came to me, one Roselle. Her uncle, Crequy, is tavern-keeper on Paul's estates.—It seems the people, before murdering Paul, had assassinated his steward, an old man. They thought they had also killed his granddaughter. But they failed in this. Crequy rescued her, and she lies hidden in his house, close to death. He dared not leave her. So, he sent his niece to me with the horrible news."

His voice failed him.

Gaston did not speak. His brow wrinkled, knotted itself. Under that shelf, his eyes gathered fire and fury.

"They burned the château," Arsène went on, after a long interval. "Now, the peasants lurk in their village, terrified, but still full of madness. They prowl like animals. Reason is beginning to return to them. They await vengeance. But the man responsible for this is safe from attack—"

Gaston turned to him. Though his face was so malignant, so terrible, his voice was very low: "What can I do?"

Arsène hesitated. But he looked fully at the young prince.

"This crime must be avenged. I, and my friends, are prepared to avenge it."

Gaston lifted his hands, palm up. He looked at them steadfastly. Then, with a gesture more eloquent than words, he let them drop heavily upon his knees. But Arsène seized his arm.

"Private revenge can have no effect. These foul swine, these peasants, must be made to understand that their crime is against all authority! If they are not thoroughly and mercilessly punished for their treachery, their revolt against their lord, who knows what will be the end? Who knows what excesses the canaille will accomplish next?"

Even in his anguish, his torment of grief, he used this artfulness in appealing to the proud and haughty young prince. Gaston turned to him again, alertly listening, glowering, clenching his fists.

"Moreover," said Arsène, softly, closely watching Gaston, "the Cardinal must be made to feel that there is another power in France beside his own—the power of justice—and that he cannot flout this power forever without feeling its weight."

Gaston stood up, as if stung. An exultant wave of dark blood washed over his face.

"My friends," said Arsène, "are willing to accomplish this double revenge"—against rioters who defy the power of authority, and against the Cardinal, who abuses his office, and the trust of—the guileless, the weak. But they will not attempt to accomplish this revenge secretly and furtively, like brigands, like fleeing marauders. This would also be against established authority. They are lawful gentlemen. You know many of them, Monsieur. They wish to do this thing, in vengeance for many others, humiliated, humbled and injured by the Cardinal."

Gaston turned, seemed about to speak, was silent. But the fire in his eyes increased.

"Moreover," said Arsène, "they wish, after the vengeance is accomplished, to be immune from vindictive acts on the part of the Cardinal—for a little while at least. They wish to show that the things they will do were a due process of law, sanctioned by ones in supreme positions. They will have a double justification, then—against the Cardinal, against the people of Paul de Vitry."

Gaston walked to the window. He tugged distractedly and murderously at the draperies. Without turning, he said, in a muffled voice: "What do you wish?"

Arsène grasped the back of the seat. "An order, Monsieur. An order for the just execution of the rebels."

Gaston did not answer. His hand froze on the draperies. Then he said: "I cannot give this order." His tone was full of heavy humiliation, and rage.

"But the Queen Mother, her Majesty, can give this order," said Arsène, very softly.

Gaston wheeled swiftly away from the window. His mouth opened, closed tightly and grimly. His shaken breath escaped through his dilated nostrils.

Arsène approached him, and Gaston watched him come with suddenly veiled eyes. Though he did not retreat, he stiffened.

"It will not be hard to secure this order," said Arsène. His face was contorted with his fierce and remorseless determination. "It needs only to be an ambiguous order. It needs only to say that Arsène de Richepin has been empowered by her Majesty to accomplish a certain mission, and that he is under her protection."

Gaston was silent. He looked steadily down at his feet. "That is impossible," he said coldly.

Arsène stopped in his approach. He drew a deep breath. "Then, Monsieur is perfectly willing that this latest atrocity of the Cardinal go unpunished, that he laugh exultantly to himself that no one dare oppose him, that all else in France is powerless, helpless before him?"

Gaston looked up. He put his hand to his throbbing throat. Then he said: "Wait a moment. I shall not be gone long."

He whirled away towards the door, walking with a rapid and disordered step. Arsène, exhausted, sank on a chair. Then, after a moment, he lifted his clenched fist, and cursed aloud.

But Gaston did not return for a long time. Half an hour passed, another half hour. Unable to contain himself in his growing anxiety and despair, Arsène took to pacing the room. "If I get no order, I shall do it, nevertheless," he said, aloud. Within a few days, he would have fled to La Rochelle. But there was his father, who would remain, and who would feel the full weight of the Cardinal's vengeance. There were those, also, of Les Blanches, who would hesitate to accomplish this thing, for fear of reprisals on their relatives, even though they, themselves, would also have fled to La Rochelle. Arsène's distracted misery increased, but his savage determination did not lessen.

Then, in his pacing, he stopped short, wheeled about. The door had opened almost soundlessly. Gaston was entering. In his hand was a folded paper, sealed with a certain significant and flamboyant seal. He extended this to Arsène, without a word. But his face was moist, and there were deep purple clefts about his mouth.

CHAPTER XLIII

THE CARDINAL HAD JUST COMPLETED a long and arduous morning of audiences upon affairs of State.

Usually, after such a morning, he was prostrated, returning to his bed and remaining there the rest of the day and night, and not rising until late the next day. But he was not prostrated on this day. In truth, he felt an old resurgence of his earlier vitality and youth and exhilaration. His pains had almost vanished. His limbs did not feel weak or flaccid, and the ancient agonies of his mind had lifted so that he could operate in the present. For the first time in many weeks, he felt that France, the world, was of some importance, that they had taken on themselves, once more, the firm and solid outlines and substance of significance. Momentarily, he thought: this is the delusion of petty men. But he had the strength today to push this thought from him, to refuse to look back on the dark and shifting country in which he walked so often. He rejoiced that he could descend to the pettiness of lesser men and believe that the world was worth manipulating.

Moreover, there was the affair of La Rochelle. He intended to lead the campaign against that arrogant and embattled city, himself. For the first time, he mouthed the aphorisms of the Catholic reaction, asserting that the Protestants were attempting to counter-attack against that reaction, an attack which he could not countenance. But in fact, this alleged defiance of the powerful Huguenot magnates against the Catholic reaction did not give him concern. He was really uneasy because of the growing power of the Huguenot cities, and their continued threat against the unity of France. In defense of that unity, he had placated and tolerated them. Now that that very unity was threatened, he had decided to move against the Huguenots.

He walked slowly up and down his chamber with a sense

of growing excitement. He had always possessed a prophetic eye. Today, it was sharper and keener than ever, seeming to plunge far into the future. His vision of a great French Empire seemed to lie before him like a golden dream, floating in luminous mists. But it was no longer a dream to him. It was an approaching reality.

He was no longer imbued with a passionate patriotism. That patriotism, at its best, had been an expression of his deep egotism, a fact which he had recognized but had tried to conceal even from himself. But now he did not conceal it; he rejoiced in it; he exulted in it, acknowledging it with free and untrammeled delight. This France, this dream, was his own! It was his own hand which had carved and shaped its future. It was his monument. It was the work of Armand-Jean de Plessis, Cardinal de Richelieu. Working at last in a full acknowledgment of his supreme egotism, he was hampered by nothing.

A messenger came in with a missive elaborately sealed. The Cardinal, engrossed in his visions, took it impatiently, and tossed it upon a table. He resumed his pacing, which began to take swiftness upon itself. He paused a moment, in knotty cogitation. His eye fell upon the missive, and he took it up, idly. He read it, without grasping the meaning. Only when he came to the agitated signature of Madame de Tremblant, blotted with tears, did he reread the letter with close attention.

He paused, after reading, turning the missive over and over in his fine narrow hands. His brow contracted. He tapped the envelope against his teeth. Once he sighed a little. Then he rang for his secretary, Louis de Richepin. Louis, always close at hand, entered immediately.

The Cardinal studied him for a long bemused moment. That calm and marble countenance had become attenuated, immobile, yet not rigid. It was as if the sharp and stony outlines had been softened by the rains of ages, so that they were less harsh. Yet, in those large blue eyes, so full of glacial tints and remote lights, there was a haunted shadow, an abstraction.

"Ah, Louis," said the Cardinal. He glanced at the missive in his hand, then he moved quickly to a chest near his bed, opened it, and appeared to be absorbed for a moment or two in its contents. "Ah, yes," he murmured. For the first time in some long period he did not know what to say. He turned to the young priest, who was waiting, calm and respectful as always, and appeared to return to the trivial subject at hand. "Ah, yes," he said, still again.

"Your Eminence wished to see me?" asked Louis.

"Yes, yes, of course." The Cardinal paused. He played with his golden cross. "It is nothing of much moment. But Madame de Tremblant informs me that her daughter, Mademoiselle Marguerite, is unwell, and she requests that I send someone to Mademoiselle—a confessor." He did not add that Madame had requested his own presence.

Did the young priest start, or was that a passing shadow through the heavy draperies? Did he pale, or was that again the effect of the shadow? When he spoke, his voice was low, and slightly hoarse: "Mademoiselle—she is very ill?"

The Cardinal hesitated. He touched his fingers to his frail mouth. Then he shrugged. "Who can tell? I doubt it, however. Ladies are subject to frequent humors from which we are happily more immune. Nevertheless, I should deem it a favor, Louis, if you were to go at once to the Hôtel de Tremblant."

Louis approached a step. There was a blue cast over his countenance, in which his eyes were alive and tormented. "Monseigneur, you are certain that Mademoiselle—"

"Louis," interrupted the Cardinal, stabbed by an unusual pang, "I have said I do not know. Madame has asked for a confessor for Mademoiselle. Her daughter has not been able to make her confession recently, and Madame, as you know, is a rigorous Catholic."

Louis did not speak. He wrung his hands. Then, with a bow, he backed away and left the chamber. Sighing, the Cardinal watched him go. Then he reread the missive from Madame:

"I implore your Eminence, who has always been such a kind and affectionate friend to this family, to come at once to the Hôtel de Tremblant. My daughter, Marguerite Marie, is at the point of death. She suffered a hemorrhage of the lungs at midnight, and our physician has informed me that she cannot live to evening."

Louis, impelled by some subconscious command, returned for a moment to his chamber. He gathered up the necessary articles for administration to one in extremis. When he came out of his dark abstraction, and saw what lay in his hands, he drew a sharp groaning breath. "No!" he cried, aloud, staring about him at the bare walls.

When he left the Palais Cardinal, he found the Cardinal's own equipage waiting for him. He never remembered that devious drive through the streets to the Hôtel de Tremblant.

He sat huddled forward, his clenched hands on his knees, his eyes fixed starkly before him. A strange sensation he had never experienced before had him in its grip. He felt that he was dying. Black mists swirled before him, and salt water rose continually to his mouth.

He had no sooner seen the reddened eyes of the man who opened the massive doors for him than he knew that death was in this house. He climbed up the great gilt and marble staircase, holding to the banister with a hand as cold and numb as ice. He felt nothing beneath his feet. He was walking on endless shifting clouds.

He was met at the door of Marguerite's chamber by her weeping mother and sisters. He looked at them dumbly. "I have come," he whispered.

"Ah, Monseigneur, then his Eminence is indisposed?" asked Madame, her hoarse voice muffled and dull.

Louis regarded her with sudden sharp concentration, and his pale lips parted soundlessly.

But Madame saw nothing strange in the young priest's white silence. She leaned upon his arm, as she reentered her daughter's room. They were followed by the sobbing and tearful sisters, so pretty in their subdued gowns and fluttering curls.

Louis had entered only one woman's chamber in all his life, and that chamber had been his mother's. He had an impression, confused with his suffering, of gold and silver and ivory tints, of masses of pale silk drawn across the windows, of a lovely small harp of ivory standing mute in a corner, of a prie-dieu against one wall, fluttering with dim candlelight, which blew fitfully on a large and exquisite crucifix of gilt and ivory, of a white canopied bed floating in white lace, and, upon the silken cushions, a coppery mass of curls framing a still marble face. Two distinguished physicians were bending over that slight and motionless form, which hardly lifted the gleaming white coverlet, so fragile and small was it.

As Madame, the young ladies and the priest entered, the physicians glanced up and inclined their heads. Their faces were full of grave anxiety, and in their eyes was no encouragement, no hope. Louis approached the bed. He looked down upon the dying girl, whose golden lashes touched the dim colorless cheek, whose lips were parted on the painful and feeble breath. He did not move. He might have been made of snow, so expressionless was his countenance, so darkened and in shadow his eyes.

465

"She is becoming conscious," whispered one physician. Madame knelt beside the bed. She dropped her large head, with its great, coarse and brutal features, against her daughter's shoulder. She did not weep. But her arms extended themselves over the poor body of this frail child, and tightened in a desperate embrace. Her daughters disposed themselves about the bed, applying wisps of lace kerchiefs to faces already swollen and blotched with tears.

The dying girl stirred, with a faint moan. The fluttering eyelashes lifted, and the golden eyes stared out blankly, suffused with fear and pain. They touched each face briefly, restlessly, and wandered on. At last they reached Louis. As they did so, a wild and ineffable light flashed into them.

The elder physician whispered something to Madame, and, weeping with the hard dry torment of the strong, she rose, motioned to her daughters, who, with the physicians, followed her from the chamber. Louis and the girl were alone.

They looked at each other. The candlelight fluttered on the crucifix. A faint wind blew the pale draperies at the window. Something bright and shining seemed to fill the chamber.

Louis knelt down beside the girl, and, without a word, laid his head on the pillow which supported her own head. Her hand, lifted with enormous effort, came to rest against his cheek, to press it feebly. Now the cold palm warmed; the finger tips trembled. The girl turned her head, and her icy lips pressed themselves to his brow. They remained like this in a long silence. From Marguerite there flowed that sweet and powerful radiance, comforting and tender, which once before had reconciled Louis to life, had fused him into oneness with another human being.

The sick and fainting anguish in the young priest became quieter, but, mysteriously stronger, more immense, more piercing. He took her hands, and held them to his lips. There were no tears in his eyes, no cry on his tongue. And the girl looked at him with that strong sweet smile of complete faith and love. So pure was it, so resistless, that health and vitality seemed to have returned to her, and faint rose banners fluttered in her transparent cheeks.

"My love," he said, "my dearest love."

She sighed. Her lips moved; then, with a touching gesture, she turned on her side and crept into his arms. He held her against his heart. He looked over the gleaming curls at the prie-dieu and saw nothing but his own desolation.

Marguerite stirred at last. She lifted her mouth, waiting.

He kissed her gently at first, and then, with sudden agony, sudden frantic denial, his kisses became frenzied, and between them he groaned. He held her to him with increasing despair and passionate agony. He was beside himself, distraught.

"You cannot leave me, Marguerite," he said, his lips pressed deeply into her soft white throat. "No, you can never leave me. Did you not promise me this? On that night, Marguerite, you swore to me: 'I shall never leave you.' Do you remember this, Marguerite?"

"Yes," she whispered, clinging to him, looking into his wild eyes with her tender smile. "I shall never leave you, Louis. I shall always be with you."

He understood her. His expression became dark and more wild. "No, Marguerite, if you die, you shall have left me! There is nothing beyond the grave, my sweetest one! Am I not a priest? Do I not know? It is a lie, Marguerite. The priests know it. It is a delusion, a falsehood, spoken out of pity to those who are suffering and despairing! Do I not know? Do we not confess it among ourselves, some with scorn, some with pity, and some with contempt? If you leave me, Marguerite, you will be gone forever! There is nothing —nothing—"

His voice, hoarse, distraught, frenzied, tore through his throat, inflicting pain and twisting torment upon it as though a knife had entered. His hands feverishly held the girl. Between his tortured and incoherent words his lips kissed her, over and over. He kissed her throat, her breasts, her poor emaciated arms, her hands, her forehead and her lips. As on that night of their love, he cried out: "Have pity on me, Marguerite!"

She submitted to his caresses, to the clutching terror of his arms, and listened to his groaning. She forgot her own suffering, her own sinking and fear, in one last supreme compassion and love. When he was quieter, she held him in her arms, and his head lay upon her bosom. She could not speak aloud; her voice came only in a whisper, and her eyes, smiling and full of poignant sweetness and faith, fastened themselves upon the distant crucifix.

"Louis, I shall never leave you. You must not doubt this. Even if only one soul ever lived beyond death, that soul will be mine. Believe it; if you do not, I cannot come to you. I cannot wait for you."

She put her hands under his head and lifted it, and with one last effort of her sinking and dying strength, she forced him to look at her. Now there was no fear in that deathly young face, no sadness. It was all tender smiles and steadfast courage. She drew his head to her. She kissed him slowly and eagerly upon his mouth. Her eyes closed, and she sighed.

He held her to him as if in his own strength, his own savage denial, his own will, he could defy and hold off the supreme enemy of mankind. She lay in his arms, still smiling. Slowly, that smile became fixed, lofty and remote. No breath stirred her breast.

He laid her back upon her pillows. Her eyelids had half opened. A gleam shone from between them. Slowly, with fingers as stiff and rigid as stone, he closed those eyelids. He folded the cooling hands, so frail and small, upon the quiet bosom. The slight wind blew through the draperies, and stirred the copper curls.

He stood up, and looked down upon all that he had ever purely and selflessly loved, all that had brought the world closer to him and had made him a man, all that had given him glimpses of heaven and ecstasy. He stood there, his hand against the post of the canopy, and he did not move.

In his past, there had been no joy; in his present, there was no consolation; in his future, there was no hope. The world rolled away from him like a raveling ball of mist, vanished into eternal fogs. Now he was face to face with the last mute agony of man, confronting the nothingness, the horror, the dread and the despair of eternity. A black and frightful pain transfixed his heart, too profound for words or tears. And it was an enormous hatred that embraced God, that, in its intensity was the last accusation, the last groaning contempt and loathing of man tormented to the death, and seeing his tormentor fully for the first and last time.

All at once, he remembered that he had not administered extreme unction to Marguerite de Tremblant. Remembering this, he began to smile, a most dreadful and contorted smile. That smile widened. He laughed aloud, hoarsely.

A moment later, Madame de Tremblant, her daughters and the physicians entered. Louis did not hear them. His laughter was no longer audible. But it remained on his face; it shook his body.

CHAPTER XLIV

FEAR HAS A LIVING and visible reality, like a gray and steaming fog, like a coiling miasma, like a cloud blotting out the light. It lay over the huddled village, over the vineyards and the dun hills, over the river, pitted and scarred by the cataracts of rain. The very aspect of the heavens, filled with boiling gray and black clouds, the mist which twisted over the fields and meadows, the pools of water which formed in the cobbled streets, the glistening roofs and walls of the low houses, the wind which bent the tall poplars and turned them white as driven ghosts, all seemed of the substance of fear, its very emanation. Everything seemed to shudder, to cower, to writhe, in the storm of fear. Occasionally a serpent of pale and livid lightning leapt over the hills, parted the tempestuous skies, followed by a dull hoarse roaring like the distant tumult of giants.

Not a soul stirred in the streets. Not a faint yellow light glimmered behind the shuttered windows. The small gardens were torn and flattened, petals rising like battered butterflies on the wind, leaves whirling down from the trees. The cross on the church caught wild and brilliant reflection from the lightning, so that it flashed balefully. The river was rising; its heavy and uneasy voice could be heard in the intervals of the wind and the thunder. The desolation was complete. Fear, and its follower, the storm, ruled over the earth.

It was slightly past dawn. For days, now, the villagers had lived in terror. Cooled of their unreasoning, their monstrous madness, they knew that the ferocious law of France would soon beset them. They had killed a great noble, a magnate; they had destroyed his château, the evidence of his power. They had assaulted the power, the law, of France. Punishment would soon be upon them in the shape of the gallows. The priest they had expected to uphold, to exonerate them, was dead. No argument would be allowed, no justification. The

469

walls of France had heard their blows and their imprecations. It would be enough that they had lifted their hands against established power. Now, for the first time, they realized the enormous force arrayed against them. They, the canaille, the disinherited, the helpless, the nameless, had dared to assail authority and privilege. They would die for it.

They huddled together in their fright. Some of the most desperate talked of presenting a formidable front to the coming avengers, but even the most sanguine smiled drearily at this. Some wished to flee with their wives and children. But, where? So long had they been free to think as men, to plan as men, that they evolved all manner of wild plans, with desperate strength. Now, they realized that they had no strength. With the death of their defender, their protector, they were open once again to the savagery of established power.

They still felt no remorse, no sorrow, no grief, for Paul de Vitry. They dared not feel these things. They knew if once they did, they would completely disintegrate. So, they invented among themselves a sustaining thought: he was part of the power which now menaced them, which would destroy them. So, they hated him still. In such fashion does the craven and devious human mind defend itself.

Few slept in these awful days. They waited, and listened, for the avengers. But the storm had been furious that morning. So it was that they did not hear the pounding and rumble of scores of horsemen riding into the village. They did not see or hear the forty young and resolute nobles with their grim countenances, wrapped in their cloaks against the rain, and their two hundred anonymous followers, with coarser faces and more ferocious eyes. These two hundred and forty men drifted like violent hushed shadows into the village, armed, spurred and dripping. The forty crowded into the tavern and the house of Crequy. The two hundred huddled under the eaves of outbuildings, or under the lashing shelter of straining trees.

Crequy had been expecting them. On the pommel of Arsène's horse the young Roselle had ridden. She rushed into her uncle's arms, sobbing. He kissed her, put her from him, and commanded her to go to Cecile Grandjean, who was still in a grave condition. Then the bald and sinister giant turned to Arsène and saluted him respectfully, but with a malignant grin. "You have come, Monsieur," he said.

A great red fire blazed on the hearth. There was another fire in the kitchen. The young nobles crowded about these fires, shaking their wet cloaks pettishly and vigorously, so that the fire hissed at the touch of the flying drops of water. The firelight rose and fell on their young hard faces, on their quick eager eyes, on their white teeth. They talked briefly, questioning Crequy with remote condescension. They filled the tavern and the house with orderly violence and harsh purpose. As they warmed their hands, the firelight caught the flash of jewels on narrow fingers, the glare of an alert eyeball, the dull gleam of the hilts of swords, the shine of wet and streaming hair on young shoulders.

Crequy brought forth the best wine, hams, breads and poultry which he had been hoarding for this day. He lumbered among his guests. They stood about the fires and ate with hearty but preoccupied abandon. Now one or two of the more volatile laughed a little. The scene was full of vivacious movement, all in umber, brown, black and scarlet, the glistening of bold eyes. Crequy looked at them with venomous and contented satisfaction. He was filled with excitement.

Arsène stood a little apart, his face still haggard and sunken, heavy with the apathy of grief, but somber with coming vengeance. He drank wine, but did not eat. Finally, he approached Crequy, said a few words. Crequy nodded. From a hidden place he brought forth coils of rope, went to the door. Arsène waited, and listened. Finally, from a place near the tavern came a dull and ominous hammering. Arsène felt the blow on his heart, and he breathed with difficulty.

Then he had the strangest and most terrible sensation. He felt that Paul de Vitry was suddenly present in that crowded and steaming assemblage, that he was gazing upon them gravely, with a pale countenance and despairing eyes. So vivid was that sensation, that Arsène turned away, and cried vehemently in his heart to that silent and watching ghost: "No! Go away! This is not for you, Paul! No, I shall not listen to you!"

His breath came in painful gasps. He drank deeply of the cup he held in his hands. "Go away!" he cried again, and now with enraged despair.

The rain suddenly halted. But the skies grew darker. The wind was silenced. Now the distant groaning of the river could be clearly heard. Crequy re-entered the room, rubbing his enormous hands. He was a massive figure of evil, the firelight glittering on his naked skull.

Arsène glanced at the narrow wooden stairway near at hand, and Crequy inclined his head. They moved away from the talking and drinking young nobles, and climbed upwards in the dusty darkness. They entered a small bedroom under the eaves, where the dim wailing and whistling of wind and the sharp cracking of crows could be heard. A candle glimmered on the table, striping the walls with broken shadows. Young Roselle, her curls disordered and wet, was seated on a stool beside the trundle bed. Her cheeks were running with crystal drops. Two elderly nuns, black robed and veiled, with pale calm faces and steadfast eyes and long pale hands, were bending over the bed ministering to the girl who lay there, sunken in profound unconsciousness. They looked up as Arsène and Crequy entered, but did not speak or move. Basins of water were at hand, and fresh dressings.

"Monsieur," said Crequy, "these are Sister Eloise and Sister Michele, good nuns of the abbey, sent to nurse Mademoiselle by the old abbess, who was much devoted to Monsieur le Comte. They have done what they could. Sister Eloise is much learned in the arts of medicine."

"The rest is in the hands of God, Monsieur," said Sister Eloise, with a sigh.

Arsène glanced about the poor bare room, which was like a cell under the eaves. He approached the bed with a sinking heart. He stood in gloomy black silence and gazed down at the young girl who lay there, motionless in her white shift. Her light brown hair, tinged with gold, was braided, and lay on the coarse pillows in a supple frame about her thin pale face, drawn with suffering. Her golden lashes swept her hollow cheeks; her white lips were parted and the breath hardly drifted between them. But even in her painful sleep, there was a nobility about that young chin and mouth and closed eyes, an aloof and reticent withdrawal, a coldness on the smooth wide brow, which even the hovering shadow of death could not dim.

A thick and pulsating agony sprang up in Arsène's heart, and an overwhelming passion. But his expression was closed and dark, for all his internal upheaval. Here, wounded and crushed, almost done to death, was all that he loved, all that he had ever truly desired. A bursting fire flashed before his eyes. He gripped the bedpost in one wet hand, and that hand crawled and clenched like a murderous thing. Now, in the candlelight, his teeth glistened between his pale lips.

Cecile murmured, drew a deep and shivering breath, and half turned her head. Then, on the top of that small and shining head Arsène saw the wound, still oozing through its fresh dressings. A muffled and terrible sound escaped him.

The nuns, Roselle and Crequy looked at him with compassion.

He knelt down beside the bed, and lifted the cool slack hands of the girl. Their delicate fineness was scarred with toil. He turned up the lifeless palms and pressed his lips to them, at first feebly and slowly, and then with wild grief and torment. He held them against his cheeks, in a numb desire to warm them with his own warmth. He kissed the thin veined wrists, the white soft arms about them. He abandoned himself to his fear and his love. He touched the smooth brow with his fingers, and then his mouth. He laid his cheek against hers. His shaking lips approached her ear, and he cried aloud: "Cecile!"

She stirred uneasily at his broken voice and appeal. Her head turned slowly in his direction, as if even in her unconsciousness she knew he was there. A dim smile fluttered on her lips. She sighed.

He could not restrain himself. He wept. But they were the iron tears of rage and hatred. He rose and looked at the nuns. "They who have done this shall die," he said.

Sister Eloise regarded him with white sorrow. "Monsieur, you are not God."

But Arsène gazed down again at the young girl, and his face was an evil thing to see. There was a raucous sound in the room, and it was his breathing.

"God in His mercy can still save this poor child," said Sister Eloise. "But He may punish you, Monsieur, if you allocate His powers to yourself."

But Arsène saw nothing but Cecile. The smile still lingered in a fugitive light on her dwindled face. He bent and kissed her lips, and they quivered feebly under his. Then he turned away. He stared before him, with a fixed look, and his nostrils were so dilated that the red membrane was visible in his dark pallor.

He descended the staircase, with Crequy at his heels. "Take comfort, Monsieur, she is no worse," growled Crequy. "The bleeding has almost stopped. She has swallowed wine today. Yesterday, she could take not even water. The nuns have been good."

But Arsène said nothing. If his hatred or his lust for vengeance had ever slackened, they were stronger now.

The gray and coiling heavens still darted with lightning in a frightful dim silence, broken only by the constant threatening mutter of the river. No rain fell; even the trees were hushed. The young nobles were resuming their cloaks. Now their faces were hard again, and secret.

Arsène swung on his dripping cloak. They followed him outside.

A strange crowd awaited him. While the young nobles had been drinking and eating, orders had been given by Crequy to the two hundred followers. They had, at the point of sword and pistol, gathered up the villagers, who had been cringing in the dark depths of their cottages. They had anticipated some beastlike resistance, and had been surprised at the despairing docility of their prisoners. Now they had herded them before the tavern, which commanded a view of the whole length of the village street.

A wan and spectral light, glimmering, evanescent and uncertain, lay over the earth, which crouched in its drenched silence away from the heavens. Only in those heavens was any movement, and that was darting, writhing, glittering with serpentine lightning. The baleful flashes lit up the thronged faces huddled together. Their bodies were lost; only those pale ovals were visible in the flashing light.

Arsène stood among his companions, looking down upon the faces of the villagers, whom Paul had loved. He could hardly recognize them. Only a little while ago, those faces had been filled with simple pleasure, simple and ingenuous happiness, simple affection and contentment. Now, as he looked at them, in the shifting darkness and vivid light, he saw how natural human emotions can change the false aspect of benevolence and peace and simplicity into primordial visages. He gazed at them steadfastly, with a slow rising burn in his heart, and saw them for what they were in truth: dull, sullen, wary, defiant, sly, terrified, blank and hating, and a fierce pang rose from that burning into a frightful flame.

"Liberty, enlightenment and mercy!" Paul had said, with his pure exalted virtue bright on his ingenuous and gentle face. And so, he had bestowed these upon his people. How they must have secretly writhed under them! How, under their apparent affection, they must have hated him for declaring that they were men! In the consuming rage and hatred that mounted in Arsène, so that the dark and spectral scene shifted before him in a bloody mist, he forgot everything except that Paul de Vitry had been a fool.

For he saw in these crowded countenances before him all the mean viciousness of mankind, all its cupidity, lust and eager cruelty, all its bestiality and hatred, all its uncleanness and treachery and degradation, all its ingratitude, savagery and contempt for kindness and gentleness, all its virulency and violence, all its debased evil. And as he saw, he was filled with a passionate loathing, a kind of horror and repulsion, a wild denial that he belonged to this unspeakable species, and a wilder shame at the confession that he did so belong. No man, he thought, dare say: I am apart from these! He shared the common heritage. He belonged among these hideous creatures that must set God vomiting among His clean and fiery stars.

And then he was seized with a pure vast hatred for his kind, hatred which is necessary to create the great soldier, the great statesman, the great tyrant, the great priest and the great criminal. And, as he so hated, he felt an enormous liberation in himself. Acknowledging his oneness with these other men, he was yet freed from them. Their malignant littleness became in him a malignant immensity.

By these beasts, by these unformed and degraded horrors, by these dogs and swine, the Comte de Vitry had been done to death. Paul de Vitry, so ingenuous, so kind, so tender and merciful, so full of sweetness and gentleness and peace and justice, had been mercilesly trampled by this cattle, this herd of hogs. Their ravening fangs had torn away the life of their benefactor. They had destroyed the only hand in France lifted to succor them. They had silenced the only voice that had cried out against their suffering. For this, then, he had deserved death. For this, he, the aristocrat, the lord, the man of letters and tenderness, had been befouled by the touch of their stinking corruption.

As these ghastly thoughts raced like lines of fire through Arsène's mind, the villagers, watching him frenziedly, were transfixed by the glittering ferocity of his eye. Involuntarily, each man and woman shrank back, defiance and cunning lost in a voiceless terror. For they saw in that eye a full understanding of them. They wet their lips; their hearts pounded. They glanced about them in hunted despair. But they were surrounded by drawn swords and smiling inhuman faces. Then, for the first time, one of them discerned the hasty gibbet set up before the door of the tavern. A wooden beam had been nailed at a sharp angle against the trunk of a tree. From it dangled a rope swinging in the heavy gusts of wind.

The one who first perceived this set up a great animal cry, and pointed with a shaking finger. Others saw, took up the cry. But their captors were silent. Behind Arsène stood Crequy, grinning, flexing his hands in eager and monstrous anticipation. The crowd swayed, pushed, heaved and milled against each other, each desperate eye fixed in nightmare horror upon the gibbet.

Arsène watched this upheaval of bestial terror with virulency. He waited until it had subsided a little. He heard the sobbing of women, the groaning and whimpering of men. Then he advanced a pace, and, in the thundrous gloom, he said clearly and quietly:

"Dogs, I have come to do justice to you."

A sick and portentous silence fell. Arsène looked at his companions. They were regarding the villagers with the aristocrat's loathing, disgust and contempt. They had known Paul de Vitry, and had loved and followed him. But they had not come to avenge his tragic death. They had come out of the aristocrat's rage at the rebellion of the canaille against the power of the privileged and the noble. Arsène, pondering this, felt as if a fist had been struck hard against his chest. He had come to avenge Paul. These had come to destroy a rebellion which threatened themselves. They did not know this, themselves, but the evidence was there on their narrow fine faces and hooded eyes.

It does not matter why they have come, thought Arsène. It is enough for me that they have come. But for the first time he felt a peculiar illness, a trembling of his flesh.

He spoke again, his voice hollow and echoing in the windless gloom and silence:

"Your lord was gracious and just. He was kind and benevolent. He freed you, shared what he had with you. He liberated you, and administered mercifully to you. In return, you murdered him. You have struck against France, in striking against the Comte de Vitry."

He paused, and from his doublet he withdrew a roll of paper. "I have here a warrant for your deaths. You shall die ignobly and speedily. Thus, then, all like you will beware forever of lifting a hand against the majesty and authority of France."

There was a silence. Then, from the depths of the trembling and pallid throng, a man cried out: "It was the priest!"

The others stirred thankfully, hopefully, murmuring. But Arsène smiled grimly.

"The Comte de Vitry liberated you many years ago. This priest was among you for a few short weeks. Yet, how easily you were seduced! Had not the wicked desire been strong among you, this thing would not have happened. You are to die. I regret," he added ironically, "that there is no priest at hand to shrive you."

They gazed up at him with abysmal despair. But they saw only the iron sword of France standing against them, the iron power of the magnates and the oppressors. The women sobbed and clasped their hands; the men groaned. Some of the women cried out: "What shall become of our children?"

As he looked at them, Arsène saw no remorse, no bitterness, no sorrow, but only the frenzied fear of the hunted. His hatred grew more uncontrolled. He looked at the faintly smiling faces of his companions. Their followers, ringed about the villagers, moved impatiently.

"One out of every ten men and women shall die for the murder of the Comte de Vitry, his steward, Grandjean and the cruel assault upon Cecile, the steward's granddaughter. However, it is fitting that you deliver up your leaders first. Name them."

Hoping despairingly that in some way they might be saved, the craven villagers searched each face eagerly. Then frantic hands seized a young man, who, of all of them, had retained a black composure. But he shook off their hands contemptuously. He thrust those about him aside. He walked towards Arsène with a quick firm step, holding his head high. Arsène, in spite of himself, felt some surprise, for this young man, in his white shirt and woolen britches, his brown muscular body and strong swinging arms, had dignity and pride. His square and belligerent face, burned deep brown by the sun, his active black eyes, filled with passion and fierceness, and his heavy stern mouth betrayed no fear, no cowardice. He had a presence, commanding and strong.

He paused below Arsène, and spoke quietly, his uplifted eyes glistening in the wan light: "I am Jean Dumont, Monsieur. The priest persuaded me, who have some influence among these wretches, that Monsieur le Comte de Vitry had evil designs upon us, that his merciful measures were merely designed to delay the liberating doctrines proposed by his Majesty, the King. I have discerned there was another, and more evil plot, Monsieur, and that plot was against Monsieur le Comte, and ourselves. I am guilty of my part in arousing these contemptible wretches. I have perceived that they are not worthy of any liberation, however small. Nevertheless, I seek no mercy for myself. I am guilty. I deserve to die."

He spoke with such pride, such somber sadness, such weary contempt, that Arsène was taken aback. He looked down into those unswerving black eyes, that coarse but intelligent face, strong with health and youth. He saw the dark disillusion in that grim and quiet expression. Then he turned away, with an uplifted hand.

Crequy seized Jean Dumont by the arm, but the young

peasant shook off his hand with a look of blazing outrage. He walked calmly beneath the gibbet, and waited. Crequy tied the rope about his neck. The crowd watched, holding their breath. Then Crequy took hold of the rope, after spitting on his hands. Jean Dumont turned slowly, and he looked upon those thronged pale faces, contorted with animal fear. He suddenly closed his eyes, as though sickened and revolted.

Crequy tugged on the rope. Jean Dumont was jerked swiftly into the air. His convulsively sprawling figure jerked against the gray and shifting skies in a contorted black silhouette. With horror, the people saw the convulsions slowly begin to diminish. Everywhere was utter silence. In this hushed cemetery of human passions there was only that feebly declining movement of the hanged man, the man, who, in his small and turbulent way, had hoped to succor them, and who, at the last, had ended by despising them.

Crequy lowered the rope. The body fell in a contorted heap upon the ground. Crequy lifted it, flung it aside.

Now there were wild frantic cries in the center of the mob, and struggles. Several eager men dragged forward two others, crying aloud, incoherently. One was Guy La Farge, the former overseer, and the other, Pietre Dubonnet, the former steward.

Arsène looked down upon the first struggling man, whose mouth was open on a long delirious scream. He saw the emaciated leanness of La Farge, the attenuated grayness of his countenance. He looked upon the other, Dubonnet, that small rotund and formerly ruddy man, whose face was now like streaming tallow. The two men struggled and bent their knees, dragging their feet like animals led to the slaughter, striking out feebly and desperately, their last human instincts lost in the welter of primitive terror. Somewhere, in the press, a woman was shrieking with a prolonged and insane howl.

"These are your leaders?" asked Arsène.

The mob nodded eagerly, shouting, raising upclenched fists, pressing closer in their shameful treachery to Arsène, hoping to obtain favor in him for their delivering up of those who had led them. Dubonnet, having, in his mad strength, momentarily shaken off the hands of his captors, fell on his knees before Arsène, and lifted his hands.

"Monsieur," he groaned, "my good lord and master, have mercy on me! There is no priest here to shrive me. I am a good Catholic—I cannot go to my death unconfessed. I am a man with a wife. I am a poor man."

His voice dwindled and died in his stricken throat. He whimpered, made disordered gestures with his hands. His eyes, the glittering eyes of a terrified animal, implored the inexorable Arsène. The shrieking of the woman in the background became an unbearable sound.

"Why did you lead your people against their lord?" asked Arsène.

The man's whimpering lips gibbered. He rubbed his hands against them. His voice, when it came, was a squeak:

"Monsieur, it was the priest. I am a good Catholic. He put it into my mind that Monsieur le Comte was part of a Huguenot plot to destroy the Church—"

Arsène turned away. Crequy seized the wretch. Arsène did not look on the final struggle. He heard the blind screaming of the plunging man, a scream which was abruptly broken off after the quick screech of the rope on the gibbet. Now even the distant woman was silent, as all but Arsène watched the death of Dubonnet.

A sulphurous stench pervaded the air, and from the earth rose a fetid odor as of decay and corruption. Arsène looked about him. The drumming of the thunder had become a close howl. Deep within himself, Arsène heard that howl, and a numb paralysis, voluptuous in its weakness, encased him. A kind of frightful and broken-hearted joy, vicious in its whirling intensity, caused him to laugh aloud with a savage sound. Now a horrible and fateful quiet seemed to fall on every one. It was a pantomime acted by deaf mutes moving in a nightmare.

Then Arsène fixed his eyes starkly upon the second figure of La Farge writhing against the sky. Crequy, the huge giant, stood at the flapping feet of his last victim, looking upwards, grinning. A nebulous quality floated about him, so that he seemed formed of dark fog and mist, through which an eternal malignance glowed. The villagers and their executioners stood motionless. The quickening lightning flashed over pale and bloodless faces, over staring empty eyes, over open imbecile mouths and blowing hair. Once an especially fierce blaze revealed the gutted broken walls of the château on its hill.

Arsène felt that he could bear no more. He looked away from the gibbet. He saw the gray and misty village street beyond the crowd and the tavern. What he saw made him blink incredulously. A small horse was approaching, with exhausted bent head and limping hoof. And on that horse was seated a quiet figure in a cloak and a broad low hat. The vision moved in a heavy and melancholy preoccupation.

No one else saw for some moments. The figure dismounted.

It came forward, seeming to float in a gray dream. It was the Abbé Lovelle.

No, said Arsène, to himself. His companions turned idly and stared at the priest. Now the villagers perceived his approach. Great broken cries broke from them. A convulsion rushed among them, like stagnant waters agitated by the dropping of an enormous stone. Over their tortured faces, torn and wild, a vivid light of joy flashed and rippled. They struggled to reach their priest through the circle of their guards, but were hurled back by violent blows. But they persisted, not feeling these blows, extending their arms to him, moaning, sobbing, groaning with joy, bubbling appeals for mercy rising in shrieks to their lips. Many fell on their knees, stretching forth stark and trembling hands, kissing the air frantically. Their eyes glowed with a phosphorescent glare.

The priest stood for a moment and looked at all these things, at the gibbet, at the newly hanged man jerking in his agony against the sky, at Arsène and his companions, at the wolfish faces of the executioners. He did not move. He was a small black image, bent and tragic, with a quiet face. He put his hands to his eyes, after a long time. Then his hands fell away. His old and withered cheeks were running with tears.

Then without a word, and, very slowly, he approached Arsène, looking up at him with a long and steadfast gaze. Arsène watched him come, in utter silence.

The abbé halted before Arsène. Now silence fell once more, and there was no movement but the last dying jerks of the last hanged man, grotesque and awkward against the sky. There was only one far sound: the snarling growl of Crequy, hungry and deep.

The lightning illumined the abbé's face. It was stern and still, and waiting. Arsène tried to speak; then, impotently, he lifted his arm and pointed to the ruins of the château. The abbé, following that gesture, looked aside and upwards. He started so violently that his shabby black garments fluttered as though a wind had struck them.

"Yes," said Arsène, very softly, "these sheep of yours did that, Monsieur le Curé. They murdered their savior and their protector. They did their friend to death, as a just payment for his mercy and his justice. And to this end, to this gibbet, they were led by your dear brother in Christ, the priest de Pacilli."

Very slowly, the priest returned his gaze to Arsène, and then to the peasants. He uttered no cry, made no gesture. But he gazed at those haggard and distraught men and women, and his face expressed his broken sorrow, his grief, his bewilderment and agony. His lips trembled. He bent his head. He seemed as if praying.

Then, very softly, he said, looking up at Arsène: "Seven nights ago, I had a dream. It was a most frightful dream. I dreamt that my people were in danger, that some holocaust was upon them because of a nameless guilt. A voice urged me to leave my dear niece, to arise and return to this place. In the morning, I left at dawn."

The peasants stared at him in heavy silence, as if fascinated. And then their own faces, which had been filled only with terror and cunning, changed, became torn and contorted. One by one, they began to weep, to sob, and the sound of their grief rose upwards like an arching wave, clamorous with anguish and despair. They cowered; they covered their faces with their hands. Their lamentations, now low and hoarse, struck on the hearts of even the hardest with unbearable force. All fear for themselves had gone from them. They mourned simply and movingly, with sorrow.

Then, slowly, one by one, they fell on their knees, kneeling with bent heads, still weeping. A peasant nearest the priest spoke hoarsely, lifting up his hands with humble abandon:

"Father, we do not know why we did this thing. We have killed our lord, our friend. Do not ask us why. We do not know."

The priest listened. Then he held up his hands over them, lifted his face to the stormy heavens and prayed in silence. His tears rolled over his face.

Arsène, watching as if in a dream, felt a tug on his arm. Young de la Royale whispered to him with painful impatience: "Let us be done with them, and this tattered priest."

Arsène stared at him unseeingly, then turned again to the Abbé Lovelle. The abbé was regarding him, still weeping. He said: "Monsieur, where is your authority to execute these helpless people?"

Arsène gave him the order in silence. By the light of the rapid lightning, the abbé read it. He handed it back. His small old face was paler than ever.

He said, and his voice was quiet: "There was a man who died on a cross. He said: 'Forgive them, Father, for they know not what they do.'"

His words fell in the dark silence like a distant echo. He clasped his hands, and looked only at Arsène.

When Arsène spoke his voice was a muffled croak: "Do you think I rejoice in this, Monsieur le Curé? Ten years ago, there was a similar murder of the lord of certain estates. He was cruel and depraved. Nevertheless, the law demanded that every peasant be put to death for this murder. If I do not avenge the Comte de Vitry, the law of France will do so."

The priest, after a long last look at him, turned his gaze to the heap of hanged men and women, to the corpses who had been butchered by sword and dagger and thrown aside. He shuddered, as if struck.

Arsène spoke again: "You may shrive them, Father, but the vengeance must take place. Do you think the law will be more merciful than I?"

The abbé lifted his hand, and pointed slowly at Arsène. "Monsieur, you have in your possession full authority to do as you desire. If you wish to murder these poor wretches, authority is given to you. If you wish to spare them, the authority grants this also."

His words, trembling, but full of strength and stern accusation, filled the air. The peasants' sobs and groans had subsided to a low lamentation, without words or prayers.

Arsène's face tightened, became grim and darker. "Monsieur le Curé," he said, "I do not wish to spare them." He added: "They killed my friend."

The abbé's countenance quickened, became alive and passionate. He clasped his hands together. "Monsieur, they killed their friend, and mine, and yours! But ask yourself in your heart, if he would have wished you to do this thing!"

Arsène did not answer. The abbé lifted his eyes and cried out: "The soul of that good man stands in denunciation before you, Monsieur! He would have forgiven these poor people! He would have understood them. You are not worthy to be his friend, Monsieur. You dare not call him 'friend'."

Arsène's companions, wrapped shivering in their cloaks, smiled faintly. They looked down upon this weary old man with the tears upon his face, his voice ringing in the somber and hollow air. Their faces expressed their impatience and disgust. But Arsène did not see their smiles.

The abbé, seeing Arsène's dark silence, approached nearer. He seized a fold of his dripping cloak. He fell on his knees. His seamed face was bright with his grief and despair and pleading.

"You have done enough, Monsieur. Will these murders bring back our poor and devoted friend, who was filled only with mercy and compassion? See how they weep! They are not afraid, not terrified. They wish for death, in extenuation for their blind and ignorant crime. If you execute them, one and all will go humbly to his death, understanding that it is a just punishment. Can further murder do more, increase their anguish and their sorrow and regret? You will take vengeance on men already punished, already prostrated and undone. Is that not enough? More violence will destroy only your own soul. It cannot inflict greater punishment on these poor people."

His trembling hands wound themselves feverishly in Arsène's cloak. He tried to step back. But the priest's despairing grip only tightened. He embraced Arsène's knees. He wept. His face, passionate and wild with his pleading, was a moving thing to see.

Arsène spoke brokenly: "How can I spare them? I wish them to die. I cannot command myself to wish anything else. They deserve death." And then a madness took hold of him, and he cried out: "All mankind deserves death! I wish that I might inflict it on all the world!"

The priest's arms tightened about Arsène's knees. He looked up at him, streaming with tears. But his face was sorrowful and fixed as he gazed earnestly at the young man.

"To speak so is to speak against Almighty God, who made these poor creatures. Monsieur, reflect on the dark and nameless beginning of mankind. Reflect on its former oneness with the beasts of the forest and the wild plains. Reflect how it first looked dimly on the light and began its slow and tortuous ascent from the abyss. A thousand times has the beast's torn foot slipped, and a thousand times has he returned to the pit from which he came. But always, he climbs again, impelled by only God knows what strange, terrible and immortal urge—Monsieur, we must remember that urge, even in our most distraught and hating moments. Who knows but that the day will come when that eternal and holy stirring which lies even in the barest soul will not burst into universal light? For the sake of that hope, we must have pity, we must have mercy, we must have prayer and hope and faith. We must have the long patience of God."

And now it seemed to Arsène that the old man was no longer pleading for the lives of the miserable peasants, but for his, Arsène's, own soul. His urging, his passion, his tears and his solemnity was for the spiritual saving of this young man alone. A thousand thousand lives might be lost, and it would be nothing. But to this old priest the loss of a single soul was greater than the destruction of a whole universe.

"I implore you to reflect, Monsieur! I implore you, in the name of God, in the name of the Comte de Vitry, who loved you, in the name of your soul, to spare these poor creatures!"

A spasm convulsed him. His strength failed. He fell at Arsène's feet, and laid his head helplessly and humbly on those muddied boots. His gray hairs covered them. His hands embraced them, with all the iron and convulsive grasp of a dying man. Then, moaning, he kissed those boots, crying over and over: "Spare them. In the name of God—in the name of God."

Arsène could not endure it. He tried to raise the old man, but the priest clung to him with superhuman strength, as if he felt that in imprisoning Arsène in his arms he could stay the executioner. Arsène gasped. He could hardly breathe. He looked about him with swimming eyes. He looked at his friends. Their eyes fell uneasily away from him, and they seemed to recoil. He looked at Crequy.

The giant was regarding him with a strange and lowering look. But now there was no evil in it, only confusion and a coarse pity. He looked at the peasants. They were no longer sobbing and groaning. They knelt in silence, their heads bent on their breasts.

An iron band tightened about Arsène's heart. He lifted his hands; they fell impotently to his side. He looked down at the groveling priest who still embraced him so desperately. The wind, returning with increased ferocity, struck every figure, lifted every garment like a misshapen and batlike wing. The thunder rolled closer. Now everything was lit continually in lightning.

Something seemed to open wide in Arsène, to bleed and throb and ache with an intolerable anguish. He gently disengaged the priest's arms. Those arms fell away, like the arms of the dead. He lifted the priest to his feet and held him against his breast. The gray head dropped on his shoulder, as if the old man had expired.

"I spare them, Father," he said. "Let them go in peace."

Now the rain came in gray and battering cataracts, sweeping over the kneeling peasants. The wind caused the last hanged man to dance grotesquely from his rope. Arsène lifted the priest in his arms and carried him into the tavern.

In his will, Paul de Vitry had left to his friend Arsène the whole of his fortunes and his estates, to do with them as he wished.

Before he left Chantilly, Arsène appointed Crequy and the priest as administrators of the estates.

"On the one hand will be sweetness and mercy, on the

other hand will be suspicious justice and sternness," he said, out of his new and aching wisdom. "This will be good." He added: "Men must earn and understand liberty. If it is given to them before they understand, it will be despised."

He had sent to Paris for a carriage. In this, he carried away Cecile Grandjean, with the young Roselle.

CHAPTER XLV

THERE WAS ALWAYS a quiet hour, just after sunset, when the Cardinal sat in his chair in his chamber and drowsed, or read, or meditated, his eyes closed, his delicate and aristocratic hands lying palm upwards on his knees in a drained and impotent attitude. Near the windows would sit Louis de Richepin, writing busily, frowning coldly over tomorrow's appointments, composing the formal letters of his Eminence, and reading the missives that had come that evening. Then there would be utter silence in that room, except for the whisper of paper, the slide of Louis's quill pen, the sifting of sand over the wet characters.

Even in quiescence, the Cardinal loved the sound of activity near him, and the potentialities of all those letters read and written by his secretary gave him a sense of dynamic continuity even as he rested. He could sit aside, meditate or drowse, but the vast wheels he had set in motion continued to revolve with increasing acceleration. His was the kind of character that cannot utterly rest, and allow rest to pervade the atmosphere about him. He could relax completely only when the enormous thunder of activity resounded in the air that encased him; he could breathe easily only when that air was charged with the echoing thunder of his own past activities. His weary eyes were soothed by the flash of lightnings he had evoked. Tranquillity descended upon him when he could hear the distant reverberations of events. But if those about him rested and meditated or drowsed also, he was filled with feverish restlessness and a sense of horrible waste, a fury against the impotence of apathy. It was then that his tormented body would rise again as on the arch of a cry, and create tumult about it.

But he could not rest tonight, for some mysterious reason. The torture in his flesh was like a febrile pain, but nameless. Supersubtle and supersensitive as he was, he felt that in that chamber was an agony greater than his own, however much, in his selfishness, he had struggled, for hours to ignore it. (He had one unfailing conviction: that to sympathize, to identify oneself with the pains of others was to disperse a large measure of one's own strength, with disastrous consequences. The wise man lived in his own fortressed universe, into which no cry, no despairing hand, could enter.)

He obstinately forced his eyelids to remain closed over his strange and brilliant eyes. But they jerked uneasily. The slack hands lifted, and twitched, as if in a spasm. He moved against the back of his chair, as an animal, incensed by an unscratchable itch, rubs his spine. He was annoyed with himself; he fumed that the soundless groan that emanated from his miserable secretary should echo in his own austere and aloof ears. What was the misery of such as Louis de Richepin, that obscure and glacial priest, that bewildered and voiceless little soul, to Armand-Jean de Plessis, Duc de Richelieu, the most powerful man in Europe? He had seen such misery, such majestic and illimitable misery in his life, beside which the anguish of this frozen-lipped young man was nothing, nothing at all! He had seen the despair in the faces of great and powerful men; he had seen the death of friends and momentous enemies, and if he had felt regret, it had been the regret of an academic man who found something of the artistic in such despair and such deaths, something of dignity. He had been pleased at the perfection of these, for there lived in him the love for that which had grandeur and operatic gestures.

Louis had been his secretary for some years. In idle moments, Louis had amused him. Too, he had amused himself often at Louis' expense, as a man teases a humble dog, or a caged and clawless bird. He had played with Louis. And Louis, after a very few moments, had completely bored him, as the unstable, the inflexible, inevitably bored him. Even Louis' occasional vehemence, his narrow theological passions, had caused him to yawn and smile. Only when Louis had manifested the strength and vastness of the hatred which devoured him had the Cardinal become interested. He was always interested in tremendous human passions, though it was a cynical interest in which his own hatred was the dominant ingredient. He confessed, candidly, that only those passions which duplicated his own could command his respect and attention. I am an egotist, he would think, and would be pleased. What man, even Jesus, had ever succeeded, except by virtue of his powerful egotism? To become the center of things, it was necessary that a man convince himself that he was already the center. The easier move, thereafter, was to convince others.

He meditated upon these things, as he lay in his chair, and was consoled that a pleasant drowsiness was overcoming him. His thoughts drifted away from him like great shadowy ships putting out in gray silence upon misty and boundless seas. The allegory pleased him; it was his favorite method of putting himself to sleep. He liked to watch the vague and majestic star-shine gleaming among the ghostly folds of the sails, and the sliding mountains of the waters that had their source in his own soul.

And then he heard a sigh. The waters and the ships vanished, and he was acutely and angrily aware once more of his mind, his consciousness, the aching confines of his own flesh. The acrid feverishness of his body tormented him again with its old insistence. He refused to open his eyes. He heard the sigh once more, and all at once it had a terrible sound, overwhelming in its desolation. He remained inert. Louis thought he slept, as usual. The sigh had come from a naked spirit, believing itself alone.

The Cardinal partially lifted his eyelids, and looked at his secretary. The twilight had become thicker. A single golden taper burned on the table at which Louis had been writing. The windows were shrouded in their heavy draperies. All was silence, heavy and brooding. Louis sat in his chair, his elbows in the table, his head in his hands. The sigh came from him repeatedly, and it had in it the essence of the last breathing of a dying man.

Louis had a strong body, full of the rigid grace of the humorless but handsome man. His back was straight and firm, in its black garments. He had a certain lofty splendor of shoulder, carriage and bodily formation. Always, he had carried himself with a stately and princely air, not affected, but a manifestation of the glacial quality of his frigid spirit and hard virginal mind. The Cardinal, in his idler moments, had often amused himself with speculations as to what might happen to that carriage, that large frozen countenance, that blue and icy eye, when the mind and heart behind them was smitten and utterly undone.

Now, he needed not to speculate, or to wonder, with smiling cynicism. He knew, and saw. For the young man before him had the appearance of a marble statue that had been crushed and distorted under the hammer blows of a destroyer. His outlines were misshapen; the cold grandeur of his body was dissolved, as a statue of ice is dissolved under a devastating sun. His head was bowed, sunken between his shoulders. The strong white hands, which in their cold formation had seemed incapable of any latent tenderness or softness, were clenched in agony against his eyes. His back writhed; he rocked on his chair. And from his hidden lips came those long dying sighs, like heavy gusts.

The Cardinal understood that agony. Since Marguerite de Tremblant's death he had observed the almost imperceptible disintegration of Louis de Richepin. He had been like a mountain, apparently changeless on the surface, which was disintegrating and collapsing within, dissolving into dust, giving only to the most observant eye the faint manifestations of an occasional falling stone, a slight shifting against the sky, a far muffled murmur, though its outlines remained the same. And, as to the inner ear of that astute observer had come the profound inner whisper of immense dissolution, and to his eye the dim fog of drifting dust that mantled that mountain, so to the Cardinal's ear and eye had come the signals of the inner collapsing, the ruin, that was taking place under the immovable and motionless surface of Louis de Richepin.

He had been regretful. But, at the end, he had been bored, as he was always bored by those things which did not imminently concern himself and his enormous designs. Too, he had that contemptuous impatience for the wretchedness of little humanity which is an attribute of the man who hates his kind, and furiously resents being identified with it, even to sharing the formation of its members. After his first pang of compassion for his priestly secretary, he had been annoyed at what he saw. Good God, the fate of France, of Europe, depended on his, the Cardinal's plots and intrigues for the next few years, and this miserable pale man could be so absorbed in his petty yearnings and achings, his mewlings over an insignificant girl whose passing had not evoked a single word at Court!

But, for some strange reason, as he watched Louis now through his secret eyelids, he could not feel annoyance or impatience. An unfathomable sadness pervaded him, a nameless warmth and terrible sorrow. And that sadness, that sorrow, was like a violent convulsion in him, a breaking-down of walls and barricades. He could pause, even then, for wonder that he could feel so, for he had had no love for Louis, and hardly anything even so strong as occasional liking.

He had so despised mankind that the sight of its suffering

had seemed to him a petty and shameful thing, much below the suffering of a noble and humble dog. But all at once Louis de Richepin's agony was no longer petty and shameful to the Cardinal. All at once, the Cardinal reflected that no agony was mean, whether it was the agony of a man or a woman. In suffering, all things attained grandeur, fatefulness and dignity, commanding the respect even of God. Man, and worms, participated not at all in the ecstatic transports of God, in His mighty cognizance of the future, nor in His joy and peace and sublime satisfaction. Blindly wandering, and mute, they had no prescience, no encompassing comprehension. They lived outside the glowing and fiery circle of knowledge. But in suffering, they were one with God. The tendrils of universal pain quivered in God and man and worms, and the last despairing convulsion of the last was felt in the heart of the first.

These were strange thoughts for his Eminence, the Duc de Richelieu, to be entertaining, and a curious excitation pervaded a body which had believed it had experienced all emotions, and was tired of them. It had been so long since he had felt sadness, or gentleness, or sorrow. Echoes of his early manhood resounded in his ears; the strong compassion he had once known for all living things stirred his heart once more, and it ached, as an unused and atrophied muscle aches upon violent exertion.

With compassion comes the impulse to alleviate, to console, to comfort. This, the Cardinal felt. His mouth opened to utter gentle words, and then was dumb. For it suddenly overwhelmed him that he, a prelate of the Church, a prince of Rome, a priest who was first of all a minister to men, had no words of consolation or comfort to give this suffering man before him. He had too much knowledge! He was too wise! Sanctimonious words, however impelled by sincerity, had, even in rehearsal, too much puerility, a childish and mean quality, a foolishness. How, in the face of this anguish, could he say: "God will give you comfort, my son?" All the trite and worn phrases of priests sounded shameful to his inner ear. Who but a fool, or a cynic, would have the effrontery to insult such anguish with silly words?

Words of comfort implied a smug superiority on the part of the utterer, a detachment from the pain of the recipient. Insult was implicit in them, a self-satisfaction. Unless they came from the deepest faith and humility.

And Armand-Jean de Plessis, Cardinal and Duc de Richelieu, prelate of Rome, vested in holy garments and standing before the monstrance of gilded religion, had no faith, no humility. He had known this for a long time, but had not felt it. Now, he felt it in its full enormity. He was moved by an impulse to bitter laughter. I have no true words, for I have no faith, he thought.

Had he ever had any faith? He ran back through the long dim corridors of the years, and opened a thousand doors, querying, seeking. But he found nothing at all, nothing but expediency, ambition, hatred and cunning, nothing but a contemptible knowledge of other men. Where, even in the most narrow and obscure chamber, had he dwelt even for an hour with pure faith and humility? He could find no such chamber.

And now he asked himself: Do I believe in God? And after a long moment he answered himself: No. I do not know.

And then he confessed to himself that he had believed that faith was a convenient attribute for the fool, an idiot's gesture, the mumbling of medicine men. It had no part in the character of the wise man. Intelligence was above faith. Remembering, with acuteness, Père Joseph, the Cardinal came to the penetrating conclusion that the Capuchin had no faith, either. He had rapture, he had orisons, he had convulsions, he had ecstasy. But these were self-intoxication. He had no true faith.

And now he knew that only those with faith could speak words of comfort, without insult. For in faith was an awareness of universal anguish and grief, the oneness of all creatures in the all-pervading agony of living. Faith cried out: "I have no consolation for you, but I have no consolation for myself. I have only my tears, which, while shedding them for you, I shed them for myself, also. In weeping, we weep for God, who weeps for us." Thus, in the universal participation of mutual grief, man approached God, and they clasped hands together.

Sunken in his thoughts, the Cardinal forgot all else. He sighed deeply. There was a floating and dimness in his vision.

He looked at Louis again, and his tigerish eyes no longer held in them their usual baleful gleam, but were soft and diffused. He called out, gently: "Louis."

The young priest stirred, as a tree stirs at the movement of wind, but without conscious motion. He dropped his clenched hands from his eyes. But his profile, frozen and rigid, remained turned away. He looked blindly before him.

Again the Cardinal sighed, and again he called out. And this time, Louis turned his face towards him. The Cardinal's

491

heart plunged downwards on the sword of pain. For Louis' countenance was empty and stark, fixed in the rigidity of agony. It was like one of those Greek masks, fleshless, but bearing in the gaping eyeless sockets and the stark and open arch which was the lipless mouth, all anguish, all tragedy, and all dreadfulness. In its every emptiness, soundlessness, was the epitome of mankind, which, in the final moment, could open its bloodless lips only on speechless horror.

The two looked at each other in the awful silence of that moment. And they saw each other completely. They could not move, could not speak.

And after a long time, the Cardinal lifted his hands, and let them drop heavily and impotently on his knee.

He said, and his voice was hoarse and low: "Louis, I know. And I have nothing to say to you. Nothing at all. I have no consolation, no words. I cannot tell you of God, for I know nothing of God. I cannot comfort you, for there is no comfort in me. I can only offer you my sorrow." He added, in a still lower tone: "Forgive me."

Humility, sadness, sat strangely on the delicate and bloodless face of that terrible man. He seemed smaller and feebler, as he sat in his great crimson chair. He appeared to attain enormous and fruitless age, and somber futility. And yet, in the loss of his terribleness, in his humility and despair, he attained grandeur.

Louis listened. And then, very slowly, the hard mask of tragedy softened, crumpled, and the bleeding flesh overcame the layer of cracking plaster, and a cry issued from his lips. He rose, and staggering, caught the back of his chair. Slowly, painful step after painful step, he approached the Cardinal, weaving from side to side as a wounded man walks. He held out his hands, as if feeling his way in impenetrable darkness. And then, reaching the Cardinal, he fell suddenly before him and dropped his stricken head on the Cardinal's knee.

The Cardinal was silent. His hand had automatically risen to lay itself on that tragic head. Now words of rote had risen to his lips: "Be comforted, my son. God understands your grief, and will send you consolation."

But he quelled the foolish words before they could be spoken. Even in that moment he could smile at them with heavy bitterness. How easily habit could destroy the dignity of truth! How easily words rose to insult that dignity!

At length, he said, in such a gentle voice: "Louis, I, too, have suffered. I, too, have known the deepest of sorrow. This is all I can offer you. This is the only comfort I can give you: that all men have known this pain."

And then, after these words, he could raise Louis' head, and lay it on his own breast. And he could embrace him, in the simple communion, the voiceless sadness, of all that has suffered.

Had he comforted this poor priest? He felt that he had. For in Louis he had perceived that devastating loneliness and terror which had always dwelt in him. In this embrace of another sufferer, he came again into the communication with humanity which Marguerite de Tremblant had given him. The Cardinal heard the sound of his weeping.

CHAPTER XLVI

ARSENE ESTABLISHED CECILE GRANDJEAN and the young Roselle in Paul de Vitry's small hôtel in Paris. The servants, grief-stricken over the tragic death of their kind master, were eager and delighted to administer to the young girl who had suffered in that calamity. There, in the house of the young and ingenuous man who had loved her, guarded by the dim portraits of his ancestors, the girl fought her slow and painful way back to life.

Each day, a discreet messenger came to Arsène and told him of the girl's progress. But he did not go to her.

He was fighting an heroic and desperate struggle in himself. Until, in his confusion, he had come to the place where he could endure himself, where he could clarify the turbulent passions and dark chaos that devastated him, he dared see no one. He locked himself in his apartments, receiving only the messenger from the Hôtel de Vitry and those who were secretly admitted to him by Pierre, his lackey, to convey to him plans for the impending campaign to defend La Rochelle.

Simple and ruthless and unsubtle of temperament, he found himself assailed by a thousand passions and doubts. The affair at Chantilly had shown him to what depths the human heart could plunge. He regarded himself with heavy distrust and vehement disgust. Nevertheless, he could not persuade himself that he had been unjust or unduly vengeful. He knew that the first reaction to attack was a violent counter-attack. But doubts came to him that he had been inspired by an impulse to justice. Justice and vengeance, he perceived, were entirely opposed to each other. But where did one begin and the other end? Did not all the virtues, after all, have their roots in the vices? Did mercy rise from weakness and expediency? Was compassion the attribute of those who were abysmally selfish?

He could not rid himself of hatred. Now he knew that in

all men lived hatred for all other men. From the single root of hate blossomed the poisonous fruit of all the vices. But how could a man destroy natural hatred in himself? He saw that man's great conquest, great crusade, great adventure, was in the destruction of the hatred which was born in his own heart.

To a man of his kidney, it was an appalling thing to be precipitated into a country of a thousand lights and shadows, filled with obscure whispers, and the gestures of countless doubts and bewilderments. This world which once to him was a thing of sharp blacks and whites, shadowless and firm of outline, and very simple and uncomplex, was revealed to him to be a world of endless shades and tints, in which the human soul questioned in perplexity and at length gave up in impotent despair, overwhelmed with unanswerable enigmas.

Had Paul de Vitry confronted these enigmas and had he known the answers? For a brief dazzling moment Arsène conjectured that men like Paul refused to see the tints and the shades, closed their ears to the whispers of devious and clever doubts. In much questioning, he saw, was much confusion. One must look clearly and steadfastly at the simple necessity: to conquer hatred in oneself. With that shining and fragile thread in the hand, one could walk safely through the labyrinths, guided along the edges of pits and chasms.

But still, he could not rid himself of that hatred which was part of the blood and bone and spirit of man. He struggled with it, but at every subduing, it sprang up in another area in his heart, as strong and triumphant as ever. He found himself regretting that he had been so weak as to be diverted from his purpose at Chantilly. At these moments, the fire roared up in him again, and he longed to destroy all mankind.

I know the truth, he would say to himself, but I cannot force myself to believe in it. If I destroy my own hatred, I shall be destroyed as were Paul, the Abbé Mourion, the Duc de Tremblant and François Grandjean. It seemed to him that the world was the graveyard of all noble and selfless souls. To survive, one must build hatred like a fortress.

It was not for some days that the thought came to him like a whisper from the graveyard: The world of men shall be saved from their hatred only by those who have conquered hatred.

I care nothing for saving men, he thought, in the midst of his grief for his friend. But his new knowledge, like a

495

feeble but living plant, struggled for life in the midst of poisonous weeds.

In some obscure way, he realized that this battle must be fought in himself before he could undertake objective battles. The campaign at La Rochelle, his whole subsequent life, must await the ordering of his own passions and the formulation of his own unshakable philosophy.

But one day a hurried messenger, covered with dust and with a strained and haggard face, appeared at his door, accompanied by the wary Pierre. This messenger had come from the Duc de Rohan, and he brought with him the hasty and exigent demand that the time had come for all the members of Les Blanches to appear at the beleaguered city of La Rochelle. "I implore you to come at once," the Duc had written grimly. "Every wasted hour is an hour of danger to us and our cause."

Arsène immediately sent Pierre to his friends. No later than that night, they must set forth for La Rochelle. England had declared war on France. The Huguenots were supporting this enemy, for they saw in the triumph of Protestant England the assurance of liberty and tolerance for themselves. Richelieu, therefore, perceived that the first blow to England must come in the subduing of the Protestant French nobles at La Rochelle, for these nobles were the Achilles heel of France, the port of invasion open to English military assault. That port must be closed.

Richelieu, who by temperament preferred the good offices of the purse and diplomacy to that of the sword, in spite of his constant conceit of himself as a soldier, had determined, with secret aversion, to lead the campaign himself. By the time Arsène received the message from the Duc de Rohan, the Cardinal had left that morning for La Rochelle, where a dyke, or mole, was already in hurried construction to prevent the entrance of English men-of-war.

Later in the day, by way of his passage through the cellars of the Hôtel du Vaubon, Arsène hurried to the Hôtel de Vitry, for the first time since Cecile Grandjean had been installed there. A servant admitted him to the small drawing-room, where Mademoiselle sat in sad contemplation before the fire.

Arsène, engrossed with the single-minded man's absorption in his present problem, suddenly found himself shaken at the sight of the girl. His heart began a furious pounding. He, who always precipitated himself with graceful dexterity into any room, entered falteringly, and with diffidence.

The girl did not immediately perceive him. She sat alone, before the low fire, a white shawl over her knees. Her attitude was one of deep despondency and sadness, but there was strength also in the quietness of her young body, and the nobility which was an integral part of her seemed more evident than ever. Her plain black gown made more emphatic the whiteness of her neck and her still hands. Her light brown hair, glistening with radiant threads, was plaited in long shining ropes which fell over her slight straight shoulders. Her head was bent, her face composed and meditative. Arsène saw her profile, clear and silent. The firelight glimmered in the lucid blue of her eyes. Her lips, of the most pale and delicate rose, were folded firmly, but without tightness. If her thoughts were sorrowful, they were also courageous, and without bitterness.

As Arsène watched her, a tide of the most intense love and ecstasy washed over him, mingled with grief. This was the girl whom Paul de Vitry had loved. Arsène was no longer jealous. Paul's love mingled with his own. He had no doubt, now, that the proximity of that gentle and noble man had impressed itself upon Cecile Grandjean, that if she had not loved him with passion, she had loved him. If she grieved for him now, Arsène felt no wild resentment. Had she not grieved, he would have loved her less. It was good that she was in Paul's house. Perhaps his spirit felt that goodness, and was content.

Arsène knew also that Cecile loved him, as he loved her. But in their love was anger, irritation, resentment, antagonism and obstinacy. Perhaps all these were the very essence of passion, after all, and, without them, passion was impossible. Purest love, devoid of passion, was a noble but raptureless thing. Strife was necessary for complete joy.

Cecile felt his presence. She turned her head slowly and looked at him.

A thousand darts of light passed between them. For an instant, Cecile could not control her expression. It softened; it kindled; it became enormously excited. Her lips parted, turned to deep rose, and trembled. Then, controlling herself, after that instant, she forced her face to assume a look of boldness and reserve, and even hostility.

He approached her across the shining floor, and she watched him come. Her hands were no longer quiet; they clenched together upon her knee. But she said nothing. She did not offer him her hand. Her deep blue eyes regarded him with a formality in which there was something of dread,

497

and much of withdrawal. In their depths an icy spark became brighter.

He bowed before her. There was a dryness and tightness in his throat.

"Mademoiselle, allow me to commiserate with you over the death of your grandfather," he said, and his voice had a dull sound in it which he despised, helplessly.

Her clenched hands moved. Her whole figure became imbued with something that was inimical and alert.

"And allow me, Monsieur, to commiserate with you over the death of your friend," she answered. Was that a tone of contempt under her quiet and formal voice? A quick but nameless anger seized Arsène. The girl was bloodless, heartless! She had expressed no grief, no softness, over those tragic and innocent deaths. Her eye revealed no trace of past tears.

Hardly knowing what he did, he held out his hand to her. She looked at it long and meaningfully, and then raised her eyes to him. The spark was a bitter blaze.

"Is Monsieur to be congratulated for the affair at Chantilly?" she asked.

He was silent. But he was filled with fury. He looked at her with narrowed gaze and tightened lips. The signs of her illness, and her recent suffering, were still clear in her thin pale cheeks and the somber purple that stained the skin under her unshakeable eyes, but he was not moved by these. He wanted to strike her.

"So, you have heard, Mademoiselle?" he asked, ironically. "Who was the informant who so distressed your sick-bed, where you were recovering from the kind ministrations of your recent friends?"

Her fury rose up to meet his, and if it was quieter, it was not the less violent. A vivid light exploded on her face, which was now drained of all color.

"Roselle, who today returned to Chantilly, received this information from her uncle, in a letter. Let me assure you, Monsieur, that you have a deep admirer in Crequy, who wrote gloatingly about his part in that shameful crime. No doubt Monsieur is flattered that Crequy admires him?"

Her voice, ringing with contempt, breathless with passion, struck at him like a brutal fist. She half rose in her chair. Her hands turned white on the arms, with her straining efforts. Now scorn blazed at him from her face, from the teeth that glittered between her lips, from the straining muscles of her throat, from the illuminated blue eyes.

Before that scorn, he felt a sudden daunting, and then

wild anger. His heart roared in his ears. He was overcome with shame, and with rage.

He could not speak for a moment, then he said, in a voice hoarse and heavy with his emotions: "Would Mademoiselle have preferred that I shower honors on the murderers of her grandfather, and my friend? Would she have been delighted if I had assured them that they had done a just and noble thing? Mademoiselle appears to have disdain for justice."

"Justice!" she cried. "Does not Monsieur mistake justice for revenge? Was Monsieur activated less by grief than by hatred?" She rose now, leaning against the chair, and her face was white as death.

He clenched his hands at his sides as he looked at her. His lean dark face was convulsed, and the sharp black eyebrows drew down over his sparkling eyes.

"Mademoiselle's words and actions betray that she feels no grief for either her grandfather or my poor friend," he said. "She is less concerned with their horrible deaths than the fate of their murderers. Mademoiselle will pardon me if I do not understand, if I suspect that she is hard of heart and insensible to natural emotions."

Her face changed. It became lined with suffering, but, strangely, it also became harder. She drew a deep and quivering breath. She could hardly make her voice audible when she answered: "If I grieve, it is without hatred. Do not mistake that I feel no bitterness, no despair, Monsieur. But I cannot perceive that Monsieur is more worthy, nor greater, than those he executed. They were activated by what they believed was a just revenge on the Comte de Vitry. Monsieur was activated by the same revenge, on his murderers. But Monsieur was inspired by no love for the Comte. Had he paused to consider, to reflect, he would have known that the Comte would have desired no such retribution on those he had loved. He would have known that the Comte understood all things, even cruelty, and had long perceived that the cruelest acts come from ignorance, fear and confusion. But Monsieur did not consider, or reflect. In his revenge on those wretches he exercised a hatred which must long have been latent in him. That is what cannot be forgiven. That is what the Comte de Vitry could not have understood."

Now proud tears rushed to her eyes. She bit her lip to prevent a sob that rose from her breast. But she did not bow her head or turn away. She looked straightly at Arsène, and without flinching.

"I had thought that Monsieur was incapable of that hatred, and that revenge," she added, and her voice shook.

Suddenly, all his fury was gone. He approached her a step, understanding. She recoiled slightly, but her eyes did not leave his face.

"Has Mademoiselle thought that if I had not done justice, the law of France must inevitably have accomplished it?" he asked, with much gentleness.

But she was not softened. The scorn was enkindled in her eyes.

"France, then, owes a debt of gratitude to Monsieur, for his accomplishment of an act it would otherwise have been compelled to exercise itself?"

She cried out: "I cannot endure it that Monsieur did this thing! Speak no hypocrisy to me, Arsène de Richepin! Do not tell me that the vengeance of the law would have been more merciless! I do not care for this. It is nothing to me. But I cannot endure it that Monsieur in his own person sought such a frightful revenge, out of the urging of his own heart!"

Arsène gazed at her meditatively, and with great softness. Seeing this, she uttered a faint but desolate cry, made an impotent gesture, and turned away proudly and with grief.

He went to her and took her hand. For an instant, she resisted, strove to release it. And then it was quiet. Now she bent her head and wept, as she had not wept at the death of her grandfather and Paul. There was a heart-broken sound in her weeping.

Arsène lifted her hand to his lips, and kissed it deeply, pressing it against his mouth, and then his cheek. The fingers were chill and lifeless at first, then suddenly warmed, became like soft tendrils winding themselves about his own. But she did not turn to him, or cease her weeping.

"At the last, Cecile, I was merciful," he said. "It is true that I was revengeful." He paused. He had almost said, so devastatingly: "But what are these wretches to us, this low-born canaille, this scum, this anonymous refuse?" He bit them back, and was depressed that even now he could think these things. Did the noble, the high-born, the powerful, the privileged, return, in moments of stress, inevitably, to old habits of thoughts and compulsions?

He continued: "You must not forget, Mademoiselle, that I was, at the last, merciful, that I held back my hand. You must comprehend that I now regret that I was motivated by hatred and revenge. But you must understand that these came from my love for Paul de Vitry, and I acted only in a human manner."

She did not speak, but her weeping was softer, as she listened.

He felt a fond impatience for her. But he spoke even more gently:

"I saw Mademoiselle at the inn of Crequy. She was at the point of death, because of the injuries visited upon her by her savage assailants." He hesitated, then whispered: "Had I been on that bed, instead of Mademoiselle, would she have had more lofty thoughts than I?"

She tore her hand from his, and turned to him impetuously. And then, as she met his eyes, penetrating and gentle, she was silent. A deep flush ran over her face. Her lips parted. But her eyes were fixed on the vision he had invoked. Now she turned pale again. She looked at him with passionate honesty.

"Monsieur," she said, in a low tone, "I most probably would have felt the same." Then she cried out: "You are guilty, then! But certainly, I am guilty, also!"

She was innocently overcome with grief. She regarded him with wild horror. When he drew her into his arms, she dropped her head on his shoulder and sobbed aloud. He held her tightly against him, kissing her hair, her forehead, her cheeks. She clung to him in abject despair.

He was overjoyed. Now, he felt only peace and fulfilment. He could face whatever the future brought, however terrible and convulsing, with srength. He had not thought it possible to love like this, with such protectiveness and gentleness, such wisdom.

He said, so moved that his voice trembled: "Our poor friend wished us to be together, my dearest one. He knew that we loved. Not long before he died, he said to me: 'Take what joy can come to you, in each other's arms, no matter what the morrow brings.'"

He was silent a moment, while the girl, clinging to him so desperately, listened:

"Tonight, Cecile, I go to La Rochelle. Shall I live or die there? Shall I flee in exile, in ruin? To what strange land shall I go? Only God can answer it. My beloved, will you go with me, to share whatever comes to me?"

She lifted her head. Her eyes, luminously blue and full of courage and passion, fixed themselves upon his face. Never had she appeared so beautiful and desirable to him.

"What else is there for me, Arsène?" she whispered.

CHAPTER XLVII

IT HAD BEEN a relief to Arsène, embarrassed and ashamed, that during his last days at the Hôtel du Vaubon, his young wife, Clarisse, had been at the home of her mother, Madame de Tremblant, consoling her for the death of Marguerite. Madame had evinced a passionate grief which astonished her friends, for surely there could have been little rapport between that coarse and brutal lady and the silent and docile young girl. A strong and vicious mare had given birth to a lamb, the ribald of Paris had often asserted. Now it appeared that this mare was inconsolable over the passing of this pretty lamb, who had lived and died insignificantly and gently in the shadow of her violent and lewd mother.

Clarisse, her favorite, therefore was necessary at the Hôtel de Tremblant. Madame clung to her, lying in her shaded masculine chamber. Her collapse was complete. Arsène, who had been fond of Marguerite in a careless way, found himself grateful to her for removing the embarrassing presence of his wife from his house. He remembered Clarisse with sheepish regret, but he had no doubt that his permanent removal from her side might some day be of considerable relief to her. He could not believe that she loved him as Cecile loved him. In truth, in conjecturing on this, he was uneasy and annoyed. He had removed her from his life, with ease. He wished her to remove him from hers with the same casualness. That Clarisse was with child, a fact that she had carefully concealed from him until such time as she could reveal it with proper grace, did not occur to him. However, the Marquis, who was much in her confidence, knew, and was delighted. The news was to be broken to Arsène after Clarisse's return from her mother's side. The Marquis, who was simple-minded in many respects, was certain that when Arsène knew, all the darkness and doubts and malaise which seemed annoyingly to be engrossing him these bewildering days would pass away, and he would immediately become more composed, and lose all the moodiness and abstraction which was so distressing to more orderly and realistic persons. Such as the Marquis. Deep in the Marquis' mind lived the fatuous belief that obstetrics answered all problems, including those perplexing and obscure ones which tormented the human soul. They had never solved his problems, but he had an invincible conviction, sentimental and foolish, that they inevitably accomplished this pleasant result in others.

Having done with his old life, and now confronting a hazardous and gloomy future, fraught with violence and death, Arsène was irritated that no one else at the Hôtel du Vaubon, except Pierre, perceived his withdrawal. He did not wish the Marquis to be confronted with the inexorable fact that his spiritual withdrawal was a prelude to his actual withdrawal, but he did wish that the Marquis was less obtuse to the distress and despondency which agitated him. There was much of the theatrical and the dramatic in Arsène. He was an actor in a terrible drama, but the Marquis, the audience, was serenely oblivious of this. Yet, had the Marquis suddenly understood, no one would have regretted it more than Arsène, for all his egotism.

He had disliked his father, but had been fond of him in a careless and indulgent fashion. He had endured him, laughed at him, been annoyed by him. And now, in these last days, he loved him. How was it possible to love such a malicious and shallow creature, full of affectations and frivolities and malevolence? He was a brittle old chameleon, colorful in a silly and pretentious way, but of no value whatsoever. Yet, Arsène now found his attitudes endearing, and pathetic. He was a fool, and a malignant one, but he was amusing. There was pathos in this, too. Also, he loved Arsène, and it is impossible to be indifferent to a creature who loves one.

The Marquis had not been unaware, however, that Arsène was changing under his eyes. And changing much too ominously for the Marquis' peace of mind. But he was convinced that if one ignored unpleasant things, the unpleasantness atrophied and disappeared. So he ignored Arsène's moods so flagrantly and obstinately that the young man was more convinced than ever that his father was an old fool who never saw further than his nose.

On this last stressful day, he was uncommonly affectionate to the Marquis, and showed a tendency, in the last two hours, to be possessed of a deep love for him. The Marquis was

503

going, later, to the gaming tables. He had been complaining that since the Cardinal had left, the tables were no longer the same. He complained incessantly, with a kind of feverishness. Arsène had said nothing about going to La Rochelle, and the Marquis forced himself to believe that if Arsène had thought of this, he did so no longer. Surely, Arsène, the voluble, would have mentioned it!

They were together in the Marquis' gay and frivolous but tasteful chamber. Candles blazed everywhere. Lackeys, burdened with colorful satin and velvet garments, brought armfuls to be inspected and pettishly discarded by their lord. A fine array of curled wigs was set out before him on an inlaid table, and he examined them irritably. Another lackey was laying out the Marquis' immense collection of jewelry. Still another was tentatively extending buckled and jewelled slippers and hose. The heavy but delightful odor of the Marquis' latest scent pervaded the warm room. Arsène, smiling and dark and unusually quiet, sat nearby, affected to be interested in the wardrobe. The Marquis could not make up his mind. He sat before his dressing table, trying on one shade of rouge after another, plucking his eyebrows, preening, pressing his painted lips together to spread the paste, and wafting a handkerchief, impregnated with his new perfume querulously across his nose. But at each whiff, he smiled a little, with arrogant pleasure.

While he complained about the Cardinal, who had so incontinently left the gaming-tables for the arduous and miserable campaign against La Rochelle, the Marquis insisted on obtaining Arsène's opinion as to the evening wardrobe. "I am slightly pale today," he said. "The purple would give me a look of jaundice. Do you not think so, Arsène? Would you prefer the yellow? Or the blue? Madame de Chevrois complimented me upon the blue at the last soirée. She declared it gave me a vivacious appearance."

He preened. A lackey, very alert, came forward and laid the soft and radiant blue of the coat against the Marquis' cheek, for effect. It served to cast a corpselike shade over his raddled and painted face. "Curse the blue!" said the Marquis, violently thrusting the lackey and the coat away from him.

"If Madame de Chevrois admired the blue, wear it," said Arsène. His heart was very heavy, for he knew that this was the last time he would ever see his father. However, he smiled indulgently. "Nevertheless, I prefer the black velvet. It has an air."

The Marquis, who knew Arsène possessed considerable taste, contemplated the black with a thoughtful frown. "Perhaps," he murmured. "The diamonds with it, certes. Drops of dew scattered among the laces. A glitter at the instep. Severe but elegant. And interesting, suggesting a romantic melancholy. Yes, no doubt it must be the black."

The lackeys sprang forward eagerly. The black was laid out, smooth and sleek. The laces were fluttered. The other garments and jewels and shoes were whisked away like magic. The black hung over a chair in aristocratic austerity. The Marquis regarded it with satisfaction, and stretched out a leg to admire it in the delicate black hose. Ah, there was no better leg in Paris! And with that sparkle among the ribbons at the knee, the effect would be devastating. Curse Madame de Chevrois and her penchant for blue! What a hag it was, with those crowfeet. Now, young ladies adored elegance, especially if it suggested intriguing melancholy. There was mystery in black, as well as elegance, and a certain nobility known to be irresistible to ingenuous girls. He must remember to have dignity and gravity tonight, as if a certain fatefulness hung over him.

He turned to Arsène and smiled at him fondly. "I must consult you more often, my fine bravo," he said. He added, with returning pettishness: "It is so long since you came to the tables. Have you not recovered from the death of that foolish friend of yours?"

Arsène's smile became somewhat fixed. But he said: "I have no desire to lose money, tonight." He rose, restlessly, and walked slowly up and down the chamber. The Marquis watched him with uneasiness. For a moment he contemplated telling Arsène that he was soon to be honored with fatherhood. But a strange impulse forced him to be silent. Nevertheless, his uneasiness and his efforts at control, made his painted face appear wizened. Wrinkles sprang out over it, like heavy cobwebs. He bit the nail of his right little finger, then hastily cursing the damage done to it, scrutinized it with infuriated dismay. He was proud of his fine effeminate hands, and was convinced that the slightest flaw ruined them.

A lackey produced a pot of solidified oil, which Armand vigorously rubbed into the ragged nail, then wiped with a fine silk kerchief. This absorbing and important task occupied him for several moments. However, the seams deepened in his raddled countenance. He held the injured finger to the light of the lamps, and studied it. He said:

"I understand that the death of Paul de Vitry caused you

sadness, Arsène. Nevertheless, will you forgive me if I confess that it has released me from much worry? Too, he was a young man without taste. He lacked a certain noblesse oblige, a certain aristocracy and elegance."

Arsène did not answer. At first an impetuous and angry look had flashed into his eyes. Then, after a glance at his father, he smiled to himself. The Marquis' casual words and air of deep absorption in his nail did not deceive him. He replied with considerable mildness: "You refer, of course, to his affection for the wretches who murdered him. I prefer to believe that he merely lacked discernment, and not taste."

"It is the same thing," said the Marquis, lifting a silver mirror and examining a pimple near his mouth. "Taste extends to a discernment of others. The obtuse are vulgar fellows."

He put down the hand mirror, and his eyes met Arsène's in the larger glass. For an instant or two Arsène thought that he saw in his father's eyes a mournful sympathy. He turned away.

"You are careless in your dress, lately, my fine cavalier," said the Marquis. "Am I to understand that you are going nowhere tonight?"

Arsène was silent for a little space, then he answered: "I may visit Clarisse." He spoke the lie with reluctance, but was rewarded by his father's smile of approval.

Impulsively, Arsène laid his hands on the Marquis' shoulders, and they smiled at each other in the mirror. Then Arsène bent, and carefully touched his lips to the painted cheek. A strong emotion passed over the older man's face. He laid his hand on one of the hands on his shoulder and pressed it with deep affection. A tear came in his eyes; he winked it away, bending forward a little to see that it had not smeared the kohl on his lashes.

"You are a rascal," said the Marquis, in a light but changed voice.

But Arsène had lost his smile. His expression had become stern and grave. He said, looking full and sadly into the mirrored eyes that held his: "I know this. I ask you to forgive me."

A cold sensation passed over the Marquis' heart, a sensation akin to nameless terror. Arsène's look, his manner, his voice, his words, struck at him icily. He turned about, and caught his son by the arm, and cried out: "I was jesting, you fool! What happiness or satisfaction I have had in life have been in you!" The grip on Arsène's arm strengthened, as if with overwhelming fear, and the Marquis exclaimed: "Come with me, tonight! It has been very long since you accompanied me."

Arsène hesitated. Then he said: "It is possible. I have been distrait too long."

There was something in his manner which did not reassure the Marquis, but he put the thought from him and smiled. He resumed his toilette. Arsène pretended to be concerned with it also. They haggled over the wigs. Arsène declared that a too elaborate wig would ruin the effect of the black austerity and richness. "Those excessive curls are frivolous," he argued, as the Marquis insisted that a particularly intricate wig was devastating. Finally, after exhaustive tryings-on, a dignified wig of long lustrous hair, slightly curled at the ends, was chosen. The Marquis stood up and pirouetted on one dainty heel, extending his arms, the hands drooping elegantly, head turned haughtily over one shoulder, while Arsène and the lackeys volubly admired. One lackey sprayed perfume over the entire costume as the Marquis rotated. Another whisked a brush over the deep and glistening velvet. The Marquis was all graceful splendor, glittering at the throat, wrist, finger, knee and instep. He had a manner, and a leg. He was as egotistically delighted as a child at the admiration of his son and his lackeys, but he maintained a lofty and reserved expression.

The carriage was waiting. A plumed hat was set carefully on the false curls. A cloak was tenderly draped over the black velvet. From beneath its folds the jewelled hilt of his slender rapier gleamed. A cane was given him, the knob glittering. The Marquis struck a last attitude in the mirror, then left the room with Arsène, laughing lightly at one of his own ribald jokes.

But Arsène never learned the point of the jest, for, as they reached the head of the curving white and gilt staircase, they were confronted by Louis, who was rapidly ascending.

All three halted, and a deep silence fell. Louis stood there, half-way up the stairs, his hand on the balustrade, the light of the great crystal chandelier that hung from the ceiling shining down into his wild blue eyes, distended and strained. There was a fierce and disordered air about his flowing black robes, his white and contorted face. When he looked at his brother, that face became a blaze of evil and hatred.

So intense, so mad, was that blaze, that Arsène involuntarily stepped back a pace. But Louis came on, like an avenging fury, distraught and beside himself. He looked only at his brother, and all his lifetime of humiliation, despair and loathing stood like a flame in his eyes.

"So!" he cried out, loudly and hoarsely, "you are to go to La Rochelle, you traitor, you mountebank, you liar! You are to betray your country, in the company of scurrilous heretics and foreign malcontents, against the arms, the religion, the safety and the throne of France!"

The Marquis was stupefied. He looked first at his younger son, and then at Arsène. But his stupefaction was less at Louis' words than at the delirious ferocity that radiated from him.

Louis had reached his brother. He did not appear to see his father. He caught Arsène by the upper part of his doublet, and shook him savagely.

"But, you shall not go, even if I have to kill you with my own hand!"

They looked in each other's eyes. He is mad, thought Arsène. He is mad at last. He was overcome with such a horror that he could not release himself from his brother's grip. He fell back against the balustrade. He felt himself shaken like a mouse in a terrier's mouth. Yes, there was no doubt about it: Louis was mad.

Louis, with a strange loud cry, flung his brother from him, so that he staggered backwards, and had to catch the upper curve of the balustrade to keep from crashing to the floor. He was seized with dizziness, and put up his hand before his face as if to defend it.

Now the Marquis came to life. He caught Louis by the arm; he lifted his hand and struck him violently across the face.

"How now, you brute, you dastard, you malignant priest!" he cried. "Leave my house at once, and never enter it again. I have always detested you. I loathe you now, you puling fool, you priestly imbecile!"

The blow, the cruel words, the look of detestation, halted Louis, whose mind was only a cauldron, whose tortured heart was being consumed to ashes. He looked at his father, and for an instant or two the madness, the wildness and deathly hatred, died away, and it was a dying man who stood there, motionless, with dying eyes.

Arsène had recovered himself. He saw that he must escape at once, while his father held his brother. He slipped past them, hurrying as if in a nightmare. He wished to be out of this house with all speed, away from this horror and sickening scene. There was no time for a last word with the Marquis, as he had planned, no last embrace or smile. He knew that if he was ever to leave, it must be now.

The stairs, in the strong and glittering light, seemed to extend beyond him into bottomless depths. He was trembling uncontrollably. His sweating hand gripped the hilt of his sword.

He had reached the bottom, when he heard a great and savage cry from Louis, a cry that was a loud hoarse scream. Some compulsion made him halt, and look back. Louis was descending the staircase. He seemed to be of enormous stature. His black robes flew about him. The chandelier made a golden halo about his large head. And in his hand was his drawn sword.

Unable to move, frozen into stone and ice, Arsène waited. It was an archangel with a flaming sword who was descending upon him. It was an archangel with a terrible face.

He did not know when he drew his own sword, but all at once he heard the clash of steel. Louis had flung aside his cloak. He was no longer a priest. He was an enemy with a fixed and frightful smile, on guard. Arsène had a dim impression of the Marquis, who had half descended the stairs, and who was standing there, motionless, with open mouth against which he had pressed the fingers of one hand. And beyond him, at the head of the staircase, crowded the gaping lackeys.

It is a dream, a ghastly dream, thought Arsène. He looked at Louis, and the dreamlike sensation increased. No man could have worn such a malignant and appalling expression; that was no human light in those glaring fixed eyes. Arsène dropped his sword, and instantly he felt a sharp pungent pang in his left shoulder not far above his heart.

This is death, said Arsène to himself. It is either my brother or myself. The horror made a thick nausea rise in his throat, and he swallowed to keep the salt water from spewing from his lips. He forced himself to cry out, as he parried aside that deadly glittering sword which lunged swiftly towards his heart:

"Louis! You are mad! You do not know what you are doing!"

But Louis only smiled again, that most frightful smile. Arsène saw the sharp gleam of his teeth between his drawn lips. The mad light in the blue eyes danced. Now he had his enemy before him, and between them was naked steel! Now all his lifetime was to be avenged on this symbol of his loneliness, his agony, his grief and fear! Now he was face to

509

face with his supreme foe, and he would kill him in one last gesture of rage and hatred and despair!

In one awful instant, Arsène, with the prescience of those in deadly peril, understood. It was his life, or his brother's. There was no retreating.

Now he was silent. He gripped his teeth on his lip. This was an enemy to be killed, and he intended to do it with dispatch. His sword darted and flashed like a tongue of cold flame. From somewhere came a strangled cry, and then utter silence.

The wound in his shoulder ached and bled. He felt its dripping down his left arm. He concentrated on the horrible task at hand. He would need all his strength, all his energy, all his skill, for Louis was one of the most accomplished swordsmen in France. Many a time, long ago, the two brothers had fenced, and Arsène had only one victory to his credit over Louis.

Yet, as he fought, with that fixed and frightful face before him, he could not shut out his awareness of the terrible aspects of this scene. He could feel, with intense sensation, the soft carpet under his feet, the portraits on the white and gilt walls, the face of his father on the steps nearby. A numbness began to pervade him. He shook his head to clear the mists from his eyes. Suddenly, he could not endure it.

He cried out: "You are my brother!"

And then Louis, as he stepped back for a moment's breathing space, threw back his head and laughed aloud. The laugh started softly, and then became a most appalling howl, broken into tremulos, quivering like the howling of a wolf. Arsène's heart rose on a wave of sickness, and he retched.

He felt a plunge of Louis' sword not two inches above his heart, and very near the first bleeding wound. He fell back. His head whirled. Instinctively, he lifted his sword, and struck aside the darting blade reaching for a vital spot.

I must be done with this, he thought. I must be done with this, or I shall surely die of very horror.

He decided that he would wound and disarm his brother. He could not kill him! No, please God, he could not kill him! Let me not kill him, he prayed silently. Tears rose to his eyes, dazzled him.

The sword flashed a murderous beam within an inch of his throat. He struck it aside. The steel rang like a sharp bell. Louis fell back. Now was the time! A plunge over the right breast, and before Louis recovered a hurling away of his sword!

510

Arsène advanced upon his brother, his eye fixed on the very spot where he would wound and cripple him. But on that very instant, while Arsène's sword darted towards him, Louis' right ankle turned, throwing him sideways. And the sword plunged deeply into his left breast.

There was a sudden dreadful silence. Louis' sword arm dropped. The fingers slowly loosened. The sword fell at his feet, its tip stained with Arsène's blood. Louis looked at his brother, and the white fire slowly quenched itself on his face. His mouth and eyes opened wide in an expression of intense preoccupation and surprise. He stood there rigidly, not moving, and moment by moment, he turned to a pillar of snow.

And then, while Arsène, paralyzed, watched, the priest swayed. A faint moan came from him. His eyelids dropped over his eyes. His hands lifted with a helpless and irresolute gesture, as if he had become blind. He swayed heavily. And then, with a muffled cry, he fell forward on his face, his head striking Arsène's feet.

Arsène, weighted down with stone, could not stir even a finger. He heard cries about him, confused, far-off cries. He felt his father's arms about him, heard his father's sobs. He heard the Marquis' voice: "Oh, mon Dieu, mon Dieu! My son, you are hurt! That foul beast—! My son, my son!"

But Arsène looked only at his brother, silent and motionless, like a fallen statue, at his feet. A thin red trickle of blood writhed away from him from under his left arm. And then Arsène looked at the sword still in his hand. With a convulsive cry, he flung it from him. It struck against the far wall with a clanging and ominous sound.

Arsène thrust his father from him. He knelt down beside his brother. He lifted him in his arms and turned him over. Louis' face was already gray with approaching death. But his eyes were open and steadfast. And very quiet. He tried to speak. Blood gushed from his mouth. Arsène wiped it away with his own kerchief. He began to weep.

And then Louis saw his tears. He struggled to speak once more. He whispered thickly: "You have always hated me."

"No! No! In the name of God, no!" cried Arsène, drawing his brother closer to him. "I have never hated you, Louis. I swear it. Believe me, for Christ's sake!"

In those dimming eyes, on those purple lips, a strange expression dimly appeared.

"I have even loved you, Louis," said Arsène, and he felt as if his heart was dissolving within him with pain. "I have

511

wanted to be friends with you. You would not allow this. I did not hate you, Louis. But you have hated me."

"You have not hated me?" repeated Louis, and a look of wild surprise blazed up in his dying eyes, and incredulous joy.

Arsène could not speak. He bent over his brother, lying so heavily in his arms, and he kissed that cold wet brow, and pressed his cheek against the fair hair, now wet with blood. "O, forgive me," he groaned, when he could speak again.

Louis stirred in his arms. Finally, with a last supreme effort, he lifted his right arm and let it fall feebly about Arsène's neck. He smiled, and closed his eyes. He drew a long and shaking breath, and then appeared not to breathe again.

The two brothers remained like this for several endless moments, clasped in each other's arms. And then at last Louis' arm fell away, and he sank into unconsciousness.

Arsène looked up at his father, who was watching them with a strange expression. Streaks of wet black kohl ran over his painted cheeks. He was an old rouged man, trembling and undone.

"I have sent for my physician," he said, meeting Arsène's eyes.

"It is too late," replied Arsène, speaking with difficulty. "He is dying."

He gazed down at the dying priest in his arms. Louis seemed to be sleeping. There was a faint chill smile on his gray face.

Arsène laid him down, very gently. He saw the gaping and terrified lackeys behind his father. He stood up. It was almost midnight, and he could delay no longer. The wounds in his shoulder were nothing to the aching wound in his heart.

"Stay with him, to the last," he said, turning to the Marquis. "He loved you."

The Marquis, not comprehending, nodded his head. He approached his younger son, and stood, looking down at him. And then, with a dwindled sound like a whimper, he knelt and bent over Louis. He did not see Arsène slip away. He heard no far closing of a door.

The hotel was dreadfully still. No life seemed stirring in it. The faces of the lackeys were a painted back-drop. And the Marquis knelt beside his son and chaffed his unconscious hands, which were now as cold as dead stone.

At last Louis stirred, and sighed. He opened his eyes. He

512

looked fully at his father, who bent his head as if in shame. But the Marquis felt a tremor in the hand he held. And now in that malicious and frivolous heart, so malevolent and greedy, a peculiar emotion stirred, as if of boundless grief.

He said: "Louis. Louis, my son."

At those words, a long quiver passed over the dying man. He tried to raise himself. The Marquis caught him in his arms and pressed him against his breast, and he wept aloud, with a hoarse sound.

But Louis was speaking, in faint gasps: "He must not go! He will be killed. You must stop him, and bring him home. La Rochelle—it will fall, and he will die."

The Marquis listened, and cried out. He felt Louis' hands, with a last strength, gripping his own.

"Tonight—he is going. He will die!"

A deathly rattle sounded in his throat, and at that sound, the Marquis' attention returned to his son. He raised his head upon his black velvet knee. He looked down into the glazing eyes.

"Louis," he groaned. "Ah, my son!"

With much wildness, he kissed that stony brow, and then the cold lips. A far marble smile appeared on Louis' face, a smile of supreme happiness. And then, he looked beyond his father, and those filmed eyes suddenly quickened, became alight with ecstasy.

"Marguerite," he said, clearly and lightly, and his hands lifted for a moment, with humility, with unbelieving rapture.

The Marquis cast a wild confused look over his shoulder. But he did not see what his son was seeing. When he returned to Louis, his son was dead.

CHAPTER XLVIII

ACCOMPANIED BY FOUR trusted lackeys, the Marquis du Vaubon rode furiously down the dark midnight road towards Longjumeau, which Arsène must inevitably have taken on his swift journey to La Rochelle.

The lackeys were armed, as was the Marquis, for the road was infested by highwaymen. There was no moon, but the stars, swarming like millions of silver bees caught in a silver net, lighted the way with a fugitive and spectral gleam.

The Marquis' equestrian exploits during the past decade or two had been confined to elegant canters through the Bois on languid steeds. He adored the picturesque aspects of a gentleman upon a horse (with appropriate attitudes). But he knew that the arduous pursuit of his son could not be accomplished on animals intended for effect. Therefore, the horse upon which he grimly rushed through the night had been created by nature for speed and endurance, with the accompanying physical characteristics. Thus, added to his anxiety, his grief, his confusing mental upheavals, was the imposition on tender parts of his anatomy of bony rib and narrow hard saddle. Hardly ten miles had passed before his gloved hand was sore from the reins, and a certain portion of his torso was well blistered. Nevertheless, he did not decrease speed, in spite of a melancholy foreboding that he would suffer abominably later. Moreover, he became aware that he was an old man, for he could hardly breathe in the smothering wind, and exhaustion soon threatened to overpower him. Inclined to asthma, his lungs labored. All his detestation for the country seemed well justified, and he looked at the lonely trees, standing in their star shadows, with disgust and loathing.

So well did he ride, despite these various handicaps, that the lackeys were hard put to it to keep up with him. The necks of the horses strained forward, long and lean, so that they appeared to fly. Their thudding hoofs sounded like drums on the thick soft dust of the road to Longjumeau, and their diffused shadows flew behind them in a disorderly fashion.

As he rode, the Marquis raked the vague dim distance with feverish eyes, for a sign of Arsène. But the road continued to be empty, except for threatening shadows. Arsène had had not more than an hour and a half in his advantage. However, there was not the slightest indication that he had passed this way.

But, thought the Marquis, desperately, he could have taken no other road. Unless, of course, for purposes of concealment, he had taken one less travelled. In that event, the Marquis' gloomy thoughts continued, he would be compelled to pursue his son to the very gates of that accursed La Rochelle.

It was very bad, that flight, but in the light of Louis' death, it had its advantages. The fatal conflict between the brothers had been inevitable. But it would have had its very serious consequences. Duelling was forbidden, by order of the King. A murder charge against Arsène was not improbable. The Marquis no longer felt aversion and dislike for Louis, but only a bitter sadness, a feeling of mournful futility. Other, and more spiritual things were bruised in that mad pursuit besides his body.

Two hours flew by in the wake of the galloping horses. Now the animals were panting, for the speed had not abated. The road wound and twisted under the crouching trees. The starlight was so spectral that at times it seemed that they had lost their way.

Then, in the distance, the Marquis saw the faint light of a little tavern, near the roadside. It was possible that Arsène and his companions had paused there for a moment's refreshment. As they came near the tavern, the Marquis uttered a cry of relief. He saw a number of tethered horses at the side of the tavern, and their heads were hanging low with weariness. One of them he could just barely identify as Arsène's horse, for there was a vagrant gleam of white about the rump and upon one leg.

The Marquis swung down from his horse, groaned aloud as his buttocks winced with pain. Staggering from side to side, he ran towards the tavern, and flung open the door.

It was a small mean place. A wide fire seemed to fill the dirty room. At various bare tables sat a group of grim young men. Talking rapidly to one or two, was Arsène. By his side sat a young girl. The Marquis' eye, in spite of his agitation, observed that she had a certain noble beauty. He perceived, as he entered, with a burst of sound, and some curses, that she turned a brilliant blue eye upon him. She wore a heavy dark cloak, and the hood had fallen upon her shoulders, revealing lustrous light hair gleaming with threads of gold in the fire and candlelight. Before all of the men in that tavern stood bottles of wine and tankards, and a half of ham and some crusty bread.

Arsène looked up, and when he saw his father, he started to his feet with an exclamation. His face was dark and haggard, his lips bloodless. His wounded arm was bandaged, hanging in a sling.

"Ah, now, my fine rascal!" shouted the Marquis, "I have found you at last!"

Arsène looked swiftly at his companions, who rose and bowed, somewhat sheepishly, and with indications of alarm. They glanced at the door, as if expecting that the Marquis was accompanied by a formidable detachment of armed men. The Marquis looked at them, his little black eyes sparkling with anger. He recognized the young gentlemen, whom he knew were members of Les Blanches.

Arsène came forward, trying to scowl, but succeeding only in appearing disturbed. "Father! Why have you come?" He hesitated, then said in a lower voice: "Louis?"

Irate, still panting, the Marquis turned to him. "Your brother is dead. But before he died, he told me your abominable plans, and urged me to pursue you and bring you back, lest you die."

Arsène did not speak. He looked steadfastly at the floor, and a deep sorrow passed over his face. He sighed. The young gentlemen, and the girl, regarded the Marquis in watchful silence.

"You will return with me at once," continued the Marquis, and his voice, in spite of its efforts to remain stern, quavered. "But not, certes, to Paris, unless you are desirous, you fool! of arrest and trial for murder. You will go to Gascony." He fixed the girl with a long hard stare. "In the company of Madame, your wife, who is about to bear you a child."

Arsène paled still more, if possible. He stared at his father, who stood there before him, in a state of complete disorder. The rouge and kohl were streaked in red and black lines on his wizened face. The wig, which he had neglected to remove in his haste, was tilted rakishly under his hat. He still wore the sleek black velvet and diamonds, but over it was a dusty cloak.

"A child," muttered Arsène. He did not see the sudden rising of the girl nor did he hear her dim cry. He did not see the faces of his companions, nor the glances, amused or disturbed, which they exchanged with each other.

He, at last, drew a deep and audible breath. He looked at his father with grim resolution.

"I cannot return, my father. I am committed, with all my heart and soul, to this campaign. I attempted to leave, being unwilling to cause you grief and anxiety, without a last word. Nevertheless, all preparations were made. Clarisse is in possession of the keys to my commode, in which you will find letters and directions." He paused. "I leave Clarisse—and my child—in your hands, and in your care. Do well by them I implore you. Some day, perhaps, I may return—"

"You abandon your wife and son?" exclaimed the Marquis, beginning to tremble. "You foreswear your vows? You will leave them desolate, for a mad adventure, which can end only in death, ruin, or exile? You—you will abandon me?"

"I abandon no one," said Arsène, through dry lips. "But I am committed to this. I have told you before—there can be no peace for me, until this thing is done. If I am to die, or to flee, it is my fate. I can say nothing more."

There was silence in the tavern. The Marquis, in despair, implored every cold and obdurate face which was turned to him. Then he cried out, in furious grief:

"You will go with these traitorous wretches, and take up arms against your own people, in the company of foreign malcontents—Germans, Spaniards, English and Italians? Can you not understand that if you do this, you shall see Paris no more, nor those who love you? Do you know this is the end for you? What is Protestanism to you, you foolish adventurer, you bravo? A silly political religion, which has disturbed France for generations!"

Arsène regarded his distraught father sternly. "My grandfather, and your father, died for this silly political religion.' You, yourself, fought for it. It is no religion to me, but a struggle between darkness and light, between slavery and liberation. I am committed to it with my heart and soul. But you have known this. I can only go forward."

He suddenly cried out, like a man in extremity: "Is history nothing to you? Cannot even you perceive that the fate of millions of men awaits the decision at La Rochelle, that unborn generations shall know freedom and life if men like me do not retreat, do not abandon the fight? If expediency were the law of all men, the world would continue to wallow in slavery and depravity. Shall I die? I do not know. But it is enough for me that I have fought, and that in my death, some unborn man shall live!"

The Marquis opened his lips to reply furiously, then, seeing how strange, how dark, how moved, was Arsène's face, he was silent. This was not his son, this stern and resolute man with the fiery eyes and the impetuous gesture. This was not the joyous and frivolous Arsène, the easy cavalier, the laugher, the man of attitudes and postures. This was a stranger, and before him the Marquis felt confused and full of consternation.

Then Arsène held out his free hand, as if in somber pleading: "Do you wish me to live as you have lived?"

The Marquis dropped his eyes; his painted lips twitched. Then, with a last desperate appeal, he turned to the girl, who, so pale and silent, was watching him with fixed blue eyes:

"Mademoiselle, I do not know you! But I have discerned that in some manner you are attached to my son. I implore you to consider! I implore you, if you have regard for him, to return him to his wife, and to the child which is coming."

The girl did not recoil. Her pallor became even more intense. But she looked at Arsène in silence.

Some pity stirred Arsène for this depraved and broken man. He took his arm gently, and smiled into his face.

"Do not grieve; do not distress yourself. You know I cannot return. You know I must go forward. I ask you to go to the side of Clarisse, and comfort and sustain her. I have done wrongly by her; I should not have married her. I cannot forgive myself. But there are greater things than wife and children. I am committed to them. I beg you to understand."

The Marquis did not speak. He looked at his son. He moistened his dry rouged lips upon which the paint had dried in ugly flakes, and was peeling. He staggered a little, as if suddenly overcome with weakness. He groped for support, then fell upon a bench. He covered his face with his hands.

Arsène sighed. He looked at his companions, at Cecile, as if for assistance. The young men regarded him with silent reserved faces, but watchfully. Cecile was weeping, her head bent, the tears running down her cheeks. No one helped him. His decision was left in his own hands. Every one was moved, yet no one spoke. The tavern keeper, in a far corner, blinked his eyes in bewilderment, not understanding this strange scene.

Then the Marquis dropped his hands. He had suddenly taken on the aspect of dignity and quiet resolution. Even the streaked paint upon his sunken cheeks could not disperse that dignity, that resolution, and the pride and stillness which accompanied them.

"I cannot move you," he said, quietly, gazing at his son with brilliant eyes. "Be that as it may. But, if you go, I must go, also."

Arsène exclaimed incoherently. The Marquis rose. He looked at each and every face in a profound silence. An inscrutable expression appeared on his own. He said, in a hollow but meditative voice:

"Clarisse shall not go without comfort, without sustenance. Madame, her mother, will not fail her. There is nothing for me in Paris. There has never been anything there for me, except you, my son. Do you not understand what I have endured, in myself? Do you think I have had no thoughts? I am old, but I am still not impotent. If you go forward, then I must go, also."

Arsène opened his lips to protest, then seeing his father's face, the ghastly pallor of it under the rouge, the strange and unfamiliar firmness of the malicious mouth, the sudden heroic set of his shoulders, and the resolute gleam of the weary eye, he said nothing. But he put his arms about him, and they clung to each other in stern and feverish strength.

Later, as they rode side by side in a darkness which was paling towards dawn, Arsène spoke of his dead brother. His voice was low and heavy with sorrow.

"I did not wish him to die. I prayed that I would not kill him, though he tried to kill me."

"I have learned many things in one hour," replied the Marquis, in a peculiar tone which was faint with weariness. "He hated you, Arsène. Nevertheless, it was a strange hatred, born of his loneliness. How were we so blind, you, in your amusement, and I, in my detestation? We must bear the knowledge of our indifference, our cruelty, to our graves. But how was it possible to approach him? He was fortressed in his terrible but lonely and desperate soul. What mysterious knowledge is now given to me! I am a foolish and wicked old man, but now I understand so many things."

"I always knew," said Arsène, in a low voice, broken and exhausted. "It is my crime that I did not care, except at the last. I tormented him, all his life." He looked at the milky east, already streaked with fire. "I had no time! But I should have liked to have heard him forgive me."

"He forgave you, Arsène. He implored me to make you return. He feared for you, for my own grief. How strange it is to realize that he loved me! I must have known; assuredly I knew. But it amused me, and I tortured him for my own pleasure."

The Marquis paused, overcome. His horse slowed, as his hand slackened on the reins.

"If there had been only a moment's joy for him, in life," said Arsène.

The Marquis sighed, then suddenly lifted his head as if a thought had struck him. "Before he died, he said one word: 'Marguerite!' And in such a voice, so full of love and delight. I had forgotten this. Was it possible that he loved some woman after all?"

Arsène turned to him, with an odd and startled look. "If he perceived that woman, when he was dying, it is evident that she had died before him. Who is 'Marguerite?' " He paused, then his face changed and kindled. "Is it possible that it was Marguerite de Tremblant, the sister of Clarisse?"

They looked at each other in a momentous silence. Then Arsène said:

"Yes, it must have been poor Marguerite! Ah, then, he was happy once. He loved, and was loved! We must remember that, for our own consolation."

CHAPTER XLIX

THEY CONTINUED THEIR journey with all dispatch. Arsène rode as one possessed, as if attempting to flee from the sorrows and anxieties of the life that lay behind him. He paused long enough, the next day, to write a letter to Clarisse, full of affection, regret and grief, and imploring her to love and cherish their child with all her heart, forgetting the desertion of her husband, and remembering him with all charity. "Some day, perhaps, we shall meet again," he wrote, "and I shall have the joy of embracing my little one."

His heart was heavy, but he allowed himself little time in which to contemplate or regret. All his apprehension, now, was centered in the young Cecile, who never complained, nor sighed with weariness, despite her white face and the disability she must still have felt because of her recent dangerous illness. Little passed between them but silent and eloquent smiles, a touch of the hand, a courageous flash of the eye, but understanding was there and a passionate and undeviating love. Arsène marvelled at the steadfastness of this young female heart, that could face coming danger, and even death, with the single-minded fortitude of a noble man. It is the women who are the true fanatics, the truly dedicated, he would think. They lacked the prudence of the more realistic sex. They could give themselves up to martyrdom with joy and simplicity. Men who possessed this joy and simplicity had, in themselves, something of the essentially feminine nature, and, something of the hysteria and transports inherent in that nature. No man, he understood, approached martyrdom and immolation with passion and faith unless there was a femaleness in him. The complete man tended more to conservative battles and compromise.

He admitted that he, himself, did not possess this tender but invulnerable touch of femaleness, that only a supreme

521

act of will, battling with caution and prudence, enabled him to go forward resolutely. Even in his resolution lingered doubts and hesitancies, and an enervating weariness. Finally, with some pride, he came to the conclusion that those who truly deserved the accolades were not the fanatics and the heroes, but the realists who faced death and danger without illusion, and only by the power of will and reason. They rode forward in a cold and bitter light, hearing no orisons, and harkening only to the chill and steely voice of a comfortless but necessary duty.

"Once," the Abbé Mourion had said to him, "I tormented myself in conjecturing whether I loved God enough. Now I only torment myself with the conjecture whether I love men enough."

In those words, to Arsène, was the very essence of true Protestantism. He knew that he had far to go, to awaken in himself a complete love for his fellows. Hampered by the traditions, hauteurs and contempts of his caste, the struggle was monumental. But he was cheered that he had at last discerned the shining shore of the far distance. Nor was he deluded that to love men it was necessary to idealize them, and believe that they were fair and noble creatures. An understanding of their rapacity, stupidity and cruelty did not, in the real lover of mankind, dim his love. It might arouse his anger, but it also aroused his pity, quickened his resolution to awaken other men to a knowledge of every man's responsibility to his fellows.

Of all this, he could make only Cecile understand. His companions were impelled only by hatred of the religion which would limit their intelligence and their personal liberty, and would reduce them to mental serfs. The Marquis, with only dim perceptions of his own father's passionate dedication, and vaguely tormented by conscience, accompanied his son from love and an inability to live without him.

Sometimes Arsène was depressed by all this. But slowly he realized that, in the beginning, it was only necessary that the leader understand. The followers trailed him blindly, listening to his leading footfalls. But at last the end would be accomplished, and the blind would see to what glory they had followed him.

They dared waste not even an hour, for they must not only overtake the Cardinal, travelling on the main road in slow pomp and circumstance, surrounded by banners and martial music, but must pass him and reach La Rochelle before he arrived there. They knew that at every town the

Cardinal must wait impatiently for news of the vacillating King, to learn whether or not that personage had decided to follow. Half-way to La Rochelle, the welcome news arrived that Louis had finally determined to follow the Cardinal, jealous of any triumph which might come alone to that implacable man. He could not endure that the Cardinal accomplish the fall of La Rochelle, while he, Louis, lurked sulkily in Paris. So, the messenger came to Richelieu that he was to wait at Tours for him. The Cardinal, enraged and disappointed, fumed in silence, expressed his joy in public. He hoped that Madame would accompany the monarch, in his luxurious train, for then the ardors of the journey, and the campaign would be much alleviated.

That fool, he thought, referring to his King, is making of this campaign a holiday, a festival, a Roman triumph, travelling in splendor and music, and excitement, setting up his Court in the byways and the highways, noisy with revelry. He knew that every bravo and adventurer accompanied the King, and also a number of avaricious and dangerous priests.

Now the Cardinal frowned with real anxiety and anger. He thought of the Spanish Armada, filled with its thousands of priests and all manner of torture implements, attempting its famous invasion of England. God, or the devil, had intervened, and priests and their hellish implements had disappeared in the gray and boiling waters of the Channel. What if the deity had not intervened so advantageously? What frightful things might not have taken place in England, then! Moreover, the face of the world would have been changed. The Cardinal did not delude himself that the change would have been salubrious.

He thought of the Rochellais, and he grimly resolved that the priests would not have their way among the Huguenots. A Frenchman, first and always, he thought with impatient anger and sadness of the Frenchmen beseiged at La Rochelle. He must conquer them, for the sake of France. But, for the sake of France, he must reconcile them and make them understand that their duty lay in the attainment of a complete unity in France, against the threat of the Habsburgs, and Spain. Frenchmen, against all the world, and let the priests be hanged!

He had planned this campaign at the instigation and seductions of Madame, Anne of Austria. But now he went forward upon it with the sole purpose of welding Frenchmen, Catholic and Protestant alike, in a devotion to France alone. There were no limits to the glories and the powers of

France if all Frenchmen served her with single-hearted love and determination. There must be no memory of a new civil war, of victory obtained by cruelty and torture. Such memories destroyed a nation.

While he waited, idly and angrily, at Tours, the entourage of Arsène de Richepin passed him on a distant and obscure road, hardly a cattle-pass, at midnight. By dawn, Arsène and his companions were leagues away. The Cardinal lying sleepless in his bed, thought he heard the far dim thunder of hoofs, but he finally decided it was only the wind. He was filled with his musings: Why could it not be possible for men, of one blood, to live in harmony though bedevilled by different creeds? And, carrying this further, why was it not possible for men of different races, as well as creeds, to live in peace together, owing a single devotion to one ideal, one political philosophy? Individuality was necessary to create a whole man. But to the common good all men should be dedicated, individuals though they were.

It is not possible, thought the Cardinal. But a strange prescience urged him that it was possible, and that, perhaps, some day, a great nation of men might live in harmony and peace together, dedicated to common good and common humanity, though composed individually of differing creeds and races. Was this not the essence of true Christianity? Without this essence, the world would be lost in a holocaust of wars and ruin.

CHAPTER L

THE FLIGHT TO La Rochelle was of necessity most furtive and secret. The highways must be avoided, travelled only fleetingly at night, and then with drawn pistols. Then it was the gloomiest, as they fled like muffled shadows under the moon or the ragged black clouds, clinging to the nebulous shapes of the trees, watchful alike of Cardinal and highwaymen. Some travelled ahead on a dangerous stretch, then whistling softly and shrilly, heartened their companions to come on. They rode through the most desolate country, wild with ravine and rock, starved, blasted and blackened under spectral moons that etched strange sharp shadows on barren cliffs, and stretched lean pale fingers over empty plain, or glistened wanly on marshland threaded with writhing lines of silver. They heard, as they rode, the dolorous thunder of heavy wind in the dark trees, felt the uneasy breath of the ponderous and giant earth. They wrapped their cloaks closely about them, and shivered, sensing their insignificance in the enormous face of nature.

These hours were the worst. They dared not sing to lift their spirits, nor were they able to while away the black hours with jests or laughter, for fear of enemy ears. Like phantoms, like exiles, they drifted by little hamlets and villages, seeing the night fires, the squat chimneys, blooming like agitated red towers against the darkening purple skies, seeing the dark steeples and towers outlined with the first stars, or the last, hearing the chiming of pious bells sweet against the rising fragrance of wood and harvest-land and vineyards, or the distant call of a child and the laughter of a woman, frail and musical in the evening. Often, crouched in a thicket, they saw the peasant girls bringing in the cattle, heard the lowing of the beasts and the echoing tinkle of their bells and the munching of their jaws, and sometimes the joyous bark of rollicking dogs. They heard the Angelus over fields like beaten and serried gold, and saw how the peasants humbly bent their heads and clasped their hands, their figures heavy and dim and earthy against the burning sunsets. They watched the dawns rise like an army with blue and scarlet banners over the formless horizon of the night, heralding the approach of the sun, which, like a young warrior carrying a shield of blazing gold, stepped on the highest hill with a waking shout. They passed these lovely and simple and majestic things, feeling their exile, feeling their hearts grow heavier and sadder, knowing that they had no part in all this, might never again have part. Even the rivers beside which they paused, to lave weary eyes and sick pale faces, seemed to be alien rivers in an alien land. This was France, but they felt no longer like Frenchmen, and many were the secret tears hastily wiped away unseen on the back of trembling hands. They felt in themselves the separation of all that was flesh of their hearts and substance of their souls. They were like souls forced violently from their bodies and wandering disconsolately over the earth they had so greatly loved, shut away forever from the warmth of loving and living and the voices of kinfolk. Long before they had indeed become exiles, their spirits had felt the crushing weight of exilehood, beyond which there is no greater agony.

Many there were like Cecile, accepting the exile with stern fortitude, but feeling that this exile was in itself a sacrifice to greater things. There were times that Arsène felt this also, but many more times when his anguish of mind seemed more than he could endure.

He rode through the countryside at sunset, all through the night, until the passionate dawns made further travel too dangerous, and he looked about him and his heart said to him with a solemn conviction which he could not deny: I shall not pass this way again. It is done with me, and I am done with it. Then his sorrow became like a sword in his breast and he longed to lie down in the soil of France and never rise again. All his sleeping love for his native land rose up in him, and he looked about him with wild and streaming eyes, and sometimes thought that nothing in heaven or earth or hell should dare come between the heart of a man and his country. A man could lose all else, even his soul, but so long as his feet stood upon his native earth and his eyes dwelt on familiar and beloved things, his fortitude could not be shaken, his spirit never crushed.

He thought to himself that he could not speak of these things, and then suffering became endurable. The shapes of his companions became unreal in the moon-steeped darkness, and they had no faces, no forms, no blood and no flesh, not even Cecile. And it would seem to him that he was accompanied by ghosts riding thinly by his side over the rim of the earth, out into the everlasting night of exile and homelessness. How could he know that so many thought these things also, and that to them, he, too, was a ghost?

Adventure was no new thing to him, and he had always loved it. But it was a different thing, this real exile, to night adventures that led inevitably in the morning to a warm sweet bed within familiar and beloved walls, and the sound of kinsmen. Adventure of that kind was a play, a spectacle, the sport of young men, heedless and gay. But this was the hard dark road travelled by grim men, without hope, without consolation. And Arsène found the process of maturity a painful one, and sometimes he revolted with passionate despair, and felt himself surrounded by dour and menacing strangers.

He grew to hate the night, which once he had loved. Now it took on itself the substance of all his anguish, his desolation, and his abandonment. Never had he known that the night could be so long, so silent, so empty, and so cold! And when the morning came, and they hid in thickets, woods and copses, and in ravines, and in caves, he would fling himself unspeaking upon the earth and give himself up to oblivion.

But there was one morning that he never forgot as long as he lived, for it was the kind of morning which comes once in a lifetime to all men, when things became lucid and filled with a strange and solemn light.

The night had been unusually cold and long. After midnight, a cold rain, accompanied by icy lightning and tearing wind, made the torments of the travellers unendurable. Only the beat of their horses' hoofs on the dusty or stony paths could be heard above the sound of the wind and the roaring of the wild trees. They had had to seek shelter in a lonely inn, and spent the rest of the night in the dirty drinking room, where the host yawned and eyed them with apathy. The man built a fire for them. Its red and wavering light glimmered over their haggard faces and sunken eyes, their disordered dress, their streaming cloaks and sodden hats. The wine was abominable, but its fiery warmth penetrated their numbed bodies at last. They ate the tough rabbits and fowl the host set before them, and broke the dry stale bread. Now they were slowly becoming men again, and could look at each other with faint smiles. The Marquis, who found the intimate inconveniences of the travel the most insupportable, had persuaded the inn-keeper to heat water for him, and, behind the high back of a settle he had taken off his crumpled clothing and was luxuriously bathing. Once or twice he lifted up his voice and bewailed the condition of his hands, and a certain other portion of his body much in contact with the saddle, and did this in such rich and lusty language that the others burst into laughter, and even Cecile joined in the general merriment. But to Arsène, his father's uncomplaining endurance over the miseries of the flight seemed the most moving and saddest thing of all.

To what have I brought him? he asked himself, with hatred. He was inspired not even by the spurious gallantry and impulsiveness which animated myself. He had not even the consolation of a woman, as I have. He is an old man to whom music and candlelight and a soft bed must be more than any firing of the heart. Thinking this, he said aloud, his voice grating and hoarse and strange against the laughter which still rang through the room:

"My father, you ought not to have come with me!"

The others became suddenly silent, and their faces turned on Arsène darkly and alertly, for they had heard a breaking sound in his voice. Cecile paled; she reached out to touch Arsène's hand, but, with a distraught gesture, he repudiated her, and addressed himself to the settle above which, like a decapitated head, the staring face of the Marquis could be seen. How old and tired was that wizened and narrow countenance, and how exhausted those red-rimmed eyes! Arsène did not see the sudden gleam in the latter.

He repeated: "You ought not to have come with me!"

The Marquis continued to stare at his son, and they saw no one else but each other. Then the Marquis said: "So, you would deprive me of the illusion that I have become significant?"

There was an ominous silence in the room, in spite of the lightness of the Marquis' tones. Arsène rose abruptly. He looked at the fire, at the faces of his companions, and his own face worked. He struck his hands together. Now he could hardly control himself.

"What is all this to you?" he cried out, and his voice broke even more.

"In truth," replied the Marquis, "it has taught me one thing: the ineffable luxury of a bath and clean towels."

He then emerged from behind the settle, the towel wrapped about his middle. His body showed every rib, every sunken bone. It was the body of an old man. The face that confronted Arsène was an old man's wrinkled face, unshaven and haggard, webbed with years. No one smiled at this apparition, grotesque, shrunken and creased though it was. There was a sudden dignity about the Marquis now, such as he had never possessed in the days of richest velvet and finest lace and perfume. Clad only in his nakedness, with the towel as a mere concession to Cecile, he stood before Arsène with a strange and unfamiliar majesty, and he spoke only to him:

"Is it to yourself you speak, my son, or to me?"

Arsène's pale lips parted in his unshaven beard, then closed again.

"If it is to me," continued the Marquis, "then you have offered me an insult. If it is to yourself, then I can only despair."

Cecile stood up, disheveled and white as death, her wet hair streaming about her face, her colorless lips trembling and proud. She stretched out her hand to Arsène, and said with stern imploring: "Come with me."

Arsène did not move. He looked at the others, who sat like streaming and haggard statues, then at his father, and finally at Cecile. Her eyes, sunken and feverish with exhaustion though they were, yet sparkled with an intense blue light. The power of her soul was stronger than his own rebellion and despair. Moreover, something was cracking within him, and he felt the weight of weeping in his chest. He took her hand, and, like a blind child, she led him out of the inn.

The night had passed. Earth and heaven stood in clear crystal light, in which there was no color. Their footsteps echoed on the flagged path. They walked alone into the morning. On and on Cecile led him, opening a rustic creaking gate, descending a steep pathway, brushing by shrubbery and trees that showered down drops of diamonds upon them. The air was permeated with the sweetest and most poignant smells, and birds were whistling in the trees, and darting from bough to bough with soft rustlings and flashes of wan light upon their glistening wings.

They found themselves in a tiny glade. The grass under their feet sparkled; warm breaths floated in gentle breezes into their faces. The far trees stood in luminous mist. Now there was only profound silence about them. The sun had not yet risen. There was no color on the earth, only that mist, only that radiant half-shadow sweeping over the pale and distant hills beyond the trees like the ghostly heralds of the sun. The peace that fell on them was like the whisper of an angelic host, and Arsène felt the hot fire smoldering in his heart, then disintegrating.

Cecile stood at his side and they looked together at all this silence, this crystal motionless, this fleeting bright shadow. She still held his hand. Then, very slowly, she turned and faced him.

How clear was that young and exhausted face, those steadfast blue eyes, and how stern yet understanding were those pale young lips! Her cloak was heavy on her firm shoulders. Her loosened light hair tumbled against her neck and over her weary brow. She was bedraggled and soiled. But she had majesty and pride and Arsène gazed at her with a little fear and a new adoration.

"I have heard your thoughts, all these long dark nights, Arsène," she said quietly. "I have understood all your thoughts. Monsieur your father is right: you did not speak to him, you spoke to yourself."

She turned a little and looked into the far distance. The rims of the spectral hills were outlined with bands of blowing gold.

"Do you think I do not love this, too?" she whispered. "This is my land, as it is your land. We leave it, for a strange city, for strange people. We shall hang precariously on the battlements that overlook a strange sea. Where shall we go from that place? What is our end to be—?"

"I have brought you to this exile, to this hopelessness, to this death!" cried Arsène, hoarsely. He tried to put his arm about her, but she stepped aside. Now the blue light was so intense in her eyes as she gazed at him that he was taken aback.

"This is your hour of decision, Arsène! You must decide in this hour whether personal life, and personal safety, are more than greater things! You must decide whether there is not something more sacred than life, or, you must return to Paris. There is time no longer for any further hypocrisy."

As he stared at her, dumbly, he was overwhelmed with her sternness, her beauty, her steadfastness, and her extreme and piteous youth. There was no contempt in her eyes, only a bright waiting and calm aloofness. He thought, incoherently: Shall I return, and take her with me, back to peace and quietness and security? And then he knew that if he returned, he returned alone.

He said, in a shaking voice: "You are hard, my poor little one."

She smiled then, and her smile was less gentle than it was swift and flashing. But she said nothing, and only waited.

He cried out: "What can I say to you about my thoughts, and my pain? My longing for peace and cleanness, my hatred for flight and exile and this misery which shall never end? I have thought so much! Do you not understand, you child, my dearest one, that we cannot win, that we must fail? That we can only fight, and die, or flee ignominiously, again and again, until we fall, exhausted? This is a lost cause!" He could not speak again, and fell silent, with a groan.

Cecile drew a deep breath. She approached closer, and gazed steadfastly into his eyes.

"My grandfather," she said, in low and thrilling tones, "once told me there are no lost causes. There are only lost men."

Her voice, clear and penetrating, echoed back from the clear and colorless air. And now Arsène wished only to escape her eyes. He turned aside.

"I am a lost man, then, perhaps," he said, so deeply that the tones were like a moan.

When he could control himself once more, he began to speak discordantly, his words tumbling with incoherence over each other.

" 'There are no lost causes!' That is the stupidest of all things. The world is heaped with dead and ruined causes. The graves of martyrs are piled so full that their bones can be seen bleaching in the earth. I have no love for martyrdom— I have no true idealism. In the beginning of this journey, I had delusions to sustain me. But now they are gone. I have nothing left but fear and weariness, and hopelessness. Noble words are only noble words. They are no substitute for fires and peace, for security and quietness, for cleanness and the smell of unthreatened vineyards—"

His voice choked in his throat, and no sound could come from it.

This strange and unshaken girl, this girl so very young and unbroken in spite of weariness and desolation, looked at him deeply and said:

"And you believe these things still exist in France, in Europe? Once my grandfather said to me that Europe was rotten with history, that its centuries were too heavy and crushing upon it, that its cellars were gutted with filth and rats, that its beams were broken and bending. It has too long a memory. He said that if all men could forget history there might be hope." She paused, then said: "If one could only go to a land where history did not yet exist, where life was new—. But there is no such land. We must live in our ruined city, and rebuild its broken walls."

There was a long silence between them now. Arsène bent his head. His face became more haggard, more distraught. Then he flung out his hands. "I find no strength in myself to rebuild, to live, in this desolate place."

He turned to her, as if imploring her: "My darling, how can I labor and fight in dust? I know this cause is lost from the beginning. I know that we have no hope that we shall overcome the Cardinal. We can do nothing to destroy the growing Catholic reaction in Europe. There is nothing but death—"

She clasped her hands convulsively together, but this was the only sign of her desperate agitation. Her face was still calm and cold, and her tone quiet, when she said: "You would wish to go to England, perhaps?"

"No! Not to England! The old men are there, also! The old men are everywhere, in their mouldering grave cloths, and their voices echoing in their dead bony skulls like ancient doom. They have no new books to open, but only the hoary lying ones, full of sickness and disillusion and decay. Can I not tell you, Cecile," and now his voice rose higher, became more full of agony, "how I long for a land where the old men have not yet come, have not yet filled the graves, and where there is no history? Where there is no hatred, no lies, no cities of filthy intrigues, and no tombs of tales and rotten bones? All these things are here. We can build nothing clean and living upon them. Whatever new is built must fall into broken sewers and reeking kennels."

Now his anguish was so extreme that the girl could not endure it. She put her warm arms about his neck. The wet and bedraggled sleeves fell back from them, exposing their white and tender flesh. He pressed his cheeks against them, holding them closely with his hands against his face. She lifted her lips to his, and they clung together like two alone in a rocking world.

When they finally released each other, her eyes were wet, and more gentle than he had ever seen them. He saw her lips, moved and trembling. It was some moments before she could speak.

"Arsène, my love," she said, with more than a little humility in her voice, "this only do I know in truth. That one must have faith. One must believe that the individual is nothing in the long tasks of the future, but only men. The work at hand may appear hopeless, doomed to failure. But assuredly, it has not failed, in the end! Let us do what we can. When that single task has been accomplished, we will look further, to see what has to be done."

She paused, and now the blueness of her eyes had intensified, become a deep glow, as though she contemplated something still unseen by him. She smiled a little.

" 'A new world!' " she said, very softly. "Who knows, there may be a new world for us!"

Her words seemed mysterious and inconclusive to him, but Arsène suddenly felt a strange uplifting of his spirit as though he had heard an exciting and heroic promise. He was comforted. His heart rose. He pressed her hands to his lips. They returned to the inn together, and when the others saw his face they smiled as if some unbearable pressure, some fear, had been lifted from them.

CHAPTER LI

Now THEY RODE with more spirit, and more fleetness, for their leader had taken heart, and though he did not know for what he hoped, he was hopeful. The nights grew more dark, and much colder, but now they sang a little, and jested in low voices. When they arrived at obscure and wretched inns, far from the main roads, the hosts exerted themselves to put before them the best their poor larders afforded. For these travellers seemed no furtive fugitives, as they had done before, but a gay company travelling on honorable business, and seeking modest lodgings and tables because of modest purses. Heretofore, they had crept into taverns, hats pulled far over feverish eyes, cloaks tightly wrapped about them, and betraying every indication of pursuit. This had inspired uneasiness in the hosts, and wary truculence. But now, this was changed. The gaiety came with spontaneous light-heartedness, for the leader was no longer beset by his own fears, but revealed fortitude and firmness and a new faith.

Cecile, with her new wisdom, understood how volatile was Arsène's nature, and did not extravagantly expect too much. She knew that he would demonstrate new depths of despair, new morbidities, new distractions. This, then, was her task: to watch for these moods, then offer consolation, faith, courage, and gentleness. When the dark shadow appeared in his eyes, and his lips became heavy and somber, she would reach from her saddle, press his hand, smile humorously, and in a short time the vehement pendulum had swung back again on its too-large arc.

The Marquis knew all this, also. Though his old frame creaked and ached agonizingly, he was mute. But he complained lavishly about the minor and more intimate discomforts of the journey, and kept the company in bursts of ribald laughter. Cecile, with her needle, maintained his decency. Her industry was endless. Torn cloaks and breeches and hose passed regularly through her busy fingers. The company was soon reduced to adoration for her. They marvelled at her endurance, her steadfast smiles when her face was drawn and white with exhaustion. They picked wayside fruits and berries for her, helped her tenderly over stones, literally carried her into inns. She was "Madame la Duchesse" to them, and she pretended, in the spirit of the thing, to wield haughty court over them.

He thought to himself: There is nothing she could not face with fortitude and faith, no hardship, no pain, no weariness, no hopelessness. Ah, this was a woman for a new world!

A new world. The words became familiar to his thoughts. And then, with amazement, he thought: I have been seeking a new world, and it has already been discovered, and is waiting for us!

It was a world of wilderness, of wild places, of unexplored forests, of unbelievable vastnesses. But his own people, and the English, and the Spanish, had already gone to that world, and it was even rumored that in many places respectable cities had already risen, and commerce had taken root.

America! But his heart shrank from it, for it was still engaged with France, with his home, and his kinsmen. The largeness, the immensity, of the new world terrified his insular spirit. But even as it terrified him, his heart began to beat with passion.

Each time his thoughts fearfully approached the idea, they came with more confidence, more hope, more fortitude. Once, riding beside Cecile, he looked at her, and she was startled by the dark glow of his haggard face, the contemplative and dilated expression of his eyes. And then she thought: he has thought of it also! And she smiled deeply upon him.

And now, as they approached closer and closer to La Rochelle, they increased their speed, for they must reach the city before the Cardinal. Once he had arrived, the city would indeed be besieged, and it would be almost impossible to gain entry.

Arsène thought much of the Cardinal these days, and he no longer seemed a malignant plotter, but a tired old man, fit to arouse pity and compassion. Surely, he, too, felt the pressure of the centuries of history upon him. Surely, he too, was sick in the midst of the pestilence. Why, then, did he labor so enormously? Was it because he had no hope, that he knew himself a prisoner? But then, intrigues were for sick men; they were the unnatural stimulants necessary to the alleviation of the pangs of disease.

Once, as they travelled, they saw the lights of distant campfires, and knew that yonder lay the cohorts of the Cardinal. They passed in the night, fleet and swift as shadows. But Arsène looked back, smiling. What did the Cardinal know of the hopes of a new world which so dazzled and intoxicated him? What could he dream of such a world, of such a radiant and giant land?

Arsène could not know that at that very instant the Cardinal was thinking these things, and staring sleeplessly into the dark about his bed. He did not know that the Cardinal heard the distant hoofbeats, and that the sound of them had awakened these strange and mysterious thoughts. Across the black chasms of the night, the hands of the old man and the young man met, unknowingly, feeling only the momentary thrill which passes between the dying and the living at the instant of dissolution, and farewell.

Arsène began to think of Paul de Vitry, of the Abbé Mourion, of the Duc de Tremblant, and he wondered if they, too, had thought of the new world with passion and longing. And then he knew that if they had not actually thought of it, it had lain strangely in their souls, and they had given up their lives for it. Their faith, their hope, their invincible belief in the future, had been the wind in the indomitable sails that had set forth for the new and living land.

He knew that the spirits of these noble men, and the spirits of countless thousands of others like them, were present on the ships that sailed courageously to the west, and that the cargo these ships carried were not only the bodies of the exiled and the hopeful, but the hearts and faiths and passions of those who had died that other men might live in peace.

With such a cargo, with such light in the sails, with such illuminated figure-heads, how else could it be but that the world ahead would be a justification of all their dreams and their faiths? Who would dare to betray them?

Who would dare to allow the coming of the old men, the old lies, the old bloody religions, the old pestilences, and the old diseases, the old hatreds and the old cruelties?

Ah, said Arsène to himself, with passionate dedication, let it be in my hands, and the hands of my children, and my children's children, to keep that world inviolate and beautiful, faithful and indomitable, a new hope and a new joy for a world of men still unborn, so that they might dwell in freedom and peace forever.

The extravagance of his nature seized upon the new thoughts. Before his mind's eye rose the visions of dazzling cities, of vehement and passionate men living in peace, exhilaration and hope, of new governments of justice and freshness and peace, of mountains incandescent with light, of vast seas sparkling beneath endless white sails of commerce and adventure. He was overwhelmed. The wilderness fell away, the valleys, chaotic and strewn with boulders, became green and filled with multitudes of fat and peaceful cattle. The bright and glittering air rang with the sound of new cities rising where only silence and eagles lived before. He saw great roads, and heard the turmoil of a new empire. He saw the strange but shining faces of a new people, in which his own blood was mingled with countless other bloods, forming this race of hopeful and vigorous men. Winds, not of close and teeming France, but of fresh and limitless spaces, blew in his face, and he smelled strange and vital odors. Ah, this sweet great land of no torturous history, of no vile persecutions and rotten books, of no memories of dark hatreds and furies, of no hoary churches built by bloody hands, of no mercenary armies engaged in vicious quarrels and treachery! Of no kings and statesmen, gray with ancient lore and ancient disease!

Thinking these things, he became dizzy, had to clutch his pommel to keep himself from falling. Tears filled his eyes; he heard the wild beating of his heart. Here was a solemn adventure set in motion by God, Himself! Here the wilderness waited the happy firm tread of men who believed in the future!

And now he knew that in his heart he had not believed in the future of France, that hag-ridden land in a hag-ridden continent. Men were too heavy with history; their memories were too long. They could not forget, surrounded and choked with the past as they were. Tradition was a labyrinth in which Europe was forever caught. Hatred was a perpetual miasma. He must have done with it. He must leave it, if he was to live.

Now his intoxication grew. The difficulties, the shrinkings of his spirit, the gloominess, fell away from him. So many of his own kind, the Huguenots, had gone to that new world. What they had done, he could do. Surely they were not greater men than he! Dimly, he remembered the tales of the Englishmen who had sailed the terrible seas to the young world, to escape the vengeful hatred of the old men of Europe. He had learned this, with the indifference with which one listens to an unbelievable legend. Now he recalled, very faintly, the stories of the cities they had founded in the wilderness, of the strange things they had encountered, strange races, fruits, trees, birds and animals. He had shuddered with amused delicacy, upon hearing them. Now, they became close and vital to him. He felt new and excited blood in his veins. The last ragged shreds of satin, the last costume of the courtier, fell from his spiritual body.

These Englishmen, these Frenchmen, these Germans, these scores of old races, had gone to the new world, and welded themselves into one new people. Now a new vision rose before Arsène. Who knew but that, in the strange and tumultuous future, this new people might not cut the umbilical cord which bound them to Europe, and create a unique and invincible empire of their own? Freed forever from the old men, the old faiths, the old traditions, the old lies and the old hatreds!

He could hardly contain himself, so turbulent, so passionate, were his thoughts.

Once, he turned to Cecile, and she looked at him in silence. But he saw, on her face, the reflection of his own passion, his own dreams. He said, reaching for her hand, and speaking in a choked and trembling voice:

"My sweet one, will you go with me, even to the ends of the earth?"

She pressed his hand, and said, so softly, that he could barely hear her:

"Oh, not to the ends of the earth, but to the beginning!"

A strange kind of siege had been in progress in La Rochelle for several months before the arrival of the Cardinal. Though the land approaches to the city were still fairly open, a dyke, or mole, had been slowly and remorselessly in progress across the harbor, to prevent the entry of English men-of-war. The Rochellais had watched this building with despair in their hearts, praying that the English would arrive in sufficient time to enter. So far, no hostilities had taken place between the Huguenots and the Catholics. There was no sign of approaching combat or struggle, except for that mole.

Every vantage post facing the sea was watched constantly, with straining eyes and hopeful spirit, for a sail, for the battleships of the English. But the sea remained empty, while the mole grew longer, stone by stone. And with the growing

538

of the mole, the bitterness and disappointment, the conviction of betrayal, grew stronger in the besieged. The churches were filled hourly with those praying that the English might arrive to save their co-religionists, that the promises of England might be fulfilled. But as the days passed, murmurs and open expression of hatred and distrust became more frequent. There were some who declared that the English, as ever, promised, but betrayed at the end, that it was her eternal scheming against France which had set Catholic brother against Huguenot brother, for her own crafty ends. Many declared that the English had become apprehensive and jealous of the growing power of France, and in order to cripple France were hoping to stir up civil war, in which the hopes and ambitions and very existence of Frenchmen would go down in a sea of blood.

But still more could hardly believe that the English would betray them. Sentries and watches stood motionless, their faces fixed on the gray ocean, hope still sustaining their fortitude. Children watched, and women with streaming hair in the wild salt gales, and every rampart, every tower, every wall and rock, had its watcher. And, the Cardinal and the King, with banners, music, silken tents, armed adventurers and soldiers, approached steadily upon the desperate city.

The city had less than twenty-eight thousand inhabitants, including over a thousand Germans, Spaniards and Italian Protestants, or heretics, who had come to assist in its defense. Among the Spaniards and Italians were many brave men of noble blood, who had voluntarily exiled themselves from their rich estates, where the Church had not dared to attack them, in order to devote themselves to the cause of free men, and to die in that cause. It was a strange thing, but among these Germans, Spaniards and Italians was nothing but the sternest resolution and devotion, and if the murmurs of distrust and rebellion and dismay were heard in La Rochelle, they did not arise from the foreign defenders. With hands unaccustomed to toil, they helped build the forts that were to protect the city, and during their labor it was not unusual for many of them to collapse, their hands bleeding and torn beyond recognition. They appeared on the ramparts, working with passion and silent fortitude, so that the grumbling and fearful French were shamed into activity and courage. They watched these foreign defenders and friends with amazement and gratitude, and even adoration. But their amazement was the greater. To the French mind, it appeared incredible that foreigners, with nothing to gain and everything to lose, should be dedicated to an ideal which was somewhat vague in their own minds. In the more stupid, distrust began to grow. Why had these men come, these gentlemen with the fine faces and the delicate hands, to face privation, hunger, pain, ruin and death? What were Frenchmen to them? The French, never famous for altruism, sacrifice or allegiance to a noble ideal, could only gaze at their friends in astonishment, and with doubt, and, many times, with suspicion. Some of the bolder whispered that it was intolerable that these gentlemen were to kill Frenchmen, even if they were the abominable Catholics.

The city had provisions sufficient only for two months, with the greatest care. Farmers, hurrying against time, drove their laden carts over the one or two causeways still open. Because of its low and marshy position, the city was almost impregnable on its land side. The causeways were well guarded, surrounded by forts and fortresses. The citizens were men of a proud and independent nature, complacent over the reputation of their city, maritime and vigorous. Many of them were descendants of the privateers who had ranged the seas, raiding Brittany and England. They had long enjoyed the privileges of refusing admission to royal garrisons, if they so desired, and had a very democratic government in which they elected their own Mayor.

The city was not unaccustomed to siege. In 1573, the Catholics, taking the city, had perpetrated horrible outrages upon the defenseless population, who had starved for months. Many of the older inhabitants remembered this massacre of disarmed men and women and children, and they moved among the people in this second siege exhorting, pleading with them, and recounting to them the dreadful things which would be visited upon them in the event of the fall of the city.

"Remember, the Scarlet Woman never changes," they would say. "Bloodthirsty and merciless, rapacious and ungodly and without humanity, she will wreak her hatred and vengeance upon us with gloatings and joy. If she destroys us, Rome will order a Te Deum to be sung over our mangled corpses and the slain bodies of our children. Let us, if necessary, die in our homes, of starvation and disease, but never, so long as one last man remains, must we surrender."

Their faces were so stern, their exhortations so passionate with memory and resolution, that even the most vacilating kept silence. But nevertheless, whispers began to grow. Would the English indeed keep their promise? It was remem-

540

bered that Charles I, King of England, had, as his wife, Henrietta Maria, the sister of the King of France. Would her pleas be sufficient to break his promise, and abandon the Rochellais to the death and fury of their Catholic enemies? Terror began to blow through the city, remembering the last siege, remembering the Massacre of St. Bartholemew, when Catholics slaughtered thousands of Huguenot women and children, and babes in the cradles, and flung their bleeding corpses into the rivers. They remembered the unspeakable tortures afflicted upon the young and the tender, the burnings and the stranglings, the hangings and the brandings. Now, with the terror came a wild hatred, a lust for revenge. Where an ideal could not sustain the common populace, fear did yeoman duty.

Some of the Spaniards, Germans and Italians had at one time been members of the Catholic priesthood, but had either been excommunicated in their own countries because of their mercy, indignation and true Christianity, or had abandoned their calling to sustain the strugglers for liberty and enlightenment in France. Some of the more stupid and malicious among the Huguenots whispered that these men were spies.

Among these foreigners were several Englishmen with pale devoted faces. They were fervent in their belief that their countrymen would come to the aid of La Rochelle. They watched tirelessly, their sea-blue eyes fixed far out over the empty waves. Never did they doubt that the English would come.

The Cardinal and the King had not yet arrived. The King had been taken with a fever on the road to La Rochelle, and had been compelled to pause at Villeroy, to await recovery. So, taking advantage of every moment, the defenders of the city refortified and strengthened every fort, gathered food to sustain them for the coming siege. Every hour gained was an hour in the balance of victory. The Huguenot farmers worked feverishly to garner their harvests, which they then carted into the city. The fields and the vineyards were heavy with grain and fruit, and to the Rochellais, on the warm winds of September came the rich scents of the ripening countryside. The people were well armed, with muskets and artillery. They settled down to await the siege, gazing fearfully at the causeways and the forts which guarded them, and watching endlessly for the English ships. The populace were sustained in their belief that the land approaches were impregnable. The only entrance to the city was the free sea, and, as France had few or no ships of its own,

541

the Rochellais were confident that the sea lanes would remain open. But slowly, as they watched the stretching of the mole, their hearts sank into despondency and dread. Of what use were the fortified islands in the harbor if the dyke spread far enough to close the sea-roads of these islands?

Among the Senate the whisperers were active. They were not traitors for the most part; they were merely expedient and fearful. Among the one hundred men of the Senate, however, there were less than ten whisperers. In a body, each day, the Senate inspected the defenses. Their appearance inspired the builders and the people, for they represented to them the freedom and democracy of Protestantism, the bulwark of enlightenment. They took heart from the repeated assertions of the brave and noble that though the mainland was fetid with marsh and malaria, the city itself was safe from disease because of its well-drained soil. Moreover, the tides were to their advantage. The chain of towers that guarded the narrow port lifted their battlements grimly to the warm blue heavens.

But slowly, and inexorably, the mole being constructed on orders of the Cardinal, was built on the shallow bottom of the sea near the harbor, within actual sight of the Rochellais. The builders worked calmly, and, apparently, as oblivious as beavers to the besieged city. No word passed between the enemies, though at frequent intervals the ships of the Rochellais slipped through the harbor on errands of communication with the English ports, passing within sight and sound of the builders of the mole.

Buckingham, before his assassination, had stormed the Isle of Rhe, and had been defeated by the Catholics. The Cardinal, realizing that sea power was necessary for the survival of France, after this experience, ordered the building of a navy.

The defeat of Buckingham, and his subsequent death had been a terrible blow to the Rochellais. Their only prayer now, was that Charles I would remember the promises made by Buckingham, and fulfil them. Watching the construction of the mole, fortified by boats chained together with great logs, they knew that it was a race of time between the completion of the mole and the arrival of the English.

In the meantime, the heroic Mayor, Guiton, sustained his people. Extremely squat in appearance, broad of body, with a large erect head and indomitable blue eyes constantly flashing and lighting, his quiet faith and strength were as effective as the fortresses.

It was to this city, then, that Arsène de Richepin, his

father, Cecile, and his companions, arrived two weeks in advance of the Cardinal. They rode over one of the guarded causeways, and billeted in the town. Arsène, his father and Cecile were received as guests in the home of the Duc de Rohan, and graciously made welcome by his indomitable and noble old mother.

CHAPTER LII

HERE IT WAS, thought Arsène, as he walked through the streets of La Rochelle, that my grandfathers died, slaughtered by the shrieking minions of Rome, and one of my grandmothers perished of starvation in the siege, and another sank to her grave with a broken heart.

Here in this maritime city, in this proud town of merchants and ship-masters and sailors, this habitat of men with far blue eyes and brown faces, was the last fortress of Protestant Frenchmen. The struggle about to take place would decide whether France was to rejoice in a future of constantly expanding glory, liberty and enlightenment, or subside into the morass of oppression, darkness, slavery and ignorance.

He recalled something which the Duchess de Rohan had told him: "Do not despair. If we are overcome, do not believe that the fight is lost, that the faith is gone, that the day shall forever be obscured. A dream has been born in the hearts of men, and all the blackness of hell, all the scarlet torture of Rome, shall not destroy it. Today, perhaps, the defeat. Tomorrow—O always tomorrow! the victory!"

Nevertheless, he could not be so sanguine. What did it matter, to him, and to those he loved, if one hundred, or two hundred years hence, France might be free, might overcome the oppressor? He did not have the faith of great men, that one ought to work for the future of humanity, even if they failed to live to behold it. Impatient and impetuous, he wished to see the work of his hands accomplished today. Only the saints, and the heroes, fixed their eyes on the faint gleam of tomorrow, the while they died in the darkness.

Meditating sadly, he walked through the winding cobbled streets of the sea-guarded city, over which hung the ancient houses and narrow bridges. He saw the towers of the fortresses, vigilantly guarded, strong and squat against the warm

544

blue sky. He heard the sound of the sea, smelled the pungent salt of the great winds. He passed the market place, where the hurried farmers haggled with shrewd women, and cattle lowed and chickens squawked, and geese evaded the clutching arms of little boys. He saw small flowered gardens, bursting their confines, under the very shadow of wheeling gulls. Here was the hoary church of St. Margaret, serene and gray, throwing its painted shade over the streets and over the walls of crowded houses. Arsène was compelled to dodge donkeys, carts, geese, scampering children, dogs, cats, goats and creeping old women, and galloping horses, so that he was often thrust into the gutter and against the walls. La Rochelle was much cleaner than Paris, and if it possessed any stenches, they were purified in the salt gales, the brilliant sunshine, the polished light of the heavens. A feeling of hope, resolution and fortitude was in the air, a busyness, an activity and motion. If the hearts of the defenders failed, it was not visible, except in the faces of the old, who remembered.

When he climbed the battlements, Arsène saw the blue silk curtain of the sea, glittering and trembling in the distance. He also saw the mole, spreading its inexorable length, like the body of a serpent, across the harbor. He turned his back and looked landward, to the low gray marshes, steaming in the hot sun, the causeways across them, and the distant green and gold of fields and forest, the mauve of low hills shimmering in light. The incandescent air was full of vitality, color, and excitement. He looked down at the steaming, winding streets, cobbled and bridged, filled with hurrying people.

Here, in this air, was the burnished reflection of freedom, liberty and courage. Nothing, but that mole, appeared to threaten it. The gray and brown walls of the city, streaked, speckled and fretted with dazzling sunlight, seemed peaceful and full of the contentment of ages. Here and there large green trees appeared, bending in the salt winds, glittering with light. He allowed himself to hope. The English might —must—come in time! Even if they did not, the city was impregnable from the land side. But how long could it stand a siege? Arsène forced himself to believe that Richelieu would soon tire of this stubborn people, and return to his luxurious palace to ease the pains of a rheumatism made much worse by the marshy dampness.

He left the ramparts, after a long conversation with its cheerful defenders. But not until he had talked at length with Count Alfred Von Steckler, a German nobleman, Don Carlo da Santa, of Spain, and the Conte Luigi di Brizzini, of Italy. These illustrious gentlemen, none over the age of forty, were the officers in command of this fortress.

Arsène had made their ceremonious acquaintance in the Hôtel de Rohan. Nevertheless, he felt uneasy in their company. He looked at the handsome figure and face of the German, with the thick hair like wheat in the sun, and at his fiery blue eyes. He scrutinized the countenance of the Spaniard, for indications of the craft and subtlety which distinguished the Spanish character. As for the Italian, he was too insouciant, too gay, too light-hearted, in Arsène's opinion, for this arduous task ahead. Small but delicate of face and body, with dancing black eyes, glittering white teeth between black mustaches and imperial, brown of skin, and ribald and merry of expression, he was more like a bon vivant than a soldier who was to face torture or death within a very short time.

The German dressed simply, his sleeves rolled back on great arms as white as milk, but the Spaniard and the Italian seemed bent on outdoing each other in sartorial splendor. Apparently, they had come to La Rochelle with inexhaustible wardrobes, and each possessed three adoring lackeys. In the evenings, relieved of their duties, they spent hours upon perfumed baths and unguents and curled wigs. They changed their garments a dozen times, fretfully, and with intense concentration, until they had made a choice and could sally forth arrayed like the lilies of the field. The Hôtel de Rohan was their favorite destination, and it was amusing, even to the sad Arsène, to see how they scrutinized each other with open hostility and affected derision, and languid envy. The Marquis de Vaubon, as serious and dedicated arbitor, would slowly circle about each posturing young man, comment softly on admirable points, nodding his head with deep and sincere gravity, and finally, after long thought, would concede the prize of the evening to one or the other. They appreciated his taste and elegance, and never contested the decision. The loser would then, during the balance of the evening, retire a little distance and give himself up to the imaginary assembling of a devastating wardrobe for the next night, in which he so outshone his rival as to make him appear a veritable cow-herd, a watcher of geese. No one had the levity to intrude upon this brown meditation. Only when, with a deep and satisfied smile did the loser arise, his eyes gleaming with triumphant anticipation, and engage in the conversation, did they include him in the company.

Arsène found this very frivolous. But the old Duchesse smiled wisely and said: "Frivolity is often the affectation of a brave and noble man. Do you believe Carlo and Luigi are less heroic because they prefer sweet smells to foul? Or affect to pretend that the most important things in the world are the fragility of lace collars or the exact width of knee-ribbons?"

When the Marquis, in amusement, asked her why she did not appeal to the Cardinal to abandon his campaign, she stared at him in speechless outrage and imperious pride. It was some moments before she could speak, and then she said in a voice trembling with anger: "Monsieur le Marquis does not comprehend the dishonor of his suggestion!"

Others, in fear, exhorted her to use her influence, and excited such fury in her that they feared that she might collapse. Nevertheless, in her proud heart she was dismayed, for she knew that many priests, among them the frightful Capuchin, were accompanying Richelieu. She feared no ghastly and unspeakable reprisals against the Rochellais on the Cardinal's part, but she had no illusions about the priests. However, she did not speak of her dismay. She was chronically exhausted with her unremitting efforts to maintain the courage and inflexible resolution of those about her.

And, it saddened her that she found less courage and pride and determination among the Rochellais, themselves, than among the two thousand foreigners who had come voluntarily to the beleaguered city, to give their arms and their lives to it in the name of freedom. These, above all, would suffer the merciless punishment of the Cardinal, even if the Rochellais were spared. And spared she believed they would be; they were Frenchmen.

CHAPTER LIII

THE DUCHESSE DE ROHAN bitterly believed that for all the Frenchman's protestations of noblesse oblige, he was the most deficient in it. She found this heroic and aristocratic spirit more in evidence among the foreigners of La Rochelle than in her own people.

She did not find it even in Arsène de Richepin. She found something greater; in its strength was a sustained rage, sorrow and vengefulness. Yet she deplored the absence of that finer, more steely and delicate spirit. She knew that noblesse oblige was the essence of a gentleman, and Arsène, in spite of his illustrious ancestry, was no gentleman.

Prudent and far-sighted, the Duchesse served only the simplest and most frugal of viands in her hôtel, even to the Mayor, whom she greatly respected, and to her numerous and constant guests. Her cellars were full, but God only knew how long they would remain that way, and she knew that, at the last, the aristocratic must be sacrificed to the mob, if La Rochelle was to withstand the siege. She had no delusions about the common mass. Under stress, and fear and starvation, they could be expected to become treacherous, stupid, panic-stricken and mad. Gentlemen could endure all sufferings, with silent smiles and graceful fortitude.

Once she said to Arsène: "You have asked me what sustains me. Is it Protestantism, a heroic ideal? I must confess it is not. But only in freedom, in Protestant liberalism, in the light and air of liberty, can the superior man exist, and bring enlightenment and peace to lesser men. Therefore, we must fight for these things, and die for them. The world must be made a secure place for the habitation of the superior, and to this end, the inferior man must be succored and saved."

Another time she said: "Examine the blood, tradition and ancestry of the hero, and you will discover that, however

548

apparently humble his origin, there is, in the background of his body and spirit a noble and lofty ancestor."

She did not believe that the canaille had any virtue in them by the very fact that they were vulgar, as did some of the more enthusiastic and idealistic. Poverty, ignorance and stupidity did not argue a superior soul. In truth, these manifestations were the very essence of the creature hardly above the level of a swine or a dog. "As a spring, however deeply buried, encompassed about with stones and earth and rocky mountains, will find its way to the light and the sun to give refreshment to men, so will the superior man, however crushed by circumstance and suffering and adversity, break through his environment and rise triumphant," she would say.

She was fond of mentioning a grizzled and elderly man who acted as her advisor and steward, friend and confidant, and who was now with her in La Rochelle. This man had been born on her father's estates of a peasant wench and a travelling singer. Nevertheless, from the earliest day that he smiled, he displayed great talents, audacity, cleverness and wisdom. In some manner, he had induced a local priest to educate him, and when, in his enormous daring, he had broken into the library of the old Duc, that gentleman had been so impressed by the clear logic and grim courage and intelligence of this youth, that he did not have him hanged or even whipped, as the brutal old gentleman might easily have done as he had done to many others for less crimes. He became the youth's patron. The best tutors were obtained for him. The Duc began to trust him in vital matters connected with the estates, and so honestly, wisely and fairly did his protégé conduct himself, that the Duc finally trusted him completely, and treated him as a son. When he died, he left a large fortune to the man, leaving him free to abandon the estates and make a greater fortune in the world. But the man refused to leave, and remained with the Duchesse when she married.

This man, Alphonse, who, nameless, had been given the surname of Champaigne by the Duc (who liked his jest), was now at the Hôtel de Rohan, devoted as always to his mistress, whom he served as advisor and friend and not as servant. He sat at her table, mingled with her guests, and entered all conversations. He was grave and respectful, yet full of pride, displaying none of the unpleasant arrogance of the vulgar man elected to a high position, and when he spoke, so astute were his words, so penetrating and logical, that all

549

listened with admiration and thoughtfulness. And, as he spoke, the Duchesse would gaze at him with a proud and indulgent smile, glancing occasionally about the table to garner in the moved and aroused eyes of her guests as one gathers flowers to be presented to a noble personage.

Under a different delusion entirely, the Rochellais were grateful for this manifestation of tolerance and democracy in their Duchesse, for had she not received as a friend, as a diner at her table, one of the lowest among them? So, laboring under this delusion that the Duchesse had raised up one of these lowest, they argued that she had, for the poor and the dirty, the tenderest heart and most open regard. The Duchesse was wise enough to keep her true opinions to herself, for she knew how vital were morale and delusion for the canaille, if they were, at the final moment, to act as men and not beasts. Yet, she guarded her cellars. At the last, food would be a more persuasive argument for the canaille than any grand ideal.

She presided at her table, lit as it was by her great twin silver-gilt candelabra, and her guests were served on the finest of gold plate, and honored by the snowiest and most satiny of damask and the most brilliant of sparkling crystal. They were waited upon by corps of liveried servants. Only in one thing was the Duchesse lavish: the best of wines were invariably served, for, though she was willing to dine on dry crusts and fragments of stale meat, if need be, she would drink nothing but good wine. Gracious and noble, she would sit in her tall carved chair, like a queen, watchful of her guests' comforts, skillfully directing the conversation in the most amiable and witty of channels, smiling and inclining her imperial head, and fanning herself lightly. The Marquis sat at her right hand. On her left sat Cecile, beautiful and radiant as only a young woman in love can be beautiful and radiant, arrayed in the gorgeous garments presented to her by the Duchesse. Next to Cecile, Arsène was seated. The other guests, including the Mayor, whom the Duchesse deeply respected, were seated in long lines about the balance of the table. Here were the prettiest and most aristocratic of the women of La Rochelle, the finest gentlemen, including many foreigners, and Alphonse Champaigne.

However fatigued and sad the Duchesse might be, she never canceled a dinner, for she knew the value of constant stimulation for the leaders of the people.

Tonight the German, Count Von Steckler, whom Arsène did not like at all, was deeply and agitatedly in strong argument with Arsène. Perversely, out of Arsène's constant nagging grief for Paul de Vitry and his brother, out of his malaise and weary heaviness of spirit, he was in a quarrelsome and contemptuous mood, hardly skirting the dangerous borders of courtesy and tact. Even the presence of Cecile could not divert his loud and too impetuous manner, nor soften his words, though she touched his hand under the tablecloth at intervals, in a soft and imploring manner.

Arsène had begun his attack on the German Count with exaggerated politeness, lifting his sharp black eyebrows sardonically over his dark and restless eyes. He had expressed his ironic surprise, which he declared was constant, that such as the Count had come to La Rochelle to fight and die for Frenchmen. Not, he added, lifting his hand with a viciously sweet smile, that the Rochellais, and himself, did not appreciate such noble self-sacrifice, but he confessed that he could not imagine himself in a similar position. It may be, he admitted, that he was first a Frenchman, and he had not yet arrived at that supreme state when politics and ideals could obliterate that fact.

Von Steckler had listened to this heavy irony in silence, but with vehement breathlessness, fixing his strong blue eyes intently on Arsène's face. His milk-white skin became even more pale, so that it was translucent and one could feel the beat of his emotions under it. There was something heroic and grand about his large blond handsomeness, something eager and touching.

He answered: "Monsieur, men of good will have no race. They belong to the brotherhood of man. In this struggle, which is only the prelude to more enormous struggles in Europe between the forces of liberalism and reaction, is a symbol. We doubt, all of us, that we shall be successful in the combat about to come, and we know that we shall surely die. But there is no other way of life possible for us. Should we surrender without a fight, the generations coming after us will surrender to the tyrants and oppressors of every age. But, remembering our devotion, our immolation, they shall take heart, lift up the swords fallen from our hands, and fight on to the ultimate victory of peace, liberty and fraternity."

He glanced imploringly but with gentleness about the table, where the candlelight gave the illusion, as it flickered over the faces, that every one was either smiling or grimacing. But every eye seemed brighter and more living for that light.

He gazed, now, at the Spaniard and the Italian. Da Santa's

subtle narrow face, so handsome and clever, was suddenly enkindled, and his frivolity was gone. The Italian smiled, but in the fire of his eyes was a passionate affirmation of the German's words. The Frenchmen listened politely, and with visible gratitude, but it was evident, with the exception of the Duchesse, that they remained somewhat mystified.

"I cannot be elated," said Arsène, "at the thought that I may die in misery, or in exile, but that men yet unborn shall profit by my sacrifice."

No one but the clever Duchesse saw the wondering grave look, full of sadness, which Cecile bent upon her lover, nor heard her stern sigh.

"And I," said the German, in a low and deeper voice, "receive my elation from that very hope." He looked at Arsène, and now a scarlet flush ran over his face, and his voice trembled: "Monsieur, may I ask, then, why you have come to La Rochelle?"

Arsène stared at him in affront, and replied coldly: "The Rochellais are my people. They are Frenchmen. I am a Huguenot. I come to defend my own."

The German looked at the Spaniard and the Italian, and then gazed deeply and meditatively into space, as though he contemplated a great and shining vision. "And I," he said, very softly, "have come to defend my own."

There was a sudden silence in the dining hall, as if every one were stricken with a little shame. The Spaniard, with a slight and graceful gesture, lifted his wine glass to his lips, and smiled upon the German and the Italian, as though he drank a toast to that unseen vision.

Arsène was moved. He understood perfectly. But the perversity that bedeviled him in his grief and wretchedness, impelled him to shrug his shoulders lightly and smile.

"I confess that I see in this coming struggle only the weariness of the old religious wars. But there is some stubbornness in me which compels me to fight for my own brand of religion, against those of another whom I despise. For I shall not, by any man, be forced to conform to his convictions, or serve him with docile servility, or accept his superstitious and tyrannical dictums designed to destroy my soul and my mind—" He paused abruptly, and flushed.

The Duchesse smiled irrepressibly, and even among the less acute a smile appeared. But the look the German bent on him was suddenly tender and compassionate, and the Spaniard and the Italian looked at each other with sparkling eyes of intense amusement before they regarded Arsène with wise approval.

"Monsieur," said the German, in that same soft tone, "we comprehend each other, do we not?"

Embarrassed, but still perverse, Arsène exclaimed: "This is but a series of religious wars—!"

"Impossible, Monsieur," said the Count, with new relief and courage in his voice, and comradeship. "The terms are contradictory. No war is a religious war. Nor is this. It is only the age-old struggle between the oppressor and the oppressed, with God leaving the decision in the hearts of those who hate tyranny and cruelty. If their hatred is not strong enough, then they must go down in ignominy, with the knowledge that they have betrayed their children."

But Arsène, for all the acknowledgment in his own heart, continued to bicker, as a man afflicted with a great pain displays petty irritability in order to hide his suffering. The German listened, always gently, understanding. The Marquis yawned. The others resumed conversation among themselves. The Spaniard bent amorously towards Cecile's beautiful profile and whispered with adoration: "Madame is simpatica!"

The girl was uneasy before all this gallantry, and kept glancing pleadingly at Arsène to deliver her. But he was engrossed in his obstinate quarrelsomeness. The Duchesse frowned a little. She had begun to love Cecile, who, though deprived of the graces of a courtier by the necessities of her birth and her former life, had a native dignity and aristocracy, and the instinctive breeding of a grande dame. Cecile, arrayed in shimmering golden silk, with her white bosom daringly exposed, and her light lustrous hair piled in waves and curls upon a small head poised gracefully on her slender snowy neck, was no peasant wench but a gracious and delicate lady.

"It is not the sort of sweet stern creature to take a lover, in consolation," thought the Duchesse. "Ah, that is a pity! She will be miserable with that perverse and vital young scoundrel."

Nevertheless, when she looked at Arsène, her clear direct glance, so uncompromising and disingenuous, would soften.

This, then, was La Rochelle, with the Cardinal approaching the walls and causeways of the city, with high hopes and determination among the people, with devoted and dedicated foreigners to lead, inspire and fight side by side with those they had come to serve out of pure high-mindedness and a passion for justice and liberation.

The Marquis, after a discreet knock, entered the apartments of Arsène and Cecile. One glance at the young people confirmed his pessimistic belief that all was not well. Cecile sat before a long pier mirror brushing and combing her shining hair. She was clad in a loose gown of white silken stuff, and, as she rose at the Marquis' entrance, her hair mingled with the foaming whiteness and gave her the look of a proud young angel.

Arsène was standing near a high window, whose diamond panes looked out upon the dark night-shrouded gardens. He was gnawing a finger restlessly. His white shirt was open at the throat, and his brown neck was visible. He turned at his father's entrance, and favored the Marquis with a scowl and a complete silence.

The apartments were beautiful, if austere, and the candles flaming at the walls and upon graceful inlaid tables picked out the curve of a chair, the glimmer of a commode or wardrobe, the rich colors of the Persian rugs. The Marquis, as always, cast an approving glance about the great room. Then he said irately:

"Your conversation, my rascal, was not edifying this evening. Had you seen the smiles, you would have retired in confusion."

"My conversation is my own!" exclaimed Arsène, with anger. But misery stood starkly in his eyes. The Marquis looked at the girl. She was very pale, but retained her silent dignity. Is he weary of her, so soon? asked the Marquis anxiously of himself. But when he saw her expression as she gazed fleetingly at his son, his anxiety was dispelled. For, if reserved, that expression was compassionate.

The Marquis loved Cecile with a father's affection. He favored her with a loving smile, to which she replied with a sudden softening and the appearance of tears in her eyes. The Marquis seated himself, with a sigh. Despite the splendor of his dress, he appeared, all at once, to be an old and withered man, too tired for speech, sick of living, and futile. His face fell into dissipated and exhausted lines, and he blinked as if his vision had become dull. He took a pinch of snuff in his fingers, stared at it as if he had never seen it before, then, with a despairing gesture he replaced it in the enameled box the Cardinal had so admired, and put it back in his pocket. He flicked his perfumed kerchief across his nose, and sighed again. He leaned back in his chair, and closed his eyes.

Arsène watched all this with knitted brows and jerking lips. Then, unable to maintain an obdurate and disdainful pose any longer, he approached his father and laid his hand contritely on the other's shoulder, and pressed it.

The Marquis did not open his eyes, but asked, with unusual and weary softness: "What ails you, my son?"

Arsène was silent a moment, then he cried out with vehement passion: "I do not know! But I shall not listen to your reproaches, as I have not listened to Cecile's!" He added, in a more temperate tone, but one still filled with despair: "All appears useless to me. I am weighted down. I have no hope, for La Rochelle, for France. I feel the age and stony heaviness of all Europe upon me. I long for freedom, for air, for light, for new adventures and new opportunities, for a new land where a man can breathe and start afresh!"

The Marquis, sighing, opened his eyelids, and looked with fathomless eyes upon his son. Those eyes were like burned-out coals, from which no new life or fire could be enkindled. They were the eyes of the old, which had looked on much evil, and had rejoiced in it, and much malice and frivolity, which had finally disintegrated the soul. But he took a momentary comfort from the fact that Cecile had approached Arsène, and that, though he looked at his father with such despair and wildness, he had put his arm about her and had drawn her close to him, and that she was clinging to him with the warm white arms of a consoling mother.

"Where is that land?" repeated the Marquis, in a murmur. "Ah."

"It is not in Europe!" cried Arsène, and he ran his hand feverishly through his long black hair.

"I do not long for any new lands, or Arcadias," muttered the Marquis, with a glance crushed by exhaustion. "But, I am no longer young."

"I am tired of philosophy, of discussion, of argument and tiredness," said Arsène, as if he had not heard. He became excited again. "I long for action, but not on old battlefields, and among the dusty ruins of cities where men have philosophized and discussed and argued, and grown more tired through the ages." He flung out his arms. "I must be free! Of what avail is this struggle, in this old land?"

No one answered, but he finally turned and pressed his lips passionately to Cecile's forehead. She gave him a glance eloquent with love and understanding.

The Marquis, curiously, seemed to sink into a revery, in which he regarded his son with slowly burning eyes, in which the fire began to leap. Once or twice he muttered, shook his head, with a darkening countenance, and then the fire would glow again.

"The struggle will always continue, in this ancient world," said Arsène, his voice rising.

The Marquis appeared not to have heard, but he still regarded his son with that curious look. Finally, as if his mind had been made up, he rose. He put one hand on Arsène's arm, and the other on Cecile's. The girl regarded him through her tears, but she smiled a little.

Then, without another word, the Marquis bowed to Cecile, and left the chambers.

Arsène sank into gloom and feverish despondency again, and Cecile kissed him with wordless compassionate understanding.

"What can I say to him?" asked Arsène, at last, in the greatest melancholy. "How can I say to him that I must go, that I cannot remain in France, in Europe, when this sorry tragedy is done? He is an old man. He has given up the world, his life, for me. He would brave all danger and death again, as he has braved it now. But I cannot bring myself to continue his suffering."

"He would understand," said Cecile, smoothing his forehead with gentle hands. "It is strange, how much the old can understand. And forgive."

He thought of his wife, Clarisse, and into his face came a stronger frenzy. To hide this from Cecile, he turned away.

"We must do what we can," said Cecile, in that low stern voice which he had not heard from her in many months. "And then, we must trust in God."

He smiled slightly and drearily, as at the words of a child. Because he had wronged her so deeply, he was enraged against her.

"God!" he cried. "No God of man's imagining could endure the spectacle of these long centuries of cruelty and death, of hatred and persecution and torment! We must believe then that God is more monstrous than man, or has died, or has never lived."

He would not be comforted. He knew that he was imposing a greater burden upon Cecile by his transports, and some tortured perversity in him would not allow him to beg forgiveness. When he turned to the girl again, he saw that she had left him.

What have I done? he thought, wretchedly. There is no fortitude in me. There is no firm and abiding purpose. I am blown by a thousand winds.

This, the Marquis knew, very shrewdly. If Arsène were to step into the future he must be thrust hence by the hands of those who loved him. So, after he had left Arsène and Cecile, he made his way to the chambers of the old Duchesse, and upon her imperious voice bidding his entry, he opened the door and entered.

The old woman sat with strong serenity before her fire, meditating. She looked up at her friend, and then, seeing his face, dismissed her women. She indicated a seat for him. He sat down, groaning a little, as if, all at once, he felt his age and fruitlessness. They regarded each other in silence.

Then the Marquis said, hesitatingly: "I have come from Arsène. My son is ill. There is a sickness in his heart. Perhaps Madame has observed this?"

The Duchesse smiled faintly, and her lips twisted. "You do not believe Arsène a poltroon? But certes, we know this is not so. A man like this should not love, but, inevitably, he loves the most. I have observed him." She paused, then continued meditatively: "You and I have nothing left but pride. That is because we are old. But what have the young to do with pride, the young with their warm hearts and their running blood? It is pride, and love, which are destroying Arsène. There is a thought in his mind, but in some manner, you, and the young Cecile, interfere with it, or he fears for you."

"If he fears for me, then he is a fool," said the Marquis, with grave humility. "Each man choses that path which is easier and less painful for him. I have chosen that path. I cannot force this comprehension upon Arsène. He believes I have sacrificed for him. He does not understand that what I abandoned was less valuable than what I gained, in following him. But, pardieu! He is not to be blamed. The evidences of all my life were his to read."

The Duchesse compressed her lips as if to conceal a smile. "You cannot persuade him you were activated by the noblest motives?"

The Marquis saw her attempts to conceal her smiles. He smiled wryly in return. "Morbleu, Madame! You are cruel."

"Forgive me," she said. Then her thoughts semed to stray away and she gazed at her hands, sparkling with gems.

The Marquis leaned towards her, holding his hand against his back, which creaked painfully of late. He grimaced somewhat. "He spoke to me tonight of a new land, and seemed overly excited by it, as if some mysterious thing prevented

557

him from attaining it. I swear that I do not understand this son of mine!"

The Duchesse glanced up alertly. "Ah, a new land! I comprehend. I have thought of it also, for those who are still young and strong. It is inevitable that many of us must flee France, and all of Europe." She added, impatiently, as the Marquis stared at her uncomprehendingly: "I am speaking of America."

Had she said "the moon" the Marquis could not have been more astounded. His mind reeled. Now he knew that deep in his soul he had believed that La Rochelle was but a passing event, that Arsène must, of necessity, of fact, return to the life of France in the future. But in the Duchesse's words finality was implicit. He saw that Arsène might never return. For a moment or two he could not endure the thought. He had never been involved in any matters or ideas except those pertaining to France, and he had not thought of America at all, except to regard it as some fantastic and horrible wilderness at the ends of the earth. The idea of Arsène fleeing to such a place was equivalent to death. The vision was too terrible, too fantastic, not to be squared with reality.

"America!" he cried, incredulously, staring at her as if she had gone before his eyes. "My son? Arsène? Madame, you are jesting!"

"No," she cried, composedly, "I am not jesting." The sudden sparkle in her eyes was more brilliant than the sparkle of her jewels. "Do you not understand that this is an old world, without hope in it for young men? Do you not understand that the old men's hands are cruelly restraining their sons, and their grandsons, who yearn away from them, and the ancient corruption and dust?" Her face kindled as she looked at him. "Do you not comprehend that this is of what Arsène is speaking, and this is the cause of his misery and his frenzy? He has done with all this. You cannot, you dare not, attempt to imprison him any longer."

The Marquis' face became more wizened, more narrow than ever. He was appalled. He shook his head, numbly. Then he muttered: "But America! That is the wilderness, the unexplored, the frightful, the abandoned, the last refuge of the criminal and the adventurer and the hunted— Madame, you believe my son longs for that horizonless horror?"

Now she softened. "My dear old friend, there is one final sacrifice demanded of you. You will not turn aside from it."

CHAPTER LIV

THE CARDINAL WAS ENCAMPED beyond the causeways of the city. At night, the defenders on their walls and ramparts could hear the distant sound of revelry, of music, of trumpets. They could even see the distant scarlet banners, the smoke of the luxurious camps. It was an army of vicious decadence and frivolity and silken cruelty that was besieging them, a laughing enemy merciless and bland.

An ominous stillness grew among the Rochellais, and, among the common people, fear. There was no laughter or gaiety in the city. Dread was mingled with the sunshine and the warm blue winds. As the riotous festivity increased among the besiegers, so did the heart darken and grow cold among the besieged. Had there been a grimness in the Cardinal's camp, a silence and fatefulness, the Rochellais would have felt their own confidence rise.

The city had settled down to its siege. The weeks went by. There was little actual combat at first. The besiegers were content to prevent all entrance into the city.

Hourly, with growing despair, the watchers on the ramparts looked seaward, for the English. But the seas remained empty, full of moods, sunshine, storm or serenity—but always empty. Was there to be no rescue of those who represented the spirit of the Reformation in France? Was God to abandon them to their inhuman enemies, as he had abandoned the Huguenots to the fury of the Catholics on St. Bartholomew's Day? History reeked with stories of such abandonment. There was no promise that this day would be different, that the siege might not end in fire, on the gibbet, in corpse-strewn streets within the embattled walls, in agony at the hands of blood-thirsty priests.

Beyond France, the religious wars were raging. This, the Rochellais knew. But they derived no particular comfort from the knowledge that all Europe was being torn apart in agony in the name of God, Christ, the Virgin, and innumerable male and female saints. They preferred that the eyes of the world be turned solely upon them, so that their own sufferings might possess singular grandeur, and the sympathy of their co-religionists. Aid, too, might be spared, before the mole strangled the city. But, instead, La Rochelle was only one small spring of anguish in an ocean of torment.

The mob was afraid for its bodies. But the leaders, Frenchman and foreigner alike, were afraid for their minds, their souls, and their ideals.

"Thus it has been, and shall always be," commented the Duchesse de Rohan on this inexorable truth. "Tell the people that the enemy threatens their dining, their breeding, their vineyards and their lives, and they will fight to the death. But they will compromise eagerly with the enemy, if that enemy promises them that these shall be preserved to them as the price of surrender."

She added, with cool bitterness: "At the last, we must depend upon the bellies of the vulgar for the continued existence of the soul."

So it was, when the people began to complain in terror that their food was dwindling, that she opened her enormous cellars to the somber Mayor and bade him take what he willed for the people. She cajoled and threatened her friends into this also. "Retain your wines and fat hams," she said to them, "and prepare to surrender the holy things, if you will."

Nevertheless, with contempt and sadness, she observed how the people eagerly and fearfully read the broadsheets prepared by the terrible Capuchin, Père Joseph, which were smuggled into La Rochelle by real and potential traitors, and broadcast in the streets. "Surrender," urged the sheets. "Do it today, then you can be assured of the King's mercy and pardon, and all that you have, your homes and your commerce and your peaceful pursuits, will be retained by you. It is your leaders, your Mayor, the hateful foreigners who plot secretly to destroy France, who are betraying you, and who will look upon your death and your starvation and your punishment with cynical eyes." Other sheets cried: "You are hungry, but the cellars of your rich and plotting leaders are filled to the rafters, and they dine and carouse while you starve!"

Other sheets, shrewdly appealing to the lower emotions of the mob, luridly described the punishments, confiscations and hangings which would take place if the Rochellais remained obdurate. Others, understanding the bestial hatred which lurks, waiting, in every man, asked: "Who is one of your leaders? A German, the immortal enemy of France, the brother and mercenary of England! A Spaniard, a man of a nation who looks covetously at France! A dancing Italian, creature of a nation famous for its craft, villainy, stilettoes and murderers! A Mayor, whose grandmother was a Jewess with a yellow badge! A Duchesse of the House of de Rohan, an open despiser of the poor and the oppressed! A nobleman, Arsène de Richepin, who recently perpetrated one of the foulest crimes in human history when he hung three leaders of the helpless in Chantilly, in revenge for the death of another oppressor! Men of La Rochelle! Deliver these traitors, these despoilers, to their doom, open the gates of your city to your friends and liberators, and only clemency and love shall be extended to you, Frenchmen, by your brother Frenchmen!"

"Most certainly," said the German, Count Von Steckler, to the Duchesse, "the people laugh at such lies?" For he was an idealist, who believed that other men were as devoted and faithful as he.

But the Spaniard and the Italian, more subtle, more cynical, more realistic than this, lifted their eyebrows and twisted their lips in an ironic smile.

"They do not laugh," said the Duchesse briefly. "The superior man laughs at lies, even if he is starving. But the inferior laugh only when they are swollen with food."

With the utmost artfulness, the sheets refrained from any religious issue, and God was not even mentioned. They merely stressed the lie that "foreigners and the powerful" were using the poor besieged simple Rochellais for their own sinister ends, which was to set Frenchman against Frenchman for their ultimate destruction.

In one thing was the Duchesse in error: it was not only the mob which was being seduced. Among the rich and landed of the leaders in La Rochelle plans for treason were furtively discussed. They knew that even if La Rochelle successfully resisted the siege, their own estates, properties and wealth in other parts of France would be confiscated, in punishment. What would they gain, either in victory or defeat? They began to whisper of "compromise," and, with dignified and noble faces, began to discuss why it was not possible for Frenchman, Catholic and Huguenot alike, to live in peace and amity. Who, in the beginning, had set them against each other?

Hunger began to strike the people, despite the open cellars

of the more honorable. For the others, already breathing treason, locked their stores against the poor. The worst occurred when, during a brief battle on the outskirts of the walls, Père Joseph's cousin, Feuquieres, a man deeply attached to Catholicism and the King, was captured by the Huguenots. In some strange manner, this Feuquieres had smuggled to him the finest of foodstuff from the King's own table, brought to him under a flag of truce. The jailors who received them were most cordial to the King's men, and, after the laden trays and baskets were passed on to obsequious lackeys within the walls, the jailors remained to converse in the friendliest fashion with the Catholic soldiers and officers.

"Never has a siege failed without the aid of the besieged," said the Duchesse. But she was without power to punish the traitors, and the sad Mayor dared not do so.

And now the mole, far out of cannon shot, almost strangled the harbor. Seven miles of trenches enclosed La Rochelle on the land side, with twelve forts. The Rochellais, from their own battlements, saw all this calm and unhurried preparation, in which there was something inhuman and ominous. They, themselves, hungered, but they saw that the besieging army was well-clothed, well-nourished, and gay. Winter was upon them, with violent, sea-borne gales, icy spume, rain like needles of penetrating ice. The houses in the narrow cobbled streets were cold. Rain coated the windows, and froze there like a thick layer of crystal.

And still, they watched for the English, who were to rescue them.

In the meantime, conspiracy and treachery raged in and without the walls of the city. Agents, Catholic and Huguenot, passed in some secret fashion through the walls. It was Père Joseph who received them, gave them their instructions, paying them the price of their perfidy. Thereafter, he gave himself up to endless prayer, rapture and orisons.

He was having his own difficulties. The Cardinal appeared to show no enthusiasm for this siege. He made many sarcastic and witty comments about it to his old friend, and often yawned, smilingly, in his face. When the Capuchin passionately launched into diatribes against the Huguenots, prophesied that the city symbolized the struggle between the Catholic holy culture and peace in Europe, against the forces of disruption, state-domination, heresy, confusion and war, not to mention the worst, blasphemy, the Cardinal would gaze at him with his tigerish eyes gleaming, and a faint smile at the corners of his delicate and fragile mouth. At these times, waves of exhaustion and despondency would sweep over the Capuchin, and he would be near to fiery tears.

The King, himself, was horribly bored by the whole proceedings. He yearned to return to Paris, where he could be alone with his gloomy thoughts. He did not even pretend any enthusiasm. He looked with a lacklustre eye at his troops, listened to the Capuchin, and the lines of his mouth settled in obstinate lines. Sometimes he invaded the Cardinal's quarters and complainingly upbraided him for a thousand and one trivial things, while the Cardinal listened, stifling his yawns and playing with his cross. As for Madame, she had long ago returned to Paris, pleading indisposition, which the King hoped presaged an heir. With her going, the Cardinal was overtaken by a very paralysis of ennui.

They lived in comparative comfort. Gaming tables had been set up. But beyond the tents and the barracks the melancholy swamps and marshes spread away, full of mist under dim stars and pallid moon. Every one avoided that scene as much as possible. They dined luxuriously. Père Joseph ate cold dry bread and drank the water from the ditches. Never a decadent gourmet, he castigated himself more and more, as if to balance the casual and rich living of the besiegers. The strong huts of the soldiers disgusted him; their revelry affronted him. They seemed imbued by no holy ardor, no godly exhilaration. They talked of loot, and the fun they would have among the Rochellais after the surrender.

Despite the Cardinal's casualness, he was much worried. Among the Catholic nobles of his train, he knew there existed astute men who realized that a strong Protestant minority in France guaranteed that the power of the King would not become absolute, and that should that absoluteness finally be obtained, they, themselves, would be curtailed and hampered in the management of their own provinces and estates. He also knew that in some mysterious way provisions had been smuggled into La Rochelle, and he needed to ask no questions from whence they came.

The King's desire to return to Paris now became stronger than a furtive suggestion. This alarmed the Cardinal. The Queen Mother presided in Paris like a waiting black spider, hoping to enmesh the King and withdraw him from the Cardinal's influence, and thus obtain once more the old power of which the Cardinal had deprived her. Let the King once return to Paris, and the work of long years would be undone.—He knew, that in his absence, the Queen Mother was surrounded by hating malcontents and enemies who would plot unceasingly to destroy him.

Finally, the King abruptly bade the Cardinal farewell, and returned to Paris. He promised to return after the winter passed, but it was a promise given with a sly sliding of the eyes, and surly pouting of the lips. The Cardinal, overcome with dread and worry, would have followed precipitously, had not Père Joseph been present. But under the fixed glare of those terrible eyes, even his fear dared not betray itself. He was caught in this disgusting debacle whether he wished it or not. His only hope was in the continued insistence of his advisers that La Rochelle could not be taken. He frequently called in the Capuchin to hear these pessimistic reports, hoping that the dread monk might, himself, be convinced.

But the Capuchin looked at Cardinal and advisers and said in a loud and most frightful voice: "It can be taken! Nothing is impregnable, before God! We shall remain." The Cardinal shrugged, and smiled, but groaned internally. For the first time he had a real desire to smite his old friend very firmly and consign him to hell. But some shame withheld him from announcing that the city could not be taken, and returning posthaste to Paris. He began to curse Madame, the Queen. On such an ignominous venture, jeopardizing himself, he had come at the behest of a miserable Spaniard whose pink and white flesh he could not resist. He had many sour meditations with himself on man's vulnerability to woman, and most of them were obscene. His former idle scorn and wonder at himself for his weakness in being enmeshed in the ancient trap now became active detestation. With it, the first shaking of his self-confidence came. When might his body not betray him again into such abysmal folly? He could control its achings, but he could not control its itch. This placed him again in the detestable pen with all of the mankind he loathed.

Now, perversely, he began to pity the Rochellais. He felt himself one with them. He had been betrayed by a woman into this ludicrous degradation, and, indirectly, they had been so betrayed by the same woman. He saw himself and them as victims of a silly Spaniard's nether regions. How many worlds, how many deaths, had disappeared into the bodies of foolish women? he questioned himself. It infuriated him, with appalling disgust, that he was so absurd, so weak, so contemptible, that he could aid in the universal conspiracy, and be caught in it.

His respect and admiration for the Rochellais became

almost extreme. He meditated upon the Mayor, the Duchesse, Arsène, and all the others, with surprised pleasure. What ideal sustained them? He, who had no ideals, had found them ridiculous in others, had believed they were pretentious affectations, either the vaporings of fools or sly intriguers. But apparently idealism sustained the Rochellais. It shocked him. Did men actually exist for which some philosophy was bread and honey, and the wine of heaven? He knew that the Rochellais had been seduced with promises of clemency, therefore it was no fear that kept them obstinate within their walls. He knew that they knew that continued resistance would have terrible consequences for them. Yet, they preferred to starve and die rather than surrender. For the first time in his life a dim respect for some element in mankind, unknown in him, began to dawn in his mind.

From his acquaintance with the Capuchin, and others like him, he knew that there was some intoxication in religion which sustained them, made them insensible to suffering. But he knew that the Rochellais did not have this kind of religion. Protestantism, in the majority of the Huguenots, was a cool and liberal thing, more attuned to logic and reason than ecstasy. And logic and reason were usually the first to succumb before assault, despite their vaunted power. What was it, then, that sustained them?

When the thought came to him that some men might be willing to die for the right to think and act as they willed, that there might be a kind of pride in a few men which refused slavery to another man's ideas, and demanded liberty and honor and enlightenment, not only for themselves, but for others who cared nothing for it, he was astounded. He repudiated the thought. It was not possible! Where lived the man, who, without the intoxication and irrationality of religion and superstition, had the fortitude to believe that freedom was the most precious possession of all men, and was willing to die for it? How could such a man operate steadfastly in a chill and bitter light, not enraptured, not drugged?

The evidence was before him, beyond those scowling battlements that guarded the exhausted and starving city. Despite the traitors, the expedient, the soft and the opportunistic who dwelt among the Rochellais, there were many who believed that the rights of man were the holiest things on earth, beyond chants and churches and altars and an unknowable God. He was more and more astonished. It shook the evidences of a lifetime. It shook the knowledge of men which he had acquired in his long and embittered years. He was compelled to believe that some men were above the beasts of the field, above the love of self, and the thought humbled him.

Now he vowed that when La Rochelle fell, if it did, he would treat the surrendered with all courtesy, all admiration, all wonder, as strange creatures of which he would like to know more, in order to complete his education.

Men had killed and been killed in the name of religion, in a miasma of rapture. They had been drugged, debased creatures, as were all creatures robbed of reason. But how many had died because they had loved other men, and demanded for them the same liberation and reason, the same right to live in peace and knowledge which they demanded for themselves? So few. So very few! A Socrates, here and there, stood like a pillar of light in the black desert of history, which was strewn with the ruins of those who had only hated in the name of dead gods and forgotten deities.

Yet, those pillars had not fallen from heaven. They had been raised by countless dusty hands; they had been born of the sucking muck and slime in which all humanity struggled.

And now some strange passion was born in him that the Rochellais would resist to the death. Should he retire? No, he would not retire! He would observe this humbling, this glorious miracle, to its end. Perhaps, then, the sickness that lived in his flesh and his soul would be relieved, and he might dare hope that all men were not vile. It became a necessity in him to believe this. If he lost this belief, then the remainder of his life must be a thing of evil, of blood and death, of fury and madness and hatred.

He, who never prayed except before an altar, before a multitude, found himself praying that the Rochellais would prefer death to surrender to superstition and slavery. To what God did he pray, who believed in no God? He did not know. But he seemed to pray to a vast and universal spirit, who had a thousand faces, yet had none.

CHAPTER LV

THE TERRIBLE WINTER slowly passed. The condition within the walls was most frightful. But it was not yet hopeless. The aristocrats, the leaders, suffered the most, but they suffered with white faces and resolute hearts, and in silence. Their courage still intimidated the people, and shame was still strong among them.

Then, on a certain day, when the spring winds blew softly, and the fields beyond the towers and the walls were green and shimmering as new emeralds, when gulls flew with the sunlight on their wings over the harbor, a feeble shout from the heart rose from the watchers of the sea.

For, in the distance, the thronging white sails of the English could be seen, approaching the desperate city. Fifty sails there were, strong, smooth and serene, seeming to touch the distant clouds that floated through the polished young sky. They cast their shadows on the opalescent sea. The gulls wheeled about them, like the doves of heavenly messengers. They came under the direction of Denbigh, the brother-in-law of the assassinated Buckingham.

Of the more than twenty-five thousand inhabitants of La Rochelle, ten thousand of the weak, the old, the women and the children, had died of starvation and misery and disease. The winds and clouds and storms of winter, the hunger and hopelessness, had lain in the streets like a poisonous fog, stifling and strangling. Grief and agony had resounded in every house. But, with the coming of the English—the blessed English!—joy awoke again with irresistible brilliance, and the streets became alive with singing, weeping, rejoicing crowds. Now, they were to be rescued! Now the troops and the priests of the foul Catholics, the murderers, were to be routed, driven away! God had prevailed.

Thousands crowded the battlements like skeleton birds. Thousands of famished and sinking faces, radiant with joy,

567

turned seawards. Inexorably, the English approached. Then, the ships appeared to move no more. They stood like a bowing tall barrier near the harbor, the sinking sun red on their upper sails, the last light sparkling on metal and on the wet and glistening hulls. Triumphant pennants streamed in the breeze. But they did not come on, though they crowded the sea.

"Tomorrow," said the Rochellais, "they will attack, and deliver us."

They went to bed, gnawed by terrible hunger, but their hearts uplifted.

The watchers remained at their posts all night, their eyes fixed without rest on the ships. They could hear the far and distant sounds of those on the ships. They could hear the wind rushing between the fairy sails. They could hear the plunging of the anchored keels, the shriek of ropes. They could see the glittering restless lights, and they could just catch the thin brilliant notes of trumpets.

The night passed. Then, one by one, the watchers began to blink. Where were the lights? Were their eyes too strained? Had they become blind? Only darkness now rested on the ocean, profound and smothering. Now there was no sound. No man dared speak to his neighbor of what he discerned, lest a wild scream of agony arise from him. Oh, it was only that the English—the clever unpredictable English!—had extinguished their lights in order that their nearer approach to the harbor might be concealed. It was a narrow channel, that, between the curve of the harbor and the mole! They must slip between them, dark and unseen. At dawn, they would be within the harbor, beyond the mole!

The dawn came, gray and floating, as unreal as a dream. And then the watches saw that the ocean was empty. The English had fled.

No man spoke. No man looked at his neighbor. But they gazed out upon the sea with dead eyes. There was no question in their hearts, no asking if the English had found it impossible to enter the harbor. It was enough that they had gone, that La Rochelle was doomed, that the English had taken with them the souls and the courage, the hope and the faith, of Frenchmen, of a whole continent, of dedicated men and heroic hearts. They had taken with them, in their fault, or their lack of fault, the banners of freedom and peace. A world had gone down in the wake of their fleeing ships. For countless generations, for centuries, that world would be submerged, its lights drowned, its banners lost, its brave spirits mute and sleeping. They had taken with them all reason, all the hope of deliverance, all the ghosts of noble men who had died in the ruck of centuries that other men might be free. They had taken the shades of Luther, of Huss, of Erasmus, of Knox and Calvin, and those shades were dumb and weeping. The flags of freedom were gone, and there was only the scarlet dawn presaging a thousand thousand scarlet dawns of slavery and death and blood, of hatred and fury.

There was no need for the watchers to descend and inform the city. While they stood there, like statues of frozen snow, the city knew.

No sound arose from the cobbled streets, from the houses. There was no word. There was no outcry of denunciation or despair. There was only the staring of dead faces, the feeble touch of dying hands.

The siege continued. The dying dropped in the streets. Children wailing for food were suddenly strangled by a merciful death. Now the spring storms came, beating over the silent and deserted city. Hundreds thronged to the churches, but they could not pray. They could only kneel there, with bent heads and hanging hands, their lightless eyes fixed unseeingly on the stones beneath their knees.

The old Duchesse, as indomitable as ever, but with her old face sunken and gray, summoned the Mayor. She sat in her gaunt splendor before her empty fireplace, and looked at him with eyes that still glowed.

"My dear Guiton," she said, her voice still clear but very feeble, "we must do something for the children, for the weaker women."

He inclined his head. He was almost beyond speech, so famished was he.

"Open the gates sufficiently for some hundreds of them to leave. The Cardinal will be merciful. He will feed them. And just now," she added wryly, "food is more important than freedom, to these poor bewildered ones."

Her heart, always so cold and majestic, was touched by the sufferings of the anonymous people, as it had never been touched before. She, like the Cardinal, had had to revise much of her former convictions.

"I will ask them," said the Mayor, hoarsely. "Perhaps they will not desire to leave."

The Duchesse smiled darkly. "They will," she said.

So, within a week, over six hundred women and children received the last kisses of their weeping husbands and fathers, and the gates were opened.

569

Now hell itself must have been plotting. The Cardinal had had a very bad night. He was sleeping late. He knew nothing of this exodus. But the priests knew. They gave their orders. The women and the children, ragged, fainting, staggering, accompanied by their old men, crept through the gates between the lines of the silent troops. The women carried their babes in their arms, and other of their children unable to walk. They passed through the lines of troops, their haggard faces searching for one eye of pity and compassion, one eye of mercy. But they saw only burly red-cheeked men with lifted pikes and swords and ready muskets.

The last of that most dolorous procession trickled through the gates. A promise of mercy had been given under a flag of truce, a promise of gentle Christian succor. Ah, but the priests had promised everything!

The gates, groaning and creaking, closed. The procession went farther from the gates.

Then, at a given signal from some horrible creature in the robes of religion, the troopers fell upon those hundreds of women, girls, babes and old men and massacred them in swift and frightful silence. They did not bleed much, as they fell, with one last sigh, one last groan, one last lifting of skeleton hands. There was not much blood left in their tortured bodies. The corpses were piled up, like tossed fragments of wood and cloth. Babe after babe died in its mother's clinging arms. Between the trenches and the walls they died silently, old men collapsing on new life, the hair of women mingling, face crushed into face, empty body seeming to dissolve into other empty bodies, staring eye fixed into staring eye.

The sun, bright and gay in its springtime splendor, looked down on that dreadful and piteous scene. The arms of the Christian murderers rose and fell, until they were exhausted, and their swords ran with red rivers. Only those faint sighs and groans, and the occasional firing of a musket when sword-arm could no longer be lifted strongly, had broken the morning calm.

The Church had been triumphant! Let the Te Deum now sound from every gilt and scarlet church! Let Rome rejoice! The helpless and the innocent, reason and enlightenment, had suffered another death, another assassination! The tide of liberation had been forced to retreat once more into the dark and formless future. The sleeping ages still slept in the womb of time, awaiting the avenging hour, awaiting the foolish voices who would declare: "But that was long ago!"

Awaiting the form and the substance of heroic men who knew that tyranny and hatred never slept, and watched only for the hour to arise again.

The Cardinal, when he awoke at noon, was appraised of what had taken place by the Capuchin, Père Joseph. He went mad. He was beside himself. He raved like an insane man. Then, he became very calm and cold, and the Capuchin rejoiced that at last reason had returned to his friend. He was none too easy, himself. He was angered that he had not been consulted, but that his subordinates had perpetrated this thing. Nevertheless, the Church must not be attacked, nor denounced.

There was a fatal light in the Cardinal's eye, which the Capuchin, in his relief, did not discern.

The Cardinal called the officers and questioned them in a quiet voice. He gave his commands, over the protestations of the sickened commanders, who had declared that orders had been given the troops without their knowledge. It had been the priests—

That night, at sundown, one hundred of the murderers were ruthlessly selected and shot against the very walls of La Rochelle. The agonized defenders heard those shots, the sounds of the vengeance done in the name of their murdered loved ones. They paused in their weeping long enough to listen. They did not know that the Cardinal had forbidden the administering of the last sacrament to the executed, that the priests smoldered in their huts and whispered among each other, that the Cardinal witnessed the executions with a fierce and contorted face. They did not rejoice at these deaths. Their anguish was too great.

"Your priests," said the Cardinal to Père Joseph, in a tone which had never been addressed to him before, "are guilty of the deaths of the murdered and the murderers. Nevertheless, it is apparently impossible to punish them. Let them be happy, therefore—for it may not be long."

"I do not know you in this mood," said Père Joseph, sternly.

The Cardinal lifted his unfathomable and peculiar eyes to the other's russet face, and they were very calm. "You never knew me, Joseph," he replied.

He sent his own Captain, Bassompierre, alone, to the gates of La Rochelle, with a message for the Duchesse. "I weep with you, my dear old friend," he had written. "Hold it not against my soul in the final judgment, that I have approved or ordered this thing."

The Duchesse, sitting alone that night, held the note in her hand. She had never wept since her early childhood, not even at the deaths of those she dearly loved. She did not weep now, though her heart was like a wound, for she had already wept too much that day.

That day, she had ridden slowly through the desolate streets in her great gilt carriage. At every door where she saw the signs of mourning, she alighted, and without the assistance of footman or friend, she entered each house, her tiny majestic figure erect and quiet. She went in through the door like any humble townwoman, offering no platitudes, no exhortations, no pious consolations, no urgings to courage. She had stood with the mourners and had mingled her tears with theirs, in silence. "I have nothing to give you but my tears,' she had said, over and over, in the final moments. Had the Cardinal heard this, he would have started, remembering another whom he could not console but with whom he could only weep.

The people received her apathetically at first, instinctively shrinking away from the expected words of noble hypocrisy. But when she merely extended her hands, and her tears ran down her face, they crept about her, knowing that she suffered as they suffered. She saw their pathetic faces. But where she had once seen slyness, fear and stupidity, she now saw the courage that only death can bring, a simple courage so noble that it broke her heart and inspired her soul.

Now she sat with the Cardinal's note in her cold withered fingers, and looked at her cold fireplace. That haughty and imperial face was old and softened. There was a knock on her door, and her friend, Alphonse Champaigne, entered, a strong short man, once burly, but now completely emaciated. There were furrows on the face from the tears he had been shedding for his adored mistress. He knelt before her, and laid his clasped hands on her knees, imploringly.

"Madame la Duchesse," he said, in his weak and failing voice, "I beg you to flee, either seaward where small boats may still make their passage, or landward, to the Cardinal who is your friend. He will receive you with kindness. Flee, before it is too late, and you have died with us."

The Duchesse did not speak. Her expression did not change. In his fear, he began to speak with rising passion:

"Why does Madame remain? Who will be grateful? The canaille who would betray her eagerly, if it would save their cattle-hides? The canaille who would leave her to starve, so long as they had a crust of bread to satisfy their bellies? The canaille, who are the natural enemies of such as Madame? Who bear a natural hatred for her, and would destroy her for a centime? What loyalty does Madame hold to these? She has always despised them, with justification. Surely Madame will not remain with them?"

So weak from hunger and grief was she, that it took almost superhuman strength for her to turn her old stately head and speak to him, very gently, but absently:

"I have changed my mind."

The man was astonished. He felt that she hardly addressed these words to him, but to herself. He wrinkled his exhausted brow.

"Then Madame has contemplated fleeing? I did not know this! But I rejoice. Let Madame consider again."

But she only repeated: "I have changed my mind."

This seemed heroic sacrifice to him. He did not comprehend.

Later, the fat, well-fed and sleek Feuquieres begged admittance to her to offer his condolences. She received him with a rigid but punctilious courtesy, as befitted one aristocrat to another. But strangely, as she looked at him, after he had sought permission to sit near her, her face changed as if with astounded horror and revelation. He, too, after she had listened to his condolences in silence, implored her to flee, to go to the Cardinal.

Then he saw a mysterious thing happen to that imperious countenance. It became the face of an old peasant woman, acquainted with the fields, acquainted with hunger and suffering and long patience. It was no longer the face and the eyes of the Duchesse de Rohan that were turned to him.

"Why should I flee?" she asked, and even the intonations of her voice had changed. "My sisters and my brothers cannot flee."

After a long embarrassed moment of confusion, he offered to supply her with the rich viands of his own table, which were sent to him by the Cardinal. Now her eye lighted. "Bring me as much as you can spare," she said. "My people are hungry. They are starving."

He was not affronted, for he had seen her face. Huge baskets of food were brought three times a day to the Hôtel de Rohan, and the Duchesse took only a morsel. The rest was distributed among the people. The Cardinal remarked to Père Joseph that Feuquières seemed to have developed an

573

enormous appetite lately. "Probably from comparison," he said, wryly. "He demands enough for ten men."

But as the summer wheeled towards winter, scores, hundreds, of the Rochellais died of starvation and disease in the streets and houses of the city. The animals of the city, the donkeys, the dogs, the cats, the horses, the doves, had long ago been devoured. The people ate rats when they could catch them. They stripped the trees of their green leaves; they dug up the grass that grew in the gutters, in the squares, between the paving stones. They boiled leather, harnesses and hats and belts. They picked among offal for scraps.

If possible, those of the Duchesse's household, and her friends, ate less than the people themselves. Their misery was indescribable. But they did not complain, as the simpler people complained. They came to her table, to dine off gilt and silver plate on which reposed stews of grass, leaves, mice and rats, resplendently dressed as always, punctilious in their courtesy, deep in their bows, witty in their jests. Never had Madame's remarks and epigrams been so dry and devastating, for she was of the old and noble Lusignan blood. The people were brave, but they whimpered. The Duchesse and her friends were brave. And they never whimpered. They might be too weak even for a laugh, and only smiled. Their bodies might be so shrunken and emaciated that their rich and splendid garments hung on them like clothing draped on sticks. Their voices might not be able to rise above a whisper. But they remained gallant and composed, if they had only a twinkle of a sunken eye to answer the Duchesse's quips and naughty remarks.

Now only half of the Rochellais remained alive. The Duchesse visited them on foot. Her horses had been eaten by the people, the harness boiled. She walked proudly, even if she staggered, and had to support herself by touching the adjacent walls. But she visited constantly. If she had no smiles left for her friends, she had them for her people.

"Though we die," she said to her household, "the world shall not forget this siege. It will remember. It will remember the enemy, and be fortified against him."

Now more broadsheets were distributed among the Rochellais by the Catholics, and they had a genuine note of distress in them. "Frenchmen!" they implored. "Surrender. Our hearts are breaking for you. The massacre of your innocents was done by those already punished by our own hands. This shall not happen again. Open your gates to our bread, meat and wine, and your friends. We swear by all that is holy to us that we shall treat you only as brothers, and that nothing shall be taken from you but much given."

The Duchesse read these broadsheets with darkened eyes and heavy heart. She went among the people. She would have had no blame for them, but only a sigh, if they were wavering, if they desired to surrender. But to her amazement, and her broken-hearted tears, she saw only fortitude, only resolution, in those dying and skeleton faces. They touched her garments, these fainting people, and gazed at her humbly. She returned to her hôtel, and broke into a wild storm of weeping. She fell on her knees. She dropped her old white head to the rich rug on her floors. She whispered: "Forgive me!"

But those who heard, in silence and astonishment, did not know for what she implored forgiveness.

CHAPTER LVI

To ONE OF ARSÈNE'S active and ardent temperament, the long slow torture of the besieged city resulted in apathetic despair, and a kind of frozen inertia. Though he was now the acknowledged leader of La Rochelle, he was compelled to force himself to listen with attention to complaints and suggestions. Slowly, he began to acquire a poisonous hatred and aversion even for his friends, and he looked upon their sunken and exhausted faces with a momentarily wild repulsion. He despised their patience, but even this despising had in it a sick weariness and indifference.

Once the Duchesse said to him reprovingly, after he had delivered himself of an incoherent and rebellious tirade: "What would you have us do? Sally forth and attack the Cardinal? We, who are starved and weakened, our defenders decimated? Our hope is from the sea. If it does not come—"

"If it does not come?" repeated Arsène, bitterly.

The Duchesse lifted her little hands in an eloquent gesture. She regarded Arsène in cool silence.

"We die, then, like rats," continued Arsène, with that dark wrath which was so evident in him these days.

"Not an original remark," said the Duchesse. She paused, then fixed her eyes sharply and piercingly on the desperate young man. "It did not occur to you, Arsène, to say: 'We die, then, like men?'"

"It will not be hard for me to die," Arsène said, after a somber moment, and after a slight flush had receded from his cheek. "But what of Cecile? My father?"

The Duchesse rose, and diminutive though she was, she appeared to tower over the other. She gazed at him with cold but passionate contempt. "Have they complained? It seems to me that they possess more fortitude than you, who profess to love them." Then she softened, for she understood him so well. "It is action you desire, Monsieur. Take it, then. But it will accomplish nothing."

She knew she had judged him aright, for his eye suddenly flamed, and the most malignant smile touched his lips. "A dead Catholic is a dead enemy," he said. "It is true: I wish for revenge, retribution for the death of our innocents. Madame is willing?"

"You are the commander of La Rochelle," replied the Duchesse, quietly. Her imperial face had paled, become very still. "Have you thought, in the event of your death, who would defend Cecile?"

"I shall not die!" cried Arsène, exultantly. All his inertia had vanished. Life came back to his lips and his eyes. His hand gripped his sword.

In her heart, the Duchesse was pleased. She had perceived Arsène's wild disappointment at the lack of spirit among the body of the Rochellais. She had seen his disgust, which had dwindled to apathy with the disappointment. She said to herself: Disappointment because of the stupidity, ugliness and bestiality of men is very painful, but it is worse not even to feel the disappointment, and not to endure the pain of it. For such men as Arsène, too vehement, too exuberant and passionate, action was necessary. Waiting and patience were for the calm, for the disingenuous.

He went to the Spaniard, the German and the Italian, and hardly had he spoken hesitatingly, than they grasped his meaning and went mad with enthusiasm. They assured him that their followers would be delighted at the venture. Within less than two hours, five hundred men had kissed their swords, primed their pistols, gathered about Arsène. That night, there would be a foray. Now Arsène had calmer moments. This would not only be a raid of revenge. It would also be a raid on the food stores of the Cardinal's camp.

He went to Cecile's apartments the hour before the foray was intended. She lay supine and silent on her bed. He saw that she gazed at him quietly and sternly, as so often she gazed at him these days. He knelt beside her and lifted her hands to his lips. She felt a new vibrancy in him, a new excitement, and her poor aching heart was lifted.

He wondered if he dared tell her of the coming adventure. Cautiously, he began. The people were starving. She, herself, his beloved, was dying for lack of food. That night, he intended to obtain it.

She raised herself on her pillows, and under the pale and bloodless skin a bright color ran. She breathed hurriedly.

577

She stared at him with unspeaking agitation, and her lashes were suddenly wet with tears. He misunderstood her. He exclaimed: "Certes, you do not disagree, ma cherie? You would not have me do nothing?"

"No. Oh, no!" she whispered, and drew his head to her breast. He heard the wild beating of her exhausted heart.

Never had he adored her so much, or loved her so profoundly. He could not embrace or kiss her enough. He thought: It is possible I shall never return. For a moment his courage dwindled. Who would protect her, then?

As if she understood his thought, she said. "You will return. I shall pray."

He went to his father, but before he could speak the Marquis said: "I have a charm for you." And from his purse, somewhat sheepishly, he withdrew a tiny ivory figurine which had come from China. It was grotesquely carved, the image of a little fat old man with a round grinning countenance and a smooth jovial belly. There was something more than a little obscene in the nakedness of the image, and its rolling posture, but something also of lusty merriment and ribald cynicism. Arsène, taking it, could not restrain himself from laughing aloud, and he felt much relief, for his spirit had become heavy upon leaving Cecile. The Marquis smiled.

"It is said that he who laughs remains untouched by death," he said. "That is very subtle. I prefer to think, in this instance, that it has a less clever meaning, and one more practical. This image is very old; it has survived a thousand years, while many prettier and more lofty have been destroyed."

Then he took Arsène's face between his hands and kissed him gently on both cheeks. He could not speak again.

After Arsène had gone, the Marquis entered Cecile's apartments. Calling upon the last morsel of her strength, she had arisen with the help of her women, had arrayed herself in a crimson velvet gown, and had seated herself near the great windows. There she had taken up her vigil. From her bemused and withdrawn expression, from the tears on her white cheeks, the Marquis knew that she had been praying.

He had never prayed in his life. The sight of others praying had made him feel excessively foolish and irritable, as at the sight of childish and meaningless exercises. But now he was touched beyond speech. He approached the girl and sat down beside her. Then he saw that she held a rosary in her hands, and that in her open palm the cross lay, limpid gold and glimmering.

The Popish symbol took the Marquis aback. The girl said, very softly: "It was given to me by the Abbé Mourion. Monsieur le Marquis has heard of him?"

"Yes. Arsène has told me," replied the Marquis.

They both gazed in silence at the cross.

Then the girl spoke again, in a trembling voice: "He was such a good man. This came from his hands. When I hold it, so, I receive strength, as if he had sent me a message of courage and faith. Only an hour ago, I thought I heard his voice, so gentle and kind."

After a long moment, the Marquis said in a peculiar tone: "I have always thought that the beloved objects of the good and the resolute partake of their qualities, that some mysterious essence is imparted to them. And, perversely, that the objects of the vicious and the malevolent retain their own poison. I have touched the relics of the wicked, and have sensed the vicious vibration that remains in them even after the centuries. Perhaps, in this rosary of the Abbé Mourion there is some virtue, some indestructible power for good. Perhaps Arsène ought to have carried it—"

At this, the girl began to smile. Her blue eyes lit up. A faint dimple quivered at her lips. "I offered it to him, and he was aghast. He cried: 'What if I were taken, and this were found upon me!'"

The Marquis burst out laughing, and Cecile joined him. But the Marquis noticed that her transparent fingers clung to the cross with an involuntary passion, as the fingers of the drowning clutch.

They found comfort in each other's presence. They spent the night together at the windows, gazing out into the night, seeing the reflection of the candles on the dark glass and their own stained faces.

It was not until almost all the watchfires of the Cardinal's camp had been extinguished that Arsène led his followers to the foray. They knew the gates were guarded not only from the inside, but the outside, by the Cardinal's men. They dared not let their own sentinels know, for fear of traitors, or unwarranted excitement. They circled the city, and waited until the guards had moved away. It was a dark night, lit only by the spectral light of the crowding stars.

The wall loomed above them, thick and solid against the teeming sky. Some of the more agile swarmed on the shoulders of their companions, holding knives between their teeth, and fastened knotted ropes at the top. Then, so silently that not even a breath could be heard, the rest of the men swung themselves up the ropes, reached down helping hands, crouched at the top, then dropped the ropes on the other side. Some were delegated to remain at the wall to assist those who returned.

Now the soft thump of feet sounded on the dangerous and open side of the wall. The men lay where they fell for some moments, holding their breath. The watchfires near the marshes flickered and glowed redly in the black night. There was a faint sound of music, of far laughter. The figures of sentinels passed between the watchfires and the raiders. Slowly, now the latter crept on hands and knees to the far side of the watchfires. Once they passed so close to a group of guards that they could plainly hear their yawns, the exchange of an indecent story, and the subsequent hoarse laughter.

Reaching a safe spot in the marshes, where the cold water oozed around their hands and knees, the raiders waited. The music ceased; the laughter was gone. One by one, the watchfires flickered out, and now there were less than half a dozen at scattered points. The camp was guarded in a scattered manner, for no one dreamed that the starved and exhausted Rochellais might dare to attack.

Arsène suddenly lifted his head in a signal, which those behind him imitated by also lifting their hands to those behind them. Then, rising in a body they swept down, as silent and shapeless as ghosts, upon the camp. They had already discerned where the foods stores were secreted, for these stores had several guards about them, distrusting the Cardinal's own lusty and rapacious soldiers. So swift was the attack, so unexpected, that not even a cry escaped the guards when Arsène and his men fell upon them, throttling them with one hand while they drove home their knives with the other. There were only faint grunts and heavy breathing, for the attackers lowered their bleeding victims slowly upon the ground so that not even the clank of a sword or the thud of a fallen musket might be heard.

One hundred and fifty men had been delegated to carry the stores to the wall. The others were to advance deeper into the camp on their mission of vengeance, and to cover the operations of the raiders of the stores.

A terrible excitement seized Arsène, giving his emaciated body superhuman strength. When his knife had entered the plump bodies of the guards, he had had to bite his lips to restrain a savage and exultant cry. His appetite was only whetted. There was bloodier and more important work to be done.

The Cardinal's soldiers slept in scattered improvised barracks and tents. It was an easy matter to attack each small unit separately, and in a concentrated manner. Within a few moments fifty sleeping men, surprised and dazed upon a swift awakening, died swiftly and easily, even as their hands stretched out to seize musket or sword. Within the next five minutes, fifty more died. The attackers had not lost a single man, though the attack had taken place in total darkness.

Emerging, blood-stained and covered with sweat, and panting heavily, Arsène saw a distant small house which had once belonged to a local farmer. There were several guards pacing about the house, stopping to converse indolently. A campfire burned near them, and Arsène could see their sleepy and truculent faces, and their distinctive livery. Here, then, slept the Cardinal, himself.

He had a sudden mad thought. Why was it not possible to seize the Cardinal, take him prisoner, drag him within the beset city as hostage? Or, at the most desperate, to kill him? Nothing seemed impossible to the aroused young man, whose head was giddy with weakness, hunger and excitement.

He communicated this to his emerging companions in a stifled whisper. They thought him mad, and dubiously shook their heads. They were doing splendidly so far. But it would be no easy, and silent matter, to approach the house of the Cardinal. There were many guards. Some would immediately give the alarm. Arsène was enraged. His thoughts were turbulent and delirious.

"Let us return to the stores," said the Spaniard, whose natural lust had been excited by the sight of food. "Let us take what we can, and return."

"I am not done," said Arsène. He was muffled up to the nose in his cloak, and they saw the mad gleam of his eyes in the light of the far watchfires.

The German, Von Steckler, hesitated, shaking his head slightly. The leaders stood in the shadow of low thick brush. Behind them they heard the crowded breathing of their followers.

Giddy, seized with mounting delirium, Arsène stared unblinkingly at the house. There lay the Cardinal, the Monster of Europe, sleeping. He could be destroyed! With him would fall the persecution of Frenchmen, the mounting horror and cruelty of the Catholic reaction, the creeping pestilence of the world. It could be done!

He turned to his officers and whispered: "Fifty men can do this! Let the others return to the stores and hasten to the walls."

The Spaniard, the Italian and the German were silent for several moments. Then they whispered to those behind them. The whisper sped on almost soundless lips to the others. In a few moments all but fifty men had melted away into the night. Those that remained were not convinced, but Arsène's excitement had communicated itself to them. It was a mad, an impossible scheme, but they were caught up in their leader's insanity, and wild recklessness rose in them. If they failed to carry off the Cardinal, there was still the possibility, before they were seized, of killing him.

They crept forward, stepping lightly on the balls of their exhausted feet. Now they were in terrible danger. The firelight would soon betray them to the guards. They spread out in a thin line, closing in towards the house.

Suddenly they halted. A faint strangled cry sounded not too far in their rear. Hearts roaring, they listened. Was that the sound of stealthy feet at their rear? They looked backward, straining into the darkness. They saw nothing, heard nothing.

They turned back to the little house. And then they saw that the door was opening. The Cardinal, fully dressed in his uniform, his plumed hat upon his head, appeared in the doorway. His guards came to attention, presented arms. He glanced at them abstractedly. He was looking in the direction of Arsène and his companions. The watchfire lay between them. The Cardinal's vision was bedazzled by it, so that the wall of flickering red light must have prevented him from seeing what might have been seen.

Arsène raised his musket desperately. There was a slight movement, as if of involuntary protest and uneasiness about him, then silence. He pointed the musket directly at the Cardinal's heart. But his hands shook. He caught his lip between his teeth and bit it so violently that it bled. He did not feel it. His whole being was concentrated in his hatred, in his purpose. He blinked his eyes furiously for the firelight and his own weakness made the Cardinal's figure dance before him.

The Cardinal stood there, cloaked and uniformed, unprotected, calm and still, gazing towards the brush where the attackers stood. He did not move. His guards had begun their pacing again. Nothing could have been more composed than that slight regal figure, the night wind stirring his plumes and blowing his cloak. His expression was lofty and removed as usual, his terrible tigerish eyes glowing in the firelight.

And then, all at-once, the wildest and strangest thought seized Arsène. He was convinced that the Cardinal knew everything, had discerned everything in the moment that he stood there, that he saw Arsène as clearly as though he were standing in the blaze of the noonday sun. Was that a faint sardonic smile on that narrow ivory countenance, or was it only the effect of the blowing firelight?

Arsène's hands became wet. The musket shook more and more. His numb finger fumbled for the trigger. He could hear his heart, like a caged thing, leaping and roaring. Somewhere, some time in the past, he had heard that the Cardinal, like all felines, could see in the dark—

Then the Cardinal lifted his hand with a delicate and negligent gesture. He smiled, as if pleased. His clear strong voice sounded in the night:

"Is that you, my dear de Bonnelle?"

Arsène started. It must be now, or never. He exerted all his strength in his shaking finger curled about the trigger. But some paralysis held him, some nightmare.

Then he heard a faint thick exclamation behind him, a dim confusion. A horrible sickness welled up in him, though he did not swerve from his position or drop the musket. From the sounds of his companions, he knew that they were surrounded. Yet, there was no uproar, no shout, no shot. They were undone. They were lost.

But he, Arsène, was still free, the musket still pointed at that figure which appeared to be jigging and dancing wildly in the firelight. Now it had become a tiny distant figure, a marionette, jerked by the strings held by a drunken man. The ground swayed under Arsène's feet; he felt the drops of his own sweat dropping into his eyes. But the paralyzed finger would not stir in spite of his superhuman efforts to jerk it.

"De Bonnelle?" called the Cardinal, and now his smile was broader. He advanced a pace or two. "Come forward. You are recognized."

Arsène felt a strong hand on his arm, and the Spaniard's indolent and amused voice in his ear. "We are lost," he said. And then the musket, in some way, had fallen from Arsène's fingers and had dropped at his feet.

A strange and dreamlike coldness engulfed the young man. He looked behind him. Beyond his companions were a host of silent men, armed and waiting. He could barely see them; he sensed, rather than saw, their presence.

He heard the light sound of approaching feet in the frightful and ominous silence. The Cardinal was advancing. Three of his guards fell in behind him. Arsène watched him come. The firelight threw vivid red shadows upon him. He walked with calm grace and certainty. Now the smile was more fixed upon his attenuated countenance, as though he were contemplating something which amused him. Some one threw more wood upon the fire. It sprang upwards with a scarlet roar, and bathed the surrounding countryside. It revealed, completely, Arsène and his companions, and the shadowy outlines of the enemy behind them.

Arsène thought: It is finished. He sighed. His madness had gone. He thought of Cecile, and his father. At least, they would have food for a while. A deep grief and weariness assailed him. He waited for the Cardinal's exclamation of recognition and final betrayal.

But still the Cardinal said nothing. He continued to advance. He paused only five paces from Arsène, and the two men gazed steadfastly at each other.

He knew from the beginning, thought Arsène, with a kind of dull wonder. He still waited.

The firelight was now behind the Cardinal, and his figure was silhouetted against it. Arsène could no longer see his face clearly. He felt, rather than saw, the strange glimmering light in those frightful eyes, a fiendish and sardonic light. He advanced a pace, then waited again.

There was utter silence all about him. Arsène's companions were caught in a strange numb amazement. Why did not the Cardinal speak, denounce their leader, order them all to be seized? They gripped their swords. They waited for a signal from Arsène. They would sell their lives dearly, even against overpowering odds, if he gave them the word.

But Arsène did not move or speak. He and the Cardinal were regarding each other like statues, eternally turned face to face.

Then the Cardinal spoke softly, and affectionately: "Ah, so it is you, my dear de Bonnelle. I have been waiting a long time. I had come to believe you might never arrive."

A long murmur broke behind Arsène. He heard the rustle of his companions, the relaxing of their waiting executioners.

The Cardinal extended his hand. Arsène stared at it, incredulously. Was it possible that the Cardinal had not recognized him? he thought, his mind swirling. But as he looked again at his enemy, he knew this was a foolish thought.

For the Cardinal was laughing softly, his hand still stretched forth.

Arsène, convinced now that he was in a nightmare, took that hand. He felt the pressure of the fragile and delicate fingers. The Cardinal's eyes regarded him with long slow amusement, and there was an irrepressible movement about his bearded lips as if he could hardly restrain his laughter.

"You have brought few bravos, my dear friend," said the Cardinal, in a light reproving tone, as his eye flickered on Arsène's companions. "But even a small detachment is welcome. Spaniards, I presume, of course? How unfortunate! They will not be able to converse and make merry with my own men."

Arsène heard the caught breaths of his companions, the shifting of their feet. I have gone mad! he thought. This is a dream. He felt his head nodding.

"Yes, unfortunate," he murmured.

"But not doubt you have others encamped at a distance?" urged the Cardinal, in a careless and friendly tone. Arsène nodded again. The Cardinal still held his hand.

"And you will wish to return to them almost immediately?" said the priest.

"Yes, Monseigneur," said Arsène, in his dull sick voice.

"But first," said the Cardinal, in a tone of affectionate enthusiasm, "you must rest a while, and join me in a glass of wine."

He glanced beyond Arsène to his own soldiers.

"You, Bretonne, take Monsieur de Bonnelle's men to the fire, and feed them well, and give them some wine. They cannot converse with you, but food has an international language. Monsieur de Bonnelle will return in a few moments, after we have had a brief conversation."

He dropped Arsène's hand. Arsène looked at his companions. Their eyes, in the firelight, were amazed and bewildered. But the Spaniard and the Italian were smiling faintly. They did not understand, but they were supple enough to move cautiously wherever the Cardinal directed.

Arsène found himself following the Cardinal towards the house. How soon would the murdered men be found? His thoughts were confused, swirling in alternate darkness and redness. This was a mad play. It was not happening. The Cardinal waited for him, until he stood abreast.

"You have had a hard journey?"

"A very hard journey. A long and painful one," replied Arsène, hoarsely.

The Cardinal nodded, with sympathetic understanding. They entered the house. It was simply but comfortably furnished. Candles were lighted on a long oaken table, and a fire smoldered on the hearth. The Cardinal's orderly, whom Arsène did not recognize, was moving about with agility, setting out plates of stewed fowl and rabbit, bread, pastries and wine. The Cardinal removed his cloak, flung it aside, sat down with quiet grace before the table, indicating that Arsène was to do so also. Then he ordered his servant to leave. He spoke in the friendliest and most casual manner.

"Doubtless, you did not come this far without some— murder?"

"Doubtless," said Arsène. His head was throbbing with his weakness. The warmth of the little house, the excitement of the night, his capture, his fear for his father and Cecile, and the unaccustomed exertion of the past hour, had completely undone him. Everything swam in snapping bands of light and color before him. He saw his blood-stained hands as they rested on the white damask cloth of the laden table. Suddenly a slow shudder passed over him, and his chin dropped on his breast.

He heard the Cardinal's light amused voice.

"Yonder there is water in the bowl, and towels nearby. You would, of course, prefer to wash before dining?"

Arsène forced himself to his feet. He staggered, passed his hand over his eyes. The Cardinal, smiling so casually as he sat at the table, waited. Arsène's footsteps wavered on the way to the bowl. Now there was no sound in the room but the splashing of the water, the crackling of the good fire. The touch of the cold water on Arsène's hands and face revived him. His mind still swirled, but here and there a poignant thought and lucid conjecture forced themselves through the mist. He had no doubt that the Cardinal was playing with him, in his famous cruelty, and enjoying himself in the process. Then, certes, he could play, too. It was a grim comedy, but such comedy had always appealed to him. He was certain that he was lost. His only uneasiness now was in the fear that he would suffer the ignominious death by hanging. He resolved that he would appeal, as a soldier, . . . death by shooting.

He had seen death so often, had looked into its fatal countenance on more than one occasion. Like all the young men of his caste, he had regarded death with indifference, as a regrettable inconvenience. But now he had become older. Life had taken on new and vivid values. He did not want to die. He suddenly clutched the silken linen towel in desperate hands.

He returned to the table. The Cardinal had heaped Arsène's plate with luscious food. Arsène smelled the hot wine sauces, and his mouth watered. He would play to the end. In the meanwhile, he would eat, to recover his strength for whatever ordeal still lay before him.

With a graceful and most courteous gesture, the Cardinal filled the sparkling wine goblets. He lifted his own and waited. Arsène lifted his goblet. They looked into each other's eyes for a long moment. Then the Cardinal inclined his head with a grave smile, and touched Arsène's rim with his own. The little clink in the silence had a portentous sound. Arsène drank deeply, his hand trembling on the stem of his goblet.

He put down the goblet and again gazed into those tigerish eyes, which were now so hooded and inscrutable. The Cardinal silently indicated Arsène's plate. The young man could not resist. He seized knife and fork and ate ravenously. He hardly tasted the food, so rapidly did he gulp. He did not look at the Cardinal as he devoured the excellent fowl, pastries and salad, and gulped the wine. When he did glance up, his eye touched a huge golden crucifix which hung over the fireplace. The Cardinal did not speak. He sat at his place, one narrow ivory hand drooping slackly over the back of his chair, his attitude one of remote contemplation, as if he were alone. His profile was presented to Arsène. His expression was withdrawn, stern, yet still faintly sardonic. He appeared less frail, less terrible, less majestic, in his general's uniform than he did in his ecclesiastical robes. He was more of a man, less clothed in terror, more approachable. Though the moulding of his narrow and aristocratic head expressed his natural pride and hauteur, its contours, without the Cardinal's hat, were singularly defenseless and delicate. To the casual glance, that head and that long melancholy countenance belonged to a scholar full of sadness and weariness. On one attenuated and bloodless finger his Cardinal's ring winked and flashed in the firelight and candlelight.

Finally, Arsène could eat no more. He was replete. Strength had come to him. But his mind reeled with the wine. He felt the warmth of the room and the warmth of the wine in his body and his veins. He became reckless, but also cunning.

The Cardinal sighed. He appeared to arouse himself with

an effort. He turned his face to Arsène, smiling. But that smile was like invincible armor.

"Monsieur is refreshed?" he asked, gently.

"Yes, thanks to Monseigneur's hospitality," replied the other.

The Cardinal placed his thin elbows on the table, cupped his chin in his hands and regarded Arsène with the most extraordinary friendliness.

"I was excessively attached to Louis," he said.

Arsène's wan face suddenly flushed deeply, and he bit his lip.

"The law," continued the Cardinal, delicately, "is very particular about—"

"Fratricide," said Arsène, in a dull voice.

The Cardinal lifted his eyebrows in painful remonstrance. "Dueling," he protested. "There is the penalty of two years in the Bastille for that offense. It would distress me to see Monsieur in that uncomfortable prison."

Arsène heard these extraordinary words, but they did not convey any immediate meaning to him. He had resolutely pushed all thoughts of Louis aside in the past few months, for his endurance had been solely tried by the siege. But now all his old grief, sadness and desperate regret flooded him. His face changed, twitched. He looked at the Cardinal with miserable pleading.

"It was my life, or his," he whispered. His hands lifted, dropped impotently. "Almost, now, I wish it had been mine."

The Cardinal said nothing. He still smiled, but the smile was dark and thoughtful, as if he was thinking of something else. His hands dropped to the table. The right fingers beat a soundless but rapid tattoo on the cloth.

Then he said, very softly: "Do not regret. There was no happiness implicit in that strange and mournful heart. It was conceived in tragedy; it lived in tragedy; it died in tragedy. Only for a brief interlude was there joy, and even that joy was tragic. Those who loved Louis should rejoice that he died. I rejoice."

Arsène started. A moved expression passed over his features. He felt a burning under his eyelids.

"I had no consolation to offer him," mused the Cardinal, gazing at his beating fingers. "That is my tragedy, singularly my own. But Monsieur does not comprehend this?"

Arsène was silent. His lack of subtlety was no aid to him in this. He was bewildered. Then the faint obscure thought touched him, and threw him into confusion. He saw the

Cardinal's face, swimming before him. There was a sudden pang in his breast. He cried out, with involuntary vehemence: "We were reconciled, before he died! He understood—!"

The Cardinal's brows lifted. "Be consoled, then, Monsieur," he said, and Arsène did not hear the irony in his words. "You have had a most extraordinary experience."

His tapping fingers halted. The hand relaxed as if exhausted. Now his smile was gone. His strange eyes glowed and welled with an inhuman light, as they fixed themselves piercingly on Arsène. He scrutinized the young man as if he were some mysterious and provocating object, which puzzled and excited him. He remembered this bravo, this adventurer, this gay and reckless courtier so well! But where, now, was all that color and that vitality, that heedlessness and flamboyant courage? This man appeared no longer young. He drooped with weariness and profound tiredness which was not only physical. His emaciated body was sustained by some fortitude it had never possessed before. That dark beard was close and shadowy over that haggard jaw and those sunken cheeks. The aquiline nose appeared larger and sharper, the nostrils more red and distended. His eyes seemed to have fallen deeper into their sockets, and burned steadfastly with an unfamiliar expression of power and steadfastness. What had sustained him? The Cardinal became much excited and curious. He knew, from old acquaintance, that Arsène professed no faith, no fanaticism, that he had always been motivated only by hatred, resentment and a lust for dangerous adventure. But these qualities appeared to have gone, and left strength and hard firmness behind. At the corners of those pale lips, at the corners of those eyes, there was a mysterious residue, a faint luminosity, which lingered on the lips and in the eyelids of those who had dreamt a noble and ecstatic dream.

The Cardinal inclined his head whimsically. "'It is Monsieur Arsène de Richepin, in truth, that I address?" he asked, gravely.

Arsène colored, and his eye flashed with anger at what he believed was some mockery. "It is," he answered, with great coldness.

"I meant no offense," said the Cardinal, smiling once more. "For a moment I thought I might be mistaken. Monsieur has changed. Would it be discourteous if I inquire, with genuine interest, when this change took place?"

Arsène was still angry, and perplexed. He stared resentfully at the Cardinal, and did not answer. His confusion grew.

The Cardinal resumed his scrutiny. His eye lingered thoughtfully on every feature of the young man's face. Then slowly, he raised his hand and passed it over his mouth, as if to hide a smile.

"I perceive it is still Monsieur de Richepin," he observed.

Arsène stared.

"Monsieur has revealed unexpected traits of character," resumed the Cardinal, after a moment. "It is my stupidity which failed to observe them before."

There was silence in the room. The Cardinal's expression became increasingly friendly, but very curious.

"There is another question, for which I must beg Monsieur's pardon. I do not ask in vulgar curiosity, but in real interest: What sustains Monsieur in that wretched city?"

Arsène did not speak. His brows drew together.

"Remembering Monsieur, of whom I have long been fond," continued the Cardinal, "I may be pardoned for being somewhat puzzled. Monsieur had no faith, no profound convictions." He became more eager. "Again, I must implore Monsieur's pardon. I am a student of men." He paused. Then he added impatiently: "Certes, Monsieur understands what I am asking?"

Arsène was silent.

"In that city, Monsieur must find his endurance sorely tried. He must suffer, not only for himself, but for those to whom he is attached," continued the Cardinal, fuming at this apparent stupidity, but determined that his curiosity be satisfied. "He must know the cause is lost, that the city must fall. He is the leader. He must observe the torment, the hunger and despair of his fellow rebels. He must, by now, have realized that the English, as always, have betrayed their promise. He must know what the inevitable end will be, and that there is no hope. I wish, then, to know, with all amazed sincerity, what sustains Monsieur."

But Arsène was still silent. His eyes were fixed upon the Cardinal's face. Is it my imagination, asked the Cardinal of himself, with profound excitement, or is there in truth a strange and poignant light in this bravo's bold eyes?

"Monsieur comprehends," went on the Cardinal, "that each day's continued resistance lessens our patience, and the possibilities of our mercy. Yet, Monsieur has ordered that the city continue to resist. I wish to know why he has come to this desperate conclusion. It is not in keeping with Monsieur's shrewd character, which I believed I knew so well."

Arsène stirred on his seat. The strange light increased in his eyes. It cast a luminous glow over his emaciated features. His voice was hoarse and uncertain when he spoke, and almost humble:

"Monsieur le Cardinal remembers Paul de Vitry, my friend? Paul had faith; I did not comprehend this faith. It is still uncertain in me, still wavering. I did not see his dream, while he lived. Now, it is given to me to catch faint far glimpses of it. I cannot put it into lucid words," he said, lifting his hands impotently. "There are no words for it. I still hardly believe——. But I know: that I must recreate in myself the faith of Paul de Vitry, if only that I might hope again."

There was a long silence in the room. The Cardinal looked down at his hands. He regarded the sparkling ring on his finger with a withdrawn and musing look. He turned it around and around, like a jeweler scrutinizing wares offered for sale. Now his expression was masked and hidden.

" 'If only that I might hope again,' " he repeated, almost inaudibly.

He glanced up swiftly. Arsène's face was moved and working. He appeared about to weep.

What a terrible spiritual coming-of-age this bravo must have experienced! mused the Cardinal. What agonies he must have endured, and none of them physical. Men began with hope and faith, and slowly lost them. But this man had begun with nothing but his own shallowness, recklessness and obtuseness, and had acquired, in desperate and frightful jeopardy, in succorless ruin, the hope and faith which sustains men, and which cannot be comprehended. Then, certes! there must be something divine, something untouchable, something selfless and heroic, noble and majestic in the souls of men, after all! There must be something indestructible under all the bestiality and foulness of mankind, some nugget of beauty and self-abnegation and loftiness. The Cardinal, with much puzzlement, had observed that civilization was the conquest of some mysterious will over man's natural inertia. He had believed it was rapacity and lust. Now, he was not so certain.

"I am not so certain," he said, aloud, and started at the sound of his own voice.

He was moved and stirred. Some dark and bitter core in him was shaken. Yet he could smile at himself. Is my ingenuousness so great that I must seize eagerly on any

591

evidence that there lives in men some obscure and tender virtue? he asked in his heart.

A peculiar lightness pervaded him, a relaxing, a relief. An odd delirium rose to his head. Hope, then, and faith, existed, could manifest themselves inexorably and with supernatural strength even in such as this bravo!

His narrow and delicate hands clenched themselves convulsively on the table. His eyes pierced Arsène's face like twin lances of lightning.

"Monsieur knows," he said, very softly, "that resistance is hopeless, even with faith. I will not dishonor Monsieur by asking him to order the surrender of the city. But I ask him to reflect."

"We have reflected," said Arsène in a low voice. "But, we cannot surrender. For our own sakes, we cannot surrender."

"Continued resistance will bring terrible retribution," whispered the Cardinal, still hardly believing.

Arsène gazed at him steadfastly. "For our own sakes, we cannot surrender, no matter what the end," he said. "If we surrender, and live, how can we endure the living?"

The Cardinal leaned back in his chair.

"And the others, they feel so, also?"

Arsène hesitated. Then his expression kindled once more. "Not in the beginning. There were many who bewailed; there were many who were treacherous, cowardly and expedient. But these have already escaped from the city. Those who remain believe as I do, that we cannot surrender."

He stood up, as if his thoughts impelled him to urgent activity. He clenched his fists, and leaned them on the table, fixing the Cardinal with a passionate look.

"Monseigneur, La Rochelle may fall. The cause of Protestantism in France may fall. The hope for the rights of man, for liberty and enlightenment and peace may be darkened. This hope cannot be destroyed! It may be stamped into the ground, buried under the fallen walls of La Rochelle, be silenced by the noose or the sword. It may be assailed by a thousand barbarous foes, driven from gutter into attic, into cellar or sewer. It may lie supine under the stones of centuries. But it cannot be destroyed! The dream has been dreamt, and the swords of a hundred armies, the cannon of a multitudinous force, cannot obliterate that dream! If it shall not be dreamt again in France, it shall be dreamt elsewhere, and then again, elsewhere, until all men know it, and have liberated themselves."

And then, in himself, the doubt and the uncertainty, the

bewilderment and confusion, were flooded away in a wave of exultation and conviction. He looked at the Cardinal with a great and dawning joy in his heart, as though he had received an invincible message, an invincible promise.

The Cardinal looked at him, unspeaking. His frail fingers clasped themselves tightly. His face became very grave.

Then he rose, and began to pace up and down the warm bright room, his hands clasped behind his back, his head bent in deep meditation. His slight figure in its somber soldier's uniform seemed taller than it was, and very reserved and finely wrought. His fragile countenance, with its imperial, took on the aspect of carved and delicate ivory. Arsène watched him, and he was overcome with a dim wonder. Could this elegant and exquisite gentleman be in truth that mountebank, that malefactor, that ruthless murderer whom all Europe regarded with terror? Could this be that Roman plotter, that lecher and Machiavelli whose intrigues had set a whole continent to seething and whispering? It was incredible. This was some aristocratic thinker, some philosopher, who was less engaged with armies and courts than in the profound study of man, an inexhaustible subject which called forth all the powers of his mind and the metaphysical conjectures of his unknown and terrible soul.

He returned to Arsène, and smiled absently. Arsène believed that he did not really see him. His words, too, were very strange and inexplicable.

"Monsieur, it has occurred to me just now what might happen to the kings, the generals, the princes of the Church, if the peoples, confronted in hatred and war with each other, should suddenly regard each other with complete understanding, complete awakening. How aghast they would be, how stricken with dumbness! Can you not imagine how they would stare, each man into his antagonist's and enemy's eyes, and how their hands would drop and the swords clatter to the ground? And now they would whisper to themselves: how is it that I have come to this place, to kill?"

Arsène was silent. The Cardinal paused in front of him, and there was a blind fever in those fathomless eyes.

"And then," continued the priest, in a peculiar voice, "there would be a sudden echoless silence all over the world."

It was only in moments of passion that subtlety and intuition could flare up vividly in Arsène. Too, he was so exhausted by weakness and his own emotion now that he could feel and think nothing. So, he merely stood and regarded the Cardinal in exhausted silence. However, he knew that the Cardinal did not resent his lack of response. He was too engrossed with his own thoughts.

The Cardinal continued to stand near him, and to look at him. Finally, he said:

"Monsieur, I have known you for many years. I have known your father, and esteemed his gifts at the gaming table, his miraculous perfumes, his exquisite taste. Your brother had served me, and had acquired my fondness. I ask you now, what favor can I grant you, in these sad hours?"

Arsène lifted his head eagerly, and moistened his dry lips. "I prefer death by the musket, to the noose," he said. "I am a soldier, and ask a soldier's death."

The Cardinal's brows rose delicately. The thin and brittle mask darkened his features again. He appeared to sink into thought. At last he moved to the door and opened it upon the darkness. The captain of his guards appeared, and saluted.

"Bretonne," said the Cardinal, "Monsieur de Bonnelle prefers to take his mercenaries to their own camp immediately. You will please to assemble them."

He closed the door. Arsène stared at him, white as death, and trembling. The Cardinal smiled. He laid his hand on the young man's shoulder.

"May I give Monsieur a message for my old friend, the Duchesse de Rohan? Please assure her of my endless admiration and affection, and inform her that I have great need of more unguents for my rheumatism, and that her last vial of herbal remedies for indigestion has cured me."

Arsène was speechless. Tears blinded him. Through the blur and dazzle of them he could see the Cardinal, smiling with the utmost candor and friendliness, and with a hint of amusement.

"Some prescience warns me that we shall never meet again, Arsène," said the Cardinal, in a lower tone. "I regret this exceedingly. In parting, then, I wish you all godspeed. And peace."

Arsène tried to speak, but his pale lips could only move without sound. The Cardinal pressed his shoulder strongly for an instant, then turned away. The door opened, and Bretonne appeared, and saluted.

"The mercenaries are awaiting Monsieur de Bonnelle, Monsieur le Cardinal," he said.

Arsène still strove to speak, but now a cold and warning look had entered the Cardinal's eyes, for all his smile. So, with a deep bow, the young man bent his head and lifted the

Cardinal's hand to his lips. Then, turning, he stumbled out into the night.

His companions were waiting for him near the watchfires, excited and anxious, but as silent and alert as himself. The Cardinal's men saluted briskly, and were saluted in turn. If they were curious, or doubtful, it was not evident.

The old dreamlike quality beset Arsène as he led his companions away. They, too, did not speak. They began to hasten. They passed the bodies of the guards they had slain, still undiscovered. They reached the walls of the city. There they found the others waiting, fuming and overcome with apprehension. They began to whisper furiously. But those who had returned shook their heads in silence. Now they moved even swifter. They dropped like heavy apples over the wall.

Arsène, in climbing, reached the top. All at once, in the far distance, he saw the sudden agitated flaring of torches, heard the distant shouts and cries, discerned the leaping of fresh fires. The murdered men had been discovered, the alarm had been given.

He dropped over. In the safety of the city, torches had been lit. He saw the huge piles of foodstuffs, gleefully piled up, and the hurrying men who carried them away.

"It was a great and involuntary gift of his Eminence," laughed one young man, ironically.

"Yes, it was a great gift," said Arsène.

CHAPTER LVII

THAT WINTER WAS most horrible. Ten thousand Rochellais remained alive. By the time the first spring breezes blew, less than seven thousand remained.

There was no fuel. Now, there were hardly any children, for they had been the first to succumb. A sickness invaded the starved and desolate houses, and when starvation did not kill, the disease released the people of their sufferings.

Among the people, the expedient still remained, and the traitors. No one knew how they obtained food, but they continued to be singularly plump, though they protested their agonies. Feuquières, less from treachery than from compassion, went among the leaders, pleading for surrender. He was sickened. He never forgot this siege, and the scenes in the city. To the end of his life, he remained a liberal Frenchman, though in the beginning he had been as intolerant and cruel as the others of his class and religion.

Now the Duchesse gave orders that even suspected treachery was to be punished by hanging. The Mayor ordered dozens of executions every week. One night an attempt to assassinate him took place. The Duchesse commanded that he move his family and himself into the Hôtel de Rohan.

At night, the Rochellais, in their empty and stricken city, heard the loud prayers for them uttered by Père Joseph's Calvarian nuns directly below the walls. None was touched. If anything, they were stiffened. The sound of those incantations horrified them, with a mysterious horror. The Cardinal denounced it as "mummery," to the Capuchin's indignation. "Do you think the prayers of cloistered women will move emancipated Frenchmen when the cries of their own dying and tormented wives and children will not do so?" he asked.

He was suffering as he never suffered before, and he was not suffering for himself. Behind these walls, beloved

Frenchmen were dying, and he, so jealous of every drop of French blood, cursed the foul fate which had brought him here to inflict so much agony on his countrymen. Was this a way to unite Frenchmen, Protestant and Catholic alike? Would not the hatred inherent in such bloody seed live to grow a dread harvest through countless centuries?

"Who knows but that, hundreds of years hence, when all Frenchmen are faced with the supreme hour, this harvest may not then bear its ghastly fruit, and destroy France?" he asked himself. "For then Frenchmen shall not trust Frenchmen, and all will be lost."

Only six thousand men behind those walls now, but they were writing an epic. Strong souls such as this aroused his pride. They were needed to set the vines and the trees of life-giving orchards.

He wrote to the Duchesse: "I have not implored you in the past to order surrender, for you and I have honor. But I am tortured by the thought of the sufferings of your people. Before your gallantry I kneel, and ask that you order the gates to be opened, in the name of humanity. I cannot endure this. I am racked with agony, my bed sleepless."

The messenger, with his white flag, brought back an unguent in a little gold box, and a letter from the Duchesse. "I recommend that your Eminence rub a portion of this upon your brow before retiring, in order that you may sleep," she had written, wryly.

No one had displayed more fortitude in all this horror than Cecile Grandjean. Though she was wasted to a transparent skeleton of herself, she said no word of complaint or fear. She was confined to her bed, for she could no longer walk. Moreover, she was enceinte. No one but the Duchesse knew this. The old grande dame brought morsels from Feuquières' baskets for her, urging the girl to eat for the sake of the child. But Cecile gently refused. "My child and I die together, if need be," she said, with a stern look. Arsène was not to be told, she said. This, above all, might shake his fortitude.

Each day Arsène, the German, the Spaniard and the Italian took their watches on the rampart, though so fainting that they were hardly conscious. There were white patches at Arsène's temples. He looked a man of forty or more, rather than his true age of barely past thirty.— Then, one day, a ball, coming from no one knew where, struck the German in the heart and he died as bravely as he had lived.

This did not awaken any wild fury in Arsène, as the

Duchesse believed it would do. He was very quiet. "Our Arsène," she said to the Marquis, "has had too much food for thought forced into him, and he is suffering from indigestion."

"I believe he is digesting only too well," said the Marquis, in the whisper which was the best he could summon these days.

The Marquis had displayed a fortitude and simple heroism which amazed every one. He worked with the other townsmen in burying the dead, in standing watch. Now he was in truth an old man, uncomplaining. His hair was white and thin. He no longer wore his many curled wigs, though, when he appeared at the table, his garments were as rich as ever, though shabby. The malice had left his soul; it had almost left his wizened face. Only the thin web-like lines about his sunken mouth and eyes betrayed his past frivolity. The Marquis, too, was thinking.

No one knew that there was joy in his heart. He had lived for so many years in self-disgust, triviality, self-betrayal, and contemptuous ribaldry. Now, he was his father, his grandfather. Sometimes he dreamt of them, standing by his bed, their hands on their swords, their heads proud and high, bending their proud smiles upon him. Once he heard his father say: "Soon, my son, you shall be with me in eternal glory. You have redeemed yourself."

He had come because he could not bear to be parted from Arsène. He remained, because he could not bear to be parted from the souls of his ancestors.

His hands, once so fine and delicate and perfumed, were calloused and torn with toil, from digging the graves of the dead. His body was bent. He shuffled feebly through the streets and the houses, helping drag the carts loaded with corpses, until even the suffering could forget their own suffering and take compassion upon him. But one look at his quiet and uplifted face, his shining eyes, and they could say nothing.

He could still make epigrams. Around that dolorous table, on which there were no longer any candles, he and the Duchesse, in their whispering voices, matched wits, for the sad amusement of the others. Only Arsène did not smile. His face was perpetually darkened and closed, but full of intensity. He no longer had strength for words of love, for his father or his mistress. He could only touch the Marquis feebly on the shoulder or the hand, and kiss his cheek. He could only kneel beside Cecile's bed and lay his head on her shrunken breast.

The uncomplaining sufferings of the girl, her steadfast smiles, tore him apart. But he dared not urge her to flee. He loved her too much to have been able to endure her scornful bright anger. He dared not let her know how his heart was failing, not for himself, but for her. Sometimes, he prayed that when he awoke in the morning, she would be dead, and free.

He thought he moved in hopelessness. He did not know that strange things had permanently taken root in his soul, and would never die. His calm, which he believed came from fatality, came, instead, from his new and unshakable fortitude.

The Spaniard and the Italian died the same night in their beds. It was thought at first that they had died of starvation, but the dread signs of pestilence were soon discerned on their bodies.

Hardly was the horror felt, the bodies buried hastily, when the Marquis sickened.

The old magnate, from the onset of the first chill and shiver, knew that he was dying. A supreme thrill of joy convulsed him. He called for his son, and asked to see him alone. He lay on his silken bed, hardly more than an outline of bones, and the linen was no whiter than his hair.

Now a new strength was given to him. He could speak clearly and firmly. He held Arsène with his burning eyes. "I have talked with Madame la Duchesse, my dearest one, my scapegrace, my vagabond," he said, with a smile that did not lessen his seriousness. "She will speak with you when I am gone. I urge you, I pray you, not to refuse her. What she will ask will not be for yourself alone, but for Cecile, for your children, for me—and our fathers."

He appeared so happy and so serene, that Arsène could feel no grief. He sat beside the bed and held his father's dwindled hand. Sometimes he lost consciousness, for he was weak. But when he looked up, the Marquis' eyes were still fixed upon him, smiling and unafraid, and full of love. "Not only you, my son, but I, have been born again," he whispered.

There was no candle in that room, but the moonlight, brilliant and full, streamed through the open windows so that the first airs of summer could enter. Now it seemed to Arsène that the chamber was full of ghosts who did not know him, but only his father. So engrossed was he in his sensing of these ghosts, that he was unaware of the silent coming and going of the Duchesse. Cecile begged from her bed to be allowed to say farewell to the old man, but this was not allowed.

The moon sank to rest, and when it was the darkest of all, and the ghosts most imminent, the Marquis died, without a last sigh or murmur. Arsène knew he had gone only when the hand he held grew cold in his.

When they had arranged him in his bed, the dawn was clear and gray in the sky. He lay there, rigid, seeming to have grown taller, nobility obliterating forever the last lines of malice and shallowness of heart. Now there was much in his lineaments that reminded Arsène of the dead Louis. There was the same loftiness and coldness and dignity. For some reason, Arsène began to weep.

The Marquis was hardly in his grave, when a letter came from the Cardinal to Arsène. It began on a note of affection and personal regard, and slight raillery. Then it became brief and somber.

"A messenger has just arrived at our camp bringing me a missive from Madame de Tremblant, your *belle mere*. It is a sad message, one which I know will cause you much sorrow. Madame de Richepin died a month ago in childbed, leaving to you a handsome young son, who has been given your name, and your father's."

It was some hours before Arsène could absorb this message, and its portent. Then he was overcome. He did not speak of it to Cecile, but to the Duchesse, and his words were wild.

"It is too late to ask forgiveness of my poor Clarisse," he said, distraught.

"You could have done nothing else but what you did," said the Duchesse with compassion. But she eyed him thoughtfully, with a brightening eye.

She was relieved that there was no sign of love in Arsène's grief, but only regret and remorse. She was even more relieved when he went to Cecile for consolation.

Several weeks later, she sent for him on the ramparts, and believing that Cecile was at last about to die, he rushed through the streets with the last strength he could summon. But he found the Duchesse in company with the parson of the nearby chapel, one Monsieur de Duvois, the Mayor, and several other of his friends. The Duchesse greeted him with a roguish smile. She was arrayed in the last of her splendor.

There was the last of her good wine waiting in crystal goblets. She kissed him upon both cheeks, rising on her toes to do so. Every haggard face was radiant with smiles.

His relief was so great that he staggered, and would have fallen but for ready arms.

"I have plans for you, my bravo," said the Duchesse. "But they first demand a wedding ceremony. Go, then, to your rooms, and prepare yourself. Cecile is being dressed by my women for this most auspicious occasion."

He stared at them dumbly. He could hardly comprehend.

"Time is imperative," said the Duchesse, firmly. "Hasten, and then there shall be news for you."

Her face and manner were so full of authority and resolution, that he obeyed, and climbed feebly to his rooms. He had never thought of Cecile as anything but his wife. It seemed strange and improbable that others had not thought so. It angered him, in his hunger-ridden confusion. He heard the faint sounds of preparation behind the doors which led to Cecile's apartments, and her sweet weak voice. A lackey entered to assist him.

When he arrived downstairs again, they had brought Cecile to him, supported by her women. She was arrayed in blue and ermine, her hair wound high upon her head. Rouge had been skillfully applied to her white face, and touched to her lips. A semblance of health radiated from her. She gazed at Arsène softly.

Arsène took her hot thin hand, and looked deeply down into her eyes. His face was so moved that others felt tears rising in their throats. He thought: I have brought so much pain and suffering to this poor child, as I brought them to Clarisse. I have brought her to starve and to die, I have given her my heart, but it is nothing to what I have inflicted upon her.

The ceremony was brief but dignified. Arsène supported Cecile in his arms. They drank wine, and the young couple was congratulated. Then Arsène carried Cecile upstairs to his apartments and laid her in his bed.

Now he could feel joy. There was no escape for either of them from this doomed city. But still, there was joy.

He lay beside her, and his tears came. She held him in her arms and murmured to him softly. At last he was still, and he slept for exhaustion. But she gazed into space with a far brilliance in her eyes, as of hope and resolution.

CHAPTER LVIII

THAT NIGHT THE DUCHESSE sent for him in her own apartments.

He found her as always, alone and tranquil, composed and contained. She asked him to sit near her. She poured a glass of wine for him. Over its rim, she studied him thoughtfully and shrewdly. He saw that she held a paper in her hand.

Then she said in a very quiet voice: "La Rochelle will surrender in two days."

He started to his feet so violently that he overturned the chair. He staggered, and caught hold of the edge of a table. "No," he said. "No!" Now his face took on a terrible and enraged expression.

But the Duchesse was not disturbed. She still studied him. She nodded her head. "It is so. We cannot go on any longer. There are only five thousand of us left. I have decided. I have the Cardinal's promise that these shall be spared and he has never broken his word to me."

She seemed mysteriously calm, and not despondent. Arsène looked down at her with a convulsed face.

"Do not be so desperate, my poor child," she continued, in a softer tone. "We shall surrender. But, we are not defeated. We have given an epic to the world, and it shall not forget."

She paused and said: "However, there is no place for you in France, in Europe, any longer. Your father spoke to me long ago, and then before he died. We made our decision. There are other worlds which need you, your blood, your fortitude, your courage, your faith. We shall send you to those worlds, not for your sake, but for all time to come."

She indicated the chair again with her imperious gesture, and he was forced to seat himself. But he was trembling uncontrollably. He bit his lip to stop its shaking, and the blood came. The Duchesse did not appear aware of his emotions. She looked before her and spoke tranquilly:

"Europe may blaze up once or twice more in splendor. But its day is done. The pestilence runs too deeply in its murky veins. It is a place no longer for the young and strong of heart. It is old; it is a land of old men, who remember only the past, and believe there is no future. Nothing can destroy the plague in its body, the disaster in its soul, the blight on its face. The evil ones have done their work too well."

Now she turned to him, and her steadfast eyes were full of stern light.

"But there is another world, a new world, still a wilderness, but a plain where great harvests can grow, where new governments, new philosophies can flourish, where young men can be born and mighty things can be evoked. Not, perhaps, in your lifetime, or the lifetime of your sons, but your blood shall run into the future and beget other men and women who shall not forget, who shall prevail against the enemy of all men."

She leaned towards him with stern enthusiasm. "Before evil deeds are done, there are first the evil, perverse and twisted thoughts. In a house of pestilence, one acquires the pestilence, no matter how healthy the body. This is true, also, of the mind. The pestilence lives in Europe! It cannot be washed or burned away. It would rise in its full strength as a plague whenever there is the opportunity. One must flee to a clean place, to escape it, one where the pestilence has not become the fungus of infection. And in that world of which I have spoken, the fungus is not yet deeply rooted, though its spores have been scattered in the north, and in the southern continent."

She stood up suddenly, her wide and brocaded gown rustling about her, and he was forced to rise with her. The words came from her lips, but he felt them rushing from his own heart, and hers were only an echo.

"It is a wilderness still, that world, beyond a few sea-coast towns and raw small cities. But it is not a barren wilderness. It is full of the promise of life. To that world, that wilderness, you are to go, Arsène, with your wife, your blood, your hopes and your faith."

He passed his hands over his face. He felt giddy, like a man who has been confined in a narrow prison and finds himself suddenly freed. But still, he was incredulous at the words he was hearing, and astounded.

"What is Madame saying?" he muttered, but more to himself than to her.

He dropped his hands. "I must stay here to the end, no matter what comes," he said.

"To the end," she repeated, thoughtfully. Then she turned to him, ablaze with such scorn that he was startled.

"It is the end!" she cried. "And you will die and fester here, betraying all that we have hoped!"

She was like a seeress, bright with passion and prophesy.

"You dare not refuse!" she exclaimed. "You dare not let us surrender in hopelessness and darkness. With you go all that we have fought for, suffered for, and died for! Refuse them, and you are not one of us any longer."

He could say nothing. He was violently bewildered. But she held his attention, and now he felt the beating of his liberated heart.

She gazed at him fixedly. "Do you know that you are about to have another child, my dear Arsène? Do you not know that Cecile is to give you this child?"

Arsène was silent.

But the Duchesse continued inexorably: "Remain, and your children will inherit the pestilence and the ruin and the hopelessness of Europe. Leave, and a new world is their inheritance. Dare you refuse?"

It was a long time before Arsène could speak. His face was pale and moist.

"I, too, have thought of it, Madame la Duchesse. Long ago, I came to the decision to leave this place, when my work is done. But it is not done. To go now would be ignominious flight, and dishonor. It would be betrayal, abandonment. The work of a coward and a traitor. I know of this new world: America. I know that thousands of us must go there, to escape the things of Europe. But I have work here still to be done. If I die in the doing of it, then it is regrettable. I cannot go."

There was a profound silence in the room. Their eyes held together, and it seemed that a strong dark current, gleaming with surface light, ran through the chamber.

Then the Duchesse said gently: "There is a time for honor, and a time for discretion, a time for valor, and a time for retreat, a time to fight and a time to flee."

She touched him lightly on the arm: "Think of us as a besieged army, defending the fortress, while those armed with a message go out to sea. Think of us as covering your retreat, guarding that precious and indestructible message. You are not abandoning us. We are sending you out with all our hopes and our prayers and our faith, and we will keep the enemy at bay until you are safely gone. You have taken the jewels with you. The enemy will find only an empty casket when he breaks into the fortress. We shall be comforted, knowing that he is balked, and the jewels are safe."

But Arsène's face remained dark and obdurate.

"And what of those who remain behind?"

The Duchesse shrugged, and smiled. "I am not afraid. I know Monsieur le Cardinal. There have been the strangest implications in his letters to me of late. There has been mention of you. You have done inexplicable things to that frightful man, Arsène. I tell you, we are not afraid." And she appeared amused.

Arsène did not speak. He rubbed his clenched fists together, and compressed his lips. His whole soul revolted at the idea of flight. It was indeed flight, in spite of the Duchesse's fine and heroic words.

The Duchesse was speaking again. "America," she said. "The shadow of the mitred head, the shadow of the enslaving hand, the shadow of the old men, have already fallen there. Shall America be devoured, also? Shall the pestilence of hatred, oppression, slavery, intolerance and despair flourish there?—In many parts there are men of English blood, of your own blood, also, of your own faith and courage, of your own resolution and dreams. Go to them. Give them your strength and your hands. Give them your belief in the rights of man and the dignity of freedom. Give them your sons."

Now she became more passionate. "Keep that new world safe from us, the old and the done, the cynical and the cruel, and the venomous!"

Arsène remained silent. A dark gleam wavered across his face. He sighed heavily.

The Duchesse glanced at the paper in her hands.

"At a seaport in Holland, your other son awaits. I have arranged it all, through the Cardinal. You seem astonished. I have long ago lost the capacity for astonishment, for I know that all things are possible. Your son awaits with part of your fortune, cared for by valiant others who will accompany you. You will take the child into your custody there, and assume command over those devoted men and women who are only the vanguard of thousands of others. Within a short time, you will set sail for the new world."

Now she became very gentle. She reached out and took Arsène's cold hand. She saw the moisture in his haggard eyes, the trembling of his lips. She saw the hopes that passed and repassed across his face.

"Tomorrow will be too late. Tonight, a small boat waits in darkness for you, in the harbor. Tonight, and tonight only, will you be allowed to pass. I have a passport from the Cardinal—."

"Cecile," said Arsène.

"She has new strength," said the Duchesse. "She has been told, and understands completely. She has forced herself to eat of the baskets which have been brought in for Feuquieres. More of those provisions await you on the small boat. I have not deprived my people. In two days, they shall have sustenance enough."

Then Arsène, fully realizing, cried out: "You ask me to be a coward, to flee, to leave my people! I cannot do this."

The Duchesse's expression became cold and scornful. "It is you who are the coward, Arsène de Richepin! It is you, out of your egotism, your fear of the opinions of others, who will deliver yourself and your sons to slavery. You cannot delay the surrender of La Rochelle. If you refuse to go, I shall order the surrender immediately. Then, you will be forever lost."

She faced him with implacable grimness.

"Have you no thought, no mind, you fool?" she cried. "Have you no compassion on us? Would you deprive us of our last hope?"

They gazed at each other in an impetuous silence. Then, very slowly, Arsène fell to his knees. He embraced the Duchesse, feeling the slightness and steeliness of her small body. And then she enfolded him in her arms. She smiled. There were tears on her short and faded lashes.

CHAPTER LVIX

Two DAYS LATER, La Rochelle surrendered. Hardly four thousand of the people remained alive.

The Cardinal and Père Joseph entered the city at the head of the singing and victorious troops. Père Joseph walked in his ragged habit, his russet head and russet beard catching the light of the dying sun so that they seemed to be imbued with a fanatical fire of their own. The Church had triumphed. The blasphemers were conquered! He saw visions of the future, when this Protestant heresy would be driven from the world forever, and Rome should, as of old, be the supreme arbiter of mankind, the servant of a victorious God.

The singing priests were jubilant. They looked at the haggard faces who watched them pass with evil anticipation, thinking of their tortures, their whips and other gentle persuaders. But there was no fear in the faces that watched them, no shrinking. They had looked too long on death. Now there was only pride in those quiet eyes, sunken so deeply in the bones of famished skulls.

The Duchesse de Rohan came herself to greet the Cardinal. She walked on foot. She had no carriage. But at the sight of her, the Cardinal alighted from his horse and approached her. He took her hand and kissed it passionately. For an instant she thought that those terrible eyes were clouded and moist. She stood before him proudly. Her lips parted. He, himself, could not speak, so moved was he.

"I trust," she said, tranquilly, "that Monseigneur's sleeplessness has been cured?"

He looked into her face, and he said, so low that no one else caught his words: "Madame, I shall never sleep again."

He led her into the Hôtel de Rohan, and there he told her that he contemplated no punishment for her heroic people, "though others," he added sardonically, thinking of the priests, "had urged otherwise." Nor would the soldiers be allowed to loot or massacre. Death would be visited upon them if they did so.

"I have seen a strange vision," said the Cardinal, in a peculiar voice. "For the sake of that vision, La Rochelle shall not suffer."

He continued, telling her things which astonished her heart and blinded her sight with tears.

The Rochellais were to be pardoned. They were to continue to hold their property, and exercise freedom of worship.

"I ask," and now his voice rang with sincerity, "only that the Rochellais shall be faithful to France."

And now he looked full in her eyes: "Faithfulness, for unity of all Frenchmen. Until the end."

"Until the end," repeated the Duchesse.

And now the two old friends were silent, and they saw, without delusion, the end that was approaching Europe with the inexorable doom of a hurricane.

The next day the sick and gloomy Cardinal sang Mass in the ancient church of St. Margaret. The bells pealed joyfully. The Rochellais, fearing all horrors, remained in their homes. The sound of the bells shattered the sunlit air over empty and devastated streets.

The Duchesse attended that Mass, seated in a place of honor. She listened to the Cardinal's faint voice, in which there was no note of triumph. She heard the rolling of the music, the surge of the choristers' voices. She had come here at the urgent invitation of the Cardinal, and, understanding him, she had accepted that invitation. It was as if he had invited her to hear his cry of despair.

But, in truth, she heard neither Mass nor singers. It seemed to her that she was listening to the sound of wind in sails that were bearing Arsène, his wife, his son, and his unborn child into the future.

The voices of the choristers were the voices of unborn men, raised in hope and triumph, in victory and freedom, in ever-lasting conquest over the forces of darkness and evil, super-stition, ignorance and fear and hatred.